Critical acclaim for
Different Women Dancing

'Brilliantly successful: the previous novel
that *Different Women Dancing* most
reminds you of is *Brighton Rock*.' *Sunday
Times*

'A smashing new crime novel.' *New York
Times Book Review*

'Light years away from the jovial roguery
which Gash has made his own, but just
as distinctive.' *Literary Review*

'A woman doctor and a streetwise gigolo
make an offbeat pairing in a brilliant
thriller.' *Peterborough Evening Telegraph*

'Gash is in top form as he introduces Dr
Clare Burtonall . . . Promises further
entertainments to come.' *Publishers Weekly*

'A smooth, sexy suspenser . . . The
promised series is cause for rejoicing.'
Kirkus Reviews

different
women
dancing

Jonathan Gash is the author of the hugely successful Lovejoy novels, which were adapted into the long-running BBC TV series *Lovejoy*, starring Ian McShane. His latest Lovejoy mystery, *The Rich and the Profane*, is available in Macmillan hardback.

Jonathan Gash is also a doctor specialising in tropical medicine and lectures worldwide on the subject. He is married with three daughters and four grandchildren and lists his hobbies as antiques and his family.

The second novel in his series featuring Clare Burtonall and Bonn, entitled *Prey Dancing*, will be published in October 1998.

JONATHAN GASH

different
women
dancing

PAN BOOKS

First published 1997 by Macmillan

This edition published 1998 by Pan Books
an imprint of Macmillan Publishers Ltd
25 Eccleston Place, London SW1W 9NF
and Basingstoke

Associated companies throughout the world

ISBN 0 330 35287 3

9 8 7 6 5 4 3 2 1

A CIP catalogue record for this book is available from
the British Library.

Phototypeset by Intype London Ltd
Printed and bound in Great Britain by
Mackays of Chatham plc, Chatham, Kent

Susan, with thanks

1 Goer – a male hired by a female, implicitly for sexual purposes.

Bonn liked to stand at the corner before his next woman.

He loved the decayed city square. Girl stringers touting at the station, bike couriers arguing over piston performance, pickpockets comparing skills, a lone temazepam flogger hoping to sell his yellow jellies before Martina's standers caught him. The traffic was a snarled-up maelstrom, some lunatic taxi creating mayhem. Sheer beauty, Bonn's world.

The next woman was new. He had no need to check the crowded bus station. Rack would be there, giving out some barmy theory to whoever, but ready. Clockwork.

The traffic surged a yard or two. Horns blared, drivers shouting real anger.

Bonn shook his head. That taxi, daft as a brush, cutting in front of a great old maroon Humber. Somebody would get killed.

Dr Clare Burtonall was in a temper. She hauled her heavy maroon Humber Supersnipe aside, giving a stupid cab room to misbehave, and stabbed her foot at the brake.

'Oaf,' she muttered. 'You'll kill somebody.'

She had been displeased right from early morning. Had she realised that Dr Shacklady was going to be off duty, she never would have done the locum job. Not that she hated Dr Therle Bettany, whose endless saccharine-sweet charm swept all before her, but enough was enough. Clare felt conned. The locum bank had specified 'Locum to replace Dr T. Bettany . . .' And who should greet her, as she'd pulled in to the Farnworth general practice's forecourt, but the charming Therle Bettany herself, saying charmingly, 'Oh, Bert's *so* grateful you could locum for him!' Inevitably, Dr Therle Bettany had brought in, with her own lily-white hands, a charming cup of coffee. Cow.

Clare gritted her teeth, knowing her anger was unfair. If Therle spent a little less effort on being so bloody charming, she'd get more done. But Therle Bettany's charm was purchased at the expense of others. Inevitably, Clare had to cope with an extra five patients, all from Therle's list, while the wretched woman spent hours sighing on the phone to friends about her 'positively *staggering* workload. Bert's away again.'

'Next time, lady,' Clare seethed, as the lights changed and the cars inched forward, 'you do your own *charming* bloody locum. At least Bert pulls his weight for the patients.'

Five – repeat, *five* – times this morning, Therle had 'just liked to mention that in Aberdeen we *always* . . .' Or 'in Aberdeen, we *never* saw a thyroid scan as anything other than a . . .' Clare had never been to Aberdeen, now hated the place.

That impossible taxi. Pedestrians crowded the pavement. The London Road station concourse was disgorging more passengers. Splendid, Clare thought, abandoning bitterness for resignation, I'm here for the duration. She turned on the radio.

Drivers were leaning out, calling irritated what-the-hells as the taxi stopped to let its passenger alight. In stalled traffic, yards short of the traffic lights, would you believe. Clare was tired, and paid little attention.

She would be needed soon.

'Better get out here, sir,' Oz said over his shoulder. 'Looks like we'll be here all day.'

'You think so?'

'You'll make it before the lights change, but watch it.'

The man paid casually, like he knew that money made the world tick. So different, Oz thought, from new-money folk. Their stingy disdain kept the city down.

'Tall building, near the shopping mall, okay?'

The man alighted. The door clunked shut. Oz breathed a sigh of relief. The passenger was out there, vulnerable, with his briefcase. His pockets were sewn, as all new off-the-pegs. A meticulous man. Oz had done his time at Seven Dials among London's best subtle mongers.

'Come on, Salvo, Christ's sake,' he muttered.

Salvo, the burke, ought to be among the waiting pedestrians. That was the plan. Sometimes, Oz thought Salvo was out of his pond.

He saw him at last, the lazy sod, chatting up some bird. A goon tried to flag Oz's taxi down on the amber. His former passenger dithered between vehicles, should he go for it or backtrack.

Salvo knew his job. The scene was kaleidoscopic, a pattern of bits, the Warrington exit signed for the coast, the white van in front of Oz's taxi dowsing its tail lights.

The lights greened. Oz's nightmare at this millisec was a stalled engine. Salvo came from nowhere, clumsily nudging a little old dear carrying shopping. The marked man hesitated, tried for the pavement as the traffic moved.

Oz gunned his engine, shoving at the startled fare and his briefcase. The cab's nose lifted him and his astonished face hard against the rear of the van. The image froze in Oz's mind, Salvo yelling and hauling the old lady to the kerb, pedestrians gaping, the man abruptly aware, trying to look round, maybe demand what the fuck, then realising the horror, staring at Oz as he slid smudging dark-red blood down the van's white doors.

Predictable sounds began, screams and shouts, Salvo's crazed roar. Oz heard his own yell, double-stamped the accelerator so the cab almost stalled before kangaroo-leaping onto the body on the ground.

Salvo was nowhere. Oz opened his door, shouting For-Chrissakes and OhmyGod. It wasn't a bad act, though not new. Salvo always pulled his leg about it, mimicking Oz's stock phrases in falsetto to annoy.

Oz bawled that he hadn't stood a chance, that man just rushed forward, dramatic shit he should have got an Oscar for.

'Get an ambulance!' he was going. 'The police! Quick!'

'It's the man who pushed me,' the old lady said, unforgiving, an instant star witness, brilliant.

Some moron grasped Oz's lapels, shouting right into his face, 'Reverse off him, you fucking idiot,' over and over, as if Oz was deaf. There was always one hero, a barmy fucking breed of their own.

'Call an ambulance!' Oz yelled. 'Anybody!'

He wondered if he could sob convincingly, except he'd tried it that time he did the Liverpool girl in the St Helens canal and tears failed, so he decided to keep up his babble for ambulance, police, simple hysterics always the safest.

The hero in disgust shoved Oz aside and restarted the stalled engine, reversing the taxi off the crushed man with a sickening crump.

'I can't look!' Oz whimpered, hands covering his face but taking a quick shufti. The destruction wasn't clean. This was major blood on his front bumper, the wheels all gristle and bone flecks. It would be a bastard to clean, two fucking days at least.

'It's the man who shoved past me,' the righteous crone was giving it as Oz was spectacularly sick over his own rear mudguard, no acting needed. 'Poor man,' the old lady said. 'He's the cabbie.'

'Help him. Please,' Oz blurted between retches.

'No helping him, mate,' from the hero.

'There's too much of it these days,' the old bat said. 'Hurry, hurry, hurry.' She had them all nodding, a consensus Oz would have paid bag money for.

'You the driver?' some plod asked, materialising at last.

'I think he's the fare I just dropped. Insisted on getting out in the traffic.'

'He tripped,' Oz's favourite witness announced, proud of her senile prominence.

'I swear to God I never saw him,' Oz said, trying to look grey, retching busily, bored stupid, angry about the mess on his mudguard. He hated solvent cleaners.

There would be no comeback, maybe an inch in the local rag. It would be forever accidents, the need of a by-pass, the council idle, the usual crap they could print weeks before anything happened, lazy sods. Acting away, Oz almost yawned.

*

Clare saw the man go down, the taxi's horrid leap, heard the din. Quickly she got out, grabbed her emergency bag, and pushed through. A young man was kneeling by the injured figure, touching its face though it was covered in russet blood. He muttered quietly.

'Please let me pass. I'm a doctor.'

The news was taken up. Folk spread arms to allow her through. A sweating man climbed out of the taxi, telling the young helper it was no good.

'No helping him, mate.'

Clare arrived just as the policeman banished the young man. 'Shift, you. Sod off. Leave it to the doctor.'

The taxi driver was making a show of feeling sick. An old woman was reciting her favourite litany, people never taking their time so now look. Clare made a cursory examination. The crushed man almost bisected. The young kneeling man had risen, and seemed to melt into the crowd.

Something was not quite right. She wanted to ask who'd seen it happen, but everyone was talking. She shook her head at the policeman. He was painstakingly taking notes.

Oz felt aggrieved. That bitch of a doctor didn't take the slightest notice of him, when he was all but fucking dying from shock, real hysterics, Christ's sake. Still, it was a clean job in one sense. His taxi was crapped up, but you couldn't have everything. He'd dun the wallet for extra. Money was always paid on the nail.

'See, constable,' he started up, 'I wanted to drop him at the kerb. . . .'

The briefcase was gone. In its place, a new one of the same colour and type. He hoped Salvo, fucking mental age of eight, had had the sense to take the price ticket off before pulling the swap.

2

Stander – one who protects a goer during the hiring period.

Rack fell in with Bonn as he crossed to the Vivante Hotel. 'See that, Bonn?'
'The accident?'

Rack barked a laugh. 'You talk like everything's got no answer, Bonn.'

'You talk like anything has.'

Rack fell about. Women got on well with Bonn, though nobody on Martina's syndicate ever knew what Bonn was talking about. Rack called half-insulting greetings to Grellie's line girls. Until dusk they had nothing to do but chat up the motorbike messengers who were waiting to zoom up the Affetside moorland road.

'I didn't see it.' Rack sounded aggrieved, still calling out cheery jibes to Grellie, who was eyeing Bonn as usual. 'Know why he got topped?' Rack demanded, walking backwards to challenge Bonn better.

Bonn could have done with a few minutes' quiet. If it was simply seeing one woman, it would be easy. But a stranger, every time? You needed a moment's solitude, to gather yourself.

Rack bounced along, black widow's peak shorn close, pudgy, short, black leather jacket, thick corrugated-sole boots a questionable tan, offering non-stop theories. All his notions invented for the instant, then forgotten.

Bonn gave up. 'Why, then?'

'He was thinking about holidays.' Rack yelled something in numbers to a girl, listened to numbers called back, turned to walk normally. 'Was he smashed up? They're saying a taxi and a van.'

'I didn't see much, Rack.'

Rack gave him a look. He had seen Bonn come from the crowd, slide into the gents' by the newsagent's. Bonn had bloodied hands. But saying nothing was Bonn's way, and you didn't ask.

'Leave now, Rack. What's the room number?'

'Four-oh-seven, Bonn. You got nine minutes.'

Bonn went to the lifts without a word, pressed the button. Rack had never let Bonn down. Best stander in the business.

Two shoppers drifted chatting from the hotel's foyer. The lift came. Bonn stepped in, glad to be alone. From now until the woman left the hotel, Rack would be invisible, but close by.

Room 407. He was there when the woman arrived.

She was younger than others Bonn had seen lately. He smiled, moved towards her as she entered, took her coat, did the essential ordinary reassuring gestures.

Mousey, plain, nervous almost to the point of panic, she was steeling herself. She stood as if waiting to be asked at a dance. Mid-twenties, maybe? It was easier when there was more of an age gap. Like actors; age up is easy, down near to impossible.

'Phew.' Bonn smiled to mock his relief. 'Can I offer you a drink, something hot, coffee, tea?'

She said no thank you, formal, smoothing her dress. He took her hand and drew her in, taking charge.

'I'm glad you came, Devina.'

'Yes.' She said it shrilly, as if expecting derision at her false name.

He gave her a quick embrace, immediately releasing her. Her hair was newly washed, her twin set brand-new. She was spotless, must have planned this for weeks.

'And I'm really pleased you chose me, Devina.'

Words were hazardous. She was not merely treating herself, as some women did, using him as self-rewarding present. He sensed that this Devina was desperate to learn, perhaps fighting some complex, maybe paper over some emotional disaster.

'Oh, I didn't . . .' She coloured, broke off.

Bonn went gently over her anxiety. 'Then it was just my good luck.'

The balance, he knew, was between words and silence. Smiling, he led her into the bedroom, the curtains giving just enough daylight. Progress would be inchwise, deliberate enough not to offend yet steady enough to reassure. Pace was everything with women. Hesitation might give her screaming hysterics. Go too fast, she could just as easily assume she was being ravished against her will.

'I've never done this before.' She pulled back, wanting to explain.

Bonn remained with her. 'Whatever you wish, Devina, and however you wish it.'

He shrugged, to disarm. Her silence was all to the good. Let her solve her own doubts, while he created none.

'I'm here for you, Devina, to do what you want. Is that all right?'

She stood, desperate to speak but panicked by lack of words. Bonn went to the window, adjusted the curtains, and stepped away as if gauging his efforts. 'Can I tell you what I would do?'

Devina's mouth pursed. She gave a stiff nod, her gaze fixed on the carpet. Bonn started speaking, giving way, recognising her fear.

'Security, and all the reassurance a lady deserves. They are my responsibility, Devina. The risk of interruption, somebody tracing you? No. With me, you're perfectly secure. Those terrible consequences you've heard about? Also no, Devina. There can be none. The lady must be protected at all times.' He let his slow words linger. 'I want you to know that. Stay only if you believe. It's a belief in your right to life, as much as in anything.'

She finally spoke. 'I've always felt that.'

'It's all up to the lady.' He smiled. 'If the lady was hesitant, perhaps starting to wonder what she was doing' – he went on over her sudden look – 'then I would take her handbag, like this, gently, to show her that she was completely in control.'

She saw her handbag go onto the occasional table.

'Everything is just to please her.'

'I . . .'

He gave her the chance to speak, then stepped in. 'Because where's the harm?'

'It's only that I'm not sure . . .'

'Then I would lead her.' Bonn moved her, holding the fingertips of one hand. 'Only so we might sit down if we wanted to, nothing ominous.'

He stood still, not too fast.

'Maybe then I would ask if she wanted the curtains drawn, something like that, wanted to talk. It's anything for the lady. Our meeting is for you, Devina.'

'For me,' she said dully.

'Of course. I am yours, the rooms, hotel services, my time. You alone. Nobody else.'

Devina's gaze was almost childlike in its wonder.

'Like,' he went on, sitting on the edge of the bed, taking her down with him, 'what if the lady wanted the bedroom dark? Or brightly lit? Or flowers, something she'd always imagined? My only question is, why not simply please her? There's no harm in it.'

Devina shook her head, an inch each way. He looked at her fingers. She tried to draw them away, but he smiled and kept gentle hold.

'Lovely hands, Devina.'

'They're not,' she said. 'They're pudgy. My nails are terrible. They used to mock them at school.'

Bonn wouldn't have it, but didn't make an issue. 'You talk yourself down, Devina. Nice name, nice hands. That's why I say, if the lady has definite ideas, then they become my duty. Ideas about what she wanted, maybe to chat, be made love to, just about anything. She doesn't have to *do* whatever. She might like to say it right out. Or just be here.'

'I'm . . . I'm . . .'

Like that, Bonn finished mutely for her.

'Then I'd wait in case she decided,' quietly confiding now. 'Maybe talk about her life, something going wrong, her hopes, dreams out there. I have to respect that, Devina, because in here she's utterly secure. Here, the lady is queen.'

'Secure.' She spoke in a whisper, glancing round.

'A lady deserves listening to. It's not too much to ask, is

it?' He answered himself just as quietly, 'It's only fair. Some people have marvellous lives, nothing ever wrong, people admiring them. Others . . .' He shrugged. 'Well, not everybody has that kind of life. They deserve something better.'

'It's just that lately . . .' she started bravely, then petered out.

'Soon, I would rub her shoulder, not hard. She would hardly know.' He touched a light hand to her shoulder to explain where. 'After a while, no hurry, I'd help her off with her cardigan, if she wanted.'

He'd turned up the heating moments before Devina had arrived.

'I'd try to fold her cardigan just right, though I'm hopeless at that. Place it on the chair, hope I'd not creased it.'

Devina followed it with her eyes, started to say, 'Oh, no. It's fine,' before her voice faded.

'Then I would admire her form. You can't help it. A man can't avoid wonderment. It's only natural. It's simply her. She might think nothing of herself, yet her presence still overwhelms him. A woman *does*. It's night following day.'

His eyes took in her features, her eyes, cheeks, her mouth, the contour of her face, openly marvelling. Her eyes watched.

'Then I would let my finger touch her cheek, just once, and move away after an instant, but showing how she'd impressed me.'

She showed no alarm at what was happening. He passed his hand, slightly firmer, over her cheeks, down to her neck.

She said huskily, 'I haven't got a nice figure.'

'Devina, every woman has her own beauty. It starts within. A man sees the truth in a woman's form. Don't you see? She's the emblem of loveliness.'

'Every woman?' She was honestly asking.

'Of course. I believe it from the bottom of my heart.'

His palm cupped her breast briefly, and moved away.

'Then I might take her breast, not making a movement that might disturb its magic. Pass my fingertips to touch the inner thigh, hardly at all, careful not to break the spell that her loveliness casts.'

'I was never . . .'

'I would shush her,' Bonn whispered, closing her eyes with his fingers, 'when she believed in her woman's power over me. I would stroke her, not roughly. It would be absurd to disturb so much attraction.'

'I'm not . . .'

His finger pressed on her lips. 'I would place a finger there, as a child quietens a loved one, then gently pass a finger along her lips. . . .'

His mouth descended to hers, quickly moved away, came to her cheek.

'The vital thing is for her to know how compelling she is, know her allure.'

Her eyes opened, filled with mistrust. 'People said I—'

He shook his head, and spoke with quiet fervour.

'People aren't here, Devina. *You* reign here. I want to see how much she means, so desirable, so fetching. To prove how irresistible she is, by drawing my hand down her lovely form, moving to her.'

He half closed his eyes in wonder.

'There can be nothing else, Devina. Thrilled by beauty, admiration that she engenders.'

'Bonn,' she said eventually, breathless, then asked, 'Bonn?'

'The sense of her woman's beauty envelops me. She would see that she fills my soul. It simply *is*. And where is the harm, when a woman is suddenly so precious to a man she is all he can know?'

'Bonn. I never meant to go through—'

'Her presence replaces the whole universe. The world vanishes away. I would take her down, softly reach for her sacred perfection. . . .'

'You went over time,' Rack told Bonn in annoyance. 'What was it, a benefit match?'

'It needed time.' Bonn was never impatient.

'Martina keeps on at me.' Rack always caught it, like Bonn was sacrosanct. 'Paid by the fucking minute. Piece work.'

'It needed time.' Nor exasperated. 'Please mind your talk, Rack.'

Disbelieving, Rack shook his head. 'You're hired to shag some tart stupid, and I've to watch *my* talk?' They crossed into traffic noise.

Bonn slowed and halted, gazed steadily at Rack until Rack felt uncomfortable. 'That's it exactly, Rack.'

'Sorry, sorry. Martina wants you, urgent.'

Rack never knew what the hell Bonn was on about. They resumed their walk to the Shot Pot. Bonn was the only person on earth could make Rack go red, except Mama, but she was as evil as Bonn was. . . . Rack's thought-words ran out. Maybe there was no opposite for his troublesome Catholic once-Italian mother. Seconds later his embarrassment had run its natural course.

'Hey, Bonn,' he said. 'Know how women learn to shag? It's a joke, from Jogger Hemming.'

'Please pay in the money for me, Rack.'

'She paid in *money*?' Rack was aghast.

'Yes. To Jay this time.'

'The silly bint never heard of credit cards? Martina oughter set a rule. Money's going. Y'know why, Bonn?' Rack was relieved. Bonn always forgave in two-three beats.

'No,' Bonn said resignedly. 'And get Grellie, please.'

Rack was delighted. He'd failed to pull Grellie himself, so reasoned that Bonn should dick Grellie, home use. Going without a bird crippled a bloke. Bonn slipped Rack Devina's money.

'Only for a chat, Rack. See you at the Granadee.'

'Shag Grellie, Bonn,' Rack said seriously. 'She'd do you proud. Know what happens when a bloke goes without a bird? His skin turns colour. Know why?'

'Go now, Rack.'

Bonn turned through the bus-station gardens. Five minutes of Rack's wild talk, he was exhausted. Grellie was watching him from her position by the football stadium's shuttle bus. He quickened his pace. Martina was dynamite on punctuality.

3

Upper – a female who hires a male for one episode of sex.

CLARE DROVE SOUTH ahead of the city rush, holding the Humber aloof from the traffic's jousting, the duck-and-drive churning races with the huge slab-sided pantechnicons with their menacing rainspitting wheels. Today's lesson was, you didn't need to rush down a motorway to kill.

The accident had begun innocuously enough, from what little she remembered. That poor businessman – had she seen him alight? – crushed in an instant between the taxi and the van. Police had taken statements, made arrangements for her to clean up in a nearby hotel, though her hands still felt tacky and blood-soiled on the steering wheel. The victim hadn't stood a chance. Firmer images eluded her.

A Ford crowded her. She sighed, gave way. A young male driver roared past, rejoicing. She felt in a fret, something nagging and she didn't know what. Young males died in and killed with cars, a steady statistic. Which made her recall the kneeling figure so peremptorily dismissed by that policeman's 'Shift, you. Sod off,' when everybody else was allowed to remain, talk silliness, give witness. Except that one. Why?

The traffic loosened, flowing steadier. She kept pace, signs white on green instead of the motorway blue.

Her image clarified as she drove. The young man, kneeling, had looked up. Pale, slim but not too slim, brown hair a thatch over blue eyes, his clothes nondescript but not quite, hands bloody. Was he talking, possibly giving reassurance, the meaningless ritual of the would-be helper? Not handsome, not ugly, though why should she even classify so? Wasn't it sexist or something, these days?

Another thing. He had gone without demur. He had expected dismissal. She ought to have asked was the youth a pickpocket, ghoulishly robbing a victim. She abandoned the problem.

Clifford would be home by now, tapping finance details into his latest computer. Keeping abreast of technology, in he would come, with, 'Clare! Come and see! I got a twenty-nine-per-cent reduction!' Then would follow an incomprehensible hour while he extolled silicon-microchip gigabytes. Medicine used the blessed things, of course, but why extol their inert innards?

She tried to drift left for the A6, a racecourse. She blessed her episcopal trundling saloon car, of which Clifford was so proud. Its maintenance cost a fortune, but he justified it. Teenage joyriders would never steal a tardy, elderly motor. Traceable, its maroon colour unmistakable.

And other motorists did make allowances. She abused her status, of course. A woman driver could always gain concessions, making irate men grin their what's-the-use by flinging her hair about in exasperation. Her car phone rang. She pulled into a layby. The locum bank. It was the same girl who'd conned her about charming Dr Therle Bettany's locum earlier.

'Are you available to do a locum at Breightmet, Dr Burtonall?'

'I'm sorry, but I can't manage.'

Clare's anger evaporated. She clicked off, judged the traffic for re-entry. Let them whistle, find some other doctor. She'd done two days out of the last four. Enough. Her always-on, never-off, period at Farne was over. She was married now, 'got a life', in the phrase currently making the rounds.

Fifteen minutes, she was home.

The Ashdun Road house was not quite grand. Six windows, two bayed, set off the front door, some stonework about but no ugly soffits to the windows, thank heavens. No awnings or external blinds – she'd hated those at Farne's scrimpy little surgery.

Clifford's newish saloon car was parked. The house had been Clifford's when they married two years before, she the interloping wife. His mother was still sceptical.

She drove the Humber in, garaged it with a cosy sense of relief. No more today, that accident the last straw, poor man. She gathered her case and handbag to take in. Her useless attendance at the scene meant paperwork, reports, giving professional witness at the coroner's inquest.

'Hello, Mrs Kinsale.'

'Hello, doctor. Mr Burtonall is already home.'

The housekeeper was capable, smiley, always in the pinafore. It looked a grannie's hand-me-down, blue-black with dimming orange flowers. She too had come with the marriage. Clifford's family menial, who would wear the same apron all her life, proving stolidity, here long before Clare upset the routine. You needn't count the silver teaspoons after Mrs Kinsale had done her day. Always that distancing 'doctor', for Clare.

'Thank you, Mrs Kinsale. Could we have tea now, please? I'm gasping.'

'You must be! Mr Burtonall has one of his engines going.'

Clare inspected the mail on the hall stand. Two letters, one from the Chief Medical Officer in outer space. Probably about the side effects of hypotensive drugs, the consistency needed to define abreactions. She felt a disgraceful twinge of relief, at being a locum doctor of no fixed medical abode. Administration was still there, but responsibility was lighter.

Clare had space now. No clothes in the hall except sudden weather-changers, raincoats, plastickery, umbrellas. Really heavy wear, like hoods, wellingtons, was kept by the side door for garden forays. This had been her first edict, and Clifford, with a reluctant Mrs Kinsale, had obliged. A home's orthodoxy made easy.

She showered and felt better. Separate changing rooms were a feature of this house – were they a constant of Edwardian design? They made love, no longer with the same pallyness of newlyweds, but with satisfaction. So far they hadn't had any of those sniping rows that passed for marital exchanges. God, how some couples ever even got together!

Before the dressing-table mirror, Clare inspected today's damage, and set to work with moisturiser. Surgeries were all so dreadfully overheated.

She remembered a middle-aged couple at a Walkden day surgery. Each demanded her support against the other. She had listened, appalled, an impotent referee, as they'd decried, accused, harangued. When she'd finally got rid of them, the unconcerned receptionist blithely told her that the couple always did that, came to brawl before an impartial listener, and invariably left blaming whatever doctor they'd seen. 'They'll be back in a fortnight,' Clare had learned, 'just the same.'

People mystified Clare. She remembered that police constable's curt dismissal of the kneeling youth, who'd only been trying to help – hadn't he? Maybe everyone had some little mad core that kept them going in a malevolent world.

Mrs Kinsale called that tea was ready. What was Clifford's miniature lunacy? He had none, except perhaps his obsession with finance. She examined her reflection. She looked tired. Accidents were an ordeal. Skimping, she managed to be downstairs before Mrs Kinsale called a second time.

'Clare.'

Clifford came to her smiling, kissed her in greeting. On the rear lawn a morello-cherry tree had sadly gone wrong at the roots. He'd had a high old time making bonfires, for days coming in stinking of smoke. He was so natural. In fact, it was his easy manner that had appealed at first, that and his tousled handsomeness. They had met at a medical fund-raiser – bitter white wine and inedible biscuits – at which she'd been astonished to learn that this boyish looker was the principal benefactor. He had visited the paediatric unit where Clare was a locum the week after. Matters then took their course, with Clifford's humour eliminating every doubt and obstacle.

Everything about the house was familiar to him. This chair his sister Josephine tried to set on fire aged six; over there he'd failed to espalier plum trees sent by cousins in Hertfordshire. Clare was still learning. Did an incoming wife make changes to have less to catch up on?

'Planning the garden, darling?'

'Just thinking what a shame February is.'

'February? But Easter's come and gone.'

'February lingers, like a bad taste.'

Clifford had lived in Italy two or three years before she had met him. He mentioned Florence, Rome, Venice, but only as a duty, get the reminiscence over with. Her attempt to decide a Tuscany holiday had failed abysmally, though the Norwegian cruise a year after their Gibraltar honeymoon, with a Greek afterthought, had been successful. Clifford was pleasing company. They were both professional people who matched well, thank you. She could talk to him.

She told Clifford about the accident, not giving details that might disturb. Mrs Kinsale brought in the tea tray, started clinking saucers. There was a ration of biscuits, a practice Clare detested. The woman would never bring in the biscuit barrel, but laid out two Peak Freans apiece – no more, never less. Endlessly told about this, Mrs Kinsale only laughed, 'Oh, I'll forget my head next!' and did the same tomorrow. Clare hadn't decided if it was mere forgetfulness.

'What happened in February?' Clare asked.

Clifford went to the window, a small surprise.

'Those visitors. Endless. First Josephine and hers, then those others. Don't you remember? The Year of the Rat, we had the Month of the Visitor.'

'So we did.' Clare poured. Stingy Mrs Kinsale had doled out miniature creams. It *was* a campaign. 'Some road contract?'

He sat opposite, took the tea. 'I felt like a chef whose food went wrong.'

Clare sipped, decided that it was time the whole suite was re-covered. It would be costly, but the only problem would be finding a good upholsterer.

'Nothing sporting, then?'

It was a jibe, and he smiled, remembering her gratification that he was a wholesome bachelor, not a divorcé, when they'd met. His interests were swimming, and watching sport. He went to the races, though he'd abandoned York after a calamitous hotel booking. He gardened, more to fume about old Stan than take an active part.

'I don't like you lingering in February, Clifford. You should be here.'

'I am, I am.' He talked with less than his usual enthusiasm about the day. She knew so few of his staff, but their professions ran on separate lines.

February? Vaguely, she recalled his secluded hour-long calls. He hadn't slept for several nights. Clifford always had simultaneous contracts on the go. She'd once studied under a chief – the consultant doctor heading a 'firm' of junior doctors – who drifted round his wards with seeming indifference. Later, he would accurately summarise every patient's condition, treatment, laboratory investigations, in brilliant detail. But he had to stick to the order in which he had examined the cases. Deflect him, and he lost it. It was a fluke of mind. As a crystal handles light, so some minds treat facts. Clifford's mercantile mind must be like that.

She felt disturbed this evening, something wrong that she couldn't fathom. Perhaps she ought not to have mentioned the accident. Medical events did make him squeamish. Not that she gave names or locations. Reticence came with the diplomas, the endless medical training.

'Is it the central development?'

He started on about it without preamble, proving to Clare's relief it was that all along.

'The notion's fine,' he said. 'A central lake, connections with the ship canal, bridges, shopping malls, big medicine

– sorry about the pun. The fringes of a thing are always the worst.'

She knew he loved abstracts of an enterprise, hated the essentials.

'They can be settled, though, can't they?'

His problems were all one pattern, she now knew. First, he excitedly showed her plans, maps, charts of some project. Then came doubt, and finally this phase of self-analysis, even gloom, and not a sod turned or a brick yet laid. The city's central redevelopment was unavoidably political.

'Will it matter if you don't get the consultancy?'

'Oh, we'll get it, no doubt of that.' He seemed surprised by her question. 'It's just the bits that go along with it.'

They separated with banter. It was warming, despite Clifford's worry. Clare went to see Mrs Kinsale off, and returned upstairs. Once, she had conducted a series of intelligence tests on a little boy. Simple multiple choice, tick one of the three answers. The boy was ten years old. His teachers knew he was bright, yet he failed every time. Sure enough, he got every one of Clare's questions wrong. Zero. Nil. Even a gorilla would get at least one-third correct, simple random chance. The little boy was deliberately failing so he could stay with his family. They'd intended to send him to boarding school.

'The problem was,' she remembered telling Clifford the punch-line, 'once they realised, they sent him off to boarding school anyway. I almost cried.'

'Why were you so upset?'

'Well, it just shows,' Clare had explained lamely. 'I blew the gaff. I felt a traitor.' Too much honesty could damage families, marriage, even a conversation.

She changed into gardening clothes. A tweed skirt, a

thick cardigan from her Farne Island days that she was too sentimental to throw out.

The garden was becoming a shared interest. Those disastrous herbaceous borders. Lady's-mantle was a godsend. Daphne, candytuft, scabious (perhaps a dark-crimson variety), penstemons – she'd had a rather sour relationship with those, so they were non-starters – and the usual Solomon's seal. She had decided this year to go for pinks and reds, really make a show. Safe plants – wallflowers, pansies – were utter cowardice. Happy, she decided to abandon cowardice in everything, including the slight matter of Clifford's parents and his sister Josephine.

Her own parents were great ones for duty and 'keeping going'. Duties, though, were controlled by others. That was the rub. Clifford's parents were safely – or not so safely – in Altrincham, in visitor range, and held strong views on reproduction. Meaning it was time she started a family. Clifford's mother emitted this, as Farne's lighthouse had beamed its signal.

What were Clifford's views, though? From her window she saw him by the hedge. Worthy professional or not, a new wife was always under test. Within days friends called, sweetly implying the wrong distribution of her furniture, nowhere to put a cup down. It was the wife's job to dispose, and get the blame for housekeeping faults. At the time she'd been working a seventy-hour week. Soon, Evadne and Arthur, Clifford's parents ('Now, we positively do not mind. Use first names, my dear!'), would come asking again about offspring with that urbane enmity of in-laws.

'What about schools?' Clare asked no one.

A stupid thing to blurt out. Before schooling you had to produce a child.

She thought she heard a noise downstairs and paused to listen. Nothing.

Words were silly games, and her a career woman. Those tiresome antenatal classes, being weighed, urine for albumen, and the rest, erythrocyte sedimental rates every two seconds, the whole Rhesus business – though wisely she'd been born O Rhesus positive, no problems there until proved otherwise.

Another noise?

'Clifford?' she called.

No answer. A card falling off a shelf, or perhaps the wind. Except there were no cards on the mantelpiece. Clifford was still out there in the garden, doing something with a hoe.

The sound had come from inside. Had Mrs Kinsale come back for something?

'Mrs Kinsale?' Clare listened.

The evening was drawing in, not yet the vigorous even-tide of summer. She only minded autumn's remorseless heel-dragging into cold winter.

'Darling?' A footfall. Downstairs, definitely downstairs.

She rose, went to the window, wanting signs of normality. Clifford was still at it. Four people waited by the bus stop opposite. The distant church with the blackish tower where she went to evensong of a Sunday. She watched. Nobody on the gravel drive.

Clifford wasn't much of a gardener in truth, a snip-and-tuck clipper. He turned to inspect some japonica leaves, his campaign against parasites –

And something downstairs went over with a small thud. They had no cat.

Mrs Kinsale had clearly returned. Clare slowly went down the stairs, giving whoever it was time to escape. She called out Clifford's name, the doubter's is-that-you. The hall was empty.

On the hall stand was a briefcase. It had not been there when she'd gone upstairs. It was scratched, as if it had been dragged, whitish scags along the dark-brown leather. Clifford was in the garden. Therefore?

'Hello?' she called out. Absurd to feel her heart banging so, with people at the bus stop, occasional cars, her husband so near.

The kitchen door led out into the small herb garden. A field was visible over her feeble soft fruit canes, nothing doing this time of year. That door now stood ajar. A man's head showed briefly at the field's edge, ducked out of sight. A motorbike sounded, dopplered away to nothing.

'Who is there, please?' she called, querulous and frightened.

She walked quickly out of the front door and round into the garden. There was no gate, just an ornamental trellis that must go when she finally got up enough courage to confront Evadne. Old Stan would also have to be argued down and his sabotage quelled.

'Clifford?'

Her husband straightened, holding some spray gadget. 'Catastrophe here, darling,' he said. 'Bloody greenfly shouldn't be out so early.'

'Were you in the house just now?' He couldn't possibly have been.

He questioned her with a brief look, dismissed the problem. 'What do you reckon? I didn't think they went for quinces, greenfly. The old gardener used Jeyes Fluid, tablespoon to a quart of water. Swore by the stuff.'

'I thought I heard somebody. You weren't expecting a

courier or anything? There's a briefcase on the hall stand. I didn't hear anybody ring.'

'Briefcase?' It brought him up short.

'I heard somebody come in. At least I thought I did.'

'Perhaps Newton stopped by.'

'Wouldn't he have rung the bell or something?'

Clifford smiled, shrugged. 'Maybe he sent a courier, those motorbike lads who pretend they're in the Tourist Trophy.'

'I suppose that was it.' No relief came.

'Did you leave it where it was, darling?' He was a little too casual.

'The briefcase? Yes.'

'Let's go in.' He took her arm. 'It's getting chilly.'

It wasn't as cold as all that, but Clare went along. The briefcase was still there, its new pale marks suggestive of having skittered on some rough surface.

'Better take a look, I suppose,' Clifford said lightly, 'see what rubbish Newton's letting me in for.'

Clare, restless, felt compelled to suggest something different.

'I wondered if we could walk to the old church after supper,' she offered, out of the blue. 'Mr Torrance practises organ pieces until nineish.'

To her disappointment Clifford declined. 'I ought to give this a glance, seeing Newton went to all the bother of sending it over.'

Moments ago in the garden a total surprise, yet now he knew all about this special delivery from Newton. And didn't they come in bags? They always had before, as did her own medical manuscripts. This damaged briefcase was uncovered.

'I'll not go on my own,' she decided. 'It's rather a walk from Old Seldon across the fields.'

She was preparing supper when she realised her self-trickery. The dead man had somehow seemed familiar, crushed as he was. Not merely the situation – accident, frantic observers, police, the gore, her despairing resignation that she could do nothing.

It was him, the fatality. She should remember him. In life, he'd been sweating and uncomfortable. But when and where? February came to mind, a printed word on some invitation, ornate engraving on a cream-coloured card.

Supper would have to be simpler than she had planned, commonplace, nothing more than a background to a pretended conversation. That would give her time to think, make some good guesses about the killed man.

Tomorrow, first thing, she would buy newspapers. At the hospital, she would call on the pathologist before he got round to the autopsy.

4

Key – a goer who controls a group of goers, usually not more than three in number.

THE SNOOKER HALL was a hundred yards down a side street off Victoria Square, its tables islets of green-shaded lights in a sequence of cones. To Bonn, snooker players were somnolents moving with the reverence of devoted acolytes. No nights, no days, mere zones of timelessness. Osmund was playing patience.

'Red six, black seven, Osmund,' Bonn said.

'I see it.' The old man never cheated, maddening everyone.

A row broke out, coloured Moss Side lads riled at someone playing for baulk. Canno howled in a phoney Kingston, Jamaica, tone Bonn liked, 'We gotta *flower*, man, yo playin' lak ee bamba claat.'

Someone took a swing. Two ponchos – the only swingers allowed and thrilled to prove it – moved in. They had pride, reputations to keep. Bonn wanted to reach Martina, but watched the riot quelled.

'Know what's done for yon game, Bonn?' Osmund asked. 'Telly.'

Osmund believed in Bonn, right from the day he'd walked in out of the rain and stood waiting for someone to ask what. Osmund kept playing, black ten on a red jack, in his glass booth. Bonn thought the snooker hall quite beautiful, an enchantment that painters should be painting instead of three-minute blotch-and-liners. He never said this.

Bonn was in awe of brawls. Tooth, the player who wasn't fighting, leant on his cue. His opponent was folded over holding his belly. The ponchos wandered, affably cuffing resisters insensible, moving with grand pride, hulks held in suits by stretched stitches. Two minutes, Bonn'd see Martina.

Osmund was old. Bald, skeletal, waistcoated, watch chain, sleeves cufflinked, black shoes highly polished of a morning. He'd worked at a loom back when the mills had thrived, hived, and finally dived in cotton.

'Look how they dress theirselves,' he said. 'Ponces.' And was immediately contrite. 'Sorry, Bonn. Snooker on telly, though, what d'you see? Fine damask, bishop sleeves, Jap silk, hair like tarts.'

The racket was over, the ponchos shyly lumbering off, conversations starting, what was the score, my turn on the yellow wernit, moaning about Oldham tonight.

'Martina sent for me, Osmund.'

The old man couldn't stop a grumble. 'Davis – greatest ever – bought the world cup with his own money, won it himself year after year. People forget that, Bonn.'

People don't even know it, Bonn thought sadly. The players resumed. He watched Fortress, erstwhile aggressor miraculously recovered to jauntiness, line up on the black, trying to screw into baulk for an easy red. Fortress missed by a mile. Osmund chuckled.

'See, Bonn? Useless. Aye, Martina's already seen Rack.'

Martina astonished Bonn. Osmund pressed something. The door, overtly a coat rack holding the same clothes month and month about, slid back. Clever, except it opened with a screeching melody, the noisiest secret door on earth. Bonn often thought to say something. Osmund once allowed Bonn to press the button, but the clothes rack hadn't budged. Maybe lean over it worked okay, sit upright it didn't, something like that?

Bonn stepped inside the little space. He read the grubby Safety First notice on the wall as the door squealed shut. *In the event of fire . . .* Count five, then the side opened, right-angle turn into the world's smallest corridor. A door swung.

'Is this really necessary? Black Hand Gang of the Lower Fourth?'

'It's as I like it, Bonn.'

Martina was beautiful, and lame. He tried not to be put out by her spectacular smile. She sat at a desk, clearly from a Macclesfield government-surplus auction, four quid top weight and your own transport.

Worse, the room was on the kilter, every plane skewed. Existentialist? Not an honest rectangle there. On her desk a small tin filing cabinet, a phone, a picture of her dad, Posser. Bonn liked Posser.

'When will you get a proper office?'

'Mind your own business.' Martina smiled, worth waiting for, dimples, lovely colour. Anyone else, Bonn would have wondered what she was doing in the business. He didn't even know where she went for meals.

Her silence became a prompt. 'The councillor's wife from the Wirral?'

'Yes. The complaint.'

'I've explained.' Martina was always fair, and trusted Bonn's account.

'Now, she wants to book you again. How do you feel?'

'Feelings don't come into it, Martina.' Her dad, Posser, established the rules when he'd started the syndicate yonks since. Now Bonn said it as doggerel.

Martina wafted his words away with a shake of her glinting hair. 'Take your time with her.'

'Very well.'

Martina didn't pause. Any of her other goers would have said yes or okay, right, sure. She looked up from her one sheet of paper, forever blank. Martina made no notes, her sharpened pencil, he'd swear, unused since he'd joined. There was nowhere to sit, never anything in the wastepaper basket, Martina's empire a sham from which she might do a moonlight flit leaving no trace.

'How long have you been with us, Bonn?'

She knew, but he answered. It was her game. 'Three months.'

No way she could forget that interview at the Rum Romeo in Tibb Street, him lost and sweating, Martina unsmiling, Posser asking questions to gauge Bonn's possible usefulness to Pleases Agency, Inc, Martina's syndicate.

'Have you thought up anything new?' she asked.

'The logo? No. It's daft making it an acronym. Why not leave it?'

The best so far was Personal Leisure Enhancement And Satisfying Ease Service. Grellie said it was silly, Pleases Agency, Inc, being enough for anyone with half a brain.

'It isn't as if we'll neon it on the Bolton-to-Macclesfield, is it?'

She smiled, and he saw it had been her lead-in to his summons.

'I'm moving you, Bonn.'

He was unperturbed. It wouldn't be Sheffield, Birmingham. It'd have to be local. She read him.

'Not as in distance, Bonn. Promotion. You've made key from midnight.' He shifted one foot to the other in question, and she answered, 'Complete today's goes. You've done that Devina?'

'I have one more client.'

'Your pay doubles. You can stay a regular goer, or go piecemeal.'

In the trade's terminology, one session with a client lady was a go, Bonn was a goer. A key was the head of a 'firm' of three goers. It meant money, influence, power on the street. He drew breath, but she was quicker.

'You also get a weekly one-bonus dollop direct from syndicate funds, weekly averaged. Draw from the Rum Romco's till.'

Best be frank. He had doubts about Martina's casino. He got ready. 'I don't like that, Martina.'

'Don't like what? Key, money, the bonus grossed out?'

He said bluntly, 'Leaving with a wadge is trouble.'

Martina was annoyed at this quibble. 'No cheques, no parcels you didn't come in with, Bonn?'

'That's elementary,' he said politely, 'but word spreads.'

'You're worried how I'm to pay you, right? You win it in the casino. Choose your game. Roulette, cards, horses, cricket.' She spoke the last dryly. Astonishing that cricket, new to the Romeo casino, had outstripped every non-table take. It was weird. Bonn sensed that Martina knew something was wrong.

'Every week, like Friday's payday?'

She let her pleasure show, Bonn still an innocent. She adjusted herself on her chair. Did her crippled leg get sore, he wondered, in this dead-and-alive hole? He never knew how long she stayed here. Five minutes? Half a day?

'It has drawbacks, Bonn, but I never use a cran.'

A cran would be unwise – a lockup garage, hole in some wall, the payee snooping up for his illicit dosh. The whole city would know, slope along for a laugh to see the lurk's face when he discovered it nicked.

'An intermediary?' he suggested, saw her face darken.

'Who? Osmund's out. I won't have Rack doing that sort of thing – he's too valuable. Grellie's got her work cut out running the street girls.'

'One of the crowd?' The syndicate owned the three Babylon game parlours, a score of low-graders with five section bosses in each.

Martina was unsure, as convincing a negative as he would ever get. 'They're reliable. Is default likely?'

'Not from thievery. Forgetting's different, especially after some dicey match.' He chanced his arm. 'You?'

She eyed him in astonishment. 'Are you serious?'

'Why not?'

'That will do, Bonn.' His mother used to say that after he cheeked her, next time a clobbering. 'Not me, nor Posser.'

He gave in. 'Then it's the Romeo till girl, but erratic.'

'I agree. The sums are not inconsiderable, after all. Weekly?'

'At good intervals,' he said. 'Ring the changes. Use bikers, switch dates.'

'This must come out as my suggestion, Bonn,' she warned.

Martina's syndicate had several firms, with four goers in each, Bonn's now the ninth. They both waited, one question to be settled, in his court.

'You choose three for your firm, Bonn.'

'I won't have Penner or Frankie or Blakeston.'

She was surprised. 'Not Penner? I'd pencilled him in.'

But not on her blank sheet, he observed laconically. 'He's as good as . . . most.'

As good as you, Bonn, she'd almost said. Bonn let nothing show. There was rivalry in the goer game. He'd once seen Penner drunk, yapping his head off in the Bottom Quarter. Bonn would have enough problems without Penner's big mouth, drunk or sober.

'Not Penner, please.'

She was taken aback, but it didn't slow her. 'Galahad and Lancelot?'

'Is it take or leave?' He didn't exactly jump at the names.

'Galahad's beautiful!' she exclaimed. 'Every woman's dream.'

'Of a goer, aye.' Bonn didn't make too much of opposing Galahad. It would call his promotion into question. Galahad was a body builder, Lancelot your effete ballroom dancer. Both had a following, no problem, but he was uneasy.

'Recruit as you like, but no rival outfits.'

Everything was settled. She nodded dismissal. He wondered when, if, Martina herself ever . . .

'You've got tomorrow, until four o'clock, Bonn.'

'Very well.' Her business after all, in more ways than tax returns knew.

He left the snooker hall, on the way out telling Osmund he wanted Rack soonest. He hadn't gone a furlong before Rack fell in beside him, grinning.

'Key man, eh, Bonn?' He did a spin. 'Doing auditions? Who?'

'Please stop, Rack.' Rack instantly mimed an exaggeratedly staid walk, hands behind his back like a queen's consort. 'Galahad, Lancelot, we suss out first. Walk properly, please.'

Rack obeyed. Anyone but Bonn would have said cut it out or jack that in. From Bonn you got walk properly please.

'Galahad's pumping iron. Lancelot's having dancing shoes fitted.'

Bonn paused at the newsvendor's. Police kept warning Fat George about his billboards' obstructing the pavement. Bonn bought a paper. Rack was incredulous.

'You *paid*,' he accused. 'The fucking *Evening News*.'

'Mmmh.' Bonn read, slowing, Rack steering him among the pedestrians.

'You listening? Martina *owns* Fat George, you *pay* him for a paper?'

'That accident, Rack. He died.' Bonn gave Rack the paper. He only glanced at the victim's photo. They walked on. 'Have you seen him before?'

'No.' Rack dug Bonn's arm. 'Thought you wanted to see Grellie?'

'Thank you. But I must get my firm. Do please apologise to Grellie.' He smiled. 'Better do as Martina says.'

It was the nearest Bonn had ever come to a joke, Martina's word being harder than law.

'Galahad'll be at the Troc tomorrow.'

One day, Bonn vowed, he would ask Rack how he knew everything.

The news had a curiously dulling effect. Bonn went for a coffee in the Butty Bar. It was only a wedge of converted warehouse in Victoria Square, an afterthought, some pre-occupied Victorian merchant absently squaring one last circle. It faced the bus station, which was why Bonn liked it.

A few people nodded to him as he entered. Crump the racing tipster gave him half a smile. Packster, leader of a courier squadron, didn't look across, but his black leather swaggered as he passed Bonn. The counter girls whispered. Word was about. They must share Rack's osmosis trick for news.

'You're a celebrity, Bonn.' Zen slid into the seat opposite, accepted the coffee one of the girls hurried over unasked. 'Word spreads like a moor fire.'

Zen had been a second-hand car salesman, but built up such a lucrative sideline among women customers that it had come to the attention of Posser. Within two weeks the young entrepreneur was a goer. One year to the day, Zen made key, with a firm of four goers, and never looked back.

A pleasant round-faced bloke with brilliant teeth, Zen, the ideal goer, had to slog to keep his pludges under control. Bonn got the dazzling grin.

'Thank you. It was unexpected.'

Zen leant forward. 'A tip, Bonn. Get Evelyn to do your savings. She's got National Savings off pat, index-linked, flat-raters. And unit trusts. Every month she gives you a printout. Multo money from now on.'

'Thank you, Zen.'

'Another tip. Don't choose your goers for flash. Them kinky buggers down Blenheim Street are more trouble than what they're worth. They look good, but you're into serious psychotherapy.'

'I'll bear it in mind.'

Zen had more to say. 'There's talk of two goers getting involved. Irons, subbos.' Meaning guns and drugs. 'You'll hear all sorts, Bonn. But none of them's my goers. If I hear any mother about your goers, I'll tell you within minutes, okay?'

Bonn nodded thanks. It was a kind offer, to pass on solid news.

'It's good of you, Zen.'

The other sipped his coffee, grimaced, made a Latin gesture of helpless appeal. A counter girl immediately flew across with a fresh cup.

'Don't underestimate my selfishness, Bonn.' Zen opened his palms, his old selling manner. 'See that lass, swapped my coffee? She did it fast, sure, but she smiled at you. It's the difference, Derby winner and any other thoroughbred.' He grinned, shrugged away the admission. 'I've common sense, youth, I like the birds, do a decent turn for Martina's syndicate. And I'm not daft. Best living I'll ever have.' He laughed, shaking his head in disbelief. 'You're supposed to say "But . . .?" with a knowing air, Bonn.'

'Am I?' Bonn considered this, complied. 'Very well. But . . .?'

'I don't *believe* you, Bonn. It's like you're just out of the egg. Other times you're . . .' He gave up before Bonn's curious stare, allowed three school lads to move past on their way to the caff's game machines.

'I hope I don't give offence, Zen.'

'You fucking wear me out, y'know?' Zen eyed the ceiling in mute appeal, resumed. 'What I'm saying is, there's only one of us who's within a light-year of getting further. And that's you. See the lads knocking about the square? They'd give anything to become a goer, money, all the crumpet they could want.'

'I do know we are privileged, Zen.'

'There isn't a goer in the kingdom wouldn't give his teeth for promotion to key.' Zen leant back. 'But you're the only one who'll make the syndicate.'

'This is kind of you, Zen. But you are addressing one who doesn't exactly know what the syndicate is. Or who.'

The other became serious. 'Remember your first day as

a goer? There was me with Grellie, waiting to say hello at the Shot Pot?'

'Yes.' Bonn smiled. He felt shy, remembering.

'Three months back. Grellie'd never met you. Know what? I've never told you this before. She groaned out loud. I asked what's up. She didn't say a word.' Zen candidly inspected Bonn. 'You're not handsome, average mark.'

'But . . .?'

Zen grinned at his hands. 'Tooshay, Bonn. It's there, like you'd been here before, done it all. Know what Grellie told me later?' Zen tapped the table gently. 'She said, "It's like I already know him." It's the bit a woman can't buy, Bonn.'

Bonn waited. 'I don't understand, Zen.'

'Nor do I,' Zen said, wry. 'But hang on to it, Bonn.'

Bonn was lost. 'Thank you for your advice, Zen. I shall see Evelyn.'

'Good luck choosing your goers.' Zen stood a moment, went for it. 'Is it true Martina's marked two of your cards?'

'Yes.' Zen must already know, Galahad and Lancelot.

'Didn't you squawk?' Zen was curious, wanting detail. 'I've never known it before. But not straight off.'

'To protest is not my privilege, Zen. Thank you for stopping by.'

Zen laughed, and went shaking his head, giving a wave, the girls smiling at him. Bonn suspected that Zen found his manner quaint. He thought *But . . .?* again and went to change. He had another go soon, his very first after being made key. He felt unable to meet the girls' eyes as he went among the tables, just called a quiet 'Thank you.' They stared after him, then bent to whisper.

*

Parents, Rack knew from a lifetime's experience of one, were a pain. Papa had taken off the instant Rack showed.

The one was Mama.

You wouldn't look twice at her in Old Seldon market, her black shoes, her cane straw hat's Ping-Pong hat pins, just write her off as some old git. But you noticed her eyes, and thought, Whoops, better not get in the way of *that* when it's moving. Close to, Mama was straight out of some old black-and-white movie of Marshall Tito with maybe Trevor Howard, a British major, looking down on an un-suspecting enemy column. Rack saw Mama as a partisan, the one that took your breath away. Compelling attention because she *knows* the .303 Lee Enfield bolt-action, carries it like a piccolo. He'd seen other folk take one look at Mama and go, Oops, don't jump *her* place in the queue.

Mama was Rack's Italian cross. He'd never been further than Southend. She had a personal line to Almighty God for the sole purpose of giving Rack earache, and had ears like a frigging bat.

He arrived at the old folks' flats where Mama lived. She was sitting stony-faced in her rocker, an Oriental potentate awaiting terms from redcoats while her tribes massed in the hills. Rack said hello. She punished him with silence.

Rack told her how holy he'd been this week.

' . . . sent money to the Saint Don Bosco, Mama. You know, Pendleton?'

'Uncle Gianni,' she said.

Rack halted. Who the fuck? Mama's words were shellfire. You had to guess the direction.

'Oh, Uncle Gianni!' Why didn't he have a load of sisters, help him survive Mama? 'I can't keep track.'

He'd conned her that he was a computer wizard at ICI, Runcorn. She blamed him for not being married. She could insult a daughter-in-law, for breeding children to row with him about.

'What does he want?'

'Come from Calabria to say hello.'

Mama proved how the Inquisition pulled it off. Deadening repetitions, then the switch. You agree to anything so they'll shut the fuck up. Rack never asked much of Il Signore up there on his almighty cloud, except maybe pull the frigging plug out of this Calabria and let these uncles glug into the ocean.

'Your toys too important to help Uncle Gianni, spit in his face?'

Christ, was this a yes or no? Rack'd tried to teach her to talk proper when he was five. Another winner. This Goldoni must be yet another scrounger from Back 'Ome. Like the others, he'd be smart-suited, handmade shoes, wanting free lodging, somehow too poor to buy bog paper.

He plunged into gloom. He promised, and Mama intoned reproaches. Martina would never give him time off. Even if she did, it would drive Bonn into one of his forgiving silences. Which would nark old Osmund, who never wanted Bonn riled. Which would infuriate Martina, because she was secretly crazy for Bonn. Which would ruffle the lads, because Bonn was made key now and they wanted to be among Bonn's new goers, because Bonn had that magic pull that guaranteed superlative life here on earth and, who knew, maybe life ever after. Which would piss off Posser, Martina's poorly dad, who hadn't to be narked at any price. Which would send Grellie spare, because she'd split for Bonn, and the girl street stringers'd go berserk, because God in His infinite wisdom sent the girls nuclear when the smooth-running prostitution at the railway station got ballsed up. And it would all be Rack's fault for not finding this Uncle Gianni a free living.

He started damage limitation.

'Holly Mass, Mama.' He smiled. Her lips stayed welded. He'd heard that Italian daughters were shit hot at quelling maternal friendly fire. 'I'll take him to church this Sunday.' He let that sink in. 'Unless he goes with friends?' Fat chance. The chiselling bastard would want a free car. Mama stared. 'He want a car, Mama? On the firm?'

A nod. Mama knew about milking organisations. Her wayward son was learning responsibility.

'Good boy. Your belov' papa . . .'

She started to weep. Rack never had a beloved papa. He'd ask Grellie, maybe Jenny, if mama tyranny was everywhere, sonhood a perennial crucifix. He really wanted to ask Bonn, but you didn't ask things. Questions wounded him, and not even Martina did that.

'And a free flat, Mama.' He was desperate to hit the vicious street, where it was safe. He left in abject misery.

5

BRADSHAWGATE WAS NO longer a city gate. Now it was a mere triangular recess where children played tap footer with a frayed ball. Unemployed men hung about. On clement days elderly women went through to the supermarts. Here Posser observed the city, strolling his four laps.

Northern unemployed men lean on walls, Posser noted, and drink bottles of sour clag. They were doubly deprived, by wage and booze – the latter the cheapest source of calories. He'd had his spell of both. Now it was the vitamin E, obeying the doctor's stern admonition, and sickening cod-liver-oil capsules. And the precious TNT, little white jobs, for the chest pain.

He liked Bradshawgate. He'd been born here, only because nobody would look at a house numbered 13. He squinted, breathless on a bench facing his old home. A lawyer's office now, for God's sake, knocked into one with Mrs Mason's, the Townsons', the whole run of 15, 17, 19, and 21. Travel agents gaudied up the corner. A council hut stood where Maggie's shop used to be, for council workmen to smoke fags and play pontoon. They didn't bring their lunch baggins. Now they had a pub session. Traffic roared round the main square.

'Dad?'

Martina came and sat by. Posser had moved away to Rivington moors, raised her single-handed in a cottage overlooking Bowton. Eventually, affluence struck, a bolt from the blue. He'd moved back to Bradshawgate, appalled by the changes but determined. Him and the city, with their wonky hearts and all.

'Hello, love. You did it? Promoted Bonn?'

'Yes. He was taken aback.' She paused. 'I can't ever tell with Bonn.' She laughed openly at a little lad cheating, moving the ball slickly with his hand as he dribbled past. 'I wish I knew him, Dad.'

'We don't need to. We only need to guess right.'

She changed her approach. 'Promotion gives all that power.'

'Some are naturals, love. Worth their weight in gold.' Posser smiled on his beautiful but lame daughter, not liking her resentment. 'Women sense trust. They respond to him.'

With frank curiosity she inspected her father as he spoke on.

'When old Mrs Ainsworth died, I saw myself for what I was, a kept man, a *cicisbeo*, nothing more than a *damigello*, a "walker" in London cant. A Jemmy Jessamy. Ridiculed, a pub joke. You were still at school. It must have been hard on you, love.'

'You had a proper job! Mrs Ainsworth's estates, Dad!'

He patted her hand. 'Aye, the stables, rent-free cottage. And, when she'd passed away, her land and investments, God rest her loving soul.'

Martina watched him. He had never before admitted his feelings for the old lady. For her father to have such emotions seemed improper.

'Her family contested, frauded most of it!' Martina grew heated.

Posser wheezed, having a hard time breathing out. In was easy.

'This country has no law against general fraud, love, only specific. Settling for twenty-six per cent was wise, or we'd still be in court, lawyers worrying me into my grave, you unprovided for. No, love. Pragmatism's the game.'

More than pragmatism, though. Mildred Ainsworth had once lent Posser – lent as in *lent* him – for a single night to a sick friend. He'd consoled the lady, then returned bitter with accusations. It was the closest he'd come to leaving her. But Mildred's gratitude had been so touching, filled with compassion. The other lady had died not long after. It had taught him something new about humanity.

'Dad?' she asked, as if she'd just that minute arrived.

He leant forward, hands pressing down on the bench helping to lift his chest. 'I'm wondering about selling, love.'

She was startled. 'Selling *out*? Have we had an offer?'

'Not yet. I'm trying to out-guess time.' He grinned rue-fully. 'We've only muscle enough for local purposes. The city centre is being redeveloped – marinas, leisure com-plexes, theme parks, God knows what. They'd bring regiments to force the sale.'

'Can't we go on just as we are?' She seemed frightened.

'Not if heavy money moves in, love, no.' Posser tapped his chest for emphasis. 'Our syndicate's just you and me, when all's said and done. I know we talk as if there's a giant power in control. But our syndicate's an ailing bloke with his daughter, and a few willing scrappers.'

'We've expertise, Dad!' Martina was offended; her cheeks were red.

'Which they might want to use for a while.'

'And then we do what?'

He looked at her sadly. The afternoon light was starting to fade. Lights were on in the insurance offices.

'Me? Doesn't matter, love. You? Become respectable. Go where you wish, move in different circles.'

She tried to concentrate. Coming to meet him, she'd been so pleased. Now look. 'I'm scared when you talk like this, Dad.'

'I'm trying to plan ahead, that's all.' He looked askance. 'I started with two goers, set up the snooker-hall office. Bought freehold when I could, leased short when I couldn't. Took on Osmund.'

She had heard the story a hundred times. 'The five tough lads, arrangements with three hotels.'

Posser chuckled. 'I must say I guessed well. A standing start, but not as ramshackle as it might have been. And you did brilliantly, love.'

'Then what's new, Dad?'

'The city, love. Its decay is over. This is as bad as it'll get. She'll redevelop. Whoever's in the way'll get blammed. It'll be real hoods, money men, who'll make an offer.' He pulled a face. 'Oh, it'll be genteel enough – to start with. As long as we accept and leave.'

'We can refuse, and make a fight of it.'

'They'd laugh. Then get angry, and simply take everything. We're obsolete. Like the old films they made yonder.'

'The Granadee Studios?' Martina could just see where the huge fluorescent sign blinked night and day. She bridled. 'They use our services, Dad. Three uppers, regulars, not counting occasionals.'

Uppers being lady clients, Posser was not impressed. Martina smiled.

He caught her look. She'd been defiant and brave even when small. He'd been scarred by poverty, she never. Immunity from hunger allowed luxuries like freedom.

'I'd die before I'd be poor again, love. Nowadays, poverty's only putting your hand out for the dole, three pints a night instead of eight, smoking twenty, not thirty a day.' He took her hand. 'Face it. We're miniatures, collectable like some ornament.'

'You'll accept when the offer comes,' she said quietly, trying not to hurt.

'We'll have no choice. A foreigner's coming from the Continent.'

'Very well, Dad.'

Posser smiled. He spotted her new catchphrase. An indicator of a possible boyfriend? Very well, indeed.

'How's Angler doing?'

'Leading the pack. I'm pleased with him.'

But no change of breath, no sudden quickening, so it wasn't Angler. He said, idly, 'Wigan through and through him. He used to do pub imitations of Angelo Dundee, y'know, boxing promoter who cheated Henry Cooper.'

'Rack says he's fine.'

'Then they must be doing right.' Posser's hopes, he realised with a canny inward look, were on Bonn. It was time he brought them together to find their valency. Christ's sake, the village matchmaker at his age.

'We need another blower, Dad.'

That took him by surprise. 'Five, on one switchboard? That's a hell of a lot.'

She counted on her fingers, like homework from the convent school. 'Miss Janet does days, Miss Rose tea to midnight. Miss Merry and Miss Hope alternate days. I spell them, front at the snooker hall. It's too thin, Dad.'

He'd chosen them for their honesty, and their mellifluous voices could reassure at a hanging. They were tact personified, could reassure any lady client who was losing courage. Their judgment – when to call in Martina, somebody trying it on – was cast iron. They were paid a fantastic salary, with perks unknown to tax gatherers. Posser's latest perk was overseas holidays, two fortnights in one year. They lived rent-free, with investments. Now one more?

'The question is who to hire, love.'

Their one failure was a treacherous girl who had tried to set up her own service. Posser had sent Akker. She now languished in gaol on a three-year sentence for arson of a derelict mail-order warehouse in Stockport. Posser had been pleasantly surprised – Akker's perjuring witnesses had been so cheap. He'd kept Akker on ever since that success.

'When do you see Dr Winnwick?'

'Nine tomorrow.' Together they rose and walked haltingly from Bradshawgate towards Victoria Square. 'Let me know who Bonn chooses, eh?'

'I will. Sometimes I wonder if he's very bright.'

He knew better than argue. There was encouraging asperity in her voice.

Martina said without heat, taking his arm, 'He can't converse, as if he's some idiot boy scout.'

'Doubt he was ever in those, love.'

'How do you know?' Martina was too sharp.

'A guess. See you in an hour?'

'Right, Dad.' She stood at the kerb. 'I'll wait until you're across the road.'

Christ, Posser thought, here's my dotage, but he took it gamely and waved back when he'd survived the traffic. He saw her limp off and thought, Martina needs something more than an ailing dad, that's for sure.

'Never known a noisier nick,' Hassall complained, reading the list. Sergeant Younger had known him years. 'Nor a gungier noticeboard.'

'Always the case, Mr Hassall. Every spare bit of paper, up it goes.'

'Who's next?' Hassall never expected the best. 'Don't give me some freak who's playing for the police college at Hendon.'

'Tim Windsor. Accident fatal.'

Windsor came up. 'There's a ton of witnesses.'

'Here,' Hassall asked Younger. 'Why say everything backwards?'

'Excise ledger system,' Windsor cut in. 'Nouns go first, qualifiers next. Like: cup, coffee, officers, for the use of.'

'Bright bugger,' Hassall said. 'Old, this accident fatal?'

'Middle-aged businessman.'

'Wasn't pushed, was he? Get the camera tape.'

'The camera at that corner of Victoria Square's been vandalised,' Windsor said, blinking his sandy eyes. To Hassall they looked scabby, the trouble with pale redheads.

Hassall said heavily, 'It's odd squared.' Hassall asked after the taxi driver. 'Let's have him looked at.'

6

Punter – gambler, a prostitute's client, a customer.

CLARE WAS UP early. She had slept badly, wanted nothing to do with anything. She'd made breakfast with disguised amiability, talked to Clifford about the garden, those tall white romneya flowers attractive enough but don't they travel so, that inconsequential patter that means so much in marriage. She left the things for Mrs Kinsale, and against her intentions faxed the locum-doctor bank. She felt restive.

By the time Clifford was ready for off, the locum bank had answered, allocating her to Farnworth General. Not her first choice – what would have been, today? – but frankly she felt out of kilter, her vague unease recurring. Clifford had collared last night's *Evening News*, and it hadn't been evident since. Things seemed odd. She wondered if Clifford was as unperturbed as he seemed. It was lucky that she loved him.

On the way in she stopped at a convenient layby and bought the morning papers. The man's photo was speckled and grainy, the accident baldly reported. Leonard Mostern was his name, identified from credit cards and driver's licence. She remembered meeting him at one of Clifford's firm's events. Pinning down dates was always hard, but it was around last bloody February, that month so much on Clifford's mind last night.

Faithfulness was a marital problem, that and deceit. She ought to simply ring Clifford and say outright, 'That accident was Leonard Mostern. We met at that do, didn't we? Poor man. And to think that I attended his accident, how terrible. . . .' And so on. Bring it into the open.

She knew she wouldn't do any such thing. This morning was certainly not the time, she with her hospital locum to get through, Clifford with his – presumably his – briefcase filled with financial documents. An odd compulsion was on her to get away, ignore Farnworth General, drive up to the moors and sit watching the shifting colours on the fells in emblematic escape. But she folded the newspapers, put them carefully into her bag, and drove to work.

The hospital had seen better days. Clare had been in worse, but why did they always smell of cabbage and ether? She entered the main corridor, conscious that today she had chosen the wrong shoes, too noisy on the imitation-tile flooring. Once, in this same hospital, a patient's little girl had told Clare, 'These are my hammer shoes!' The defiant six-year-old had clacked her heels about the consulting room until Clare, striving to hear the mother's systolic murmur through the stethoscope, had got Sister Ellison to stir herself and distract the child.

So today here she was, walking with undue diffidence into the Admin offices to scan the allotment board. Here too she'd drawn the short straw. Locum-tenens doctors were cannon fodder, invariably Admin's easy way out. Therefore they had to suffer. Inevitably, the nursing staff would be irritated at having their precious routines upset.

Clare had even met with frank abuse from nurses whose sacrosanct rituals were to be observed at all costs.

'You're in neoplastic counselling, Dr Burtonall,' the overweight secretary informed her airily. 'Starting ten minutes ago.'

Clare swallowed at the unfair criticism. She turned to look. Why did secretaries adopt that nasal whine? Did they speak so with their husbands, on holiday with friends, or was it taught in secretarial school?

'Who of the regular staff is off duty, please?' she asked. 'And which clinic?'

'Dr Daubney's down with flu. His wife phoned yesterday.'

'I think you have grounds for complaint, then, Mrs Wensford,' Clare said, frowning. 'It is your Admin's own rule that locum-tenens doctors like myself must be fully informed of clinic, identity of physician for whom they are to deputise, time of start, patient numbers, at the time of notification. I was told none of these.' She took up the hospital contract forms and moved out as smoothly as she could manage in her clamorously wrong shoes, saying over her shoulder, 'It's that sort of inefficiency that gives Hospital Admin its bad name. I'll complain for you to the bank locum agencies.'

She set off down the corridor, her heart sinking. What a way to begin a day. The 'Neoplastic Support Clinic', in the jargon of hospital classification, was more properly the Patient Counselling Service. It was a job shunned by many doctors, a punishment posting. She quite liked Dr Daubney. She could have done with a quiet clinic day, to think things out, make a few discreet phone calls. Her unreasonable irritation at the cancer specialist's bout of flu worsened her feeling of guilt. And that wretched Mrs Wensford would of course get her own back. Sooner or later the fat cow would engineer some default, lay it, sweetly and with utmost regret, at Clare's door instead of her own plodding ineptitude.

No illusions, she cautioned herself despondently. Those were for saints, who had never slogged through the six years of medical school.

'Morning,' she said with determined brightness to the desk nurse. 'I'm Dr Burtonall, standing in for Dr Daubney. Just give me a moment to settle, please.'

'Morning, doctor.' The nurse followed her in. 'Nurse Minnie Jarndiss, second year. The X-rays are alphabetic, lab reports here. . . .'

Despite Nurse Jarndiss's second-year status, she was aware of any locum doctor's usual temptation to perform a swift scan of the laboratory reports to see how time-consuming each patient was likely to be.

Clare decided to try to match the other's cheeriness, and left the lab results untouched. 'I'd like time to consult the notes between cases, please.'

'That's fine, doctor. Dr Daubney takes ten minutes, but just bell us when you're ready. I'll quell any riots.' She hesitated. 'There's one patient Dr Daubney wanted to see himself. Personal reasons. He's due in an hour.'

'A relation, or somebody in the profession?' Clare's misgivings were justified. Doctors and nurses made foul patients, and relatives were notorious complainers.

'No, Dr Burtonall. He used to teach Dr Daubney when he was young.' Nurse Jarndiss blushed at her gaffe.

'Dr Daubney's old teacher? Better blip me when he arrives.'

Clare could see that was a problem. Still, cross that bridge as and when. She took up the first folder, with its accumulation of pink, blue, and yellow laboratory, radiology, and histopathology forms thickening the back inserts. Social, family, and past medical history, then the present clinical problem, and the terrible finalities of the diagnosis itself.

Ninety minutes later she had seen three patients. They had all been straightforward. A follow-up patient with colonic cancer was doing well after a two-stage operation and managing his colostomy with his wife's help. The district nurse had been sound. Then a breast-cancer patient, calmly facing irradiation therapy and cytotoxic drugs, no trace of nausea now, and without evidence of a recurrence. The last was an elderly woman with a rodent ulcer by the outer canthus of her right eye, bright as a button, making a complete recovery. Clare let the talkative lady chat a while, giving her extra moments to reassure. Something she said caught Clare's attention.

'I still go to St Benedict's, doctor, from being a girl. Not many can say that, now the school's closed! I'm sure I remember that elderly gentleman outside.'

'Do you, Mrs Lacey?'

'You can't tell who's what nowadays, can you, doctor? I remember when the infant school was where Leghorn's new store is. . . .'

Mrs Lacey was ushered out. Nurse Jarndiss entered.

'The old teacher you mentioned is a reverend, Nurse Jarndiss?'

'Yes, doctor. He's retired now.'

'The biopsy reports have Dr Daubney's initials,' Clare pointed out. So he had already perused them.

Clare flicked to the first page. The notes were sparse, as if the compiler had been keener to conceal than inform.

The patient came in with a diffident smile. First

impressions are best, Clare remembered being taught by an opinionated surgeon, because they come before educational baggage clutters up the picture. Mr Crossley was thin, almost cachectic, with a slight stoop. No clerical collar, no black suit, nothing to suggest the clergyman. His manner was apologetic yet confident, an unusual mixture.

'How do you do? I'm Dr Burtonall. Mr Crossley, isn't it?'

'Jonas George Crossley.' He had a dry, flutey voice. 'Sixty-two, perennial cigarette smoker. I'm sorry.'

She tried to give a reassuring smile, but faded. 'Your occupation?'

'I asked Dr Daubney to fudge it, Dr Burtonall.' He suddenly smiled, an engagingly brisk grin taking over his features. 'Priest, if I were in clergy-friendly country. Here, I'm lucky if people misunderstand and think me a clerk in a bookie's betting shop.'

'Retired?'

'Yes.' He sighed, but showed no dismay. 'A seminary theologian. I retired from teaching a year since.'

'A year? But . . .'

He was abruptly less inclined to humour. 'My illness came on after the seminary closed. I wasn't invalided out. Too few recruits for the priesthood, materialistic claims on the youth of today, put it how you will.'

'Retired for non-medical reasons.' She reread the histo-pathology of the type of the man's lung tumour. 'Your GP—'

'He has told me the cancer is inoperable, doctor.'

Clare found it hard. The pathologist's account of the histology sections implied the most serious outcome. Cancers took many forms. This biopsy revealed columnar cells interspersed with varied spheroidal cells. In this patient's thorax there would already be soft friable masses of pinkish-grey cancerous material. The range of cell size, and the intensity with which the cells took up the histopathology stains, were ominous indicators. The disparities in nuclear sizes at high-resolution microscopy signified a poor outlook.

'Please, Dr Burtonall.' The man was pale but composed. 'I can guess what you must be feeling. Dr Daubney made quite firm predictions.'

'Thank you, Mr Crossley.' She hesitated, feeling lost. 'Am I to call you by a title?'

' "Father" would be inappropriate, seeing you are probably not of my persuasion.' He did his sudden grin, so full of inappropriate merriment.

'Can I ask where you live? The address given—'

'A boarding house. Folks on social security, commercial travellers.'

She went for frankness. 'Are there homes for retired clergymen, that sort of thing?'

'There *are* residences for retired priests.' His eyes wrinkled as if against smoke. 'I honestly can't see myself stuck in such a place, atrophying among the derelict. At Turton, my boarding house, there are occasional new faces, and I like the city.' He winced at a reminding pain. 'This is the only area I know.'

'Forgive me, Mr Crossley, but I'm unsure . . .'

He helped her out. 'Finance? I'll be funded until I need, how is it phrased, terminal care.' He opened his hands. 'I'd like an accurate prediction, doctor.'

'I'm sorry, but the lung tumour is a primary malignancy, meaning that it originated there. It is a type that usually advances at speed.' She had viewed the radiographs, gone over the radiologist's report. 'Given the size, position, the type of tumour cells.' She saw his unspoken question. 'Some four weeks. But occasional cases—'

'Except you don't believe that I'm such an "occasional case," Dr Burtonall.' His look was sharp. Just for an instant she glimpsed how he would look with gaunter features as the tumour disseminated and took firm hold. 'One question, please. Can I ask to be under one doctor, or is that not done? I mean, these days is it just pot luck?'

'A lot depends on the care that's needed, but, yes, you can usually get the doctor you want.'

'Thank you.' He seemed relieved. 'Theology isn't much use when it comes down to it. More than times have changed, doctor.'

'Mr Crossley, I think I should go over some practical points. I will pay a domiciliary visit, make an assessment in your home, if that's all right?'

'Certainly.'

'We shall contact your GP. I want you to drop in at the clinical-pathology laboratory, haematology division, for blood tests . . .'

Clare finished the clinic at noon. Near the hospital buildings a park had been improvised from industrial clearances. It wasn't much, a few nondescript acres, but the trees were established now about a docile river. With ornamental bridges between flower beds, it was a place where waiting relatives could pass the time. She had left her car near the bus stop there.

It promised a bright sunny afternoon, with people moving along the riverside. A small cluster congregated to watch the swans.

A young mother had a twin in its push chair. As Clare

watched, the other child tottered in its reins towards the water. There was a weir, but the mother was within a yard, so Clare, like everybody else, smiled hearing the child's excited squeals. From the corner of an eye, Clare saw a young man suddenly start forward in a smooth fast run. He sprinted with intent face, urgent eyes on the toddler. Clare was too astonished to call out. A great cob swan rose hissing from the water's edge, seeming to swell as it moved against the infant. The baby girl went into the water with a splash. It happened all in a second.

The huge bird stood, slamming its wings, the alarmed crowd retreating before its fury. The mother screamed as the push chair fell over with the child strapped inside.

An older man yelled, tried to wave the swan away with his cap. Something splashed. Clare thought, where was the little girl? The cob charged, hissing in outrage, its wings massively thudding the air. Clare was thirty yards away but could feel the wafts on her cheeks, so powerful was the force.

The running youth – no, man, twenty – hurled himself through the crowd, took a flying leap, and kicked out at the swan as he passed it. Something cracked in the old man's arm as the swan's wing caught him. He shouted, scrabbled back, hauling himself away one-handed. People were shouting, the frightened mother was hysterical, almost running on the spot, impotent.

The runner splashed into the water fully clothed, his kick having shoved the great bird off a couple of yards. Two young lads threw stones at it. A dog, barking frantically, tried unconvincing rushes but lacked courage. Clare saw the young man in the water. No heroics there, the river moving him along as he swam towards the weir, the little girl splashing half submerged. He caught her.

'Get a rope! Get a rope!' some woman was yelling.

A lad threw a stick at the male swan, which was now back in the water and beating along the surface, feet splashing, wings flapping, towards the swimmer.

The other lad took hold of his dog and urged it floundering into the water, yelling to create distraction. The young man took hold of the infant and swam obliquely downstream towards the weir away from the chasing swan. Clare realised his coolness, using the current to gain yardage by angling across.

The crowd joined the lad and the barking dog, shouting and throwing anything that came to hand to deflect the giant bird. Two ambulance men came at a run. By the time Clare reached the water, a uniformed security man was already slithering down the slope and the little girl was being brought out on the riverbank to the mother, people excitedly telling each other how it had happened, thanks mingled with reproaches, all admiring the mother's tearful exhaustion and her astonishingly thrilled child. Everyone was talking at once.

Clare, amused and relieved, went to sit on a bench as the cacophony subsided, in a way charmed by the outcome. The security man was pleased with the two lads and their noisy dog, which was still barking loudly at the swan, but did no more than take the young hero's name. With hardly a glance the drenched youth left to sit on a bench, and left it at that. The small greensward returned to normal. The little girl and her overwhelmed mother were hurried in to Casualty, while the cob swan serenely returned to patrolling the waterway, doing occasional theatening sneezes. People were still explaining, imagining fearsome outcomes a million times worse. The old man's bravery was being extolled. He was already inside being examined by the Casualty surgeon.

A doctor's fate, Clare told herself wryly, was to be indispensable one minute and superfluous the next.

She gathered up her handbag and coat. Her exit took her past the young man, still thoroughly soaked. He was sitting hunched, elbows on knees, looking dispassionately at the river. People had dispersed.

'Are you all right?' Clare asked, smiling.

'Thank you.' He didn't look.

She tried again, a little put out. 'I did tell the security man it was you and not the others who did the deed.'

'The lads were instrumental,' he said, 'but thank you.'

His detachment peeved her. Instrumental? An odd word for a pandemonium. 'You kept so calm, Mr Whitmore. Quite admirable.' She'd heard him give his name. 'The only one of us.'

'I'm not Whitmore.' He seemed shy, caught out. 'I give the names of Hollywood actors, old ones.'

Give, so therefore habitually? Was this sort of rescue usual?

'If you wish,' she said, piqued, about to write him off. 'It doesn't alter what you did.' He didn't speak. 'Have you offended the security man?'

'Yes.'

She was taken aback. 'Yes what?'

'Yes, I offend the security man.'

His flat replies reminded her of witnesses giving prepared evidence in court. Yet he didn't seem in any way perturbed, more mildly amused.

'It was the same at the road accident, Mr Whitmore. That policeman?'

'Yes.' Unconcerned. He must have recognised her, as she him.

'Seriously? You offend them both?'

'Both would say yes. I cannot regard it in quite the same terms.'

Clare felt she ought to go, yet she persisted, irritated by his detachment. 'Quite the regular rescuer. The policeman didn't take to you one bit. Remember?'

Fishing, of course. He didn't care either way. She felt an intruder, ask questions all day and get nowhere. Yet she had a vested interest in hearing an impartial view of yesterday's accident, and wanted to prolong this, even with this wet youth who didn't even have the sense to dry himself.

Slowly he looked up, level blue eyes, brown hair a wet slicked thatch. 'I remember, of course.'

'Might I ask how you, the archetypal do-gooder, give offence so readily?'

He said evenly, 'I'm a goer.'

'A . . .?' She wondered if she had possibly misheard. What was a goer?

'Goer, street slang. Gigolo, walker, troller, cicisbeo, jessamy. Meaning a male hired by ladies for their own purposes and use.'

That was pretty stark, she thought with wonderment. A . . . one of those people, here, in this hospital park?

'You,' she said stupidly. 'You?'

'I.'

Education, Clare thought in the warm daylight, doesn't really fit you out. Convent nuns should have prepared her. A drowning child's rescuer responds to a polite enquiry by saying blithely that he is a, what, a goer. His manner is condign; such an occupation is bound to anger propriety, it's only natural, thank you and good day.

She had a sudden absurd image, herself in the convent school, Manners and Etiquette with Sister Immaculata. *Now, girls, introduction to a goer: with a ladylike inclination of the head one extends one's hand, but only when the gentleman's hand is fully offered. Let's try that. Clare . . .?*

'The policeman and the security man recognised you.'

'Or guessed.' He nearly smiled at her concern. 'Please don't worry. The old man deserves the credit, and the lads with Rin Tin Tin.'

'Do you, ah, work alone?' she asked on impulse.

'For an agency called Pleases Agency, Inc.'

He raised his head to follow a rising kite and added, 'I like the colours on the tail.' She glanced up. A child with his granddad was flying a multicoloured kite, concentrating. 'They say the longer the kite's tail the better it flies. Is it true?'

'No. Weight is a limiting factor.' She paused, knowing she should go.

'A limiting factor.' He nodded agreement, eyes on the kite.

'Are there many of you?' But where, though?

It was extraordinarily difficult to ask. She wished she'd had an hour's warning of this, to work out what to say.

'Not nearly enough.'

'I'm sorry. I didn't mean to intrude.'

'I don't mind your being intrigued.'

Which, she thought a little tartly, was hurtful. 'Intrigued', as if she was nothing more than a voyeuse, nothing else to do all day. He really was a high scorer at offending people. How on earth did he get along with those women who hired him for 'their own purposes and use'?

'I suppose your public often are.' Now she sounded combative.

'I have no public,' he said simply. Did he mean no one?

In the nick of time she held her next cutting remark in check and forced a smile, wanting to sit beside him but not knowing whether it would be right. The security man was bound to be watching from the window. Sister Immaculata hadn't done her job. Clare felt in a mess. He had begun to shiver. The sunshine was watery, a low breeze rising. Why didn't he leave?

'Hadn't you better get home and dry out?'

He gave that shyish look about the park. 'Perhaps. Thank you for your company.'

'Do you need a lift?' Against his painful politeness it was like an assault, sounding at least boorish. Quickly she amended, 'Could I offer you a lift somewhere? You will look conspicuous on a bus, Mr Whitmore.'

He made no move. 'You will look conspicuous in my company.'

'I'll bring my car to the bridge. Five minutes?'

'I am grateful.'

'The least I can do. My motorcar is maroon.' She paused. 'Have you a name, Mr Whitmore? One I could use?'

'Yes,' he said, with apology. 'People say Bonn.'

She paused a moment for him to ask hers, but he didn't. She got her car, found him waiting at the bridge gate.

Their conversation was stilted as she drove, because she felt baffled. He said the central bus station in the main square would be fine, and there asked if 'it would be convenient' for her to drop him by the textile museum. He thanked her. She said not at all, and immediately pulled away. Ineptly, she had disclosed nothing of herself, and had learned nothing more about him.

Why had he been at the hospital? Outside, sitting waiting for a patient perhaps? She would never know.

That evening she scanned the newspaper. It was reported that a Mr Whitmore had assisted two local lads and their dog to rescue a child, who was pictured, from the hospital river weir. Questions were being asked in the local council about the presence of swans in the grounds of Farnworth General. Swans were known to be highly dangerous. An elderly gentleman was the 'city's real hero', and was pictured recovering in hospital from injuries sustained when he had courageously battled the vicious bird.

The twins and the mother were pictured. The hospital security services were praised.

Bonn, a goer at the agency with the lugubrious name, had been there when Leonard Mostern had been killed – no, Clare corrected, had *died* in that accident. She looked in the phone book. The agency was there. She was astonished.

That evening she described the swan incident to Clifford in general terms, but said nothing about Bonn.

Sleeping together was vital. It's what marriage was, is, should consist of. Other rituals were fine, even necessary, but sleeping – meaning lying, sweating, snoring, rutting, all of it – was the essence.

They made love that night. All right, Clare admitted, she was impelled by the accident's consequence, that brief-case, but so? Nothing wrong with feeling the need of a little security, which is what tonight's sex was.

She lay awake, seeing the ceiling shadows darken against the grey. Now, why had she thought *consequence*, instead of *aftermath*? The former meant a related, the latter an un-related, event. A subconscious mistake, or a truth?

Love was odd. She was sure she loved Clifford, and he her. There was a theory that it was an invention of trou-badours in twelfth-century Provence with fancy rituals written down in those oddly sexless codes. Yet magazines were emphatic enough about it: 'romantic love' flourished in 89 per cent of mankind's cultures, said researchers (and much *they* knew!). Lying there, her leg still over her hus-band's recumbent form, Clare almost giggled. She and her friend Beth in medical school used to compose ridiculing rhymes when 'research' was cited. Most nations, tribes, cultures, throughout history – as now – distinguished between arranged marriage and love-based marriage. Simi-larly, there was a sharp difference between sexual intercourse for an ulterior motive – money, getting a part in a film – and sex for 'love'.

Nowadays, though, body chemistry seemed to have a say. Break it down to stages. One, encounter with sight and smell, like animals. Hadn't there been some odd experiment, when male or female pheromones were rubbed onto seats in a cinema, then people admitted to take their seats at random – and most sat on seats secretly smeared with the pheromones of the opposite gender? Secondly, after the sniff factor came phenylethylamine, the 'rush' chemical, with neurochemicals like norepinephrine and dopamine, which like amphetamines fired up elation and different excitements. This chemical response to one sexual partner lasted maybe forty months, said experts, then dwindled. Sad, really, but just as some drugs have to be given in ever larger doses to produce the same effect, so with phenylethyl-amine – our human chemistry factories simply get worn out producing it in response to one lover. So it fails, and with it our sexual fever. Was this why, Clare wondered, moving Clifford's hand to her breast, divorce rates soar during the third or fourth year after marriage, because our bodies get bored turning out the right chemicals? And, incidentally, wasn't something like phenylethylamine there in chocolate, promoting its randy-candy fame?

Stage three overlaps in the nick of time. Morphinelike endorphins tickle up the brain, inducing comfort and tranquillity. Oxytocin does its cuddlesome stuff, batting orgasms along to the climax. Hence satisfaction, hence peace of mind.

But competition creeps in. Maybe growing sexual confidence coincides with the chemical fade-out? Anyhow, other contestants enter the field, amorous encounters begin – and of course newcomers bring their own stimulus to rekindle the body's chemical boilers. Stage five is nothing more than resolution. Either responsibility wins out, or moral weakness chucks in the towel – the husband succumbs to his secretary's sexual enticements, or the wife scampers after some passing new male. Over and out.

Feeling suddenly alone in the gloaming, Clare decided that it was all too ornately biochemical. Sleep together, you got through the biochemical barrier. Simple as that. She pulled Clifford's somnolent weight on her, and slept.

7

Bunce – money, profit, illicit or otherwise.

THEY ENTERED THE hall, the entire place echoing with clangs and grunts. To Bonn it was a menagerie.

'Incongruous,' he told Rack.

Bonn's judgements disturbed Rack. There was no need for them. Bonn was like somebody seeing secret football scores in everything, to gladden or deplore. Rack couldn't understand it. Rubbish activities like pumping iron were just stupid. Finish. Bonn hadn't got the hang of life.

They stood watching. The seats were sparsely occupied, though a scattering of body builders packed the front rows, ogling those already on the stage. A good two dozen men were pumping iron; the air was thick with male sweat plus the scent of ironmongery that hung where men laboured to no purpose. Bonn stared in wonder, fellers dedicating their lives to lifting metal chunks. It was an addiction crazier than drugs or booze.

'What is it for, Rack?'

Another thing, Rack couldn't see the point of Bonn's thoughts. He should think less, sleep sounder. He'd be more cheerful. But, then, Bonn had the magic, so it was okay. Charisma, he would have thought if his mind had allowed.

'I might ask Galahad,' Bonn said, finding a seat.

And he would too, Rack marvelled. Only Bonn would demand of an obsessed mountain like Big G why the hell he behaved like a prat, shoving steel nowhere.

'Go careful, Bonn,' Rack warned. He didn't want Martina asking how come he'd let her prize goer get crushed.

Rack, Bonn's stander, was there to protect. Fall down on the job, Martina'd go into orbit. As for Grellie, well, best not to think of the effect losing Bonn'd have on that particular knife-bearing female. Luckily, Bonn could avoid setting off the fuses in people, including these great oafs thrusting, flexing, oiling, or leaning spent in glistening exhaustion.

'Bonn,' Rack said, seeing his caution got no answer. 'Everybody knows they're nerks, but don't tell them, okay?'

There was an area of cork matting near the tea machine where you stocked up on kilojoules after wearing yourself out. Small tables, white-painted, chairs with fawn covers. Bonn was brought Earl Grey tea unasked. The girls were in awe, ever since Bonn tried to pay at the counter, first visit. They even put his picture up on their kitchen wall, until Martina heard and sharply banned that sort of thing. Rack reckoned it was typical birdthink, girl helpers now hating their boss but giving Bonn still greater aura.

Rack found Galahad oiling himself. The pumpers called it the machine room, as if it was filled with engines, when it had nothing but space and a coir flooring. He called to Galahad, returned to Bonn.

A smiling girl brought him a cola, ruffled his spiky hair. He paid no attention. She really wanted to ruffle Bonn's. He found Bonn eyeing him.

'How's your ma, Rack?'

Rack looked away from where a middleweight failed his snatch lift.

'Some relative's coming. She wants me to fix him up with lodgings.'

'His firm doesn't give expenses?'

'Don't know. Maybe he's milking the sheet?'

'I wonder if I can help.'

There it was again. Another bloke would have nodded, meaning fuck off.

'I can't go to Martina with this crap, Bonn.'

They watched Galahad approach, a looming alp. 'She'd understand.'

Bonn held up a restraining hand for Galahad to hang on a sec. And, unbelievably, Galahad actually did pause. The girls eyed his physique as Galahad used the full-length mirrors for a quick self-appraisal. He flexed, bulging and forcing, on the ball of one foot, head back. Let anybody else put him on hold, though, he'd have gone berserk. Bonn could do that, make an insult an apology.

'Tell you what, Rack. I could ask Martina, allow your visitor some free lodging, a courtesy.'

Bonn frowned as if it was a problem, when Rack had been screaming inside for salvation. Rack told him yeah, fine, ta, relief washing over him.

By now Galahad was into a routine, the girls clapping, when Bonn raised his hand for Galahad to stop that crappy posturing and get over here. Ironers would kill for an audience, yet Galahad came like he'd got a knighthood and didn't even blink in outrage when Bonn came right out with it, Rack's heart in his mouth.

'Hello, Galahad. I assume this muscle business has a purpose?'

Rack tensed, waiting for the mighty figure to go kong

at the mortal insult, but Galahad only said, 'I'm glad you asked, Bonn, Got a minute?'

'Aye, Galahad.'

'Well,' the hulk began, meek as a lamb, 'it's body image. . . .'

Rack marvelled, and settled to boredom while Galahad, the goon, expounded on muscles, but meaning his own glorious physique that the whole world had a solemn duty to adore but which looked like a bag of fucking spanners.

'This is the corac.' Twenty minutes, and the big blond was earnestly showing a ripple under his armpit Rack wouldn't have bothered with.

'Corac?' Bonn repeated, serious.

'It's a forgotten muscle left over, Darwin, you know, monkeys? The corac was huge, in caveman days. We were all birds.'

Rack almost cackled but hung in there copying Bonn's sober inertia, this moron redeveloping fucking muscles to out-fly what, some pterodactyl? If Bonn had guffawed, Galahad would have taken ridicule on the chin, yet he'd crucify Rack for an honest laugh.

From Bonn, 'You have judges? How?'

'That's it!' Galahad cried. He paced like a wrestler about to go for it. 'That's the *art*, Bonn!'

'A most serious question.' Bonn, forgetting global warming with death zapping through them ozone holes.

'Judges *judge*, Bonn!' Galahad flexed, copying Rodin's *Thinker* postered on the walls. The girls went, 'Oooh!' Galahad beamed.

'But it's unreliable, Galahad.'

For God's *sake*, Bonn, Rack urged inwardly. But never

no need when it came from Bonn. Galahad shook his head ruefully.

'It's science, who's got the sharpest cuts, the max mounds.'

'Cuts?' Bonn, risking annihilation. Rack slid in his chair, casual.

'Where the muscle ends, see?' Galahad, desperate to make a convert of Bonn, who led the world. 'Flab stops it being sharp like my lats here. . . .'

Rack listened to the muscle-hussle crap. A small audience of other ironers had assembled to hear their gospel propounded. Rack wondered, was he the only one who saw Galahad was a prat.

'Will you tell me more later?' Bonn asked. He rose, took Galahad a step. 'Martina's made me key. You're on my new firm.'

'Me?' Galahad was stunned. Rack watched the effect. Galahad had been single-trigger, a reserve. Only had one request for his services, and that had proved a real Balkan, no gain but mighty effort. Bonn himself had had to rescue that time. 'Me, Bonn?' Galahad's eyes filled, to Rack's disgust. 'But that time—?'

'There was no time, Galahad.' Bonn looked the big man in the eye. 'I want no votes, no backchat. Martina picked two of you.'

Rack winced. Wiser to keep shtum, but this was Bonn talking.

'Thanks, Bonn.' For instant wealth plus status.

'Meet at the Café Phrynne when I send.'

The ironer looked about to shake hands, didn't, stayed humble, in unknown territory. 'You'll have to tell me what to do, Bonn, eh? I'll give it my best.'

'Thank you for the talk about muscles. Really interesting.'

'Cheers, Galahad,' Rack said, adding silently, you boring misshapen fart, but he grinned as Galahad clasped both hands over his head like a boxer. The other ironers clustered for the galactic news, slapping his shoulder.

'That crap they talk,' Rack said as they left. 'Even with their girls in bed. Jammy bugger's never been so lucky.'

'Rack. Will a studio flat over the Phoenix Theatre do?'

'Thanks, Bonn.' Rack really meant it. He'd be able to give Mama the news for her visiting creep. Jews grumbled about mothers. Give the bastards Italian mothers, they'd really know suffering. Italian mamas, you had to make Pope *and* give them a prial of grandbabbies.

Grellie was waiting for them outside, pleased about something. She wore a new cobalt-blue dress, a king's ransom. Rack knew it was for Bonn alone, but Bonn couldn't see these things, probably thinking incongruous or, yesterday's word, icono-something.

'Bonn? Some flowers came for you.' Grellie walked with them. 'You should *see* how many.'

Rack stared. This was new. 'Somebody having us on?'

This was his area. Martina's syndicate couldn't get dissed, not in this city. Respect was down to Rack's war team, ten minutes, if need be.

'No. A client, silly!' Grellie tutted Rack down, him firing off half cocked. 'From a Wirral florist. I had Libby check back. The whole place is packed out like Chelsea Flower Show. Cost a mint!'

Rack subsided, disappointed. There hadn't been a rumble for weeks.

Grellie linked Bonn's arm. 'Who sent them, Bonn? The girls are agog.'

'Nothing to tell, Grellie.'

' "A grateful client, for services beautifully rendered," ' Grellie quoted.

Bonn moved off up Coffee Alley without speaking.

'I'll make up a story, then!' Grellie called, annoyed, her idea of threat.

'Best thing you can do,' Bonn said, but Rack it was who turned and raised one warning finger. Grellie tossed her head and strolled into the square, by the Royal and the Grand. 'Rack. Lancelot in thirty minutes, Café Phrynne. I'll check with Martina. The studio flat will be on the second floor, the exit stairs.'

And Bonn would take the fallout, if Martina put on her frown that could kill.

'Ta, Bonn.'

'Done nothing.'

That was Bonn's eternal reply, whatever favours he'd shown, which was truly weird for a person who was climbing fast up a whole syndicate.

The pity was that the Café Phrynne was in a narrow back street in the old city centre. Impossible pavements, slender shopfronts, creaking pubs, and new fast-food joints trying to belong. Fashionable in parts, grotty in patches. Bonn thought it down-at-heel without being sordid, his home patch. A Huguenot church, dedicated to the memory of some ancient king who had given the Continent's Prot-estants succour, stood behind railings that made nonsense of the inches of pavement. Opposite, a bookmaker's, then shops trying for the boutique image selling handbags and fashions, delicatessens, shady bookshops, and a street market of barrows strung with electric lights brilliant through the brightest day.

Phrynne was a lady of the ancient world who'd got up to no good.

'Carol? I'm here.'

'Right, Bonn.'

Carol was on the door, a slim smiley girl with long black tresses. The café was genteel, its decor feminine and fetching. She was a talented interior decorator. Trellises that seemed ridiculous when carried in from the pantechnicon suddenly became exactly right when she'd done. Impossible vines took on a warming air. Grotesque wall hangings became Mediterranean. Scarey lopsided pots became submerged amphoras. It wasn't travelogue, either. It stopped short of excess. Carol was class.

Most tables were set back in alcoves. Small wall bays, as for statues, refused to become illuminated grottoes by careful-casual settings of incidental shows, haberdashery, perfumes, sewing mementoes. Each week Carol had her 'performance', as she called it, a wall showing garments – Japanese, Old English, Damascus embroidery, muted by discreet floral arrangements.

Carol was a sort of genius who kept waiters in their place, brooked no nonsense, and reported in secrecy to Martina. Bonn approved.

'Lancelot,' he said quietly to Carol, pushing through the curtain. It was never quite drawn, open just enough to invite.

He took in the ladies who were there, walked through, passing where Yoff ruled his environmentally controlled kitchen – no cooking aromas, no sounds of culinary slog.

Bonn went down the corridor's right branch. Ladies' rooms and a lounge were set apart, Carol's instinct deciding the feel. A disguised office stood at one end, Carol again earning her crust. Bonn marvelled. It felt welcoming, but homely would have repelled women entering alone for illicit solace. Excess luxury would have challenged. The balance was friendly acceptance. Carol spent a fortune on flowers, to Rack's ridicule. Bonn countered that Carol always got it right, so where was the problem? Get the flowers.

The office was Spartan. He sat. The wall opposite should have opened to the Dickensian alley, with a fire escape backing the video-rental shop next door, but didn't. It couldn't. Bonn had worked it out, never tapped the wall wondering where the missing pieces of the café were. Martina designed what she designed. He only spoke his mind when asked, the rates of return, Grellie's girls' conduct, the risk of competition from the Dutch ZeeZees in Stratford.

He waited. No clock, a radio playing, never anything raucous, the background signal that all was well. Any interruption meant aggro, Rack's flash team urgent, Poncho and the lads if they were handy.

The trouble was Carol's replacement. Time off, Lynne and Liz coped, though neither was up to much. Carol he trusted, though lady customers found Lynne likable. Liz was too brassy, too ready to grin, out of place.

'Bonn?'

The coloured lad entered. Lancelot was the ultimate in companionability. He had everything Bonn would have said was right for the job: the wickedest grin, teeth with it, swift recognition of moods. Today's gear, a bolero, cummerbund, click heels of the dancer ready for off.

'You came through the kitchen, Lancelot.'

'Yes, Bonn.' He looked injured, sat, crossed his legs with not quite a pout. He wore gloves and a huge thumb ring with a yellow stone. He knew what Bonn meant – You didn't come through the caff dressed like that? – and showed petulance at the implied rebuke. Others wouldn't need to be told. Lancelot needed watching.

'I'm made key, Lancelot. Martina says to set up a new firm. I've got Galahad so far, and she wants you in.'

'Me? Goer? On a firm?' Lancelot seemed dazed. His eyes glistened. Lancelot's spectacular tears had to be tolerated or you got nowhere.

'Galahad's at the Rum Romeo. You can celebrate.' Bonn smiled. 'In a restrained manner, please.' One of Martina's admonitions, but Lancelot was away into his own dreamery.

'Me!' he kept saying, over and over. 'Me! I made goer!'

'It's the difference between not much,' Bonn said, to cool him, 'and being a millionaire in ten years. House, motor, one side business. As long,' he added, for Lancelot's proclivities, 'as Martina rules every breath.'

'Without saying, Bonn.' Lancelot rose, flexed his arms, did a sidestep, looking down over one shoulder. Bonn guessed a tango, some formation dance?

'I'll have a key meet soon. Have you anything on tonight?'

'No.' Lancelot was instantly defensive. 'But some enquiries.' Others wouldn't have needed excuses, another worry. Lancelot posed, undisguised camp, fist on hip. 'Who's the other goer? Three plus the key, right?'

'I shall tell you later.' Bonn wasn't going to be interrogated, not even by Martina's appointee.

Lancelot's grin finally burst. 'We're rich, Bonn! Motors, mansions!'

'One of each, Lancelot.' Bonn made his warning a shared joke. Martina forbade employees to hold more than enough, and she defined sufficiency. Millionaires couldn't be choosers, Martina's words.

'Bonn.' The other was suddenly diffident. 'I appreciate this. I really do.' He pursed his lips. 'Would you like to see me dance? The Palais Rocco. Veeree Hip's playing, y'know? Big band.'

'Is it that mogga dancing?' Bonn put on a show of interest. 'I like that.' He didn't, but it was Lancelot's speciality. 'Thank you. I'll be delighted.'

'I'm sixth on. Starts at eight.'

'Half past, then?' Four minutes or so would give Bonn a margin, after which he could respectably leave. Mogga dancing was the city's most yawnsome event. 'I look forward to it. A treat.'

'Thanks, Bonn.' Lancelot pivoted, gave an extravagant bow.

Bonn watched the door close, none too happy. The stick-and-bush trade was no place for a loose cannon, however elegantly it moved. He would say nothing to Martina. Another thing to worry about.

He should settle Rack's problem of that visiting uncle. Then time for a light meal with Grellie before wasting time seeing Lancelot dance. Rack would sulk. Bonn wondered about those flowers.

On the way out he told Carol he wanted to meet Grellie, please. Carol never jumped to conclusions like Rack. She had a sense of the long term. Maybe ten, a dozen, ladies were in the Café Phrynne having tea, two pairs and the rest singles. The lads waited graciously on, Carol never looking but seeing they never overstepped. What better place could a lady visit, tired from a day's shopping, to rest over tea, the cakes sumptuous, the café discreet, the serving lads ever willing to smile and share a mild exasperation or two?

'Bonn?'

He'd hardly gone a yard when Oliver fell in, pace for pace.

'May I speak?' Oliver, a regular-army man once, betrayed his ultra-conformity by double-breasted suits, shoes gleamingly ready for inspection. He somehow went about older than he was.

Bonn didn't slow, nodded, knowing what was coming and thinking, Oliver, for heaven's sake, lighten; it would do you a power of good.

'Just wanted to say congrats.' Oliver was nervous of speaking out of turn.

'Thank you, Oliver. I'm just lucky.'

'No. Promotion due where it's earned, where it's earned.'

Some military axiom? Bonn wondered, pausing at the intersection. Oliver, incongruous among the street barrows, only needed a bowler hat and upper-lip sweat to complete the picture of the ex-officer.

'Bonn, ah, a question, right?' Oliver rocked on his heels. 'Heard you'll have three goers, what?' Only the world's Olivers still said 'what?' like that.

Bonn smiled to put the man at ease. 'I never gossip, Oliver.'

'No! Understood! Only,' he drove on, almost at attention, 'you know my success – fair only, first to agree – in that area.' He fixed Bonn with desperate eyes. 'I'd appreciate being considered for any possible position.'

'I shall take you into consideration, Oliver. Thank you.'

Bonn stepped away, escaping. Oliver tried so hard to integrate, yet stuck out like a sore thumb. His military service had ended in some minor scandal, leaving him lodged in a corner upstairs flat in Cotton Street, where he was kept by an imperious Chester lady mad on bridge, investments, and golf. Oliver's chances as a goer were nil. If Martina put Oliver's name forward, Bonn would have to refuse.

Rack came. 'Want me to tell Oliver to sod off?'

'Find Grellie, please.'

'Already here.' Rack waved to Jodie and Elise by the private porn cinema and called cheerily, 'I never said a word, Jodie!' and resumed conversationally, ignoring their catcalls, 'What you want her for?'

'Just a quiet minute.'

Rack cackled, his plan working, Grellie and Bonn pairing off.

'Hey, Bonn. A joke. A little sadomasochism never hurt anybody. Good, eh?' He roared. The market folk laughed along, shouting he was a noisy git.

'Very good,' Bonn said, unsmiling.

Bonn was enough to make a bloke give up, and that was a fact. Still, Bonn with Grellie was okay. Martina shouldn't find out, for safety.

DOMICILIARY VISITS WERE not within Clare's purview, but the old gentleman's place was on her way home, so it was quicker in the long run. Granny Salford used to say, tight of lip: 'If you doubt whether to do something, there's *no* doubt!' Here I am, Clare thought, still pleasing the old lady, gone these twelve years.

She smiled to herself, standing there looking from the address card in her hand to the long low building with its herbaceous border, early mixed wallflowers, and the lawns closely cut. White paint predominated, the bright-red brickwork looking new. Bedsit land, this faded suburb hoping to be mistaken for a chunk of holiday resort. Vaguely she wondered about developers, like Clifford. She might ask him, is it a kind of subtle hysteria that changes all architectural fashions in synchrony, or do they all simply get the same magazine?

Then she remembered that Clifford was behaving oddly. Something was awry. Light-hearted chitchat was out until this strange unease left her.

She saw the listed names, went in, 'J. Crossley', on the name board. Third floor. She noted the stairs, narrow and carpeted, holes with the edges worn. Somebody was cooking, one radio getting the best of its competitors along the second landing, an elderly lady trilling along in forced vibrato.

She knocked. The door surprised her by opening quickly. Crossley stood there in slippers and dressing gown. His face looked imploded from lack of teeth.

'Come in, doctor. I saw you arrive. Grand motorcar you've got.'

She entered. 'It's my one distinction. It's my husband's.'

'Must be marvellous.' He showed her to an armchair and offered her a cup of coffee. 'Go wherever you want, day or night.'

'Among the city traffic?' She wanted no comparisons, his past and her present. 'There are days I long for public transport.'

He was pleased at her acceptance of his offer, and set an electric kettle going while she looked about. He did an apologetic sleight-of-hand for a moment, and smiled with teeth miraculously restored, full-face.

His place was basically one room, with a curtained alcove that held a shelf cooker and a sink. A closed door presumably led to his bathroom. One window, old-fashioned sash type, looked out onto the front lawn and across to a housing estate. Crossley saw her looking at the distant church.

'Wrong denomination,' he joked. 'God's little trick. They'll all go to hell, and serve them right!'

She smiled along. 'Just a little milk, please, no sugar.'

'I'm glad you're willing. Since word got round, everybody's rather shunned me. Contagious, am I?'

He asked it quite seriously. She shook her head. 'No. Some neoplasms have viral elements, but that's stretching aetiology impossibly far. Your scared friends are more in awe of the words than anything.'

He went for cups. 'It's odd, doctor, but I've always thought how atrociously bad – intrusive, accusatory even – counselling is.'

'Like what?'

'Like the sort of counselling that is so fashionable these days. Get your flat burgled by some yobs, and some counsellor comes calling with a dose of solace. Divorce, they send counsellors to say it's really all right. Lose a lottery ticket, you write to your MP demanding a public enquiry, and counsellors rush to appease your grief.'

'I'm not here for that,' Clare said quickly.

'You're clearly not in that category, and I'm glad. Stay cool.' He explained with a twinkle, 'I learned to say that at the seminary. We had some day scholars, and depended on them for slang, to face the new millennium!'

'The seminary ended, then?'

'Yes.' He sighed, stood staring at the faded lavender flock wallpaper. It was horrible; stripes on magnolia, badly stained by the cooker. 'That's our final photograph, two days before dissolution.' He smiled sadly at the word.

There were two photographs on the window wall. Clare looked about from politeness. The furniture was oldish, worn and knocked. A divan bed stood along the nearside wall. A television, a small portable radio. No plants, one vase. A single shelf of books, looking homemade and put up slightly askew. She guessed there had been no bookshelf at all when Crossley had come. He had done the best he could.

'No family photographs, you see, doctor.' Crossley shrugged, bringing the coffee and sitting opposite. 'We didn't have cameras. Autobiographies always puzzle me. Where on earth did they get childhood photographs?'

He was trying to make it easy for her. Gratefully she took the opening. 'Your family is?'

'Parents long since, I'm afraid, though I'm relieved they're spared the consequences of my cigarette addiction.' He gave a wry smile. 'My sister's not well. She has a large family, but I'm merely the quaint northern uncle who's dropped from the Christmas-card list. I phone her every so often.'

'You haven't told her?'

'Not really. Nearer the time I'll perhaps drop her eldest daughter a line.' He looked anxiously at her cup. 'Is that all right? I can thin it down.'

'No, it's fine, thank you.' She showed willing, but it was the worst brew ever. 'The question I raised the other day, about looking after you.'

'This is it.' He gestured at the room, his few possessions. 'I'm paid up here, so to speak, until . . . There'll come a time, I suppose.'

'Can I ask about particular friends? You say they know your diagnosis.'

'I know them only incidentally, staircase meetings, corridor conversations. There're fourteen here, not all elderly. The council warden does a daily visit. He reports to some office or other, heaven knows why. That's about it.'

'Have you read the literature we gave you?'

It was usual to give terminal patients documents covering disposal of effects, making wills, as well as guidance with symptoms as diseases progressed. Crossley nodded.

'Yes, thank you. The hospice, though?'

'I've already notified the St Helen branch hospice—'

'I know it.' He smiled, added with a mock grimace, 'From exercising my calling. I know the senior lady there quite well. Mrs Peggs. Might I be able to go there?'

Clare spoke calmly through a wash of sympathy. 'It seems likely.'

'Thank you.' He looked about, measuring sadness. 'I shan't be terribly sorry to leave here, doctor. I'm lucky to have sheltered accommodation. But after a life of communal living, this is like community without the community. Do I sound ungrateful?'

'Not at all.' She rose casually to examine the photographs. It was going so smoothly because of the old gentleman's resolve, not from anything she brought to the visit. 'Is this you when you entered there?'

The larger photograph was in a silver hanging frame. It showed some two dozen young priests in black cassocks standing behind a row of seated older clergymen. All were smiling, posed on an expansive lawn before the ornate façade of a pale building. It was not quite sepia.

'I've worn well, don't you think? Pick me out.'

'Standing, third from the left.' She looked at the next photo.

'That's the final year. The world had rolled on by. I'm not at all sure that we noticed time's passing. I rather wish we had.'

The smaller photograph showed a very different scene, though it had been taken in the same spot. The pale elegant building was scruffy. The bushes, curving from the balustraded walk to the ornamental gardens, were now gone. Two modern bungalows obtruded. The row of smiling young priests was reduced to two, the older clerics with their soprano capes and birettas only five.

She looked, looked harder. The light was not good, of course. Crossley was in the centre.

'You were the big boss, then?' she asked conversationally.

It gave her the chance to look closer at the two young males.

'Bursar's the word you're looking for, doctor. The one with the money, feathering his own nest. Sorry.' He looked shamefaced as she slowly rejoined him. 'You become defensive, living so unproductively when the country's struggling to earn a living, in clover while the rest suffer, all that.'

'The seminary wound down rather, from the look of it.'

'Mmmh. We had to sell off parts here, bits there. The grounds shrank. The school couldn't stand the changes. And the age of religion is ended. Our recruitment dried.'

'That last day must have been sad. Do you keep in touch?'

Bonn, that day he'd rescued the little girl in the river, had been possibly waiting for somebody attending the hospital. Like, say, his former teacher, this sick old gentleman?

'Nothing is immutable,' Crossley said, lightening the conversation 'Especially croaking old relics! Keep in touch? Hardly. Before, one was an epicentre. After, one became a free-floating bubble. I found it impossible to be on the lookout for other bubbles. It was,' he ended gently, 'a major transition.'

'If I could arrange the St Helen by next week, would you accept?'

'So soon? Can you?'

'I'll give it a serious try.' She drew breath, wondering if she dared raise the question of the identity of the young face she had seen in the photograph, but put it aside. If the young man had witnessed Mostern's accident it would be reassuring to know his full name and home address.

'Would you mind if I had a smoke, doctor?'

'I'm leaving, Mr Crossley.' She stood, smiling. 'There'll

be some documentation. I'll send you a copy tomorrow, then we can get on.'

Crossley came with her to the door. 'Thank you for your kindness.'

She didn't turn to wave. On the drive back into the city she thought of the pathologist. She'd phoned in about the accident victim. The autopsy was a coroner case, but the pathologist wouldn't mind her calling, especially as she had been the first doctor at the scene. It might lessen her sense of uncertainty about Leonard Mostern.

It was inconceivable that Clifford could have forgotten, when she could remember. She felt an urgent new responsibility, to explore this odd feeling about Clifford, and thought of Bonn.

9

Wallet – a person who commissions a crime for payment.

GRELLIE WAS BY the bus station, Rack cooling his heels somewhere. Bonn cut through the queues to the stand caff, where podgy drivers had tea between runs. He felt only scorn for the inspectors, in and out of their bunko booths.

'Good day, Grellie.'

She looked up, smiled. Bonn was the only person she knew who used the old fashioned 'Good day', Australians excepted.

'All's well, Bonn.'

Grellie made room for him on the bench. She was admiring a crocodile of children winding through the ornamental gardens. They carried drawing pads, satchels. Bonn smiled, remembering satchels, buckles, the leather straps furry on the inside. When he was seven a little girl pinched his new blue cap.

Bonn genuinely did like Grellie. Only twenty-three, yet she headed the girls on Martina's strings. Who headed up each section was up to Grellie, but their power was meagre. It was as Grellie wanted, loose connections everywhere. She ran the street girls really well, had a flair for it. There were sparks between Martina and her, for no known reason. Just as Rack had to know drifts among the betting-shop slicers, the ackers, collers, foggies, skid sellers, meats, the whole 'buildings', as a syndicate's operations were called in this left-handed bit of the North, so Grellie bossed the girls. She usually gave Bonn the best and the worst, knowing she pleased him thereby.

'I'm finding it hard today, Grellie.'

'Really?' She stared. Complaint was not in Bonn's vocabulary. 'I heard you've got special favours from Martina. Not everybody makes key.'

'Martina nominated two goers.' Admittedly it was a superb concession, an all-time first. 'She's letting Rack have a studio flat for some uncle.'

'I heard.' Grellie fondled a small dog that tried to barge in. It got whistled on by its impatient owner. 'Got your third?'

Bonn replayed Grellie's words. She wasn't angling to have some boyfriend taken on. Good.

'What do you think of a pickpocket?'

Which astonished her. 'A subtle monger? Will Martina wear that?'

He sighed. 'Heaven knows, Grellie. I shall soon find out.'

'Be careful.' Inconsequentially she added, 'They're going to build a giant chess game over there for the old cocks. Plastic, not too heavy.'

'Won't they get stolen?'

'No. Rack's passing the word.' She smiled at a small lad spinning on a skateboard, clapped her hands in delight when he scooted down the path between the bushes. 'I wish I could do that, don't you, Bonn?'

He waited. There was more. Grellie didn't speak like this.

'That man you saw get run over?' She made it a question. 'Salvo was a mite close when the taxi hit.' She looked away, careful now. 'You were there.'

'Salvo? He's that gofer at the Ball Boys disco?'

'More than that. He's putting in for a goer. Angler's firm.'

Angler? Bonn conjured up a dark-haired, smooth-skinned twenty-two, natty, dapper, crazed on football, who went on a bender every time United did a cup run. But which cup? Nowadays there were as many trophies as there were sponsors. Once there'd been only The Cup, when trophies deserved capitals.

Angler had been a key for a year. His firm had suffered lately, one of Angler's goers being crippled in a bar fight over at Walkden. The goer was sacked, Martina's instant judgement. Bonn knew Angler but little. Sly? Too embroiled in clubs? But he did the business, got through the clients on time.

'Salvo do something, did he?'

'He's overspending. The girls are talking. He gambles over the top in the Rowlocks.' It was a small casino, not Martina's, in itself a warning.

'Do we know why?'

Grellie became uncomfortable. 'I'm not condemning anyone, Bonn. Salvo and Marla, she's one of mine. He's jealous. You know the Ball Boys. It's promoting homs lately.'

Slowly he understood. 'Salvo's Marla has taken up with some girl?'

'Yes. It's Lana. Where's the harm? Five of my girls have women regulars.' She smiled half a smile. 'Martina hasn't put an embargo on.'

'That's no excuse for a money angle, Grellie.'

'Tell Salvo that.' She looked at Bonn, saw he hadn't quite

caught her up. His background too restrictive, though why and where were unknown. Bonn needed looking after by somebody like herself. 'He hires out.'

No good asking to whom, not even of Grellie. What Grellie meant was, Martina didn't know this.

'How far has Angler got in replacing Ferdie?' The goer who'd got knifed, then sacked.

'Look, Bonn.' Grellie drew breath, then paused as she saw one of her girls among a crowd of football supporters, yellow scarves and bonnets. She tutted angrily. 'That Irina. If I've told her once I've told her a hundred times.'

Bonn curiously watched Irina, a slight dark girl, vivaciously mingle with the boisterous soccer fans. Grellie's orders were never to take the initiative.

'The girls say Salvo's offering gate money.'

Bribe? Bonn almost blurted it out. Nobody was stupid enough to bribe a key to be taken on as a goer. Unless there was something deeper, long-term payment beyond day-to-day body work.

'To Angler?'

He was reluctant to put Grellie on the spot, so spoke softly on.

'Is this it, Grellie? Salvo asks, but gets binned. So he starts putting in the word. Angler responds. Do this, do that, maybe something really naff.' He stroked a cat that came on the bench. 'I'm only surmising.'

'More or less, Bonn.'

'Angler makes Salvo a goer, and Salvo gives him a cut? Then why hasn't it happened? Rack would have heard.'

'Angler got cold feet.'

He wanted to know what the payment would have been, but his relationship with Grellie was the most fragile plant in the city, and was not to be risked.

Had Salvo helped the accident along, for money? A man that money-hungry was dangerous to all. Bonn told Grellie of the incident with the swan, said he'd given his name as Whitmore. They argued about old film stars for a few moments before Grellie faltered.

'Bonn. If ever, you know, you wanted some girl, would you come to me?' It took her four attempts to say. She'd never been this frank. 'I'm careful. I don't go mad with the punters, nothing like that.'

'Thank you, Grellie.' He rose as Rack hove jauntily into view. 'I am grateful. There might come a time.'

'Them buses'd run cheaper on waste whisky.' Noisily Rack closed in. He wore floral zigzag braces like edelweiss-toting prancer. 'Know why?'

'Carburettors,' Bonn said, to shut him up.

'You don't know a carburettor from a carrot,' Rack gave back. 'Greater piston velocity.' Rack interdigitated his hands. 'Know why?'

Bonn gave up with a look at Grellie. 'Why?'

'Pistons are like tin cans, see? The spark plug . . .' And Rack was off, gesturing, talking, inventing ignorable crap, his alternative to thought.

'Ta for the time, Bonn,' Grellie said.

They separated, Grellie to vent anger on Irina, Rack coming with Bonn.

'No more goes,' Rack told him. 'So we pick your third goer, right?'

'Yes. A pickpocket.'

'He'll be drunk. Okay, okay,' Rack said. 'Just so you're warned.'

Today was turning out all warnings, Bonn thought.

*

'Forget it?'

Salvo almost spat the words back at Oz, who was cleaning his fucking taxi, ducking round it like somebody under fire. Oz hated flecks, saw them everywhere on his old crate.

Oz sighed. Salvo would bring it down on them both, him and his crazy temper. The yard, Oz's, behind a pub, was almost derelict. The council had forgotten it – a faltering school, rotting terraces, the frittering Fox and Stork pub, rubble and rusting springs. Keeping a motor spotless was uphill effort. Now his pal – loosely, him being mental – was going to cripple some tart.

'Salvo. Women have women friends. So? They talk, hold hands.'

'She's getting shagged.' Salvo threw a spanner. It clanged on the wall.

Oz wearily went to retrieve it. 'Have you asked her?'

Salvo gaped at the innocence. 'You think she'd tell me?' He went falsetto. 'Oh, sure, Salvo. Me and that dyke Lana's at it night and fucking day.'

Oz was fed up with Salvo's macho crap. 'You've no evidence, right? Lana's her pal. See it like that.'

Salvo paused for a train on the viaduct. Then, 'I'll do her. No woman fucks me about.'

'Don't.'

But Oz's heart wasn't in words, not when his wing mirrors were spattered with fly carcasses. Priorities were priorities.

'Switch that light on, Salvo,' Oz called from under the taxi, but the idiot was already stalking out of the slanted wooden gate.

Oz couldn't believe some people. For hours Salvo'd smoked, paced, fumed about his tart Marla, who was close with some bird Lana, who worked the hotel saunas. Okay, a couple of girls shared a wank. So?

His taxi gleamed. It ought to, after the work he'd put in cleaning it free of grease and bone fragments after Salvo'd put that fat prat under the wheels. But wheels were a problem. You took bleach, washed the tyres. Then soap, then one egg to half a gallon of water to neutralise the bleach, or the fucking tyres rotted. He'd be finished by now if Salvo hadn't stopped by to talk of killing some girlfriend.

Night coming on, and still he hadn't done. That's what comes of listening to friends. Good money, and still Salvo grumbled. It was a daft world. Nothing made sense, except his lovely machine.

He knelt to his tyres. The world was unspeakable filth, and that was a fact.

10

Drop – to take or pass on stolen money or goods.

THE MORTUARY WAS at the rear of the hospital. Clare called on the off chance of seeing Dr Wallace, the taciturn old pathologist.

'Always my turn for forensic. Notice that, Dr Burtonall?'

'You haven't quite as far to go, Dr Wallace.' The standard sour joke, an aged pathologist without many years left.

He laughed at that. He still liked to smoke his pipe, but had forbidden it in Pathology. He bore his abstention like a cross.

'Is this that accident?' Clare asked.

'Mostern,' Bruno the mortuary technician said. He was an elderly refugee from some forgotten European catastrophe, chunky and weathered, never took a holiday. 'Taxi, Victoria Square. Funny.'

Funny? Clare gave him a look, but knew the reputations of mortuary attendants: being crude simply to shock, stoics with elephantine memories.

'Multiple injuries. A depressed fracture, temporal artery, did it, but take your choice.' Dr Wallace pointed with a Baird Parker scalpel. 'Remember your anatomy, young Burtonall? The temporal artery – not the biggest or hardest-walled in the world – runs in this bony depression. Such are the appalling design flaws of the Almighty, that the pterion – the temple, to one from *your* inept medical school! – is paper-thin. Hold the dry bone up to the light, the damned thing's quite translucent. An idiot could have designed better.'

'Haemorrhage,' Bruno said. 'His clothes no good at the pawn shop.'

'Poor man,' Clare said.

The cadaver lay on the slab. Always running water, always drenched flagged floors, and the sort of impedimenta they never showed you in feature films. Here in the real world, it was depressingly sordid, carnage and mementoes of carnage. What was it made the living more acceptable, when all the risks and tribulations were still with them? This inert mass of damaged muscle and bone, the skin mottled and pitted ugly pebble dash, had no problems now. Those were ended. It lay there, its own solution to its problem of existence.

The pathologist saw her looking.

'Skittered along the road, no distance. Take a shufti. Bad luck, really.'

He held the calvaria up, the skull cap neatly cut and dissected away to present a shallow bowl. The grooves where the blood vessels ran were distinct.

'See this side?' He squeezed his forceps, as all pathologists did for use as an improvised pointer. 'The skull splits literally like a potato crisp, slices the artery. Always does. Wish we'd a quid for every time we'd seen that, eh, Bruno?'

'Dollars. Only one side, though.'

Dr Wallace grinned to indicate Bruno's disagreement. They'd obviously had this out before Clare arrived. '*That* was the bad luck.'

'Bad luck?' Clare asked. She'd come hoping for good.

'The taxi kangarooed over him again as he lay, poor chap. Fat as hell. What's his Quertelet Index?'

'*Guinness Book of Records*,' Bruno said impassively, earning a chuckle.

'Come on, Bruno. He's not as fat as all that.' Dr Wallace put his head on one side, judging the cadaver. 'Thirty-two?'

'The taxi hit him twice?' Clare examined the deceased's effects, briefcase, clothes, shoes, all bagged and ready to go.

'The cabbie must have panicked.'

Or not, Clare thought. Funny.

'Compression injuries to the chest. Spleen ruptured to buggery, liver also. Death certification when the coroner says,' Wallace said primly. 'What's your interest, young visitor?'

'I attended. He was already dead when I reached him.'

'He never stood a chance.' Wallace laughed. 'Were you checking up that I'd read your scribbles? Caught out again, Bruno. She'll have it all over the hospital by coffee time.'

He started sewing up the cadaver's chest, placing the brain in the pleural cavity as usual. She watched him haul the stout twine through the skin with the triangulated hagedorn cutting needle, decided that she wanted a word with Bruno. To temporise, she asked about his request for better facilities.

'Those stingy bastards – pardon me – on the finance sub-committee. Never noticed that hospital mortuaries are always hidden in the woods, with Venereology?' He grinned. 'I heard you declined Dr Hodding's offer of a permanent post. Pity. We'd have liked you here.'

Clare blinked. Dr Hodding had sworn her to secrecy.

'You must be loaded, the fees Hodding pays.' Dr Wallace looked shrewdly from her to the wall chart, pathologists on the rotas. 'Not expecting, are we?'

The Fifer was a grandfather and could say these things. 'Not yet awhile.'

'My youngest grandbab set my books afire last night,' Wallace said reminiscently. 'How the hell did she get hold of matches? Incendiarist aged two, what tomorrow?'

The phone rang. The pathologist stripped off his gloves, stamping on the phone cue to put it on hold.

'Coroner's office,' he called over his shoulder. 'Always the wrong time.'

Bruno chuckled, took over the sewing. It's their gloved hands, Clare realised, that are so repellent. Rubber gloves underneath loose canvas bloodstained gloves, once white, to prevent undue slipping while they handled the organs. They wore wellington boots and a long plastic apron. He washed the scales noisily.

'Bruno, why funny?' She couldn't bring the words out for a moment. 'The taxi made a mistake, didn't it? The driver panicked. That's how it must have happened.'

'That's what is funny.' Bruno indicated the briefcase. It was in a plastic bag tied with a kitchen twist.

Clare went to look. 'This?'

'An executive, carrying an empty briefcase? That's very funny.'

It could have been identical to the one in her house, on the hall stand.

'How come?'

'That's what Dr Wallace said.' Bruno's expression was a picture of disgust. 'Too many books. Too much learning. You doctors don't see the obvious.'

'And what is obvious?'

'Somebody stole his real one, swapped it with this new empty thing.'

She stood there. On the wall were different histopathology sheets, investigations colour-coded. The postmortem sheet was white, name and address inked in, next of kin, family history, occupation, distribution of this report to . . . *Insert Designations Here.* Wording she'd seen countless times. She read the details painstakingly, getting colder, memorising.

'Is this complete, Bruno?' she asked the old man.

He had almost finished sewing up, tilting the head back to get to the angle of the jaw.

'In America is more difficult,' he said laconically. 'They make a scoop incision, low collars, necklines for cosmetics, put on a show. Real morticians, America.'

He shot a glance at the lists.

'The BID details? Unless you know more than Dr Wallace.'

Brought In Dead. The next of kin was a brother in Barrow-in-Furness. Marital Status: single. Offspring: Zero.

'No,' she said quickly. 'Just came from interest. Bruno, why is the briefcase . . .?' She knew that she had already asked once too often.

'Brand-new, doctor.' He pivoted the cadaver's head as she'd seen rugby players on television handle a ball. 'The price tag inside.'

'So?' she said blankly.

'So somebody switched the briefcase. He was going along okay. Some hoodlum shoved him under the wheels, does a swap, leaves him the empty new one.' Bruno laughed towards the office where Dr Wallace was visible through the glass. 'We make up stories. Sometimes they feel right.'

She raised a smile to show how amused she was at their games, keeping themselves sane in the most macabre task on earth.

'Thanks, Bruno. Please tell Dr Wallace thanks also.'

'Funny, though, eh?' Bruno said. 'My idea.'

She left the hospital to drive home, but found herself taking
the oddest route, through Victoria Square, by the textile
museum, turning left by the Granadoe TV Studios with its
ectopic soap-opera set. Several street girls were standing
near the bus station.

It was here that she had dropped Bonn. Did his sort
simply hang about? He'd implied that client ladies telephoned – what, placed an order? Bonn, a strange nickname.
She might ask – if she ever ran into him again, she amended
quickly.

And drove on home, thinking all the while about
Leonard Mostern, deceased, of the brand-new briefcase
with its price tag still inside.

Where had she met him? Among investors in a hotel.
She'd just driven past that same hotel in the circling traffic.
Mostern came alone, she vaguely recalled. Wives had striven
to laugh and be memorable, brittle from pink gins, wearing
jewellery like contestants displaying their husbands' financial attainments.

Some politician had been guest of honour, she remembered with sudden clarity, London. Clifford had joked about
Trade and Industry. Under-Secretary sounded so mediocre
but, Englishwise, was frighteningly pre-eminent. One of
the man's quips came to mind: 'You must come to London
and see the sights, Clifford. Well, *some* of the sights,
perhaps!' to roars of in-on-it laughter. Even I'd laughed
along knowingly, knowing nothing, toadying, hating to be
left out, proving how pathetic we all are, Clare thought at

the intersection where the accident had happened, this traffic easy if you beat the rush hour.

Mostern, though, had listened, not contributed. She remembered now that twice, not once, he'd dropped his wine glass, nervous. She'd felt sorry for the man, harshly out of breath from stoutness. And of course his chair went over with a crash after dinner. Sweaty, worried about the effect he was creating.

If she could recall so much – she was trying like mad, of course – then Clifford could do the same. Wasn't that reasonable?

Home after a slick journey, Mrs Kinsale affably in action, Clifford due back in a while, Clare bided her time. She struck after supper.

Clifford was in a reflective mood, Clare thought. Things must have gone well in the Exchange building. They had been talking of their wedding, her folks thin on the ground, his cohorts plenteous, both sides of the church eyeing each other across the aisle. She felt happy, truculently so, and mentioned her days on Farne Island.

'Do you think back to there a lot?'

'Often.' She smiled. He looked so content this evening. 'It's incidentals, mostly. The shop, the village hall, the sea trickling in, then suddenly engulfing the strood road to the mainland. The monastery, of course. It's a very small place.'

'You don't have pictures.'

Playing into her hands, or maybe something linked their minds.

'Like me. Teams, university. You never go to reunions.'

'I was never unioned in the first place.' She wanted to say it lightly, but it came out too sharply. Clifford raised his eyebrows. She hurried to make amends. 'Sorry. I can't recycle. The very thought of reunions chills my spine.'

'Not even a leaving party? No send-off? Woman of mystery!'

She laughed. 'Keep that image, darling! Every woman wants that!'

Clare had made instant coffee, wanting to get down to it.

'Your old acquaintance won't be attending any more,' she said, too quick a switch but knowing she had to try.

'Acquaintance?'

'Poor man. I remember he looked so hot and dishevelled.'

He had red wine after supper now instead of whisky, which was Clare, thinking cardiac. The glass paused. 'Who're we talking of exactly?'

'Mr Mostern. It was on the radio. I was at the PM.'

'Local radio?'

'Mmmh? Who knows? I can never find the same wavelength twice. Poor man.'

'Tragic.' Hesitation, then, 'You went to the postmortem?'

Those pauses, Clare thought in despair, tracking the conversation like a spy. She felt guilty as sin. 'Well, I was there. Quite hopeless, like I said. Has he a family?' She was treacherously innocent.

'Wife and two kids, I seem to remember.'

Longer lag phase still, for a non-existent family? Clifford was chatting, true, but looking into himself somehow, his newspaper on his lap.

'Will they be provided for?' To his blank gaze she said, 'Insurance?'

'Oh, I should imagine. It was his field.'

'Did you know him well?' As he refocused she added, 'I never know if your business acquaintances are temporaries.

Mind you, there's no reason I should, is there?' She smiled brightly, overdoing it.

'No.' Clifford came smoothly back on course. 'From the start, I vowed never to bore you with work. I saw myself boring you with details about properties and exchange rates, while you screamed inside.'

'A vow of secrecy.' Clare wished her words were less ominous, heard from within.

'We both did that.' His smile was easier, reassuring. She felt stupid, worrying about fragments of a puzzle that was all in her imagination. Christ's sake, she told herself irritably in Clifford's defence, accidents do happen.

'Secrecy?' She sighed, wanting to lessen the peril in this banter. 'Come to my clinics. You'll find secrecy enough. Hullabuloo, children running amok, nurses on the sulk, tortured parents, notes scattered to the four winds.' She gave him a half-serious glance. 'Would you like to?'

'Fly on the wall?' He laughed openly. The strange mood had passed, her interrogation ended. 'Don't forget how squeamish I am! The thought of that postmortem . . . ugh!' Then he said, quite out of character, 'Was it all right?'

'All right?' she asked, concealing her dismay. 'Well, yes. The man died instantly.'

'Do you do the death certificate?'

'No. It's the coroner. When he's satisfied.'

'But it will?' He caught her apprehension and smiled. 'Just thinking insurance. So there's no delay for his family, I mean.'

'Yes, as far as I know. It seems a closed case.'

He relaxed at that. She went on, 'What I've been wanting to say, darling, is maybe we could spend more time together. Mary Fenham meets her husband Tuesdays and Thursdays.

Of course, it's on her way to picking up the children, but we might meet in the midday somewhere.'

'Mary doesn't work,' he cautioned. 'And she lives for shopping, hordes of her cousins in retail.'

'You're right,' she said, stung, thinking, That's it, then. Had there never really been anything amiss, except Clifford's preoccupation with work and her own misunderstanding? Now her questions were out and settled, she felt warm towards him.

'Must we go to his funeral?' she asked on impulse. 'Perhaps I should give Mrs Mostern a call?'

'Better not, Clare. I will, tomorrow, from the office.'

She knew he wouldn't, couldn't, because there was no Mrs Mostern. She could make her own phone call tomorrow, maybe speak to Bonn.

'Oh, Clare. I forgot to tell you. Mother said she'll be phoning. She wants a chat. Seems het up about something. You know what she's like.'

Clare felt relief. *That's* what was wrong. Clifford's concern about his manipulative bitch of a mother had somehow touched Clare.

Yes, she thought, I know what she's like. And what she's het up about. Imagination could safely take a rest, with the elder Mrs Burtonall on her way to fuel troubled fires. Reproaches, reproaches, every minute.

She went out in the half light, ostensibly to take a walk. There was a coin box at the corner near the three shops. She rang Pleases Agency, Inc. A woman's controlled voice answered, quiet reassuring.

Clare didn't speak, replaced the receiver, and slowly walked home.

MARTINA FELT WAR was overdue. She explained this to Posser, her father. Mercifully, he'd had a good night.

She found him sitting by the window waiting for the four-thirty television word quiz, reading his eternal history books. His colour looked really good. She made tea. Even with Dad, she tried to disguise her lameness. He went for the biscuits.

'Dad, I've got to clog Grellie.'

'Have you, chuckie? Saw a Jowett Javelin in Bradshawgate. Took me back.'

'Did you, Dad?' She showed interest. 'Why not buy one? Old vintage car, go round Bowton moors, if you wrap up.'

The problem wasn't old cars. It was what if something happened to her. He'd be alone, wheezing, blue as slate, coughing up phlegm, rotting in some charity home in the tender care of idlers.

Exactly, she knew, as Posser worried for her.

'There's a choice, Dad. I can scrap it out, or sack Grellie and let Jaycee or Freshie or Reenie take over.'

'Can they run the strings?'

'One hand behind their backs.'

'And keep Grellie on how?'

'Demote her to a street stringer? Possibly, at London Road station, if she'd agree to keep clear on big race days or Cup Final.'

'She never would agree.'

'I don't want to lose her, Dad. She's a clever bitch. Cause more trouble than soft Mick, if she was let loose with a grievance.'

'She's got the girls' sentiment behind her,' Posser warned.

'That wouldn't count for much if I pulled her peg out, Dad.'

Posser sometimes forgot that Martina could be hard as nails. 'I know, love.' He made room for her in the window seat. It overlooked the small triangle of green. 'But times are past for motors now.'

'Don't talk like that, Dad.' She felt the pot, replaced its cosy, needed a minute longer. 'I can't let Grellie go on as she does.'

'Go on how?' He was curious.

Martina let her annoyance show. He was too quick to question.

'It's Bonn, your favourite,' so he saw her acidity. He said nothing. 'She's developed more than a passing interest in him. I can't have it.'

'Meaning what, love?'

It was at times like this Martina wished she had an elder brother. It was unfair. The agency would go to pieces if she let it.

'Meaning she's got to back down.'

'You'll forbid her to move on Bonn?'

'Dad,' she said, patient because he wasn't a well man. 'We're in a ticklish business. Grellie runs the girl houses and the stringers. We're lucky.' She held up a hand, let her make the point. 'Grellie's excellent. The girls like her. But crossing over's not allowed. It's always hell to straighten out.'

'Crossing was all right, once,' Posser said mildly. 'Never did us any harm.'

'That was then, Dad.' Martina poured the tea, no sugar for him on doctor's orders and skimmed milk, but what happened the minute her back was turned? 'Times are new. Relationships between the girls and the goers are forbidden. You, Dad,' she said with asperity, 'forbade it.'

'Maybe we should change?'

'Nowadays it isn't a simple police payoff, a kiddie scampering to the plod's back door of a night with an envelope. That was the Dark Ages, nursery tales.'

'More's the pity, love. But you'd be surprised. The city council still takes.'

He meant recent bribes, to allow a house concession at the proposed new marina. She almost smiled. They'd had a row about that.

'We're getting off the point. Grellie must be heeled.'

She was determined. Posser sighed. Grellie was a lovely girl. Twenty years younger, and half a lung more, he'd have been in there.

'Which will you do, love? Throw or blow?'

'Stamp on her fingers. Just talk,' she corrected, when he grimaced.

'Can I have another biscuit?'

She recognised the bargain. 'Yes, Dad. But no more when I've left. I've got a pudding for later. Leave space for your breath, like the doctor said.'

They talked of this and that, drifting to the old days she'd never known, when people were all-round better folk. She didn't believe his remembrances. It was transparently clear to her that Grellie would have to be put in check, so why delay? The old poem she'd had to learn at convent school, what was it now, talking about being over and all that?

From the moment Grellie entered, Martina could tell that she hadn't a clue why she'd been summoned to the Rum Romeo.

She came among the casino tables with her smiling eyes everywhere, checking the girls, seeing how they worked on the clients, scoring, dropping, promoting each other. A natural, was Grellie. Born to rule stringers galore. Very valuable.

She was petite, slender, but in Martina's opinion too heavily breasted, 'pert' she supposed was the word. Martina watched her come, feeling something near hate for the bitch. Pleasantry was an art she favoured only for its ability to deceive. Grellie's dress sense proved that she used every groat of her allowance from Martina, never patronising back-street shops, the markets, never in a million years. She lived in ladyland, saved little, swung spending through major shops in Edwardian mahogany-and-crystal thorough-fares, wearing guinea-an-inch, as the local saying had it.

Grellie plunked herself opposite, miming fanning her-self.

'Hello, Martina. I'm exhausted!' She leaned forward. 'See that Shani? Four weeks since I took her on, horrible in yellow, Aussie working her chit?'

Since 'I' took her on? Martina didn't pick her up, but noted it in smouldering cinders.

'Mmmh. What about her?'

'I'm bringing her in full-time, off railway work.'

'Is she that good?'

'No,' Grellie surprised her by saying. 'But she's red hot at numbers.'

'It's too soon.'

Martina saw somebody pull a five-carder at a game three tables nearer the door. Two silly women applauded. Old George was banker there, unchanging of expression, with the stupidly slick girl who called herself Abba, pretty in plum velvet with her hair piled absurdly Carolean.

Grellie digested Martina's opposition. 'Well, I think she's ready.'

'I want trust, not speed.'

It was only then that Grellie understood this was no routine peck-and-check coffee. Her expression changed, but only to surprise. Wariness would have elated Martina, given her direction, for treachery meant punishment. Grellie's expression showed only honest concern. Innocence?

'Is anything wrong, Martina?'

'Who's your feller, Grellie?'

'Feller?' Martina got the woman's instant hooded gaze that defied intruders. 'I take what I want from punters. I need the mood. Why?'

'I've a feeling there's something on your mind.'

'Me?' Still honest, despite those leave-my-sex-alone eyes.

Martina gave her a pulse or two, a chance to offer more, then came out with it. 'It's policy, Grellie. No crossing. You know that.'

'Who's been crossing?'

Grellie still didn't see, or was cleverer than Martina thought. 'Have you?'

The girl's cheeks coloured as she realised. 'Me? See the goers? You know the answer to that, Martina. No.'

'Can I be sure?'

'Yes. Besides, who would I . . .?' Grellie watched two floorwalkers exchange signals – shoulder hitch for too slow, pocket tap for a rush of punters on the way soon – and slowly drift on. 'You think I book Bonn, don't you?'

'It had occurred to me.'

'Then let it un-occur.' Grellie's anger was deliberate. She caught somebody's eye, smiled, waved, pooh-poohing the idea of a chat just now, tapped her wrist to say maybe later. A rather plump girl taking drinks for the fantan table, where the Cantonese girl was doing well with her graceful wand and pile of white Go buttons, waved back. 'I've never hired Bonn. Nor had him spike me. In private hours I do my own life. Those are your rules, Martina.'

Their eyes held, level.

'Then I needn't ask Bonn.'

A vague realisation was dawning in Grellie's gaze.

'Ask him what you like.' She spoke just short of rudeness.

'All right, Grellie. I had to ask. You understand.'

'Yes, I understand.'

All this understanding, Martina thought. But as talk shifted easily to whether Grellie could staff the new moorland motel with girls of the right sort, Martina couldn't help wondering if Grellie's annoyance hadn't been just that little bit too careful coming and a mite too extreme. For a fleeting instant Grellie had looked almost venomous.

It was important, though, to show only friendliness to Grellie. They talked of the new boutique in the main arcade that Posser had insisted on buying, against advice. Martina let Grellie win that one, agreeing not to exclude the goers from the syndicate's two hair emporiums for the whilst.

But she decided to have Grellie's sidelines watched round

the clock for a couple of weeks. Akker would do that well, and what harm could it do?

By four Clare had finished the notes, summarised the laboratory investigations – cervical smears were problematic, because histopathologists had their tumour grades instead of cast-iron standards. She coded the follow-up cases, and said goodbye to the midwives.

She decided not to phone from the hospital's Out-Patients Department. Instead, she drove a mile, stopped near a newsagent's. These days, one phone button recalled the source's phone number, so she used her own mobile phone.

'Pleases Agency, Inc, good afternoon. May I help you?'

With a start Clare realised that she was quite unprepared. She felt her heart thump, as if she was doing something illegal. It was absurd to feel so. Wasn't she making a respectable enquiry?

'Hello? Yes, please,' she said with unnatural loudness. To her anger, she heard herself almost stammering. 'Could I ask what, ah, services you provide?'

The woman was unfazed. 'Have you ever contacted this agency before?'

'No. This is my first time.' Definite, steadying her voice.

'May I ask how you came to ring?'

'I wondered if a person called Bonn worked . . . was on your staff?'

The woman's quiet voice said, 'Might I ask why you mention that name?'

'I . . . I encountered Bonn at the scene of an accident. We both went to help, and naturally exchanged a few words.'

Clare held her breath. This was the moment. She'd been as frank as she dared.

'Then that is quite in order. The service you require?'

Another pause. Why the hell hadn't she thought, gone through this in quiet rehearsal? The girl made it easy with practised matter-of-factness.

'You do not need to be explicit, ma'am. But there is a fee, and the question of exactly when.'

'Fairly soon, if possible,' Clare found herself saying, suddenly calm as you please and determined to take one thing at a time. After all, she only wanted to ask a few questions. Could it be more mundane?

'Do you have a particular venue in mind?'

'No.' Clare was alarmed. Did they send their Bonns to your home, or what? 'I'm not exactly sure what your arrangements actually are.'

'The lady can decide whereabouts – city centre, a hotel complex perhaps. We then advise you if the place of your choice is secure.'

That hadn't crossed Clare's mind. 'Secure against what?'

'We protect our lady clients scrupulously We can suggest a venue . . .?'

'Yes, please.'

'Some location in the city centre? There are several secure and respectable venues.'

'I think that would be all right.' As a doctor, she could visit any hotel she wanted, and claim at a pinch that she'd been called there.

'Any particular time, or day?'

Her knees were trembling, Clare realised. Yet she'd negotiated the minefield, and got there.

'Today, if possible.'

'One moment, please.' After a brief silence the woman said it would be fine. 'Does madam know the Vivante Hotel? It's in—'

'Yes, yes, I know it.' Clare wanted to ask more, but the clerk was already booking things down with professional briskness.

'One hour from now, ma'am?'

'Right. I shall . . .' Shall what, exactly? Walk in and ask where a hired man was waiting? For an insane moment Clare almost asked the girl what to wear.

'Could you give me some identification, ma'am?'

'Identification?' Clare said sharply. Wasn't the woman bragging about ultra-confidentiality a moment ago?

'I mean a name or designation by which you wish to be known. A first name is adequate, if you prefer. Not necessarily your own.'

'Clare,' Clare said stupidly before she could think that through.

'Now please give me any three-digit number, for coding. We like you to remember them.'

'Oh. Three-Nine-Five,' Clare answered, her medical student number.

'Very well, Clare Three-Nine-Five. In one hour, the person you named will be waiting in room . . . a moment, please . . . four-oh-seven.'

Clare repeated the number. 'Thank you.' She waited. Was that it?

The woman's finish was smooth, quite a patter. Clare listened. 'All future service orders will require that forename and number. Please regard it as your own personal code. Pleases Agency, Inc, runs a twenty-four-hour service, and accepts cheque cards. Standing bank orders are not advised . . .'

The prattle went on. The agency desired to please. Comments on the service were welcome. The line was open except between midnight and . . .

Clare put her phone into the glove compartment, marvelling. Why had she thought it would be any different? Men must go through this when booking some girl. Or maybe they didn't have a woman's ingrained self-criticisms? Or didn't they mind the social stigmas, was that it?

One hour! She stupidly found herself hurrying when she had time to kill.

RACK WAS PUT out. He'd been narked a lot lately.

'Don't, Bonn. Doob's a drunk. You know what shrinks say? Winos are hooked on tits. They're all orphans. You never get a wino isn't an orphan.'

'Get Grellie and the girls to help.'

'Already pinned him.' Rack didn't give Bonn a glance. This was the shortest Bonn had ever been, doubting Rack's prowess like that.

'Before Martina changes her mind.' Bonn's joke erased his brief but wounding curtness. Martina was the oracle. You got yes, or got no.

Rack calmed down. 'You got a new go in half an hour.'

'Clare Three-Nine-Five? I know.'

Two minutes later, Bonn was admiring Doob's skill in the Butty Bar. He had seen the drama evolve scores of times. Doob never came out of his pickpocket gambit with less than a full day's dossing and grub money. It was beautiful, a whole play based on the assumption of honesty in others.

The woman would soon have her handbag stolen. She was mildly surprised that the man, Doob, sat opposite when the café was only sparsely occupied. Doob always looked the part for a steal. His hair was combed, white shirt, clean nails, quick and ready grin, but a little worried. He did the whole scene – absent-mindedly taking the woman's bread, his embarrassment remarkable. It was the whole monty – blushing apology, rushing for replacement roll and butter. The woman, so soon to be robbed, ended up laughing.

Her handbag was on an adjacent seat, safe enough. She became engrossed in Doob's tale. (Bonn's favourite was Doob's sorrow at a girlfriend's cruel expellation of her aged father. Doob couldn't live with that, it was too cruel, you see. He'd chucked her yesterday because of it.) Doob had a series of lines, each with a wry smile. Women can live without a man, but a man can't live without a woman. Then the generous smile and 'I'm hopeless, really. . . .'

Big on phoney, high in skill. Bonn had first seen Doob's con in this very nosh bar, and known he was in the presence of a master. He saw Rack signal outside the window. Time was passing. He couldn't be late for this new one, Clare Three-Nine-Five.

The woman was eager to talk. They always were, after one of Doob's tales, the perfidy of young females, such disrespect of parents, liking Doob's self-deprecation, capti- vated by the lost-without-a-woman sentie, or the parents- deserve-*some*-consideration. The woman was married, wedding ring, looked a parent. Bonn didn't recognise Doob's scarper today, the accomplice who entered and sat with his newspaper at the next table.

The scarper left after barely tasting his coffee. Maybe he was from the bookie's round Tibb Street. He'd be doing it for a fiver, less if Doob pulled the gulp, did the steal without trouble.

It was only when Doob was exchanging addresses with the woman, wanting to take her out somewhere, art gallery, theatre, whatever, that she saw her handbag was gone. Doob did the swift burn to anger – laying it on thick this afternoon, Bonn thought. Egad! There was only one explanation, the man who'd left so swiftly! Bonn watched, fascinated, Doob's superb denunciation, a whole Chaplin melodrama gestures, downright fury. Finally, the dash out to recover the lady's handbag while she fretted, helpless, explained to the bored waitress who'd seen it all a hundred times, nodding yeah, you get all sorts.

The lady became agitated, checked her watch, but no less worried than Rack at the window. The woman began to suspect the worst, looking anxiously at Bonn, should she phone the police. She'd all but given up when in came Doob. He was having difficulty breathing. Who knew what battles he'd had to fight to recover the lady's handbag from the forces of evil out there?

Typical Doob, though, his final touch: no dramatics now. He simply sat, nostrils flared for air flow, and shyly met the lady's eyes. Bonn put words into their inaudible interchange.

'Is this your handbag?' (Doob, gently.)

'Yes! Oh, thank you! Was it . . . well, *hard* to get it back?'

'Oh, you know . . .' in modest disclaimer.

'I'm so grateful.' (Swift examination of the handbag's contents.) 'Everything's still here!'

'I was just lucky . . .' etc., etc.

Doob was a quiet hero, alone worthy in this terrible city. Bonn walked out, waving to the counter lass.

Moments later Doob caught him up as he made for the hotel.

'How did you leave things?' Bonn asked, curious.

'Expressions of gratitude, mutual support should we ever meet again.'

'Nothing more tangible?'

'Is there ever?' Doob smiled. 'I've given up the booze, Bonn. On my life.'

Bonn said outright, 'I've made key. Lancelot, Galahad, and you.'

'Me? Definite?' He didn't take Bonn's silence as an affront, and stuttered thanks, overwhelmed. 'Ta, Bonn.'

'Rack will say when to meet. Depends what I have on.'

He made it to 407 with eight minutes spare. Bonn felt Rack's displeasure, though he was nowhere to be seen. Best stander in the world, Rack.

Bonn settled in.

Clare felt almost faint, waiting in the station buffet. Which made her cross. Hadn't she been trained to meet, treat people from all walks of life? Why was she behaving like a schoolgirl entering her first dance hall?

Amid the cries of parents and the beeping of the café's space-war machines, she'd gone over her reasoning. A pro fessional lady needed to keep abreast of social changes. It's necessary for her work, to examine Bonn's particular occupation.

And to get him to find out about an accident.

Oddly, she remembered the time she had tried a ciga-rette. Was this the same sense of guilt? She rose and left, passed the investment offices. The hotel was not dowdy. She vaguely knew of it, but became more doubtful as she approached. But confidence was nine-tenths of everything. She walked calmly through the foyer, seeing no one she recognised.

Four minutes to go. People were in the lounge having tea. Somebody was booking in at Reception, pretty flower arrangements there. Nobody was interested, she was just one more person crossing the carpet. Her heart was pounding. She felt like ice. Her first operation came to mind, the dreadful awareness that it would be *her* scalpel that did the incision. But this? A mere social enquiry, nothing like serious surgery. She closed her mind to doubt and took the lift, alighted in a bright corridor among ferns and paintings of hunting scenes.

Arrows said this way to 410 to 440, that to 409 to 400. She stood, irresolute. What if he wasn't there? She almost turned to run, the ghastly image of herself tapping at some door while hotel guests came to stare.

Anger saved her. For heaven's *sake*! A professional lady doctor has a perfect right to engage somebody for a particular line of enquiry. If she hasn't, who has? It was perfectly above-board.

The number faced her far too soon, but delays sapped courage. She knocked. The door opened, and there was Bonn. For a moment she was amazed. The system had worked.

He stepped back, nearly smiling. She hesitated, then made herself go forward.

'I'm so glad you came.' He spoke quietly. 'Thank you.'

Not at all was her reflex, but she stopped all that.

'I was wondering what if you weren't here.' Did that sound too imperious? She stood, inspecting the room. He had recognised her.

The place was pleasant. This surprised her, though she wasn't sure what she had been expecting. A sitting room with doors off – bedroom and bathroom, she supposed. Fresh flowers in a vase of admirable plainness, couch, matching armchairs, coffee table, paintings of Rivington moorland scenes. The window overlooked a small triangular green with terraced houses. Bradshawgate?

A horrid thought came unbidden, what the hotel staff would have thought had she asked for directions. Was 407 reserved for this kind of encounter? Delete that 'this kind'. She was legitimate.

'There is no other view,' Bonn remarked. 'Can I offer you a drink?'

'Drink?' She advanced hesitantly. How odd. Things hadn't occurred to her. That he would be here to welcome her, engage in social niceties. Foolishly, she wondered was everything included in the price?

'There's tea, coffee, wines, spirits.' He almost managed a smile, his look she was coming to recognise. 'Except I should warn you. I'm hopeless at cocktails.'

'In a moment, then, please.'

She sat on the couch, her action a sort of statement. This was an interview after all. The ball was in her court. She must not forget that for a single instant. She could leave at any time, just up and go.

Which meant it would be quite proper to make him explain what usually went on.

He sat on the other end of the couch, a distance away. Suddenly she panicked. There was something nebulous about him that left a space in the memory where Bonn, that person whom she'd already met twice before, should have been. He had a chameleonlike quality that she found scarey. Sitting here, wooden, she worried he would suddenly assume too much, move on her, expect her to start undressing for goodness' sake, be aggressively masculine, 'Right, you've got fifty minutes, get on with it. . . .' Or, even more appalling, ask her what she wanted him to do to her? She cringed inwardly, thought, My *God*, this is utterly ridiculous—

'May I call you Clare?'

So the agency functioned, its communications intact. 'Yes.' Did she sound relieved?

'Bonn is hopeless.' He grimaced. 'I made it up, not realising that it means something actually quite bad in French argot.'

'It does?' She caught his anxiety. He was asking had she known. 'I didn't know.'

'It means good for nothing. Worthless.' He seemed rueful. 'Names worry me. Choosing a new one's such an opportunity. I messed it up.'

'It was a shame,' she blurted out. 'That security man, by the river.'

Bonn really smiled. She watched, intrigued in spite of herself. It began slowly, spread until it lifted his mouth. 'He thought he recognised me. The policeman.'

'Do they all? In the city?'

'Recognise me for what I am? No.'

There. It was out, in his somewhat stilted speech. He spoke like from another world.

'Something past, I suppose.' He seemed to come to some resolution, possibly abandoning one tactic for another. She warned herself not to have any illusions about him. This was a fee-for-service contract hiring, after all.

'You could have walked by,' Clare said. 'Attracted no attention.'

'Could I?' he asked gravely. 'Given a choice, yes.'

So he had no choice but to help? 'That accident was odd, wasn't it?' she said, too quickly. This was her purpose, to find out more.

'I didn't see it, only the consequences.'

'Do you—?' She got no further. Hire out for jobs other than . . .? Any expression risked insulting him. Just for one minute she'd love to be a man, clumsily uncaring.

'Do I?' He made his question create a little amusement.

'Do you hire out for additional purposes?' Almost as bad.

'Not really. There are rules.'

'Not for anything at all?' Her dismay made him weigh her up.

'You mean while,' he became careful, 'your friend watched, that sort of thing?'

'Of course not.' This was cross-purposes. Silly to feel peevish, for no reason. 'Not related to, well, what you normally do.'

Hopeless, Dr Clare Salford Burtonall, she raged inwardly, women's euphemisms at this stage. And did she know 'normally'?

'I'm sorry. Some days I'm just so slow.' He was honestly puzzled. She thought, Is he thick?

'I want something found out. Need.'

He went still. The only creature she had seen so motionless was a heron, on a canal once, a longboat holiday in Cheshire, the bird a statue reflected in the gleam of early morning. Now it was in the clear, she found it oddly difficult to go on. 'You know the city. I suppose there would be a fee?'

'I would have to see.'

'Haven't other women . . .' Just as bad. 'Have you not been asked this before?'

'Sometimes. But not relating to non-sexual matters.' He shook his shoulders as if freeing himself of some encumbrance. 'Once I was asked to discover whether a lady's friend had ever hired a goer.'

'Goer.' That word. 'And did you. Had she?'

'I never disclose a lady's confidence.' In gentle reprimand. 'This "something" is unrelated, I assume.'

If he can do it, why can't I? she thought. He managed to be oblique, yet precise. Was it practice?

'Unrelated to anything, as far as I know,' she said, trying. That was better. She rose, crossed to stand opposite, demonstrating her right to remain uninfluenced. The interview was over and done with.

'Very well. I shall ask general permission. Will that be enough?'

'Not really.' She felt on surer ground. 'I must know if there will be any disclosure.'

'None from me,' Bonn said courteously.

'And your . . . what are they, bosses?' Mentors? Rulers? Pimps couldn't be right. Guv'nors, perhaps?

'One person whom I would have to see. Can I be told more?'

Clare hesitated. 'I want to find something about a recent event involving one person, locally, near the square. Once you've told me what you learn, that would be the end of it.'

'The consequences would be entirely yours.'

'All of it will be my responsibility.'

'And the police, if it came to concern them, would be . . .'

'My problem, not yours.' She became firmer the more she went on.

'I'll say a provisional yes, then.' He didn't rise with her, leaned his head on a hand, half sprawled in his corner of the couch. 'The accident?'

'Yes.'

She paused, and suddenly lost it. He was waiting for some explanation, but what on earth did she want to know? It was their only point of contact, except for that aggressive swan. The taxi driver was identified, after all, hadn't made a run for it. It was all in the newspapers.

'Give me a day, maybe two. Tell me how I get word.'

'I had better ring you. Can you give me a number?'

'No.' No apology, just that. Nope. He caught her surprise. 'You will have to say.'

'Then I'll call the agency.' She found her handbag, remembered in the nick of time and said rather breathlessly, her new firmness frittered by having to fulfil her part. 'I must pay. I'm sorry, but I'm not quite sure how I go about it.'

'However you decide, Clare,' he said, rising with a man's angularity.

In near anguish at her incompetence, she left money, notes she had previously counted out, on top of the small television.

He seemed not to notice, and let her out as if she had been for afternoon tea. She walked off in a daze, still aware of the risk of being seen but now relieved and almost exhilarated. Success felt warm. One thing made her really glad. Bonn had looked at her, really *at*, instead of vaguely in her direction. She had been given his complete attention throughout. She must have been really worried, deep down, about being treated as if nothing more than a passing client, spoken at instead of with.

Patients must feel the same when seeing doctors. How horrid. Her relief stemmed from Bonn's concern. *Show* of concern, perhaps? No, no pretence. Back there, Bonn had been genuine.

It was odd to realise that the concealment was all his, yet she knew more of him than he did of her. She felt it ought to be the other way round. But she would soon know more about the accident than even the police. It excited her, like the acquisition of a new and potent strength.

13

Mogga dancing – that type of ballroom competition dancing where each couple changes their dance rhythm to a different style every few bars – usually four or six – throughout a single melody.

P OSSIBLY SOMETHING IN his religious past made Bonn embarrassed to watch the dancers swirling onto the floor. Cymbals crashed, lights flickered enough to set off epileptics everywhere. The MC screamed announcements in his glitzy suit, wriggling and exultant.

'Mogga dancing!' he screeched. 'It's . . . here . . . *now!*'

Except it wasn't, yet. Bonn sat at a balcony table. The Palais Rocco lived in gloaming, its splashes of light too fleeting to give eyes a chance. They flashed, rippled, dazzled, wheeled overhead, the dancers below under attack from a celestial dogfight.

'You know the rules!' the compère boomed, whipping his mike's trailing wire like a lash. 'The dancers randomly draw one dance . . . *each!*'

Please don't say *eacheroo*, Boon prayed silently, please, please.

'And I do mean . . . eacheroo!' The compère laughed inanely. Unbelievably, people at the tables applauded. 'One dance only! That's *how* many?'

'One . . . *dance!*' the audience screamed. The girls twirled their skirts, their partners waving boxer fashion as if they'd floored somebody.

'You *gad* it!'

The pseudo-American accent was obligatory. Bonn was astonished by the enthusiasm. He'd only been here a couple of times before, and wondered if Martina knew of mogga dancing's mad popularity. Spectators were rushing about the dance floor to touch their favourites for luck. One group at tables near the band had bouquets ready.

'What hap-*pens* now?' the compère bawled. The mike whistled deafeningly. 'Here's the great . . . mo*ment*!'

He marched about, generating tension.

'The couples draw a dance. Old-fashioned waltz for one luck-eeeya couple. Cha-cha-cha for another. Maybe the ga*votte* for some, who knows? And so-o-o-o *on*!'

The audience fell about. Bonn squirmed. Everybody clapped and stamped.

'Our super . . .?' The MC cupped his ear, face enraptured.

'*Dooper!*'

'Orchestra, big-band sound, everybodee, is Merry Jerry Doakes! And what do our finalists do, everybodee?'

'Dance-dance-dance!' The place thundered.

'With this proviso.' The MC hunched, grim, talking with hushed intensity. 'The dancers must ex-ee-cute as many dance styles as possible before the music ends!' Tumultuous approval drowned his climax. He waved a card.

'First couple, let's hear it . . . Lancelot and Guinevere!'

To roars, Lancelot and a girl Bonn didn't recognise walked with stateliness onto the dance floor. They wore matching electric-blue costumes, shimmering with sequins.

Rack slid into the next chair. 'Put-up job.'

'The MC said it was random.'

Rack grinned. 'Dance competition's rigged worse than wrestling.'

'Lancelot has drawn' – people hushed to hear – 'the tango!'

Whistles, jeers, catcalls, and boos met the announcement. Lancelot grinned and waved. Guinevere pouted.

Rack whispered as the pandemonium subsided, 'The tango is Lancelot's favourite. He'll win hands down.'

Bonn didn't know if Rack was having him on.

'Straight up. You'll see.' Rack made sure nobody could overhear. 'You have a visitor. A wannabe, Salvo.'

'Is the girl one of ours?' Bonn asked. Salvo?

Rack choked back a laugh as the old 'Blue Tango' began and Lancelot and Guinevere swept into the dance.

'Leave off, Bonn. She's a pro dancing teacher. Lancelot doesn't want to be lumbered with some scrubber all left feet.'

Bonn watched Lancelot swoop, the girl draped languidly over his arm. After a few steps they snapped into a synchronised tap-dance routine, then into the English slow waltz.

'Foxtrot!' He recognised that, been taught as a lad. Now into a mad jive, quickly abandoned for the military two-step, all to the tango strain.

'He'll get another twelve in,' Rack predicted, engrossed as he counted. 'They've to finish back on the tango, six bars min. I had to clobber this bandleader.'

All round the ballroom people were already arguing. Rack rose to shout at a nearby table. They gestured back. The band was hardly audible as the racket worsened.

'Bonn?'

He stood before their table trying to look at ease.

'Salvo,' Rack said in Bonn's ear, then stalked off to bawl insults.

Bonn went through the red plush door, Salvo following.

*

From the moment Salvo saw the one they called Bonn he guessed the interview might go bad.

He saw Bonn's stander, called Rack, a short stocky bloke who was arguing, poking people in the chest – what a prat. Salvo had seen him telling some street bint how weather came. Who'd believe such a pillock?

But this Bonn, Salvo had never seen a bloke like him.

He'd tried to get to talk to Bonn outside earlier in the day, every city prick excited about a new key man going to recruit, but suddenly Rack had appeared from nowhere and shunted Bonn aside like he was secret fucking royalty that mustn't be bothered. For a minute Salvo wondered whether to do the noisy little nerk over, but finally swallowed his pride, put the word in while Rack talked to some goojer who'd pulled a fake-pickpocket dop in a caff.

Salvo could hardly keep his eyes off Bonn. A furlong off you noticed nothing special, really spit average. Closer, he seemed a pillock, casual, at a loose end and maybe unemployed, no home to go to. Step closer, your eyes began to stare until you wanted to look away in case somebody got the wrong idea and thought you wanted a scrap.

Cool, maybe, was it? Definitely weird. Not the sort you'd scrap with, though, because he wouldn't scrap. He'd stammer sorry, be worried he'd narked you some way. But inside his fucking head he knew things. He was like somebody sad for nothing, heartbroken for fuck all. He'd be a good mate, be there when the fucking graves opened. Not fashionable, dressed real mankie, definitely no mode. But the birds looked at him, made moves told you they wanted next, any price. It was more than fucking weird, it was sort of sick. Only time he'd felt this was seeing his dying auntie.

'I'm Salvo,' he said before he was asked.

'How do, Salvo,' Bonn said.

They stood leaning on the corridor walls. A couple of dancers pushed past. He heard Rack's voice, loudly telling somebody about music and trees, fucking lunatic. The door closed with a hiss. The noise went to a distance.

Bonn looked direct, right at you, not trying to fix you, just seeing in. Like going in somebody's house, you look about, walls, the windows, furniture. It astonished Salvo, seeing interest. That was it! Interest! He felt important, and wondered if it was some trick.

'I heard you're key, Bonn.' Like they were friends.

Bonn, still looking round in Salvo's skull, shrugged, apologetic. Applause sounded, dancers coming off. Salvo suddenly knew, but had to go on despite. People knew he was in here, asking, birds itching to spread word, bitches.

'Say where you are, Salvo, please.'

Which felt odd, because Salvo had never been asked that, yet he knew exactly what Bonn meant. Should he tell Bonn outright what he thought of birds – including his own Marla and her queer girlfriend Lana, their giggles excluding him? He'd get laughed at, and nobody laughed at Salvo.

'I handle birds okay. Before, I did labouring, driving.'

So he started telling Bonn about his girlfriends, mentioning Marla but not by name, giving Lana some stick as he went.

'And you do like older women too, Salvo,' Bonn said. Salvo had said nothing of the kind.

'I had one or two.' Salvo's face broke into a grin. 'Holiday camp, near Skegness. It paid, until a pal got me city work.'

'It proves satisfactory,' Bonn said. Weird.

'My job's part-time. Cars, helping my mate. Oz sees me right.'

'Your pal, who is married and settled down.'

Salvo, duped by this style of talk, almost agreed before

he caught himself and said no, Oz was a loner, daft about his bloody engines.

Bonn said, as the music struck up for a new couple, 'Salvo. I can't take you on, but I am grateful that you considered asking.'

'Can I go on your waiting list, Bonn?'

'I keep none, Salvo.'

Salvo was sure this Bonn admired him. 'Maybe you'd put in a word with, like, Ton Atherton or Fret Dougal? They'll listen to you. I'm dead keen.'

'They do not know me. I have nothing to do with anyone, Salvo.'

Which Salvo could not believe. 'Can I get in anywhere, Bonn?'

Somehow Salvo had calmed. He'd been ready to erupt. Instead he was calmer than in a pub. This Bonn talked it like it was, for all his sadness beyond that calm. Did Bonn ever gamble? Odds to follow, if he did.

'I do not know, Salvo. I heard rumours, but gossip is only that. You know as much as I.'

'Thanks, Bonn.'

'No, Salvo. Thank you.'

Clare found the two policemen waiting for her in the doctor's office. It wasn't allowed, and she withdrew to chastise Sister Bristowe.

'Be with you in a moment,' she said, heartier than she felt, beckoning the senior nurse aside. The last patients had gone from Dr Fettisham's afternoon GP surgery. It had been short and straightforward, one problem of late-onset diabetes for investigation.

'Why did you let them in, please?' she asked Sister Bristowe, cold.

'They're police, Dr Burtonall!'

'They cannot be left unsupervised where the patients' confidential notes are kept. They have no right, and well you know it!'

'They said they're investigating a death. A man's been killed—'

'Which leaves us with responsibilities for the living, sister!'

Clare wished before she'd gone a yard that she had had a better exit line. She entered her office. The two men rose.

'I've met you before, by proxy,' she said, taking her place at the desk.

'We didn't touch a thing, Dr Burtonall,' the older man said. He wore a thick overcoat, too heavy this mild weather, and looked balding, tired. His younger colleague was a natty dresser, coloured shirt, sandy hair waved. 'This is Windsor, who's no help. He wanted to rifle your belongings. I'm called Hassall. I've heard all the name jokes, and I'm past the pilfering stage.'

He'd overheard her lambasting Sister Bristowe. Which was fine.

'Mr Hassall, Mr Windsor.' She ignored their identification cards.

'You were first medical assistance on the scene of an accident in Victoria Square, Dr Burtonall. A man died, one Leonard Mostern?'

She almost smiled. Converting statements into questions by a casual inflexion was a trick every doctor learned in embryo.

'That's so. I attended the autopsy in Morbid Anatomy.'

'Was anything unusual about the incident, Dr Burtonall?'

Odd how names intimidate, Clare thought. You see name tricks used daily on TV talk shows, interviews. *But can't you see, Mr Blenkinsop, that . . .?* Sister Immaculata's put-down all over again. Hang on – incident, not accident?

'Dr Burtonall?' Hassall was diffident, cool. Windsor was fed up, all this routine.

'Have you any specific question, Mr Hassall? I'll try to answer.'

'Right.' He waved away his assistant's notebook. 'Can you describe exactly what you saw? Brief as you like.'

'Very well. I was driving my motor – it's a maroon Humber Supersnipe. There was traffic thrombosis, so to speak. A taxi cut in front of me, then went two cars ahead. It was all very slow, you must understand, inching forward.'

'Would you say the taxi was driving recklessly?'

'We were hardly moving.' She thought a moment. 'No, I wouldn't say so. Maybe jerkier than the rest, but it was all stop-start-stop. He was trying to get through, that's all I'd say, like everybody else.'

'Did you see anybody at the scene?'

Her throat constricted. She pretended to dwell on Hassall's question.

'Many. It was the rush hour. I remember seeing a lot of pedestrians coming from the railway and thinking, Oh heck, another swarm to block the lights.'

'Did you notice any one person?'

'The taxi driver, behaving rather stupidly – though it was possibly excusable. An elderly lady kept saying it was the victim's own fault for pushing. A middle-aged man told the cabbie to reverse, and finally did it himself. The policeman.'

Hassall waited patiently, all benign. Windsor was desperate to butt in.

'You don't remember anyone else?'

'In the crowd? None in particular. Can you not be more specific?'

'The answer to that's a plain old-fashioned no, Dr Burtonall.' Hassall smiled. 'The Stockholm Effect – isn't that it? Create the answers you're after?'

'Aren't there cameras, like in the shopping precinct?'

Windsor looked away, tricked to anger. Hassall heaved a veteran's sigh. He'd been a troubled parent in his time.

'The camera by Warrington exit wasn't working. Pity, really.'

'Not nicked, but broken,' Windsor cut in, blaming everyone.

'All right, Windsor.'

Hassall held out his hand. Windsor hauled him up. Clare wondered if it was an act they'd seen on TV reruns and felt clever copying.

'Is something wrong, Mr Hassall?' she asked. Suddenly she didn't want them to leave without more explanation.

'No answer to that, doctor, even for Jack the Ripper.' He smiled, edged towards the door. 'All sodding stairs, these clinics. Thanks for your time.'

'Not at all.' She stood in the corridor to watch them go, then asked Sister Bristowe, regretting her earlier asperity, 'How long were they waiting, sister?'

'Not long, Dr Burtonall. I'm sorry about—'

'Sorry. I shouldn't have snapped. What did they ask you?'

'Nothing, doctor.' The nurse seemed surprised. 'It was you they wanted.'

'That's done, then, thank goodness.' Briefly she told Sister Bristowe about the accident. She'd read of it in the local paper. It didn't seem odd to her.

*

The house was more of a chalet bungalow set back in a short cul-de-sac. Rack had whizzed past – 'I did a one eighty, second gear, transed up to first and slided out, four seconds!' – and said it was secure enough to post Bonn through the woman's letterbox.

'Thank you, Rack,' was all Rack got, as he stopped sedately to let Bonn off within two doors. 'Fifty minutes.'

'Here, Bonn,' Rack said, all serious. 'Know why homers are always quicker than in hotels?' And when Bonn didn't reply, 'It's because the bird is scared you'll pinch things, see? Give us a yell if, eh?'

'Certainly.' The car moved off to the end of the road.

Bonn walked along the pavement, up the path. No dogs, a small Ford before the garage. Plants tied back so as not to straggle, neat pots with begonias, reds and yellows, cleverly increasing the size of the lawn.

The door opened. A man stood there, looking almost surly.

'Are you him?'

'Hello. I believe I'm expected. Is that right?'

'You don't look like one.' The man held the door for Bonn. The only way when doing a homer was to seem routine. Humour was out.

'We do vary. Have you any requests, Clint?'

The man had made the booking, his woman speaking once for authenticity. Bonn's use of the man's assumed name had the right effect. The man swelled with importance.

'I want to see you start.' Clint was more assured. 'And you stay while I ask her questions after. Okay?'

Bonn detected a little uncertainty. He nodded, not quite frowning.

'You're the boss, Clint. Make sure I don't overstay.'

The woman was nervous, standing by the bedroom

window. Bonn guessed that she'd tried every position in the room, finally settled for something resembling the Gainsborough Lady without the ostrich-plumed hat. She wore a dressing gown. Wedding ring, heavy cosmetics, hair freshly done.

'I told her to get ready,' he said.

'Like your hair,' Bonn said to the lady. 'Where do you go?'

She said quickly, 'I've been going to Vernon's. You know, Eltham Street? They're dear, but the girls are nice and never pester you to have different.'

'It's a risk,' Bonn agreed. 'Find a hairdresser that you like.'

'That's it.' She seemed astonished that she was actually holding a conversation, and in her bedroom.

Posser said the thing was to distract them from examining you, make sure you got that out of the way straight off, because a woman looked at a man different. A woman did it piecemeal, face, contours, hair, eyes. Then and then only – Posser's expression – did they take the man in, find his motives, kindnesses, his passions. A man saw the whole woman, then only later registered her breasts, her face, maybe threw in her eyes for good measure, and all only after she'd made her total impression.

'It's harder for a woman,' Bonn said. His glance checked with Clint. Such power in that name! 'Dresses, fashions changing, colours.'

'That's so true!' she cried softly, pleased. 'And we haven't got the shops—'

'That'll do,' the husband cut in. 'There isn't all that long.' He gestured to his wife, who went obediently to the bed.

She looked at her husband. He wafted a hand, and she

slipped under the bedclothes. He tutted irritably, yanked the dressing gown off her, and beckoned Bonn.

'I want it orthodox, nothing unusual.'

Bonn smiled at the woman. 'Can I call you by your name?' he asked.

'Vanessa,' she said hurriedly.

'Lovely name.'

Bonn shed his jacket, and smiled the man out of the room. Clint went, with a backward look. Bonn closed the curtains, glancing casually round the room. Two cameras, on angle supports in the top corners. It was par for the course, he thought with sorrow. They could be ignored.

He started to strip, sitting on the bed and looking at her. She sat with the sheet raised to her chin, staring. Bonn wondered how long it had been for her. The children's photographs in the hall had given little clue. Wiser not to ask.

'You know, women have it made,' he said with a sigh.

'How?' Her voice was defensive.

'They look so lovely, undressing. Look at us men. Bag of frogs, however we're seen. Front or rear, top or side, we look ridiculous.'

'Not always.' She hesitated, and he looked over his shoulder at her, smilingly denying it. 'Some women aren't at all pleasing. I mean, I'm . . .'

'You are beautiful,' Bonn said, stripping off the rest of his clothes. 'So it's easy for you to say.'

'I've been on a diet since—'

He rolled under the bedclothes, and put a gentle hand on her mouth.

'You, Vanessa, are a delight. Believe it. I have the evidence of my own eyes to prove it. Say what you want.'

She had tears in her eyes. 'I don't know what to do.'

'Bonn.' He smiled. 'I'm called Bonn. I'm yours, to do what you want. This is your hour.'

'What did . . . Clint say I had to do?'

'You, Vanessa,' Bonn whispered. 'I do whatever you decide.'

Her eyes were round, staring. He placed a hand on her knee, gently moved his palm to the inner side of her thigh.

'I don't know what to say, Bonn. I never do. Is that ridiculous?'

'No, Vanessa, love. There's another way. Just close your eyes. Simply let go, Vanessa.' He was looking into her eyes along the pillow. 'Slip away. Feel the coming love. Think of yourself for once.'

'I want to tell you,' she said, lips near his ear. 'There's a camera—'

'Forget them, darling. Forget everything. Shhh . . .'

Bonn got in and shook his head at his stander's interrogative look.

'Cameras in the bedroom. Two that I could see.'

'They'll be camcorders on auto. Any stillers?'

'I don't know, Rack.'

''Kay.' Rack drove to a phone box.

Bonn switched on the radio, retuned, listened until Rack returned.

'What's that crap?' Rack demanded, glaring at the radio. 'Listen to something proper.' Rack filled the car with a heavy-metal band. 'Know what makes this better than that old stuff you had on, Bonn?' he asked as they drove on. 'They put codes in, like trigger words in adverts—'

'Excuse me, please, Rack. Did you obtain—?'

'I obtained.' Rack grinned. 'Akker's on his way to nick the cassettes. The bugger won't even know.'

'He's utterly reliable?'

'No,' Rack said unexpectedly. 'But I make him.'

14

Cicisbeo – a male paid by a female for sex plus, usually, regular companionship.

S OME GOES WERE doomed, or dangerous. This was one. Bonn felt it the minute he stepped to meet her. Open plan, Rack called this sort of encounter, never liked them.

The woman was practically purring. Bonn was being amusing, chatting, but it was hard work. She was not at all fazed by his youth, her middle years.

The Conquistador Bed and Grill had been unfairly described as a misplaced motorway service station. Converted from a derelict cinema, it now did for salesmen, passengers seeing a halt between London and Glasgow, and visitors to the International Free Trade Hall's concerts.

He had twice asked Rack to be sure to be on time, a sign that something felt bad. Rack was talking overloudly to the sparsely populated lounge's bar staff. It had enough mirrors. He talked his theories, but watched Bonn.

'It isn't a lot to ask,' the lady told Bonn. 'It's for somebody else.'

He'd already decided that she smiled too much, preening herself.

'Not for you?'

'Why, no!' She still wasn't in the least put out.

Comfortable, other women would have described her.

Sensible shoes, makeup a little overdone with wrong colours for her complexion. Hair newly permed, handbag from a weddings-and-funerals wardrobe.

'A friend?' The commonest fiction. Bonn never minded.

'Yes. Does that matter?'

The armchairs in the lounge were not quite facing. Bonn regretted offering her coffee. It was unwise to prolong this. Being hired for her friend was one thing. Being hired to create trouble was something else entirely.

'Not at all. In fact,' he introduced carefully, 'it's commoner than you might expect. It's surprising how often people want to give a person like me as a gift, to a lady friend. Or husbands pay for it, for their wives, a celebration. Nobody would think twice if it was a present of, say, a necklace, a bouquet, or a new dress, so why should pleasure be looked down on?'

'Is it really? Common, I mean.'

He talked quietly into her fascination. 'It's a new tradition.'

'How, exactly?'

This was outside the lines, Martina's phrase when she was niggled, but he played it through, the woman hired him after all. If it came to nothing it wouldn't be his fault. He was simply there until the clock ticked out. Expenditure and expense, Martina's law.

'It varies,' he said in his steady hushed voice, the one that got the best results. 'I can't disclose any details of ladies who . . . you understand.'

'Oh, certainly!' she cried softly. 'I wouldn't want it any other way!'

Which raised the question, Bonn thought, why this meeting was taking place in an open hotel lounge at this time of day.

'Confidentiality is everything.' He reflected a moment, stories he could risk. 'Some ladies want to fix up a friend.' He had the words off pat. 'You can imagine. Girls at work, having a plain friend on, a cruel joke.'

'What happens?' She was still as a stoat. Sadly, he'd guessed right.

'Strangely, I always enjoy the company of such plain ladies, even if they are hoax victims.'

'Do you tell? Own up?' She meant herself, but he was not to know this.

'I obey my instincts. Sometimes I concoct stories, so the plain lady in question can extricate herself without being embarrassed.'

'Extricate herself?' She didn't like the sound of that, and lost drive.

This was it. She was into something personal, destructive. He was relieved it was the Conquistador after all, Rack talking, mirrors full of eyes.

'Well, think of the emotional scars a vulnerable lady might suffer. A cruel joke, her ashamed, her friends laughing at her.'

'Joke.' She tasted the offensive word. She'd wanted an automaton, a malevolent one at that, and got Bonn.

'Or some hurtful game.' He winced, so sad. 'Maybe somebody wanting evidence for a divorce, or to do some other lady down.' Then he smiled, at his best. 'I'm to give love. As you know, I am expensive.'

'Well, of *course*!'

'If it's for some neffie purpose . . .'

'Neffie? What's that?'

'Neffie, nefarious.' He reached for her hand, disclosing terribly clandestine secrets. 'Like, suppose some lady wanted me to see her, to damage her, by getting back to the wrong person. It wouldn't be fair.'

'Aren't you paid for that?'

Here it comes, Bonn thought in despair. What street lads called luck-fuck-buck sessions were the norm out there. But in the real goer trade two out of every seven were this kind, the client wanting you to ruin some other woman.

'For love, yes. The ideal,' he said, frankly now willing her to cut her losses and abandon her sorry plan, 'is for an attractive lady to hire me for herself.'

'And this . . . this neffie thing?'

He groaned inwardly. She would make complaints, vicious ones.

'It is unacceptable. To provide evidence, disrupt her life, like that.'

'But you're hired!' She came back to it. Furious any second now.

'For you,' he said. 'I would be disappointed if it was for somebody else.'

'It's my friend.' Her lips set in a rigid line. She forced herself on. 'She isn't suitable for my Eric. She's known for doing all sorts.'

Bonn started his countdown, Rack there.

'Eric and I are real friends. We met two years after I was divorced. It was *right*. Then she came along. We go to this club.'

'You hired me for her?' He made himself utterly disappointed.

'Yes,' with non-negotiable truculence. 'I've arranged to meet her here in half an hour. She's always punctual.' She was bitter even about that.

'And you want me . . .?'

'To take her out, and . . . *do* it with her.' She swelled with rage. 'I asked most particular if I could. The telephone woman said yes.'

Thank you, Miss Rose. 'Love, could I make a suggestion?' She was a one-woman wrecking crew, focused on ruination. 'I like you.' He was so apologetic, wanting no more to do with her but acting anguish at missing the chance of serving her personally. 'It's the agency makes these rules. I'm so disappointed.'

Bonn put both hands to his cheeks, the universal sign of alarm.

'When I saw you I was really pleased—'

A crash sounded, to Bonn's huge relief. Rack was throwing glasses.

'One,' Rack bellowed. Crash, crash. 'Two! Three!'

'Good heavens! Quickly, darling.' Bonn stood, took the woman's arm, urging her up, out, away. 'There's a disturbance!'

'Get the frigging manager!' Rack bawled. 'I've got the wrong drink! What sort of a fucking place is this?'

'This way, love.' Bonn made a real drama, darting with her down a corridor and through the restaurant. 'The police will be here.'

'*Police?*'

Bonn got her into Quaker Street, where he disengaged.

'Please look casual, darling. Phew!' He smiled, confident and helpful. 'There'll be newspaper photographers along soon. Disturbances always bring them. You don't want to be arrested with a stranger.'

'No! No! That man started throwing, breaking things!'

'Some drunk,' Bonn intoned gravely. They walked towards the shopping mall, safe on crowded pavements. 'Football supporters, who knows?' He drew her into the multiple store. They moved among shoppers, stood at the leather-goods counter, drifted on. 'There are better places, darling. The Conquistador isn't as secluded as it might be.'

'Where?' She gathered herself, conscious of the risk she had taken.

'Where you and I could meet? Not for anyone else?' He timed the hesitation. 'You see, darling, you deserve pleasure. I think it's silly.'

'What's silly?' she asked sharply. 'Do you mean me?'

'No, love. Wasting your best years worrying about some other woman.' He made sure nobody could overhear. 'I'll bet you always put others first.'

'That's true. I have.'

He was at least halfway.

'Naturally, I'm disappointed, because I took to you straight away. I'm sorry about that drunk. I'll tell the agency there's no charge.' He hesitated, obviously wanting to take his leave in a more intimate way. 'I just hope that you place an order. For me. For yourself.'

He pressed her hand, and they parted. She stood a moment, not quite sure what had gone on. Bonn walked away, wringing with sweat.

Outside, Rack was sitting on the pedestrian barrier by the kerb.

'It's okay. She's heading for the Tibb Street exit. Well out of that one, eh?'

'Ta, Rack.' Bonn spoke with feeling. 'She wanted me to wreck her friend. You did excellently.'

Rack barked a laugh, shaking his head. Nobody like Bonn for adding '-ly' to words that didn't need.

'Martina's barking mad, Bonn. The bill's a fortune, and it's down to you.' To Bonn's gaze he said, guffawing so much he rolled about the pavement. 'Ted the manager's dropping an invoice.'

'Didn't you explain?'

'Me?' Rack paused to help some woman fold a push chair while she put her infant into her car. 'Me?' He walked on. 'When have I had the fucking time?' He laughed so much he could hardly get words out.

'I want to speak to Tuesday and Glazie. They on duty?'

'Now? Sure. Why?'

'Tell you later. Do I have to see Martina?'

'Wouldn't be in your shoes, for half Grimsby.' Rack left, laughing.

Bonn went to investigate the death of the man Leonard Mostern. Two workmen were replacing the surveillance camera at the corner of Victoria Square.

The Weavers Hall was a palatial remnant of the city's industrial wealth. One floor held banqueting rooms, with an elite club. No more than twenty night guests, with sitting rooms overlooking the square's shopping mall. Inside, an ornate balcony ran round the great central well of the lounge. The man on the desk, Glazebrook, was a stoutish blond bloke whose appearance belied his record. He'd done time for knifing two men over some forgotten trifle.

'Glazie,' Bonn greeted him.

The receptionist, Glazie's live-in girlfriend, Harriet – 'Hattie' at your peril – moved away to defend their conversation. Bonn smiled his thanks.

'Bonn. Still no chance?' Glazie's eyes gleamed in his specs.

Bonn checked the lounge, old jewel-drop chandeliers,

leather armchairs. He'd asked Glazie if they really did iron the morning papers before laying them out for breakfast, been told yes. Details fascinated Bonn.

Glazie was too eager. He had heard about the promotion. Glazie's dream was to become a goer on Martina's syndicate. He did endless favours, though Bonn would never recommend him and Glazie knew it. No AC-DC goers were wanted, and that was it. Needle histories and sexual shifts were too risky these permissive times. Bonn let Glazie hope. The fiction sufficed.

'Anything, Glazie.' Bonn wanted information.

'Two football managers in one-oh-nine fiddling fixtures. Remember the Midland club relegation? Same blokes.'

'Referees again, I take it.'

'That's it.' Glazie had his facts ready. 'And some Norwegians on a scam Harriet overheard. Only buying Olympic results.'

Harriet said candidly, 'Lovely bums. Skiers, I'll bet.'

'Wait until Bonn gets me into Pleases,' Glazie said waspishly. 'That'll cost you guinea a word.'

How Glazie found things out – or Harriet, for that matter – was not Bonn's business. Time to go. Nothing about Mostern.

'Thank you, then.'

Glazie, Bonn thought, was becoming a risk. He wondered whether to see Harriet on the quiet, get as much gossip from her without Glazie. But what about payment? He couldn't service Harriet by way of fee, as Martina forbade that, though once, in Glazie's absence, Harriet'd asked Bonn outright.

He had time to cut through the alleyway to the Worcester Tea Rooms. Nothing like as elegant as they once were, with their wall tapestries. Now the élite name was a jibe, for it had become a place of bevelled mirrors where live models rotated in tableaus. Bonn was embarrassed, often felt himself go red.

With a preoccupied air he walked through the lounge to the decorative trellises, and found Tuesday. She stepped into the clerker's cubbyhole.

'Hurry, Bonn. I've only a sec to change. What?'

She was a pleasant dark girl topping twenty, thin as a lath and always out of breath from being in a desperate rush. Her father was a Barbados cricketer who'd got religion. She lived in terror of his hellfire morality.

'Just time of day, Tues, no more.'

'Bonn, I'm *late*, for heaven's sake!' She caught sight of herself in a mirror among pinups over the desk clerk's locker and started a busy primp. 'News? I never know anything! There's some insider-trading thing, French, their government owning some company, who knows? One of the girls shagged one last night, really boring, talked of that Yves Thing's finance on the wobble, French Cabinet ministers moving fortunes. Musical chairs. Well?' she demanded.

'Ah . . .' Bonn, blank, wondered, Well what?

She glared, whizzed round in the confined space. 'What do you think?'

'Oh. Lovely, Tues. Anything's superb on you.'

She pouted, knowing the effect it had. 'Some cow from the SFO, her bin going three *days*. Ever heard anything so crazy?'

'Three days.' Bonn simply spoke the words and she winced.

'I forgot! For he'n's *sake*! You make me feel *bad*, Bonn! So I forgot you a goer, is it a crime?'

'Please don't worry, Tues. Serious Fraud Office are heavy.'

'I oughta told you. I heard him outright. The SFO woman, a bitch with a long voice, y'know? Sent Jefferson's black-pepper steak *back*! The ultimate mare.'

Tuesday giggled. Jefferson, her reputed cousin and the club's comi chef, was also her lover, and a man of jubilation.

'We were doing it, y'know? Jefferson has this gadget for lissnin'. Some man called Mossern wanted out, like what man wouldn't? That Antrobus mare got teeth like a fucking carn-ee-*vore*, Bonn. So Miss SFO Bitch of the Year wants a pile to let him off, him mighty scared, Section *Two*, for fuck sakes. Jefferson has me in fits, wagging his dick at the wall.'

'Thank you, Tues.' Bonn bussed her to show her delay didn't matter, he was pleased.

She darted out squealing at her lateness. Bonn considered her news; Mossern was Mostern, most likely. And a Serious Fraud Office woman called Antrobus was supposed to be trapping other people's fingers in the till, not dipping in herself.

Reassuring to know this and that, especially bits that even Rack might not learn. The ideal was a balance. Out here, gossip gave an understanding of scale, of pace, and news, tattletales, were a lifeline. Clare Three-Nine-Five wanted the news.

He adjusted his features, and drifted to keep his appointment. Hilda, did Rack say? Martina's anger about the invoice for the Conquistador's wrecked bar would have to wait. Cheap at any price.

15

IT HAD BEEN drummed into Clare that the need for a confidante was a weakness, a failing likely to lead to revelations that should be reserved for parents. Her one friend was Dr Agnes Ferram. They had met at Breightmet General some eighteen months before.

With Agnes, it was always light-hearted arguing, a real bonus. Her friend was from a severe northern university, not some plush ghetto of idleness – Agnes's words, to needle her – and was unrelenting in her pursuit of data, numbers, statistics. They ruled her attitudes.

'There's no question,' Clare was giving Agnes back. 'Every unit in the country must recognise that atherosclerotic renovascular disease scores high among causes of acute and chronic renal failure.'

'Figures, figures.' Her friend's mantra.

Clare could do with Agnes, but the paediatrician made these incursions into adult medicine with impunity. She proved herself right every time by adopting a punitive air – *you* can't draw a quick histogram on the cuff of your white coat showing percentage incidences, so *I'm* one up, so tough luck. Clare was thankful that she hadn't been a house doctor partnered with Agnes Ferram. It would have been intolerable.

'These ACE inhibitors have been implicated in some twenty per cent of renovascular acute cases,' Clare said, risking it.

'Some. "Some"? You mean maybe?' Agnes laughed her melodious laugh. A passing nurse smiled as she herded three toddlers and their mothers to the hospital reception area.

'And fifty per cent in chronic.'

'Possibly, or not?' Agnes taunted. 'Come back full-time, Clare. You have a responsibility to medicine. Hone your bone. Abandon suburban housewifery.'

'My heart's not in it, Agnes.' But was that true? 'It's different once you're married.'

'Wrong, Clare.' Agnes could be firm about anything. They had finished their work less than an hour late, and surrendered their lunch break. 'Doctors can't exit. Leaving is for nurses and radiographers.'

'Look, Agnes. If you're going to ask—'

Agnes had the remarkable facility of making notes, checking the enormous X-ray folders, filing complex metabolism updates, while chatting. 'Once a doctor, always. Medicine never lets go.'

Clare recognised the cause of Agnes's irascibility. It was about now that her friend needed a smoke, one of her customised secret cigarettes.

'Medical problems follow you, that's for sure,' Clare said ruefully.

Agnes appraised her. 'I *thought* you were looking peaky. Is Clifford well?'

'Fine.' Clare told her about the accident. 'I had the police along. I didn't mention something I ought. I'd met the dead man once. Some function of Clifford's.'

'Why didn't you?'

'It slipped my mind, I suppose. I'm not sure.'

'See?' Agnes checked her watch. Clare wondered if Dr Ferram had some way of neutralising smoke alarms. Her temper would sour soon. Then she would eel into the ladies' room, and smoke herself into a coughing fit. 'You shouldn't let thoughts like those haunt your pathetically narrow life.'

Clifford had left the house unbelievably early this morning, long before Mrs Kinsale had arrived. It was the sort of start he only made when leaving for the city's Ring-road Airport, but he had said nothing.

'You're feeling guilty, Clare.' Agnes could be too astute sometimes.

'There's nothing wrong, Agnes. The accident was at a notorious black spot.'

'You women with husbands.'

Agnes handed Clare six sets of notes. More than a year before, Agnes had co-opted Clare to help with preliminary scans of possibly cystic-fibrotic children. Clare put them away to take home. Her friend was a crusader against the stuffed owls of Admin, who, cruising to awards for long service, packed the committees of the Regional Hospital Board. Her grievance was that Clare shirked the fight against such forces of darkness.

'We ought to have the resources,' Agnes grumbled, waiting for Clare to pack the clinical details and go. 'One in twenty with the CF genes, as far as we know. About one in four hundred couples have both parents featuring it.'

'Surveys are all right, as far as they go, Agnes.' It was old ground. 'Chromosome Seven is the pig. A hundred wonks, the gene on Seven. They should fund research on the delta-F-five-oh-eight mutation, get down to where the business bit does its stuff.'

'Hire more cleverclogs?' Agnes demanded. 'That's the modern myth, invest more in "research". Research does little except raise bureaucrats to ever snootier heights. Ivory-tower research is empire building in lucrative black-magickery. Come back to medicine, where you belong.'

'Maybe I've given up the struggle.' Clare zipped the folder, got her things.

'You've no right. We need simple things. The country has six thousand of these patients who need looking after.'

'You're right, Agnes.' Clare felt tempted. Was this what Agnes was leading to? 'Autosomal recessives get the short end of the stick. It's as if people are somehow to blame.' She went into the corridor. 'See you, Dr Ferram.'

'Fine. And,' Agnes got in, 'tell Clifford your dark secret. He could fund me a survey unit, lend me his wife to run it!'

Clare laughed and left. It wasn't the first time Dr Ferram had given that hint.

She put her files on the old Humber's passenger seat, and sat a moment watching. Should she tell Clifford, or was that making too much?

That man she had seen behind her house on the evening of the accident came to mind. She had since inspected, actually examined, the footpath that curved towards Old Seldon church. The footpath was merely that, inadequate even for a motorcycle. In parts it was troublesome to walkers, with puddles, and a small brook undercutting the path opposite the hedge.

The man had been dark of hair, no beard or moustache in that brief glimpse, wearing a fancy jacket – tall collar, the jagged cut. And the glint of a gold earring! She felt satisfaction at the small detail, as if she had come across some clues. But what was she compiling, for heaven's sake? Any why?

She had work to do on the patients' notes. She would use the city library, work through them there maybe. Then she might phone Bonn's agency. It annoyed her. She would have to pay for Bonn's time merely to ask questions that were probably pointless. But if she had hired – fanciful, but just suppose – a private detective, she would have had to pay, wouldn't she?

The maroon motor started first time. She drove sedately into the city, thinking of Agnes's insistence that it was high time to return to full-time.

It proved to be the heaviest day since Bonn had joined. It made him recollect how he'd begun.

The girl Hilda was a sudden order, Rack racing to find Bonn watching the players in the Lagoon, a sombre place where cards were played for nods and winks, settle up elsewhere before the pubs got going.

Hilda was pert, brisk, surprisingly sure of herself in a way clients were, once they became regulars. Lovely long hair – astonishingly, a natural blonde dyed jet-black. She certainly achieved a look. It made her even more lissom, conveyed a languor you had to notice.

'You've got connections, Bonn,' she said, getting dressed.

'I have connections,' he said.

'Don't be so wary, darling.' She was all smiles, having reached the ascendancy in their forty-minute relationship. What was she, eighteen, nineteen? 'I'm good in the sack. You can testify, right? I'm educated. Get me a chance with a good working house, I'll prove my worth. Give better return than any of the slags round here. You can do it. You know the way in.'

He dressed. True, she was skilled and strove to please,

with just enough sexual deviance to excite further, and had come with him laughing when he'd hurled them together off the edge of sanity. Fine. But she used in-words – 'houses' for brothels, 'return' – suggesting she knew trade. She'd probably once been a prostitute. Martina said once meant always.

'You don't live near, Hilda.'

'No. But I hope to.' She drew a stocking over her hand in casual inspection. Stockings, not tights. She looked at him unsmiling. 'There'd be a slice, Bonn, permanent as you like, if you'd fix it.'

'Slice' meaning an illicit backhander. This dark-dyed girl was a veteran.

'I know what syndicates do, Bonn. They take your money, money that should be yours by rights.'

This would go down brilliantly with Martina. Bonn was enveloped by sadness, at what this would lead to.

'Say where and when.' She didn't answer immediately, so she also knew the risks. He cleared his throat. 'Where can you be reached?' He added to allay suspicion, 'I can't promise, Hilda. They might, they might not. There's always plenty of girls on hope.'

'The First Drop, Affetside, room eight-six. I'll wait two days, okay?' She posed, showing off. 'You can visit me, if you like.'

'Thanks, Hilda. But they'll have contacted you by then.'

She found her shoes, four-inch heels, laughing. 'You sound like a teacher.'

'Wish I was,' he said in apology, thinking, God help you when they come knocking, Hilda. And may God forgive me.

He kissed her forehead, bringing a surprised cackle out of her. Then he went to phone. Rack intercepted him, told him of an urgent take. Hurrying to the Vivante Hotel, Rack trying to interrupt, Bonn told him about Hilda.

By seven that evening Bonn was ready for a rest in the Volunteer, where he appeared to read the sports news, races at Doncaster, football scandals, while watching the rain fall on the central gardens as the night drew in and the traffic shone. He liked the old Volunteer tavern, with its amber lights and dark alcoves. He saw Rack, told him of his misgivings about a second client, Nicolette, said something queer was going on. Rack said he'd let Martina know.

The Nicolette lady had sounded Italian, or maybe French? Nicolette had also been an expert lover, capable and demanding, needing a second time before she lay back replete and ready to talk. She was correct in manner, yet oddly posed more threat. He had been warned about these risks by Posser: 'Some clients who aren't really clients. They are exploiters, journalists exposing the trade, revealing all to bored readers. Others are simply trawling for information to sell to rival syndicates, the police, forces of righteousness keen to eliminate city sin.'

Two oddities in one day? One was chance, but two?

Women never ceased to surprise. When he was first made a goer, his second take was an older woman who insisted on mouth contact only, kneeling to him, leaping away in alarm when he'd reach for her breasts, and only resuming her busy fellating when he was supine. He'd been firmly repulsed as she'd worked harder, squirming to a climax, concentrating on her remote passion. Only when he had spilled did she rest, lying there, untouched, purring.

She had paid by credit card, a platinum gleam from several in her expensive handbag. Wealthy, brisk as any younger woman, checking the time and saying things like, My God I'm late, all that. Parting, she had kissed him, told him she really loved his company, and departed with a gay wave. He wondered what she had gained from the encounter, why she'd even bothered to go to such expense.

The TV news came on in the saloon bar, some boxer fined, a racing driver fiddling his weight for better octanes, the usual. A man came between him and the screen, just as Bonn caught sight of Rack's face by the frosted-glass door.

'You the one they call Bonn?'

'Yes.' The crowd in the Volunteer magically thinned. 'Can I help?'

The man flashed some authority. 'Windsor. You can call me sir. Bring your drink.'

Bonn went with him to the iron table, sat in the attitude of one under interrogation. He wanted the others to know. He left his mineral water.

'Leonard Mostern. You were first on the scene. Tell me about it.'

Bonn narrated the bald details. 'I wasn't first. I didn't see what happened. A lady screamed. I saw a man tell the taxi driver to back his cab off. The cabbie was sick. The man himself reversed the cab off the dead man. There was nothing I could do.'

'Then?'

Bonn knew the technique, made a demand however vague, then criticise the answer. It got people flustered, the old courtroom trick. In a way, Bonn almost enjoyed these encounters. A religious training in mediaeval rhetoric did wonders for the composure.

'Then a policeman came,' Bonn continued, 'and said piss off. A lady doctor came. The station slope was crowded.'

'Your job?' Windsor's sandy eyes looked dry, slightly inflamed, with a hating opacity. 'Be precise.'

'I am an observer for an agency.' Bonn had the party line ready. 'Precision Counts and Counting, Ltd. I survey pedestrians. Proportions of female to male shoppers, numbers of motors going through Victoria Square. Last week it was old-car registrations.'

'Who uses the information you collect?' Windsor asked.

'You'll have to ask the bureau. I just get told where and what hours.'

'Where's your information now?'

'Back there.' Bonn went to fetch the folder that had mercifully appeared underneath his newspaper. He handed it to the plod. 'Should have been in an hour ago, but I wanted to hear about the championship.'

Windsor's sandy eyes scanned the folder. He handed it back.

'What's it about?' Bonn didn't need to act to appear intrigued. 'There must've been a hundred witnesses.'

Windsor leaned forward. 'Mind your own fucking business. Precision Counts means cunts unlimited. We'll have you. I mean that.'

Bonn did a surprised stare as the man left. Rack came in after a few minutes, when the bar had returned to normal.

'Thank you for the file, Rack. Glad you were on hand.'

'Martina would have killed me if I hadn't been. She wants you.'

They left together and made the Shot Pot with only minor distractions. Rack told Bonn he had a go booked for the next afternoon, Clare Three-Nine-Five, plus the councillor's wife from the Wirral. Bonn asked Rack to be by when he'd seen Martina. He had too much to think about for the minute.

The pool hall was in uproar when they arrived, the home team losing badly to Oldham. Already a couple of fights were being settled by the ponchos over wrong bets.

'Is there a right bet?' Osmund said. 'Go through, son.'

Martina was waiting in her tilted office. She was as angry as he'd ever seen her.

'Forget Hilda Two-One-Four,' she ordered without preamble. 'What about Nicolette Nine-Two-Five?'

Bonn summarised the encounter with Nicolette, sexy, post-coital talker, asking about the trade.

'To which you replied?' Martina demanded.

'Nothing to write home about. I think she's investigating us.'

'Like your Hilda? Rack said you thought Hilda Two-One-Four was wrong. How wrong, and why? A partnership?'

'Hilda is a prostitute, maybe a loater, or a stringer. She's accomplished.'

'Sussing for?'

Bonn's ideas had formed on the way over. 'Big money, new in town.'

'Nicolette was also a working girl?'

'Doubt it. She's high time, posh resorts, foreign money, not like us.'

Martina bit her lip. 'Have you any further thoughts, Bonn?'

'Very well.' He hesitated. 'Please don't have Hilda injured, Martina. A warning will be enough. Promise?'

She agreed. 'I promise. Is all well otherwise?'

'Police asked me about that accident. Hundreds of witnesses.'

She watched him go, waited a burning minute, then buzzed Osmund and told him she wanted Akker. The

Burnley lad came in smiling, a pale thin form. He appeared a lazaroidal fourteen, but was twice that age. Martina told him of Hilda.

'Make it look a chance thing, Akker. Do not – repeat not – be seen.'

Akker licked his bloodless lips. 'How far do I go?'

'Something moderate, just so she'll limp.' She spoke with great calm. 'No traces, nothing to investigate. I have enough trouble.'

'Can I take Tooth?' Akker's mate, the Jamaican snooker player.

'No. Tooth can alibi you. And don't touch her – you know what I mean.'

'Hilda, room eighty-six, First Drop, Affetside. No traces, on my own.'

Martina saw the door close. Which, she thought, leaves only Nicolette.

The Worcester Tea Rooms consisted of two separate parts, a lounge of Edwardian tranquillity where meals and teas were served to the city's affluent élite, and a kitchen filled with flame and unholy din. Bonn found Jefferson there, exuberant as ever, to suss out Clare Three-Nine-Five's mystery.

'Antrobus?' Bonn repeated the name while Jefferson almost reeled into the fish chef. 'Are you sure?'

'Am I sure? Tuesday couldn't stop giggling. I shut Tues up with my spe-shull giggle stoppa!' Jefferson slapped his thigh. 'Funny voice, that lady.'

Bonn was actually scared among the kitchen's clashing trolleys, the heat, the clang of ovens, the mass of cooks. He'd seen chefs actually clobber helpers. He had asked

Jefferson to slide out into the alley. The comi chef had stared, then been convulsed when he'd realised.

'Man, *we* is normal here! It's the fuckin' *world* that's crazy!'

So they stayed in the mad carnage while Bonn asked about Mostern.

'Him and that Antrobus woman? Jeez, Bonn, she talk like a fuckin' graveyard. Bass voice like my dad, she.'

'Made you laugh, though.'

'She talkin' Section Two, that Mostern prick. They shagged, but it came to paper and money.' Jefferson paused to yell abuse across the kitchen. Jefferson laughed to his mate, watch this hero here, scared of a fucking *roast*. Bonn was desperate to get out of the place.

'Tuesday got scared – worse'n you, man! Told me to stop listenin' at the wall. That Mostern's mate come with his wife. Posh doctor, she. Your luck's in. He's inna the lounge.' Jefferson mimed taking tea, very grand.

He pretended to glide on spread wings, out of the kitchen. Bonn came on the chef peering from portholed doors.

'That he, younger honk. Dunno the name.'

Bonn looked through, memorising Clifford Burtonall. 'Thanks, Jefferson.' He made to go. The chef held him.

'See the far corner, Bonn? That Antrobus, man.'

Bonn inspected the large-boned severe woman dining alone. So that was the SFO lady. 'Thank you, Jefferson. I'm indebted.'

'Hey, Bonn. You make key?' And Jefferson struck. 'Look, man. I know you, never ask no favours, right?'

Well, maybe. A door went as they made the kitchen. Jefferson saw something wrong, leapt through screaming abuse at a lass about to decant some unspeakable fluid. The girl staggered away into the steam.

Jefferson resumed conversationally, 'My friend, a Kingston 'laat, you seed him, Gyearbourn? Plays blower, Goon Hoppa, them studios?'

'Tall trumpeter.'

'That's Gyearbourn.' The chef had to keep pushing Bonn out of the way of waiters.

'You need Askey and his paper team for Mostern. Gyearbourn wants *in*. Y'know? Give him a tryout. He's my fren.'

'No tryouts, Jefferson. But I'll see him, he finds me.'

'Thanks, man. Let him down light. Mention me, the good mouth.'

Bonn spent a few minutes recovering from Jefferson's kitchen. Then he caught Disco, the suavely quiet dong domo at the reception counter, and went through the club registers, noting times, dates, who. He reached the pavement in Victoria Square, where the team of bikers were talking revs. Askey was on pavement singing.

'Askey.'

The diminutive man resembled the long-dead comedian, large head on a frail body, black hair with a calf-lick, spectacles big enough for the night sky.

'Yes, Bonn.' Askey bounced to his feet, quivering to carry messages.

Bonn tilted his head, walk along. Askey fell in. 'Things are bad, Bonn. I need dosh.'

Askey lived with a frail elder sister in Pendleton. He only went home once a week, to see she was all right and neighbours were still doing her shopping.

'That accident was terrible luck, Askey.'

Askey snorted with derision. 'Police couldn't tell the frigging time, Bonn. Salvo did the shuff with the case.'

'I hadn't heard that. They said a taxi.'

'Ponce, he is, double switcher. Has this bird Marla, quite nice.'

The little messenger eyed Bonn, eyes bottled in those great specs. Bonn believed Askey only wore them for effect. But what effect exactly?

'You need more messages, Askey, I think.'

Askey had never seen Bonn nod before, and watched the grave process with admiration, at once a promise and a reward. He felt rescued.

'Ta, Bonn. I'll get agate. Oz did the wheels, heavily built feller, uses a girl in Waterloo Street, on Grellie's string.'

'Thank you, Askey, for your assistance.'

The messenger grinned, years falling off him. He could only be twenty-eight, behaved a tired fifty. Bonn was saddened, the world too worn by anxieties. Askey should have a parcel of children, a wife, hobbies.

'I'll send a slider into the Ball Boys, where Salvo's lass goes. Pell's the best. He won't charge, get word in an hour.'

'Do I know Pell?' Clare Three-Nine-Five's task was more complicated. Too many asking the same thing made the wrong noise.

'He's given up night walks.' Pell, Bonn remembered now, the cat burglar, a slider who could enter anywhere without trace. 'Just alters tom – jewellery and such – in his brother's workshop.'

'Fine, Askey. Soon, please. I'll see that you're used more. One thing.' They stood at the corner by the Volunteer. The traffic was crowding the lights and damming back pedestrians. 'If it turns out to be the real mother – the genuine truth – you give me it all, and point Salvo out, please.'

Bonn wanted no mistakes.

'How is your sister?'

'Still got her bad legs. It's the stairs, see.'

Bonn said to pass on his regards, and watched Askey eel off towards the Triple Racer, where the bikers and the skateboard messengers hung out, cramming the pavement with their gadgetry, motorcycles, stacks of leather boxes.

'Bonn?'

He found himself looking almost vertically up at Gyearbourn, trumpet man of the Goon Hopper. It felt coming on to rain.

'Jefferson told me you'll listen a sec, you making key and all.'

'Would you care for a cuppa, Gyearbourn? Out of the rain.'

'Bonn, man. Why you so fuckin' po-*lite*? It get a man down, y'know? Done wanna tell yo business, but you'll get no takers, that polite.'

'Thank you, Gyearbourn. I shall heed your advice.'

'Jeez, Bonn. You never say fuck off, once in a while?'

'No, Gyearbourn.' They went for tea, chatting.

16

String – an organised group of prostitutes, esp. female.

THE NAME WIGAN PIER was perpetuated buffoonery, for Wigan was miles from the sea, and even in industry's heyday was served by a network of canals. Except now the joke was on the jokers, for Wigan Pier had become, in a witty tour de force, exhibitions, restaurants, a centre of unmatched excellence. It was also the fashionable place to dine out.

Clare had chosen it as a neutral place to meet Clifford. Not without guilt, the sense of betraying a surely innocent husband. Unfair, she scolded. 'Neutral' suggested a treaty between warring factions, not a meeting of loving spouses.

Clifford seemed in high spirits. They chatted, watching the school parties, children among the museum sets, and all the young actors and actresses cavorting in eighteenth-century costume, hearing the laughter, the muted chug of engines. The sun did its stuff, shone on Clare's lunch table as she chose her moment. Salmon, a curry with rice, vegetables just undercooked, thank God, white wine diluted to extinction by soda, and the weather unseasonably warmish, a loving, loved husband.

'The police came to see me, Clifford.' She didn't give him time.

'The police? That child in social care?'

She had mentioned having to go into the Wirral, a little girl with a drug-addict mother.

'No. The accident, that Leonard Mostern, insurance or something?'

'Mmmh? Yes, I remember.'

Too studied, her mind shrieked. How many fatal accidents did she mention in one week, for heaven's sake? She smiled the waitress to refill his glass.

'Some policeman called Hassall and a callow tempest called Windsor trying to show off in a rather shop-soiled way. They asked who was there. Can you imagine?' Her trill of disbelief fell short of a laugh. 'The London express was in. People were pouring out!'

'What were they looking for?' he asked.

Would an innocent husband ask exactly that? She was being unfair. After all Mostern was Clifford's business acquaintance.

'Heaven alone knows!' She smiled at two children in linked push chairs, probably twins. Their older sister, maybe six or seven, pushed them vigorously, the father vigilant between them and the canal, the mother telling him a tale of scandalous prices. 'You'd think they'd have better things to do.'

'Than ask about what? Who?'

Which gave her the chance to defuse the conversation. 'Don't you start!' she said, with proper exasperation. 'Bad enough having them! Their constable had told them about some young man.' For the first time, she described the irate man who'd angrily urged the taxi driver to back the cab off Mostern, then did it himself.

'Did they say what they were looking for?'

'No.' Her smile was now concealment. 'And I didn't

want to keep them from their social club, or wherever it is police go.'

Clifford chuckled at that. 'It's a pity they bothered you.'

'Isn't it.' Clare felt a kind of grief, but made herself say it outright. 'Is there something wrong, darling? You looked so worried when I mentioned it.'

'What's this "it"?'

Reasonable, first define your terms. She thought a moment, conscious of breaking new ground.

'Leonard Mostern's death.' He didn't answer. 'I thought you looked shocked.' Still nothing back. 'Was he close? I remember him. He doesn't have a family, no next-of-kin. The police,' she invented quietly, 'said so, I think.' A get-out clause, in case he challenged her on it later.

He nodded, eyes on the opposite bank, a festive fairground mood to the whole Pier concourse. The sun chose that instant to go in.

'I didn't know him well, Clare, just business. Some days I see dozens.'

'Have the police been to see you?'

He stared at her in alarm. 'No! Did they mention me?'

'Certainly not.' If only she hadn't made the negative so defiant, failed to think this out. Was she an accomplice now? It felt like it.

'Darling.' Her hand went to his. To anyone watching, it might have been a tender anniversary moment. 'Is there anything I can do? I've read of people absconding with office records. There was that investment bank, wasn't there? Is it like that?'

'No. It's caused ripples in other companies, nothing serious.'

'Thank goodness! I was starting to worry.'

'It'll blow over. After a person's gone, it's a dickens of a job unravelling their data. Reports start flying about. They can go on for ever.'

'If there's anything I can do, darling, you will say?'

He smiled at that, really smiled. 'Do you think I wouldn't come screaming?' he said. 'My one and always ally!'

They drank to that, then Clare told him about Agnes Ferram's insistence that she return to medicine full-time.

'I'm not sure I want to,' she confessed.

Clifford looked askance. 'Would there be advantages to you at all?'

'You don't like the idea?' She was pleased. 'I've had part-time offers.' Deliberately she became coquettish, joking her way out of that mistrustful feeling, making up to him.

'One benefit is that you aren't embroiled in the city's innards,' he said. 'It's a relief. Everybody I talk to all day long is in finance, analysing subplots.'

'Then I'll not go back full-time, darling. Every doctor I work with knows what's best for me – except me!'

They toasted their resolve. Clare hadn't yet broached the question of the briefcase, or of the man who she might – *might* – have seen among the pedestrians in that freeze-frame instant memory at the scene of the accident, but who, she tried not to remember, she had seen over her garden hedge.

But she had done the loyal thing, talked it over with her handsome husband the way a loving wife should. Now she could tie up those loose ends with a clear conscience.

Martina was in her worst possible mood when Bonn arrived at the control office. Bonn disliked the name for its preten-sion, sounding like Bomber Command Operations when it was only elderly ladies on a switchboard over the Pilot Ship

Casino. Martina was checking a recorded voice. Miss Rose was in floods of tears. She'd been a headmistress, and did not wilt easily.

'It's a Dorie, with a false number. She gave Seven-Seven-One.'

All double digits were out. It was a foray, God knew where from. Newspapers, drunken office jokers, who knew? After Hilda and Nicolette, this was one too many. Bonn listened to the voice.

'It's that broadcaster, Verity Hopeness,' he said. 'Relinquish it to me.'

'Relinquish?' Martina snapped. 'What is this, Certificate English? To? For? Why?'

'I shall solve any problems that might arise.'

Martina thought, I need Rack here. Bonn talked like a fairground guess-your-weight machine. He took the cassette, hesitated.

'A lady client wants to hire me for a job, Martina. Nothing sexual.'

'What else can you do?' She was aware of her rudeness.

Bonn seemed not to notice. 'It's to find out about some accident. Clare Three-Nine-Five. One hiring so far, just to ask.'

Martina stared. Unusual, but not unknown, that a client wanted only talk.

'Very well. Don't become a private detective service, though.'

'Thank you. And I have appointed Doob for my third goer.'

As he turned to leave she said, rage thickening her throat, 'I wouldn't have let Rack hurt this Verity. I want you to know that.'

He nodded, waved to Miss Rose. Martina slammed the

door after him and sharply told Miss Rose to make up her lost time at the end of her shift. Bonn must have got wind of her orders to Akker about that Hilda.

Time she spoke with Dad about her future. It was overdue.

17

Straightener – an illegal disciplining, by financial or physical punishment, of one who transgresses.

AKKER WAITED IN the dark. Moorside blackness was rotten stuff, miles from anywhere. Only ten o'clock, and so remote he was sick from isolation.

He was impatient. His mates told him that impatience buggered things up. But what was a bloke to do? Do the girl, then scarper.

This Hilda bird was shagging her way through a whole run of blokes. Three so far, trolled up from the saloon bar. He'd sussed her game. She allowed herself fifteen minutes after each fuck before clipping down to the taproom to hook a new shag, ten minutes flat. Clockwork. Why didn't Martina hire her for Grellie's strings? That wasn't his problem.

The bedrooms at the First Drop were arranged along a balcony, wooden steps outside. Cars came and went, the car park lit by two burning torches. Doors slammed, women shrieked, blokes laughed. Music sounded, a right hubbub. A posh restaurant glowed with golden light. Akker waited.

The bloke emerged, about time, called something back. Christ, he looked tired, staggered down the steps. For a moment Akker was tempted. This Hilda must be rattling good to drain a man like that in, what, twenty minutes top whack. But Martina had to be reckoned with.

He let the bloke vanish into the bar, then walked up the steps and along the dark balcony. He knocked. Nobody followed. No answer.

Akker knew she was in there. He did the lock – old heavyweight, the sort a babby could do with a buttonhook – and slipped inside. He stood blinded by the light. She was in the bathroom, running water, something clacking into the sink. He looked for a weapon, to his disgust found nothing.

The bathroom door was closed, not locked. For a second he paused, then shoved the door, and there she was sitting on the loo. Akker thought her surprisingly young. She gazed at him in astonishment, the pair of them frozen.

No good hanging about. She was drawing breath to speak, scream for somebody, so he leaned forward and fisted her head to keep her quiet, then raised her left leg and stamped down on her kneecap.

He had to do it twice before he heard the proper snap, after which it was safe to let it flop. She cried out, even though she should have been unconscious, because he'd given her a hefty thump.

Her arm he pulled out, straightened and broke it with a thrust downwards over the side of the bath. Its sound was sharper, better.

A moment later he was in her bedroom. Birds had so many clothes, beyond fucking belief. Jesus, but it was tempting. Who'd know, if he nicked a few quid?

Except computers checked banknotes, bankers too idle to read the fucking things, lazy gits. He'd used household gloves. And Rack, Martina's chief stander, was a fucking animal. He ended up not taking a penny, a fucking saint, which was a pig.

He switched off the lights and left as Hilda started to whine away in there. Untouched! He wasn't seen. Martina'd be pleased.

An hour later he was in the Shot Pot, challenging Toothie to a game, being noticed, there half the night anybody asked. But they wouldn't.

'Mr Burtonall? How do. Hassall, rhymes with tassle.'

Hassall entered Clifford's office acting weary. Windsor introduced himself formally. Clifford was easy, willing, had Beatrice in with her pencil and pad.

'Just that Mostern accident, Mr Burtonall. Needn't detain you long. He was an associate of yours?'

Tautology, Clifford's mind scored. 'Detain'? He wasn't being detained, but delayed. 'Long' meant these police defined *how* long, for their own purposes. Which purposes, exactly?

'Yes. We need an insurance broker now and then.'

'Always Mostern, was it, this brokerage?'

Brokerage, not broker? This Hassall had some terms off pat.

'We make several compete, to get the best value.' He shrugged, forced into disclosing the ruthlessness of commerce. 'We shop around. If some pal can't give us better rates we let him go. That's business.'

'Pal?' Windsor barked while the older man sighed and glanced apologetically at Beatrice, scribbling away. 'Mostern was a "pal" of yours?'

'No. Just knew him.' Clifford expressed surprise at being taken up on this. 'Beatrice, how many brokers do we use?'

The girls in the outer office kept glancing, thrilled by the police visit.

'Seventeen, Mr Burtonall, fourteen different firms, six in the city.'

Clifford spread his hands. 'Mostern was one of many.'

'Who had been here just before his accident,' Hassall said casually. 'Had a new briefcase, nowt in. Did he take anything.'

'Don't think so, Mr Hassall. Beatrice?'

'No, sir. The canal-marina contracts were to be couriered to Mr Mostern the day following. We heard of the accident, and instead contacted' – she flipped pages – 'a Mr Rohan, of Bettany and Barclay's. Who,' she added in prim disapproval, 'has yet to appear.'

'Did he have his briefcase with him?' Windsor demanded.

Clifford thought. 'I can't remember. Do you, Beatrice?'

'Yes, Mr Burtonall. He took it in with him.'

'New, old?' Hassall got in before Windsor did one of his shouts.

'His usual, I think,' Beatrice said. 'Brown, a bit frayed, heavy.'

The rest was all repetitious and inconsequential. Clifford showed them out after more of Hassall's platitudes. He mentioned about his wife, Clare, at the accident. Hassall told Clifford about the video camcorder's failure, a pity.

Clifford thanked Beatrice and told her, as casually as he could, to file her notes of the meeting. He faffed about the office for a while, gave the police time to clear off, then drove to the sports ground.

*

Clifford met Goldoni hours before kickoff. They walked among straggles of fans to stand beneath the awning of a food stall. Goldoni accepted a cola and a rock cake with distaste. He hated the cold damp weather, the pokey little flat found for him by some young lout of a relative. He hated this weak man.

'I take it your action was necessary?'

'Yes.' Clifford mouthed the word because a tannoy suddenly started up, blaring news of the coming evening match. Girls were among the drifts of spectators, scarves, hats, red-and-white favours. Boisterous fans charged past, arms linked.

'So defensive?' Goldoni asked. 'Clifford, if your action was essential then you did the right thing.'

'He was grassing. I had to get the documents back. It's down as an accident.'

Goldoni sighed. It was the same old carousel. 'A miracle of organisation, Clifford.' He detected the instant sharpness in Burtonall's glance. Weak, but no fool, so patronise at your peril. 'You have earned my thanks.' He let the other find his ease, the doom of weak men. 'You met your friends?'

'It's set. Half of a per cent's needed by tomorrow.'

Goldoni pursed his lips. 'Formidably more than we agreed. Such a bribe!'

'Can it be done, Gianni?'

So weak, this example of a declining race. Goldoni looked round for somewhere to throw the inedible cake. What digestions! Had they truly once ruled the world?

'I've given commitments.'

A coach arrived, spilling cheering fans. They looked so forlorn in the wide macadam spaces.

'Then I had better guarantee the transaction!'

'You will?' The weak man's eyes shone with gratitude. 'Thank you.'

Goldoni timed his remark. 'A private angle, Clifford. I want a personal investment. The city has a small syndicate, a casino here, snooker hall there, girl strings, an escort service. Not much.'

Clifford's lips were dry. 'A private one, Gianni?'

Men without balls even think sterile, Goldoni thought with contempt.

'You and I will finance a buy-out. I will be your sleeping partner.'

Clifford dithered. 'What if they won't sell?'

Goldoni smiled. 'They will. You will see to it. I shall give you details in the car. Shall we go? You know what will do the killing, Clifford?' he asked mischievously as they left among the thickening crowd.

'Killing?' Clifford thought he had misheard, but it was only his visitor amusing himself.

'It's your catering. International chefs have voted your cuisine to be Europe's most interesting, yet you serve crap. Is this civilisation?'

Clifford did not answer the jibe. He had to find Salvo, check that nothing was about to jeopardise Goldoni's new sideline.

18

Slider – a cat burglar, who burgles without trace.

BONN HAD ASKED for the end room of the longest corridor in the Vivante Hotel. Rack said where the hell was a stander to wait? You could see into the next *county*, the stairwells noisy as a race crowd, people up and down in streams. Bonn typically said nothing, assumed it would all be as he said.

The councillor's wife from the Wirral arrived pretending outrage. Bonn knew it was nothing of the kind, silently helped her off with her coat. Pouting was never angry, he knew, oil and water. It merely invited attention for the lady who'd complained volubly to the control office. Martina ordered this go, so it was unavoidable.

Exactly how absolute *was* unavoidable, when a troublesome client had insisted on having Bonn this evening or she'd sue, bring the world tumbling about Martina's ears? Hysterical overstatement, true, but Martina had said, quote, the cow's threats had to be taken into account so Bonn must get the syndicate out of the scrape, unquote. The scrape that he, Bonn, had got them into, thank you.

Rack brought the 'unavoidable' message. Which was all very well for Rack, that cosmic black hole of non-information. Bonn was here in pole position, confronting this woman's vengeance. She was an attractive fortyish.

'You were angry,' she said, her eyes enlivened as she accepted the sherry she'd brusquely demanded.

So far neither was even sparring. Bonn guessed that sex would come slowly. He knew to go with her, not dictate.

'Angry.'

Considering the word. He'd somehow learned, osmosis his teacher, that women liked repetition. They saw it as a kind of confirmation. And they liked opinions firm, nothing conjectural. Appetites were, after all, their stock in trade. Babes, men, hungers were the stuff of life, what they coped with by joy, rewards, duties.

'I can tell,' she told him, quite jaunty.

'All right, then.' He injected a smattering of truculent don't care.

'Say it.' Her eyes watched, bright.

'Very well.' Agree, agree. He said, all reluctance, 'Yes, I was angry.'

'Were you punished?' When he nodded. 'How?'

She bade him sit beside her. He made sure the length of the sofa was between them. She budged closer, turning to inspect, full of curiosity.

The silence became a cue. She was within reach, staring into his eyes, devouring his expression.

This was new to him. He'd had a client once, Dorsetshire or somewhere, who'd quite blithely come in and stripped, lain down naked, brisk as you please, told him to beat her. Startled, he had obeyed, delivered several smacks, gentle and somewhat trusting, wanting her to say that would do. She'd been disgruntled, risen after his gentle blows, wanted nothing else, and left in disgust without paying. She too had complained to Martina, drawn comparisons between 'the gigolo' – using the taboo term openly – and a 'worthwhile' service in Birmingham where they 'knew how to'.

Bonn was sent to discuss the Dorsetshire lady with Posser, who'd put him straight. Bonn used Posser's advice now.

'Punish me? I'm not allowed to say.' Look away, assume inner torture.

'Did it hurt?'

The councillor's wife – was she really such? – was thrilled. Bonn said nothing. If the client said she was a councillor's wife, then she was.

So, 'Yes, it hurt.'

'Bad?' She accused, 'You don't want to talk about it, do you?'

'I can't.' Nostrils flared, pent-up anger simmering in there.

'I did it. I *caused* it, Bonn.' She was excited, provoking.

He turned and fixed her, cold. Her jacket had slipped from her shoulders. Her blouse was buttoned. He had to control his quickening breath to keep himself steady. She was exhilarated.

Only two ways to go. The crux, in Posser's words. Transmute into action, or shunt swiftly into different emotions. Social chitchat had a million alternates, but here? Here it was act or leave the arena. And guess right.

She edged closer. 'I had bruises, Bonn, from last time. You made them.'

'I was careful.'

'I told you what to do with me. Then blamed you.'

'That was bad,' Bonn said.

'I sent you the flowers. Did you guess it was me?'

He recognised taunt in her huskiness. She seemed to melt before his eyes, almost sprawling onto him. He resisted the urge to clear off. But what then, blue murder, and more complaints? Act or leave the arena, but guess right.

'You had no right.'

'I know, Bonn. But I had to.'

'It got me into more trouble, all those bouquets.'

'I meant to, Bonn.' A hint of yearning in there? 'I did wrong.'

Sadness moved him. But there was no time for that.

A month earlier, a woman from Strasbourg had wanted to take him into the Lake District, and had been astonished to be told it wasn't on. She'd been furious, she had the money, proved it in three currencies for heaven's sake, *she* had hired *him* and he'd better not forget it.

The average lady, he thought, looking at the Wirral wife, kept to the one hour, two at the outside. Posser said they planned orthodox sex by the clock. That, and having a hair do, which necessarily stuck at one hour or, perm time, ninety minutes. Women thought the hour was defined by the Almighty, another Posser dictum, instead of a candle cut by Alfred the Great any old how.

'Why have you gone quiet, Bonn?' she asked. Her mouth trembled.

'It simply isn't good enough,' Bonn said, tight. He clicked his fingers once. Her eyes darted down.

'What are you going to do?'

'I won't put up with it.' Posser advised contradiction, in the right place.

Her hand fumbled at her blouse. She glanced as if looking for a way out. Bonn remembered the first time, her casual demand for hurt, and took strength from it.

'No. I can't stay. I'm meeting somebody.'

In that instant Bonn decided to act, not leave the arena.

'There's no escape, not for a bad girl like you.'

'My husband will be here soon.'

He ignored that. 'Do you really think there's any excuse for being bad?'

She tried to laugh, scale things down. 'Good heavens!' she cried softly. 'Sin? What I did can hardly—'

'Stop it. I haven't said you can speak.' He reached for her blouse, took hold of the flimsy material, and savagely ripped it downwards. 'Get stripped.'

Frantically she started to obey, shoes off with that quick effortless grace women did, the hurried problem with the skirt waist.

'Do I have to get my toy?' she asked, anxious.

Toy? 'No.' He cuffed her so she almost fell over, righted herself. 'Last time was only playing. I have to give you what you deserve.'

'Bonn, darling, I think I'd—'

Never change an act, Posser's law. She almost undressed, Bonn quite still.

'What do I have to do?'

She went into the bedroom, pulled the bedclothes away, sat upright looking in terror that was nearly pretence.

Bonn moved slowly after, undid his jacket, then fed his belt out to its full length. The buckle clinked mutedly. She groaned, her tongue wetting her lips.

'I told you to stay silent.'

'You didn't! You didn't say anything about—'

He lashed the bed with his belt, making her squeal. 'Don't argue. You'll wish you'd never told those lies.'

She was weeping. 'It's my fault. I know, I know.'

He hurled his clothes away, flung the bedclothes off her, shoved her onto her face, kicking her legs straight and deliberately pausing after each swing of his arm. He used the belt's free end, hitting her gently in spite of her hoarse exhortations and keeping the buckle in his palm.

She wept, groaned, laughed once aloud even, her moans rising after each blow. When she was whealed and red he straddled her hot frame and gently entered her, letting the act take over.

Almost instantaneously she started to move with him, reaching back to pull him deeper.

Later, as she left, embracing him at the door while she made him promise to reserve time for her in exactly a week's time, he reflected that Posser was correct. Guess right was the rule for all life's choices.

Dr Ferram had left a message for Clare when she reached the small surgery at Westhoughton, please to ring urgently.

Agnes was even more peremptory than usual. 'Clare? Get over here and sign on the dotted line. You've got a plum position itching for you to fill it. No. Something you could do standing on your head.'

'Look, Agnes. I have the GP's surgery here.'

'Cardiac, male, preventative care of. Interested, or do I go and eat humble pie with people I loathe?'

Clare said, troubled, 'I've not answered any offers—'

'But I have, dear,' Agnes told her sweetly. 'I forged your name. I have their lies – and mine, incidentally – right here in my hand.'

'Agnes, what on earth have you done?'

'I've told them you will commence work at Farnworth General in two days.'

'You have no right—'

'See you in the staff canteen, my dear. Where the soup is a foul sea of *Klebsiella*, though of relatively low pathogenicity—'

Clare disconnected, and belled the first patient. She was in no mood to show compassion towards an elderly posthysterectomy lady, but forced herself to postpone her annoyance at her friend's presumption.

She let the nurse bring the patient in, and started scanning the notes, concentrating. The problem of that desirable cardiac post could wait until afterwards, when she would find reasons for refusal, Dr Ferram or no Dr Ferram.

Bonn reached the Vallance Carvery after getting Askey's message from Grellie and found Pell the slider, ex-burglar, now mender of stolen jewellery in his brother's workshop. Bonn hardly knew the man, found him difficult to assess as they found a place to sit. He felt worn out.

So far today he'd had two clients, both pleasant, one a little worried, but those were often easiest. The second was irritated at learning he would not be able to spend time on a cruise. She vowed to ring the control lady. 'I'll get round that little problem, darling,' she'd told him, bright with confidence. 'I always do!' Next time would be her fourth time with Bonn.

'Pell,' he told the ex-burglar, 'pass word I've asked Osmund to use Askey for snooker messages.'

'Ta, Bonn. He'll be pleased.'

Pell had the shakes, a heavy drinker and his usefulness short-lived. Also he was old, hands becoming transparent. Somebody Pell's age craving drink didn't need chitchat. Bonn cut to the point.

'Askey said Salvo did the accident.'

'Aye. Oz did the wheels. Taxi. Oz has a woman, in Sale, down in Cheshire. He does Grellie's girls in Waterloo Street betwixt.'

Which relieved Bonn, one woman less to worry about. 'Salvo, then.'

'The Triple Racer lads, the paper team, all saw it. Oz wheeled Mostern down. Salvo shuffed the briefcase. He'd already slit the camera.'

'The briefcase?'

Pell winced. 'Look, Bonn. I'm out of the game. Too old.'

'Don't worry. I won't ask you to burgle anywhere, Pell.'

'It went to the wallet. Called Burtonall, somewhere out on the A666, wife a quack. Salvo and Oz done him straighteners before, one that St Helens canal job.'

Mostern was wheeled, his briefcase was nicked and taken to the man who'd funded the killing. Burtonall, husband of a doctor. Clare. A straightener could be an inexplicable fall under a train, a crushed hand, or a quiet word.

'Detail, please.'

'None, Bonn.' Pell was crestfallen. 'Salvo's girl Marla's seeing Lana, an eachway lass. Salvo's playing hell at Marla getting dyked on the sly. He's an idle sod,' Pell said with distaste. 'Earns round the halls, fiddles deliveries. A knit man.'

A small-time thief, from the joke saying: knit one, purl one, drop one.

'But troublesome, Bonn.' Bonn sent a waitress to Molly on the desk for a pencil and paper. 'Salvo shacks up in her flat, Marla's.'

'You've done well, Pell.' Bonn thanked the girl for the notepaper, wrote, handed it over. 'This is a promissory note to Osmund. At the Romeo, ask for Fay. She will pay you. Please thank Askey.'

'Ta, son.'

For a long time Bonn sat there. He accepted a drink from Molly, made a deferential apology when a woman tried to converse.

He finally rose, thanked Molly with a glance, and left.

Molly looked after him. She didn't like the thought of Bonn being in that horrible syndicate business, even if it did mean him getting made key and everything. He was the sort that life ought not to go wrong for, but life wasn't fair and she had the grief to prove it.

19 Walker – a male paid to escort a female regularly to social functions, whether or not he provides her with sexual services.

CLARE SPOKE WITH Dr Porritt of the Farnworth General's cardiac unit as he was going over the electrocardiographs from Male Out-Patients. Clare was admitted into the aquarium gloaming of green and fluorescence. A registrar greeted her, resumed his goggles before the radiograph.

'No criticism, Burtonall,' Paul Porritt warned. 'We're old-fashioned.'

'I've not said a word, doctor.' Clare perched on a stool, careful lest the roller ferrules carried her violently aside, the newcomer's mistake.

'She'd better bloody not, eh, Ashcroft?'

'Advisable, Dr Porritt,' Ashcroft said, concentrating on the P-A and left lateral X-rays of a patient with cardiomegaly and expansion of the aortic knuckle. Clare's eyes were drawn to the translucent areas of the radiograph.

'See?' Paul Porritt complained. 'All I get is diplomacy. I want serious sloggers who'll work for pennies, not smart alecs who can't utter an opinion. They say, "There is a school of thought. . . ." I want yes or no.'

'We were too indoctrinated, Paul,' Clare said equably. 'They aren't.'

Ashcroft cheerfully gave her the thumbs-up sign behind Dr Porritt's back.

'I saw that, Dr Ashcroft,' his senior said. 'Consider yourself sacked.'

'Yippee. Can I go?'

She had known Paul Porritt at medical school. Even then he had been a semi-joker, though the most industrious student. His interest lay in the technological aspects of medicine as long as they could be proved to set morbidity tumbling, get people to their feet all the faster. Research purists opposed him at finance meetings, on the grounds that fundamental research at molecular level was true progress. Understanding, the boffins claimed, was everything. Porritt's view was, let the molecules take care of themselves, just shut up and prevent or cure, get on with it.

'He needs you, Dr Ashcroft. He only pretends he doesn't.'

'Know what I do need, Clare?' Dr Porritt showed her a strip of an ECG as Ashcroft sniggered with deliberate loudness. 'Take a look. I need you to come and do a heart-fitness survey, that's what I need.'

Clare held the strip obliquely to the green glimmer, straining to see. She went through the PQRST sequence, judging the intervals, the heights and troughs of the trace's pitch.

'No cardiac infarct—'

Porritt took the strip. 'Nine traces, Clare. *Nine!* For a case who's well on the way to jumping in the next Olympics. Know why?'

'No.'

'Because the patient was a hospital bloody administrator, that's why. Can you imagine? Fit as a flea, so some bloody registrar puts on a show of concern. Spends a fortune of my unit's money doing it, too!'

Clare said laconically, 'You once did the same, to impress a junior nurse.' Dr Ashcroft whooped with glee, laughed outright.

'That was different!' Dr Porritt said huffily. 'Times – and research funds – were a world away.' He grinned unexpectedly. 'She was gorgeous.'

'I'm in no position to judge, doctor. Why me?'

'Needing you, Clare? Because you speak up for yourself. Gumption. At least, you used to have.'

'Have you—?'

'Been talking to Agnes Ferram? Of course. She says you're desperate for a proper full-time job.'

'She's lying, Paul.' She paused. 'What *is* the post, exactly?'

'Surveying a block of male patients in general practices, double-ICGTM. It'll have all the mumbo-jumbo, quality-controlled, cohorts levelled and ranked, codes done, lab support, industrial links.' IICGTM stood for If I Can Get The Money, every hospital doctor's wry joke.

'How many?'

'One doctor, namely you, plus technicians, choose two nurses. It's a WICGTM survey, doctor.'

'When,' Clare said. 'No date?'

The cardiologist sighed. 'I'll come clean. I used your name on the fund form. Hope I got your qualifications and dates right, incidentally. Deal?'

Ashcroft stopped checking the radiographs, lifted his goggles, and looked across. Clare shook her head, feeling sad at having to refuse.

'Paul. I'm happy as I am, but thanks.'

They both resumed work as she left. 'Hey, Burtonall,'

Dr Porritt called, 'I guessed your age at fifty. How close'd I get?'

Clare heard a nurse stifle a laugh in the outer office, and found herself smiling as she cut through Casualty. She was right to refuse. Four sessions a week was enough, whatever friends might say.

The three goers were waiting for Bonn. Pencey the Ghana display stroker was showing off fancy cue work, running the white along the cush, then dropping the pink, top right pocket, in an actual game. Tonto, Toothie's Guadeloupe cousin, was disbelievingly screaming fresh odds against any of this, and losing time. The crowd was engrossed. Osmund was disgusted.

'Know the trouble with Pencey, Bonn?' Rack was close to despair. 'Can't do it in championships, see?' He glared at Galahad and Lancelot as they followed to one of the alcoves where Rack could get a beer. Doob was already waiting, spick-and-span, edgily on parade. The other two were contemplating themselves in mirrors.

'Thank you, everybody,' Bonn began. 'You all know each other. Martina's rule is, you each get your own stander. You never – that's never – do a go without your stander. Rack, please.'

Rack was delighted. He caught Bonn's glance, no theories.

'Sooner or later your stander'll not turn up,' he said round the table. 'You think, Oh well, sod it, I'll do it anyway. So you go ahead, the hotel room's booked, all safe, okay? No! Because that's the one time she'll panic, scream rape, fire. Worst is, there's no records when that happens, see?

Martina lives by Posser's book, and Posser's law is, all screamers get ditched straight off.'

'Doesn't the hotel work for us?' Lancelot asked.

'No.' Rack was enjoying himself. He should have brought a cigar, maybe got cufflinks, say 'City desk!' Like on the pictures. 'The hotels do nothing for you, me, Bonn even. You go without your stander, you're done for.'

'The other problems, Rack.'

'Coming to that, Bonn,' Rack said grandly. 'The lady's bloke might follow her. Your stander protects you and her, see? Stander does his job, you never know there's been a disturbance, and she's in the clear. It's up to her what tale she fobs him off with when she gets home. Hotels get things wrong – double-book rooms, mistake floors, we seen everything.'

'Who do the standers report to?' Galahad asked.

Rack leant, arms on the table. 'Mind your own fucking business.'

'Thank you, Rack. Very succinct.' Bonn regained their attention. 'I'm setting up rules, beginning today.'

'Martina is rules.' Lancelot shuffled in his chair, looking at Galahad.

'Martina's rules stand. I want a couple more.'

'Does Martina know?' Lancelot, pushing it, Rack slowly turning to stare.

Bonn kept it cool. 'It's up to me. No question. If you object, say now, and depart.'

They considered depart. Rack had never heard Bonn so blunt. The three new goers watched him and each other.

'First rule.' Bonn spoke with slow precision. 'Fret Dougal's firm, I hear, sometimes take clients on with no stander. Rack's boss stander. Disobey Rack, you disobey me.'

Lancelot said, wanting Galahad's backing, 'It's not just Fret's goers.'

'Not on my firm, Lancelot. This rule is without exception.' He let it sink in. 'No scruffs, heavy drinkers, pals taking your stander's place, because it's the Two Thousand Guineas.'

Doob asked nervously, 'Can we get good standers?'

'Rack can,' Bonn said. 'The city's got plenty working the ladies' clubs, reception desks. They want in, and to serve their apprenticeship.'

They digested this in silence. Galahad swigged his fluid. Bonn gave them time.

'Next rule: no homers unless your stander's within earshot.'

'When homers are so easy?' Lancelot was now frankly rebellious.

'Are they,' Bonn said with inflexion.

'Well, yes.' Lancelot shot defiance around the table. 'You simply get the address, meet the mark. It's usually a husband, who takes you to his missus. You shag her, whatever. Collect, and off out of it.' He did his dancer's imperious so-what, which worked so well with ballroom judges. 'She won't cut and run because she's seen some friend in the foyer. Homers are easy peasy.'

It was too pat for just hearsay. Lancelot would be trouble. Bonn suppressed his irritation. Did Martina know? What was Rack doing? Lancelot really was doing amateur homers. . . . A dancing career cost.

'Thank you for pointing it out, Lancelot,' Bonn said kindly, to Rack's wonderment. 'Yet such a lady, who loses courage, is good money. Invariably she becomes angry at herself and regrets her defection for denying herself a treat that she's paid for, after all.'

'Hey,' Rack said, thrilled at psychology. 'That's true! Remember—?'

'Well done, Rack,' Bonn cut in. 'I want us all to understand this. No talking about ladies, even among ourselves. Not with the standers, not even in your sleep.' He smiled, shy. 'Especially not then!'

'I'm talking about homers.' Lancelot stuck sullenly to it, his argument filled with grudges. 'They're a cinch. There's only the husband to consider.'

'A gander job,' Galahad said, pleased to contribute. 'I did three in a month once, shags with the husband looking.'

'They are acceptable.' Bonn could sense Rack stirring, wanting to lash out, bawl at the goers that they were on Bonn's firm for fuck's sake and do as they were frigging well told or piss off back to the street. 'I am pleased you're enthusiastic, but my rule is, no homer unless the stander is on hand, on watch.'

'How do we fix that?' Galahad wanted to know. 'Where does he wait?'

'Hangs on the rafters?' Lancelot suggested, sarcastic, a dancer's twirl at the ceiling.

Rack lost his rag. 'Watch it, cloggie.'

'Thank you.' Bonn defused it. 'It is your stander's problem, not the goer's. If your stander's in doubt – like the house is in a tree-lined avenue a mile long – then send your stander to ask Rack.'

Rack looked sideways at Bonn, wondering if there was a barb in there because he'd once sent Scal along as sub, when Bonn had had that difficult Wirral masochist woman who sent forests of fucking flowers, silly cow.

'Please agree.' Bonn smiled at them. 'All or none.'

'You mean it's agree or the firm's finished?'

'Yes, Lancelot. I won't continue as key. My way, we

shall succeed and survive intact. Disagree, we part, no hard feelings.'

Bonn showed no amusement as Lancelot came to heel.

'I know. But I want absolute safety. You read the papers. The wife talks, persuades, ultimates. Then it's ructions. Your stander saves skin.'

'Sometimes it's the husband,' Doob put in. 'He brings in some extra bird, or a pal. I've heard that.'

'The stander copes.' Bonn had to be firm. 'Maybe he's the driver, which is Rack's favourite method, has a cup of tea in the kitchen while the goer does his job. There are scores of different ways of going about it.'

'Third parties, though, Bonn.' Doob had been brewing this anxiety.

'No third parties,' Bonn answered. 'No threesomes.'

'Why not?' Which took Bonn by surprise. 'A feller wants his wife while she has you. Sharing.'

'I've done a couple of them,' Galahad said, morose. 'It puts you off.'

Bonn said, thinking it out, 'The Soho. I won't have it.'

'Are there *more* rules, Bonn?' Lancelot asked, foot tapping.

'Girls for your own use. You have one. Change her, that's allowed, but stick to one.'

'That's a bit much.' Lancelot again.

'One,' Bonn explained patiently, 'will understand that you have to work, will see it as that and nothing more. A decent goer has his own girl on the side.' He caught Rack's hooded glance meaning Grellie, but did not rise. 'It's what we goers are for, to make love, please a client. A girlfriend accepts that. It's you bringing in the bread.'

'Then where's the problem?'

Rack had had enough and pointed a finger to shut the

dancer up. Bonn shook his head, but it was coming that close.

'The problem is two girls on the sly.' Bonn smiled, how patient he could be. 'Your girl will see a second non-paying girlfriend as a bitch cutting in on her man. Then it's knives out, and people getting split.'

Lancelot asked silkily, 'You mean me?'

'Yes.' Bonn took his time adding, 'And you, Galahad. And you, Doob.'

'When does the firm start?'

'Now.' Bonn stood, waved to Beth, beckoned Rack with a tilt of his head, and they left, Rack whooping at Pencey, who played a spectacular bounce shot over a black and three reds as they passed. Bonn called his admiration. Rack snorted.

He said dolefully, 'Pencey can't hack competitions. Here, Bonn.' Rack became surreptitious. 'What *do* blokes do while you shag their missus?'

'Watch television, the pub, wait outside.' Bonn shrugged. 'It's life, Rack. Who's on the Worcester?'

'Now? Jefferson, and Tuesday. Know why girls like being on show in them glass cases? They're poor when they're little. It turns their minds—'

'Mmmh,' Bonn said.

Rack was thinking, He's fancying Tuesday, maybe wants her on the side? He really ought to be shagging Grellie, who'd give her teeth. He decided he would have to work, pair Grellie off with Bonn once and for all. Should he ask Martina about it? Maybe not. Mention Bonn, sometimes Martina hit the frigging roof. He'd not worked out why.

The room reminded Bonn of his former place. That was the reason he had chosen it when first he'd taken up the life. Here, he cooked beans, oven chips, vegetarian pasties, made tea with skimmed milk. Profligacy a milestone down some half-forgotten lane. With it had gone greed, and with that ambition.

He switched on the lights, one each side of the boarded-in fireplace. Here, he had just the traffic, the coloured patterns made after midnight on his ceiling, and the racket of Grellic's girls bickering with crude raucousness before the passion in motorcars, doorways, alcoves, on church steps.

It was one room, Spartan clean, with a curtained alcove over a sink hiding a miniature electric stove, minuscule refrigerator. No pictures, because of what? No photographs, because who? A sliding door let onto a boxed-in landing, six by four. Miniature bath, a toilet, no handbasin.

He brewed tea in his one mug, stoneware – never visitors here – and eked out the milk. Less left in the bottle than he'd thought. He would have to go down to the all-nighter near the Triple Racer. He never minded these discovered tasks. Each confirmed his status as free, and alone. He might consider change, but it would be spontaneous, abstract. His room was, well, an intellectual problem.

With his mug of tea, he went to the window and saw Bradshawgate, the grassy triangle that petered out into tilted paving stones. He saw Posser on the bench. He liked Posser. The old man looked ill.

For a second he imagined Posser's eyes glancing his way, and drew the curtains as a politeness. The past was there, the city's enormous churning vitality somehow enshrined in that vestige.

He shelled his jacket, his shirt, singlet, trousers, underpants, his socks, and lay naked on the divan bed. He was tempted to switch the television on but news seemed made up, coined by redundant sixth-formers, to be marked for 'originality and dynamism' once handed in.

How much longer would he be here? He paid a pittance for rent, nothing for electricity, water rates. It was a haven, a monastic cell, given as a gift almost as from God. His mind drifted.

The seminary was closing, due to be sold, and the furnishings were already gone. Three brothers, none yet ordained, were leaving for the sister seminary in Tuscany, where the Order had been founded. The nineteen remaining priests were dispersed. Last week, each had received the Letter of Submission, made his peace with the novice brothers, and gone. The Rector, and the lay Brother Francis with the starched collar and pinstriped suit, were the only ones remaining.

It was not exactly a tearful diaspora. The seminary had existed since 1898, when emancipation reached its, what, third generation among the reformers of the sinful island. 'Let us pray for England', was the Sunday admonition, the country doomed by Reformation, with the blissful *for Thine is the Kingdom* pointedly omitted.

Bonn had felt singular, among those brothers who had convinced themselves that they should leave the Order for a life outside among the laity. It was escape to perdition. Bonn had been adjured to go to Tuscany, for a life among the religious devout. Bonn closed his mind, and left the other two brothers to it. One went to the Midlands, the other to Tenby, to search his soul.

There had been occasional defections before, individuals who suddenly decided to leave. Bonn had no real friends among the four who had left like this during his time at the seminary. As they had said their goodbyes they had seemed merely tired. Bonn still worried about them.

He himself had reached the city, also tired out, after saying his own goodbyes when his time came. Father Crossley had been kind, asked if he had the fare, joked about The Great Wen with its Protestant sinfulness. Bonn had pretended to be amused, and that had been that.

In the city he had gone into a hotel, trying freedom, eager to experiment.

He had sat in the hotel lounge at four in the afternoon. His idea was to sleep on the London train, rouse in tomorrow's dawn, and embark into life. A waitress asked him if he wanted tea. He said yes, too ashamed not to conform. He instantly started worrying about money. Tea, scones, crumpets, marmalade, all were brought.

He felt obscure, a distance from the foyer, where people talked in idleness so complete that he found it offensive. Had they no jobs, no families?

The mood changed quickly. Pouring his tea and daring himself to look at the folded bill laid beside his saucer, he felt on display, as if he was a prison escaper. Then a smiling lady seated herself opposite.

'Could I share?' She beckoned a waitress, who provided an extra cup with a strange look at Bonn. 'I *know* I'm early, but it's since I've had the new car. The *traffic*! I'm not *terrified* exactly, you know what I mean.'

She laughed, shaking out her hair. Pleasant, smiley, thirtyish, expensive clothes. He was disturbed to see that she wore a gold ring and a large diamond, ring finger. Married. And speaking without introduction to a stranger. And asking the stranger to share his tea. Was this how the outside world behaved? He had heard of liberated normality.

'Well,' she said, amused, imperious. 'Aren't you going to pour?'

He reddened. 'Certainly.' He shook, managed to serve her tea, offered her cake, cut it with feeble inaccuracy.

She watched, even more amused.

'Your first time?' Was she laughing at him?

'Here, yes.' His smile cracked and he felt absurdly shy.

'That means yes,' she said. 'I'm Chelsea Five-Four-Eight.'

He realised he was expected to say something, hesitated, wanting a clue. Hers was an odd name. Nickname, some club membership, perhaps?

'Do you mean my name?' he offered nervously. 'They call me Bonn.'

But who were 'they'? Nobody had called him that since his childhood. He'd been astonished to learn that it was spelled with a double n. He did not know who decided these things, spellings, etiquette in hotels where ladies commandeered the food of strangers.

'I thought Hame.' She was surprised.

'No,' he said in weak apology. Who was Hame? 'Bonn.'

'I rang for four o'clock, Bonn.' Chelsea glanced meaningfully at the lounge clock, ten minutes to. 'Barely time.'

Did she know the times of trains too? Bonn's train was at quarter past.

'Thank you,' he said politely for her reminder. He struggled to find conversation. 'Er, did you have far to come?'

She was immensely amused. 'Bonn, darling!' she exclaimed softly. 'You needn't be so . . . *scared*. Heavens! I won't *eat* you!'

Which caused her even more inner laughter. He felt made fun of, and coloured. He wondered how you made the excuse to leave. The mental reservation, which neo-Thomistic theologians now called an outright deception, was sometimes justified. But in this baffling encounter?

'Though,' she ended coyly, 'who knows what chance might force me to do?' Her smile faded, became speculative. 'You really *are* concerned, aren't you? Maybe they should give you some preliminary training. I mean, it's rather a responsibility.'

He was shocked at her recognition. She must have identified him as a seminarian leaving for the outside world. He felt obliged to offer a defence.

'An acceptable one, however,' he began, thinking of other seminarians.

'Chelsea,' she sang in a chant.

So names were quite proper. 'Chelsea,' he repeated obediently. 'I believe we must enact spirituality, honestly see it as a prime duty. It's the basis of all love. Do you not think so?' He took her stare as agreement, or at least understanding, and went gravely on, 'There is no more solemn duty than love of that kind.'

'There isn't?' she asked as if mesmerised.

He lowered his gaze, wondering if he had gone too far, mentioning spiritual implications of duty on so short an acquaintance. 'I believe that we complicate our inner life unnecessarily.'

'You do?' she was saying, staring, when they were interrupted.

'Chelsea Five-Four-Eight? I'm Hame.'

A youth stood by their table. Chelsea looked up, her face suddenly pale. She glanced from him to Bonn. The young man glared at Bonn.

Chelsea appraised the newcomer, then Bonn as if seeing him anew. Her colour slowly returned and she smiled.

Without looking away from Bonn, she addressed the newcomer.

'Go up and wait, Hame.'

Hame turned on his heel and strode off through the lounge. Chelsea inspected Bonn, cool and analytic.

'It seems I jumped to conclusions, Bonn.' She took in the tea table with frank amusement. 'And leeched onto your private tea party.'

'I'm sorry.' Bonn was worried about the effect his presence had on the lady's friend. 'Should I try to explain to, er, Hame, perhaps ameliorate—?'

'Darling, don't ameliorate.' She was now vastly amused, and reluctant to go. Bonn wondered if the language had altered during his seminary sojourn. 'I must say I am rather disappointed.' She extended her hand. He shook it awkwardly. Her fingers pressed his.

'Er, thank you.' His face reddened, felt uncomfortably hot.

'Please.' She opened her handbag, gave him a card. 'My home address. Do call, please. I would like to continue our conversation.'

'How kind.'

'And here.' She dropped a note on the table. 'Let me pay.'

'Certainly not.' This encounter had got out of hand. He was lost.

She leant forward and kissed his cheek. He was overwhelmed with perfume, a sense of closeness, the touch of her mouth. He almost leapt away, but stayed. She went, smiling, almost swaggering, to the lifts.

He sat staring at the money, not sure what had happened or why. The world out here had mutated out of all recognition. He had never been in a hotel before, which worsened his confusion.

An elderly man, wheezing with some chest complaint but respectably dressed, approached and stood nearby.

'Good day,' he said politely. 'Might I ask if I could take this seat?'

'Please do,' Bonn said warily. Now what?

Bonn almost wanted to breathe for him, so hard was it for the old man. His eyes were rheumy with age and effort.

'Please indulge an old man who has greater experience of life than yourself.' It took a minute to get the words out. Bonn nodded, responding to the other's weary smile.

'Is there anything I can get you?' Bonn asked.

'Thank you, no.' The old man composed himself, came to the edge of his chair in preparation. 'I was at the next table. I couldn't help overhearing.'

Bonn said he was not offended.

'The misunderstanding was the result of the lady's assumption that you were her escort, her personal escort.'

'Escort?' Bonn thought a moment, wanting to point out to the old gentleman that the lady had followed Hame, her 'escort', into the hotel lifts, and not been escorted at all. 'That can't be so. The lady failed to recognise him. And I don't think I ought to be discussing a lady in her absence.'

The sick old man wheezed into a pause for a moment, then politely extended his hand. 'I wonder if I might introduce myself, Bonn? Posser.'

Bonn rose. They shook hands formally. 'How do you do?'

'Do you have time for me to explain a few vital matters, Bonn?'

'Ten minutes only, Posser.' Bonn found himself warming to the other.

'There are, Bonn,' Posser began, 'a few truths in current society. One is this: There are only three sorts of people. Earners, thieves, and spongers.'

Posser waved Bonn's interruption down. 'Please. Nine more minutes. Another truth is that a woman craves to be a nun *and* a prostitute – life's extremes. Why? Because she wants to know the difference!'

Embarrassed, Bonn interrupted. 'Sir, I'm not sure—'

The older man abandoned it as futile, and said bluntly, 'I need you to come and work for me. You may enter at any stage, Bonn. Either be a field worker – we call them goers – or an administrator. Frankly, a job.'

'A job,' Bonn repeated. 'Goer?'

'A slang term, I'm afraid,' Posser said. 'Some individuals appear to be naturals, Bonn. Shall I go on?'

20

SOME PLACES IN this city Salvo hated. One was the Ball Boys. It was 'Our City's Finest Disco', it said in lights with two bulbs missing. Its paint was chipped, the boards were weathered, one of the five broad windows was cracked, and another taped over like cladding on a seaside stall. It stood in a side street. Once the alleys had echoed to the rattle of clogs, mill folk hurrying against mill hooters. Now the terraced cottages were gutted and inhabited by cardboard-city mumpers burrowing to make some corner secure. The top end, near traffic lights in Victoria Square, shed patchy coloured light onto the pavement. The bar's entrance was a foyer transplanted from a defunct Salford cinema. It dazzled with swivelling bulbs.

'Ponces,' Salvo said, fuming even before he saw Marla.

They were all ponces, in designer jackets. They looked crap. He could take on any dozen.

Tonight Marla was wearing her red. He'd watched her dress. Going out to see her mother, she'd said. Red, with the frothed hem proving her legs were smashing, her claim. Lana was the bugbear. If he found her with Marla, that would prove it. Lana the dyke, Marla the feather. Lana was a vicious cow. They said she'd stabbed a bloke once, everything bad round Lana.

He stood by the entrance, glowering. All very well for Oz – fucking name *that* was – to say leave off, it's normal. Not with his bird it wasn't.

A queers' bar, studs-and-buds mockery. Blokes arrived giggling like tarts, red hankies hanging from their gob-jobbers' pockets, silver alchemical jewellery for mash-and-bashers. It made Salvo ill, his tart one of these queers.

He couldn't wait any longer. He'd seen Lana in here. It was her place. He shoved in through the press, got stalled by a bruiser who made him pay entrance. A whole note, for this? Inside, the place was hot as hell, air thick with enough scent to gag you. All sorts were bounding to the deafening music, some snogging. Two girls embraced, whispering. A DJ was giving it the falsetto.

No sign of Marla. That made him angrier. Somebody spoke to him. He pushed the ponce aside, plenty of elbow, and blundered to the side tables. Went through the gloaming, came to a great red curtain, realised he'd gone all the way round the dark turmoil. Maybe she was in the loos?

He stood by until the women emerging were the ones he'd seen go in, then gave up. Six dykes sat guffawing at the bar, competing loudly for one feathery mincer who Salvo pinned as a trans, their lookout, not his.

The bar staff tried chatting him up. He snarled them away, hauled himself through the bobbing dancers, ripped aside the entrance curtain. Three bouncers grabbed him and slammed him against the admissions counter. One forced his head back against the paybox amid excited squeals.

'What're you up to, feller?' one bruiser asked.

Salvo croaked. 'Looking for my bird.'

'Here?' the bouncer said, incredulous, looking about to prove Salvo's mistake.

People screeched, the joke repeated by the foyer crowd.

'Get him out,' the head bouncer said. 'Don't come back.'

Salvo was thrown onto the pavement. He intended to wait opposite, but saw one of the bouncers coming after him and walked away towards the square.

He was almost blind with fury. His face was bleeding, his eye feeling tight. Marla. Would she cheat him with a dyke? He'd been cunning, sussed the bitch out. Some women did cheat.

But would Marla?

Inside, Marla emerged from the loo with Lana. She was white-faced, and spoke to one of the bouncers.

'Jesus, Marla.' The bruiser was solid cuboidal. He was the one who had held Salvo's face in one crushing hand. 'Could have started a fucking war.'

Lana said, 'That Salvo's off his fucking head. A psycho.'

'I can handle him. But let us know in future.' He looked sumo-fat, beringed, balding, but was respected for ferocity. 'Lie doggo a night or two, okay? Pacify the mad bugger.'

Lana objected. 'Marla's better off with me, Postie. I can take care of her.'

'Lots say that, Lana.' Postie shrugged, went back to the paybox.

Lana coaxed Marla back to the dance floor, to the cheers of friends. Marla felt better as her sense of security returned. It was pleasant, without that frantic anxiety she always got with Salvo. With Lana she felt in control, could withhold or give, submit, or award pleasure.

The music came on, an eighties rehash. Marla forgot Salvo.

*

'I'm sorry about this, Evadne,' Clare told her mother-in-law, leading her into the hospital cafeteria. 'Will here do?'

'Don't mind one bit, dear!' Evadne gushed. Her long-suffering husband, Arthur, trailed behind, trying to guess the specialisms from the various uniforms. 'We can rough it, can't we, Arthur?'

'Let me get coffee for you both.' Clare found them a table. 'Unless you would like something . . .?'

'Allow me.' Arthur went off to join the queue.

To Clare, her mother-in-law looked only half dressed without numerous packages from expensive shopping expeditions. Evadne always seemed too elegant. She whispered, 'I mean, eating in this sort of place is, well, rather macabre, don't you think?'

'Not really.' Clare got the point, and deliberately showed surprise in retaliation.

'With those diseases so *close*, I mean to *say*.'

'Don't worry. You're quite safe.'

'But are *you*, dear?' Evadne Burtonall leaned back, gazing with distaste at the table's laminated surface. 'Time's getting on. Clifford is so eager to start a family. There are better uses for your time.'

Clare kept control. 'When did he say that?'

'A mother knows her own son's mind.'

'And what does my husband's mind say?'

'He desperately wants to be getting on with raising a family, Clare.' Evadne leant away from a couple of radiographers passing in their white dresses. They carried trays holding plates of pasta.

'We've never discussed it, Evadne.' Clare thought, One day we'll meet and not fight. But one day is none day.

Evadne patted Clare's hand. 'But isn't it *uppermost*, dear?'

She waved away Clare's reply. 'Time waits for no man. Or woman!'

Her mother-in-law drained Clare. It had been like this from the start. Arthur wasn't so bad, but was completely swamped. He'd been defeated years ago, lost the battles and the war in one go.

'Evadne, we'll make our own way, thank you. It's up to Clifford and me—'

'Coffees!' Arthur arrived with three cups. His wife looked at hers with ill-concealed distaste. 'I was talking to a most interesting man in the queue—'

Evadne wiped her palms together as if ridding herself of a noisome contaminant. 'Did you check the cups were clean?'

'Of course, of course.'

Clare thought, The man sounds positively humbled. 'We'll let you know when we decide anything, Evadne.'

'Mind if I interrupt, Dr Burtonall?' Dr Porritt stood beside the table, smiling. 'Sorry,' he said to her in-laws, 'but I've only a minute. About the offer, Clare?'

'Still thinking, Paul,' she answered. 'I'll reply very soon.'

'Drop in.' The cardiologist pursed his lips. 'The whole thing's set up, everything a cardio survey needs.'

'Good. Perhaps I shall.'

'The subvention might come through any day. I'd want a flying start.'

'I really do appreciate it, Paul.'

'It's the room by the old surgery. Sister Gascoine has the key.'

'Ta, Paul.' Clare prayed that he would leave.

'The night staff know the key's in Sister Gascoine's office.'

Evadne took the offensive the instant he went.

'Offer, my dear?' she cooed. 'Offer of what?'

'Oh, some enterprise or other.'

Arthur began to look uncomfortable as his wife pressed on.

'It didn't sound at all casual, Clare. It was more like the offer of a job. Might it interfere with family plans?'

'It's a scheme Dr Porritt wants to set up,' Clare said, exasperated. 'It isn't even off the ground yet. Nothing's fixed. They haven't even the money to start.'

'Any day,' her mother-in-law quoted in reprimand. 'And fully equipped. He as good as said so.'

'What if it is, Evadne?' Arthur said, in sympathy with Clare.

'Don't carp, Arthur!' Heads turned at adjacent tables. 'I'm being perfectly reasonable. Some things are best said!'

'Look, Evadne,' Clare tried, anything for peace. 'Perhaps it was a mistake for me to invite you here. Come for tea next Sunday. How about that?'

'Fine!' her father-in-law said heartily. 'We'll be there. Make some parkin, we'll never leave!'

'I see we've outstayed our welcome,' Evadne said frostily, rising. 'You have your new unit to inspect – and your new contract.'

'No, Evadne,' Clare said. 'Please finish your coffee.'

'Another time, Clare.' Evadne swept out, Arthur following, turning to mouth a miserable apology.

21

THE RAGE WAS like being ill. A year back, Salvo had been under the doctor for flu, but he'd felt like death, three whole days. Take everything lying down, she the ball breaker, you were a laughing stock. Rather be shot at than laughed at. Salvo recalled Marla's lies – see you at the Domino or the Shot Pot eightish – but never the Ball Boys, where she'd really be with that Lana. It was vital to stand your ground. Bonn telling him thank you, Salvo was great. A bloke like that, paid to dick birds one after another, polite, hinting – hadn't he? – that one day Salvo would make it. Gelt plus grumble meant heaven.

He'd lost Marla near the Waterloo Street junction, the old mill in Oberon Street, where the shops began. She'd changed direction twice, but all the time doglegging to the Ball Boys. He headed for Marla's flat. He'd wait there.

Climbing the stairs, he felt proud. Oz would be impressed, hearing how Bonn himself had talked to him. Better than Angler, better than Faulkner from Horwich, better even than the tall Commer from Liverpool, everybody's front runner until Bonn came.

He paused on the landing. Not much noise, but what was it?

A muttering telly next door along. A babby wailing. A bloke shouted up the next stairwell, something about his bike, Christ's sake, this hour, night already out there with half the fucking bulbs missing from lads laying throw-stone bets. He deserved better, folk stacked like fucking sardines.

Somebody inside? The crack near the hinges showed nothing, which it would if there was a light on. Somebody hurting? He looked about.

The landing showed droppings from the flying years: dust, paint flakes, ceiling plaster heaped like snow drifts smoothing out corners, fragments from imploded light bulbs. He stood listening, the shitty life he lived. Bonn's firm would have been his way out. The noise couldn't be in the flat. Marla was out. He'd followed the bitch, hadn't he? So who the fuck was inside, that keening noise? It wasn't the babby. The little bugger had finally shtummed.

Why had they asked that moron Lancelot, the mogga dancer? And that prat Galahad? Everybody knew muscle hustlers were poofters. Bonn wasn't to blame, poor bugger, syndicate keeping tabs on him.

He turned the key, the door chain not on, went in.

The notes had changed to breathless grunting, chugging. Except it wasn't pain, as he'd imagined out on the crappy landing.

No sense closing the door now he was in. His one good burglary – a solicitor's office after hours – he'd been helped by an experienced mate who'd done time, so everybody knew he was good. The old tea-leaf told Salvo, never shut the door behind you. Good advice he heeded now.

He moved quietly down the narrow corridor. Bathroom, kitchen, the broad room for bedroom and living. There he'd watched racing from Haydock this afternoon, losing a few quid, Marla nagging and slamming things.

The bed was down from its wall position, as he'd left it, except now the bed held Marla and Lana, with Marla, whore that she was, making all the chugging any tart had a right to, her legs spread like Marble Arch and Lana's head working like a fucking excavator between. He could see in the light from the windows, the whore not even the decency to pull the curtain.

In the strange orange light he saw Marla reach for her dyke's hand, Lana grunting and Marla's head thrown back, the cow, like she wanted to lose it over the headboard.

He stared, rage swelling. The most insulting thing was Lana hadn't even bothered to un-fucking-dress, just down to the waist for tit work before really getting down to doing it to Marla.

So how many times had Lana dyked his Marla and made a right prat of him? Maybe ten times a day, then everybody at the Ball Boys sharing what a good fucking joke it was?

Which meant the syndicate must already have word about him not being able to keep a bird, not even from a dyke as rough as Lana. It was this dyke who'd burked his chances of goer, picking rich.

A bubbling fury filling his throat. He took his time, silent on the stained carpet. Lana, to start with. He stared down at them. This one-sex act in the weird neon light was loathsome. At school, the roughest area, he'd been punished by one of the schoolmasters – and who the fuck called them *that* now their glory days were done and they had to do what they were fucking well told? He had this saying, the cunt, chanting while he lashed out, 'You have the arrogance of ignorance', like fucking Holy Writ. Salvo never did know what it meant, some insult.

He was curious in spite to see how she managed it, where

the tongue went, how fast, the other hand slowly doing what, flicking ahead of Marla's whimpers or, in time, details.

Stupid, he cursed himself, standing silently there. Time they paid up. His fury filled him and he moved on them then, ready steady. One of Lana's shoes had come off and was on the bed, spiky heel a mile long, glitter down the back.

For a moment, his knees touching the bed, he stood looking down onto the features of his Marla. Her mouth was agape, her protruding tongue lashing one corner of her mouth to the other like she was taunting, going carnie over some street bint who sold her arse for a quid. He'd never seen Marla this far over. For him, she just lay there like a fucking plank. Habit, she'd given him. She'd conned him.

Habit, for him. But this Lana bitch got the real thing, this bitch slavering and chewing, grazing in his field.

Lana's shoe was in his hand. He prodded Marla's face with it. For a moment she didn't understand, opened her eyes to smile, maybe ask Lana what now. It would have been funny, given him a laugh, as the bitch started thinking, coming to, horror in there, caught redhanded, redcunted, under her slobbering dyke.

For just an instant he wondered whether to do an Oz, let them get on with it, who cared. But then what? They'd giggle, decide it was Lana's turn, his Marla doing the gob work while they gave the whole city a laugh, him not having the nerve to raise a finger. Not this time.

'Surprise,' he said, causing Lana to squeal and jerk back, head lifting, mouth dripping. The arrogance of ignorance? For a fleeting instant he felt the fury of justified disgust and lashed out.

*

In the office Clifford had little to do. So he told himself. He shifted files, got letters written, Dictaphone stuff that could wait anyway. The girls were gone, that Mona, calling irritatingly cheerful reminders, do this, don't forget that, before six o'clock. He'd faffed about. In the morning there'd be gales of laughter. 'He'll forget his head next!' and such-like whimsies.

There didn't seem any road round his problem. Hassall and Windsor were moving slowly through Mostern's acquaintances. He had to do something. Some *thing*. Inactivity was out. Goldoni had seen that straight away.

The police were nearing, plod by sombre plod. The question was, were they moving randomly, or did they have a list for the killing of Leonard Mostern?

Every deal had weak links. The woman Jane Antrobus had been well paid. He'd seen to that himself, the master of currency. She'd been grateful. He'd seen the light in her eyes more than once, the rapture of gratified greed-lust, the money paid over. It was Jane Antrobus who had told him the statistics: the Serious Fraud Office's conviction rate was 71 per cent. 'It sounds impressive,' the large-boned woman had told Clifford when he'd met her for a drink with Mostern, RIP. 'But the number of *alleged* frauds that are *dropped* is in the thousands!'

And, later, after a few drinks, 'The SFO wants a crime of fraud, when our legal system has no such thing.' Gales of laughter, then she and her sweaty boyfriend Leonard had retired to her bedroom to discuss how much to take Clifford Burtonall's development scam for.

Clifford sat in his great black swivel chair, genuine Dakka leather, as the office lights faded in and the city darkened. The picture window gave him a view of the city's centre,

Victoria Square. God, he'd developed a good tenth of it even in the few years since he'd started. He couldn't lose it now.

Odd, yet interesting, how a deal tied your hands. This new deal, in every way routine, forced Clifford into taking steps he'd never imagined.

Once before, he'd had to correct somebody who had become uncooperative, a supplier in St Helens. That had been easy, some ugly canal business he really didn't want to remember. The supplier's girl had been sanctioned – he carefully thought of it in those terms.

They say about generals that they are serene once the order's gone out and the battle joined, men sent to their deaths in thousands. It had been that tense, a nail-biter. But Clifford felt absolved, sitting watching the night city. He was not – repeat not – to blame for the outcome. Salvo had exceeded his orders. The idea was simply a smash-and-grab business, that time of day. Clifford had certainly said nothing about killing. The briefcase had to be rescued, that was all.

He pondered, then took a decision. He tried the contact numbers with no success. But he had an address for Salvo. He had time. If Salvo was alone, he could instruct him should there be any police interest. If Salvo wasn't alone, Clifford could do a wrong address, off the cuff.

Morally or legally, he couldn't be blamed. Mostern's death was a misunderstanding. Jane Antrobus was still in the hotel, because he'd checked. She hadn't called. Maybe she was so shocked by the news of Mostern's death that she was stunned. The SFO didn't have a leg to stand on.

Except Salvo. Wise to visit, simply check that everything was still safe and quiet. It wouldn't take more than an hour.

Clifford left some office lights burning and locked up. He decided to walk through the square. His car, and the lights in his window, would prove he was still hard at it on the top floor.

22

Mother – a truthful warning to friends in perpetration of a crime.

THE WOMAN HAD been more pleasant than Bonn felt he had a right to expect. She was importunate, wouldn't take no for an answer. He felt fond. This was her sixth time with him. She told him stories of her children's antics, while she dressed to go. She insisted on his remaining on the bed. It was, she'd told him, something she'd once seen in a film, the heroine leaving her lover as she flitted back to propriety.

'The things children write at school!' She knew Bonn liked to watch her.

'What things?' Bonn lay on the pillows, smiling, arms behind his head the way she'd described the cinema's hero lover.

'Honestly!' She drew on her stockings, pointing her toes. 'I'm ashamed! The teachers must have a really good laugh! Children! You have to be careful.'

Bonn sensed that she was leading up to a vital question. She came slowly to the bed.

'Bonn?' She sank slowly, the bed tilting him. 'You know so much about me.'

'I wouldn't say that, Yasmine.' He added, 'You're a woman of mystery.'

She didn't smile. 'That's the point, Bonn.' She took his

hand. 'If I wanted to invite you . . . well, out, could you come?'

'Come where?' He was startled, a different request.

'I don't know, a drive in the country. Just us, I mean.'

'It would depend, Yasmine. They allow a visit to a home, as long as it won't complicate the lady's life.' He pressed on. 'And they don't mind if a lady wants to go away somewhere for a night, but they lay down strict conditions, what and where.'

'So many rules, Bonn, darling,' she exclaimed petulantly.

'Without rules, Yasmine, there'd be no me.' He raised himself on one elbow, but she pushed him back and pressed her head to the pillow next to his.

'What would they allow?'

'A cottage in the Peaks, say. But not gambling in some casino. Too many witnesses.'

'Not to a dance, then?' she asked wistfully. 'It would be wonderful, just the two of us. My husband'd rather be off drinking with his pals.'

'I wish I could, Yasmine. Honestly.' He stroked her.

Martina had called a meeting of all the keys. Rack would already be champing at the bit in the corridor, hoping to hear the door go.

'Shall I ask?' That was always a good ploy, its implications of something decided.

'Please, darling.' She pressed her mouth on his, lingering, inhaling his breath as she loved to do when nearing a climax.

'I promise, Yasmine.'

He would keep his promise, and ask permission. Of course it would be hopeless. Martina would refuse, wondering why he'd even bothered to ask. Yasmine's attitude was no longer that of the client. It was the beginning of friendship, and therefore dangerous. Were their positions reversed – he the hirer, she a prostitute – then it might be tolerated. But this way, the risk was never far from the surface. Plain fornication must not become a tryst.

'You won't forget, darling?'

'Never in a million years, Yasmine,' he said.

The Bar Owl was a floor in a converted mill that was sectioned for small enterprises. The second floor was the size of a tennis court, with carpets higgledy-piggledy and a central black-lead stove. Huge paintings, a job lot from a redundant art school, blotted the whitewashed walls between great rectangular windows. This was Martina's meeting room. Posser only rarely attended, but he was here. Martina would be the last to leave, keeping her lameness to herself.

She sat, her dad beside her on a straight chair for his breath, as the keys arrived. It didn't escape Bonn's notice that Martina's early presence effectively prevented idle chit-chat among the keys.

All the keys' appointments had been deflected to preserve the hour. Grellie entered last, shaking rain from her coat, grimacing apologies and mouthing embarrassment.

'Names, please,' Martina kept to Posser's custom, since they saw so little of each other.

Bonn spoke first, as the newest. 'Bonn.'

'Fret Dougal.' The lanky Accrington key was rumoured to be some vague relative of Posser's. Nobody was sure.

The others stated their names: Ton Atherton, Zen, Angler, Faulkner from Horwich, Canter, Suntan, and Commer the Liverpudlian beside Bonn. They were disposed in a circle, Martina and Posser completing the ring.

The old man's wheezing was audible, worse than Bonn remembered.

'Some have clients later,' Martina began, 'so get this over with.'

'Lads.' Posser sat forward, hands pressing down on his knees. 'There's a development. I want you to hear it from me first, before rumours fly.'

He inhaled, sat back a moment, glancing at them all in turn.

'There's interest in the syndicate. I mean money. We've been asked to sell out.' The sudden stir caused Martina to shoot them a warning look, them interrupting her father. 'I've more or less refused, so far. I want Martina to carry the syndicate on.'

He would have wiped his forehead free of sweat but couldn't spare a hand.

'There's no question of hiving off parts – the caffs, snooker halls, the girls, the goers as one lot, bingo corners, whatever. I've explored that.'

'And?' Canter asked, who had five goers on his firm, the largest, since he dealt with towns within a dozen miles of the city. He alone had a special phone inlet, and a part-time woman to handle calls.

'They are serious, Canter.' Posser halted to breathe noisily, and nodded to Martina to take it up.

'This approach was made some two months ago,' she said. 'The offer came through one man who knows the city, or seems to. He's anonymous. It's all public-phone communication direct to Posser. We have been given definite proof that they have the money.' She invited questions.

'How did they know of us?' Canter again, most concerned of them all.

'We don't know. Some informant among the teams, the

stringers even? He might have sent in dipsticks – that's standard practice. It certainly wasn't an advert in *Exchange and Mart*.'

Nobody laughed. Grellie spoke up with diffidence.

'What now, then? If we've turned it down.' She got no reply. 'I mean, isn't that the end of it, us going on as we are?' She looked about hopefully. 'There's no reason for this meeting, if we've said no. Right, Posser?'

Mistake, Bonn scored. She ought to have addressed Martina.

'The problem is,' Martina answered, 'we don't know who these people are. Europe is money shore to shore, and it's spilling over here. Continentals find their old exploits aren't as profitable as they used to be, and move into other areas.'

Posser, recovered, put in. 'Europe is hack-worthy. Subsidies invite scams. Heavy money wants a home.'

Bonn thought of Rack's friendly uncle who needed a quiet place to stay unnoticed. But Rack was trustworthy. The doubt was unwholesome.

'You mean they might force us?' Suntan, the one key who insisted on two standers, asked the question for them all.

'That's our worry. You know my feelings. I won't be party to a scrap.'

Suntan had been done for knifing a drinker in Leeds, and thought mayhem a part of normal life. He had taken five years to make key. Rumour said he was negotiating to move to the Midlands, for reasons unknown.

'If a rumble finishes it, where's the harm?'

'The harm is sides, Suntan,' Posser was fond of Suntan. Bonn wondered if he saw himself as he had been in youth, violent and enjoying the danger. 'People take sides. Somebody – I don't mean here – will take sides against us. That will be remembered. Words like "traitor" and "betrayal" never go away.'

'Not if we suss who they are, Posser.'

'Assuming we get it right, you mean?' Posser rasped, raising a finger so nobody would use the space to interrupt. He breathed harshly into speech. 'The odds are enormous. Nothing's easier to hide than Continental money.'

'Posser, please.' Bonn's interruption caused a silence. Heads turned. 'Do we know its origin?'

'No, Bonn,' Martina answered for her father. 'We checked as far as we could. In trades and out, they're solid.'

'Martina. What now?' Grellie asked. 'Will something more happen we won't know about?' She looked startled. 'Sorry, Posser, Martina. I didn't mean—'

'Don't worry, Grellie,' Posser said. 'If they have cannon, that will be it.'

'The minute we have details, you'll all be told, Grellie,' Martina said.

'Until then we carry on as before?' Bonn did a pantomime, hands in supplication, the others smiling at his joke, him so newly promoted.

'Please,' Posser said.

Martina looked her disapproval. It should have been a command. Bonn knew that he was witnessing the end of Posser's era.

Martina said quietly. 'If you please.' A command after all.

As they left, two women from one of the hotels nearby came out of the service lift wheeling a covered tea trolley. It seemed to be laid for two, no more. Angler started to make some joke to Suntan, but the mood was not on any of them and they went out into the drizzle without speaking.

'All right, Bonn?' Rack was at the corner. He knew it was serious news, all the keys and Grellie in one street.

'Rack, would you suss out Salvo? You know, that contender.'

'Right. See you where?'

'The mogga dancing.' Bonn paused, cars whizzing by, drizzle hazing lights and haloes round every face. 'Rather quickly, please.'

23

THE DOOR WAS shut, but Rack hadn't walked five streets to be baulked. He went through hardly breaking step, grinning. Old Pell would pull his leg unmercifully: 'You *what*? Used a comb and wire to dub through an effing prewar wood *door*?' And the lads in the Spinners Arms would make wanking gestures while he told them made-ups about special reinforced locks with them flanges.

He'd been lucky, seen Salvo come out, hurry off towards the square. That meant the place was empty. Was Bonn thinking of stuff nicked from Martina, something like that? No harm to have a quick shufti. And the way Salvo had gone, like a frightened ferret.

Rack went silently down a corridor and in the room where Salvo –

Where two girls were, who looked dead.

Except one, Marla maybe, if there'd been enough light, moaned and raised a hand. The other girl, skirt up around her waist and bruises black on her white thighs like mottled ink. Brown bloodstains on walls, spatters, a few streaks made by hands desperate for something, shit on legs and bed, puddles of piss. He thought, or maybe said, 'What the fuck?'

'Rack,' the battered thing that might be Marla said.

'Yih?' He stood, not knowing what to do.

Marla, if that slow-motion creature with the blood-matted hair and teeth hanging – teeth *hanging*, fuck's sake? – on her chin like ivory saliva and eyes that bulged in blue-black mounds, Marla lay against the wall side, one leg twisted like legs couldn't be. Her legs were soiled, her clothes ripped and everywhere, her arm was swollen, her shoulder somehow heaped up one side of her neck.

Somebody had lashed her, stripes on her face, if it was still face there. A tuft of hair, surely hers, was stuck on her left tit like for some mad effect. Her shoe, a high heel, was stabbed into her neck, the stiletto heel pronged into the skin, russet blood congealing round it, shelved on display, except it wasn't a shelf but her neck.

Lana, if that lifeless thing was Lana, was cleaner, lying with her head wrong, turned to the window. The curtains were the sort you could tell daylight through, except it was night, orange neon. Somebody had wiped blooded hands, rucked the drapes up like a lavvy towel.

'I'll get help, Marla.'

She recognised him, with her jaw sprawling out of her face, the chin pointing to her other shoulder, away from the shoe stabbed into her neck. Jesus, he thought, said, not knowing, Jesus. He felt sick, kept cool.

'Don't move, Marla.' How long had he been standing there?

'Lana,' Marla managed to get out: '*An*-a.'

'Lana's,' he said, licking his lips for the lie, 'Lana's okay. Lie still,' he added in wild inventiveness, 'both of you, okay?' This needed Bonn.

'Lana?' he babbled. 'Lie still. Don't move. And don't,'

he burbled in a burst of genius, 'don't either of you talk, okay?'

He looked about the room. No phone, but then he thought how stupid that would have been, dashed out across the concrete space with its twisted basketball circle, and rang Martina. She came on straight away sounding tired, but woke up when he gave it her.

'Call an ambulance,' she said, precise. 'Any sign?'

'Of Salvo?' he asked straight out, wondering why she tutted in annoyance. 'Nar. He's left enough traces even for the Old Bill. I saw him.'

'Do it. Then ring back.'

'Okay, Martina.' He obeyed, telling the address to some dim cow at the ambulance station in Wythenshaw, for fuck's sake, like who'd believe city ambulances had to come from fucking Mars? For good measure he rang again, demanding where the fuck's the ambulance, saying he'd rung an hour since. He told them there was a fight, two blokes injured, and there was also a fire, so get the fucking brigade out. Cursing the spluttering bitch made him better. Okay, less worse.

He got Martina, running out of money quick.

'How many phone boxes are there?' Martina was mad at him. Why?

'Four. I'm in one.' He'd only done what he'd been told.

'You've got your phone card. Switch.'

He changed to a card phone, two along, mercifully unvandalised. 'Hello?'

'Stop there.' No preliminary chat. 'Watch.'

'Shouldn't I go up to Marla? Bonn sent me—'

'*Silence!*' Him a kid in school, her the bullying teacher. 'Watch.'

Rack felt narked. He was about to explain, Bonn's orders, suss Salvo, all that, and gets shut up.

'Watch what for? I reckon Lana's been snuffed—'

'For anything you see, anyone you recognise.'

So like a fool he stayed at a silent phone while his card clicked its cost away. The odd person came and went, nothing out of the ordinary, an estate like this, the odd bloke running, bawling riots upstairs hardly noticed. One or two cars drove through the road loop, lights cutting night. Young lads shouted footer abuse to each other, scuffling, City versus United, one lot doomed to relegation. No ambulance.

Then into the light, quite close, walked this bloke. Smart suit, wristwatch gleaming. He'd never been here before. Rack could tell. He checked the numbers by the lifts, went up when he found Salvo and Marla's number. Rack got excited. He told Martina this. It was half past seven.

'He's on the balcony. Jesus! Silly cunt's *switched the light on!*'

He saw the man enter, light casting his shadow back. Rack had had the sense to wipe the doors. Then the man came hurrying out, was sick on the balcony, looked about, frightened, pausing like a kid playing hide-and-seek, left at a fast walk, too fast for honesty in rough housing estates.

The ambulance came, its crew standing doing sweet sod all while they sussed out hoax calls, the flats up there safe or not. One ambulancer pointed to the door ajar. Other folk opening doors now, the blue light jampot to fucking flies.

Rack told Martina he was off out of it. Police wahwahs sounded nearer. He struggled to yank the receiver, failed, so wiped and shattered it. He did the same to the previous phone, let them sort it out.

He slid into the dark, and was gone, side alleys by the old closed canal. He had an idea, ran for the distance, emerged into respectable lights near Victoria Square, and saw the bloke, same one, walking quickly past the Vivante. He followed, saw him go into an office block by the museum for old frocks. Rack stood outside at a bus stop, looking up. Window, fifth floor? He crossed over, checked the name. He could hardly read, funny scrolly writing.

Martina hated phones, so he went to tell her face to face. She looked knackered, lines on her face he'd never noticed. Outside, Osmund was doing his patience, some Leigh lads – third in the league table, their tails up – doing trick shots, making a racket.

'Tell it to me in order, Rack. As it happened.'

He wondered why Martina was narked. Then it hit him.

'Hey, Martina! You didn't want names talked, right?'

He got a tut-tut. Obviously didn't want to admit that he'd done brilliant, been fast and smart. He detailed his destruction of the phones, his care.

'The scene?' she demanded, really pissed off.

Rack was astounded. She wasn't like this. He still hadn't heard about the big meeting. He should be out in the street ballocking the girls for gossip. And he hadn't yet told Bonn all about Salvo, when it was Bonn sent him.

'No point me watching them cart Marla and Lana out.'

He could have said what would happen anyway: estate kids getting clobbered for fiddling with the ambulance wheels, police trying for statements, nobody seen fuck all. It was always the same.

He told Martina all about the city gent. She became headache-alert then, made him go over and over it. Then the bit he'd dreaded.

'Why were you there, Rack?'

Bright cow, Martina, he thought grudgingly. It was time she moved on Bonn. For an instant he wondered if this was the right time to say how about you and Bonn, really tactful, bring it up like, Hey, Martina, whyn't you shag Bonn? Graceful, the way birds wanted, cheer her up. Except birds wouldn't recognise tact if it slapped them in the face.

Second thought, if he got her under Bonn would he be doing Bonn a favour? A bird gets too close she starts on your teeth, nails, comb your hair every fucking minute. Maybe first thoughts were best, Grellie for Bonn? He felt really bad at the thought of hurting Bonn's feelings. Though it wouldn't matter, because Bonn's teeth and nails would be clean. Hundred to one, Bonn's teeth would dazzle. He'd look.

He ended his account, Bonn ordering him to suss Salvo. Martina was all headache-attention, eyes wrinkled like in smoke.

'Thank you, Rack. You did really well. Ring a plant.' He copped the name Martina gave.

'Am I to tell Bonn?'

'Yes.' But a pause, all was not well. Women fucking wore you out.

Rack went outside to ring the plant girl. He was gleed up, because he liked this one in Wythenshaw. Martina had seven or eight of these plant lasses, just alibi dills really, never did sex or gambling, bints on nothing but money. They gave evidence to the Old Bill to order. You worked out your tale like a menu, this ingredient, that cake mix. This was some married lass he'd used once before after some greyhound racing at Burnden Park frittered and the plod went berserk. Her husband saw no harm, and Martina paid case by case. Plant women were cheap, no retainer except a lousy Christmas bonus, did as they were told.

He was sick in the lavvy at the bus station, spewed his ring up but proud. He'd tell the lads. They'd bet on Marla, say 13 to 8. It was her neck and jaw that made him puke. He'd lay twenty on her making it.

Bonn came by as Rack was talking with Grellie's studio stringers by the bikers' stand. From his look, Bonn had already heard.

'Wotcher, Bonn,' Rack said, buoyed up with triumph, the two girls listening. 'I got that thing you wanted.'

'Thank you, Rack. It is good of you to have taken the trouble.'

'Not at all,' Rack said grandly, eyeing the girl he fancied, Liz from Pendlebury, diamond in her nose making Rack wonder did it hurt. *Not at all!* just like Bonn sometimes said it. He caught the admiration in Liz's eyes, speaking to Bonn like an equal.

'When you're ready, please,' Bonn said, moving on.

'I'll be there, Bonn.' Rack strolled after, no hurry, seeing Grellie cross quickly to intercept Bonn by where two street buskers danced, mouth organ and ricks clacking away. Life was back to normal, at fucking last.

24

Honcho – one who enforces order at a place of entertainment.

It was always going to be difficult. Bonn waited nearly an hour for Clare Three-Nine-Five. Rack was on stand somewhere, doubtless incubating theories about lateness. Bonn'd made fresh coffee twice, binned both. Mistake to watch TV, sloppiness was in the eye of the beholder. No, probably Clare Three-Nine-Five had become scared of what he might have discovered about the dead man, rationalising that she'd misunderstood, forget she'd ever doubted it.

He was halfway out of the door when he heard footfalls. She came at a breathless trot. He suddenly thought her pretty.

'I'm so sorry.' Careful to omit his name. Good.

He re-entered the room, closed the door. She grimaced at her watch. 'Does this mean you have to go?'

'I'm so sorry, but yes.'

She shook out her hair. 'I had to see an elderly gentleman. He was leaving his home today, for terminal care.'

'I must report in on the hour.'

'Can you not extend?' She had hoped the hint of Father Crossley would make a difference. 'He had old photographs of his seminary. What hell, to leave such tranquillity.'

'I wish I could stay, Clare.'

'Did you find anything out about what I asked?'

'Yes. It would take time to tell.'

'And you're going to somebody else?' It came out un-expectedly bitter.

'No. But I must clear my next hour.'

'Checking in, like a child?' More bitter still. She was astonished at her inexplicable anger. *I'm scared of what he has to say,* she guessed. He was already opening the door and stepping past. 'Wait. Please. It was your old priest made me late, for heaven's sake.'

'You will excuse me.' He left the room key in the lock. She held his arm.

'After, then? The evening's early.' *Listen to me pleading,* she blazed at herself, *like a woman ditched by a lover.* She felt obscene. 'Can I phone and book you?'

Fright. That was it. Not anger.

He waited while she phoned the Pleases Agency, Inc. Foolish, giving her code, Clare Three-Nine-Five, while Bonn was within reach.

'I've been delayed,' she explained. 'I need another hour. I mean,' she said, colouring, 'to speak.' Pause. 'No, it must be tonight.'

'I'm afraid Bonn is heavily booked this evening, Clare.' Miss Rose's soothing voice asked her to hold. Then another female voice, firmer and less restful, came on.

'Is it a mere conversation, Clare, or something more?' it asked frankly.

'What I said. To speak.' Clare felt her anger return. 'It will not take all that long.' *She could have finished by now.*

'Meet Bonn at the mogga dancing fifty minutes from now. You may remain at his table for half an hour.'

'Thank you.' Clare failed to suppress her relief. The

woman would now sense her desperation. 'What dancing, please?'

'Bonn is there with you,' the voice stated, cold, 'and will explain. You will be billed as for a whole hour. Thank you.'

Clare heard the phone purr. She looked at Bonn.

'Mogga dancing?'

It was shameful, to feel defenceless entering a dance hall. Clare found herself hesitating. Everybody seemed young, knowing the way.

It was garish. She had imagined something sedate, a scent of lavender, uniformed gentlemen holding doors. Instead, here was a wide recess of mirrors, coloured lights racing round posters, youths and girls blocking your path, everybody screaming with laughter.

Great cream letters flashed *MOGGA DANCING* on and off. Inside it was as Bonn had told her, no real throng of spectators. No embarrassing box office. She walked with assumed calm through the foyer.

There was the wide staircase with scarlet hand-ropes, crazily ornate. A young couple argued on the stairs about some dance, voices raised. Clare walked past the bored bouncer, taking her time, clearly used to being here.

Music sounded, a jerky melody with a thumping beat, far too loud. She came on a wide balcony overlooking the dance floor. Most tables were unoccupied. A corner bar served coffee, cakes. The spectators were mostly women.

Clare walked to a table midway down the balcony. Three couples were already on the dance floor, wearing everyday clothes, performing a varying routine with different degrees of slickness. Astonishingly, they changed their dance every few bars, no pattern evident. She sat to watch.

'Your coffee, missus.'

She looked up. Bonn was placing cups from a tray. She said awkwardly, 'Thank you,' wondering. Half an hour. Had it already started?

He sat, gave his attention to the dancers. 'See that couple?' He pointed. 'We're sticking up for those. The others stand no chance.'

She eyed the pair. 'We are? Why?'

'They will win.' He added, 'Unless the judges are wrongly bribed.'

'Bribed?' She thought she'd misheard. 'All bribery's wrong.'

'It happens. But it's fair.'

She thought, *He's shy here*.

'Am I all right sitting here?' It seemed important to be in charge with him. She was paying through the nose, for heaven's sake. She tried to erase that crudity, but still felt aggrieved. 'I mean, you have so many rules.'

'Then don't obey.' His eyes were on the dancers. 'You can leave.'

For a second it seemed a taunt, but he was too serious. She looked away. He brought bad news, and was inviting her not to hear.

She put her elbows on the balcony edge, looking down with him. The dancers she was supporting were by far the best. The male was fantastically supple. His partner was a showy girl, hair tightly got up, wearing a skirt that went anywhere. Their shoes were the only formal items.

'Because they need to practise in their actual performance shoes.' Bonn divined her thought. 'You never see mogga dancers without.'

'Do you do this?' she asked, biding her time.

'No. I would be embarrassed, though I am a fair dancer.'

'Fair,' she heard herself say and thought, God, I'm starting to speak like him, saying instead of asking. 'Are they your friends?'

He didn't hesitate. 'No. I know them. They are the best, are they not.'

There he went again. It could irritate. If ever a woman got close enough she'd have every right to tell him so. Except that would be hard to do.

'Is this all there are?'

'Two hundred started out. Sixteen reach the regional finals.'

Clare laughed, as did other spectators, as Bonn's couple broke into a tap dance, then changed smoothly into the palais glide. She recognised it.

'They're dancing wrong. How can they score it?'

'Dance ability, slickness of change, degrees of dance difference, partnership conformity, transition, harmony, audience captivation, flair, musical distance, overall impression. Those ten. I believe there is an eleventh.'

'You do.' She shook herself, said sharply, 'You do?'

His gaze returned, disconcerting her. 'Fix on one couple, Clare.'

She did as he said, picking a hardworking pair. 'Yes?'

'At whom do you look? Ask yourself.'

'The girl.'

'So does everyone. The girl is flamboyant, the male stereotyped.'

'That is your eleventh test?' she asked.

'Yes. Style turnout.' He spoke solemnly, wanting to be correct.

'I'd no idea this went on. What does mogga mean?'

'Mixed.'

Bonn clapped casually as the dance ended. Clare thought, His pedantry is a kind of extended care. The couples walked off the dance floor. Conversations began among the spectators. One pair argued, angrily showing each other how their steps ought to have gone.

Clare looked about. Nobody she recognised. It was all as casual as Bonn had promised. Below, several new dance couples were coming on, one doing a soft-shoe shuffle as a joke. So light-hearted.

'Sorry?' she asked.

Bonn had said something quietly that made her stare. He tilted his chair back to be shielded from the staircase entrance.

'Your fears are justified, Clare. He was killed. A designed accident.'

His news, he was telling her his news. She spoke in sudden fury.

'I told you—'

He held up a hand, wait for the music. Killed, though. He'd said killed. His expression was one of unutterable sorrow, beyond mere sadness. An old Beatles number began, orchestrated almost out of all recognition.

'I am sorry, Clare.' It was as if he wanted to take her hand. 'Mostern was killed, for his briefcase. It was replaced by an empty one by the two men who killed him.'

She tried to swallow, feeling sick. 'What are you saying?'

'I do not know who the wallet was, but he received the briefcase—'

'Wallet?' Her heart drained, cold but not shivering.

'Wallet is the person who pays for a killing.'

Received the briefcase after the killing took place, Clare repeated silently.

'Who did it?' Where had Clifford been during Mostern's accident? That afternoon he had been at home.

'One drove the taxi, the other pushed Mostern. Unfortunately, there is a further complication, evident today.'

'For . . .?' She faltered, had almost said Clifford.

'A girl, two girls, have been . . . hurt. Today. A man from the Burtonall office might have visited the scene.'

'What scene?' Too shrill. It was his mentioning her name. He gestured her to be quieter.

'The flat is where one of the men lives. Who perpetrated the killing of Leonard Mostern. You do see?'

'I do see,' she said, savagely mocking his manner. Anger at Bonn almost blinded her. Ancient emperors slew bad-news messengers.

'One of the two men was mentioned in the newspapers after Mostern was killed.' He let it sink in. 'Today's crime, the two girls, will be in the papers soon. A man went to the scene, but didn't call Emergency. He went to the Burtonall office. It's by the TV studios.'

'Everybody is identifiable, then.' She was outraged by Bonn and his horrid, detestable information, his sadness.

'The Serious Fraud Office were about to Section Two an associate of Mostern.'

'An associate,' she sneered. The music was intolerable, the dancers' rigmarole absurdly frivolous. She had no idea what Section Two was.

'Clifford Burtonall,' he said. 'Same dining club as Mostern. If *I* know, the police will.'

'I see,' she said dully. How often had she, telling a patient the grimmest news of all – some fatal cancer, some heartrending birth defect of a newborn – heard the same meaningless reply. *I see.*

'The SFO lady is Antrobus.' Bonn clapped mechanically at some remarkable dance change. 'She maybe guaranteed Mostern immunity from prosecution if he handed over documents. I have no more information.'

'Give it me all!'

'Shhhhh.' Bonn whistled through his fingers, applauding.

The dancers snapped from a samba to a Viennese waltz, did a mock sand dance, a *paso doble*. She forced herself to watch the rhythm. She could only wonder why they were dancing, when she was in hell. Clifford Burtonall. Bonn actually said the name just like that. She shook.

'Please,' she said. 'All you know. Clifford Burtonall ordered Mostern killed, to stop him helping this Fraud woman?'

'It's almost certain, Clare.'

'*Don't call me Clare!*' she hissed, suddenly furious with him, his life, his repellent status, the things he'd brought to tell.

'I apologise.'

Someone began calling out, as in mockery. 'One-two-three, one-two-three!' A row started, abuse, noise of a scuffle, running feet. People on the balcony craned. The music came to a ragged halt.

It was as if her mind was suddenly ill and unable to cope. She had no idea how long it was, but the broil below had died down and new dancers were taking the floor, the music different and now twice as loud.

'No, Bonn. I apologise. Thank you.'

'Your handbag is under your seat.' It was his dismissal. She – *she* – dismissed, by him?

She found it, appalled at her misery. In a moment she

would leave and be alone with his news. She didn't want to be alone.

'Please. Is there somewhere we could go, just to rest?'

'That is proscribed.' He made to rise, decided to let her go. 'All appointments have to be made the same way.'

'I see.' *I see* again, when she didn't see anything. 'Could I possibly ring you? I don't actually know where you live.'

'Not really.'

'You must live somewhere, for God's sake.'

He checked they were not being watched, overheard. Was his entire life so secret?

'The Café Phrynne. I might be there about this time, the next two days. It is quite in order to be alone there. It is secure.'

She repeated the name. 'What do I do if I'm there and I see you?' Quite pathetic, talking in guarded circles.

'Just say good afternoon. Or here, at the finals.'

'Thank you.' She spoke in a dreadful monotone. 'Goodbye.'

'Goodbye, Clare.'

Feeling foolish coming in, feeling foolish leaving. She walked out, knowing she must look pale as death. He had used her name when she'd blurted out that he was not to. It had been like a blessing, a forgiveness. More stupid still, she was walking away from her one ally. She found her vision blurring at his compassion, stopped in the ladies' toilets.

The mirror showed her face. Jesus, an advert for poison. How ugly, hearing Bonn say, 'Clifford Burtonall' straight out.

She went out into the street as the next tune ended. Ripples of applause followed her through the velvet curtains. The garish lights split her head. Really, she was in no fit state to drive. The wise thing would be to rest in the Humber awhile, close her eyes. Soon, she would focus them on her husband, Clifford, whose very name now sounded so alien. One might say new, and utterly unknown.

25 | Plod – the police.

ON DAYS YOU didn't want day calls, the phone issued messages like an evil oracle. Switch the thing off, it nurtured malice, splurging out terse bleats the girls would bring in. All right for them, Clifford thought. Come in, do your nails, chat, type some Dictaphone, lunch, home.

He played the message again. It lodged on his heart like a stone.

'Mr Burtonall? Windsor. We met. I'd like a word.'

Silence. Then somebody wanting currency for overnight transition in Tokyo, tied to the Hang Seng, if you please, having the unmitigated gall to demand a review of commission. Any other time, he'd have flown into a rage at the insolence. Now he listened, then closed the office.

He had the Ford today, Clare the Supersnipe. Efficiency, not style. No 'please', no 'thank you', punctuating Windsor's Napoleonic assertions. You were to conform.

Clifford felt that his hands were too large as he drove, as if the ghastly experience at the flat had changed his size. He'd touched the door. Had he touched the wall, blundering out, making himself walk, not run? He'd rested a hand by the door. Had he worn gloves? They were in his jacket pocket. No good now.

Who had seen him? He had vomited in the office loos, sweated pints, still felt sodden. Those two girls, Jesus. He'd switched the light on as he'd gone in. He remembered letting out a screech. Or had he uttered a sound? He now thought not. And nobody had come out as he'd fled that terrible place. A handful of lads had been kicking a ball in a concrete area lit by two dim bulbs. Had they looked his way? He'd heard them calling pass the ball, useless, dribble, street cries heard everywhere. No 'Wotcher running fer, mister?' Nothing to implicate.

But had he touched anything, recoiling? Did fingerprints smear?

Why was Windsor ringing? The timing device was off, that useless cow Val in the outer office forgetting. He was latish getting home. Mrs Kinsale had gone, her notes everywhere for Clare. He was relieved to be alone.

The answer device was on. They were ex-directory.

'Hello, Clifford.' His mother, who always avoided Clare's name. 'I have some information about schools you both might like to see. I'll drop it over. So many changes!' A light planned laugh, ending with a goodbye of reassuring brightness. He couldn't even remember sitting with Clare in the conservatory for almost an hour.

And, 'Mr Burtonall. Windsor. Ring this number when you get in.'

Had Clare given Windsor this number? Clifford stood in the hall, worrying. He hadn't turned on the lights, as if that would erase memory.

He went to the front door. He'd left the key in the lock, dark out there now. The trip lights were on upstairs. Clare's caution and the housekeeper's careful checking.

How had he switched on the lights at that flat? Felt round the doorway, then moved the switch with fingers?

He put the hall light on, starting to hope because he'd simply moved the back of his hand on the projecting switch. Had he done the same at Salvo's place? He repeated the trial. Maybe he'd left no fingerprints at all?

Fingerprints were from fingers. Could they take them from, say, a knuckle? He switched the light off, repeated his home-coming, only it didn't work this time, his reflex somehow lost by concentration.

He was sweating badly. He needed to bath, rest, brew up, have a drink.

Then the inner-city project. He went over it, frantic. It had started as a simple development, make a routine slice on the side, the usual dipping and swarming, squeeze this, relax that. He felt enormous waves of self-pity. It was all so unfair. It was *routine*, for God's sake.

Then Mostern got to that bitch Antrobus. On the sly, earn his own immunity while ruining others. Clifford felt contempt for the dead man. Once a fool, always a fool.

The whole thing had been compounded by hiring Salvo. The money he'd paid Salvo was untraceable. No holes there. But he'd wanted a blam-and-lam job, not a massacre. Was Windsor ringing *about the two women*?

'Clifford? What are you doing?'

He almost leapt in fright. Clare was in the hall. He hadn't even heard her motor arrive. She looked unusually pale, but what didn't look strange now? He felt so weary. His greeting seemed robotic, at a great distance.

'Sorry.' He forced himself to invent, 'I thought the light was on the blink.'

'And is it?' She kissed him, waited. 'Broken?'

'Er, no, no.'

She took off her coat, put her handbag down. It was return home by numbers. He suddenly thought, What does she know? She went past him into the kitchen, putting the lights on as she went. He heard the kettle start its low hum, crockery, the oven click.

'I'm just wondering,' he said to the space she'd left in the hall.

'About Leonard Mostern?'

This was ridiculous. What could she possibly know? She'd been to a couple of functions, Mostern simply one of scores in some hotel club months back. Anger shook him. Was he being threatened by his wife? Christ, he had nothing to do with any deaths. He, Clifford Burtonall, provided full employment to hundreds, and he was being treated like somebody with everything to hide. It was repellent.

Those two dead women were nothing to do with him. Who knew what the lower classes got up to in their seedy stack-shacks? He was clean. Let the police ask what they wished. He'd been elsewhere when Mostern had died, so tough. And tonight he'd made a simple mistake over some address, that was all. He wouldn't stand for it. He strode into the kitchen. Clare was standing there as if she expected him to come.

His tremor was gone. He confronted her, cool, taking the reins.

'Why mention Mostern?'

'Isn't he the crux in the whole thing?'

For a fleeting instant she seemed as determined as he, but he'd found a new resolve. He'd been pushed around and wasn't going to take it.

' "Whole thing" sounds so all-embracing. What do you mean?' He smiled, glancing aside before capping the remark, one of his tricks that showed his witty grasp of subjects. It stood him in good stead in board meetings.

'His accident.' Clare had as much difficulty saying it as Clifford had thinking it.

'What are you implying? Nothing sinister, I hope?'

Clare laid aside the oven glove. The kettle did its faraway whistle. She absently clicked it off. Fingers, he observed.

'I wonder if it isn't. Sinister, I mean.'

She put that in because he was waiting, eyebrows raised, for clarification. Doubt took her. Easy to accuse, and heaven knows she'd almost worried herself into a stroke planning what to say, but until this moment she hadn't doubted Bonn. His account had damned, she'd believed it and hadn't wanted to. Now that she had to get the accusation out, anxiety immobilised her. She blushed like a child.

He poured the water, slapped the electric kettle back on its stand. Nothing wrong there. Perhaps it was in her?

'Out with it, Clare. Something's on your mind.'

He found Mrs Kinsale's tray, checked the cups, milk, spoons. Calmly he crossed into the living room, elbowing the light switch as he went. Clare followed. She needed sleep, see what had gone away when she woke.

'Is it because you were at the accident, and realised you couldn't do anything?' His expression was sympathy and rue mixed. 'I understand how that must feel, all your expertise no use and some poor man—'

'Killed,' she put in dully. She sat. 'Clifford. That briefcase. Who delivered it? What for? It came the evening Mr Mostern died.'

'I explained that. Some courier—'

'Who, Clifford?' Her voice caught like a finger on a thorn. 'Salvo?'

He stared. She watched his face go pale. He started to say something she didn't quite catch.

'Salvo?' he got out finally. 'How did you hear that name?'

'I've heard it. That should be enough.'

She felt tears come, blinked them away in anger. His response proved she was betrayed. The killing was nothing really to do with whatever schemes he was involved in. It was between herself and her husband.

'From Hassall, Windsor?' He said the names, then realised.

'No. If I've heard the name, then so have others.'

'How—?'

'Never mind how!' she shouted, then composed herself. She wanted to punish his idiocy, sacrificing everything in her marriage for some stupid scheme. 'It's what's happened that's the problem. You . . .' She halted, impotent. She didn't know any word. She found one. 'You were the instigator. You paid for somebody to see that Mostern was . . .' She ran out of euphemisms. '. . . executed. In order to prevent his meeting the Fraud lady.'

Clifford sank into his armchair, staring at her aghast, his wife suddenly a complete stranger.

'I can't believe . . .'

'You're hearing this?' Clare listened as the phone rang in the hall, heard Windsor's message. 'How much do the police know, Clifford?'

His lips moved. They'd become rimmed in purple. 'I don't know.'

'And the Serious Fraud Office lady?'

'She has nothing to justify an investigation now.'

'Now?' Clare almost yelled at him, calmed with a struggle. 'Now Mostern is dead? Is that it?'

'I don't know. Honestly, Clare.' He was almost tearful, his hands spread in appeal. She'd never seen him break down. 'If I could put the clock back, I would. Honest to

God, I never meant it to happen. It was an accident. I didn't mean them to go so far.'

'Is that police message about the two women?'

He began to cry at that, tears that Clare should have shed for herself streaming down his face. 'You've not been to the police?'

She was astonished. Her emotion, she realised, was contempt, nothing less, at the man who'd been her husband all this time. As if she would betray him, as he had betrayed her. He saw her expression harden, and tried to make amends. 'They've not been at you, putting ideas into your head?'

'No. I worked it out all on my little own.'

'How? Why, darling?'

She ignored the endearment, not caring what showed. 'I knew there was something wrong the day of the accident. I saw a man by the hedge. Thieves don't bring – they take. Couriers don't creep – they roar up to the front door.'

He visibly tired. 'Had you met Mostern without telling me?'

'At your stupid investment dinners.' She was furious at his suspicion. 'You went to the girls' flat. Hadn't you better explain?'

'Jesus.' He covered his face and wept, his shoulders shaking. 'I'm not involved, Clare. You must believe me. It's God's truth. I just went to find the man.'

He wiped his face, sniffed, and sat staring at the carpet. 'I found two women. In bed. I think they were dead. They'd been beaten. I thought one tried to say something, but I ran.'

'You *ran*?' It corroborated Bonn's account. 'You didn't phone for help?'

'How could I?' he complained. 'They'd have asked why

I was there.' His eyes rounded in horror. 'Maybe accused *me*.'

'So you left them.' Clare inspected him clinically, a species beyond her understanding. 'Didn't phone anonymously.'

'I couldn't think, darling. I was bewildered, scared. Jesus, I'd have been taken into custody. Me! *Arrested!*'

The words seemed to scare him even more. He went over his account, why he'd decided to visit the flat, why he had to know what the police had asked the man Salvo.

'Who'd done it?' Bonn had told her one was dead, the other maybe.

'Honest to God, darling, I give you my word. I don't know.' She watched his self-pity grow, overcome him, tears again.

'You'd never seen them before?' She was allowed to sound callous.

'Never! Honestly!' He made a helpless gesture. 'When you came home I was trying to remember if I touched anything.' He looked up soulfully. 'I switched the light on.'

'Then ran,' she said, deliberately scoring penalty points.

'I was careful once I got downstairs.' He was pathetically eager to prove his common sense.

'They saw.' Clare met his shocked look. 'You were seen walking to your office. You went in using your key.'

'You . . .?' Points of red appeared on his cheeks. 'You've been having me followed?' He stood, outraged. 'Of all the—'

'No!' She was a deal angrier than he could ever be, with the facts she possessed. 'I wouldn't *do* such a thing. As you didn't tell me about your involvement in Mostern's death, I think I had the right to make my own enquiries.' She raised her voice. 'I think I was justified. Don't you?'

'Who is he?' Suspicions flitted across his face.

'Male, yes,' Clare said, furious at his implications. ' "Another man", no.' He had confessed to his marriage-long deception, yet had the gall to reproach a blameless wife.

'A private detective?' He was blustering.

'Nothing like that. It was a fluke more than anything.'

Hope showed. His words became almost wistful. 'You mean there isn't a trace?'

'No. It's as far as it will go.'

'But how—?'

'Leave it, Clifford, *leave* it!'

'It's medical confidentiality, isn't it?' he begged, clutching at a straw. 'Doctor–patient obligation not to reveal a patient's details?'

'Something like that.' Let him have his bit of solace.

'You're sure, darling?' His eyes shone with relief. He saw her impatience and quickly appeased her. 'Thank you, darling. You're marvellous—'

'What now, Clifford?' She moved away.

'Well, I simply . . .' He remembered the police calls and faltered. 'I suppose I'll have to speak to Windsor.' He drew breath to ask, but Clare shook her head quickly.

'I won't make your call, Clifford.'

'Please, Clare.' He showed her his trembling hands. 'What could I say? I'll have to phone soon, or they'll come here. Bloody police read whatever they like into everything you say. Please?'

'No, Clifford. I might inadvertently get it wrong, too.' And implicate Bonn, his agency, people she didn't even know. 'Do it yourself.'

'Clare. Please don't be heartless—'

She blazed up. 'Heartless? After what you've put me through?'

'I'll do it, I'll do it!' He composed himself, then gave Clare a nod as if he'd decided to do his wife an immense favour. 'I'll ring Windsor now, darling.'

Clare didn't answer. He went out to the hall phone. She heard him dial, and at last she began to think.

That Bonn'd been so apologetic at first had seemed almost insulting. Now it seemed merely sadness. He would have spared her if he could. She felt ashamed, the way she'd spoken to him. Out in the hall, Clifford lifted the receiver. She heard the clicks. He would walk about as usual, a pace or two, pause, then return, his handsome head tilted. Telling the police what he knew of Mostern, possibly what he also knew of the two women in a flat he had no honest reason to visit.

She had been used. Was this self-loathing always the same, a wife realising a husband's contemptuous betrayal? Her marriage, once so sound and forever, was a cloak for Clifford's deceit frauds. What had he been doing, all this time? Worse, how many other crimes was he involved in? She felt giddy. One death, maybe three. More?

How piteous to have wondered as she had, about the morality of asking Bonn to find out. She'd accused herself of treachery, infidelity even. How often had patients come to her with similar questions?

There had been a couple only last week. The wife had contracted a venereal illness from an incidental lover – some casual holiday affair. Mercifully, it was easily cured. But the contact tracers – health auxiliaries responsible for finding other sexual contacts – had wanted the husband to report for examination. The wife had flatly refused to admit her address, her name, the identity of her casual coital partners, and had left in outrage.

'But they may still be at risk,' Clare had explained – reasonably, she thought.

'It's *my* business, doctor,' the wife had stormed. 'Nobody else's. It'd be admitting everything.' Later she had fumed, 'Think of the effect on my husband. It'd mean I'd let him down.'

The argument had gone on. Confidentiality forbade a doctor to simply send out the contact tracers to find the sexual partners of index patients – those who first came with an infectious illness. Unless they could be persuaded, there was simply no way of finding out other people who were at risk. Patients with more conscience persuaded their lovers to come to the clinics, all under codes. Clare had been pleased to find prostitutes accepting health assessments every three months as a matter of course.

Why was she thinking this? She heard Clifford's voice in the hallway.

'No, I was with my wife.' A casual laugh then. 'Yes, certainly.'

But that was only one side of infidelity. If the husband was unfaithful – how she hated the pompous word, with its pejorative overtones! – then was the wife free from marital constraint? To be so juvenile as to retaliate? Betrayal meant dissolution, didn't it? If a firm reneged on a contract, then wasn't the contract void? Or at least unpinned?

Clifford had treated her as someone who didn't need to be told anything. She made herself listen.

'Certainly, Mr Windsor. I'm sure she has!' How calm Clifford sounded, mmmhing along, good on the phone.

'Though what records the National Health Service keeps these days heaven knows!'

Records? Of what?

'No. I'll dig it out.' Pause. 'I'm sure my wife can!'

And a laugh, mild and unaffected, nothing all that important.

'Clifford?' Clare called, worried. She went to the door.

Far from being at ease, Clifford looked in a state of exhaustion. He was actually shaking, the receiver trembling at his ear. He was a man at the end of his tether. He replaced the handset. She wanted to go to him, but stayed herself.

He turned an anguished face to her.

'Clare, darling. You'll have to help me.'

'Help how?' But she already knew, from the little she had heard.

'I've said that you were giving me a medical examination.'

She stared. 'Me? Examine you? It's never done, not in families!'

'I said you did, that you have records, tests and all that. The times.' They remained standing apart, like fencers before a bout.

'But I haven't!' Was this all in one day?

He met her gaze with desperation. 'You must, Clare. We've no choice.'

'How? *It's impossible!* You mean, for an alibi?'

'Darling.' He moved but she instinctively stepped back. He nodded as if it constituted a new agreement. 'There's no other way. It seems there's been some business involving two young women at one of those high-rise blocks of flats. Windsor wants to know my movements.'

'What did you say? Tell me exactly.' It was unreal.

'I said I was with you at a clinic, being examined.

Anxieties about my ticker.' He tried a smile, wan and tired. 'I confided in you, old girl.' He never called her *old girl*. Why now? 'You took me along to some cardiac place you're involved with, ran the rule over me. Heart, all that.'

'You said that? You're out of your mind! It simply can't be done. Dates, times are incorporated in the electrocardiograph, the ECG. It's the same with the serological tests, the lab reports, everything.'

His face set. 'You have to, darling. We've no other way. Please don't forget that I love you in all this.'

We now? She flapped her hands as if to deflect sentiment. 'Do you know what you're suggesting? I haven't a surgery of my own. I can't simply walk into some hospital or surgery and say, Excuse me, but I need to establish an alibi for my husband!'

'You're an accessory, Clare. You're in this with me.' He spoke with a new quiet firmness, suddenly belligerent.

'An accessory?' She didn't follow.

He seemed to grow, and spoke as if they both agreed on a solution.

'You and I are in this together, darling.' No tears now. 'Let me remind you that you were – what did you imply, suspicious? – *before* the two women were attacked. You could have gone to the police. You didn't, did you?'

'That has nothing to do—'

'With the case?' he said for her. 'I'm afraid it has, darling. You see, Windsor says they are linking this new event with Mostern's demise. You told the police about the accident, but said nothing that could have helped them further, did you?' He had her. 'An accessory before the fact, darling, and an accessory after.' His smile was one she had never seen before.

She said warily, 'Meaning what, exactly?'

'You are both, darling. Exactly as I am – unless you give me an alibi. Clear me, you clear yourself.'

'It's against all medical—'

'Rules, darling?' His confidence returned. 'Bend them. Not too much. Just enough.'

'It's out of the question.'

'It's what we must do. You can teach me the symptoms, then create the alibi. After all, I didn't murder those girls, so really you're helping to prove the truth.'

He drew a breath. 'I suggest we have a drink. Then we can provide the police with the evidence they need. All right?'

That night Clare sat alone after Clifford had gone up. She drank a little wine, that emblem of tolerance, to 'think things through' as Agnes would say.

Wasn't it that Clifford was simply afraid – why else would he have spoken as he did? All men were children, unable to face problems, wanting the woman to provide solutions. And he was right, of course, in that the cardiologists insisted on the maximum number of males of Clifford's age for the cardiac survey. Heavens above, under any other circumstances she might have enrolled Clifford without another thought, so why make such a fuss?

She remembered his look at their first dance. She still laughingly teased him, calling it his 'desperate visage'. Surely she was reading far too much into what was, after all, a natural anxiety? You can think too much about an event, make it into something it never was in the first place. Why, a year previously a hospital vehicle had accidentally knocked down and injured a visiting father outside Casualty.

Every single person on the staff had felt personally guilty for days afterwards.

But if she was going to include Clifford, it had to be soon, tomorrow. And was it wrong to simply do Clifford's preliminary tests and write them up? What would it matter? Somebody had to be the first. She rinsed the glass. Tomorrow, actually taking him to the hospital, her doubts might well recur, but for now she felt calmer, back in control, reasonably sure what to do.

26

Cran – a place where money, especially a bribe, may be left for collection.

THEY PARKED OUTSIDE Farnworth General. The hospital lights were on; the huge car park was full of visitors' cars. Clare yanked the handbrake on. Beside her Clifford's face shone in the gloaming.

'You know what to do?' she asked. She felt leaden, weighed down by what she was about to create, a false record for a false patient. Who was, she reminded herself bitterly, a false husband.

'Yes.'

'Tell me again.'

He crinkled a piece of paper. She had drawn directions on it for him. He held it against the light. Nearby, an anxious family noisily alighted, predicting misery for some elderly relative in the surgical division. Clifford waited until they had gone.

'I wait five minutes. I go to the second-floor corridor, bearing right. It's fifty yards. I will see ECG signs, blue on white, by the stairs. I descend one flight.'

'And if a nurse comes out of the wards?'

'I pretend I'm lost, turn back, and repeat my arrival.'

'Right. Go on.'

She couldn't disguise her contempt. It was mostly aimed

at herself for succumbing the way she had. She could simply walk away, let him stew. But she hadn't. Instead, she was perpetrating a crime to conceal his *other* crimes. It could have her struck off the Register, eradicate her life's ambitions. And she was abetting a criminal. Why? Because of an archaic ritual, that betrayal called marriage.

She took a perverse glee in thinking of Evadne. I should give the bitch a ring and say something like, 'Oh, Evadne, glad to catch you. This marvellous son of yours. How should I handle this?' And give the details straight out, the killing he'd arranged, his association with two murdered girls.

' . . . the door marked Cardiac Surveillance, which will be ajar. I check I'm not seen from the ward, and go in. You will be—'

'Waiting.' Clare finished. 'And after?'

'I wait. You will go into the ward, to prove you're around.'

'I,' she added, sleek, 'have no need for concealment. You'll give me one minute exactly, then go to the visitors' canteen, have a coffee. Don't be surreptitious. Then come for me, asking everybody the way.'

No cars arriving for the moment, an opportunity. Clare made to get out. Clifford put a hand on her arm.

'Darling. Thank you.'

'Not at all.' She wanted to punish him for stealing her world.

'One thing, darling.' He sounded nervous. 'Will it hurt?'

'Hurt?' She almost laughed aloud at the incongruity. 'Christ, I betray everything I've sworn, and you're worried about a needle?'

She shook him off and walked away, tears of anger in her eyes.

*

It went well. Sister Gascoine was not on duty. Night staff were arriving, making it easy for Clare to go to the cardiac section ostensibly to 'have another look' at the new surveillance unit, take the key from the wall, and leave the nurses to their reporting.

The room was about thirty feet square. Two alcoves, desks, couches, chairs, screens for radiography, the 'rollers', as cardiac registrars called the arteriography monitors for viewing the radio-opaque dyes inserted into arteries. It wasn't much, but it was enough.

She hung her coat, drew the blinds over the frosted glass of the doors, quickly switched all the lights on. If anyone intruded, she would have to blag it, think up some tale on the spur.

Her alcove was at the far end. The men would enter for blood pressure, height, weight, body-mass indices, body-fat measurements, and morphology assessments. Then blood samples would be taken for peripheral blood cholesterols and the high- and low-density lipoprotein factors. The laboratories did those, despite the dot-spot tests. Freezers and refrigerators already hummed, with wire baskets for shipment to haematology. Further along, the ECG, with the gels and pads by the last couch, plastic covers in place. Everything was ready to use, just as when Dr Porritt had shown her round and said innocently, 'Get a few volunteers in and give it a go. The clerk might be sober enough.' And he'd added with a disarming grin, 'Once you're back, young Burtonall, you'll never escape.'

So it was the cardiologist's idea, this caricature.

She found the sterile syringes, pulled clear the sequestrated ampoules, the needles, and, before breaking the covering seal on the three syringes she would need, freed each piston action – she'd been caught too often to omit this. She labelled the containers which would hold the blood, giving Clifford his full name, age, and carefully putting the time he'd told her. It was the exact moment he'd been at the flat. It was the time he'd told Windsor that he was with Clare, being examined for cardiac symptoms.

Behind her the door went and Clifford slipped in. For a moment it almost stopped her heart. She beckoned him over quickly, told him to strip to the waist.

Working swiftly, she placed a rubber catheter – the best trouble-free improvised tourniquet – round his upper arm and broke the syringe seals. The small white haematology tray was down to its bare essentials of cotton wool, antiseptic, ampoules. The Hazard Sharps containers for waste needles and syringes were ready, their two seals properly ripped.

'Keep your arm straight, please,' she intoned.

She cleaned Clifford's skin, and capped the syringe with the needle.

'A prick now. Stay still.' She drove the needle into his antecubital fossa, picking up the vein cleanly and aspirating blood, checking the marks along the piston.

She pulled the tourniquet, as usual letting it fall anywhere, and pressed a dry sterile swab to the puncture wound.

'Press with the fingers of your other hand.'

How many thousand times had she said that, she wondered, distributing the blood. And how wrong to be doing this. She disposed of the syringe and needle in the Hazard containers, and placed the blood in the refrigerator. They were now circumstantial evidence that she had examined Clifford earlier. If everything went right.

Even before the puncture wound had sealed, she had Clifford on the ECG, setting the terminal lead pads on his body. The machine signalled its auto-dating facility. Carefully she clicked the time to zero, then advanced the timer to read Clifford's alibi time. Time, place, date.

She took readings, switching the leads to make the tracings in the usual order. She became aware of Clifford's gaze.

'I've never seen you so rapt like this before, darling.'

Her mind screamed. *Don't call me darling.*

'I'm just taking traces of what your heart is doing,' she said. 'We have names for each of the flicks and patterns on the trace-out.'

'Am I all right?'

'So far,' she said cryptically, talking to give normality to this double betrayal. 'We do them in order. Chest discomfort makes a doctor hunt Lead Four. The electrical changes can stay there longer than other wiggles, and go earliest, especially in the Q-wave bit. Some clues are especially good, like the T wave suddenly inverting.'

'Do all doctors do this?' He was still watching.

'It's like knowing a language.' His stare disconcerted her, and she babbled on. 'I check ECGs in a set order, or I'd miss one. X-rays, the same thing, you stick to your own pattern.'

'Like the police.'

'The T wave is my favourite,' Clare said, to shut him up. 'Once the ECG goes back to normal – it can, even after a heart attack – the T wave in only one lead can stay inverted. Doctors call it the registrar's friend.'

'I've never heard you talk like this before, darling.'

'I've never done this before, under quite these circumstances.'

She dismantled the leads, and changed back the auto-dater.

'Get up. For completeness I'll do the Quertelet Index,

body-fat measurements, and BP, enter records with earlier times. I'll start a new record book.'

'You will enter seven-thirty?' he said, alarmed.

'Don't worry, Clifford,' Clare said evenly. 'I'm learning to lie superbly well.'

'Thank you, darling.'

'Don't call me that,' she said evenly. 'On the scales, please.'

Ten minutes later, Clifford came to find her as planned, and they left together. Some hurrying nurse might vaguely recall that, yes, she'd seen Dr Burtonall waiting for her husband, but that would be it.

The times and date of Clifford's blood samples that Clare had clipped into the cardiac ward's haematology baskets would be replicated in the laboratory's records. She would phone in, and make sure the false times were correctly reproduced in the lab's computer printouts.

After that, there was little more she could do to protect her husband. It wasn't foolproof, but it was the best a lying, treacherous doctor could do.

She drove home in angry silence. On the way, she made a new resolution. This time, it was for herself, not for Clifford, not for her marriage.

That night, she only half slept, and awoke with her bitterness still there, the anger renewing itself and circling. She told Clifford she would call in at the hospital, make certain his blood samples had been processed.

By nine o'clock she'd given Mrs Kinsale her day's instructions, and stopped the old Humber on the A666 before half past. She called the agency number on her car phone.

Subterfuge be damned. They answered on the first ring. Clare quickly identified herself.

'I want Bonn,' she told the voice. No diffidence now.

'Very well, Clare Three-Nine-Five. What time would suit you best? Please give a choice of three—'

'Today,' Clare almost snapped. 'This afternoon, two o'clock?'

'That is in order, Clare. Venue?'

'The same as before?'

'Vivante Hotel, suite number four-two-six. Repeat, please.'

'Four-two-six.' Clare wrote it down. 'Vivante. Am I limited to one hour?'

'No, Clare. But an extra hour is chargeable, with—'

'Then until four o'clock, with a possible extension afterwards.'

'Your order is placed. Thank you for calling the agency. We assure you—'

'Thank you,' Clare interrupted. She was nervous, but it was no longer pure anger. Betrayal was in the air. It entitled her at least to sit with Bonn, talk over the problem, maybe just watch the afternoon TV film with someone gentle, and sad enough to listen.

Who knew the pathways of city evil, where her husband walked.

LANCELOT CAUGHT BONN as Rack passed him three bookings. One double, Clare Three-Nine-Five, plus a homer, which old Posser still called a 'dommy'.

'Dommy? In her home?' A new home client was unusual.

'It's checked,' Rack assured Bonn. 'She's maybe an upper from somewhere else, finding her feet.' Bonn didn't ask the obvious. Rack said, 'The address changed hands last week.'

'Fine. That other new one, tell Galahad to do it. Lancelot does the next.' Bonn looked up through the car window. 'Yes, Lancelot?'

'Listen, Bonn.' Lancelot danced when agitated, as now, springing from foot to foot beside the car. 'Can I postpone my goes today?'

'Are you ill?' Lancelot was a picture of agitated health.

'Bonn, man, it's my partner. Stupid cow wants four leps revised.'

Bonn looked at Rack. Leps?

'Changes from one dance style to the next. Tango to moonlight saunter. Know why they lose? Wrong heels—'

'Thank you, Rack.' Enough. 'No, Lancelot. Ladies first.'

'Bonn!' Lancelot wailed, dancing as he whimpered. Passing people smiled. One raised clenched hands, wishing him luck. Lancelot beamed, returned woefully to plead. 'Christ's sake, Bonn. I've never got this far. And a second lady's booked me twice running. She's getting—'

'What she pays for, Lancelot,' Bonn said, still pleasant.

Rack in the driving seat made Fangio noises, vroom vroom.

'But Galahad closes them down,' Lancelot cried.

'Lancelot. Dancing second, clients first.'

They pulled away, Rack doing his crash start. Bonn nudged Rack – slower, please – then told him to find Galahad. Rack yelped with glee, did a lunatic 180 and screeched wrong down a one-way. Bonn said nothing. At the Rum Romeo he alighted, said thanks and he would make his own way to the General Hospital. Rack was hurt.

'I'd get you there fastest, Bonn. Honest.'

'Tell Galahad the front coffee bar, if you would.'

The muscle man came instantly, nervous, Bonn let Rack bring the problem up, just sat to watch.

'Galahad. You closing the clients down?' Rack asked straight out.

'Closing down?' Galahad looked hunted.

'Telling them you're too booked up when you're not.'

Rack leant forward, threatening. He did this very well, Bonn could see. The stander gave the counter lass a glance, don't interrupt.

'Who told you that?' Galahad's indignation was too weak.

'Why, Galahad?' Rack loved violence. He slowly lifted the table edge, and slowly let it down. The simplest threat.

Galahad gave a cough to get his voice going.

'Look, Bonn,' he said, but to Rack. 'I have to look my best, see?'

Rack didn't even glance at Bonn. He'd been given the

job. 'Galahad. You gone against Bonn's rules. You could've said your piece then, butcher di'n't.'

Bonn listened curiously to Rack's changing speech. His Cockney reversion came out in aggro. Deliberately?

'I might make the championships, Bonn.' Still pleading to Rack.

'Diggin' yer grave, Galahad.' Rack opened his palms. Bonn thought, *Oremus*, let us pray, before the Consecration. 'How many yer closed?'

'Two.' Mesmerised, what could he get away with.

'It's six, innit?'

'Well, yes. But two were repeaters, honest.'

'Galahad.' Rack sat back, sighing. 'Six ern two int four, yer stoopid cunt. It's eight, geddit?'

'Why?' Galahad bleated, sensing the verdict and no way out. The counter girls had vanished, and the customers.

'Is yer stander in on it, or just you?'

'No. Me.'

Rack nodded to the air, telling Bonn he would check that.

'I believe yer, farzands wun't.' Rack said, 'Eight, Bonn.'

'Galahad.' Bonn touched the body builder's arm sympathetically. 'You are suspended. It grieves me. You are fined a year's earnings. And please withdraw from the championships.'

Even Rack gasped at such punishment. Galahad stood, stunned.

'Where'll I get that much money, Bonn?'

Bonn spoke quietly and with compassion. 'I might reinstate you, in time. When that comes, repay the whole sum plus half as much again interest monthly, by working it off. There will be no physical hurt.'

Rack stirred. Punishment should be done proper, fists,

bludgeoning, make people understand. He'd tell Bonn his theory of straighteners.

'Thanks, Bonn.' Galahad was hangdog, in tears. 'I'm sorry.'

As they started to leave, Bonn paused. 'I am so disappointed.'

The body builder recoiled as if struck. Bonn walked out, Rack following.

'Bonn. You oughter let some carnie in,' he urged, even if Bonn would never go back on a sentence. 'Coupla kicks straightens a bloke out. Think the girls'd get up if Grellie didn't have one tanked now and again? Jesus, walloping them two Aincoats saved Grellie more trouble than—'

'No, Rack.' Bonn paused at the entrance. It was coming on to rain. 'Find if Lancelot is also closing down. And check that Doob isn't still subtle mongering.'

Rack guffawed. 'Any more?'

'Yes,' Bonn stilled him by saying. 'Check Grellie too, please.'

Rack sobered. He looked at Bonn. Cold had come over him all of a sudden. For the first time he sensed that something was badly wrong.

Rack wanted to cheer him. 'Hey, Bonn,' he asked, brightening. 'You talk to Grellie about using her regular?'

'I suppose she is at the hospital.'

'Grellie? Yeah, she's taking some of the girls.'

Bonn relented. 'Get me there, Rack, please.'

Rack dashed for the motor before Bonn changed his mind.

The General was hectic. Bonn found it daunting. Trolleys clashed, thumping doors' rubber edges. Children howled, patients blundered. Rack was annoyed that Bonn said not to come in, the plod might see him and make the connection with Marla's flat. Rack started a theory, but Bonn looked him to silence and walked in.

He asked at the enquiry desk after Marla, her real name, Marlene Patricia Lancaster, off by heart. The clerk was slow, but told him Marla's ward, A-17, intensive care. He talked the lady into letting him use the internal phone. The ward sister told him nothing.

That was it. He wandered through the corridors to suss the layout, locating the lifts, wards. He wanted to ask after Lana, but Lana had too many names and the clerk might become suspicious.

A policeman was having coffee with a nurse in the anteroom of A-17. Glass panels allowed a partial view, but the patients were screened.

He followed the main drift. Most people left through the Out-Patients concourse. Doctors were being called. It was an hour before he decided enough was enough, and gave up. Too much risk to find Lana, alive or dead.

Halting to let a nurse pass as he turned to leave, he heard an announcement over the intercom, a doctor wanted in Cardiology Surveillance, please . . .

Burtonall. Dr Burtonall, on extension six-one-four-six soonest.

Easy from there to visit the Reception. The hospital's internal phone list was cross-referenced, department and alphabetical. Ten minutes, he'd located the number. He invoked her smooth face, her air of being unsurprisable, capable of strong decisions. And her sudden stillness at his mention of Burtonall's name, the photograph that could have been her among club members by Glazie's desk. Make way for the doctor, at the accident.

'Bonn?'

His heart leapt, then he recognised Grellie by the fountain in the open area, seated on a bench. He joined her.

'I didn't see Marla, but I phoned. You?'

'She might be blind.' Grellie had been weeping. 'I said I was her sister. She's not recovered consciousness yet.'

'Dictaphones everywhere, I suppose.'

'There's a WPC in.' Grellie eyed him. 'You asked too?'

'Of course,' he said evenly. 'I'm as anxious as the rest. Lana?'

'Lana's . . .' Grellie sniffed, blotted her face, watched some children enter with their father, her eyes following the anxious little family. 'Bonn? Don't let me speak out of turn, but y'know? Like I asked?'

'Have a woman for my own.' Bonn nodded, the subject grave.

'I'm in your queue. I feel it's time I went steady. I know there's your job and everything. I don't want to find you've got some girl.' She tried to smile. 'I know I look a mess. And it's unfair, what with Marla and your goers . . . y'know?'

It was as far as Grellie could go. Making it plainer might push him away. You couldn't tell with someone like Bonn.

'Thank you, Grellie. I'm finding my way still.'

'Is it my work?'

He looked at her. 'No. I shall woo someone soon.'

Woo, she thought, almost laughing at the archaic word. Considering what they did, for God's sake, 'woo' was deranged. She'd done poetry at school, *Idylls of the King*, old talk, trysts, mysterie. Was that Bonn's charm, that he could step back centuries, behaving proper in this city of knee-trembler shags in back streets?

'May I invite you for supper one evening? Nothing, well, y'know?'

Listen to myself, she thought distractedly. *May I invite . . .* Like she wasn't the whip for Martina's street stringers, working girls all, and like he wasn't key goer shagging the arse off any woman with gelt enough. Chivalry.

'Thank you, Grellie,' he replied, smiling as a child trotted round the fountain edge tracking a goldfish. 'I'm honoured.'

'Ta, wack,' she said, slang restoring sanity. She was rewarded by a brilliant smile that became more grin than she'd ever seen any man show, not silly wide, but of dazzling intensity. 'Tell me a time, luv.'

'I shall.' He rose to go, paused, and said, 'I like you, Grellie.'

'What?' she said, startled. He moved off. 'Thank you,' she said foolishly after him. Her eyes started filling, but she instantly put a stop to that nonsense.

Rack was chatting up two girls in the car park, a risk Bonn didn't like to see. The girls said hello to Bonn, who said hello back and got in the car.

'Lana's dead, God rest her,' Bonn said, the minute they pulled away.

'Thought so.'

Rack started on how rain should be used for electric power in hospitals, save the kingdom a fortune. Bonn's mind was on Clare Three-Nine-Five.

AT THE LAST minute she volunteered to help at the Well Baby Clinic, from disguised motives. She had never felt so drained since her house jobs, when days and nights merged into a six-month blur, landmarked by tricks – like keeping the time and date you last ate written on your white coat sleeve so you didn't faint from hunger all over the place. Worn out, you had crazy suspicions that you'd missed some diagnosis, forgotten this new patient, that old case, or some patient you'd discharged last week. . . . The mad total-time kaleidoscopic year that followed doctoral qualification.

Motive, she thought, making sure of her car keys. Self-correction, possibly, chastising herself for what she was about to do. Yet what *was* she going to do exactly? Meet a younger man – okay, think it outright, a *hired* male. So? Firms hired hostesses, didn't they? And men hired women, when need arose. She had hired Bonn, to investigate her husband. With, she angrily reminded herself, good reason.

But that hidden motive might be preventative.

She shuffled the clinical-pathology forms into one lot, handed them to Nurse Bushey, whose impatience clearly announced that such tardiness never happened in old Dr Rochford's day. Clare made herself be maddeningly casual, then hurtled from the hospital without using a changing room to see that she was decently turned out. Still, she was presentable. And she only intended to talk to the man, for goodness' sake, not ravish him the moment he stepped through the door.

That thought disturbed her as she drove from the car park. The instant *he* stepped through the door – wasn't that the wrong way round? *She* was going to make an entrance into *his* domain.

The traffic was flooding up from the south, of course, just when she was in a hurry. The M6, the car radio said, had lane closures today, single-lane stretches throttling the flow. She drummed her fingers on the wheel. Her motor seemed slower than usual.

Half her irritation was that she still smelled faintly of hospital, some disinfectant which clung to your clothes and hair. You could get rid of it by leaving your blouse on a warm radiator for an hour. Her spares were in her clothes case, which she carried for catastrophes. She never took that into surgeries, in case her fresh clothes took up the disagreeable scent.

The approach to Victoria Square from the north was choked, hopeless, and thank you, God. She should have gone past the cathedral, but it was too late once you'd locked into the flow. She could have used the mobile phone, but Bonn had cautioned her. Home enthusiasts logged in and tapped messages, for psycho reasons.

Twenty minutes late, after all her rush.

It was as well, because it gave her less time for nerves. Bonn was unperturbed. He took her coat.

'I would have waited,' he said. 'Would you like a drink?'

You would have waited because you had to, she thought, oddly irritable. The aroma of coffee was about. Be perverse. 'Tea, please.'

'It's ready.'

He moved away, immediately reappeared with a tray. She felt annoyed. He must have made both. Then she warned herself. She was here in a new way.

'You have a new jacket,' she surprised herself by saying.

He sat across from her by the window. A suite, not merely one bedroom. Was this a clue to some change in her status? His jacket hung on an upright chair by a bureau, flowers in the vase. She liked that, but why was it reassuring? And his every gesture could be part of a plan. She hated the idea.

She didn't know what she was doing here. He poured the tea with routine questions about sugar, milk in first or last. Normality was needed.

'Have you been busy?' she asked, then could have kicked herself.

He paused to think, awkward as any man with crockery. *Checking what he's allowed to tell me?* she wondered. A 'client', as she now was, might be a risk.

He was unabashed, conversational. 'Yes. I have this difficulty. A stander.'

'Stander?' It sounded like furniture.

'Guardian, of the client and the goer. One who minds you, me.'

'Stander.' She savoured the word. 'A guardian . . .' Another mistake, in view of his background, from her visit to the priest's flat.

'Angel?' He smiled. 'Not quite. Standers are really rather vicious.'

A thought struck her. She asked uneasily, 'Do standers see the client?'

'Not normally. I mean, mine won't have seen your arrival.'

'But he's nearby?'

'Within call.' Bonn frowned, guiding the teacup to her. She thought, It's saucers that worry men. Why? 'Please don't be put off. He is totally committed to protecting our meeting. Nobody can intrude, invade, follow.'

'Yet you're having trouble?'

'With an applicant.' Bonn was full of apology. 'I have to reject so many.'

'You make it sound so normal.' Clare reproved herself. She wasn't doing very well, implying that he and his were utterly bizarre.

'It's our life. We have to keep it apart.'

So don't ask, is what he meant. 'You rejected him?'

'Sadly.' Bonn had Glazie in mind. 'He isn't alley-wise. Avenue-wise, yes.'

Clare couldn't help judging. Here was this ex-seminarian, with an august reputation, in a scandalous trade. She'd seen how spectators at the mogga dancing looked at him, as if he were somehow honourable. It was unnerving, the wrong way round.

His gear was less than trendy. She'd noticed this before, but not in the same detail. He wouldn't stand out in a crowd, yet once you were with him his reticence dwindled until you became struck by a sense of immediacy. Aura, was it? Impact, in Hollywoodspeak? No dangling medallions, no platinum wrist bands or startling watches, his chest hair not fungating with fashionable manliness. No buckles to be seen, no glints of power.

'Do you go to one place for your clothes?'

Or does somebody pick them for you? But did not ask. So far she'd identified at least two different voices over the phone. Those females, perhaps? Did he go to some fashion house with arty girls arguing how far to go when cladding him for a stint? From seminarian to goer. She had a mad image, him taking the Offertory collection from clients. 'Client' was offensive. She refused to think of herself like that.

'I have no dress sense.' He guessed her thoughts, off-hand.

'Do you have, well, a code of dress?'

That stopped him in mid-reach. Instead he sat beside her.

'Not that I know.'

'Haven't you asked? I mean, you've not been a . . . doing this for long.'

'I'll see if I can find out.' Closing that conversation. 'The dancer won.'

'Dancer? Your friend?' That strange dancing, from style to style to a constant melody.

Bonn was at ease. He slid to the carpet with that awkwardness of the male, several quick successive changes. 'The bribe worked. He sacked his girl, though.'

'Is he also a . . .?'

'I make terrible coffee.' It was a reminiscence. 'I tasted some Camp coffee, as a little lad. I was quite ill. I'm on tenterhooks, in case you ask for it.'

She was almost amused, but held herself in check. A gambit, was it? She decided to risk it. 'How much of you is tactics, Bonn?'

'The same as everybody else, I suppose.'

Clare digested that. 'You never ask questions, Bonn.' He

raised his head to look up at her. She went on. 'Not even about Clifford Burtonall. He's my husband.'

He didn't even nod. 'There's no reason I should. Questions are pretend.'

'They can't be, or why ask?' He said nothing. 'Pretend for whom?'

'For what.' He seemed not to want to meet her eyes. 'I don't think much of motives. Motives are pointless. All those murder mysteries, pretending that a motive provides the solution and justice follows. Motives are the pretence in questions.'

'For the women you meet? Is that what you mean?'

'For the game.'

That shocked her. She sipped his atrocious tea. 'Game' sounded hateful, not even 'trade'. She wanted to go, have no more of this charade. He'd served her purpose, found out horrid facts about her criminal husband.

'Game? The women you meet are a game?'

She'd astonished him. 'Certainly not. To me it's special.'

There was a limit to what she could ask. 'Whose game, Bonn?'

'Theirs, of course.' He rolled over and lay there, a hand propping up his chin. 'Women play question games. It's their compulsion. What if, what happens when, how do you, endless. It's almost an ailment. I don't mind.' He spoke flatly, obliged to endure. 'It's what they do.'

'It's interest,' Clare said, defensive. If he felt so strongly about it, he ought at least to be upset. His clients deserved it. 'Women are interested in such things.'

'Interest is wrong. I wish it was only that.'

Clare argued, 'Women are interested in your life, how you see them. It *is* fascinating. You must see that, especially after your earlier . . .' Career?

He answered to cover her gaffe, 'No. The question game is one gigantic risk. Their questions, but my risk. And the questions merge into one.'

'And what is women's one question?'

'Are the other women better, lovelier, sexier. They don't ask it outright, just proxy, skate round the rim hoping you'll shout the answer from the middle of the cracking ice, save them having to skate out where the ice is perilous.'

'That's offensive! It's chauvinist!'

'No. It is merely sad, and innocent.'

It was also absurd. She was so tired of his bloody calm. He should have bawled. '*You're* calling *me* chauvinist?' because after all she'd hired him. This visit was a disaster. She should never have come. What on earth was she thinking of, childishly wanting to get back at Clifford? She was ashamed for having used Bonn.

She asked in expiation, 'How long will you keep on with it?'

'The life.' He considered that. A fluke, but still a hit. He said eventually, 'I feel a constancy that is new. I never felt like this.' He gave her his apology look. 'Even finding out what you asked was quite proper.'

'It feels the opposite, to me. Chagrin.'

'Don't.' He reached and took her hand, examined the nails, palmar creases. 'It might have been worse.'

His fingers felt warm, hers cold. She began to feel nervous. Clifford, the two girls, financial roguery, were so awful that she hadn't thought beyond the facts. 'Worse how?'

'Two deaths. He might have been involved somehow in both.'

She gazed down blankly. 'Both?'

'One girl's died.' He saw her stricken look. 'The other might give evidence. The police will want Salvo.'

'And Clifford?' She said bitterly, letting the cloak drop, 'My husband could have been more honest with me.'

'Let me.' He subjected her other hand to the same intense gaze.

'Are you a fortune-teller?' Her laugh was unconvincing.

'The police might not link Mostern and Lana – the girl who died – with Salvo. If he was the one who killed Lana and blinded Marla—'

'Blind?' She was instantly contrite. 'I sound like I'm hoping.'

'They don't know yet if Marla actually saw Lana killed. . . .' Bonn halted. He still held her hand.

'They'll arrest him for murder?' Clare decided not to withdraw. If it was some tactic, she thought tiredly, then so what? It was a comfort, and she'd missed comfort lately. 'Salvo might tell the police about Clifford.'

He touched her face with his fingertips. The gesture surprised her.

'No. He has to stick to his story.'

'Are you sure?'

'Can I look?' he asked. And slowly turned her face so he could see her in profile. He gazed so long that she felt her colour begin to heighten. 'Somebody in prison has to obey once they take the wadge.'

'Wadge?' Her cheeks were prickling, her mouth feeling paraesthesia. She didn't move away.

'The money a villain gets for work. That—'

'—that Clifford paid Salvo?'

'Yes. Break the code, Salvo would be lucky to survive a week.'

'What would happen?' Listen to me, she thought, aghast, discussing the next murder with a man I've hired.

'He'd be found hanged in his cell. The verdict would be suicide.'

Does Clifford know this? she wanted to know. And does he care, that the deaths might not be finished even now? Her rage returned.

'This is unusual for me,' she said quietly. She meant that she was usually the one who inspected, diagnosed.

'I know. Except you are bonny.' He spoke as if wondering how that came to be.

'I haven't been called that for a long time.'

He looked at her as if curious and pleased with what he saw. She almost expected him to begin the inept lover litany, how she'd previously met all the wrong men, Bonn earning his fee. Instead he let her go.

He was closer now. She realised she was staring at him in something like astonishment. His eyes were blue, she saw, filled with an emotion she could not quite identify. His finger touched her lips.

She felt her throat tighten. She wanted him not to go, to explain if these gestures were a ritual that he'd been trained to perform for, on, a client.

'I wonder if it's time,' he said, almost not to her.

For a moment his meaning was unclear. 'I was wondering,' she began, but his finger pressed gently on her mouth. Not cinnamon, she thought, not quite coriander. But, then, did she still stink of hospital?

'We have the chance, Clare.' He removed his hand before she could notice. 'Here,' he said gravely, 'you are unknown. Safe. The world will neither know nor care. It is a kind of beauty, to possess a new part of life.'

He isn't trying to persuade, she thought, not quite put out. She felt becalmed. Nobody would ever know.

'It is my purpose,' he said softly, absently, 'to offer you time unknown to anyone else. I shall never remember. The memory will only ever be yours.'

'It's just . . .' She halted. *What* was it 'just'?

He stood slowly, and raised her without effort.

'I'm not at all sure whether I meant to . . .'

'Meant to be unknown? Nobody knows you here. If you decide, I shall be secret and invisible too.'

He walked with her. They entered the bedroom. It was simply furnished, bright from a bedside lamp, the sheets turned down. Flowers, freesias this time, so few as to be almost symbolic.

Without a word he sat on the edge of the bed, drawing her round to stand close. Frowning with concentration, he started to undo her jacket, taking so long that she had to help him. He caught the garment as it slid off her shoulders. Then her blouse, not pulling it from her skirt but simply undoing the button nearest his hands.

His clear wonderment was not simulated, as the blouse came free. He lifted his shoulder for her hand to rest there while she stepped from the pool of her skirt, bright amazement on his face. As the last garment went she was smiling at his transparent delight. Still sitting, he conducted her in an arc. Three paces, and she sank to the bed's fresh cool sheets.

The feel of his body against hers was a novelty, his impatience startling. It was then that she knew herself to be his accomplice. She was astonished, then gratified, when the sensation was there exactly as she'd imagined. It was as if a deep excitement had been waiting to be released. He usurped her body with her treacherous consent. The moment he entered her she felt brilliant, defiant, triumphantly serving somebody right, giving them their own back – all the childish phrases.

Gratification swamped her as he still held her before the slow movements began. That was the most astonishing thing, her body chasing his faster movements. This was effortless. She'd earned this, she almost cried out, and she made a sulky defiant decision to leap the barrier of taboo. Bought joy was her joy, her act of buying proof that she owned and deserved it.

For a moment she let him wait, lifting to ease his steady rummage in her. This too was an amazement, that he accepted her gift, pleasing himself. It was important, she told herself, breathing harder, but for later, not now.

Bonn steadied a moment, already sweating. She heard herself groan with pleasure as her hands roamed on his chest, feeling the dampness. It was tentative at first, her hand on his flank, down the slight recess of his waist. She sniffed, the doctor in her smiling inwardly at the thought of pheromones at work. Then she inhaled greedily, glad of his scent, cupping him with a grunt of ecstasy. He lifted himself to look down questioningly, relaxed at her smile, and resumed work more purposefully. She didn't mind *work* now one bit.

Somehow she'd gone through a different barrier. With Clifford, it was slow finger play first, then a gradual coupling. Good, usually, but this was different because of Bonn's otherness, removed from the ordinary. She heard herself yelping as she dragged behind to prolong the delay between his ploughing and her reception, feeling a relish that became startlingly new as they worked. The barrier was in herself, had been there like a wall. With a growl of pleasure as her concentration began to weaken under his moves, she thought, I am now able to say, with a terrible crudity, I *want*.

Perverse, she groaned and gasped, 'Wait, wait!'

He stilled, matching her groan and came to rest with a slight shudder. Obeyed. She realised she was ruining her moment, yet gaining by testing her right. That was the newness. She had procured him for this, exchanging her woman's mere presence for authority over this shoving male. He was not currying favour, persuading, paying court. None of that. He was here, for her whim. Copulating on her demand, the terms hers. She could tell him to withdraw, come now fast, or take his time. She could be serviced like a motor, used, abused, treated, or mistreated.

It was freedom, she thought, gazing up at him with astonishment, a breaking of chains.

She kept him motionless, looking down at her, by a swift shake of her head on the pillow and a tightening of her clasp about his waist. Sweat was running on them. She was almost furious at herself for tormenting this way. He tensed in query as she moaned aloud, as she clung to the terrible, baffling thought of freedom. Love was something aside. This was coupling, hers. She beckoned him with a lift of her chin, and when he lowered bit his shoulder savagely, thrilled. This inner dawn absolved. This domination was her absolution. It would not be wrong. There were no more boundaries. She registered the amazing notion, strained not to let it go.

Drenched, she sank back, tasting her own salty sweat, feeling a vast relief as he began to stir her. She pushed a hand beneath him and tugged, her rogue fingers maddeningly urging him to speed.

A keening rose in her throat. For a moment she struggled

to contain it, then gave vent and rushed with him as they beat together and dissolved.

Clare dreamed. Her dream was nothing to do with the man dozing beside her, his chest expanding, deflating, his arm heavier by the minute, her leg still cast over him. She wondered whether to move it, a weight, but caught herself. No, because I close that particular door, Bonn, bear me. Only then can you go free – until next time, when I come and take possession of you again.

She was replete. This almost made her laugh, satiety an achievement.

She felt justified, as was her right. The princesses of old donned masks and simply announced to all and sundry that they were incognito. They could then go visit lovers, theatres, anywhere, while the world politely ignored them. A token mask put recognition out of the question. How civilised, how perfect!

But love? Love nudged her mind.

Anthropologists from New Orleans, or was it Nevada, proved 'romantic love' in over 88 per cent of the world's cultures they investigated. Dreamily, she recalled a furious argument among medical physiologists over this finding. Was love poetry a mere biological stimulus, then? On the other hand, divorces peak at the fourth marital year. Anthropologists had a field-day over this, claiming it coincided with the time when a primitive tribal three-year-old child could start foraging for itself, with luck, as it wandered with its parents, who were in search of other mates.

Love, though? She stroked his body. She had the right to.

Bravely she let her dream glide into doctoral mode. The excitement of love is not – she forced the thought –

something generated chemically in the brain by phenyl-ethylamine, with maybe a slow dribble of the neurochemicals norepinephrine and dopamine to buzz you to reach orgiastic thrills with their amphetaminelike whirr. That accounts, though purely chemically, for the elation and, well, the passion of love's coupling. Her sluggish, purring, satiated body joined the argument by thinking of the love act's sheer sexual rut. The lovingness, maybe? Maybe, not to put too fine a point on it, that was the fuck quantile?

Well, okay, her dreamy mind conceded. But chemistry left out the cosiness of love, something she had never truly met before, which was really odd. The comfort should be something discovered at home, with a husband, not newly come across in bed with a hireling. Neurochemically speaking, you could call it the thirty-month kick, because it's then that the body becomes tolerant of its glandular drugs squirted in under a particular male's stimulus. As if one male was no longer enough. Like drug tolerance? The dose of heroin that relieves the intractable pain of metastatic cancer, and the appalling cough of bronchogenic carcinoma, no longer has the same effect day after day. You have to increase the dose, then double it, then raise it to erstwhile lethal quantities to give the poor patient any relief at all. So could *person* tolerance exist? It was offensive, in a world where true love 'should be' for life.

Maybe neurochemicals, weakening smartish after marital monogamy sets in, knew better?

There is a gratification seeing pairs together, hand in hand or, she almost giggled, genitalia with genitalia. Her mind delved into its memory bag and slyly brought out a memory of an elderly couple who for forty years had experienced marital difficulties – the wife's ailments worsened by the husband's countless betrayals. When, seeing them together, she had asked in detail about their perseverance, the man had expressed astonishment: 'But we're married!' The woman too had been quite indignant. 'Good heavens! The very idea!' Clare remembered having a hard time mollifying them.

Was that love longevity, then? Or was it simply a preference for endorphins, those other chemicals – so like morphine derivatives – that warmed and cocooned your mind so it believed itself 'safe' near the loved one? Rubbish magazines talked about 'cuddle chemicals', like the pituitary gland's special oxytocin secretion, but slang nicknames only meant that doctors too wanted everything reduced to a glib catchphrase that pretends to be an explanation.

She found that she had rolled into Bonn's awakening embrace.

'Yes?' she asked.

'It's close to time, Clare.'

Stretching in annoyance, she grunted, collapsed, huddled closer.

'What a pest. Are you sure?'

His voice changed. She could tell that he smiled. 'Afraid so.'

A thought struck her. 'I asked for an extension. What if I wanted the rest of the evening?' Surely things had changed?

'I would like to.' Maybe it was more complicated now. 'I couldn't. I'm sorry.'

Was he really? More complex still.

'Could you as an option?' She could have phrased that better than a clinical interrogator. Treacherous endorphins to blame? She was tempted to ask, indignant, how other women got extensions.

'No, Clare. It's time.'

She was still swaddled down, he half reclining. She moved her head to lie on his belly, freeing her face for air. Her watch was still on her wrist, quite incongruous. And look at the time.

They dressed without speaking. She felt no compunction leaving the money. He held the door for her. She did not look back.

Her old Humber was no longer sanctuary, as it so often seemed. Now it was a nuisance. Bonn was back there. She thought of a hundred questions she might have cleverly introduced, penetrating his apologetic defence.

Frankly, she'd had time for a bath, and she could have changed. But her fresh clothes were untouched, and she'd kept his sweat on her. To *wear*. He'd sweated cobs, as locals said. She'd never known a man like him. Wet through, they'd been, the pair of them. The bed must be soaked, she thought with guilt. Once he'd got going, working with that mindlessness she'd puzzled at, rivulets ran from his body onto hers. Like a meniscus in a tube, she thought impiously, that hugged the capillary glass. She settled down for the run into the Wirral and home.

Grandma had called it the man-smell. It lurked in Grampa's own sideboard drawer – which, once daringly opened, contained only old medals, three surprisingly fine old silk scarves, lone gloves, a masonic charity badge, and faded football programmes that, astonishingly, showed Grampa triumphant – moustache, long baggy knicks, folded arms, slicked black hair. The scent was thick, alien, definite. A dark pungent tree-smell. Not 'smell' either. Aroma, more like.

She'd wanted Bonn's aroma. The pity was that it faded. Did pheromones leave so soon? It might be worth looking up, some ill-remembered biochemisty.

'Perfume?' she corrected aloud. 'A smell is a smell is aroma.'

An overtaking driver looked askance, intrigued, seeing her talking away. Clare was embarrassed, pretended to be singing along with the mute radio. What the hell, she thought, 30 per cent of shoppers talked to themselves, said social surveys. Much they knew.

She had pulled something off today, a remarkable achievement. She would have time for a bath, that unwonted riddance, before Clifford came home.

Her behaviour was truly innocent. What she'd done was no more than a pastime. Other women must be doing it by the million, like having your hair done, changing an uncomfortable bra. That was it. She mustn't think of Bonn as world-shattering.

And what, she told herself, a tart anger starting as she pulled onto the Wirral motorway, if that was a lie? It was her lie, nobody else's. Everyone harboured lies. Now she too had one all her own.

She could cope, Clifford, police, and all.

Next day there was a rumble at the Ball Boys. Rack had to drag out two of Grellie's girls. They'd started it, Rack told Bonn.

'It's the disco's air, see?' Rack waxed as they walked among the street crowds, police sirens all wahwahing. 'You breathe in what other people've breathed out, you start shoving people—'

Bonn had had enough. 'Please find Doob.'

'Doob? At the Triple Racer.' Rack added disgustedly, as they angled through the traffic near where Mostern had been downed, 'Our two tarts squabbled over Drummer. He pays for a shag in scag.'

At the Triple Racer, Bonn stood under the awning listening to the couriers' tales of wheelies, donkers, and slidders, incomprehensible talk of how they did a needle and saved forty-eight seconds on a run to the Corn Exchange.

'Doob.' Bonn kept his voice civil. The new goer was pleased to be seen talking with his key. 'Please say how much you drink now.'

'Soda water, Bonn. No spirits, no beer, no wine. Honest.'

'When did you last do a dip?'

The traffic roared and chugged, a car horn parping. Traffic lights had failed on the station slope. A policeman was on point duty.

'You saw me, I think. I've done nowt since.' Bonn waited. 'Honest.'

'Very well, Doob, I want you to dip something from a lady's handbag.'

The pickpocket looked from Bonn to Rack. 'You *want* me to do a tarpaulin? You threatened—'

'I do not threaten, Doob. It will be cleared with Martina.'

'No comeback?' Doob pursed his lips. 'Say when, Bonn.'

They parted, Bonn and Rack heading for the snooker hall. Grellie waved and crossed to meet them in the bus-park gardens.

'Those two girls, Rack. Do they use scag themselves?'

'That's the trouble, Bonn. Grellie decides that, and Martina.'

'Rack, please,' Bonn asked. It had been worrying him. 'What is a needle?'

Rack was proud. 'Needle's when you drive up a one-way street the wrong direction, see? Saves you hours. Bikers like doing it. They run a book, who does most needles in a week. Know why? Petrol's like blood, see. . . .'

'There's some connection, sir.' Windsor wouldn't give up. He alone of the police loved the coffee, drank it black, some said a dozen plastic cups a day.

'Any word?'

'Somebody local gave him the mother.'

Hassall sighed, shook his head. 'I'm always tired these days. I like short cuts – when I don't land up to my knees in muck. Who warned Salvo off?'

'I don't know yet, but I'm convinced.'

Hassall had a coughing fit, eventually came to wiping his rheumy eyes.

'My age, you never get shut of flu. Lingers. Doctors, bloody useless.' He lolled at his desk. 'Salvo? How come it's all Salvo?'

'He's the tart's bloke. Lived at the flat.' Windsor ticked points off, the way Hassall hated. 'Seen nearby. Aggro over Marla. The camera when Mostern—'

'Don't count,' Hassall said heavily. 'I tried that inhaler stuff from Boots. You shove it up a nostril, squirt. I sneezed my bloody head off for two days. Cost a fortune. The camera was put out.'

'The other one showed Salvo descending the railway—'

'You're not in court,' Hassall interrupted rudely. 'Sorry. Think what some clever-dick barrister'd make of *that*. "So, Mr Windsor, you pick out a random subject from several hundreds, and make unfounded accusations. . . ." Salvo – what's his real name anyway? – must help us with enquiries. Find him.'

'Sir.'

Windsor left the office. Hassall gazed after him. Soon, Windsor would be in the canteen mouthing off about pedantic old bastards who should get the fuck out of it. Play crown-green bowls. Hassall was the wrong side of forty. He hated age. Age was what younger officers forced you to. It wasn't fair.

Grellie, Bonn, Rack stood before Martina's bare desk.

'Lana is dead. It means problems for us.'

'We're not to blame,' Grellie said quickly.

'Nobody says you are, Grellie.'

Martina was cool, still in there thinking possibilities.

Grellie rushed on, worried, 'I mean, Martina, we're not responsible for bits on the side. Marla liked Lana. So what? It happens both sides of the fan.'

'You're jumping to conclusions.' Martina hadn't yet asked Rack for new details, which Bonn thought odd. Some warning in there. 'The police are already busy-busy. It's rotten luck for Marla, Lana. Some punter battered them. Stick to the tale when the plod come. We have no idea. Understand?'

'Yes, Martina.'

'We're never mentioned,' Martina ground quietly on. 'You all go, "What syndicate? What's it mean?" over and over.'

'The girls're up in arms, Martina.'

'Keep them quiet, Grellie. They can murmur only among themselves.'

'Can we visit Marla?'

Martina thought for a moment. 'Yes. But go through the motions.'

'Right.' Grellie asked, uncomfortable, 'I want cover. A feller.'

'She means Bonn,' Rack crashed in cheerfully. 'She doesn't want the Bill reckoning her one of Lana's lez pals. Don't blame you, Grell.'

Grellie coloured, stung. 'I'll be a friend calling at Marla's.'

'No.' Martina thought a moment. 'Too chancy. Let the plod find their own clues. Posser's going to Cardiac Out-Patients. *Don't* go with Bonn.'

Grellie didn't dare make the challenge directly, but it had to be said. 'The girls'll be upset nobody from my side's visited Marla.'

'All right.' Martina made a show of being talked round. 'You go too.'

'See?' Rack brightened, Grellie and Bonn paired off at last, some good coming out of this shambles. 'It's like I told you, Martina—'

Both women interrupted him together, Grellie quickly giving way.

'Go separately, Grellie, not as a couple. Take up a collection for Marla. I'll quadruple the sum raised.'

Martina asked Bonn to stay back as the other two left.

'It's all one, Bonn,' she said after a while. She told him Rack's story. 'The man – Burtonall, is it? – called not long after Salvo left Marla and Lana. I want to know all you've learned. Is it this Clare Three-Nine-Five?'

'Yes. She's a doctor, married to Burtonall. He's grafting some inner-city development.' He hesitated. 'I can't see why it's gone through the roof.'

'This Goldoni. You asked me for a studio flat near the theatre.'

'Rack's relative? I remember.'

'He's a money man. Friend of Burtonall. They're funding our takeover.' She judged the effect her words had on Bonn.

Bonn looked at the wall behind Martina's head, returned. 'I didn't know.'

Martina seemed satisfied by his reaction. 'I don't know where Goldoni gets his information. Does this Clare know anything more?'

'No. I blew her mind.' Bonn's slang tasted awkward.

'Goldoni's able to fund our takeover with, by, Burtonall. Who is simply doing both – peeling the city councillors, and partnering Goldoni's wedge.'

'Martina,' Bonn started up, not wanting to ask outright.

'Goldoni uses renters from the Ball Boys,' she said impatiently. 'That's all.'

Bonn blinked. She watched him for signs of perfidy. He sighed, went over what he had learned from Jefferson, Tuesday, Glazie.

'Nicolette,' he remembered. 'I reported doubts about her.'

'She's Goldoni's. She susses out businesses.'

Anyone else would have instantly jumped in, professed honesty, that they'd disclosed nothing. Not Bonn. He simply waited, his honesty beyond question.

Bonn mentioned all his other sources, Askey the diminutive messenger, the Triple Racer lads, Rack, Grellie. She listened attentively, pushing her hair away from her face.

'This Clare Three-Nine-Five. What hinges on her?'

'Nothing that I can see.' He dwelt on the problem. 'She pays cash. I think she'll be back. Her husband, after all.'

'She's punishing him by hiring you?' Martina really wanted to know.

'I surmise so.'

'Then surmise what further steps we take about La Burtonall.' Immediately Martina wished she'd avoided sarcasm. 'Do we follow her? If so, why? Do we sanction this husband? If so, why?'

'Sanction how?'

She wanted to pace, show body language to make herself more assertive. Lameness was the ultimate insult to a woman. 'There's only one sanction here, Bonn.' She barked a harsh laugh. 'He could be simply removed.'

'Remove?' He could accept evils done, but not evils planned.

She said with vulgar bluntness, 'It would pacify the girls. They see themselves in the mortuary, or blinded like Marla. Can you blame them?'

Bonn gathered arguments. 'Do nothing, Martina. Let the police sort it out. Salvo is the link – we know that, they can't prove it. Burtonall too – we know that, but the police can't prove that either.'

'Where is Salvo?'

'No idea.' He considered. 'He'll have to keep going. Somebody will have to be . . . reproved.'

Martina was relieved he'd spoken out. It showed his allegiance, which she'd never doubted anyway. 'Grellie's girls would mutiny otherwise. It'd take them a year, then our whole thing'd go to pieces.' They gave each other the chance to speak, then Martina asked, 'Clare Three-Nine-Five will book you again?'

'She said so. She behaved so.' Fair to Martina, he told her that he'd mentioned the Café Phrynne, that they might meet at the mogga dancing. 'Somewhere open.'

'So.' Martina felt cold. If there was something between Bonn and this Clare, she of the don't-suffer-fools voice, then Clare could pick her own way through the minefield without the syndicate's help. 'She does pay?'

'Of course. A client, after all.' He knew what she was asking.

'See Marla without Grellie. Invent some story, you used to go out with her once, like that. Suss out what you can.'

'Very well.'

'And, Bonn?' He raised his eyebrows in query. 'Come to Posser's this evening, maybe eightish.'

Even that command couldn't faze him. 'Thank you. I shall be there.'

She passed word to Osmund that she would leave immediately.

*

Thinking what had happened, Clare relived without shame her new vehemence. The feeling of complicity did it. She'd been assertive, shoving Bonn with her heels, moving him round for herself without considering him in the slightest.

She thought of her abandon. His movements had been softer than she'd wanted, so she had drawn him close, harder, for a more rasping sensation, to achieve on her own terms. As their bodies beat to her pace, his mouth at first evaded hers, why she didn't know, but she remembered grabbing his face with her fingers brutally curved into his cheeks, talons almost, and forced her mouth to his. She even cried out coarse instructions, flailing so he had to strain to keep hold.

The noise, moans, her crudities might have been angelic voices for all she cared.

And afterwards, she'd been as replete as she had ever been, feeling astonishingly light-headed and stunningly refreshed. She had taken possession, for the first time had ruled.

That day, renewed, she drove to the hospital and found the cardiologists. She told Dr Porritt that she would accept his survey, and begin almost immediately. She visited the small surveillance unit and checked again that Clifford's results were through. The laboratory reports were on the printout, timed and dated as she'd written.

Nothing could go wrong. She left, went round to Clifford's office, and gave him the news. They made routine politenesses. Clifford took her to a small café.

'It's plain sailing,' Clare told him quietly.

'My results okay, were they?'

'Fine.' She tried a laugh, unconvincing. 'I ought to charge you.'

'Thank goodness, darling.'

The endearment did nothing to put the clock back. 'What now?' she asked. Last night they had slept together, but turned away.

'That Windsor came.' He pulled a face. 'I proved I was with you. He implied that he'd check up.'

'And?'

The café was unbearably noisy. Actors were in, one demonstrating how he'd faced down some director, to approving roars from friends.

'That's it. The news said some bloke is being sought, to help with enquiries.'

'What will you do?'

Clifford asked, 'What will *I* do? Not us any longer?'

She was ice of a sudden. 'You did everything without telling me. Why consult me now?' Yesterday she would have been all worried sick. Now she saw the gulf between them.

'I'll have to think, darling. It depends if they catch him.'

'How direct is your connection with Salvo?'

'There's no evidence. He can say what he likes. I'll deny it. It's that simple.'

'Clifford.' She almost relented. He was putting such a brave face on it. 'If you decide to, well, do anything else, you will tell me, won't you?'

'Promise, darling.' He put his hand on hers, and looked into her eyes. 'This has made us more married than ever.'

30

Homer – the hiring of a goer for coitus or other sexual purposes by a woman in her own home.

DRIZZLE CAME ON, nothing like the north's usual heavy stuff. Salvo hated it. A bloke couldn't wear the right clothes in this. Darkness turned into a shambolic slutchy seep. He told the tart this. She said it would clear. She wasn't much good, did sex like having a kip, groused that he'd left a ring round the bath. So?

'The next water'll wash it off. It's what water's for, for fuck's sake.'

Even that pissed her off.

'Don't swear,' she said, like she was some saint, selling her arse in Vaughan Street. 'It'll stop when the tide turns. Rain always does.'

Fucking tides, Salvo thought. The fucking sea meant Liverpool.

Not knowing what to do maddened you as much as anything. He'd gone to Oz's, but the taxi was gone. He'd asked at Oz's local, but he'd not been in. Oz's terraced house was locked, no life. Twice he'd been back, until some old hag next door started watching from her steps. He'd picked up this ammy tart to get a place to rest until he could find Oz, decide.

Her room was over a barber's in Moorgate Street, where

the buses started back to the square. Grellie's stringers hated ammies, casual tarts who'd shag for a drink, charge what they thought they could get away with. Her name was Robina.

Grellie's stringers were pros and proud of it, working girls. Salvo'd often heard them blamming any ammy who peddled their patches, fought them tooth and nail on the pavements, kicking and squealing. Twice he'd asked to be a ponce, used to keep Grellie's streets ammy-clean, but that bastard Rack had his own mob. Closed shop, was unfair to blokes with ambition.

Robina was bottle-pale, twitchy, a user. He'd found her on the working men's club car park, two good comedians on that night so dense crowds, raucous noise when he'd passed. No car was the swine, because wheels were everything. He'd gone to suss the motors, but there was a hawkeyed bouncer on lurk who just belly-laughed in the semi-dark when Salvo tried a car handle. It was enough warning, the lurk sure of himself even with groups of noisy drinkers six, eight, a dozen strong arriving. So no fucking wheels. Salvo knew better than try nicking one from the streets this hour of the night. The street thieves were all on frannies, the bought-and-paid-for right to steal parked motors.

Salvo had even tried to get in on that four months back, got told to piss off. A little black Salford nerk, thin as a whippet and a cough like a Mersey horn, got took on with hardly a blink. It wasn't fair, when Salvo could do anything he turned his mind to. He watched Robina.

The slut was humming, doing her face in a mirror you could hardly see through. One bulb lit the room, a flex trailing in under the door, typical whore's trick of bleeding electric from the landing. Salvo hated flies. One thing about Marla, she kept flies out of the flat, spent more on fucking sprays than on rent. He'd remember the pong of her sprays for ever – red containers, three to a window sill.

He didn't want to be with this Robina cunt. He'd only shagged to get his feet under her table. She said they'd go out, get a pizza, a drink before the pubs closed, like he was some fucking football hooligan.

'Got a phone?' He stared at the ceiling.

'You'll be lucky.' She didn't even look, just anybody on her bed.

'Got telly?'

'I use my mate's.' She did that thing they did, folding their lips in before seeing what she looked like after all that expensive beauty care.

'Where is it?' He wanted news.

'Upstairs, but she does club turns till gone midnight.'

'Turns?'

'A singer. We go halves.' Now she looked. 'It's got to pay well, or it's not worth it.'

'Can you get into her place?'

'No. We don't lend keys. You might get a psycho.'

He almost laughed at her. He'd done Mostern, thought that didn't count because Oz'd helped. He'd done Lana on his own, so she counted.

He'd a few quid left. He'd best leave the city, softer down south.

'I'll go for a pizza.' He got up.

That stopped her checking how gorgeous she was, drawing on her eyebrows. Marla did that.

'What's your game?'

'I'll bring one in.' He got his jacket. 'Not be a sec.'

She stood with quick anger. 'I'm coming—'

He clouted her down. The mirror fell forward, cracked

on the floor, a piece cutting her leg. He'd had enough, everybody giving him lip.

Her handbag was hanging on the door. He got her few measly notes.

'Where's your fucking money?' he bawled at her. The dizzy cunt hadn't the sense to answer. The insolence of ignorance. He kicked her. Enough to piss anybody off, the run of bad luck he was having.

He started ransacking the room, pulled drawers out, yanking the pictures off the wall, yelling, 'Where? Fucking *where*?,' throwing her chair at the stupid bint.

Somebody shouted, too far off to worry about, maybe upstairs. He hauled the rug up, then had a brilliant idea and looked in the microwave. A fold of notes. He crowed, waved them in the silly fucker's face, yelling.

'Think you were clever?'

She'd been trying to crawl to the door. He booted her back, rage taking over so he couldn't speak, just had to do things, make her realise you didn't use people. Get away with anything because you're a tart's all right most times, but you can do it once too fucking often.

He kicked the paraffin stove over, emptied the spare tin, half full, over her fucking useless bed, and got her cigarette lighter from her handbag. A gas lighter, thank Christ, first bit of luck. Fires burned off dabs, he'd heard, never a fingerprint that survived burning.

Its flame he clicked tall, said to her from the doorway, 'Robina, one fucking word, I'll be back.'

She said nothing, lying there still, so she'd learned some fucking sense. Salvo almost laughed out loud. The silly cunt would soon move fast enough.

He opened the door, stepped onto the dingy landing

with its trailing flex, chucked the lighter into the room, and ran.

Martina herself opened the door to Bonn. For a moment neither of them spoke, then Martina moved aside and held the door.

'Thank you for being so prompt, Bonn.'

'And you for your kind invitation.'

He went inside, stood awkwardly in the hallway not knowing quite what to expect. The scent of cooking. He hadn't known whether to have something to eat coming through the square, or whether to trust to luck. If she offered a drink and he refused, it might give offence. Drink gave him a blinding headache on an empty stomach. If she didn't, he would have to last out manfully and get some fish and chips on the way home. But even there he'd have to be careful, because Martina knew everything before dawn. She would know that he'd left her home famished. Which, he agonised, preceding her down the hall when she gestured him to go ahead, might make her think that he'd been presumptuous in assuming that he'd been invited to dinner. Had his acknowledgement of her welcome itself been an arrogance, that word 'invitation'?

The table was set for three. He tried not to notice, and went to greet Posser.

The old man was sitting upright on a straight-backed wooden chair. He waved Bonn to an armchair opposite. His exhalations were prolonged squeaks, an old leather bag at a fire that would no longer draw.

'Sorry for the racket, Bonn,' Posser breathed. 'Put up with me, eh?'

'Glad to, Posser.'

'Would you care for a drink, Bonn?' Martina limped to a drinks cabinet. 'We have sherry, wine, something short if you'd rather.'

'I,' Posser puffed. They paused. Bonn had learned from a priest who'd stuttered the art of waiting for faulty speakers. The trick was not to feel anguish, or you ruined their attempt. Sit there not worrying, just waiting – above all, no help – and they made it. Especially don't interrupt. Their struggle had a right to a silence.

'Had a liking for whisky, once,' Posser completed in a rush. 'Until my daughter here forced me to drink red wine for my health.' It took a minute or so to say.

'Red wine is better for you, Posser.'

'Don't you start, Bonn. I get enough from Martina.'

'Thank you,' Bonn told Martina. 'Have you lemonade, please?'

'There'll be wine with supper.'

Bonn saw Martina had guessed his anxiety, and felt his face redden. Now he didn't know whether to pretend astonishment that he was to stay for a meal, or to protest he'd decided against having any alcohol.

'If I had the wind.' Posser made them wait, then managed, 'I'd ask what the hell's going on. Youth, against us wrinklies?'

'It's salmon,' Martina said, amiably cuffing her father. 'Red wine, no spirits. I've told you.'

'Listen to her.' Posser sat forward, his eyes closing as his daughter went to make a din in the kitchen. 'You don't know the pleasure, Bonn.'

'What pleasure exactly?'

'Of sitting like this.' Posser now leant with his elbows on his knees, shoulders slumped, head a little projected. He could only maintain the posture for a short while, after which he had to sit up once more. 'I used to see the old men sit like that on our steps, after they'd got home from the mills. I used to envy them.'

'When you were little, you lived round here?' Bonn knew the answer.

'Aye. I love it. A vestige, though, of a once-great city.'

'A return can cause pain.'

'Don't tell me,' Posser managed to say eventually, starting to sweat. Bonn had the idea that Posser had just got up. The evening would be hard going for the old man. 'Everything changes.'

'I wouldn't say that, Posser.'

'It changed for you, Bonn.' Posser grinned, false teeth brilliantly white. 'I can see you now, that woman in the hotel lounge, baffled as a kid at a console. And her thinking, how sweet, a novice! Truer than she knew, eh, lad?'

Bonn was embarrassed at the memory. 'I was non-plussed.'

Posser beckoned Bonn. He glanced towards the kitchen door. 'I told Martina to give us a minute.' She couldn't have failed to hear his loud rasping voice. Bonn wondered how much of all this was put on. 'Different from a seminary, eh? Sussed you from the start.'

'I know,' Bonn said candidly.

'Eh?'

'Two days after we met, I went to say goodbye to my fellow tutee. He was leaving for the English College in Rome. He told me somebody had made enquiries. Answered your description.'

'Good, good.' Posser must have told Martina this, so why the charade? 'About Salvo. What do you reckon, we have him topped?'

Bonn looked into the fire. The seminary had had only

electric bars, draughts, and a simulated gas-log in the rector's study. Posser beckoned Martina, who was closing the kitchen door behind her.

'I've told Dad what we discussed, Bonn, Grellie et al.' She served the drinks. Posser pulled a face. Martina grimaced comically back, their game.

'The reasons,' Bonn said. He realised with alarm that he wasn't at all appalled. He wondered if he'd passed the point where morality called a halt, his near-crime existence an imprimatur on immorality. Or was his life simply totally new, and he'd cast off old yokes?

'Salvo's a hand grenade rolling about the city, Bonn. Anybody can pull his pin and, kaboom, we'll all go up.'

'Is Salvo anything to do with us?' Bonn phrased it carefully.

'No. You turned him down. A pub conversation.' Posser did his best to shrug, propping his thorax stiffly on his arms, the trick of chesty old cotton workers. 'But this Burtonall lady, our client, you asking around.' Posser closed his eyes, raised a forbidding hand as if Bonn had striven to interrupt. 'Fair. We allowed it. You reported in, all aboveboard.'

'Dad?' Martina gave him a glass of water. Posser obediently sipped.

'But your questions – Glazie, Jefferson, Tuesday, Askey, Uncle Tom Cobbley – are untraceable, even if the plod tried hard.'

'And the Burtonalls,' Martina added, sitting near her father.

'The subject of my questions was Mostern's accidental death.' Bonn felt forced into having to make a case for their having given agreement.

'That hasn't gone away,' Posser reminded him. 'The plod

were asking round the Triple Racer, the Shot Pot, the casinos. And the Ball Boys.'

'They know we own those, in one guise or another, Bonn,' Martina said.

'Why Salvo, though?'

'Because he *leads* to us. He mayn't implicate us in Mostern, in Lana or Marla, but he's common ground.'

Bonn tasted his drink. 'Is there something else, Posser?'

'What else exactly?' Martina demanded.

Posser gave her a rueful glance, as if he'd been outwitted, drew a bubbly breath, and answered.

'The Italian chap. He gets info about us from Salvo, and possibly from Rack. He susses us out by dipsticks – Nicolette – plus tourist blokes he ships in for Grellie's lasses. He must have quite a dossier. About buildings that I got freehold or leased for a song when you couldn't give inner-city streets away. And about franchises I quartered and sold on, renovations at government or council expense. He must know almost everything about us. We're only a dozen limited companies, after all.'

'So he's the one?'

Posser said heavily, 'He knows there's only me and Martina, and such street loyalty as we've got.'

Resistance was out of the question, Bonn could see. It was either sell out or lose out.

'Clare Burtonall makes it all one and the same.'

'Two minutes.' Martina limped to the kitchen, calling over her shoulder, 'I'm listening.'

'Goldoni's money's to buy us out. How does he know we're here, that we're unprotected? By sussing, by informers – Salvo's one, Rack's possibly an innocent other.' Posser beckoned Bonn for help to stand, puffed his way to the table. 'And why is Goldoni here in the first place? To back Clifford Burtonall, who owns city aldermen in time-honoured fashion.'

'He must be astute.'

'Businessmen are.' Posser lowered himself into a chair, leant on the table with relief, and gestured Bonn to take a place. 'Opportunity here, he wants a hack.'

'Totally.' Martina brought in the first course, mushrooms, tomatoes, black olives, pine nuts, and hot bread rolls.

They watched Martina serve. She spun it out, her woman's trick.

'Posser,' Bonn asked finally. 'I assume there's nothing other than what I know.'

'You're right, son. Nothing.'

'Then the question becomes, where can Salvo go.' Bonn spoke with certainty. 'He'll need help, money, a car.'

'Go? To Burtonall.' Martina looked about the table, checking. 'Please start.'

'Thank you.' Bonn passed the hot rolls. 'He'll have to go tonight.'

'That's what I thought,' Posser said. 'Martina, love. Who's handy?'

'Akker, two or three others.'

'God, this is hot,' Posser complained. 'It's microwaves. Before they came in, we have everything decently cold as a frog.'

'Manners, Dad.'

'Sorry, sorry.'

They had red wine; suprême of salmon, which Bonn had never had before; and a summer pudding that he hated because it was basically bread and butter. It had been Brother Anthony's gruesome special at the seminary. He told Martina it was the best meal he had ever had. She wanted to ask about his origins. He'd never had salmon cooked like that, never had that starter. He dared himself to ask what the vegetables were but his nerve failed.

After, they sat before the fireplace talking. Bonn said little. Posser said nothing would be done until the morning, by which time they would have reports in about Salvo, when they would decide. Meanwhile, the girls were up in arms over Lana and Marla, wanting action on Salvo, all saying he'd done it. Grellie had her hands full stopping them from making anonymous calls to the police.

When Martina went to make coffee, Posser knelt to poke the fire. Bonn knelt beside him, hefting the coal scuttle near, using the fire tiger. Posser checked the distance to the kitchen, the faint clash of crockery.

'Bonn. I want to know what you feel about Martina.'

'I admire her.'

'Don't flannel me, son.' Posser smiled, determined. 'As you see, I'm a picture of health.' He sighed, rested on his heels. 'This thing's brought it to a head, rather. Made me think of time running out.'

'What then, Posser?'

'I knew it might come to this.' Posser sounded so sad. 'The best daughter a man could wish for. But look now. All the money in the world, nobody to trust. Her injury, scampering about after street carts when she was little, was my fault.'

'Come to this,' Bonn repeated.

'This.' Posser looked round, indicating his place. 'Martina. The others are good lads – as long as I'm here. After that, I'm not so sure.'

'I'll do what I can, Posser.'

'Move in here, son.' Posser's eyes held Bonn. 'I need an answer.'

'Into your home?'

'It's not sacrosanct, Bonn. It's a house. The dosshouse you live in's a right fleapit. Bare as a prison cell. Others'd have their own place out on the Wirral, moorland grandeur, if there's still any about.'

'Move away?' Bonn was shocked. 'I need a city, Posser.'

'Like me!' Posser was pleased. 'Will you move in?'

'Martina might say . . .'

'I'd ask her, if you'll come. Then I'd say you'd asked.'

'That would seem as if I . . .'

'Wanted to be near Martina? Aye, son. That's my idea.'

'I would be afraid that she would want me to leave.'

'I'm too old for strategies, Bonn, like getting you two paired off. Unless you've taken against her for some reason.'

'No. I told you, Posser. I like her.'

'Then why haven't you asked before? Supper here or there.' Posser was aggrieved. 'Why not?'

Bonn stared at the flames, rising gracefully. He knew a trick to make it draw, but that was wasteful where he came from.

'I'm scared of Martina,' he said at last. 'I didn't know. Now I'm sure.'

Posser stared towards the kitchen door. Martina reappeared with a tray of coffee. Bonn helped Posser back to his upright chair. They talked of holidays, Bonn especially interested in how you went about arranging one, what you asked the travel agencies, when you paid, their reliability. Posser already knew Bonn had never had a holiday.

Bonn was shown out at eleven o'clock. He bussed Martina, Lancashire fashion, as he left. She returned to sit facing her father.

'What did he say, Dad?' she asked.

'First get Askey on the blower, love. Tell him to come here.'

'You're sending for Akker?'

'Maybe,' Posser said. 'Time something got done.'

31

Dip-and-scratch – to pickpocket for effect alone, without profit.

THE PROBLEM WAS non-existent. Clare felt calm about everything. She returned fairly late, and heard his car on the gravel drive.

Clifford was safe. His blood samples were recorded for all time, the ECG, weight, body-mass indices, her notes all showed that Clifford was a subject in the cardiology health survey of males twenty-five to fifty. His first examination had taken place exactly when those girls were attacked.

She had had an interesting and amusing time working out survey protocols with three cardiology registrars. They had given her a surveillance nurse who'd just finished her S.R.N. and was eager to start. Things couldn't be better. Some plainclothesman – not Windsor, thank heavens – came to check, strictly against confidentiality, but Clare said it wouldn't matter. Things couldn't be better.

Virtually almost nearly they couldn't, because the girl Lana was a BID, Brought In Dead, because Marla's injuries were permanent. And because Clifford seemed even more disturbed that evening.

Clare had had a meal at the General Hospital. One of the registrars wanted serial ascorbic-acid levels as a spin-off, and she opposed letting that take over her survey. She had temporised, she'd have a word with Dr Porritt. Clifford had had a meal.

'The police were round today,' she said. She'd changed, had a bath, got into a dressing gown. 'I proved what had to be proved.'

'Thanks, darling.'

He was watching a TV gardening programme that would normally have had him taking notes, getting the odd book out to check soil acidity. Tonight, nothing. The worry had worn him out, but Clare cautioned herself against sympathy. What guarantee did she have that he hadn't done worse?

'Is that it?' she asked. 'When I've risked everything to save you?'

'I'm eternally grateful, Clare. You'll never know how much.'

'It's all over, then?' She so wanted it to be.

'Yes.' He saw she was waiting, and flicked the remote control. The screen blanked. 'If Salvo surfaces—'

'He can't say anything. It's obvious.'

'Is it, Clare?' He stared across. She was suddenly uncomfortable. 'How come you're so sure?'

'His confederates wouldn't let him say anything. They have ways.'

'Ways of what?'

'Of forcing him to stay silent.'

He was quiet, assessing her. 'Who've you been talking to?'

'I overheard two patients on about it,' she said weakly. It had sounded so convincing when Bonn had said it. Under interrogation from her husband, it seemed terribly weak.

'Who were these two patients?'

'How do I know?' she said, distressed. She'd only been

trying to reassure him, and suddenly she'd become the enemy. 'Some person who works on the streets.'

'Person? One, not two now? Who is he? And what does he do "on the streets"? Barrows? Street vendor? Messenger?'

'Yes, one of those, probably.'

'What else did he tell you?'

A suspicion stirred, that Clifford knew more than he was letting on. She might have been seen going into the hotel, emerging later with spring in her step. Maybe some friend quick to gossip had . . . No. Bonn's words. Absolute security.

'I asked the patient,' she invented stoically. 'He said Salvo would stay mute about the wallet.'

'Wallet, the one who pays for a crime? How did you know it was called that?'

'He told me.' A lie is a compound fracture of truth. One lie is never enough.

'What a knowledgeable chap, Clare,' he said. 'You doctors, such funds of information walking right into your surgeries day in, day out.'

'I simply said I'd overheard him talking. We discussed the murder, the girl in the hospital. It's a conversational highlight.'

Clifford judged her. 'I don't suppose you went to see how she was getting on?'

'Marla? Of course not. No reason I should, is there?'

'Only to tell me if she'll see again, spot me in some lineup.'

'What possible explanation could I give the trauma surgeons? Or the police? They're in regular attendance, I heard.'

'More overhearing? You're a mine of information.'

'Why are you so preoccupied? You're in the clear,' she

put in bitterly. 'Who would accept the evidence of a girl who has had three major operations after massive traumatic injury?'

'I had a phone call,' he said bluntly. 'Salvo, at the office. Bloody fool.'

'Salvo? The man who came here?'

Clifford paused as he leant away to take her in. For the first time Clare realised that she too was a witness. She had seen Salvo leave the garden that evening.

'What did he want?' She wasn't afraid. 'I suppose money?'

'Blackmail?' He barked an unrecognisable laugh. 'Him? He hasn't the brains. He wouldn't last a minute.'

A threat, another traffic accident, for Salvo himself this time?

'He wants a car, some funds to get him out of the city.'

'He's still here?' Therefore vulnerable, Bonn had implied.

Listen to me, she thought wildly, just *listen*, talking over how a murderer, Clifford's hired killer, can escape from justice. She'd be offering to drive him next.

'He won't ring here?' she asked, scared. 'He won't come?'

'No.' Clifford had recovered. 'I told him the police were watching.'

'Are they?' Her hand crept to her throat. Involuntarily she glanced at the windows, curtained against the dark.

'Of course not.' He was a little unsure of that, repeated it. 'I can see that he gets money to travel. After that, it's up to him.'

'Can you?'

'Don't be stupid.' His smile chilled her with its narrowness. 'Money's what I do, remember.'

He'd never spoken to her like that, terse and damning.

She coloured at the insult. Well, she had her new confidence.

He listened as the hall clock chimed the quarter hour, got up, giving her his new smile.

'I'll do some computer work. If anyone rings, I'm in the bath, okay?'

'Very well.' She thought, Where have we gone?

'Wish me luck, darling.'

'Good luck,' she said, withholding her irony, and watched him go.

Without even having to think, but watching her husband's study door, Clare telephoned the agency, and booked Bonn for the following afternoon, for no other reason than to test how she felt about what had gone before. The alternative was to visit the Café Phrynne. There was no guarantee that he'd be there.

She read the local news. The day after tomorrow, the northern counties' mogga-dance championships. He would be there. Hadn't he said something about supporting that dancer? She could meet him there accidentally.

Was it too soon to see him again? She simply wanted to. All right, she mentally challenged imaginary gossips, it might seem odd for a practising doctor to have a goer as a friend, but so? Stupid to feel unjustified irritation, at other clients Bonn might see, be seeing, in the meantime.

Edgy, she poured herself a glass of sherry, and switched on the television. Some girl had been rescued from a burning flat, an overturned paraffin heater the cause. A passing couple had seen a man run out, and called the fire brigade. Two darts players returning from a club match had somehow got the girl out. A hospital spokesman said she would survive.

The man was being sought by police. He answered the

following description.... Clare paid attention, and wondered if Clifford had seen the news earlier.

Only from force of habit, she told herself, she checked the door locks, the window catches. Caution did no harm. She would watch television in bed until Clifford came upstairs.

Bonn met Doob by the gigantic budgerigar cage and the huge glass waterfall clock. The shopping mall was the noisiest place in the city, infants and shoppers, with the inevitable rim of elderly men by the fountain. Rack hung about. He'd given Doob a clean bill of honesty.

'How have you done, Doob?' Bonn asked.

'Not bad, Bonn.' The goer was nervous. 'Three clients, and a homer. Another tonight.'

'Did the homer go all right?' Bonn smiled apology. 'I'm always concerned.'

'It was fine.' Doob was eager to explain. 'Her feller said—'

'Thank you, Doob. No details, please.'

'Is it enough, then?' Doob was anxious and wanted to know. 'I heard Lancelot's been notching them up at a rate of—'

'Shhhh,' Bonn consoled. 'I am pleased.'

Doob coloured, embarrassed by the praise. 'Ta, Bonn.'

'Which brings me to my problem, Doob.' Bonn made space for a young mother to walk her toddler round the rim of the fountain. It squealed with delight. 'Do the dip-and-scratch, Doob,' Bonn said, making sure he moved his head often as he spoke. Directional microphones were not unknown.

Doob asked, staring, 'Me and whose army?'

'You, Doob. With me as the cackler.'

'*You* help me to do a dipper? Who's the mark? It's a bird, right?' Doob looked ready to laugh in case this was some hidden joke, except Bonn wouldn't joke.

'Yes.' Bonn held a woman's shopping while she loaded an infant into a push chair and did the straps. 'I'll be at her table in the dining room. Don't be showy.'

'What's she got, then?' Doob was still unsure. 'Coat pockets? Handbag? Purse? I hate doing a job for one bleeding credit card.'

'Language, please. I don't know what she carries.'

'What happens after, Bonn? I don't like the sound of this.'

'We shall discover in God's good time, Doob.' Bonn turned away, saying over his shoulder, 'And neither do I. Good luck.'

'Ta, Bonn.' Doob felt he'd received a knighthood, doing a special with Bonn. It was a pity he couldn't brag. He went for a coffee in the Butty Bar. He wanted a real drink, but Bonn would know, and that would be the end of it.

Martina cleared the money with something like ill grace, the nearest Bonn had ever seen to a sulk. She insisted on speaking to Posser. There was an extra, smaller wadge for the desk records, but that would be arranged by others, Posser said, when he had the whole story.

The woman Jane Antrobus entered the restaurant a little after seven o'clock, as Glazie had said. Guests were on their way out to the theatres at that hour. From behind the red velvet curtains Bonn observed her thick-set figure seat herself, lay her handbag on an adjacent chair, and consult the menu. Bonn saw Doob come from the foyer, and started his inner clock ticking. On the count of twelve he entered briskly.

Doob was just among the tables. Three waiters were quietly about their business, none with the Fraud Office woman. Bonn had tipped Glazie off, saw the receptionist stroll in.

The woman was on the point of summoning a waiter when Doob reached her. He stumbled, almost fell, but righted himself. Her handbag fell.

Bonn, pausing to read the large engraved menu between a double bank of flowers, couldn't help but admire Doob's dexterity. Elevation to the rank of goer had certainly done Doob a power of good. From a slipshod youth with frayed elbows, he had now become neat, his clothes fashionable, making him look younger. He exuded confidence. It could have been a young executive who straightened up, apologising profusely as he handed the lady her handbag back.

Bonn's count had reached nineteen, which was about right, when he reached the table. Doob was ostensibly making for the lounge bar just visible through the partition that separated the private dining suites from the main restaurant. For a moment Bonn hesitated, glanced down at the Antrobus woman.

The SFO researcher was disconcerted. 'Yes?'

Bonn, standing there: 'Excuse me a moment, madam.'

He strode after Doob, who was having to pause to speak to one of the waiters because Bonn, inexperienced, had miscalculated somewhat and took too long.

'You, sir.' Bonn went for decibels, for the few diners already seated. 'Can I have a word?'

Doob made to go. The waiter vanished on Glazie's signal.

Bonn placed himself between the exit and Doob, then

spoke to the pickpocket in a meaningless jabber. He pointed to Jane Antrobus, stabbed a finger at Doob, who shook his head, mutter mutter. Doob was excellent, pantomiming a giveaway outrage at such a false accusation.

Hand held out as if for the cane, Bonn stood in tableau. Doob shamefacedly extracted a small purse, placed it on Bonn's hand. Bonn beckoned him, and together they returned to the SFO woman's table.

'Lady,' Bonn said, frowning, 'I regret to say that you have been dipped. I saw it all. This man is already known to me.'

'My purse!' she exclaimed in horror, frantically grabbing her handbag.

'Please, Inspector,' Doob said, collapsing into a whining scrounger. 'Don't take this any further. It's a mistake – '

'Quiet, Cullingson,' Bonn ordered. 'Ma'am. Is anything else missing?'

The researcher delved, shook her head. 'Are you a policeman?'

Glazie approached. 'Excuse me, Inspector. Can I be of assistance?'

'I need you.' Bonn shot an eagle-eyed look round the restaurant. Everybody was staring. 'Make a list of all the waiters, waitresses, and clerical staff on duty at the time of the incident.' He did his best at a glacial smile. 'Note down time, place, date.'

'Yes, sir.' Glazie retreated.

'Please, lady.' Doob pleaded. 'I didn't mean anything. An irresistible impulse. Hand on my heart, I'll never do it again—'

Bonn grasped his arm. 'Shut it, Cullingson. You're caught redhanded. This time it'll be in every newspaper in the country. You'll get sent down—'

'Inspector.' Jane Antrobus's face had paled. 'Let it go.' She checked her purse, tried to look reassured. 'This poor man. I'm willing to overlook it.'

'You are?' Bonn told Doob to stay put, and lowered himself into a chair. 'Ma'am. He was apprehended in execution of an obvious theft in a hotel restaurant. I'm sure the management want maximum publicity—'

'No!' She gathered herself. 'No. Please. That would be too embarrassing. I'm a professional lady, with heavy commitments.'

It was getting easier as the process went on. You tended to lose yourself in the arguments, whether you believed in them or not. Doob had told him that. Confidence tricks were an assumption of truth, any old truth. 'Please proffer charges against this man. He is a regular pickpocket. He does untold harm. You have a golden opportunity to put him through a rigorous process of trial. It would be a deterrent.' He shrugged, sad that triumph was to be taken away. 'However, if you refuse—'

'Inspector.' Her relief was painfully evident. 'The incident is closed.'

'Bless you, lady.' Doob came round, took her hand, bent low, and kissed it, smiling into her eyes. 'Thank you for what you've done for me.'

She was nonplussed, took back her hand. 'Yes, of course.'

'Better leave, Cullingson.' Bonn looked at Doob. 'Palms up.'

Doob stood, showed his empty hands. 'Can I go, Inspector?'

'Yes. Get gone.' A failure in accent, tone, syntax, everything to do with speech, Bonn scathed himself critically. He gave her a serious frown. 'A narrow squeak, er, Mrs . . .?'

'Antrobus, Jane Antrobus.' She kept her handbag on her lap.

'Are you here on business, Jane, if I may?'

'No. I have a night or two before travelling to London.' She was looking. 'Aren't you young for a police inspector?'

'Youngest in the division,' Bonn said, on thin ice. He waved Glazie over, and told him to abandon the lists.

Which left them alone. The conversational hum returned to the restaurant, the event was over and done with.

'Might I . . .?' Bonn hesitated. 'Would you allow me to share your table? I came in for supper – off duty! Of course, if you wish to dine alone—'

'No. Please.' She had to brave it out.

'You're sure?' Bonn smiled, on home ground. 'Providing you will allow me to be the host. Fair's fair.'

He smiled, reached across the table, and touched her hand.

At nine, Bonn reached the Triple Racer. Askey was already there.

'Done, Bonn. Everything like you said.'

'Thank you, Askey. How is that sister of yours?'

'I'm hoping to take her to Blackpool, a trip out.'

Bonn pondered. 'That's a good idea, Askey. Perhaps we might run to a car, with a driver. There are orthopaedic vehicles now, aren't there, take wheelchairs.'

'That'd be great, Bonn. But I don't know. . . .'

'Leave it a moment. The photographs?'

'Camcorded the lot, Bonn. And stills.' Askey blinked, peering. The bikers were all talking noisily. 'I've got somebody who says he can edit, but you said to be careful with this one.'

'Thank you, Askey. I'll have a Granadee Studios girl edit it. She's unattached, and wants to come in with us. Rack?'

Rack left the crowd of bikers.

'Rack, please.' Bonn shook Askey's hand in thanks. 'We've had excellent service tonight. Please arrange a car trip to Blackpool for a sick lady.'

'Only Blackpool?' Rack glared at Askey. 'Not the Continent?'

'She hates being away for long,' Askey apologised. 'Thanks, Bonn.'

Rack went with Bonn, beckoning to Grellie. 'Know why they all like Blackpool, Bonn?' he started up. 'It's ozone. You breathe it, you're an addict.'

'That is interesting, but Grellie—'

'Grellie wants you to okay what the girls have raised for Marla. And wants you for supper.'

Bonn thought, another meal? He listened to Rack's ozone theory.

32

Crisper – a person burned to death, as in an accident.

Oz counted army service one of life's blessings. He even approved of the porridge he'd done in the Glasshouse, military prison, and the endless jankers, bastard sergeants.

He lay beneath the vehicle fixing the string, almost laughing.

One thing, the Army had room for anyone. Off your trolley or a bookish saint, mardy or macho, barmy or bright, the Army took you in. And it taught you. With Oz, it had been cars, tanks, anything with an engine, and the tricks that came with every set of pistons. Like this, the phosphorus-in-water that Hairy-Arse, the warrant officer who'd done unmentionable things in the Balkans, and everywhere else for that matter, called the rope trick.

Any job was gommon, common sense. Try telling Salvo that, silly bleeder, Oz thought ruefully, testing the string – more silk than cord, actually, for strength. The lunatic sod was a psycho. Four years, maybe a six-and-ten, in some boozy regiment would straighten him out, sure as God made trees. Stop the useless wanker dreaming he was 'really somebody'. The lads wouldn't tolerate a shirker. Do the job, keep the platoon out of trouble with Hairy-Arse, make sure that if any three-tonner failed in a night column it wasn't your engines, thank Christ.

This motor was one of ninety parked at the City Vehicle Saloon Auction Co, Ltd, an area of semi-dereliction beyond the football ground. Boisterous pubs, a bingo hall, high-rise blocks watching TV soaps instead of getting on with something decent, a rotting mill, and a canal's fetid turning-pool. Their security was crap, Oz thought in disgust, working on. Odd, because the majority of security blokes were from the PFI, poor fucking infantry. No pride in their engines or their jobs. Way of the fucking world.

He rolled out from under, lay there not moving for a full minute. That was how long a thicko with a truncheon and flash-light could hang on, wait to see if that noise was anything, before walking back to his ale and the telly match thinking, Thank fuck, no knacker's yard tonight. Tomorrow, if questioned by some narked Filth, he'd say he'd thought it was maybe kids, out with his standard lie that he'd searched everywhere and found sod all.

Minute up. Oz knelt, groped for the plastic bag. Still squishy, no leaks. In the water the waxy stick. A squat candle of pure phosphorus. Oz always thought it marvellous that water, that extinguisher of fires, should stifle phosphorus. He'd tested it, cut a fragment – under water, of course – in his back yard. No sooner did he lift it out of the water on the point of his knife than the bloody stuff flashed into flame and oblivion. The warmth of your hand could start the fucker.

To make sure, he'd got a safety fire-lighter. Chemical reactions were best, Oz always thought. There was a place for electric, but how often did you hear of things going wrong with electricity? Loose connection here, some damp there, even a fucking cockroach shorting a circuit, clanged alarms one end of the county to the other. No, good old chemicals burned themselves into nothing, no traces for nasty sods with their nasty sample bottles. Mind you, Middle East these days, soon there'd be no room for real bomb expertise. They got a jar of 3-acetone, and that was it, blow up the frigging skyline, and theirselves too like as not.

The fire-lighters were elementary campers' strips. Remove from pack, tear apart, place beneath the fuel, and there's your campfire.

Oz sat, going through his checklist. Phosphorus in its bag of water. String, emerging through the waterproof seal that he'd made with the iron over a double fold. A tug on the string would tear the phosphorus stick free of its water bag. Air would ignite it. But phosphorus itself wouldn't bang. It was more of your flash and smoulder, not enough for a motor like this, that he'd chosen for Salvo's getaway.

The string would also rip apart the two strips of the campers' lighter. Flames enough there, though too tiny to be any use to anybody except a girl guide. Useful second support, the regimental Hairy-Arse used to call such devices. He would bawl in your earhole, 'Dozy fuckers like you who forget one may then rely on the other doyouunnerstannnn you 'orrible man . . .'

Oz'd prepared it all in his yard. One string for both, lay them close together, the freed phosphorus doing its stuff by erupting into fire and the camper's strip ripping into a fast flame. One plus one equalled Gawd Almighty.

The nylon-silk string, which he'd filthed in Indian ink, he tied to the plastic bag's cord. He crawled to the high wire-mesh fence and tied its other end to a concrete upright. No sense in standing up to walk the short distance, careful the game. Assume everybody was watching you, not United and some unpronounceable foreign team on telly.

The motor was a mundane Ford, easy to get into, its

registration five years old ALL FULLY SERVICED AND READY TO DRIVE! the neon sign said. If the fucking motor let him down, Oz swore, there'd be fucking ructions, welshing on a promise.

He rose slowly – fast moves spelt crime. He crouched by the driver's side, and from his pocket took half a tennis ball. With a grunt he shoved it flat over the lock. Holding it in place, he slowly let it return to its hemispherical shape. It sucked air in. The car door clicked open. A rubber kitchen-sink plunger would do it, but was harder to explain to marauding Old Bill.

Quickly Oz dived in, clicked the interior light off, and sat still. No shouts, no alarm. He went to retrieve the half tennis ball. Four cursing minutes before he happened on it. He put it away, careful, careful.

There *was* another quick way, simply smash half a brick against the front bumper. If the car was fitted with air bags, all the doors would instantly spring open as the air bag exploded. Except that was hellish noisy. Fine if you were nicking the motor from outside a football ground, but no good here, the car lit up like fucking Christmas with its lights on and its alarm wailing.

If he'd not brought his half tennis ball, he'd have used a tyre lever on the window, quiet and quick. But how do you explain a tyre iron? Drop it, it makes a clang. Half a tennis ball's almost as bad, seeing everybody knew the trick, but at least you could drop it through a hole in your pocket while you were being all innocent.

Beneath the passenger seat was the ideal place to bomb a motor. Mistake to put it beneath the driver's. You wanted a sideways blast, rather than beneath, in a confined space. He placed the phosporus bag against the seat-support bars, and trailed the cord out. It led to the fence. Move the car, and you'd get a nasty phosphorus burn. He'd got the smoulder. Now for the rest.

Must be getting on for eleven o'clock. He took a silicone spray from his pocket, and sprayed his fingertips carefully, wafting his hands to dry them. Artificial skin drowned fingerprints. He pulled on leather gloves from his pocket, still more caution, and made his way to the line of three petrol pumps. He avoided using the small flashlight he'd brought, seeing by the city's sky glow. He could hear the TV commentators, see the faint reflection of the telly's luminescence from the office. That was security, he thought. He wouldn't pay them in tap washers.

He passed the pile of gallon tins at a crouch. Their filled petrol containers were the ones on the ground, never stacked like empties. He knelt by the last one, tapped it. Full. He hefted it, and returned to the car.

Over the next ten minutes he decanted the petrol into a large freezer bag, thin plastic but with a seal that would be, in a certain immortal phrase, useful secondary support. He chuckled. There would be a brief smell of petrol, but with luck Salvo would be too worked up to bother.

The bulging container of petrol had now to be carefully stroked with kitchen wipes to minimise smell. He sealed the used tissues inside a smaller freezer bag, then placed the petrol bomb inside a larger bag. More than satisfactory. His whole kit was a small plastic bag of water, four freezer bags, gloves, and a ball of string. The tennis-ball half could go into any litter bin. Silicone spray was necessary, but what could you do?

He tied a length of nylon-silk cord tightly round the petrol bomb, hourglass style, and placed it under the seat, trailing the free end to tie to the same concrete post.

Oz did a dummy run, creeping up on the car, opening

the driver's door, crawling in, sitting there in the darkness, going through the motions of hot-wiring the starter. Hundred per cent certain.

Anybody moved this car a single yard, it was good night, Vienna.

Salvo was waiting for Oz outside the station. The city was still busy, the last trains being announced and some pop concert crowd surging.

'I thought you weren't coming, Oz.'

'Don't be daft.'

'You get the wheels?'

'Remember this registration number, okay? It's a Ford.'

It took a dozen repetitions to drive it into Salvo's thick head. Oz felt contempt. He could remember cars from being a lad.

'I were you, Salvo, I'd wait until morning. Then just pretend like you're looking for something to buy, get in, and drive away. No need to hot-wire the crate, see?'

'I'm good at hot-wiring, Oz, done it a million times.'

Oz said dubiously, 'You know what you're doing.'

'That's fucking right. How'll I get there?' asked the know-all.

'City Vehicle Saloon Auction Company, Limited,' Oz said quietly. 'The twenty-eight goes right by. It's two miles, walk it in half an hour. The car's hundred yards from the end of the fence. Just run it at the gates, they're only wire and one padlock. By the time they've switched their telly off you'll be in Brum.'

'Ta, Oz. You're a mate.'

'I've tanked it up. Don't stop on the motorway.'

Salvo was uneasy. 'Give us a lift there, mate?'

'Can't risk it, Salvo. They connect us, they'd pin Mostern on you. You know the Filth.'

'I need some bunce, Oz. I got some from a bint I had to crisp.'

'I heard,' Oz said bitterly, thinking, Jesus H. Christ. 'You're more famous than a fucking Derby winner. Shake hands.' Oz still had his gloves on. He shook hands, hissed in fury when Salvo started to count the money he'd been slipped. 'Put it away, silly cunt.'

'Thanks, Oz.'

'Cheers, mate. See you in three years maybe, eh?'

Salvo grinned. Three years was the par time. After that the Filth forgot.

Alibi time. Oz went for a pint in the Volunteer, made a couple of stupid bets, argued noisily round the dartboards so he'd get ballocked and remembered, generally made his presence known. He needed a drink, though, having seen Salvo go by in a taxi. Un-fucking-believable, the ignorance. A spell in the PFI would sort the bugger out.

He made sure he lost at darts in style, missing double top four successive darts, everybody calling him a right prat. He rather enjoyed being the centre of attention, ought to treat himself to a pint more often.

The car park was in darkness. Oz had said wait until morning, but that wasn't Salvo's way. He'd hung about the city too long.

He walked along the pavement. Hundred yards. He needn't check the gate, if Oz said it was easy to drive through. Nobody about. He climbed over, walked to the Ford. He'd memorised the number, felt the registration plate, proudly got it right.

The car door was unlocked. He felt almost tearful, Oz a real pal, maybe the only one he had left now. Even the interior light was out. Good old Oz.

Salvo climbed in. Smell of petrol, but, then, Oz had said he'd tanked it up. He closed the door, pulling it silently with the handle down.

For a moment he sat there, uneasy. He'd seen it on the pictures. Wiring. Ignition. Turn the key and kaboom, the CIA killing the hero and his tart. He turned the wheel a little. Nothing. He jiggled the wires from the dashboard. Nothing.

He did the hot-wire, stripping with his thumb-nail. The motor started like a dream. No bang. Old Oz coming through, fucking security blokes doing sod all.

With tears of gratitude for Oz's help, he moved off.

For one instant he felt bewildered at the sudden engulfing stench of petrol. Something splashed wetly on his leg. A spark showed the dashboard. He looked down. He heard a fizz, getting louder. His eyes smarted.

Puzzled, he said, 'Here, wait a sec,' but it was too late. He had time to say, 'Oz?'

The car gave a muted whoomph as fire filled its interior, still rolling forward, then blew apart in a ball of flame, pieces skittering across the concrete among the parked cars, starting five more cars burning. Then the security men came running.

33

Cushy, cushty – good, profitable, easy (Romany).

Iᴛ ᴡᴏᴜʟᴅ ʙᴇ raining, Clifford thought with distaste, coming from the telephone-company offices. Get one thing right, two things go wrong. And he'd no umbrella. He seemed to hesitate, then waved down a passing taxi.

Oz was the cabbie. He slid back the safety glass.

'In a hurry, mate?'

'Traffic's bad as ever, I see. You know the Vivante Hotel?'

'Be there in a sec.' Oz laughed. 'Well, minute or two maybe.'

'You sound cheerful.'

'Won a bet, first since I were a nipper.'

'Lucky, then.'

They spoke of bets. Clifford said once you were behind in any gambling game simply give up and cut out. Oz told him no.

'Look at me, guv,' he said, taking a side street. 'Loser for donkey's years, and now I get a run. Bit here, bit there. Suddenly it's a fortune. Cushty.'

'What'll you do with it? Rub out all your deficits?'

'What do they say in romance stories? One fell swoop!' Oz chuckled. 'All right to drop you at Asda? You can cut through, stay in the dry.'

'All right. But I'll take it out of your tip, me walking half a mile.'

'Twenty yards!'

In good humour, Clifford pushed a note through the aperture, asked for change. Oz grumbled, and Clifford relented, fumblingly repaid it.

'I'll jog the whole distance in future, save a fortune.'

Five minutes later Clifford was in the Vivante lounge ordering afternoon tea. He waited until the waitress had served before he opened his leather folder.

He examined the recorded calls, the numbers he'd queried at the telecommunications offices marked. One especially troubled him. Last evening, and there it was again. Pleases Agency, Inc. Clare must have made it as soon as he'd logged on his computer. He'd actually dialled the number from the public phone. No secret of it. The address was close to the city centre, above a casino and a courier service.

He replayed the call in his mind.

'Can I enquire what services your agency provides?' he'd asked.

'Your name, sir, please?'

'I just want to know the nature of your services.'

'Can I ask the name of the client who recommended us?' The woman's voice went singsong, the typical close-down.

He'd tried the high horse. 'Is there any reason that you can't provide me with this information?'

'We operate on strictly personal recommendation, sir. Thank you for calling!' the bitch intoned cheerily, and it was click-burr.

Hadn't there been that chap from Hull, moved into the city with a motor-insurance scheme? Burgess, wife called Lisa. They'd had a row over, of all things, the colour of their new car. Lisa had got sloshed, slung abuse at Ben Burgess, and jeered that she hired somebody to dick her. That was Ben's phrase, outraged, waving his arms when he'd dropped by Clifford's office to tell the tale.

He'd said it was right here in the city centre. Lisa, sobering with remorse, said she'd invented the whole thing. They'd separated, though, Lisa back to Norwich, the house divided, civilised.

Oz had delivered the goods. Salvo was eliminated. The billboards were already shrieking of some thief who'd started a fire trying to steal a motor. He'd catch the radio news later. First he'd make a detour by way of Ben Burgess's tacky business.

'Then what?' Hassall asked. The two policemen were having a drink in their social club. 'I hate these places.'

Windsor already knew that.

'Nothing I could see. That taxi was the one that—'

'—topped Mostern, aye. But did anything go down?'

Windsor wondered what he could say to mollify the other's disgust. 'There was some jiggery-pokery, change being argued over. I couldn't see for sure.' He grasped the nettle. 'I didn't camcord it.'

'No matter,' Hassall said, adding morosely, 'They'd not allow it in evidence. And somebody slipping a wadge could be doing anything. Do you really think Burtonall paid him?'

'As I sit here,' Windsor said, in total grief.

'My younger day, I'd have cuffed this Oz's licence, got some dip artist to nick the wadge.'

'Honest?' Windsor said, curious. 'What would you've done with it?'

'The lads had this fund, back then, for retirements.'

Hassall pulled a rueful face. 'No good now, every groat triple-checked. Only investment advisers can grease gelt.'

'That's what I mean,' Windsor said. It would rankle for life. All very well for an old bloke like Hassall to chuck in the sponge. 'Burtonall's one of them.'

'He's got alibis as long as your arm,' Hassall said. 'If it isn't laboratory results it's cardiac traces. Any word from the bars, that snooker place?'

'Blank.' Windsor waited for his senior to make a decision, and asked belligerently, 'Is that it, then?'

'Unless that crisper turns out not to be that Salvo twat.'

'It'll be Salvo,' Windsor predicted. 'Oz did him, on Burtonall's say-so.'

Hassall did feel a certain sympathy.

'I were like you, once. Just do what you can. Don't get warped.'

In twenty more years, Windsor thought, taking a hefty swig of his ale. But until then I'll cheat, lie, and sooner or later get the bastards.

Hassall beckoned the barman. 'And stop thinking like that,' quite as if he'd read Windsor's thoughts. 'I might as well talk to the wall.'

Akker didn't threaten Jane Antrobus until he was carrying her bags to the train. She had not spoken a word since he'd explained. Lowering her two suitcases onto the platform, he spoke into her ear. He knew he had dog's breath, but he wasn't here to charm.

'Look. You keep that bit of gelt, okay?'

She moved her head aside but Akker persisted.

'Those photos. That video of you receiving money. You and Mostern, sworn statements of hotel operative saying how you fixed not to prosecute. It's ready to go. Understand?' He shouted when she didn't respond, 'Understand? You gotter say yes.'

'Yes,' she said.

'Then fucking well nod, for Christ's sake.'

She nodded, said 'Yes' again.

'I've to say something.' Akker's brow puckered. 'Worse than learning fucking poems at school.' He composed himself, intoned loudly, 'Silence and inertia are in your very best interests in respect of the city's services.' He beamed. 'Did it! Understand, did you?'

'Yes.'

'Right. On you go.'

He watched the train depart, ten whole minutes later, to make sure she didn't get off. That Bonn. There was such a thing as being too fucking careful, in his opinion, but he'd seen her off exactly as instructed.

34

THE START OF the cardiology unit's surveillance was not a conspicuous success. The cardiologist said as much after Clare had spent all day coping with a meagre number of male volunteers at the hospital.

'Ten is pathetic, Clare.' He was plunged into gloom.

'I'm as disappointed, Paul.' Clare went for it. 'Ten, plus Clifford.'

'Your husband?' Dr Porritt asked.

'Yes.' Clare shuffled the files. 'I used him to time the process. To see,' she added wryly, making a joke, 'how I'd cope with the hordes.'

'Let's review what we did, then.'

They left the anteroom and discarded their coats. The canteen was crowded, some union meeting among ancillary staff. Clare avoided the cardiologist's eye, knowing his feelings on the issue. For years Dr Porritt had wanted all porters made redundant, and thought the ambulance service inefficient. They sat facing.

'I've decided on three sessions a week. At this rate, we'll have enough after a couple of centuries.'

'Women are best patients.' It was another of the cardiologist's moans. 'They're more responsible. Bloody men shun

medical help. Can't come, mustn't be seen ailing. Less practical. Women face things.'

Clare wondered how this applied to Clifford's criminal
life.

'A few quid spent on posters isn't advertising, Clare.' He
was bitter. 'I killed my bloody self screwing the money for
this out of the health authority.'

'Look. This is only day one. Let's not go under. How
about we change tactics?' She went for enthusiasm, cheer
him up. 'I take the surveillance unit into the factories.
Remember the old chest X-ray mobiles?'

'No,' the cardiologist ruled. 'I'm against that. It smacks
of desperation. Men won't come forward with all their
workmates pulling their leg. Softly, softly, catchee monkey.'

'How?'

Paul appraised her. 'Repeat your advertising campaign,
such as it is.' He smiled. 'But start with the women. Advertise in the supermarkets. Use the stores' announcers. Ask
the managers' cooperation. You know the sort of thing:
"Ladies, when did your husband last go for a free routine
medical check . . .?" Persuade them to bring their fathers,
brothers, live-ins.'

'That doesn't give us a cross-section. It picks out the
married.'

'Then adapt the announcements. Get notices up in
garages, tannoys in factories. Phone the motorway service
stations, railways, anywhere.'

'And then?' Clare ought to have thought of these.

'The GPs. They're the ones with the lists. There's something else. I know somebody at Granadee Studios.'

'The TV place? My husband's office is just round the
corner.'

'Says they'll cooperate.' Dr Porritt weighed her up before speaking. 'He'll let you have a slot.'

'Me? Go on television?' Clare felt her cheeks warm.

'If you're willing.' He nodded encouragingly. 'The old times are gone, when doctors didn't announce their names in public. Now every TV screen's bulging, doctors doing everything from lonely-heart sobbers to physical jerks. We're in a scrap to get the populace fitter, make a go of health.'

'I don't like the sound of that TV thing, Paul.' Clare wanted anonymity.

'Isn't it our duty, Clare?'

'*You* do the broadcast, then.'

'I'm not doing the survey,' he said with maddening logic. 'You are. We've *got* to get the city's males in, or the survey goes down the chute.'

'I'll think about it, Paul.'

'Quickly, please.' They parted amicably, making disparaging comments about people who didn't read health posters.

They met in the Vivante Hotel, late that afternoon, in a plain room with two picture windows overlooking the station approach.

This time they talked with a casual ease, without reason to maintain a show of purpose. Though Clare found her voice shaking a little as she undressed, not looking his way as he took his clothes off in time with her, their understanding enough to carry her through.

She was surprised by her own sense of ease. It was comfortable, she realised with astonishment, yet how could this be? His occupation, her need for some sort of consolation, and *this* was the outcome? She knew she might smile if she thought of double meanings. But for now, making a reasonably neat pile of her clothes on the bedside chair, it seemed perfectly in order to be feeling the cool sheets of the clean bed, realising the inevitability of it as his weight tilted her and he lay beside her.

Almost unaffected by the emotional distance she had travelled, she wondered if Bonn would now be frank if she asked about other women. Did they respond like she was doing? Did they too have enormous difficulties explaining to themselves what on earth they thought they were doing, paying for a hired man?

One question she dearly wanted answered was whether she too was 'a client'. They had come together – one of those double-meaning phrases she must learn to avoid – had *met* – for a different purpose. Surely those other women didn't have as much excuse, with sexual appetite their ulterior motive until they, like her, reached this level? Surely this degree of intimacy was impossible with each one?

His arm reached over and he found her breast, the palm warm on her skin. She turned, smiling at his ready accept-ance, the assumptions of trust and rights, and reached for him. This too was startling. She didn't feel at all odd, making her understanding so plain. She heard his grunt with a new relish. God, but just holding him in one hand like she was, unmoving, was almost enough.

Client? Not for this. She felt his fingers touch her mouth.

'I love mouths.'

'Everybody's?' she said, immediately wanted to erase it. 'Sorry, Bonn.'

'No,' he answered unexpectedly. 'Some mouths are beautiful. They are the ones that make me love all mouths.'

'How much is tact, and how much what you mean?'

'I mean all of it.' He placed his mouth on hers.

'Women are puzzled, men liking breasts so.'

He drew back to see her better, the way he did. 'Women are the puzzlement. Can't see the obvious.'

That made her laugh. She tapped his face in reproach. 'Know what I want? Ask about you, the seminary – that *was* you in the old priest's photograph.' She shushed him when he made to speak. 'Don't worry. I won't.'

For a while he was silent. 'Why not?'

'Because I believe too many women do. Ask you, I mean.'

'So?'

'So imagine me lying here, maybe while you ran the bath for us afterwards, me throwing out casual questions. I'd never know, would I? I mean, would your replies be your usual evasions? Or be a careful gush of platitudes? I simply wouldn't know.'

'That makes it . . .'

'No, Bonn, don't think badly.' She slid her free hand behind his head and kept it there. 'If I were to ask, we'd become different. We'd become the unknown, replying to the unknowing. Could there be a greater recipe for disaster?'

'Which of us would be the unknown, Clare?'

She'd read that Lana was to be buried the following day, the coroner having released the body. That, and the cardiac scheme's dodgy start, made her think of other unknowns.

Last time had been pure revenge on Clifford, she acknowledged. There was no earthly reason to hire Bonn a second time. Infidelity was whole of itself, like honesty. Betrayal – 'cheating', in modern American parlance – was a one-off, Shakespeare's dram of bile, which spoiled the goodness in the rest. One infidelity broke all the thin ice of marriage.

'I'm pleased, Clare. You wanted me for yourself.'

Real, was that, or reflex? How often did he say exactly the same? Dozens? Only occasionally?

'You see, Bonn, there's danger.' Just listen to yourself, she thought. Asking for reassurance now, a little amateur psychotherapy?

'Danger.'

'Yes.' She felt his hand grazing on her thighs. 'If you became a person with a background, parents, your first dreams, then I would be polarised. It's the way of all human pairs, when they learn about each other.'

'Danger,' he said, testing her word.

'That attitude cries out to be developed, and made into loving. The danger is that of growing closer.'

'There is a way round, Clare.'

'Yes, Bonn. Your way.' She had to be brave to go on. 'To stay at a distance. The process worries me. Does it become a mere carnal activity, grinding out repletion like a product?'

'Yes.' He said it with a trace of sadness that moved her, until she cautioned herself. It might be his trademark, to lace confession with sorrow. 'It does become like that, in some women. They keep score, mark their mind cards, keep record of methods, levels reached.'

'What does it mean? That they've learned to use it?'

'Not it, Clare. To use me.' His sadness lingered. 'Very rarely, one woman will arrive, an absolute beginner, baffled as some new girl at the mogga dancing, not knowing what on earth is going on, wondering what she's doing. She is so overcome by the realisation of her new power that she flings herself headlong into clienthood. Maybe she'll spend a fortune, jumping from one goer to another. We call them trippers. It's fine, but it's the road to addiction. It has no turning, no place to sit and wonder how far she's travelled, why she's travelling at all.'

'What happens? Do they eventually give up?'

'It's as if they see only possession.' He tilted his palm and showed her the rising nipple.

It was as Clare had guessed. 'How on earth do they cope?'

'One or two want possession to be total, permanent union the only way.' He shrugged. She could have sworn he was sincere, but, then, he was a magician at his trade. 'If they aren't rich, some eventually see the light and hire occasionally. If they're wealthy, it's harder.'

'Harder?' she cried softly.

'Of course. They can't buy me completely. They can't understand.'

'Can't? When they're so rich?' She considered this. By now his hands were moving on her, pressing, kneading, but not hard enough. They could hire, these rich clients – she forced herself to think the words distinctly – yet not buy?

'That isn't hard enough, Bonn,' she said aloud. 'Touch me harder.'

From there, all thoughts ceased.

The envy of others, she knew as she lay exhausted under this stranger, she could do without. Let them live in ignorance. She needn't tell anyone, or give cause for speculation among colleagues. Scandal was only women's stimulus. They wanted notoriety, risk, to be thrilled by treading close to disaster, their fear an extra fillip.

She could do without the envy of others.

Her reason? This made her feel younger. It renewed her, the way Clifford's sexual attentions no longer could, after his criminal betrayals. The carnality was the catalyst. And it was not romantic 'love' – yet who could make that claim, come to think of it?

This Bonn. Unknowable, she had decided by the ferocity of their act – she was sure to have bruises, her own doing, her own asking. She could have selected others, but had chosen this unknown. The incident with the swan she laid aside, a chance meeting like on a bus going anywhere.

Shifting under his sleeping weight to breathe better, she postponed one problem. Whether to go on. Once you reached the end of a theorem, that was it. You needn't keep on proving the damned thing. Leave it. Stop picking. *Quod erat demonstrandum*, therefore, QED. She completed the logic to her satisfaction, found it without fault. Shelve decision time.

She stroked his sweat-damp head, placed his hand over her face, breathed in as if the scent of him was addictive. Her problem of Bonn was solved. She was in control. Logic was her guide, and thoughts of possession were too dangerous. She wished he was even heavier.

They slept, one crushing the other on demand.

35

WINDSOR HAD WANTED the funeral cased, but Hassall only gave him a long look. In spite of that, Windsor was sure to clock the congregation, learning their descriptions like a school poem. Hassall stood in the choir loft getting deafened by the nearby organ some old dear was playing.

'Kist o' pipes, we called organs in the old days, young man,' the crone said, jubilation written all over her. Her mistakes came thick and fast.

Hassall smiled, but sombrely. He was not here for chatter.

Down below he could see most of the congregation. At funerals, everybody sits in singular discomfort. Was it the pews? Or the knowledge that here they were, in out of the rain, relieved it wasn't them, knowing they'd go out to a cup of tea and wake cake *alive*, the guilt syndrome?

The Victoria Square girls were in. He could see them, four rows in their idea of finery. Lads, one row only. Bonn joined them. They'd left a space for him. He alone did not genuflect. Odd, that, because everybody follows the party line in church, does the decent thing.

Hassall couldn't see the last three pews, the ones near

the church porch, and decorum forbade craning. He was resigned to glimpsing reflections in the brass furnishings. Hopeless. Maybe he ought to have acceded to Windsor's bleatings, record all attenders? He was sick of the sergeant's toxic harangues. Tim'd go far, but today enough was enough. Give in on that, he'd want the Army called out next time some kid used a pea shooter. Christ knows what they do in police college nowadays. Sociology, fuck all else. Sorry, God, he said inwardly, but I'm worn out.

People coughed, shuffled feet, whispered advice about the prayer books. Some thumbed theirs, found hymn numbers. A book fell, causing heads to lift. Some at the front turned to find something, but in reality sussing out who'd come, who hadn't who ought to have.

Windsor would be out in the rain counting, muttering car numbers into the recorder he'd cunningly concealed from Hassall, all that. He'd seen on some film or other, moving with the times, CIA procedures, cops and robbers. Pity was, nobody in the police guessed any more. Statistics and legal loopholes, preparation of evidence, procedures for those detained, the PACE Act. It would be a laugh, if it wasn't so barmy. Loony definitions of what a crime actually was, how many your patch head counts were – police stats throttled the guess.

He mostly blamed America. Not for advising youngsters how to behave moronic through U.S. videos and films – all fucking cartoons anyway nowadays – but because of their Vietnam. Body counts – real or made up – became success criteria. Such an odd war, that. You used massive power, then moaned how hard life was. Except maybe that *wasn't* their trouble. Maybe their only crime was having a world-wide audience. You could make out a good case.

The congregation stirred, rose. Hassall stood. The

organist lady glanced approvingly at him. He held his hat, remained with head bowed until the priest cleared his throat and began the service. He sat to look through the oak fenestrations of the choir-loft rail.

He hadn't seen the old priest before. A frail elderly man, having difficulty speaking. Cold coming? Getting over a chest infection? His voice, low and gravelly, seemed to take the old cleric by surprise.

They sang Number 197 from *Hymns Ancient and Modern*.

Hassall was always sorely embarrassed singing, having been made to warble tunelessly at school. He'd never recovered. His trick now was to sing bass, as far down as his voice could go without entering some silent zone. Bass voices got away with murder – he silently apologised to the girl in her coffin, which stood on high trestles before the altar.

The hymn trailed to a close behind the squeaking organ. 'Within Thy house for ever,' Hassall boomed gravely, and sat.

The homily was not long. The old clergyman's voice kept giving out. Hassall smiled at the old organist. She had a mirror rigged up next to her music light, to see the goings-on at the altar.

'Father Crossley,' she said in a whisper, as if he'd doubted.

'Is it?' Hassall had been Methodist. This folderol was beyond him, statues and vestments.

She said, eyes glinting, 'He's poorly. They're surprised he's alive. They asked for him specially.'

They who? Curiosity stirred in Hassall. It would do no harm to ask, while the old man gasped on, trying to project. Funerals revealed that churches had been built too big. Congregations had shrunk.

'Who did?'

'Friends.' She mouthed, thrilled with news of disaster, 'Cancer. They brought his own doctor. She's here, but I've not seen her.' She looked into the mirror with forlorn hope. 'I'll be on my voluntaries when the coffin leaves.'

'Is he so poorly, then?' Hassall stared down with renewed interest at the old priest. He was making heavy weather of it.

'His seminary's closed. He's in care.' She spoke with awe, somebody sinking that low.

'Poor man,' Hassall said. 'Poor man.'

Who'd come to conduct the funeral service, in a strange parish, in a strange denomination, to bury a whore he presumably did not know. How come?

'Who wanted Father Crossley, then?' he asked the old lass.

But that went too far. She made a show of checking her music, adjusting the light.

'Who?' he persisted. 'Was it her parents?'

Words were a risk in church, but reticence was too difficult. She gave in as the priest's eulogy drew feebly to a close.

'Some ladies she worked with, I heard.' She flexed her fingers.

'How very kind. Father Crossley, that poorly.'

There was a moment for silent prayer. Hassall heard some of the girls crying.

The priest announced the departure hymn. Hassall noticed that he had to check the hymn number, painstakingly read out 205, words by Charles Wesley. A newcomer, really, the old guy, to the hymnal. Everybody knew 'Love divine, all loves excelling,' or did they? Battling away, fish out of water, a game old bloke. It raised questions, not like why was he here, but who *did* bring him?

To the lady organist's disapproval, Hassall tiptoed down the wooden stairs. He was in the church porch as the coffin was carried out. And he waited in his car when the flowers were taken into the hearse.

Dr Burtonall was among the last to leave. Windsor, the prat, was skulking among the tombstones like some Apache.

The car window misted up. Hassall turned the key in the ignition like he ought to have done straight off for ventilation, and peered through the windscreen. Bonn emerged. Everybody dithered between motors at funerals. Not like weddings, where a headachy best man has the power of God Almighty and makes everybody toe the line.

The rain grew heavier as people straggled out. Cars pulled away. Another vicar appeared in the church porch as the girls ran huddled under umbrellas and shrieking in that rainy voice. Windsor lurked. A fucking Restoration comedy, Hassall thought in exasperation.

Dr Burtonall left the church, shepherding the elderly priest under her umbrella, leaving the resident vicar. Bonn was there, with Rack. Hassall knew of both. Rack was a maniac, Bonn a quiet bastard from nowhere. Last, Posser himself, wheezing his head off, accompanied by a lass Hassall guessed was Posser's daughter, bonny but lame.

Engines started up. The hearse was followed off by the column. Then the really interesting thing happened. A definite tableau formed by the lych gate. Bonn faced the old priest, who was now having to lean heavily on Dr Burtonall's arm, and the two definitely hesitated. Rack was revving his motor like for a Brands Hatch start. The girl and her father also paused. In that instant, Hassall almost shouted *Collusion!* It was there, sudden and shared.

Answer one question, raise a dozen more.

They took three motors. Dr Burtonall's Humber Supersnipe, dwarfing everything but the church tower, with the old priest Crossley. Then Posser with his daughter, in a midnight-blue Bentley driven by some smarmy long-haired get. Then Rack and Bonn in an ordinary Ford. Hassall watched them leave, presumably to follow the hearse to the crematorium.

Gone. He had an address for Bonn. Dr Clare Burtonall? Coincidences were never mere coincidences, in Hassall's experience. They were always planned somethings. Happenstance always got help.

Windsor charged up, opened his door.

'Sir? I reckon—'

'Hush, please.' Hassall sat thinking, all the rain in heaven falling in on him through the door Windsor kindly held open like that so his flu would recur. 'Right, Mr Windsor. What?'

'We follow them to the crem. Some others—'

'Got an address for that Bonn?'

'No, sir.' Windsor looked after the vehicles. 'You want it?'

'No, ta. You get on. I've an errand to run.'

He saw Windsor leave on squealing tyres. Hassall let things calm down, the birds start singing as the rain eased. Then he went back inside the church, to have a word with the incumbent.

36

To blag – to invent on the spur of the moment.

How OFTEN LATELY had Mrs Kinsale already left when she reached home? Clare was too fatigued to care, flung off her clothes and almost, not quite, had a hot shower. Instead, she filled the bath and soaked herself. Clifford had left a message to say he would have something to eat on the way home, not to bother much this evening. Only when she heard the door go did she stir herself.

Clifford was downstairs, going through the day's post when she entered the living room. Odd that he didn't have the television on. He was fanatical about news. They greeted each other warily. For safety's sake, Clare started telling him about Dr Porritt.

'The surveillance has to get more takers,' she told him, getting going.

'Can't you just tell the doctors to send people in?'

'Men are always reluctant. Dr Porritt wants me to broadcast.'

'On television? Where?'

'The city studios, near you. He knows somebody.'

'Would that be wise?' Clifford laid his letters aside. He'd poured himself a drink. 'There are reasons it ought to be somebody else.'

'What makes you say that?' she asked, suddenly aware of something being quite wrong. He often assumed this air of abstraction, but usually with a glimmer of humour. Tonight he seemed ready for battle. Her throat constricted.

'You had a high old time the other evening, Clare.'

This was it. He had found something, from a guilty husband to a combatant.

'High old time?' She gave him the chance to intervene, but he won by waiting her out. 'A cardiac survey isn't that.'

'Your reproaches would have pleased a nun.'

'I don't remember reproaching you, Clifford.'

'But you did. Loud and clear. I'm the evil bastard – not in those words – who'd caused the death of another person. Your doubts would have hanged somebody less fortunate.'

'Doubts?' She didn't go on. It was true. She still harboured uncertainties, especially about the two girls. 'Can you blame me?'

He said simply, 'I wanted support, loyalty. Did you match up?'

'Yes!' she cried out. 'Who gave you an alibi?'

'You did, Clare.' He sounded cold. 'But at what cost?'

'Let *me* tell *you*, Clifford.' She was beside herself at the unfair accusation. 'I went to that Lana girl's funeral today! To take care of an old priest. He happened to be one of my patients, and was too ill to go without medical cover. How do you think that made me feel?'

'Clever.'

'What?' She stared. 'Did you say clever?'

'Yes, Clare.' He looked as if balancing her motives. 'Clever. Who is he?'

'He?' She'd risen to upbraid Clifford, but sank into her armchair. 'Who?'

'You've made several phone calls to an agency. Rather a

sordid business, Clare. Essentially, it hires out sexual solace to bored housewives.'

She made a hopeless attempt to look scandalised. 'Have you taken leave of your senses?'

'No. Come to them, I think.' He examined his empty glass and quite casually went to refill it. 'I checked.'

'And?'

'You've been in regular contact. The Pleases Agency, Inc, is operated by a syndicate with extensive possessions – cafés, casino places, a disco or two, snooker halls.'

Did it have all those? she found herself wondering. 'So? I contact various places—'

'Because you're a doctor?' Shaking his head, he went to sit on the arm of the couch. His easy manner was disconcerting. 'Saving lives all over the place? No, Clare, I think not. You're an upper, that's what you are.'

'A what? Upper?'

'A woman who hires a goer for sexual pleasure in some hotel.'

'It's not—' she burst out angrily, then halted.

'It's "not like that", Clare?' He didn't quite smile. 'It's been going on some time, from the telephone accounts. By comparison, my faults hardly invite your reproaches.'

'I gave you an alibi when you badly needed one.'

'For which I'm grateful.' He was positively enjoying the confrontation. She realised she hardly knew him now. 'Aren't you going to explain at least some of your actions, enough to let me invent some alibi for you, should need arise?'

'I hired one of the – one,' she said, desperately working out how much to reveal, what she might still get away with. 'I was worried about Mostern's accident. He was at the scene. The police were rude to him.'

'And at the time you didn't know why?'

'Yes. I'd no idea. I'd never heard of them, not really.'

'I'll believe you.' He maddened her. 'So you hunted him down, got out your purse, and . . .?'

'I encountered him by chance outside the General Hospital. He helped a child out of the river. We spoke.' She faced him and his insufferable attitude. 'He was just the person to find out about Mostern's accident. The briefcase, you see, and the cock-and-bull story you fobbed me off with. I'd seen that Salvo clear as day.'

'Ah, yes,' he said ruefully. 'Bad news, that. Very careless.'

'More than that, Clifford. It was murderous.'

'And did you? Find out all about me, Salvo, the rest?'

'What is the rest?'

'You tell me, darling.'

She said defiantly, 'Yes, I found out some. I heard that you were seen leaving the flat where Salvo stays. It suggests that he's your regular thug. Have you had people . . . hurt before, Clifford?'

'Go on, Clare. Most of this—'

'—I've given you an alibi for? Yes,' she said bitterly, 'so I have.'

'Which makes me wonder why, Clare darling, you're still hiring this prick.' He showed polite expectancy, teatime gossip. 'What *are* your reasons? Still raking over the accident? We've both agreed the death was a mistake, made by somebody I'd only hired to retrieve some documents.'

'No.' She was on the defensive, nothing to say.

'Then you are behaving in what I can only call an unprofessional manner. Am I right?'

'Whether I say yes or no, you'll assume it's yes,' she said, infuriated at his supercilious manner.

'On quite good evidence, darling. Your bank withdrawals would show two or three little holes. Correct?'

'I had to pay him for the information,' she said stubbornly, near defeat.

The doorbell rang. He started towards the curtains, then thought better of it. He went into the hall. Clare heard Hassall's voice cursing the rain, shoes stamped, a coat being shaken.

The came in together, Hassall frozen and bleary.

'Sorry, Dr Burtonall. Just a passing visit. This weather!'

'Welcome, Mr Hassall. Would you like a drink, something warm perhaps?'

'No, thank you. I'm too old-fashioned for all that caper.' He sat when bidden, exhaling like a much older man, his sly mannerism to deceive. Doubts were everywhere. 'Just been to a funeral today. Very sad.'

'You too?' She smiled in sympathy. 'I was just telling my husband that I was at the funeral of that murdered girl. I was with one of my patients, the priest who did the service.'

'Old Crossley? I know him,' Hassall lied affably. 'Nice old chap. In a hospice.' When Clare said nothing, he grunted. 'Ah. No doctor–patient disclosures.' He gave Clifford a wry glance. 'You didn't go, Mr Burtonall?'

'Me?' Clifford went smoothly on, 'No. I only just heard about it as you arrived. My wife and I,' he said, smiling towards Clare, 'practically lead separate lives these days. Rushing everywhere.'

'Very moving,' Hassall said. 'The girls she worked with, the goers – those are hired males, the equivalent of female prostitutes. Ladies,' he explained as if for Clare's benefit, 'need more secrecy for their goings-on than men. I often wonder how far they'd go, compromising their lives.'

'I felt sorry for her. Have you any idea who the perpetrator was?'

'Perp? One of our words, that, Dr Burtonall! "Suspect" is more usual, from the laity. There was a bloke. Salvo.' Hassall looked enquiringly at Clare. 'Did you say something, Dr Burtonall?'

'No.' Clare went to pour a drink. 'Sure you wouldn't like one?'

'No, ta. This Salvo was Marla's boyfriend. She consorted with Lana. It's supposed that Salvo found them together and did the deed. He went to nick a motor, hot-wired the car. Something went wrong, petrol exploded. We've identified the remains. Very messy.'

'This Salvo was the killer?'

'We believe Marla will finger him.'

'Poor girl.' Clare carried her sherry to her armchair. It would nauseate her if she drank any. 'I hope she recovers, Mr Hassall.'

'Isn't this where you say, "What were you doing on the night of the crime"?'

'What crime is that, Mr Burtonall?'

'The explosion. This Salvo's death?'

'I didn't say it was night, Mr Burtonall. But, yes, go through the motions. Just so's I can put down "Questioned suspects" on my clock sheet.'

'When was it, Mr Hassall?' Clare cut in easily before Clifford could speak.

'We may not be able to say precisely, but as a rule we have a fair idea, what with listed phone calls, and coded work data.'

'You started your survey. I remember that. I was here, and so was my husband. Weren't you, Clifford? I remember you were on the phone half the night. The cost! I'm sure they're not all necessary.'

'I was.' Clifford made himself sound regretful. 'I had a number of outstanding transatlantic calls to make, and got through them before . . .'

'Before, sir?' Hassall prompted.

Clifford stayed cool. 'Before they started calling back. It's always much easier to make the call armed with data than cope with an incoming call that catches you on the hop. They say in America: "It's your dime." '

'Clever folk, you investors,' Hassall said, rising.

'Don't you want us to sign your time sheet, Mr Hassall?'

'Not necessary, Dr Burtonall. Like me to sign yours?'

They made light humour of that as far as the door. Hassall left, looking up at the rain, ambling through the downpour to his car. Clare led the way back to the living room. She rounded on Clifford.

'Who'd you phone that night?'

He shrugged. 'You can't think I had anything to do with it, darling. If I had,' he said with dignity, 'don't you think Hassall would have asked outright? Look, Clare. You can't go blaming every crime on me because of that one accident. I never really knew this Salvo. I'd never even met him.' He displayed weariness. 'I'm tired. I swear I had nothing to do with Salvo, other than asking him to retrieve those documents. Naturally I wanted them back. Just as naturally I contacted an expert in that sort of thing.'

'Who just then decided to kill the poor man? Is that it?'

'No. Who accidentally caused Mostern to tumble over.' Clifford was indignant, far more emotional than Clare. 'God knows what the idiot was going to do – sell them to some rival, industrial espionage, who knows?'

'Why not tell Hassall?' Clare had been close to blurting it out.

'Because that would set him on me. I'd become his eternal suspect, Clare – like I've become yours. I'd be involved in court cases. You know how those things drag on.' He looked slyly at her with triumph in his eyes. 'Anyway, I have a sound alibi for both incidents, haven't I? Thanks to you.'

'Thanks to me,' she said bitterly.

'You're the only one who could finger me to Hassall.'

'What does that mean?'

'It means that I'm safe, darling. As are you. I keep quiet about your activities, whatever they are, and you remain a perfectly respectable doctor.'

'I see.' She saw him for the first time. Had she trusted him completely, she would never have asked Bonn to make the discoveries that he had. 'Are you proposing some sort of pact?'

'No, darling. Stating the obvious. We're inextricably linked. What's the cant phrase? Joined at the hip.'

He smiled, looking exactly as on the day they had met. Clare went to pour her drink away, and switched on the television. The news headline was that Marla had died of circulatory collapse that afternoon.

Clifford heaved a huge sigh. 'It's always bad news, isn't it, darling?' He spoke with ill-concealed triumph. 'I wonder if that was the reason that Hassall came round, one last despairing lunge?'

'God rest her,' Clare said, tears in her eyes.

'One thing, darling.' Clifford casually picked up a news-paper. 'I'm bidding for control of the Pleases Agency, Inc. Did your little friend tell you?'

'You're . . .?' She stared at him.

'Tomorrow, with any luck.' He winked at her, enjoying himself. 'We're sort of partners.'

Clare felt a stupefying loathing. Now she really was trapped. She would not even have Bonn to help her carry the burden.

37 | **Mogga dancing** – that type of ballroom competition dancing where each couple changes their dance rhythm to a different style every few bars, usually four to six, throughout a single melody.

T HE PLACE WAS sparse now. His few belongings were gone. Had he chosen so Spartan a room because it had the appearance of some Trappist cell? Possibly, but speculations required no answer. He was sad to leave the room, but it would be impossible to stay, the way things were.

He locked the door, left the key on old Mrs Corrigan's hall tray on the way out, and got a taxi by the drill hall.

Bonn talked with Rack fifteen minutes before he walked across to the building that held the Burtonall Investments office.

'What does it concern, Mr Fairbanks?' the receptionist asked.

'Mr Burtonall's personal investments. I have only ten minutes.'

Bonn went and stood by the fronded palms. He was taken through almost immediately.

Clifford Burtonall rose, extending his hand. Bonn evaded it.

'Would you please eliminate the recording, Mr Burtonall?'

'Recording?' Clifford gave a hearty laugh. 'I must say, Mr Fairbanks, you are certainly direct!'

Bonn waited in silence, then mouthed the word 'murder'. Clifford stilled, went through to the outer office for a moment, returned with a midget Dictaphone. He placed it on his desk. Bonn looked at it.

'No, Clifford.' Bonn stood. 'Goodbye. Take the consequences.'

Bonn was by the lift doors when Burtonall caught him up.

'I didn't come up the Mersey on a bicycle, Clifford.' Bonn wasn't exactly sure what the saying meant, but he'd often heard it used and the occasion seemed right. 'You have three cassette pods on the go. Showing me one is simply juvenile.'

'Look. I don't know who you are, but quite honestly—'

The lift came, crashed open. Bonn entered, pressed the button. The doors closed just after the investor darted in, flustered. He tried to persuade Bonn to return to the office, but Bonn said nothing, walked out into the street. He crossed over to the bus stop. Nobody else was waiting.

'Only,' Clifford was urging, 'it's regarded as normal business practice—'

'The murders, Clifford,' Bonn interrupted. 'Evidence has come to light linking you with the deaths of Mostern, and possibly with Lana and Marla. A witness saw you leave the flat, connecting you to Salvo.'

'Evidence?' Clifford went white. He was suddenly aware of Rebecca and Monica looking down from the office windows.

'Concealment will require your cooperation. You will forthwith abort the takeover of the Pleases Agency, Inc.'

'Wait.' A minibus was disembarking visitors to the Granadee Studios.

'No, Clifford. Tell Goldoni there are other groups in the city worthy of investment. He will go along.'

'Goldoni?' Clifford gaped, staring at Bonn. 'Who are you?'

'Nobody you will ever see again.'

Clifford saw the bus coming. He suddenly guessed, Clare's abrupt streetwise understanding.

'My wife. Are you a patient? Or from that agency?'

'Goldoni will comply, when you explain. The consequences will be at least as grave for him.' Bonn felt filled with lies. 'You may purchase any other business you wish. Goldoni's pleasures with rough renters can continue. And your bribes of the city aldermen.'

The bus slowed as it approached.

'What *is* this?' Burtonall was frantic to delay Bonn's departure.

'A threat, Clifford, nothing more.'

The bus left, Bonn on it and Burtonall staring after.

As he entered the main office, Rebecca and Monica were waiting. 'Who was that, Mr Burtonall?' Rebecca asked. 'Is he an investor? I ought to get his details.'

'Mmmmh?' Their expressions confirmed his guess. He went into his office.

Bonn dropped off to see Glazie and procured a blank card and an envelope. At the reception desk he wrote, 'You are invited to the finals of the Mogga Dancing. See press for details.' He numbered the card 395. She would know it was from him, the code number proof enough. He addressed the envelope to Dr C. S. Burtonall, at the hospital, and put it in the post. She would get it in the morning, and realise that he wished her to continue. Why, could be left for the future.

It felt odd, alighting in Bradshawgate. He paid the driver off and knocked.

Martina herself came to answer. She must have been waiting in the hallway, for Bonn hadn't heard her approach. There was no carpet, just a short rug thing down the linoleum. More light than there was at his digs, though.

'I bought two bulbs for Mrs Corrigan when I first went there,' he said, in case Martina had caught his glance and thought he was making comparisons. Martina's agency owned the digs he'd vacated. 'To light her stairwell.'

'Did she put them in? Or sell them?'

'I think she kept them for herself.'

'I heard that she's like that.'

'Maybe I'm maligning her.'

'Or not. Please go through.'

Bonn went ahead, measuring his pace to hers. Posser smiled a welcome.

'Thank you for letting me come,' Bonn said. He felt it important to go pedantically through formalities. 'I feel a refugee.'

'Don't, son.' Posser indicated a chair. 'It's all fixed.'

'Oh dear.' Bonn's frown made a joke of it.

'Nothing to be scared of. Martina makes the rules. I manage.'

'Which, from a picture of rude health,' Martina capped.

Bonn laughed, then felt he had to say he was sorry. Posser, amused, would have none of it.

'Look, Bonn. Make this easy as we can, eh? Martina is

glad you are here. I'm vastly relieved. We can cope with whatever happens.' He gestured, the city all around. 'I won't mince matters. I have hopes, now you've finally made the move—'

'Dad,' Martina said through clenched teeth.

'All right, love. Bonn understands. A father's got a natural worry. You're here now, Bonn, and can take part of the strain. It's only fair.'

'I'm not sure—'

'That's enough!' Martina cried in genuine anger. 'I'm not a liability to be talked about as if I'm not even here!' She composed herself, saw Bonn steel himself. 'Bonn. I'm glad the house has more company. Dad's not well, and his age. I'm relieved there's somebody here.' She made herself add, 'You.'

They waited, Bonn glad he wasn't being asked anything, Posser irritably wanting to speak but unwilling to irritate Martina further.

'In fact,' she continued, primly clasping her knees, daring her father to interrupt, 'I'm the one who suggested you.'

Bonn wondered if she was telling it as it was.

'Please note that your staying here means nothing more than convenience,' she went on. 'We have no doubts, Dad and I, that you are the right person.'

'Thank you, Martina.'

'None of us should read more into it than that,' she ended. 'It's a suitable arrangement. Are we agreed?'

'Yes.'

'For heaven's sake, Martina,' Posser said, losing patience. 'You'll be driving the lad away. Get the hooch out.'

She made no move. 'I suggest that each evening we keep one hour aside to review the day's activities, Bonn. Are you in agreement?'

'Yes. But what if I'm booked to—?'

'That can take second place to our nightly review,' she said.

'We never said anything about that, love,' Posser put in, puzzled.

'Client priority,' Bonn said, also worried.

'You have three goers, Bonn,' Martina said. 'They can manage. We must cross that bridge when we come to it.'

'What if—?' Posser started, but his daughter was there ahead of him.

'There's nothing against your taking on a fourth goer,' she said, smooth.

'There's the problem of other firms, Martina.'

'Yes, Bonn,' she said, smiling, 'but they will do as they are told.'

'It's a small problem,' Posser conceded, but with a doubtful look at Bonn.

'Your suitcase,' Martina said, closing the subject. 'Is that all you have?'

'Yes,' Bonn said. 'I'm sorry.'

It disconcerted her. She had told Osmund to have a van on stand-by. 'I hadn't realised. Perhaps tomorrow I ought to get you fitted out.' She glanced about. 'And I wonder if that armchair is really right, stuck there. Look. Perhaps we ought to settle you in.'

'When it's convenient,' Bonn said awkwardly. Pedantry had done little.

'Now is as good a time. Would you come?' She rose and went ahead. 'The small bathroom is yours. I'm afraid there isn't anywhere for you to do any secret cooking, if that's what you're into. You'll have to use the main kitchen. I'll show you it. Would you want your own phone?'

'No, thank you.'

'If you change your mind, just say.'

She stood formally at the top of the staircase.

'I'm very pleased that you have come to us, Bonn.' She avoided his eyes.

'As I am to be here.'

They stood in silence.

'Your room is to your right. What evening drink do you like?'

'Wine, if that's all right.'

'Very well.' She stood aside to let him pass, about to start down. 'We'll wait for you, and celebrate your arrival. We must learn about each other.'

'Of course.'

'If anything isn't quite to your liking here, please say.' She was a little breathless, but that must have been the stairs.

'You're very kind, Martina.'

She went down. Bonn opened the door of his room and switched on the light. He halted in astonishment.

The room was an exact replica of the one he'd just vacated. The only difference was its cleanliness, that and the door leading to the bathroom. The window, the one chair – could it be the very same one? How on earth? The bed was similar, single, narrow, except it was spotless.

He placed his suitcase on the carpet, and that too was similar to the threadbare one he had left behind, but new. It was a statement of conviction and an assurance all in one. It was his cell.

It was just right, and enough. He smiled, and said inwardly, 'Thank you, Martina.' He could go on as before. Perhaps all life was simply a kind of mogga dancing, one episode changing to another yet to one constant tune. It was a pretty metaphor. He would see Clare as and when, but be with Martina. That would be. For now, Grellie would have to wait, very much as he himself would have to see where feelings took him, now that his vows were utterly laid to rest. First thing tomorrow, he decided, he would visit old Father Crossley in his new hospice bed, and make a last farewell while the frail old theologian still had his faculties.

He switched off the light and, assured now, went downstairs to celebrate his coming to them. He lived here now.

Outside the small terraced house where Bonn had once lived, Hassall sat in his motor waiting for Windsor to come roaring up with some barmy ideas.

Bonn couldn't have been gone long. The room was empty, the key in the hall. Mrs Corrigan had no idea. The loyal old bitch would make sure of that.

He had two choices. Go to Posser's, try it on – except Posser was wily. They'd crossed swords once or twice. The sick old prat had lawyers like dogs had fleas. Or he could wait things out, see what the world spun for the city tomorrow.

The point was, what could he ask? Whether or not they had any suspicions? If they knew this or that? He could write their answers now: Heavens, Mr Hassall, no, we don't know a thing about a thing. The Burtonalls were different. He wouldn't be in her shoes for all the tea in China. Good luck to her, if she got a shag or two on the side. As long as she did nothing worse. Always hard for a wife, when her husband was into crime and justifying it every step of the way.

Very well, Hassall thought. Live your lives. Keep on. I'm here, and I'll have you, soon as there's enough evidence.

Maybe not for the crimes done, but for the ones that are to come. I'm here.

And, face it, shagging was no crime, so good luck.

If that's the worst you do, the world wouldn't be in such a bloody mess.

He saw Windsor's lights approaching, and just couldn't face all that frigging enthusiasm. He fired his engine, and drove home.

JONATHAN GASH

The Rich
and the
Profane

A Lovejoy Novel

What follows here is the first chapter from Jonathan Gash's
new novel, *The Rich and the Profane*, which is available in
hardback from Macmillan, priced £16.99.

1

SEEING A WOMAN get arrested makes you relieved it's not you. Except this time I'd really relied on Irma for today's dinner, so it was the pits. It's always the pits in the antiques game.

Irma had found me feeding my robin, a creature of psychotic jealousy. It flirted its beak, its tail, stood truculently four-square and made its kick-kick-kick sound. I told it to shut up. It took no notice, which is typical. Women, infants and animals treat me like a serf.

'Are you Lovejoy?' She gave me a photo of a necklace. 'I need your help.'

She looked beautiful and rich. I'd never seen her before. 'You want me to find an antique necklace like this? Easy. They're pretty common. Late Edwardian, semiprecious stones. Tourmaline's bonny, but these two smaller malachite greens are horrible.' I pointed to them. 'A lady's beautiful swan neck can only take so many absolute primary colours. Mind you, it's no good telling the Edwardians that.'

A cool lass, dressed for visiting a maiden aunt. Celtic, my old Gran would have said, black hair, radiant blue eyes, pale skin. Twenty, give or take, not much older.

'I don't want to buy, Lovejoy. I want to steal it.'

'Why steal something so ordinary? They're cheap.'

'This necklace is mine.' She said it with fervour, caught herself and read my tatty sign, *Lovejoy Antiques, Inc*. 'I expected your firm to be quite grand.'

I admit I don't impress. Crumbling thatched cottage, rickety porch, windows partly boarded from recent bailiff trouble, my old Austin Ruby rusting among weeds, and a workshop with rotting doors agape.

'It's in Gimbert's Auction. My aunt won't give it back.'

'Tomorrow's sale?' I tried to judge her without direct looks. 'Why not bid for it? It'll only be a few quid.'

Angrily she erupted, 'And give her the satisfaction? They said at the Antiques Arcade that you knew how to steal things.'

I sighed. East Anglia's famed reticence was in action. What with that and this girl's hate, they'd have the TV news cameras waiting for her. I still felt uncomfortable about it.

'Look, love. Once upon a time, a bloke in our next village got left his grandad's old motorbike. It was a 1954 AJS Porcupine – banned in its day for being too fast. He sold it for quarter of a million. Same day, a vicar in the next county sold a Thackeray chamber pot and went on a Mediterranean holiday from the proceeds. That famed author criticised the city of Cork, whose Victorian citizens put his face in their utensils. See? There's legit money in antiques, if you only look. But this necklace is ordinary, even if it is Edwardian.'

'Teach – me – to – steal,' she said, like to an infant.

Three things exist in the world of antiques, and only three. They're antiques, women and money. The trouble is, everybody knows – they say – everything about all three when they know nothing. In fact, knowledge is pretty useless. Give you an instance:

Last year, a famous university (don't tell anybody that it was Southampton) spent up psychoanalysing dogs. Their project: which dog is man's best pal? Their conclusion was (1) greyhound, (2) whippet, (3) the basset hound. So let's all rush to friendly neighbourhood kennels and buy, because now we know. Except there's one hitch. What if you prefer Buster, your lovable spaniel, instead of these? See? All that magnificent research can take a running jump. Knowledge is useful, up to a point. After that, it's what you *want*, irrespective that matters. That dog info, so expensively bought, is on a par with all sorts of other "essential facts". Like, the Indian elephant has a hell of a temper in the morning. And, the world's first recorded tornado occurred, guess when, in AD 1410, in – guess where? – Venice. And intrepid polar flyer Commander Richard E. Byrd, first human to fly over the North Pole, er, faked it. Didn't get within 100 miles of the Pole. The Norwegian Amundsen *really* did it in an airship less than a week later. I explained all this.

'Knowledge only goes so far, love.'

'Get on with it,' she said, lips tight.

'It's nothing to do with me, okay?' I couldn't afford another brush with the law. I'd not long squared Dunko for my last bail.

'Thank you, Lovejoy. I'll pay.' She held out a hand. 'Irma Dominick.'

We shook politely. 'Lovejoy.'

'One thing, please.' She hesitated. 'Is it true? And can you tell from a photo?'

They all ask this.

'Being a divvy? Yes.' Before she could start I went on,

'Genuine antiques – *genuine*, mind – make me feel odd. It's a rare gift.' That was a laugh. Gift? My 'gift' has caused me more trouble than any number of friends, police, fakers and dealers. 'Forgeries don't. And no, I can't tell from photographs.'

The answer seemed to be what she hoped for.

'How much will the lesson be, please?'

'Nothing,' I said, rising to begin. 'I'll teach you how to steal free of charge.' I like to spread culture.

In less than an hour I showed her how to confuse whifflers – auctioneers' grotty assistants. I explained how to obfuscate, distract, deflect, shuff – i.e. switch – items.

'Whatever you do, never protest, hit, scratch,' I warned. 'Theft is simply nicking something, which is what you're going to do, please. Robbery is utterly different. Robbery is stealing with force or fear. Law hates both, but robbery most. Got it?'

'No violence from me,' she said.

'And don't carry a coat over your arm,' I told her. 'Everybody'll just laugh at that old trick. It announces that you're a shoplifter.'

'What's the quickest way?' she demanded. 'I've not a lot of time.'

'It's called the plop. Carry a plastic bag with shopping in it.' I hadn't got one, so pretended. 'Hold it down, at arm's length, but not with your elbow flexed – that's another giveaway. Examine some trinket. Check there's nobody watching – pretend to tilt it, to scrutinise closer. Then you *seem* to replace it on the display trestle, but keep hold of it with your forefinger and middle fingers tight together.'

'And then leave?'

'No.' I struggled for patience. 'You let it slide down into your plastic bag, see? The plop.'

She was slow picking it up, but I drilled her.

'The advantage is that if anybody challenges you, go all flustered and say it must have fallen in accidentally. Don't, for God's sake, try to look cool. Make yourself frantic, shed tears, apologise a million times until they're sick to death of you. They'll let you go. Suspicions don't count.'

'But then I'll not have the necklace, Lovejoy, so then what'll I do?'

She had really bonny eyes. 'Send for me, love, and I'll do it.'

I saw her go into Gimbert's – auctioneers of no renown – and went to look around the shops bordering the town square. Pleasant, with colourful stalls and barrows, a fountain, children playing, a little band parping away. I'd only been there five minutes before I heard the rumpus, the shouts, and saw a constable extending his stride – bobbies are taught never to run, in case we realise they ought to move about more often. My heart sank. I listened to the hubbub, the excited chatter of shoppers. She'd done it wrong, and got caught.

Sad, I sat at a café table.

'No, ta, Ellie,' I said when the waitress came pestering.

'Was that you, Lovejoy? That fuss?'

'Don't be daft, I'm just passing.'

'It looked like that Irma you were with, Lovejoy.'

You have to put serfs down. 'I don't know the woman.' No cocks crowed.

'She shouted, "Tell Lovejoy to help me." I heard her. She was wrestling to get away.'

So much for my advice not to resist. 'It's a common name. Any tea?'

She glanced about the café. Porridge, her stout boss, a man of calamitous greed, stared out in case people weren't throwing money at his dingy business.

'Sorry, Lovejoy,' she said, and went on her way. Ellie's nice, but too mean to risk her livelihood for nothing. What happened to charity?

Freddy Foxheath found me. He was red-faced from running and flopped down breathless. The police van was just leaving, watched by gloaters rejoicing it wasn't them.

'Near thing, Lovejoy,' he puffed, like he'd been under shellfire. 'She'd almost got it in her handbag when that whiffler saw.'

'Saw?' I was appalled. She'd done the plop really quite well in my garden. 'What was she playing at?'

'Don't start, Lovejoy. You sent her in, not me.'

This is the thanks you get for doing favours.

'For God's sake, Freddy, it was a tiny necklace, not a Rolls.'

Irma Dominick was now a right pest. I seethed at my wasted effort. It's not like shoplifting, when you can be in and out like a fiddler's elbow. Antiques are different.

'She shouted to get you to help her.'

Thank you, Irma. 'Ellie told me.'

See what you get for being kind? And choosing Freddy Foxheath as Irma's cullet had been no great stroke of genius. A cullet's a look-out man, your protector while you're thieving. But standards are falling. Once, cullets were ten a penny. Now, you search all morning and get a deadleg like Freddy Foxheath. He's a horse-jawed dapper little bloke, lazy but with a knack of looking keen.

'What'll you do, Lovejoy?'

'Me?' I said, offended. 'For her? Nowt. Why should I?'

Irma Dominick was nothing to do with me.

'You two want serving?' Porridge's bulbous belly ballooned a yard ahead of his glare.

'Your coffee improved, has it?'

So I went to see Michaelis Singleton, a lawyer who was nearly struck off for putting sex and greed ahead of legal principles. As if everybody doesn't do that.

All Pan Books are available at your local bookshop or newsagent, or can be ordered direct from the publisher. Indicate the number of copies required and fill in the form below.

Send to: Macmillan General Books C.S.
              Book Service By Post
              PO Box 29, Douglas I-O-M
              IM99 1BQ

or phone: 01624 675137, quoting title, author and credit card number.

or fax: 01624 670923, quoting title, author, and credit card number.

or Internet: http://www.bookpost.co.uk

Please enclose a remittance* to the value of the cover price plus 75 pence per book for post and packing. Overseas customers please allow £1.00 per copy for post and packing.

*Payment may be made in sterling by UK personal cheque, Eurocheque, postal order, sterling draft or international money order, made payable to Book Service By Post.

Alternatively by Access/Visa/MasterCard

Card No. ☐☐☐☐☐☐☐☐☐☐☐☐☐☐☐☐☐☐

Expiry Date ☐☐☐☐☐☐☐☐☐☐☐☐☐☐☐☐☐☐

Signature _____

Applicable only in the UK and BFPO addresses.

While every effort is made to keep prices low, it is sometimes necessary to increase prices at short notice. Pan Books reserve the right to show on covers and charge new retail prices which may differ from those advertised in the text or elsewhere.

NAME AND ADDRESS IN BLOCK CAPITAL LETTERS PLEASE

Name _____

Address _____

_____

_____

_____

8/95

Please allow 28 days for delivery.
Please tick box if you do not wish to receive any additional information. ☐

Kipling's War

RUDYARD KIPLING

First published 2014

Amberley Publishing
The Hill, Stroud
Gloucestershire, GL5 4EP

www.amberley-books.com

British Library Cataloguing in Publication Data.
A catalogue record for this book is available from the British Library.

ISBN 978 1 4456 4043 3 (print)
ISBN 978 1 4456 4076 1 (ebook)

Typeset in 11pt on 14pt Minion.
Typesetting and Origination by Amberley Publishing.
Printed in the UK.

Contents

Editor's Note

This volume consists of a series of articles and pamphlets written by Rudyard Kipling during the First World War following visits to various fronts of the war, as well as a chapter from his history of the Irish Guards describing the first months of the fighting in France and Belgium in 1914. *The Irish Guards in the Great War* was published in two volumes (one for each of the regiment's battalions at the start of the war) in 1923. Kipling chose the Irish Guards particularly because his beloved son John had died serving with them at the Battle of Loos in September 1915, at the age of eighteen. *The New Army in Training* was a series of six articles written for the *Daily Telegraph* in the winter of 1914 about the training of the vast volunteer army that had enlisted following the declaration of war; the articles were published as a sixty-four-page pamphlet in early 1915. *France at War* is also based on a series of articles written for the *Daily Telegraph*, this time following a tour Kipling made along a part of the front line held by French troops; they were also published in the United States in the *New York Sun*. Published in the *Telegraph* in September 1915, these articles too were collected together in a pamphlet and re-issued. 'The Fringes of the Fleet' was originally published as six articles in November and December 1915; 'Tales of the Trade' appeared as three articles in June 1916; and 'Destroyers at Jutland' appeared as four articles in October 1916. These articles, originally published in the *Daily Telegraph*, were written for the Admiralty to explain what Britain's Navy, on which so much money had been spent before the war, was doing. They were published together in 1916 as *Sea Warfare*. The last of the pamphlets, *The War in the Mountains*, was first published as a series of articles in June 1917 following a trip Kipling made at the invitation of the British ambassador in Rome to see the front in the Alps where Italian troops were fighting the Austro-Hungarians.

Irish Guards: Mons to La Bassée (1914)

At 5 p.m. on Tuesday, 4 August, 1914, the 1st Battalion of the Irish Guards received orders to mobilise for war against Germany. They were then quartered at Wellington Barracks and, under the mobilisation scheme, formed part of the 4th (Guards) Brigade, Second Division, First Army Corps.

On the 12 August the Battalion entrained for Southampton at Nine Elms Station, each detachment being played out of the barracks to the station by the band. They were short one officer, as 2nd Lieutenant St. J. R. Pigott had fallen ill, and an officer just gazetted – 2nd Lieutenant Sir Gerald Burke, Bart. – could not accompany them as he had not yet got his uniform. They embarked at Southampton on a hot still day in the P&O S.S. *Novara*. This was a long and tiring operation, since everyone was new to embarkation-duty, and, owing to the tide, the ship's bulwarks stood 25 feet above the quay. The work was not finished till 4 p.m. when most of the men had been under arms for twelve hours. Just before leaving, Captain Sir Delves Broughton, Bart., was taken ill and had to be left behind. A telegram was sent to Headquarters, asking for Captain H. Hamilton Berners to take his place, and the *Novara* cleared at 7 p.m. As dusk fell, she passed H.M.S. *Formidable* off Ryde and exchanged signals with her. The battleship's last message to the Battalion was to hope that they would get 'plenty of fighting.' Many of the officers at that moment were sincerely afraid that they might be late for the war!

They reached Havre at 6 a.m. on August 13, a fiercely hot day, and, tired after a sleepless night aboard ship, and a long wait, in a hot, tin-roofed shed, for some missing men, marched 3 miles out of the town to Rest Camp No. 2 'in a large field at Sanvic, a suburb of Havre at the top of the hill.' Later, the city herself became almost a suburb to the vast rest-camps round it. Here they received an enthusiastic welcome from the French, and were first introduced to the wines of the country, for many maidens lined the steep road and offered bowls of drinks to the wearied.

Next day (August 14) the men rested a little, looking at this strange, bright France with strange eyes, and bathed in the sea. At eleven o'clock they entrained at Havre Station under secret orders for the Front. The heat broke in a terrible thunderstorm that soaked the new uniforms. The crowded train travelled north all day, receiving great welcomes everywhere, but no one knowing what its destination might be. After more than seventeen hours' slow progress by roads that were not revealed then or later, they halted at Wassigny, at a quarter to eleven on the night of August 15, and, unloading in hot darkness, bivouacked at a farm near the station.

On the morning of August 16 they marched to Vadencourt, where, for the first time, they went into billets. The village, a collection of typical white-washed tiled houses with a lovely old church in the centre, lay out pleasantly by the side of a poplar-planted stream. The 2nd Coldstream Guards were also billeted there; the Headquarters of the 4th Guards Brigade, the 2nd Grenadier Guards, and 3rd Coldstream being at Grougis. All supplies, be it noted, came from a village of the ominous name of Boue, which – as they were to learn through the four winters to follow – means 'mud.'

At Vadencourt they lay three days while the men were being inoculated against enteric. A few had been so treated before leaving Wellington Barracks, but, in view of the hurried departure, 90 per cent remained to be dealt with. The Diary remarks that for two days 'the Battalion was not up to much.' Major H. Crichton fell sick here.

On the 20 August the march towards Belgium of the Brigade began, *via* Etreux and Fesmy (where Lieutenant and Quartermaster Hickie went sick and had to be sent back to railhead) to Maroilles, where the Battalion billeted, August 21, and thence, *via* Pont sur Sambre and Hargnies, to La Longueville, August 22. Here, being then 5 miles east of Malplaquet, the Battalion heard the first sound of the guns of the war, far off; not knowing that, at the end of all, they would hear them cease almost on that very spot.

At three o'clock in the morning of August 23 the Brigade marched *via* Riez de l'Erelle into Belgian territory and through Blaregnies towards Mons where it was dimly understood that some sort of battle was in the making. But it was not understood that 80,000 British troops with 300 guns disposed between Condé, through Mons towards Binche, were meeting twice that number of Germans on their front, plus 60,000 Germans with 230 guns trying to turn their left flank, while a quarter of a million Germans, with close on a thousand guns, were driving in the French armies on the British right from Charleroi to Namur, across the Meuse and the Sambre. This, in substance, was the situation at Mons. It supplied a sufficient answer to the immortal question, put by one of the pillars of the Battalion, a drill sergeant, who happened to arrive from home just as that situation had explained itself, and found his battalion steadily marching south. 'What's all this talk about a retreat?' said he, and strictly rebuked the shouts of laughter that followed.

The Retreat from Mons

The Brigade was first ordered to take up a position at Bois Lahant, close to the dirtier suburbs of Mons which is a fair city on a hill, but the order was cancelled when it was discovered that the Fifth Division was already there. Eventually, the Irish Guards were told to move from the village of Quevy le Petit, where they had expected to go into billets, to Harveng. Here they were ordered, with the 2nd Grenadier Guards, to support the Fifth Division on a chalk ridge from Harmignies to the Mons road, while the other two battalions of the Brigade (the 2nd and 3rd Coldstream Guards) took up position north-east of Harveng. Their knowledge of what might be in front of them or who was in support was, naturally, small. It was a hot, still evening, no Germans were visible, but shrapnel fell ahead of the Battalion as it moved in artillery formation across the rolling, cropped lands. One single far-ranging rifle-bullet landed with a *phtt* in the chalk between two officers, one of whom turning to the other laughed and said, 'Ah! Now we can say we have been under fire.' A few more shells arrived as the advance to the ridge went forward, and the Brigade reached the seventh kilometre-stone on the Harmignies–Mons road, below the ridge, about 6 p.m. on 23 August. The Irish Rifles, commanded by Colonel Bird, D.S.O., were fighting here, and Nos. 1 and 2 Companies of the Irish Guards went up to reinforce it. This was the first time that the Battalion had been personally shelled and five men were wounded. The guns ceased about dusk, and there was very little fire from the German trenches, which were rather in the nature of scratch-holes, ahead of them. That night, too, was the first on which the troops saw a searchlight used. They enjoyed also their first experience of digging themselves in, which they did so casually that veterans would hold up that 'trench' as a sample of 'the valour of ignorance.' At midnight, the Irish Rifles were ordered to retire while the Irish Guards covered their retirement; but so far they had been in direct contact with nothing.

The Battalion heard confusedly of the fall of Namur and, it may be presumed, of the retirement of the French armies on the right of the British. There was little other news of any sort, and what there was, not cheering. On front and flank of the British armies the enemy stood in more than overwhelming strength, and it came to a question of retiring, as speedily as might be, before the flood swallowed what remained. So the long retreat of our little army began.

The large outlines of it are as follows: The entire British Force, First and Second Army Corps, fell back to Bavai – the First without serious difficulty, the Second fighting rear-guard actions through the day. At Brava the two Corps diverged, not to unite again till they should reach Betz on September 1. The Second Army Corps, reinforced by the Fourth Division, took the roads through Le Quesnoy, Solesme, Le Cateau, St Quentin, Ham, Nesle, Noyon, and Crépy-en-Valois; the First paralleling them, roughly, through Landrecies, Vadencourt, La Fère, Pasly by Soissons, and Villers-Cotterêts.

At two o'clock in the morning of August 24 the Battalion, 'having covered the retirement of all the other troops,' retired through the position which the 2nd and 3rd Coldstream Guards had taken up, to Quevy le Petit, where it was ordered, with the 2nd Grenadiers, to entrench another position to the north (from the third kilometre-stone on the Genly–Quevy le Petit road to the tenth kilometre-stone on the Mons–Bettignies road). This it did while the whole of the Second Division retired through the position at 4 p.m., the Battalion acting as rear-guard. Their notion of 'digging-in' was to cut fire-steps in the side of the handy bank of any road. At nine o'clock that night the Battalion 'came out of Belgium by the same road that it had marched into Belgium' through Blaregnies, past Bavai where the First and Second Army Corps diverged, and through La Longueville to Malgarni, where they bivouacked in an orchard 'having been forty-four hours under arms.' Here the first mail from England arrived, and was distributed by torchlight under the apple-trees in the warm night.

On the afternoon of August 25 the Battalion reached Landrecies, an unlovely, long-streeted town in closely cultivated country. The German pressure was heavy behind them, and that evening the 3rd Coldstream Guards on outpost duty to the north-west of Landrecies, on the Mormal road, were attacked, and, as history shows, beat off that attack in a night-fight of some splendour. The Battalion turned out and blocked the pavé entrance to the town with improvised barricades, which they lined, of stones, tables, chairs, carts, and pianos; relieved the Coldstream at 1.30 a.m., August 26; and once again covered the retirement of the Brigade out of the town towards Etreux. The men were very tired, so weary indeed that many of them slept by the roadside while waiting to relieve the Coldstreams. That night was the first they heard wounded men scream. A couple of Irish Guards officers, sleeping so deeply that only the demolition by shell-fire of the house next door waked them, were left behind here, but after twenty-four hours of fantastic and, at that time, almost incredible adventures, rejoined safely the next day. It was recorded also that one of the regimental drums was seen and heard going down Landrecies' main street in the darkness, strung on the fore-leg of a gun-horse who had stepped into it as a battery went south. A battalion cooker, the sparks flying from it, passed like a fire-engine hastening to a fire, and men found time to laugh and point at the strange thing.

At Etreux, where with the rest of the Brigade the Battalion entrenched itself after the shallow pattern of the time, it had its first sight of a German aeroplane which flew over its trenches and dropped a bomb that 'missed a trench by twenty yards.' The Battalion fired at it, and it 'flew away like a wounded bird and eventually came down and was captured by another division.' Both sides were equally inexperienced in those days in the details of air war. All that day they heard the sound of what they judged was 'a battle in the direction of Le Cateau.' This was the Second Army Corps and a single Division of the Third Corps under Smith-Dorrien interrupting our retirement to make a stand against four or more German Army Corps and 600 guns. The result of that action caused the discerning General von Kluck to telegraph that he held the Expeditionary Force 'surrounded by a ring of steel,' and Berlin behung itself with flags. This also the Battalion did not know. They were more interested in the fact that they had lost touch with the Second Division; and that their Commanding Officer had told the officers that, so far as he could make out, they were surrounded and had better dig in deeper and wait on. As no one knew particularly where they might be in all France, and as the night of the 26th was very wet, the tired men slept undisturbedly over the proposition, to resume their retreat next day (August 27) down the valley of the Sambre, through Vénérolles, Tupigny, Vadencourt, Noyales, to the open glaring country round Mont d'Origny where the broad road to St Quentin crosses the river. It was in reserve that day, and the next (August 28) was advance-guard to the Brigade as the retirement continued through Châtillon, Berthenicourt, and Moy to Vendeuil and the cross-roads west of the Vendeuil–La Fère road, while the Brigade marched on to Bertaucourt. After the Brigade had passed, the Battalion acted as rear-guard into Bertaucourt. Here No. 2 Company, under Major Stepney, was sent to Beautor to assist a section of the Royal Engineers in demolishing a bridge across the river there – an operation performed without incident – and in due course joined up with the Battalion again. By this time, the retreat, as one who took part in it says, had become 'curiously normal' – the effect, doubtless, of that continued over-exertion which reduces men to the state of sleep-walkers. There was a ten minute halt every hour, on which the whole Battalion dropped where it stood and slept. At night, some of them began to see lights, like those of comfortable billets by the roadside which, for some curious reason or other, could never be reached. Others found themselves asleep, on their feet, and even when they lay down to snatch sleep, the march moved on, and wearied them in their dreams. Owing to the heat and the dust, many suffered from sore feet and exhaustion, and, since ambulance accommodation was limited, they had to be left behind to follow on if, and as best, they could. But those who fell out were few, and the Diary remarks approvingly that 'on the whole the Battalion marched very well and march-discipline was good.' Neither brigade nor battalion commanders knew anything of what was ahead or behind, but it seemed that, since they could not get into Paris before the Germans and take first-class tickets to London, they would all be cut off and destroyed; which did not depress them unduly. At all events, the Battalion one evening forgot its weariness long enough to take part in the chase and capture of a stray horse of Belgian extraction, which, after its ample lack of manners and mouth had been proved, they turned over for instruction and reformation to the Transport.

From Bertaucourt, then, where the Battalion spent another night in an orchard, it marched very early on 30 August to Terny via Deuillet, Servais, Basse Forêt de Coucy, Folembray, Coucy-le-Château, then magnificent and untouched – all closer modelled country and, if possible, hotter than the bare lands they had left. Thence from Terny to Pasly, north-west of Soissons. Here they lay down by moonlight in a field, and here an officer dreamed that the alarm had been given and that they must move on. In this nightmare he rose and woke up all platoon-officers and the C.O.; next, laboriously and methodically, his own company, and last of all himself, whom he found shaking and swearing at a man equally drunk with fatigue.

On 31 August the Battalion took position as right flank-guard from 9 a.m. to 3 p.m. on the high ground near Le Murger Farm and bivouacked at Soucy. So far, there had been little fighting for them since Landrecies, though they moved with the comforting knowledge that an unknown number of the enemy, thoroughly provided with means of transportation, were in fixed pursuit, just on the edge of a sky-line full of unseen guns urging the British always to move back.

Villers-Cotterêts

On 1 September, the anniversary of Sedan, the Battalion was afoot at 2 a.m. and with the 2nd Coldstream Guards acted as rear-guard under the Commanding Officer, Lieut-Colonel the Hon. G. Morris. There had been heavy dew in the night, followed at dawn by thin, miserable rain, when they breakfasted, among wet lucerne and fields of stacked corn, on the edge of the deep Villers-Cotterêts beech-forests. They fell back into them on a rumour of advancing cavalry, who turned out to be troops of German infantry running from stack to stack and filtering into the forest on either flank. Their first position was the

Vivières Puiseux line, a little south-west of Soucy village:
the Battalion to the right of the Soucy–Villers–Cotterêts
road, and the Coldstream to the left on a front of not
more than a mile. Their second position, as far as can
be made out, was the Rond de la Reine, a mile farther
south, where the deep soft forest-roads from Soucy and
Vivières join on their way to Villers-Cotterêts. The enemy
ran in upon them from all sides, and the action resolved
itself into blind fighting in the gloom of the woods,
with occasional glimpses of men crossing the rides, or
firing from behind tree-boles. The Germans were very
cautious at first, because our fire-discipline, as we fell
back, gave them the impression that the forest was filled
with machine-guns instead of mere trained men firing
together sustainedly. The morning wet cleared, and the
day grew close and stifling. There was no possibility of
keeping touch or conveying orders. Since the German
advance-guard was, by comparison, an army, all that
could be done was to hold back as long as possible the
attacks on front and flank, and to retain some sense of
direction in the bullet-torn woods, where, when a man
dropped in the bracken and bramble, he disappeared. But
throughout the fight, till the instant of his death, Lieut-
Colonel the Hon. G. Morris, commanding the Battalion,
rode from one point to another of an action that was all
front, controlling, cheering, and chaffing his men. And so
that heathen battle, in half darkness, continued, with all
units of the 4th Brigade confusedly engaged, till in the
afternoon the Battalion, covered by the 2nd Coldstream,
re-formed, still in the woods, a mile north of the village
of Pisseleux. Here the roll was called, and it was found
that the following officers were missing: Lieut-Colonel

the Hon. G. Morris, Major H. F. Crichton, Captain C. A. Tisdall, Lieutenant Lord Robert Inns-Ker, 2nd Lieutenant Viscount Castlerosse, Lieutenant the Hon. Aubrey Herbert, and Lieutenant Shields, R.A.M.C.

Captain Lord Desmond FitzGerald and Lieutenant Blacker-Douglass were wounded and left with the field-ambulance. Lieut.-Colonel Morris, Major Crichton, and Captain Tisdall had been killed. The others had been wounded and captured by the Germans, who treated them with reasonable humanity at Villers-Cotterêts till they were released on September 12 by the French advance following the first Battle of the Marne. Colonel Morris's body was afterwards identified and buried with that of Captain Tisdall; and one long rustic-fenced grave, perhaps the most beautiful of all resting-places in France, on a slope of the forest off the dim road, near the Rond de la Reine, holds our dead in that action. It was made and has been religiously tended since by Dr. Moufflers, the Mayor of the town, and his wife.

The death of Colonel Morris, an officer beloved and a man noticeably brave among brave men, was a heavy loss to the Battalion he commanded, and whose temper he knew so well. In the thick of the fight during a lull in the firing, when some blind shellfire opened, he called to the men: 'D'you hear that? They're doing that to frighten you.' To which someone replied with simple truth: 'If that's what they're after, they might as well stop. They succeeded with *me* hours ago.'

As a matter of fact, the men behaved serenely, as may be proved by this tale. They were working their way, under rifle-fire, across an opening in the forest, when some of them stopped to pick blackberries that attracted their attention. To these their sergeant, very deliberately, said: 'I shouldn't mind them berries, lads. There's may be worrums in 'em.' It was a speech worthy of a hero of Dumas, whose town Villers-Cotterêts is, by right of birth. Yet once, during their further retirement towards Pisseleux, they were badly disconcerted. A curious private prodded a hornets' nest on a branch with his bayonet, and the inhabitants came out in force. Then there was real confusion: not restored by the sight of bald-headed reservists frantically slapping with their caps at one hornet while others stung them on their defenceless scalps. So they passed out of the darkness and the greenery of the forest, which, four years later, was to hide a great French Army, and launch it forth to turn the tide of 1918.

Their march continued until 11 p.m. that night, when the Battalion arrived at Betz, where the First and Second Army Corps rejoined each other once more. No supplies were received that night nor the following day (September 2), when the Battalion reached Esbly, where they bathed – with soap, be it noted – in the broad and quiet Marne, and an ox was requisitioned, potatoes were dug up from a field, and some sort of meal served out.

The Diary here notes 'Thus ended the retreat from Mons.' This is not strictly correct. In twelve days the British Army had been driven back 140 miles as the crow flies from Mons, and farther, of course, by road. There was yet to be a further retirement of some 15 miles south of Esbly ere the general advance began, but September 3 marks, as nearly as may be, slack-water ere the ebb that followed of the triumphant German tidal wave through Belgium almost up to the outer forts of Paris.

That advance had, at the last moment, swerved aside from Paris towards the southeast, and in doing so had partially exposed its right flank to the Sixth French Army. General Joffre took instant advantage of the false step to wheel his Sixth Army to the east, so that its line ran due north and east from Ermenonville to Lagny; at the same time throwing forward the left of his line. The British Force lay between Lagny and Cortecan, filling the gap between the Sixth and Fifth French Armies, and was still an effective weapon which the enemy supposed they had broken for good. But our harried men realised no more than that, for the moment, there seemed to be a pause in the steady going back. The confusion, the dust, the heat, continued while the armies manoeuvred for position; and scouts and aerial reconnaissance reported more and more German columns of all arms pressing down from the east and north-east.

On September 3 the 4th Brigade moved from Esbly, in the great loops of the Marne, through Meaux to the neighbourhood of Pierre Levée, where the Battalion fed once more on requisitioned beef, potatoes, and apples.

The Advance to the Aisne

Next day (September 4), while the British Army was getting into position in the process of changing front to the right, the 4th Brigade had to cover a retirement of the 5th Brigade between Pierre Levée and Le Bertrand, and the Battalion dug itself in near a farm (Grand Loge) on the Pierre Levée–Giremoutiers road in preparation for a rear-guard attack that did not arrive. They remained in position with what the Diary pathetically refers to as 'the machine-gun,' till they were relieved in the evening by the Worcesters, and reached bivouac at Le Bertrand at one o'clock on the morning of 5 September. That day they bivouacked near Fontenay, and picked up some much-needed mess-tins, boots, putties and the like with which to make good, more immediate waste.

On the 6th they marched through Rozoy (where they saw an old priest standing at the door of his church, and to him the men bared their heads mechanically, till he, openly surprised, gave them his blessing) to Mont Plaisir to gain touch between the First and Second Divisions of the English Army. Major Stepney, the C.O., reported to Headquarters 1st Brigade at 9 a.m. half a mile north-east of Rozoy. At the same moment cavalry scouts brought news of two enemy columns, estimated at a thousand each, approaching from the direction of Vaudoy. Nos. 3 and 4 Companies were ordered forward to prolong the line of the First Division, while Nos. 1 and 2 Companies 'with the machine-gun' entrenched themselves on the Mont Plaisir road.

In the afternoon Lieutenant the Hon. R. H. Alexander, reconnoitring with a platoon in the direction of the village of Villeneuve, which was to be occupied, reported a hostile battery at Le Plessis had fired on the Battalion and killed four men and wounded eleven. One of these, Sergeant O'Loughlin, died later. This was the Battalion's first fighting since Villers-Cotterêts, and they went into action while the bells of the quiet countryside rang for church. The battery was put out of action by our guns in half an hour, Villeneuve occupied without further opposition, and the Battalion bivouacked at Tonquin on the night of 6 September. The enemy had realised the threat to their flank in General Joffre's new dispositions, and under cover of rear-guard and delaying actions were withdrawing north all along their line.

On 7 September the Battalion made a forced march from Tonquin to Rebais, where there was a German column, but the advance-guard of the Brigade was held up at St Simeon till dark and the Battalion had to bivouac a couple of miles outside Rebais. The German force withdrew from Rebais on the afternoon of the 7th, and on the 8th the Brigade's advance continued through Rebais, northward in the direction of Boitron, which lay just across the Petit Morin River. Heavy machine-gun fire from some thick woods along the rolling ground, across the river, checked the advance-guard (the 3rd Coldstream) and the two companies of the Irish Guards who supported them. The woods, the river valley, and the village of Boitron were searched by our guns, and on the renewal of the attack the river was crossed and Boitron occupied, the enemy being heavily shelled as they retired. Here the Battalion re-formed and pressed forward in a heavy rainstorm, through a flank attack of machine-guns from woods on the left. These they charged, while a battery of our field-guns fired point-blank into the thickets, and captured a German machine-gun company of six guns (which seemed to them, at the time, a vast number), three officers, and ninety rank and file. Here, too, in the confusion of the fighting they came under fire of our own artillery, an experience that was to become familiar to them, and the C.O. ordered the companies to assemble at Ferme le Cas Rouge, a village near by where they bivouacked for the night. They proudly shut up in the farm-yard the first prisoners they had ever taken; told off two servants to wait upon a wounded major; took the parole of the two other officers and invited them to a dinner of chicken and red wine. The Battalion, it will be observed, knew nothing then except the observances of ordinary civilized warfare. 2nd Lieutenant A. Fitzgerald and a draft arrived that day.

This small affair of Boitron Wood was the Irish Guards' share of the immense mixed Battle of the Marne, now raging along all the front. Its result, and the capture of the machine-guns, cheered them a little.

The next five days – September 9 to 13 – had nothing but tedious marching and more tedious halts and checks, due to the congestion of traffic and the chaos in the villages that had been entered, sacked, defiled and abandoned by the enemy. The Marne was crossed on the 9th at Charly, where – the inhabitants said that the Germans detailed for the job had been too drunk to effect it – a bridge had been left ready for demolition, but intact, and by this means the First and Second Divisions crossed the river. The weather turned wet, with heavy showers; greatcoats had been lost or thrown aside all along the line of retreat; billets and bivouacs made filthy by the retreating Germans; and there was general discomfort, enlivened with continuous cannonading from the front and the appearance of German prisoners gathered in by our cavalry ahead. And thus, from the Marne the Battalion came by way of Trenel, Villers-sur-Marne, Cointicourt, Oulchy-le-Château, Courcelles and St Mard to the high banks of the Aisne, which they crossed by the pontoon bridge at Pont d'Arcy on the morning of September 14 and advanced to Soupir in the hollows under the steep wooded hills.

That day, the 2nd Grenadiers formed the advance-guard of the Brigade, followed by the 3rd Coldstream, the Irish Guards, and the 2nd Coldstream. After they had cleared Soupir village, the force was shelled and an attack was made by the 3rd Coldstream, the Irish Guards in support, on a steep ridge near La Cour de Soupir farm, which stood on the crest of the bluff above the river. The heavily wooded country was alive with musketry and machine-gun fire, and the distances were obscured by mist and heavy rain. The 3rd Coldstream, attacking the farm, found themselves outflanked from a ridge on their right, which was then attempted by three companies of the Irish Guards. They reached to within a couple of hundred yards of a wood cut up by rides, down which, as well as from the trenches, heavy rifle-fire was directed. Here Captain J. N. Guthrie (No. 2 Company) was wounded and Captain H. Hamilton Berners killed, while Lieutenant Watson, R.A.M.C., was shot and wounded at close quarters while attending a wounded man. Here, too, the Battalion had its first experience of the German use of the white flag; for Lieutenant J. S. FitzGerald with No. 8 Platoon and a party of Coldstream under Lieutenant Cotterel-Dormer found some 150 Germans sitting round haystacks and waving white flags. They went forward to take their surrender and were met by a heavy fire at 30 yards' range, which forced them to fall back. Lieutenant E. B. Greer, machine-gun officer, now brought up his two machine-guns, but was heavily fired at from cover, had all of one gun-team killed or wounded and, for the while, lost one gun. He reorganised the other gun-team, and called for volunteers from the Company nearest him to recover it. After dark Corporal Sheridan and Private Carney of No.

3 Company and Private Harrington, a machine-gunner of No. 1 Company, went out with him and the gun was brought in. A further advance was made in the afternoon to the edge of the wood in order to clear out the snipers who held it and commanded the cultivated fields outside. Towards dusk, Captain Lord Guernsey, who was Acting Quartermaster, reported himself to the C.O., who posted him to No. 2 Company, then engaged in clearing out the snipers, in place of Captain Guthrie, who had been wounded. He went forward to assist Captain Lord Arthur Hay in command, and both were immediately shot dead.

The Battalion bivouacked in battle-outpost formation that night on the edge of the wood, and got into touch with the 60th Rifles on their right and the 2nd Grenadiers on their left. Here, though they did not know it, the advance from the Marne was at an end. Our forces had reached the valley of the Aisne, with its bluffs on both sides and deep roads half hidden by the woods that climbed them. The plateaux of the north of the river shaped themselves for the trench warfare of the years to come; and the natural strength of the positions on the high ground was increased by numberless quarries and caves that ran along it.

The Halt at Soupir

On 15 September, patrols reported that the enemy had fallen back a little from his position, and at daylight two companies entrenched themselves on the edge of the wood. Judged by present standards those trenches were little more than shallow furrows, for we did not know that the day of open battle was ended, and it is curious to see how slowly our people broke themselves to the monotonous business of trench construction and maintenance. Even after they had dug the casual ditch which they called a trench, it cost some time and a few lives till they understood that the works could not be approached in the open as had been war's custom. Their first communication-trench was but 300 yards long, and it struck them as a gigantic and almost impossible 'fatigue.'

The enemy had not fallen back more than 1,000 yards from the Cour de Soupir farm which they were resolute to retake if possible. They fired on our burying-parties and shelled the trenches all through 16 September. Patrols were sent out at dawn and dusk – since any one visible leaving the trenches was fired upon by snipers – found hostile infantry in full strength in front of them, and the Battalion had to organise its first system of trench-relief; for the Diary of 18 September remarks that 'Nos. 1 and 4 Companies relieved 2 and 3 Companies in the trenches and were again shelled during the day.'

Sniping on Hun lines was a novel experience to the Battalion. They judged it strange to find a man apparently dead, with a cloth over his face, lying in a hollow under a ridge commanding their line, who turned out to be quite alive and unwounded. His rifle was within short reach, and he was waiting till our patrols had passed to get to his work. But they killed him, angrily and with astonishment.

On the morning of 18 September Lieut-Colonel Lord Ardee, Grenadier Guards, arrived and took over command from Major Stepney.

The trench-war was solidifying itself; for the Diary of that same day notes that the enemy 'shelled the trenches and the two howitzer-guns which were in position below.' Ours was an army, then, which could count and place every gun that it owned. As many as three howitzer batteries per division had accompanied the Expeditionary Force, and more were being sent from home.

The night of the 19th was very wet. They were relieved by the 3rd Coldstream, and went into billets at Soupir, 'having been in the trenches for five days.' There was an alarm in the afternoon, and the machine-guns and 100 men of No. 1 Company were sent to help the Coldstream in the trenches, while the rest of the Battalion marched at 6 p.m. to be ready to assist the 2nd Grenadiers on the left of Cour de Soupir farm. Only 'the machine-guns,' however, came into action, and the Battalion returned to its billets at 10 p.m.

Much the same sort of thing occurred on the 20th – a furious fusillade from the trenches, the despatch of reinforcements up a 'muddy lane,' not yet turned into a communication-trench, to help the 3rd Coldstream, while Nos. 2 and 4 Companies went out to reinforce the Oxfordshire Light Infantry and to hold the road at the back of it 'in case of a retirement,' and the rest of the Battalion with the machine-guns stayed as a reserve in Soupir market-square. But beyond shrapnel bursting over the village and the wounding of two men by stray machine-gun bullets, there were no special incidents. Major G. Madden this day had to return to England, ill.

On the 21st the Battalion relieved the 2nd Grenadiers on the left at Soupir farm at 3.30 a.m. – the safest hour, as experience was to prove, for reliefs. Nos. 2 and 3 Companies were in trenches, and Nos. 1 and 4 about 300 yards in the rear, with the Headquarters in one of the caves, which are a feature of the country. The word 'dug-out' had not yet been invented. The nearest approach to it is a reference in a private letter to 'a shelter-recess in the side of the trench to protect one from shrapnel.' The Diary marks that the 'usual alarms occurred at 6.30 when the patrol went out and the enemy fired a good deal of shrapnel without effect.' Soupir, like many French villages, was full of carefully planted spies of singular audacity. One was found in an officer's room. He had appeared from a cellar, alleging that he was an invalid, but as the Gunners' telephone-wires near the cellar had been cut and our movements had been reported to the enemy with great regularity, his explanation was not accepted, nor were his days long in that land.

Patrols, too, were elastic affairs. One of them, under Lieutenant R. H. Ferguson, went out on the night of the 21st, came on the enemy's trenches half a mile out, lay down to listen to the conversation there, were all but cut off by a wandering section of snipers, and returned to their lines unmolested, after the lieutenant had shot the leading pursuer with his revolver.

On 22 September the Battalion – both entrenched and in reserve in the caves behind – experienced four hours' high-explosive howitzer fire, which 'except for the effect on the nerves, did very little damage.' (They had yet to learn what continuous noise could do to break men's nerve.) This was followed by a heavy fusillade, varied by star-shells, rockets, and searchlights, which lasted intermittently throughout the night. The rocket-display was new to the men. Searchlights, we know, they had seen before.

On the 23rd a telephone-line between Battalion Headquarters and the advanced trenches was installed (for the first time). Nos. 2 and 3 Companies relieved Nos. 1 and 4 in the trenches, and a man bringing back a message from No. 4 Company was killed by a sniper. The Battalion was relieved by the 3rd Coldstream in the evening and returned to its billets in the barns and lofts of Soupir village, where next day (September 24) the Diary observes they spent 'a quiet morning. The men got washed and shaved, and company officers were able to get at their companies. There are so many new officers who do not know their men that any rest day should be made use of in this manner.' They relieved the 3rd Coldstream again that evening, and 'digging operations to improve existing trenches and make communication-trenches were at once begun.'

Snipers were active all through 25 September. The trenches were heavily shelled in the afternoon, and 'one man was hit in the leg while going to fetch water.' They returned to Soupir in the evening and spent the 26th standing to, in anticipation of enemy attacks which did not develop into anything more than an artillery duel, and in digging trenches for the defence of Soupir village. This work, however, had to be stopped owing to heavy shell-fire brought to bear on the working-parties – presumably through information from the many spies – and after a wearing day relieved the 3rd Coldstream in the trenches at night. The Diary gives no hint of the tremendous strain of those twenty-four hours' 'reliefs' from being shelled in a trench to being shelled in a village, nor of the inadequacy of our artillery as it strove to cope with the German guns, nor of the rasping irritation caused by the knowledge that every disposition made was reported almost at once to the enemy.

On September 27 – a Sunday – the enemy's bands were heard playing up and down the trenches. Some attempt was made by a British battalion on the right to move out a patrol covered by the fire of No. 2 Company, but the enemy shells and machine-guns smothered every movement.

On 28 September (their day in billets) stakes were cut out of the woods behind Soupir, while the Pioneers collected what wire they could lay hands on, as 'the Battalion was ordered to construct wire entanglements in front of their trenches tonight.' The entanglements were made of two or three strands, at the most, of agricultural wire picked up where they could find it. They heard heavy fighting throughout the night on their right – 'probably the First Division.' Both sides by now were feeling the strain of trench-work, for which neither had made preparations, and the result was an increasing tension manifesting itself in wild outbursts of musketry and artillery and camp rumour of massed attacks and breaks-through.

On 30 September, F.M. Lord Roberts's birthday, a congratulatory telegram was sent to him; and 'a great quantity of material was collected out of which huts for the men could be built.' These were frail affairs of straw and twig, half dug in, half built out, of the nearest banks, or placed under the lee of any available shelter. The very fabric of them has long since been overlaid with strata of fresh wreckage and the twig roofs and sides are rotted black under the grass or ploughed in.

The month closes with the note that, as it was a very bright moonlight night, the Battalion's usual relief of the Coldstream was 'carried out up the communication-trenches.' Some men still recall that first clumsy trench-relief.

October 1 was spent in perfecting communication-trenches and shelters, and 'the Brigadier came up in the morning and was taken round the trenches.' Two officers were sent to Chavonne to meet the 5th Brigade – one to bring the Worcesters to the Battalion's trenches, the other to show the Connaught Rangers their billets in Soupir. The 3rd Coldstream marched out of Soupir and took up the line to the left of the 2nd Grenadiers near Vailly, and next day, 2nd October, No. 1 Company of the Irish Guards dug a connecting-trench between those two. Otherwise, for the moment, life was smooth.

It may be noted for the instruction of generations to come that some of the Reservists grumbled at orders not to talk or smoke in the trenches, as that drew fire; and that a newly appointed platoon-officer, when he had admonished them officially, fell them out and informed them unofficially that, were there any more trouble, he would, after the C.O. had dealt with the offenders, take them on for three rounds 'boxing in public.' Peace and goodwill returned at once.

On 3 October, a platoon was despatched to help the Royal Engineers in the construction of a road across a new bridge they had put up between Soupir and Chavonne. The Battalion relieved the 3rd Coldstream in its new position three-quarters of a mile east of Vailly, and next day 'quietly improved trenches and head-cover,' which latter is mentioned for the first time. It was all casual timber picked up off the countryside.

On 5 October a patrol explored through the wood, in front of the right trenches, but found only dead Germans to the number of thirty and many half buried, as well as five British soldiers killed in some lost affair of a fortnight before. Private O'Shaughnessy, No. 1 Company, was shot dead by a sniper when on observation-post at the end of this wood. He had only arrived that morning with a draft of 100 men, under Lieutenant Gore-Langton, and had asked to be allowed to go out on this duty. In the afternoon three shells burst on the road near Battalion Headquarters, and fatally wounded Lieutenant G. Brooke, who was on his way to Soupir to take over the transport from Lieutenant E. J. Gough. He was sent in to Braisne, where he died on 7 October. The Diary notes 'he would not have been found so soon had not the shells broken the telephone-wire to Headquarters. A message was coming through at the time and when communication was stopped the Signalling Sergeant sent two men to repair the wire and they found him.' He was brought in to the A.D.S. at Vailly-sur-Aisne by his own men, who made the R.A.M.C. stretcher-bearers walk behind as they would allow none but themselves to carry him. They bade him farewell before they returned to their trenches, and went out openly weeping. When he was sent to Braisne that evening, after being dressed, his own men again got an ambulance across the pontoon-bridge, which had been hitherto reckoned impassable, for his convenience. His last words to them were that they were to 'play the game' and not to revenge his death on the Hun.

On the afternoon of 6 October, which was cold and misty, the Germans pushed a patrol through the wood and our standing-patrol went out and discovered one German under-officer of the 64th (Imperial Jager Guards) dead, and the rifle of another man.

The enemy sent out no more patrols. Men had grown to be cunning among the timber, and noticed every tree they moved under. When the Coldstream relieved the Battalion that night, one of our patrols found a felled tree had been carefully placed across their homeward path by some unknown hand – it might have been the late Jager under-officer – who had expected to attack the patrol while it was climbing over the obstacle.

On the 7th the Battalion rested in Soupir all day, and on the 8th, Lieutenant G. Brooke's body was brought in from Braisne and buried in Soupir cemetery.

The 9th was a quiet day except for an hour's shelling, and a good deal of cheering from the German trenches in the evening, evidently in honour of the fall of Antwerp. It annoyed our men for the reason that they could not retaliate. Our guns had not a round to throw away.

The Move Toward the Sea

The opposing lines had been locked now for close upon a month and, as defences elaborated themselves, all hope of breaking-through vanished. Both sides then opened that mutually outflanking movement towards the west which did not end till it reached the sea. Held up along their main front, the Germans struck at the Flanders plain, the Allies striving to meet the movement and envelop their right flank as it extended. A British force had been sent to Antwerp; the Seventh Division and the Third

Cavalry Division had been landed at Zeebrugge on 7 October with the idea of helping either the Antwerp force or co-operating with the Allied Armies as circumstances dictated. Meantime, the main British force was being held in the trenches of the Aisne 120 miles away; and it seemed good to all concerned that these two bodies of British troops should be consolidated, both for purposes of offence, command and, by no means least, supply, on the Flanders flank covering the Channel.

There were obvious dangers in moving so many men from high ground across a broad river under the enemy's eye. It could only be effected at night with all precautions, but as the western pressure developed and was accentuated by the fall of Antwerp, the advantage of the transfer outweighed all risk. Our cavalry moved on 3 October by road for Flanders, and a few days later the infantry began to entrain for St Omer. The Second Corps was the first to leave, the Third Corps followed, and the First was the last.

Orders came to the Battalion on Sunday, October 11, to be prepared to move at short notice, and new clothes were issued to the men, but they did not hand over their trenches to the French till 13 October, when they marched to Perles in the evening and entrained on the 14th at Fismes a little after noon, reaching Hazebrouck via (the route is worth recording) Mareuil-sur-Ourcq, Ormoy, St Denis, outside Paris, Epluches, Creil, Amiens (10.15 p.m.), Abbeville (3.15 a.m.), Etaples, Boulogne, Calais and St Omer, every stone of which last six was to be as familiar to them as their own hearths for years to come.

At 5 p.m. on the 15th the Battalion went into billets at Hazebrouck. It was a sharp change from the soft wooded bluffs and clean chalky hills above the Aisne, to the slow ditch-like streams and crowded farming landscape of Flanders. At Hazebrouck they lay till the morning of the 17th, when they marched to Boeschepe, attended church parade on Sunday the 18th, and marched to untouched Ypres via St Kokebeele, Reninghelst and Vlamertinghe on the 20th with the Brigade, some divisional troops and the 41st Battery, R.F.A. The Brigade halted at Ypres a few hours, seeing and being impressed by the beauty of the Cloth Hall and the crowded market-place. The 2nd Coldstream and the 2nd Battalion Grenadiers being eventually sent forward, the remainder of the Brigade billeted in St Jean, then described impersonally as 'a small village about one and a half kilometres east of Ypres.' They halted at the edge of the city for dinner, and the men got out their melodeons and danced jigs on the flawless pavé. Much firing was heard all day, and 'the 2nd Coldstream came into action about 4 p.m. and remained in the trenches all night.'

That was the sum of information available at the moment to the Battalion – that, and orders to 'drive the enemy back wherever met.' So they first were introduced to the stage of the bloody and debatable land which will be known for all time as 'The Salient.'

The original intention of our Army on the Flanders flank had been offensive, but the long check on the Aisne gave the enemy time to bring forward troops from their immense and perfectly prepared reserves, while the fall of Antwerp – small wonder the Germans had cheered in their trenches when the news came! – released more. Consequently, the movement that began on the Allies' side as an attempt to roll up the German right flank before it could reach the sea, ended in a desperate defence to hold back an overwhelmingly strong enemy from sweeping forward through Belgium to Calais and the French sea-board. Out of this defence developed that immense and overlapping series of operations centring on Ypres, extending from the Yser Canal in the north to La Bassée in the south, and lasting from mid-October to 20 November 1914, which may be ranked as the First Battle of Ypres.

It will be remembered that the Second and Third British Army Corps were the first to leave the Aisne trenches for the west. On 11 October the Second Army Corps was in position between the Aire and Béthune and in touch with the left flank of the Tenth French Army at La Bassée.

On 12 October the Third Army Corps reached St Omer and moved forward to Hazebrouck to get touch with the Second Army Corps on its right, the idea being that the two corps together should wheel on their own left and striking eastward turn the position of the German forces that were facing the Tenth French Army. They failed owing to the strength of the German forces on the spot, and by October 19, after indescribably fierce fighting, the Second and Third Army Corps had been brought to a standstill on a line, from La Bassée through Armentières, not noticeably differing from the position which our forces were destined to occupy for many months to come. The attempted flank attacks had become frontal all along the line, and in due course frontal attacks solidified into trench-warfare again.

North of Armentières, the situation had settled itself in much the same fashion, flank attacks being outflanked by the extension of the enemy's line, with strenuous frontal attacks of his daily increasing forces.

The Seventh Division – the first half of the Fourth Army Corps – reached Ypres from Dixmude on 14 October after its unsuccessful attempt to relieve Antwerp. As the First Army Corps had not yet come up from the Aisne, this Division was used to cover the British position at Ypres from the north; the infantry lying from Zandvoorde, on the south-east, through Zonnebeke to Langemarck on the north-west. Here again, through lack of numbers and artillery equipment, the British position was as serious as in the south. Enemy forces, more numerous than the British and Belgian armies combined, were bearing down on the British line from the eastward through Courtrai, Iseghem, and Roulers, and over the Lys Bridge at Menin. Later on, it was discovered that these represented not less than five new Army Corps. The Seventh Division was ordered to move upon Menin, to seize the bridge over the river and thus check the advance of further reinforcements. There were, of course, not enough troops for the work, but on 18 October the Division, the right centre of which rested on the Ypres–Menin road, not yet lined throughout with dead, wheeled its left (the 22nd Brigade) forward. As the advance began, the cavalry on the left became aware of a large new German force on the left flank of the advance, and fighting became general all along the line of the Division.

On 19 October the airmen reported the presence of two fresh Army Corps on the left. No further advance being possible, the Division was ordered to fall back to its original line, an operation attended with heavy loss under constant attacks.

On 20 October the pressure increased as the German Army Corps made themselves felt against the thin line held by the Seventh Division, which was not amply provided with heavy batteries. Their losses were largely due to artillery fire, directed by air-observation, that obliterated trenches, men, and machine-guns.

On 21 October the enemy attacked the Division throughout the day, artillery preparations being varied by mass assaults, but still the Division endured in the face of an enemy at least four times as strong and constantly reinforced. It is, as one writer says, hardly conceivable that our men could have checked the enemy's advance for even a day longer, had it not been for the arrival at this juncture of the First Army Corps. Reinforcements were urgently needed at every point of the British line, but, for the moment, the imminent danger lay to the north of Ypres, where fresh German forces, underestimated as usual, might sweep the Belgian army aside and enter the Channel ports in our rear. With this in mind, the British Commander-in-Chief decided to use the First Army Corps to prolong the British line, already, as it seemed, nearly worn through, toward the sea, rather than to strengthen any occupied sector. He posted it, therefore – until French reinforcements should arrive – to the north, or left of the Seventh Division, from Zonnebeke to Bixschoote.

Our front at that date ran from Hollebeke to Bixschoote, a distance, allowing for bends, of some 16 miles. To protect this we had but three depleted Infantry Divisions and two Cavalry Brigades against opposed forces of not less than 100,000. Moreover, the ground was hampered by the flight, from Roulers and villages in German possession, of refugees, of whom a percentage were certainly spies, but over whom it was impossible to exercise any control. They carried their goods in little carts drawn by dogs, and they wept and wailed as they straggled past our men.

The Salient and the First Battle of Ypres

The orders for the Guards Brigade on October 21 to 'drive back the enemy wherever met' were not without significance. All their news in billets had been of fresh formations coming down from the north and the east, and it was understood that the Germans counted with confidence upon entering Calais, via Ypres, in a few days.

The Brigade, less the 2nd Coldstream, 'assembled in a field about 4 kilometres along the Ypres–Zonnebeke Road, and after a wait of three hours, No. 4 Company of the 1st Irish Guards advanced to the support of the 2nd Grenadiers, who had been ordered to prolong the line to the right of the 2nd Coldstream. This company and both the advanced battalions suffered somewhat severely from shell-fire and occasional sniping.' Thus coldly does the Diary enter upon what was in fact the first day of the First Battle of Ypres, in which companies had to do the work of battalions, and battalions of brigades, and whose only relief was a change of torn and blood-soaked ground from one threatened sector of the line to the next.

It was not worthwhile to record how the people of Ypres brought hot coffee to the Battalion as it passed through, the day before (October 20); and how, when they halted there a few hours, the men amused their hosts by again dancing Irish jigs on the clattering pavements while the refugees clattered past; or how it was necessary to

warn the companies that the enemy might attack behind
a screen of Belgian women and children – in which case
the Battalion would have to fire through them.

On the evening of 21 October the Battalion was
ordered up to the support of what was left of the 22nd
Brigade which had fallen back to Zonnebeke. 'It came
under a heavy burst of artillery fire and was forced to lie
down (in a ploughed field) for fifteen minutes' – at that
time a novel experience. On its way a hare started up
which was captured by a man of No. 2 Company to the
scandal of discipline and the delight of all, and later sold
for five shillings. At Zonnebeke it found No. 4 Company
already lining the main road on the left of the town and
took up a position in extended order on its right, 'thus
establishing the line into Zonnebeke.' The casualties, in
spite of the artillery fire, are noted as only 'one killed and
seven wounded,' which must have been far under the
mark. The night was lit by the flames of burning houses,
by which light they hunted for snipers in haystacks round
the village, buried stray dead of a battalion of the Seventh
Division which had left them and, by order, did a deal of
futile digging-in.

The next day the 22nd Brigade retired out of Zonnebeke
about a kilometre down the main road to Ypres, the
Battalion and half the 2nd Coldstream conforming to
the movement. This enabled the Germans to enter the
north of Zonnebeke and post machine-guns in some
of the houses. None the less, our patrols remained in
the south end of the town and did 'excellent work'; an
officer's patrol, under Lieutenant Ferguson, capturing
three mounted orderlies. One man was killed and eight
wounded in the Battalion that day.

On 23 October 'the enemy brought up more machine-guns and used them against us energetically all the day.' A platoon of No. 1 Company, under Lieutenant the Hon. H. Alexander, attempted an outflanking movement through Zonnebeke, towards the church, supported by a platoon of No. 4 Company, under Lieutenant W. C. N. Reynolds, in the course of which the latter officer was wounded. The trenches were shelled with shrapnel all the afternoon, and a German advance was sprayed down with our rifle-fire. In the evening the French made an attack through Zonnebeke helped by their 75s and established themselves in the town. They also, at 9 p.m., relieved the Battalion which moved at once south-west to Zillebeke and arrived there at 2 a.m. on the morning of the 24th, when it billeted 'chiefly in a brick-yard' ready to be used afresh.

The relieving troops were a division of the Ninth French Army Corps. They took over the line of our Second Division, while our Second Division in turn took over part of the front of the Seventh Division. At the same time French Territorials relieved our First Division between Bixschoote and Langemarck, thus freeing us of all responsibility for any ground north of the Ypres–Zonnebeke road. Our Army on 24 October, then, stood as follows: From the Zonnebeke road to a point near the race-course in the historic Polygon Wood west of Reutel was the Second Division; on its right, up to the Menin road, lay the First Division; and from the Menin road to Zandvoorde the Seventh Division with the 3rd Cavalry Brigade in the Zandvoorde trenches. Our line had thus been shortened and strengthened; but the enemy were continuously receiving reinforcements from Roulers and Menin, and the pressure never ceased.

In the early morning of 24 October, and before the transfer of all the troops had been effected, the British Ypres front was attacked throughout in force and once more the shock of the attack fell on the remains of the Seventh Division. Reserves there were none; each battalion stood where it was in the flood and fought on front, flank, and rear indifferently. The Irish Guards had a few hours' rest in the brick-fields at Zillebeke, where, by some miracle, it found its mail of home-letters and parcels waiting for it. Even before it could open them it was ordered out from Zillebeke along the Ypres–Menin road to Hooge to help the 20th Brigade (Seventh Division), which had been attacked on the morning of 25 October, and parties of the enemy were reported to have broken through into Polygon Wood.

That attack, however, was repulsed during the day, and in the evening the Battalion was despatched to act in support of the 5th Brigade near Race-course (Polygon) Wood, due north of Veldhoek, where the Battalion bivouacked for the night in a ploughed field. This was the first time it had marched up the Menin road or seen the Château of Hooge, of which now no trace remains, sitting stately among its lawns.

On 25 October, after a heavy bombardment, as bombardments were then reckoned, the whole Division was ordered at dawn to advance against Reutel; the 2nd Grenadier Guards and the Irish Guards being given the work of clearing out Polygon Wood, of which the enemy held the upper half. They were advancing through the woods, and the trenches of the Worcester Battalion there, when a big shell burst in Lieutenant Ferguson's platoon, No. 3 Company, killing four and wounding nine men, as far as was known. Ferguson himself, knocked down but unwounded, went back to advise No. 2 Company coming up behind him to deviate a little, 'for the ground was a slaughter-house.' The Battalion fought its way to a couple of hundred yards north of Reutel and was then brought under heavy rifle-fire from concealed trenches on a ridge. The 2nd Grenadiers on the right had, earlier, been held up by a German trench on their left, and, as dark came on, touch between the battalions there was lost, and the patrol sent out to regain it only stumbled on the German trench. The left of the Battalion lost touch by nearly a quarter of a mile with the 5th Brigade, and as the wet night closed in they found themselves isolated in darkness and dripping autumn undergrowth, with the old orders 'to hold ground gained at all costs.' Meantime they hung with both flanks in the air and enemy patrols on either side. The nearest supports of any kind were the trenches of the Worcesters, 600 yards behind, through the woods; so the Battalion linked up with them by means of a double front of men, back to back, strung out tail-wise from their bivouac to the Worcesters. The manoeuvre succeeded. There was sniping all night from every side, but thanks to the faithful 'tail' the enemy could not get round the Battalion to make sure whether it was wholly in the air. The casualties this day were reported as four killed and twenty-three wounded.

At 4 a.m. on 26 October, just after the night's rain had ceased, word came from Brigade Headquarters that the 3rd Coldstream were to be expected on the Battalion's right. They arrived an hour and a half later and the Battalion attacked, again to be held up in a salient heavily enfiladed from every angle by machine-guns, and though No. 2 Company carried a couple of farm-houses outside the woods, they were forced to retire from one of them and lost heavily. An attack by the 6th Brigade in the afternoon relieved the pressure a little, and helped the Battalion to get in touch with, at least, its brigade. Lieutenant Shields (R.A.M.C. attached) was killed here while attending our wounded. He had been remonstrated with only a few minutes before for exposing himself too much, and paid as much heed to the rebuke as did the others who succeeded him in his office. The casualties for the day were one officer and nine men killed and forty-two wounded. The night was memorable inasmuch as the Battalion, which had had no food for forty-eight hours, was allowed to eat its emergency rations.

There was a German attack on the night of 27 October, lasting for less than an hour, but the advance of the 6th Brigade on the Battalion's left, together with the advance of the French still farther to the left, threatening Passchendaele, kept the enemy moderately quiet till the Battalion was relieved in the evening of the 27th by the 3rd Coldstream, and went into bivouac just west of Race-course Wood. It was shelled while settling down here and at intervals throughout the night. Major Herbert Stepney was slightly wounded in the back by a bullet when at supper in a farm-house; two men were killed and three wounded. Captain A. H. L. McCarthy, R.A.M.C., joined for duty, replacing Lieutenant Shields.

Next morning (October 28) the 5th Brigade was attacking and the Battalion was ordered to support. It was heavily shelled again in the wood and dug itself in north-west on the race-course, where it stayed all day ready to support the Coldstream, and had a quiet time. The C.O. (Lord Ardee) went to hospital with a bad throat; Lieutenant Greer was wounded while serving his machine-gun, which had been lent to the 3rd Coldstream, and a couple of men were wounded. Drill-Sergeant A. Winspear joined the Connaught Rangers as 2nd Lieutenant – one of the earliest of the army officers promoted from the ranks.

The enemy at that date were so sure of success that they made no attempt to conceal their intentions, and all our spent forces on the Ypres front were well aware that a serious attack would be opened on them on the 29th. Rumour said it would be superintended by the Kaiser himself. But, so far as the Battalion was concerned, that day was relatively quiet. The 2nd Brigade had been ordered to retake the trenches lost by the 1st Brigade east of Gheluvelt, and the Battalion's duty, with the 2nd Grenadiers, was to fill up whatever gaps might be found in a line which was mainly gaps between the left of the 2nd and the right of the 1st Brigade near Polderhoek. It reached the light railway from Gheluvelt to Polderhoek, discovered that the gap there could be filled up by a platoon, communicated with the C.O's of the two brigades concerned, sent back three companies to the 4th Brigade Headquarters, left one at the disposal of the 1st Brigade, and at night withdrew. For the moment, the line could be held with the troops on the spot, and it was no policy to use a man more than was necessary. The casualties to the men for that day were but four killed and six wounded, though a shell burst on the Brigade Reserve Ammunition Column, west of Race-course Wood, and did considerable damage.

The 30 October opened on the heaviest crisis of the long battle of Ypres. The Battalion, to an accompaniment of 'Jack Johnsons,' dug trenches a quarter of a mile west of Race-course Wood in case the troops at the farther end of it should be driven back; for in those years woods were visible and gave good cover. German aeroplanes, well aware that they had no anti-aircraft guns to fear, swooped low over them in the morning, and men could only reply with some pitiful rifle-fire.

In the afternoon orders came for them and the 2nd Grenadiers to stop digging and move up to Klein Zillebeke to support the hard-pressed Seventh Division on whose front the enemy had broken through again. When they reached what was more or less the line, Nos. 1 and 2 Companies were sent forward to support the cavalry in their trenches, while Nos. 3 and 4 Companies dug themselves in behind Klein Zillebeke. A gap of about a quarter of a mile was found running from the Klein Zillebeke–Zandvoorde road north to the trenches of the 2nd Gordon Highlanders, and patrols reported the enemy in force in a strip of wood immediately to the east of it. Whether the gap had been blasted out by concentrated enemy-fire, or whether what the guns had left of our cavalry had retired, was never clear. The Battalion was told off to hold the place and to find out who was on either side of them, while the 2nd Grenadiers continued the line southward from the main road to the canal. Beginning at 11 p.m., they dug themselves in till morning light. A burning farmhouse blazed steadily all night in a hollow by Zandvoorde and our patrols on the road could see the Germans 'in their spiked helmets' silhouetted against the glare as they stormed out of the woods and massed behind the fold of the ground ready for the morning's attack. Two years later, our guns would have waited on their telephones till the enemy formation was completed and would then have removed those battalions from the face of the earth. But we had not those guns. During the night the Oxfordshire Light Infantry came up and occupied a farm between the Battalion and the Gordon Highlanders and strengthened the situation a little. Company commanders had already been officially warned that the position was serious and that they must 'hang on at all costs.' Also that the Kaiser himself was in front of them.

On the 31st, after an attack by the French towards Hollebeke which did not develop, the full storm broke. The Battalion, backed by two R.F.A. guns, was shelled from seven in the morning till eleven o'clock at night in such trenches as it had been able to construct during the night; while machine-gun and infantry fire grew steadily through the hours. The companies were disposed as follows: No. 4 Company immediately to the north of the main wood; then No. 3 with No. 1 in touch with the Oxfordshire Light Infantry at a farm-house, next to the Gordons; No. 2 was in reserve at a farm with Headquarters.

On the afternoon of 31 October, Lord Ardee arrived from hospital, though he was in no state to be out of it, and was greeted by the information that the Gordons on the left, heavily shelled, had been driven out of their trenches. The Oxford L.I. and also No. 1 Company of the Battalion which was in touch with them had to conform to the movement. The section of R.F.A. had to retire also with the Gordons and, after apologies, duly delivered among bursting German shell, for 'having to look after their guns,' they 'limbered up and went off

as though it were the Military Tournament.' There was
a counter-attack, and eventually the enemy were driven
back and the line was re-established before night, which
passed, says the Diary 'fairly quietly.' The moonlight
made movement almost impossible; nor could the men
get any hot tea, their great stand-by, but rations were
distributed. The casualties among officers that day were
Lieutenant L. S. Coke killed, and buried in the garden of
the farm; Captain Lord Francis Scott, Lieutenant the Earl
of Kingston, and Lieutenant R. Ferguson wounded. There
were many casualties in the front trenches, especially
among No. 3 Company, men being blown to pieces and
no trace left. The depressing thing, above all, was that
we seemed to have no guns to reply with.

Bombardment was renewed on 1 November. The front
trenches were drenched by field-guns, at close range,
with spurts of heavy stuff at intervals; the rear by heavy
artillery, while machine-gun fire filled the intervals. One
of the trenches of a platoon in No. 3 Company, under
Lieutenant Maitland, was completely blown in, and
only a few men escaped. The Lieutenant remained with
the survivors while Sergeant C. Harradine, under heavy
fire, took the news to the C.O. It was hopeless to send
reinforcements; the machine-gun fire would have wiped
them out moving and our artillery was not strong enough
to silence any one sector of the enemy's fire.

In the afternoon the enemy attacked – with rifle-fire
and a close-range small piece that broke up our two
machine-guns – across some dead ground and occupied
the wrecked trench, driving back the few remains of No.
3 Company. The companies on the right and left, Nos. 1
and 4, after heavy fighting, fell back on No. 2 Company,

which was occupying roughly prepared trenches in the rear. One platoon, however, of No. 1 Company, under Lieutenant N. Woodroffe (he had only left Eton a year), did not get the order to retire, and so held on in its trench till dark and 'was certainly instrumental in checking the advance of the enemy.' The line was near breaking-point by then, but company after company delivered what blow it could, and fell back, shelled and machine-gunned at every step, to the fringe of Zillebeke Wood. Here the officers, every cook, orderly, and man who could stand, took rifle and fought; for they were all that stood there between the enemy and the Channel Ports. (Years later, a man remembering that fight said: "Twas like a football scrum. Everyone was somebody, ye'll understand. If he dropped there was no one to take his place. Great days! An' we not so frightened as when it came to the fightin' by machinery on the Somme afterwards.') The C.O. sent the Adjutant to Brigade Headquarters to ask for help, but the whole Staff had gone over to the 2nd Brigade Headquarters, whose Brigadier had taken over command of the 4th Brigade as its own Brigadier had been wounded. About this time, too, the C.O. of the Battalion (Lord Ardee) was wounded. Eventually the 2nd Battalion Grenadiers were sent up with some cavalry of the much-enduring 7th Brigade, and the line of support-trenches was held. The Battalion had had nothing to eat for thirty-six hours, so the cavalry kept the line for a little till our men got food.

A French regiment (Territorials) on the right also took over part of the trenches of our depleted line. Forty-four men were known to have been killed, 205 wounded and eighty-eight – chiefly from the blown-up No. 3 Platoon

– were missing. Of officers, Lieutenant K. R. Mathieson had been killed (he had been last seen shooting a Hun who was bayoneting our wounded); Captain Mulholland died of his wounds as soon as he arrived in hospital at Ypres; Lieut-Colonel Lord Ardee, Captain Vesey, Lieutenant Gore-Langton and Lieutenant Alexander were wounded, and Lieutenant G. M. Maitland, who had stayed with his handful in No. 3 Company's trench, was missing. Yet the time was to come when 350 casualties would be regarded as no extraordinary price to pay for ground won or held. One small draft of forty men arrived from home that night.

On November 2 the Battalion was reduced to three companies, since in No. 3 Company all officers were casualties and only twenty-six men of it answered their names at roll-call. They were heavily shelled all that day. They tried to put up a little wire on their front during the night; they collected what dead they could; they received several wounded men of the day's fight as they crawled into our lines; they heard one such man calling in the dark, and they heard the enemy turn a machine-gun on him and silence him. The regular work of sending forward and relieving the companies in the front line went on, varied by an attack from the enemy, chiefly rifle-fire, on the night of 3 November. On that date they received 'a new machine-gun,' and another draft of sixty men (under Captain E. C. S. King-Harman) several of whom were killed or wounded that same afternoon. The night was filled with false alarms as some of the new drafts began to imagine crowds of Germans advancing out of the dark. This was a popular obsession, but it led to waste of ammunition and waking up utterly tired men elsewhere in the line.

On 4 November there was an outburst of machine-gunning from a farm-house, not 300 yards away. One field-gun was brought up to deal with them, and some of the 2nd Life Guards stood by to help in event of an attack, but the enemy contented themselves with mere punishing fire.

On the evening of 5 November they located our one field-gun which was still trying to cope with the enemy's machine-guns, shelled it for an hour vigorously, blew up the farm-house that sheltered it, but clean missed the gun, though it had been firing at least one round every ten minutes. One of our wounded of 1 November managed to crawl into our lines. He had been three days without food or water – the Germans, who thought he would die, refusing him both. There was heavy shelling and about thirty casualties in the line 'as far as known.'

On the 6th after an hour's preparation with heavy, light-, and machine-gun fire, the enemy attacked the French troops on the Battalion's right, who fell back and left the flank of the Battalion (No. 2 Company) open. The Company 'in good order and fighting' fell back by platoons to its support trenches, but this left No. 1 Company practically in the air, and at the end of the day the greater part of them were missing. As the Germans occupied the French trenches in succession, they opened an enfilade fire on the Irish which did sore execution. Once again the Adjutant went to the Brigadier to explain the situation. The Household Cavalry were sent up at the gallop to Zillebeke where they dismounted and advanced on foot. The 1st Life Guards on the left were detailed to retake the Irish Guards' trenches, while the 2nd Life Guards attacked the position whence the French had been ousted. 100 Irish Guardsmen, collected on the spot, also took part in the attack, which in an hour recovered most of the lost positions. Here Lieutenant W. E. Hope was killed, and a little later, Lieutenant N. Woodroffe fell, shot dead in the advance of the Household Cavalry. Two companies, had these been available, could have held the support-trenches after the Household Cavalry had cleared the front, but there were no reinforcements and the unceasing pressure on the French drove the Battalion back on a fresh line a couple of hundred yards behind the support trenches which the cavalry held till the remains of the Battalion had re-formed and got some hot tea from the ever-forward cookers. In addition to Lieutenants Hope and Woodroffe killed, Captain Lord John Hamilton and Lieutenant E. C. S. King-Harman, who had come out with the draft on 1 November, were missing that day.

On 7 November the Battalion relieved the cavalry at one in the morning, and dug and deepened their trenches on the edge of the wood till word came to them to keep up a heavy fire on any enemy driven out of the wood, as the 22nd Brigade were attacking on their right. That 'Brigade' now reduced to two composite battalions – the Royal Welsh Fusiliers, with the 2nd Queens and the Warwicks with S. Staffords – both commanded by captains, did all that was humanly possible against the pressure, but in the end, as the Diary says, 'having failed to get the line required, withdrew under heavy shell-fire.' Their attack was no more than one, of many desperate interludes in the desperate first battle of Ypres – a winning fight against hopeless odds of men and material – but it diverted attention for the moment from the Battalion's particular section of the line and 'the enemy did not shell our trenches much.' Early in the day Major Stepney, commanding, went out from the support trenches and was not seen again alive. His body was found late in the evening between the lines. The command of the Battalion now fell to Captain N. Orr-Ewing.

Since 31 October, six officers had been killed, seven wounded, and three were missing. Of N.C.O.'s and men 64 were dead, 339 wounded, and 194 missing. The total casualties, all ranks, for one week, were 613.

The remnant were made into two shrunken companies the next day (the 8th) which was a quiet one, with intermittent bursts of shelling from French 75s on the right, and German heavies; the enemy 80 yards distant. Captain A. Perceval, who had been blown up twice in the past week, and Lieutenant J. S. N. FitzGerald were sent to hospital.

On the night of 9 November the Battalion of four platoons, three in the firing line and one in reserve, was relieved by the S.W. Borderers; drew supplies and men at Brigade Headquarters, moved back through Zillebeke and marched into bivouacs near a farm south of the Ypres–Zonnebeke road, where they settled down with some Oxford L.I. in deep trenches, and dugouts which had been dug by the French.

They spent the 10th in luxury; their cookers were up and the men ate their first hot meal for many days. Blankets were also issued, and a draft of about 200 men arrived under Lieutenant Hon. W. C. Hanbury-Tracy, which brought up the strength of the reorganised two-company Battalion to 360 men. Major Webber, 'S.R.' (this is the first time that the Diary makes mention of the Special Reserve), arrived the day before and as Senior Officer took over from Captain Orr-Ewing. The other officers who came with him were Captain Everard and Lieutenant L. R. Hargreaves, both Special Reserve, with Lieutenant St. J. R. Pigott, and, next day, 2nd Lieutenant Straker, Machine-gun Officer, with 'two new guns.' All these reinforcements allowed the Battalion to be organised as two companies instead of four platoons.

On the morning of 11 November, they were moved out by way of the Bellewaarde Lake and under cover of the woods there, in support of the Oxfordshire L.I. who cleared the wood north of Château Hooge and captured some thirty prisoners of the Prussian Guards. This was the first time, to their knowledge, that they had handled that Corps. Though heavily shelled, the Battalion lost no men and spent the rest of the day behind the O.L.I. and the Grenadiers, waiting in the rain near the Headquarters of the First Division (Brigadier-General FitzClarence, V.C.), to which it was for the moment attached.

It was here that one of our officers found some enemy prisoners faithfully shepherded under the lee of a protecting haystack while their guard (Oxford L.I.) stood out in the open under casual shrapnel. A change was made at once.

At 9 p.m. the Battalion was told it might go back and get tea and supplies at some cross-roads or other in the darkness behind it. The cookers never came up and the supplies were not available till past midnight on the 12th. As their orders were to return to 1st Brigade Headquarters at 2 a.m. to take part in an attack on a German trench, the men had not much sleep. The trench had been captured by the enemy the day before, but they had abandoned it and dug another, commanding, in the rear, whence they could deal with any attempt at recapture on our part. The composite force of the 2nd Grenadiers, Munster Fusiliers, Irish Guards, and Oxfordshire L.I. discovered this much, wading through mud in the darkness before dawn, at a cost to the Battalion of Major Webber and Lieutenant Harding and some twelve men wounded. They were caught front and flank and scattered among the shell-holes. General FitzClarence was killed by enemy fire out of the dark, and eventually the troops returned to 1st Brigade Headquarters where a company of the Grenadiers were told off to dig trenches in a gap which had been found in the line, while the remainder, the Irish Guards and the Munsters, were sent back to the woods near Hooge Château which was full of fragments of broken battalions, from Scots Guards to Zouaves.

The Battalion reached its destination at 6 a.m. of the 12th. Three-quarters of an hour later it was ordered up to the woods on the Gheluvelt road. They occupied 'dug-outs' – the first time the Diary mentions these as part of the scheme of things – on the north side of the road near the end of the wood west of Veldhoek; sent a platoon to reinforce the Scots Fusiliers who were hard-pressed, near by; and were heavily shelled at intervals all day, besides being sniped and machine-gunned by the enemy who commanded the main road towards Hooge. None the less, they were fed that night without accident. Captains Everard and Hanbury-Tracy, Lieutenant Pigott were sent to hospital, and 2nd Lieutenant Antrobus rejoined from hospital. This left to the Battalion – Captain Orr-Ewing, Captain the Hon. J. Trefusis, Adjutant R.M.C. Sandhurst who had joined a day or so before, Lieutenant L. R. Hargreaves, and 2nd Lieutenant

Antrobus, who was next day wounded in the arm by a shell. Lieutenant Walker, Acting Quartermaster, was sick, and Captain Gough was acting as Brigade Transport Officer. At that moment the strength of the Battalion is reported at 'about' 160 officers and men. A draft of 50 N.C.O.'s and men arrived on 13 November.

On 14 November they were ordered to return to 4th Brigade Headquarters and take over trenches near Klein Zillebeke from the S.W. Borderers who had relieved them there on the 9th. 'The day passed much as usual,' it was observed, but 'the shelling was fairly heavy and the enemy gained some ground.' Lieutenant and Quartermaster Hickie returned from a sick leave of two months. The Sussex Battalion relieved the Battalion in their dug-outs on the edge of the Veldhoek woods at 11 p.m.; the Battalion then moved off and by half-past three on the morning of the 15th had relieved the South Wales Borderers in their old trenches. Here they received word of the death of their Colonel, FieldMarshal Lord Roberts, from pneumonia while on a visit to the Indian troops at the front. C.S.M. Rogers and Pte. Murphy were selected as representatives of the Battalion to attend the funeral service at St. Omer. The Battalion spent the day under constant shell-fire in improving trenches, 'but there was some difficulty as snipers were busy, as they had been all day'. One officer wrote: 'Our men are very tired and the rifles are in an awful state. It rains continuously, and it is very hard to get any sort of rifle-oil.'

The 16 November, a day of snow and heavy firing, ending in an attack which was suppressed by rapid fire, was grimly enlivened by the appearance of one German deserter with two fingers shot off who announced that he 'had had enough of fighting.'

On 17 November, Brigade Headquarters were blown in by shell-fire, both of the Irish Guards orderlies on duty were injured, and both of the Battalion's 'two new machine-guns' were knocked to pieces. There was five hours' heavy shelling from 7 a.m. till noon when the enemy came out of their trenches to attack in force, and were dealt with for an hour by the Battalion, the Grenadiers on its left and the cavalry on its right. It was estimated that – thanks to efficient fire control and good discipline – 1,200 killed and wounded were accounted for in front of our trenches. Our only man killed in this attack was C.S.M. Munns who had just been recommended for his commission. He was a born leader of men, always cheerful, and with what seemed like a genuine love for fighting. A second attack, not pressed home, followed at three o'clock; another out-break of small-arm fire at half-past nine and yet another towards midnight, and a heavy shelling of the French on our right. 'Then all was quiet,' says the easily satisfied record.

They endured one day longer, with nothing worse than a 'certain amount of heavy shelling but not so much as usual,' and on the 18th their battered remnants came out. They were relieved by a company of the 3rd Coldstream (Captain H. Dawson) and marched off to billets at Potijze on the Ypres–Zonnebeke road, where the men got plenty of food. Hard frost had followed the soaking wet and downpour of the previous days; snow succeeded, but there were hot meals and the hope of rest and refit at Meteren behind Bailleul, 15 miles from Potijze.

They reached that haven on 21 November – eight officers and 390 men in all – 'desperately tired' in a cold that froze the water in the men's bottles. Not a man fell out. Captain Lord Desmond FitzGerald, recovered from his wound, arrived on the same day and took over the Adjutancy.

The Battalion had been practically wiped out and reconstructed in a month. They had been cramped in wet mud till they had almost forgotten the use of their legs: their rifles, clothing, equipment, everything except their morale and the undefeated humour with which they had borne their burden, needed renewal or repair. They rested and began to clean themselves of their dirt and vermin while the C.O. and company officers went round billets and companies – to see that the men had all they needed – as is the custom of our Army. It was a comprehensive refit, including everything from trousers to ground-sheets, as well as mufflers and mittens sent by H.I.H. the Grand Duke Michael of Russia. Steady platoon and company drill, which is restorative to men after long standing in dirt, or fighting in the dark, marked the unbelievably still days.

On 23 November the Reverend Father Gwynne, the beloved R.C. Chaplain, arrived to take up his duties; and on the 24th they were inspected by the Commander-in-Chief, Sir John French.

On the 28th a draft of 288 N.C.O.'s and men reached them, under command of Captain P. L. Reid with the following officers: Lieutenant G. Gough; 2nd Lieutenants H. S. Keating, H. Marion-Crawford, Hon. H. A. V. Harmsworth, A. C. Innes, and L. C. Lee. With this draft the strength of the Battalion stood at 700 men and 15 officers. Of the latter the Diary notes that nine are in the Special Reserve, 'seven of them having done no sort of soldiering before the war.' Mercifully, men lived but one day at a time, or the Diarist might have drawn conclusions, which would have fallen far short of what the future was to bring, from the fact that as many as twelve machine-gunners were kept at the base by the order of the authorities. There was need to train machine-gunners, and even greater need for the guns themselves. But the Battalion was not occupied with the larger questions of the war. They had borne their part against all odds of numbers and equipment in barring the German road to the sea in the first month-long battle of Ypres. They knew very little of what they had done. Not one of their number could have given any consecutive account of what had happened, nor, in that general-post of daily and nightly confusion whither they had gone. All they were sure of was that such as lived were not dead ('The Lord only knows why') and that the enemy had not broken through. They had no knowledge what labours still lay before them.

On 3 December, after an issue of new equipment and a visit from Sir Douglas Haig, commanding the First Army Corps, they lined the road from Meteren towards Bailleul for the visit of the King who walked down the lines of the 4th (Guards) Brigade and, after shaking hands with the four Commanding Officers of the Brigade, said: 'I am very proud of my Guards and am full of admiration for their bravery, endurance, and fine spirit. I wish I could have addressed them all, but that is impossible, so you must tell them what I say to you. You are fighting a brave and determined enemy, but if you go on as you have been doing and show the same fine spirit, there can be only one end, please God, and that is victory. I wish you all good luck.'

D.S.O.'s had been awarded to Captain Orr-Ewing and Captain Lord Francis Scott; and the Distinguished Conduct Medal to Company Sergeant-Major Munns, who, it will be remembered, was killed in action just after he was recommended for a commission: to Sergeant M'Goldrick, Brigade Orderly, who was one of the orderlies injured when the Brigade Headquarters were blown up on 17 November; Corporal Riordan (wounded), Private Russell (Brigade Orderly), and Private Glynn (since wounded and missing). The King decorated Sergeant M'Goldrick with the D.C.M. that afternoon. The others named were, from various causes, absent. It was the first of many such occasions where those honoured could not be present to receive their valour's reward.

The Diary notes the issue of cardigan waistcoats and goat-skin coats for each man, as well as of a new American pattern boot, with a hard toe which, it conservatively fears, 'may not stand the wear of the old ammunition-boot.' Route-marches increased in length, and the men marched as well as they ate. Indeed, they volunteered to the Brigadier, who came round once to see the dinners, that they had never been so well fed. It kept them healthy, though there were the usual criticisms from officers, N.C.O.'s and surviving veterans of the Regular Army, on the quality of the new drafts, some of whom, it seems, suffered from bad teeth and had to be sent away for renewals and refits. As a much-tried sergeant remarked: 'A man with a sore tooth is a nuisance an' a danger to the whole British Army.'

On 9 December Sir Douglas Haig came over to present the *Medaille Militaire*, on behalf of the French Government, to certain officers, N.C.O.'s, and men of the

Guards Brigade. Drill-Sergeant Rodgers of the Battalion was among the recipients. Captain Orr-Ewing was ordered to rejoin the 1st Battalion of the Scots Guards (his own battalion), to the regret of the Battalion whose lot he had shared since September – the most capable of officers as the most popular of comrades.

A party from the Brigade was sent to Headquarters of the 11th Engineering Company 'to be taught how to throw bombs made out of jam-pots, which apparently are used against the enemy at close quarters in the present trench-warfare.' There were at least half-a-dozen more or less dangerous varieties of these handmade bombs in use, before standard patterns were evolved and bombing took its place as a regular aid to warfare. The 'jam-pot' bomb died early but not before it had caused a sufficiency of trouble to its users. The others will be mentioned in due course.

'Aeroplane duty' was another invention of those early days. A company was told off daily to look out for aeroplanes and, if possible, to bring them down – presumably by rifle-fire. The war was still very young.

F.M. Earl Kitchener's appointment to Colonel of the Battalion in succession to F.M. Earl Roberts was marked on the 12th in the following telegram from Earl Kitchener:

His Majesty the King, having been graciously pleased to appoint me to be Colonel of the Irish Guards, I desire to take the first opportunity of expressing to you and through you to all ranks how proud I am to be associated with so gallant a regiment. My warmest greetings and best wishes to you all!

The C.O. replied:

> All ranks, 1st Battalion Irish Guards, greatly appreciate
> the honour conferred on them by His Majesty the King,
> and are proud to have such a distinguished soldier as
> Colonel of the Regiment.

On 13 December a further draft of 100 men and 3 officers arrived under Captain Mylne; the other officers being Lieutenant Antrobus who was wounded exactly a month before, and Lieutenant Hubbard. This brought the Battalion's strength to 800 with the following officers: Major the Hon. J. Trefusis, C.O.; Captain Lord Desmond FitzGerald, Adjutant; Lieutenant C.A.S. Walker, Transport Officer; 2nd Lieutenant L. Straker, Machine-gun Officer; Captain A. H. L. McCarthy, Medical Officer; Captain Rev. Father Gwynne, Chaplain; Lieutenant H. Hickie, Quartermaster. No.1 Company, Captain E. J. Gough, Lieutenant L. Hargreaves, 2nd Lieutenant A. C. Innes. No. 2 Company, Captain E. Mylne, 2nd Lieutenant H. S. Keating, 2nd Lieutenant F. H. Witts. No. 3 Company, Captain P. L. Reid, 2nd Lieutenant P. H. Antrobus, 2nd Lieutenant Hon. H. V. Harmsworth, 2nd Lieutenant H. Marion-Crawford. No. 4 Company, Lieutenant G. Gough, Lieutenant G. Hubbard, 2nd Lieutenant Lee.

Lieutenant C. A. S. Walker had to go to hospital with bronchitis and Lieutenant Antrobus took over from him.

Major Arbuthnot (Scots Guards) arrived on 14 December with Queen Alexandra's presents to the Battalion which were duly issued to selected officers, N.C. O.'s, and men, but at the time, the Battalion was under two hours' notice to move either to support an attack then being delivered by the Third Division upon the wood at Wytschaete, or 'for any other purpose.' The attack was not a success except in so far as it pinned the enemy forces to one place, but the Battalion was not called upon to help. It lived under 'short notice' for a week which naturally interfered with extended route-marches or training. Companies were sent out one by one to dig in the water-logged soil and to extemporise means of keeping their feet out of the water by 'blocks of wood made in the form of a platform at the bottom of the trenches.' Thus laboriously is described the genesis of what was later to grow into thousands of miles of duck-board, plain or wired.

Meantime, between the 20 and 22 December the fierce and unsatisfactory battle of Cuinchy, the burden of which fell heavily on our devoted Indian troops, had been fought out on a front half-a-dozen miles south of the Béthune Canal to Festubert. Nothing had been gained except the all-important issue – that the enemy did not break through. There was a long casualty-list as casualties were then counted, and the Indian Brigades were withdrawn from their wrecked and sodden trenches for a little rest. The Guards Brigade was ordered to relieve them, and on the 22nd marched out from Meteren. The Herts Territorial Battalion (to be honourably and affectionately known later as 'The Herts Guards') led that first march, followed by the 2nd Coldstream, 1st Battalion Irish Guards, the 3rd Coldstream, and the 2nd Grenadiers. They billeted at Béthune where, on the 23 December, the 2nd Coldstream in support, they took over their share of the Indian trenches near Le Touret between Essars and Richebourg L'Avoué, and on Christmas Eve after tea and the distribution of the Christmas puddings from England, the Battalion, with the Hertfordshires relieved the 4th Dogras, 6th Jats, and 9th Gurkhas. It is recorded that the Gurkha, being a somewhat shorter man than the average Guardsman, the long Irish had to dig their trenches about two feet deeper, and they wondered loudly what sort of persons these 'little dark fellas' could be.

The Christmas truce of 1914 reached the Battalion in severely modified form. They lay among a network of trenches, already many times fought over, with communications that led directly into the enemy's lines a couple of hundred yards away. So they spent Christmas Day, under occasional bombardment of heavy artillery, in exploring and establishing themselves as well as they might, among these wet and dreary works. In this duty Lieutenant G. P. Gough and Lieutenant F. H. Witts and six men were wounded.

Earl Kitchener, their Colonel, sent them Christmas wishes and the King's and Queen's Christmas cards were distributed. Their comfort was that Christmas night was frosty so that the men kept dry at least.

Boxing Day was quiet, too, and only four men were wounded as they dug in the hard ground to improve their communications with the 2nd Coldstream on their left. Then the frost broke in rain, the clay stuck to the spade, the trenches began to fill and a deserter brought news of an impending attack which turned out to be nothing more serious than a bombing affair which was duly 'attended to.' Some of our own shells bursting short killed one man and wounded six. Princess Mary's gifts of pipes, tobacco, and Christmas cards were distributed to the men and duly appreciated.

The impossibility of keeping anything free from mud forced them to reduce their firing-line to the least possible numbers, while those in support, or billets, made shift to clean rifles and accoutrements. The days went forward in rain and wet, with digging where water allowed, and a regular daily toll of a few men killed and wounded.

On 30 December Captain Eric Gough was killed by a stray bullet while commanding his Company (No. 1) and was buried next day in a cemetery a few miles along the Béthune–Richebourg road. He had been Transport Officer since the Battalion left London in August, but had commanded a company since 21 November, and was an immense loss to the Battalion to which he was devoted. Lieutenant Sir G. Burke and 2nd Lieutenant J. M. Stewart came from England on the same day and were posted to No. 1 Company now commanded by Lieutenant L. Hargreaves.

The Diary ends the year with a recapitulation more impressive in its restraint than any multitude of words:

The country round this part is very low-lying, intersected with ditches with pollarded willows growing on their banks. No sooner is a trench dug than it fills with water ... The soil is clay, and so keeps the water from draining away even if that were possible. In order to keep the men at all dry, they have to stand on planks rested on logs in the trenches, and in the less wet places bundles of straw and short fascines are put down. Pumping has been tried, but not with much success. The weather continues wet, and there does not seem to be any likelihood of change. Consequently, we may expect some fresh discomforts daily.

The New Army in Training (1915)

The Men at Work

> 'The ore, the furnace and the hammer are all that is needed for a sword.' Native proverb.

This was a cantonment one had never seen before, and the grey-haired military policeman could give no help.

'My experience,' he spoke detachedly, 'is that you'll find everything everywhere. Is it any particular corps you're looking for?'

'Not in the least' I said.

'Then you're all right. You can't miss getting something.' He pointed generally to the North Camp. 'It's like floods in a town, isn't it?'

He had hit the just word. All known marks in the place were submerged by troops. Parade-grounds to their utmost limits were crowded with them; rises and skylines were furred with them, and the length of the roads heaved and rippled like bicycle-chains with blocks of men on the move.

The voice of a sergeant in the torment reserved for sergeants at roll-call boomed across a bunker. He was calling over recruits to a specialist corps.

'But I've called you once!' he snapped at a man in leggings.

'But I'm Clarke Two,' was the virtuous reply.

'Oh, you are, are you?' He pencilled the correction with a scornful mouth, out of one corner of which he added, '"Sloppy" Clarke! You're all Clarkes or Watsons today. You don't know your own names. You don't know what corps you're in. (This was bitterly unjust, for they were squinting up at a biplane.) You don't know anything.'

'Mm!' said the military policeman. 'The more a man has in his head, the harder it is for him to manage his carcass – at first. I'm glad I never was a sergeant. Listen to the instructors! Like rooks, ain't it?'

There was a mile of sergeants and instructors, varied by company officers, all at work on the ready material under their hands. They grunted, barked, yapped, expostulated, and, in rare cases, purred, as the lines broke and formed and wheeled over the vast maidan. When companies numbered off one could hear the tone and accent of every walk in life, and maybe half the counties of England, from the deep-throated 'Woon' of the north to the sharp, half-whistled Devonshire 'Tu'. And as the instructors laboured, so did the men, with a passion to learn as passionately as they were taught.

Presently, in the drift of the foot-traffic down the road, there came another grey-haired man, one foot in a bright slipper, which showed he was an old soldier cherishing a sore toe. He drew alongside and considered these zealous myriads.

'Good?' said I, deferentially.

'Yes,' he said, 'Very good' – then, half to himself: 'Quite different, though'. A pivot-man near us had shifted a little, instead of marking time, on the wheel. His face clouded, his lips moved. Obviously he was cursing his own clumsiness.

'That's what I meant,' said the veteran. 'Innocent! Innocent! Mark you, they ain't doin' it to be done with it and get off. They're doin' it because – because they want to do it'.

'Wake up! Wake up there, Isherwood!' This was a young subaltern's reminder flung at a back which straightened itself. That one human name coming up out of all that maze of impersonal manoeuvring stuck in the memory like wreckage on the ocean.

'An' it wasn't 'ardly even necessary to caution Mister Isherwood,' my companion commented. 'Prob'ly he's bitterly ashamed of 'imself'.

I asked a leading question because the old soldier told me that when his toe was sound, he, too, was a military policeman.

'Crime? Crime?' said he. 'They don't know what crime is – that lot don't – none of 'em!' He mourned over them like a benevolent old Satan looking into a busy Eden, and his last word was 'Innocent!'

The car worked her way through miles of men – men route-marching, going to dig or build bridges, or wrestle with stores and transport 4 or 5 miles of men, and every man with eager eyes. There was no music – not even drums and fifes. I heard nothing but a distant skirl of the pipes. Trust a Scot to get his national weapon as long as there is a chief in the North! Admitting that war is a serious business, especially to the man who is being fought for, and that it may be right to carry a long face and contribute to relief funds which should be laid on the National Debt, it surely could do no harm to cheer the men with a few bands. Half the money that has been spent in treating, for example ...

The North in Blue

There was a moor among woods with a pond in a hollow, the centre of a world of tents whose population was North-Country. One heard it from far off.

'Yo' mun trail t' pick an' t' rifle at t' same time. Try again,' said the instructor.

An isolated company tried again with set seriousness, and yet again. They were used to the pick – won their living by it, in fact – and so, favoured it more than the rifle; but miners don't carry picks at the trail by instinct, though they can twiddle their rifles as one twiddles walking-sticks.

They were clad in a blue garb that disguised all contours, yet their shoulders, backs, and loins could not altogether be disguised, and these were excellent. Another company, at physical drill in shirt and trousers, showed what superb material had offered itself to be worked upon, and how much poise and directed strength had been added to that material in the past few months. When the New Army gets all its new uniform, it will gaze at itself like a new Narcissus. But the present kit is indescribable. That is why, English fashion, it has been made honourable by its wearers; and our world in the years to come will look back with reverence as well as affection on those blue slops and that epileptic cap. One far-seeing commandant who had special facilities has possessed himself of brass buttons, thousands of 'em, which he has added to his men's outfit for the moral effect of (a) having something to clean, and *(b)* of keeping it so. It has paid. The smartest regiment in the Service could not do itself justice in such garments, but I managed to get a view of a battalion, coming in from a walk, at a distance which more or less subdued the – er – uniform, and they moved with the elastic swing and little quick ripple that means so much. A miner is not supposed to be as good a marcher as a townsman, but when he gets set to time and pace and learns due economy of effort, his developed back and shoulder muscles take him along very handsomely. Another battalion fell in for parade while I watched, again at a distance. They came to hand quietly and collectedly enough, and with only that amount of pressing which is caused by fear of being late. A platoon – or whatever they call it – was giving the whole of its attention to its signalling instructors, with the air of men resolved on getting the last flicker of the last cinema-film for their money. Crime in the military sense they do not know any more than their fellow innocents up the road. It is hopeless to pretend to be other than what one is, because one's soul in this life is as exposed as one's body. It is futile to tell civilian lies – there are no civilians to listen – and they have not yet learned to tell Service ones without being detected. It is useless to sulk at any external condition of affairs, because the rest of the world with which a man is concerned is facing those identical conditions. There is neither poverty nor riches, nor any possibility of pride, except in so far as one may do one's task a little better than one's mate.

Duties and Developments

In the point of food they are extremely well looked after, quality and quantity, wet canteen and dry. Drafts come in all round the clock, and they have to be fed; late guards and sentries want something hot at odd times, and the big marquee-canteen is the world's gathering place, where food, life's first interest to man in hard work, is thoroughly discussed. They can get outside of a vast o' vittles. Thus, a contractor who delivers 10,000 rations a day stands, by deputy at least, in the presence of just that number of rather fit, long, deep men. They are what is called 'independent' – a civilian weakness which they will learn to blush over in a few months, and to discourage among later recruits; but they are also very quick to pick up dodges and tricks that make a man more comfortable in camp life, and their domestic routine runs on wheels. It must have been hard at first for civilians to see the necessity for that continuous, apparently pernickity, house-maiding and 'following-up' which is vital to the comfort of large bodies of men in confined quarters. In civil life men leave these things to their womenfolk, but where women are not, officers, inspecting tents, feet, and such-like, develop a she-side to their head, and evidently make their non-commissioned officers and men develop it too. A good soldier is always a bit of an old maid. But, as I heard a private say to a sergeant in the matter of some kit chucked into a corner: 'Yo' canna keep owt redd up ony proper gate on a sand-hill'. To whom his superior officer: 'Ah know yo' canna', but yo' mun try, Billy'.

And Heaven knows they are trying hard enough – men, N.C.O.'s, and officers – with all the masked and under-voiced effort of our peoples when we are really at work. They stand at the very beginning of things; creating out of chaos, meeting emergencies as they arise; handicapped in every direction, and overcoming every handicap by simple goodwill, humour, self-sacrifice, common sense, and such trumpery virtues. I watched their faces in the camp, and at lunch looked down a line of some twenty men in the mess-tent, wondering how many would survive to see the full splendour and significance of the work here so nobly begun. But they were not interested in the future beyond their next immediate job. They ate quickly and went out to it, and by the time I drove away again I was overtaking their battalions on the road. Not unrelated units lugged together for foot-slogging, but real battalions, of a spirit in themselves which defied even the blue slops – wave after wave of proper men, with undistracted eyes, who never talked a word about any war. But not a note of music – and they're North-countrymen!

Iron into Steel

'*Thanda lohd garam lohe ko maria hai.*' (Cold iron will cut hot iron)

At the next halt I fell into Scotland – blocks and blocks of it – a world of precise-spoken, thin-lipped men, with keen eyes. They gave me directions which led by friendly stages to the heart of another work of creation and a huge drill-shed where the miniature rifles were busy. Few things are duller than Morris-tube practice in the shed, unless it be judging triangles of error against blank walls. I thought of the military policeman with the sore toe; for these 'innocents' were visibly enjoying both games. They sighted over the sandbags with the gravity of surveyors, while the instructors hurled knowledge at them like slingstones.

'Man, d'ye see your error? Step here, man, and I'll show ye.' Teacher and taught glared at each other like theologians in full debate; for this is the Scot's way of giving and getting knowledge.

At the miniature targets, squad after squad rose from beside their deadly earnest instructors, gathered up their target-cards, and whisperingly compared them, five heads together under a window.

'Aye, that was where I loosed too soon.' 'I misdoubt I took too much o' the foresight.' Not a word of hope and comfort in their achievements. Nothing but Calvinistic self-criticism.

These men ran a little smaller than the North-country folk down the road, but in depth of chest, girth of forearm, biceps, and neck-measurement they were beautifully level and well up; and the squads at bayonet-practice had their balance, drive, and recover already. As the light failed one noticed the whites of their eyes turning towards their instructors. It reminded one that there is always a touch of the cateran in the most docile Scot, even as the wolf persists in every dog.

'And what about crime?' I demanded.

There was none. They had not joined to play the fool. Occasionally a few unstable souls who have mistaken their vocation try to return to civil life by way of dishonourable discharge, and think it 'funny' to pile up offences. The New Army has no use for those people either, and attends to them on what may be called 'democratic lines' which is all the same as the old barrack-room court-martial. Nor does it suffer fools gladly. There is no time to instruct them. They go to other spheres.

There was, or rather is, a man who intends to join a certain battalion. He joined it once, scraped past the local doctor, and was drafted into the corps, only to be hove out for varicose veins. He went back to his accommodating doctor, repeated the process, and was again rejected. They are waiting for him now in his third incarnation; both sides are equally determined. And there was another Scot who joined, served awhile, and left, as he might have left a pit or a factory. Somehow it occurred to him that explanations were required, so he wrote to his commanding officer from his home address and asked him what he recommended him to do. The C.O., to his infinite credit, wrote back: 'Suppose you rejoin,' which the man did, and no more said. His punishment, of course, will come to him when he realises what he has done. If he does not then perish in his self-contempt (he has a good conceit of himself) he will make one first-rate non-commissioned officer.

With Illustrations

I had the luck to meet a Sergeant-Major, who was the Sergeant-Major of one's dreams. He had just had sure information that the kilts for his battalion were coming in a few days, so, after three months' hard work, life smiled upon him. From kilts one naturally went on to the pipes. The battalion had its pipes – a very good set. How did it get them? Well, there was, of course, the Duke. They began with him. And there was a Scots lord concerned with the regiment. And there was a leddy of a certain clan connected with the battalion. Hence the pipes. Could anything be simpler or more logical? And when the kilts came the men would be different creatures. Were they good men, I asked. 'Yes. Verra good. Wha's to mislead 'em?' said he.

'Old soldiers,' I suggested, meanly enough. 'Rejoined privates of long ago.'

'Ay, there might have been a few such in the beginning, but they'd be more useful in the Special Reserve Battalions. Our boys are good boys, but, ye'll understand, they've to be handled just handled a little.' Then a subaltern came in, loaded with regimental forms, and visibly leaning on the Sergeant-Major, who explained, clarified, and referred them on the proper quarters.

'Does the work come back to you?' I asked, for he had been long in pleasant civil employ.

'Ay. It does that. It just does that.' And he addressed the fluttering papers, lists, and notes, with the certainty of an old golfer on a well-known green.

Squads were at bayonet practice in the square. (They like bayonet practice, especially after looking at pictures in the illustrated dailies.) A new draft was being introduced to its rifles. The rest were getting ready for evening parade. They were all in khaki, so one could see how they had come on in the last ten weeks. It was a result the meekest might have been proud of, but the New Army does not cultivate useless emotions. Their officers and their instructors worked over them patiently and coldly and repeatedly, with their souls in the job: and with their soul, mind, and body in the same job the men took – soaked up – the instruction. And that seems to be the note of the New Army.

What the Army Does and Thinks

They have joined for good reason. For that reason they sleep uncomplainingly double thick on barrack floors, or lie like herrings in the tents and sing hymns and other things when they are flooded out. They walk and dig half the day or all the night as required; they wear – though they will not eat – anything that is issued to them; they make themselves an organised and kindly life out of a few acres of dirt and a little canvas; they keep their edge and anneal their discipline under conditions that would depress a fox-terrier and disorganise a champion football team. They ask nothing in return save work and equipment. And being what they are, they thoroughly and unfeignedly enjoy what they are doing; and they purpose to do much more.

But they also think. They think it vile that so many unmarried young men who are not likely to be affected by Government allowances should be so shy about sharing their life. They discuss these young men and their womenfolk by name, and imagine rude punishments for them, suited to their known characters. They discuss, too, their elders who in time past warned them of the sin of soldiering. These men, who live honourably and simply under the triple vow of Obedience, Temperance, and Poverty, recall, not without envy, the sort of life which well-kept moralists lead in the unpicketed, unsentried towns; and it galls them that such folk should continue in comfort and volubility at the expense of good men's lives, or should profit greasily at the end of it all. They stare hard, even in their blue slops, at white-collared, bowler-hatted young men, who, by the way, are just learning to drop their eyes under that gaze. In the third-class railway carriages they hint that they would like explanations from the casual 'nut', and they explain to him wherein his explanations are unconvincing. And when they are home on leave, the slack-jawed son of the local shop-keeper, and the rising nephew of the big banker, and the dumb but cunning carter's lad receive instruction or encouragement suited to their needs and the nation's. The older men and the officers will tell you that if the allowances are made more liberal we shall get all the men we want. But the younger men of the New Army do not worry about allowances, or, for that matter, make 'em!

There is a gulf already opening between those who have joined and those who have not; but we shall not know the width and the depth of that gulf till the war is over. The wise youth is he who jumps it now and lands in safety among the trained and armed men.

Guns and Supply

> 'Under all and after all the Wheel carries everything.'
> Proverb.

One had known the place for years as a picturesque old house, standing in a peaceful park; had watched the growth of certain young oaks along a new-laid avenue, and applauded the owner's enterprise in turning a stretch of pasture to plough. There are scores of such estates in England which the motorist, through passing so often, comes to look upon almost as his own. In a single day the brackened turf between the oaks and the iron road-fence blossomed into tents, and the drives were all cut up with hoofs and wheels. A little later, one's car sweeping home of warm September nights was stopped by sentries, who asked her name and business; for the owner of that retired house and discreetly wooded park had gone elsewhere in haste, and his estate was taken over by the military.

Later still, one met men and horses arguing with each other for miles about that countryside; or the car would be flung on her brakes by artillery issuing from cross-lanes – clean batteries jingling off to their work on the Downs, and hungry ones coming back to meals. Every day brought the men and the horses and the weights behind them to a better understanding, till in a little while the car could pass a quarter of a mile of them without having to hoot more than once.

'Why are you so virtuous?' she asked of a section encountered at a blind and brambly corner.

'Why do you obtrude your personality less than an average tax-cart?'

'Because,' said a driver, his arm flung up to keep the untrimmed hedge from sweeping his cap off, 'because those are our blessed orders. We don't do it for love.'

No one accuses the Gunner of maudlin affection for anything except his beasts and his weapons. He hasn't the time. He serves at least three jealous gods – his horse and all its saddlery and harness; his gun, whose least detail of efficiency is more important than men's lives; and, when these have been attended to, the never-ending mystery of his art commands him.

It was a wettish, windy day when I visited the so-long-known house and park. Cock pheasants ducked in and out of trim rhododendron clumps, neat gates opened into sacredly preserved vegetable gardens, the many-coloured leaves of specimen trees pasted themselves stickily against sodden tent walls, and there was a mixture of circus smells from the horse-lines and the faint, civilised breath of chrysanthemums in the potting sheds. The main drive was being relaid with a foot of flint; the other approaches were churned and pitted under the gun wheels and heavy supply wagons. Great breadths of what had been well-kept turf between unbrowsed trees were blanks of slippery brown wetness, dotted with picketed horses and field-kitchens. It was a crazy mixture of stark necessity and manicured luxury, all cheek by jowl, in the undiscriminating rain.

Service Conditions

The cook-houses, store-rooms, forges, and workshops were collections of tilts, poles, rick-cloths, and odd lumber, beavered together as on service. The officers' mess was a thin, soaked marquee.

Less than 100 yards away were dozens of vacant, well-furnished rooms in the big brick house, of which the staff furtively occupied one corner. There was accommodation for very many men in its stables and out-houses alone; or the whole building might have been gutted and rearranged for barracks twice over in the last three months.

Scattered among the tents were rows of half-built tin sheds, the ready-prepared lumber and the corrugated iron lying beside them, waiting to be pieced together like children's toys. But there were no workmen. I was told that they had come that morning, but had knocked off because it was wet.

'I see. And where are the batteries?' I demanded.

'Out at work, of course. They've been out since seven.'

'How shocking! In this dreadful weather, too!'

'They took some bread and cheese with them. They'll be back about dinner-time if you care to wait. Here's one of our field-kitchens.'

Batteries look after their own stomachs, and are not catered for by contractors. The cook-house was a wagon-tilt. The wood, being damp, smoked a good deal. One thought of the wide, adequate kitchen ranges and the concrete passages of the service quarters in the big house just behind. One even dared to think Teutonically of the perfectly good panelling and the thick hard-wood floors that could–

'Service conditions, you see,' said my guide, as the cook inspected the baked meats and the men inside the wagon-tilt grated the carrots and prepared the onions. It was old work to them after all these months – done swiftly, with the clean economy of effort that camp life teaches.

'What are these lads when they're at home?' I inquired.

'Londoners chiefly all sorts and conditions.'

The cook in shirt sleeves made another investigation, and sniffed judicially. He might have been cooking since the Peninsular. He looked at his watch and across towards the park gates. He was responsible for 160 rations, and a battery has the habit of saying quite all that it thinks of its food.

'How often do the batteries go out?' I continued.

''Bout five days a week. You see, we're being worked up a little.'

'And have they got plenty of ground to work over?'

'Oh – yes-s.'

'What's the difficulty this time? Birds?'

'No; but we got orders the other day not to go over a golf-course. That rather knocks the bottom out of tactical schemes.'

Perfect shamelessness, like perfect virtue, is impregnable; and, after all, the lightnings of this war, which have brought out so much resolve and self-sacrifice, must show up equally certain souls and institutions that are irredeemable.

The weather took off a little before noon. The carpenters could have put in a good half-day's work on the sheds, and even if they had been rained upon they had roofs with fires awaiting their return. The batteries had none of these things.

The Gunner at Home

They came in at last far down the park, heralded by that unmistakable half-grumble, half-grunt of guns on the move. The picketed horses heard it first, and one of them neighed long and loud, which proved that he had abandoned civilian habits. Horses in stables and mews seldom do more than snicker, even when they are halves of separated pairs. But these gentlemen had a corporate life of their own now, and knew what pulling together means.

When a battery comes into camp it 'parks' all six guns at the appointed place, side by side in one mathematically straight line, and the accuracy of the alignment is, like ceremonial-drill with the foot, a fair test of its attainments. The ground was no treat for parking. Specimen trees and draining ditches had to be avoided and circumvented. The gunners, their reins, the guns, the ground, were equally wet, and the slob dropped away like gruel from the brake-shoes. And they were Londoners – clerks, mechanics, shop assistants, and delivery men – anything and everything that you please. But they were all home and at home in their saddles and 'seats. They said nothing; their officers said little enough to them. They came in across what had once been turf; wheeled with tight traces; halted, unhooked; the wise teams stumped off to their pickets, and, behold, the six guns were left precisely where they should have been left to the fraction of an inch. You could see the wind blowing the last few drops of wet from each leather muzzle-cover at exactly the same angle. It was all old known evolutions, taken unconsciously in the course of their day's work by men well abreast of it.

'Our men have one advantage,' said a voice. 'As Territorials they were introduced to unmade horses once a year at training. So they've never been accustomed to made horses.'

'And what do the horses say about it all?' I asked, remembering what I had seen on the road in the early days.

'They said a good deal at first, but our chaps could make allowances for 'em. They know now.'

Allah never intended the Gunner to talk. His own arm does that for him. The batteries off-saddled in silence, though one noticed on all sides little quiet caresses between man and beast affectionate nuzzlings and nose-slappings. Surely the Gunner's relation to his horse is more intimate even than the cavalryman's; for a lost horse only turns cavalry into infantry, but trouble in a gun team may mean death all round. And this is the Gunner's war. The young wet officers said so joyously as they passed to and fro picking up scandal about breast-straps and breechings, examining the collars of ammunition-wagon teams, and listening to remarks on shoes. Local blacksmiths, assisted by the battery itself, do the shoeing. There are master smiths and important farriers, who have cheerfully thrown up good wages to help the game, and their horses reward them by keeping fit. A fair proportion of the horses are aged – there was never a Gunner yet satisfied with his team or its rations till he had left the battery but they do their work as steadfastly and wholeheartedly as the men. I am persuaded the horses like being in society and working out their daily problems of draught and direction. The English, and Londoners particularly, are the kindest and most reasonable of folk with animals. If it were not our business strictly to underrate ourselves for the next few years, one would say that the Territorial batteries had already done wonders. But perhaps it is better to let it all go with the grudging admission wrung out of a wringing wet bombardier, 'Well, it isn't so dam' bad – considerin'.'

I left them taking their dinner in mess tins to their tents, with a strenuous afternoon's cleaning-up ahead of them. The big park held some thousands of men. I had seen no more than a few hundreds, and had missed the howitzer-batteries after all.

A cock pheasant chaperoned me down the drive, complaining loudly that where he was used to walk with his ladies under the beech trees, some unsporting people had built a miniature landscape with tiny villages, churches, and factories, and came there daily to point cannon at it.

'Keep away from that place,' said I, 'or you'll find yourself in a field-kitchen.'

'Not me!' he crowed. 'I'm as sacred as golf courses.'

Mechanism and Mechanics

There was a little town a couple of miles down the road where one used to lunch in the old days, and had the hotel to oneself. Now there are six ever-changing officers in billet there, and the astonished houses quiver all day to traction engines and high-piled lorries. A unit of the Army Service Corps and some mechanical transport lived near the station, and fed the troops for 20 miles around.

'Are your people easy to find?' I asked of a wandering private, with the hands of a sweep, the head of a Christian among lions, and suicide in his eye.

'Well, the A.S.C. are in the Territorial Drill Hall for one thing; and for another you're likely to hear us! There's some motors come in from Bulford.' He snorted and passed on, smelling of petrol.

The drill-shed was peace and comfort. The A.S.C, were getting ready there for pay-day and for a concert that evening. Outside in the wind and the occasional rain-spurts, life was different. The Bulford motors and some other crocks sat on a side-road between what had been the local garage and a newly erected workshop of creaking scaffold-poles and bellying slatting rick-cloths, where a forge glowed and general, repairs were being effected. Beneath the motors men lay on their backs and called their friends to pass them spanners, or, for pity's sake, to shove another sack under their mud-wreathed heads.

A corporal, who had been nine years a fitter and seven in a city garage, briefly and briskly outlined the more virulent diseases that develop in Government rolling-stock. (I heard quite a lot about Bulford.) Hollow voices from beneath eviscerated gear-boxes confirmed him. We withdrew to the shelter of the rick-cloth workshop – that corporal; the sergeant who had been a carpenter, with a business of his own, and, incidentally, had served through the Boer War; another sergeant who was a member of the Master Builders' Association; and a private who had also been fitter, chauffeur, and a few other things. The third sergeant, who kept a poultry-farm in Surrey, had some duty elsewhere.

A man at a carpenter's bench was finishing a spoke for a newly painted cart He squinted along it.

'That's funny,' said the master builder. 'Of course in his own business he'd chuck his job sooner than do wood-work. But it's all funny.'

'What I grudge,' a sergeant struck in, 'is havin' to put mechanics to loading and unloading beef. That's where modified conscription for the beauties that won't roll up 'd be useful to us. We want hewers of wood, we do. And I'd hew 'em!'

'I want that file.' This was a private in a hurry, come from beneath an unspeakable Bulford. Someone asked him musically if he 'would tell his wife in the morning who he was with tonight.'

'You'll find it in the tool-chest,' said the sergeant. It was his own sacred tool-chest which he had contributed to the common stock.

'And what sort of men have you got in this unit?' I asked.

'Every sort you can think of. There isn't a thing you couldn't have made here if you wanted to. But' – the corporal, who had been a fitter, spoke with fervour – 'you can't expect us to make big-ends, can you? That five-ton Bulford lorry out there in the wet ...'

'And she isn't the worst,' said the master builder. 'But it's all part of the game. And so funny when you come to think of it. Me painting carts, and certificated plumbers loading frozen beef!'

'What about the discipline?' I asked.

The corporal turned a fitter's eye on me. 'The mechanism is the discipline,' said he, with most profound truth. 'Jockeyin' a sick car on the road is discipline, too. What about the discipline?' He turned to the sergeant with the carpenter's chest. There was one sergeant of Regulars, with twenty years' service behind him and a knowledge of human nature. He struck in.

'You ought to know. You've just been made corporal,' said that sergeant of Regulars.

'Well, there's so much which everybody knows has got to be done that that why, we all turn in and do it,' quoth the corporal. 'I don't have any trouble with my lot.'

'Yes; that's how the case stands,' said the sergeant of Regulars. 'Come and see our stores.'

They were beautifully arranged in a shed which felt like a monastery after the windy, clashing world without; and the young private who acted as checker – he came from some railway office – had the thin, keen face of the cleric.

'We're in billets in the town,' said the sergeant who had been a carpenter. 'But I'm a married man. I shouldn't care to have men billeted on us at home, an' I don't want to inconvenience other people. So I've knocked up a bunk for my-self on the premises. It's handier to the stores, too.'

'The Humour of It'

We entered what had been the local garage. The mechanical transport were in full possession, tinkering the gizzards of more cars. We discussed chewed-up gears (samples to hand), and the civil population's old-time views of the military. The corporal told a tale of a clergyman in a Midland town who, only a year ago, on the occasion of some manoeuvres, preached a sermon warning his flock to guard their womenfolk against the soldiers.

'And when you think when you know,' said the corporal, 'what life in those little towns really is!' He whistled.

'See that old landau,' said he, opening the door of an ancient wreck jammed against a wall. 'That's two of our chaps' dressing-room. They don't care to be billeted, so they sleep 'tween the landau and the wall. It's handier for their work, too. Work comes in at all hours. I wish I was cavalry. There's some use in cursing a horse.'

Truly, it's an awful thing to belong to a service where speech brings no alleviation.

'You!' A private with callipers turned from the bench by the window. 'You'd die outside of a garage. But what you said about civilians and soldiers is all out of date now.'

The sergeant of Regulars permitted himself a small, hidden smile. The private with the calipers had been some twelve weeks a soldier.

'I don't say it isn't,' said the corporal, 'I'm saying what it used to be.'

'We-ell,' the private screwed up the callipers, 'didn't you feel a little bit that way yourself when you were a civilian?'

'I – I don't think I did.' The corporal was taken aback. 'I don't think I ever thought about it.'

'Ah! There you are!' said the private, very drily.

Someone laughed in the shadow of the landau dressing-room. 'Anyhow, we're all in it now, Private Percy,' said a voice.

There must be a good many thousand conversations of this kind being held all over England nowadays. Our breed does not warble much about patriotism or Fatherland, but it has a wonderful sense of justice, even when its own shortcomings are concerned.

We went over to the drill-shed to see the men paid.

The first man I ran across there was a sergeant who had served in the Mounted Infantry in the South African picnic that we used to call a war. He had been a private chauffeur for some years long enough to catch the professional look, but was joyously reverting to service type again.

The men lined up, were called out, saluted emphatically at the pay-table, and fell back with their emoluments. They smiled at each other.

'An' it's all so funny,' murmured the master builder in my ear. 'About a quarter – no, less than a quarter – of what one 'ud be making on one's own!'

'Fifty bob a week, cottage, and all found, I was. An' only two cars to look after,' said a voice behind. 'An' if I'd been asked – simply asked – to lie down in the mud all the afternoon ...!' The speaker looked at his wages with awe. Someone wanted to know, *sotto voce*, if 'that was union rates,' and the grin spread among the uniformed experts. The joke, you will observe, lay in situations thrown up, businesses abandoned, and pleasant prospects cut short at the nod of duty.

'Thank Heaven!' said one of them at last, 'it's too dark to work on those blessed Bulfords any more today. We'll get ready for the concert.'

But it was not too dark, half an hour later, for my car to meet a big lorry storming back in the wind and the wet from the northern camps. She gave me London allowance – half one inch between hub and hub – swung her corner like a Brooklands professional, changed gear for the uphill with a sweet click, and charged away. For aught I knew, she was driven by an ex 'fifty-bob-a-week-a-cottage-and-all-found'-er, who next month might be dodging shells with her and thinking it 'all so funny'.

Horse, Foot, even the Guns may sometimes get a little rest, but so long as men eat thrice a day there is no rest for the Army Service Corps. They carry the campaign on their all-sustaining backs.

Canadians in Camp

'Before you hit the buffalo, find out where the rest of the herd is.' Proverb.

This particular fold of downs behind Salisbury might have been a hump of prairie near Winnipeg. The team that came over the rise, widely spaced between pole-bar and whiffle-trees, were certainly children of the prairie. They shied at the car. Their driver asked them dispassionately what they thought they were doing, anyway. They put their wise heads together, and did nothing at all. Yes. Oh, yes! said the driver. They were Western horses. They weighed better than 1,200 apiece. He himself was from Edmonton way. The Camp? Why, the camp was right ahead along up this road. No chance to miss it, and, 'Sa-ay! Look out for our lorries!'

A fleet of them hove in sight going at the rate of knots, and keeping their left with a conscientiousness only learned when you come out of a country where nearly all the Provinces (except British Columbia) keep to the right. Every line of them, from steering-wheel to brake-shoes, proclaimed their nationality. Three perfectly efficient young men who were sprinkling a golf-green with sifted earth ceased their duties to stare at them. Two riding-boys (also efficient) on racehorses, their knees under their chins and their saddles between their horses' ears, cantered past on the turf. The rattle of the motors upset their catsmeat, so one could compare their style of riding with that of an officer loping along to overtake a string of buck-wagons that were trotting towards the horizon. The riding-boys have to endure sore hardship nowadays. One gentleman has already complained that his 'private gallops' are being cut up by gun-wheels and 'irremediably ruined.'

Then more lorries, contractors' wagons, and increasing vileness of the battered road-bed, till one slid through a rude gate into a new world, of canvas as far as the eye could reach, and beyond that outlying clouds of tents. It is not a contingent that Canada has sent, but an army horse, foot, guns, engineers, and all details, fully equipped. Taking that army's strength at 33,000, and the Dominion's population at 8 million, the camp is Canada on the scale of 1:240 – an entire nation unrolled across a few square miles of turf and tents and huts.

Here I could study at close hand 'a Colony' yearning to shake off 'the British yoke'. For, beyond question, they yearned – the rank and file unreservedly, the officers with more restraint but equal fervour – and the things they said about the Yoke were simply lamentable.

From Nova Scotia to Victoria, and every city, township, distributing-centre, and divisional point between; from subtropical White River and sultry Jackfish to the ultimate north that lies up beside Alaska; from Kootenay, and Nelson of the fruit-farms, to Prince Edward Island, where motors are not allowed; they yearned to shake it off, with the dust of England from their feet, 'at once and some time before that.'

I had been warned that when Armageddon came the 'Colonies' would 'revolt against the Mother Country as one man'; but I had no notion I should ever see the dread spectacle with my own eyes – or the 'one man' so tall!

Joking apart, the Canadian Army wants to get to work. It admits that London is 'some city' but says it did not take the trip to visit London only. Armageddon, which so many people in Europe knew was bound to come, has struck Canada out of the blue, like a noonday murder in a small town. How will they feel when they actually view some of the destruction in France, these men who are used to making and owning their homes? And what effect will it have on their land's outlook and development for the next few generations? Older countries may possibly slip back into some sort of toleration. New peoples, in their first serious war, like girls in their first real love-affair, neither forget nor forgive. That is why it pays to keep friends with the young.

And such young! They ran inches above all normal standards, not in a few companies or battalions, but through the whole corps; and it was not easy to pick out foolish or even dull faces among them. Details going about their business through the camp's much mud; defaulters on fatigue; orderlies, foot and mounted; the procession of lorry-drivers ; companies falling in for inspection; battalions parading; brigades moving off for manoeuvres; batteries clanking in from the ranges; they were all supple, free, and intelligent; and moved with a lift and a drive that made one sing for joy.

Camp Gossip

Only a few months ago that entire collection poured into Valcartier camp in pink shirts and straw hats, desperately afraid they might not be in time. Since then they have been taught several things. Notably, that the more independent the individual soldier, the more does he need forethought and endless care when he is in bulk.

'Just because we were all used to looking after ourselves in civil life,' said an officer, 'we used to send parties out without rations. And the parties used to go, too! And we expected the boys to look after their own feet. But we're wiser now.'

'They're learning the same thing in the New Army,' I said. 'Company officers have to be taught to be mothers and housekeepers and sanitary inspectors. Where do your men come from?'

'Tell me some place that they don't come from' said he, and I could not. The men had rolled up from everywhere between the Arctic circle and the border, and I was told that those who could not get into the first contingent were moving heaven and earth and local politicians to get into the second.

'There's some use in politics now,' that officer reflected. 'But it's going to thin the voting-lists at home.'

A good many of the old South African crowd (the rest are coming) were present and awfully correct. Men last met as privates between De Aar and Belmont were captains and majors now, while one lad who, to the best of his ability, had painted Cape Town pink in those fresh years, was a grim non-commissioned officer worth his disciplined weight in dollars.

'I didn't remind Dan of old times when he turned up at Valcartier disguised as a respectable citizen,' said my informant. 'I just roped him in for my crowd. He's a father to 'em. He knows.'

'And have you many cheery souls coming on?' I asked.

'Not many; but it's always the same with a first contingent. You take everything that offers and weed the bravoes out later.'

'We don't weed,' said an officer of artillery. 'Anyone who has had his passage paid for by the Canadian Government stays with us till he eats out of our hand. And he does. They make the best men in the long run,' he added. I thought of a friend of mine who is now disabusing two or three 'old soldiers' in a Service corps of the idea that they can run the battalion, and I laughed. The Gunner was right. 'Old soldiers,' after a little loving care, become valuable and virtuous.

A company of Foot was drawn up under the lee of a fir plantation behind us. They were a miniature of their army as their army was of their people, and one could feel the impact of strong personality almost like a blow.

'If you'd believe it,' said a cavalryman, 'we're forbidden to cut into that little wood-lot, yonder! Not one stick of it may we have! We could make shelters for our horses in a day out of that stuff.'

'But it's timber!' I gasped. 'Sacred, tame trees!'

'Oh, we know what wood is!' They issue it to us by the pound. Wood to burn – by the pound! What's wood for, anyway?'

'And when do you think we shall be allowed to go?' someone asked, not for the first time.

'By and by,' said I. 'And then you'll have to detail half your army to see that your equipment isn't stolen from you.'

'What!' cried an old Strathcona Horse. He looked anxiously towards the horse-lines.

'I was thinking of your mechanical transport and your travelling workshops and a few other things that you've got.'

I got away from those large men on their windy hilltop, and slid through mud and past mechanical transport and troops untold towards Lark Hill. On the way I passed three fresh-cut pine sticks, laid and notched one atop of the other to shore up a caving bank. Trust a Canadian or a beaver within gunshot of standing timber!

Engineers and Appliances

Lark Hill is where the Canadian Engineers live, in the midst of a profligate abundance of tools and carts, pontoon wagons, field telephones, and other mouth-watering gear. Hundreds of tin huts are being built there, but quite leisurely, by contract, I noticed three workmen, at eleven o'clock of that Monday forenoon, as drunk as Davy's sow, reeling and shouting across the landscape. So far as I could ascertain, the workmen do not work extra shifts, nor even, but I hope this is incorrect, on Saturday afternoons; and I think they take their full hour at noon these short days.

Every camp throws up men one has met at the other end of the earth; so, of course, the Engineer C.O. was an ex-South African Canadian.

'Some of our boys are digging a trench over yonder,' he said. 'I'd like you to look at 'em.'

The boys seemed to average 5 feet 10 inches, with 37 inch chests. The soil was unaccommodating chalk.

'What are you?' I asked of the first pickaxe.

'Private.'

'Yes, but before that?'

'McGill (University understood). Nineteen twelve.'

'And that boy with the shovel?'

'Queen's, I think. No; he's Toronto.'

And thus the class in applied geology went on half up the trench, under supervision of a Corporal Bachelor of Science with a most scientific biceps. They were young; they were beautifully fit, and they were all truly thankful that they lived in these high days.

Sappers, like sergeants, take care to make themselves comfortable. The corps were dealing with all sorts of little domestic matters in the way of arrangements for baths, which are cruelly needed, and an apparatus for depopulating shirts, which is even more wanted. Healthy but unwashen men sleeping on the ground are bound to develop certain things which at first disgust them, but later are accepted as an unlovely part of the game. It would be quite easy to make bakehouses and superheated steam fittings to deal with the trouble. The huts themselves stand on brick piers, from one to three feet above ground. The board floors are not grooved or tongued, so there is ample ventilation from beneath; but they have installed decent cooking ranges and gas, and the men have already made themselves all sorts of handy little labour-saving gadgets. They would do this if they were in the real desert. Incidentally, I came across a delightful bit of racial instinct. A man had been told to knock up a desk out of broken packing-cases.

There is only one type of desk in Canada – the roller-top, with three shelves each side the knee-hole, characteristic sloping sides, raised back, and long shelf in front of the writer. He reproduced it faithfully, barring, of course, the roller-top; and the thing leaped to the eye out of its English office surroundings. The Engineers do not suffer for lack of talents. Their senior officers appear to have been the heads, and their juniors the assistants, in big concerns that wrestle with unharnessed nature. (There is a tale of the building of a bridge in Valcartier Camp which is not bad hearing.) The rank and file include miners; road, trestle, and bridge men; iron construction men who, among other things, are steeplejacks; whole castes of such as deal in high explosives for a living; loco-drivers, superintendents, too, for aught I know, and a solid packing of selected machinists, mechanics, and electricians. Unluckily, they were all a foot or so too tall for me to tell them that, even if their equipment escaped at the front, they would infallibly be raided for their men.

An Unrelated Detachment

I left McGill, Queen's, and Toronto still digging in their trench, which another undergraduate, mounted and leading a horse, went out of his way to jump standing. My last glimpse was of a little detachment, with five or six South African ribbons among them, who were being looked over by an officer. No one thought it strange that they should have embodied themselves and crossed the salt seas independently as 'So-and-So's Horse.' (It is best to travel with a tide these days.) Once arrived, they were not at all particular, except that they meant to join the

Army, and the lonely batch was stating its qualifications as Engineers.

'They get over any way and every way,' said my companion. 'Swimming, I believe.'

'But who was the So-and-So that they were christened after?' I asked.

'I guess he was the man who financed 'em or grubstaked 'em while they were waiting. He may be one of 'em in that crowd now; or he may be a provincial magnate at home getting another bunch together.'

The Vanguard of a Nation

Then I went back to the main camp for a last look at that wonderful army, where the tin-roofed messes take French conversation lessons with the keen-faced French-Canadian officers, and where one sees esprit-de-Corps in the making. Nowhere is local sentiment stronger than in Canada. East and West, lake and maritime provinces, prairie and mountain, fruit district and timber lands they each thrill to it. The West keeps one cold blue open-air eye on the townful East. Winnipeg sits between, posing alternately as sophisticated metropolis and simple prairie. Alberta, of the thousand horses, looks down from her high-peaked saddle on all who walk on their feet; and British Columbia thanks God for an equable climate, and that she is not like Ottawa, full of politicians and frozen sludge. Quebec, unassailable in her years and experience, smiles tolerantly on the Nova Scotian, for he has a history too, and asks Montreal if any good thing can come out of Brandon, Moose Jaw, or Regina. They discuss each other outrageously, as they know each other intimately, over 4,000 miles of longitude – their fathers, their families, and all the connections. Which is useful when it comes to sizing up the merits of a newly promoted non-commissioned officer or the capacities of a quartermaster.

As their Army does and suffers, and its record begins to blaze, fierce pride of regiment will be added to local love and the national pride that backs and envelops all. But that pride is held in very severe check now; for they are neither provinces nor tribes but a welded people fighting in the War of Liberty. They permit themselves to hope that the physique of their next contingent will not be worse than that of the present. They believe that their country can send forward a certain number of men and a certain number behind that, all equipped to a certain scale. Of discomforts endured, of the long learning and relearning and waiting on, they say nothing. They do not hint what they will do when their hour strikes, though they more than hint their longing for that hour. In all their talk I caught no phrase that could be twisted into the shadow of a boast or any claim to superiority, even in respect to their kit and outfit; no word or implication of self-praise for any sacrifice made or intended. It was their rigid humility that impressed one as most significant – and, perhaps, most menacing for such as may have to deal with this vanguard of an armed Nation.

Indian Troops

'*Larai meii laddu nahin batte.*' (War is not sugar-plums)
Hindi Proverb.

Working from the East to the West of England, through a countryside alive with troops of all arms, the car came at dusk into a cathedral town entirely inhabited by one type of regiment. The telegraph-office was an orderly jam of solid, large, made men, with years of discipline behind them and the tan of Indian suns on their faces – Englishmen still so fresh from the troopships that one of them asked me, 'What's the day o' the month?' They were advising friends of their arrival in England, or when they might be expected on short leave at the week's end; and the fresh-faced telegraph girls behind the grilles worked with six pairs of hands apiece and all the goodwill and patience in the world to back them. That same young woman who, with nothing to do, makes you wait ten minutes for a penny stamp while she finishes a talk with a lady-friend, will, at a crisis, go on till she drops, and keep her temper throughout. 'Well, if that's her village,' I heard one of the girls say to an anxious soul, 'I tell you that that will be her telegraph-office. You leave it to me. She'll get it all right.'

He backed out, and a dozen more quietly took his place. Their regiments hailed from all the old known stations of the East and beyond that into the Far East again. They cursed their cool barrack accommodation; they rejoiced in the keen autumn smells, and paraded the long street all filled with 'Europe shops'; while their officers and their officers' wives, and, I think, mothers who had come down to snatch a glimpse of their boys, crowded the hotels, and the little unastonished Anglo-Indian children circulated round the knees of big friends they had made aboardship and asked, 'Where are you going now?'

One caught scraps of our old gipsy talk – names of boarding-houses, agents' addresses: 'Milly stays with mother, of course.' 'I'm taking Jack down to school tomorrow. It's past half-term, but that doesn't matter nowadays'; and cheery farewells between men and calm-eyed women. Except for the frocks, it might have been an evening assembly at any station bandstand in India.

Outside, on the surging pavements, a small boy cried: 'Paper! Evenin' paper!' Then seductively: '*Kargus!*'

'What?' I said, thinking my ears had cheated me.

'*Dekko! Kargus!*' said he. ('Look here! Paper!')

'Why on earth d'you say that?'

'Because the men like it,' he replied, and slapped an evening paper (no change for a penny) into the hand of a man in a helmet.

Who shall say that the English are not adaptable?

The car swam bonnet-deep through a mile of troops; and a mile up the road one could hear the deep hum of all those crowded streets that the cathedral bells were chiming over. It was only one small block of Anglo-India getting ready to take its place in the all-devouring line.

Screw-Guns

An hour later at — (Shall we ever be able to name people and places outright again?) the wind brought up one whiff – one unmistakable whiff – of *ghi*. Somewhere among the English pines that, for the moment, pretended to be the lower slopes of the Dun, there were native troops. A mule squealed in the dark and set off half-a-dozen others. It was screw-guns – batteries of them, waiting their turn also at the game. Morning showed them in their immaculate lines as though they had just marched in from Jutogh – little, low guns with their ammunition; very big English gunners in disengaged attitudes which, nevertheless, did not encourage stray civilians to poke and peer into things; and the native drivers all busied over their charges. True, the wind was bitter, and many of the drivers had tied up their heads, but so one does at Quetta in the cold weather – not to mention Peshawur – and said a naick of drivers: 'It is not the cold for which we have no liking. It is the wet. The English air is good, but water falls at all seasons. Yet notwithstanding, we of this battery (and, oh, the pride men can throw into a mere number!) have not lost one mule. Neither at sea nor on land have we one lost. That can be shown, sahib.'

Then one heard the deep racking tobacco-cough in the lee of a tent where four or five men – Kangra folk by the look of them – were drinking tobacco out of a cow's horn. Their own country's tobacco, be sure, for English tobacco ... But there was no need to explain. Who would have dreamed to smell bazar-tobacco on a south country golf links?

A large proportion of the men are, of course, Sikhs, to whom tobacco is forbidden; the Havildar Major himself was a Sikh of the Sikhs, he spoke, of all things in this strange world, of the late Mr. M. McAuliffe's monumental book on the Sikh religion, saying, not without warrant, that McAuliffe Sahib had translated into English, much of the Holy Book – the great Grunth Sahib that lives at Amritzar. He enlarged, too, on the ancient prophecy among the Sikhs – that a hatted race should someday come out of the sea and lead them to victory all the earth over. So spoke Bir Singh, erect and enormous beneath the grey English skies. He hailed from a certain place called Banalu, near Patiala, where many years ago two Sikh soldiers executed a striking but perfectly just vengeance on certain villagers who had oppressed their young brother, a cultivator. They had gone to the extreme limits of abasement and conciliation. This failing, they took leave for a weekend and slew the whole tribe of their enemies. The story is buried in old Government reports, but when Bir Singh implied that he and his folk were orthodox I had no doubt of it. And behind him stood another giant, who knew, for his village was but a few miles up the Shalimar road, every foot of Lahore city. He brought word that there had been great floods at home, so that the risen Ravi River had touched the very walls of Runjit Singh's Fort. And that was only last rains – and, behold! – here he was now in England waiting orders to go to this fight which, he understood, was not at all a small fight, but a fight of fights, in which all the world and 'our Raj' was engaged. The trouble in India was that all the young men – the mere *jiwans* – wanted to come out at once, which, he said, was manifestly unjust to older men, who had waited so long. However, merit and patience had secured their reward, and the battery was here, and it would do the hot *jiwans* no harm to stay at home, and be zealous at drill until orders came for them in their turn. 'Young men think that everything good in this world is theirs by right, sahib.'

Then came the big, still English gunners, who are trained to play with the little guns. They took one such gun and melted it into trifling pieces of not more than 150 lbs each, and reassembled it, and explained its innermost heart till even a layman could understand. There is a lot to understand about screw-guns specially the new kind. But the gunner of today, like his ancestor, does not talk much, except in his own time and place, when he is as multitudinously amazing as the Blue Marine.

The Mule Lines

We went over to see the mule lines. I detest the whole generation of these parrot-mouthed hybrids, American, Egyptian, Andalusian, or up-country: so it gave me particular pleasure to hear a Pathan telling one chestnut beast who objected to having its mane hogged any more, what sort of lady-horse his mamma had been. But *qua* animals, they were a lovely lot, and had long since given up blowing and finicking over English fodder.

'Is there any sickness? Why is yonder mule lying down?' I demanded, as though all the lines could not see I was a shuddering amateur.

'There is no sickness, sahib? That mule lies down for his own pleasure. Also, to get out of the wind. He is very clever. He is from Hindustan,' said the man with the horse-clippers.

'And thou?'

'I am a Pathan,' said he with impudent grin and true border cock of the turban, and he did me the honour to let me infer.

The lines were full of talk as the men went over their animals. They were not worrying themselves over this new country of Belait. It was the regular gossip of food and water and firewood, and where So-and-so had hid the curry-comb.

Talking of cookery, the orthodox men have been rather put out by English visitors who come to the cook-houses and stare directly at the food while it is being prepared. Sensible men do not object to this, because they know that these Englishmen have no evil intention nor any evil eye; but sometimes a narrow-souled purist (toothache or liver makes a man painfully religious) will 'spy strangers' and insist on the strict letter of the law, and then everyone who wishes to be orthodox must agree with him – on an empty stomach, too – and wait till a fresh mess has been cooked. This is *taklif* – a burden – for where the intention is good and war is afoot much can and should be overlooked. Moreover, this war is not like any other war. It is a war of our Raj – 'everybody's war,' as they say in the bazaars. And that is another reason why it does not matter if an Englishman stares at one's food. This I gathered in small pieces after watering time when the mules had filed up to the troughs in the twilight, hundreds of them, and the drivers grew discursive on the way to the lines.

The last I saw of them was in the early cold morning, all in marching order, jinking and jingling down a road through woods.

'Where are you going?'

'God knows!'

The Inn of Good-Byes

It might have been for exercise merely, or it might be down to the sea and away to the front for the battle of 'Our Raj.' The quiet hotel where people sit together and talk in earnest strained pairs is well used to such departures. The officers of a whole Division – the raw cuts of their tent-circles lie still unhealed on the links – dined there by scores; mothers and relatives came down from the uttermost parts of Scotland for a last look at their boys, and found beds goodness knows where: very quiet little weddings, too, set out from its doors to the church opposite. The Division went away a century of weeks ago by the road that the mule-battery took. Many of the civilians who pocketed the wills signed and witnessed in the smoking-room are full-blown executors now; some of the brides are widows.

And it is not nice to remember that when the hotel was so filled that not even another pleading mother could be given a place in which to lie down and have her cry out – not at all nice to remember that it never occurred to any of the comfortable people in the large but sparsely inhabited houses around that they might have offered a night's lodging, even to an unintroduced stranger.

Greatheart and Christiana

There were hospitals up the road preparing and being prepared for the Indian wounded. In one of these lay a man of, say, a Biluch regiment, sorely hit. Word had come from his colonel in France to the colonel's wife in England that she should seek till she found that very man and got news from his very mouth – news to send to his family and village. She found him at last, and he was very bewildered to see her there, because he had left her and her child on the verandah of the bungalow, long and long ago, when he and his colonel and the regiment went down to take ship for the war. How had she come? Who had guarded her during her train-journey of so many days? And, above all, how had the baba endured that sea which caused strong men to collapse? Not till all these matters had been cleared up in fullest detail did Greatheart on his cot permit his colonel's wife to waste one word on his own insignificant concerns. And that she should have wept filled him with real trouble. Truly, this is the war of 'Our Raj!'

Territorial Battalions

'To excuse oneself to oneself is human: but to excuse
oneself to one's children is Hell.' Arabic Proverb.

Billeted troops are difficult to get at. There are thousands
of them in a little old town by the side of an even older
park up the London Road, but to find a particular
battalion is like ferreting unstopped burrows.

'The Umpty-Umpth, were you looking for?' said a
private in charge of a side-car, 'We're the Eenty-Eenth.'
Only came in last week, I've never seen this place before.
It's pretty. Hold on! There's a postman. He'll know.'

He, too, was in khaki, bowed between mailbags, and
his accent was of a far and coaly county.

'I'm none too sure,' said he, 'but I think I saw ...'

Here a third man cut in.

'Yon's t' battalion, marchin' into t' park now. Roon!
Happen tha'll catch 'em.'

They turned out to be Territorials with a history behind
them; but that I didn't know till later; and their band
and cyclists. Very polite were those rear-rank cyclists
– who pushed their loaded machines with one vast hand
apiece.

They were strangers, they said. They had only come
here a few days ago. But they knew the South well. They
had been in Gloucestershire, which was a very nice
southern place.

Then their battalion, I hazarded, was of northern
extraction?

They admitted that I might go as far as that; their
speech betraying their native town at every rich word.

'Huddersfield, of course?' I said, to make them out with it.

'Bolton,' said one at last. Being in uniform the pitman could not destroy the impertinent civilián.

'Ah, Bolton!' I returned. 'All cotton, aren't you?'

'Some coal,' he answered gravely. There is notorious rivalry 'twixt coal and cotton in Bolton, but I wanted to see him practice the self-control that the Army is always teaching.

As I have said, he and his companion were most polite, but the total of their information, boiled and peeled, was that they had just come from Bolton way; might at any moment be sent somewhere else, and they liked Gloucestershire in the south. A spy could not have learned much less.

The battalion halted, and moved off by companies for further evolutions. One could see they were more than used to drill and arms; a hardened, thick-necked, thin-flanked, deep-chested lot, dealt with quite faithfully by their sergeants, and altogether abreast of their work. Why, then, this reticence? What had they to be ashamed of, these big Bolton folk without an address? Where was their orderly-room?

There were many orderly-rooms in the little old town, most of them in by-lanes less than one car wide. I found what I wanted, and – this was north-country all over – a private who volunteered to steer me to headquarters through the tricky southern streets. He was communicative, and told me a good deal about typhoid-inoculation and musketry practice, which accounted for only six companies being on parade. But surely they could not have been ashamed of that.

Guarding a Railway

I unearthed their skeleton at last in a peaceful, gracious 500-year-old house that looked on to lawns and cut hedges bounded by age-old red brick walls – such a perfumed and dreaming place as one would choose for the setting of some even-pulsed English love-tale of the days before the war.

Officers were billeted in the low-ceiled, shiny-floored rooms full of books and flowers.

'And now,' I asked, when I had told the tale of the uncommunicative cyclist, 'what is the matter with your battalion?'

They laughed cruelly at me. 'Matter!' said they. 'We're just off three months of guarding railways. After that a man wouldn't trust his own mother. You don't mean to say our cyclists let you know where we've come from last?'

'No, they didn't,' I replied. 'That was what worried me. I assumed you'd all committed murders, and had been sent here to live it down.'

Then they told me what guarding a line really means. How men wake and walk, with only express troop-trains to keep them company, all the night long on windy embankments or under still more windy bridges; how they sleep behind three sleepers up-ended or a bit of tin, or, if they are lucky, in a platelayer's hut; how their food comes to them slopping across the square-headed ties that lie in wait to twist a man's ankle after dark; how they stand in blown coal-dust of goods-yards trying to watch five lines of trucks at once; how fools of all classes pester the lonely pickets, whose orders are to hold up motors for inquiry, and then write silly letters to the War Office about it. How nothing ever happens through the long weeks but infallibly would if the patrols were taken off. And they had one refreshing story of a workman who at six in the morning, which is no auspicious hour to jest with Lancashire, took a short cut to his work by ducking under some goods-wagons, and when challenged by the sentry replied, posturing on all fours, 'Boo, I'm a German!' Whereat the upright sentry fired, unfortunately missed him, and then gave him the butt across his ass's head, so that his humour, and very nearly his life, terminated.

After which the sentry was seldom seen to smile, but frequently heard to murmur, 'Ah should hev slipped t' baggonet into him.'

Pride and Prejudice

'So you see,' said the officers in conclusion, 'you mustn't be surprised that our men wouldn't tell you much.'

'I begin to see,' I said. 'How many of you are coal and how many cotton?'

'Two-thirds coal and one-third cotton, roughly. It keeps the men deadly keen. An operative isn't going to give up while a pitman goes on; and very much vice versa.'

'That's class-prejudice,' said I.

'It's most useful,' said they. The officers themselves seemed to be interested in coal or cotton, and had known their men intimately on the civil side, If your orderly-room sergeant, or your quartermaster has been your trusted head clerk or foreman for ten or twelve years, and if eight out of a dozen sergeants have controlled pitmen and machinists, above and below ground, and 80 per cent of these pitmen and machinists are privates in the companies, your regiment works with something of the precision of a big business.

It was all new talk to me, for I had not yet met a Northern Territorial battalion with the strong pride of its strong town behind it. Where were they when the war came? How had they equipped themselves? I wanted to hear the tale. It was worth listening to as told with North-Country joy of life and the doing of things in that soft down-country house of the untroubled centuries. Like everyone else, they were expecting anything but war. Hadn't even begun their annual camp. Then the thing came, and Bolton rose as one man and woman to fit out its battalion. There was a lady who wanted a fairly large sum of money for the men's extra footgear. She set aside a morning to collect it, and inside the hour came home with nearly twice her needs, and spent the rest of the time trying to make people take back fivers, at least, out of tenners. And the big hauling firms flung horses and transport at them and at the Government, often refusing any price, or, when it was paid, turning it into the war funds. What the battalion wanted it had but to ask for. Once it was short of, say, towels. An officer approached the head of a big firm, with no particular idea he would get more than a few dozen from that quarter.

'...And how many towels d'you want?' said the head of the firm. The officer suggested a globular thousand.

'I think you'll do better with twelve hundred,' was the curt answer. 'They're ready out yonder. Get 'em.'

And in this style Bolton turned out her battalion. Then the authorities took it and strung it by threes and fives along several score miles of railway track: and it had only just been reassembled, and it had been inoculated for typhoid. Consequently, they said (but all officers are like mothers and motorcar owners), it wasn't up to what it would be in a little time. In spite of the cyclist, I had had a good look at the deep chested battalion in the park, and after getting their musketry figures, it seemed to me that very soon it might be worth looking at by more prejudiced persons than myself.

The next day I read that this battalion's regular battalion in the field had distinguished itself by a piece of work which, in other wars, would have been judged heroic. Bolton will read it, not without remarks, and other towns who love Bolton, more or less, will say that if all the truth could come out their regiments had done as well. Anyway, the result will be more men – pitmen, mill-hands, clerks, checkers, weighers, winders, and hundreds of those sleek, well-groomed business-chaps whom one used to meet in the big Midland hotels, protesting that war was out of date. These latter develop surprisingly in the camp atmosphere. I recall one raging in his army shirt -sleeves at a comrade who had derided his principles. 'I am a blanky pacificist,' he hissed, 'and I'm proud of it, and-and I'm going to make you one before I've finished with you!'

The Secret of the Services

Pride of city, calling, class, and creed imposes standards and obligations which hold men above themselves at a pinch, and steady them through long strain. One meets it in the New Army at every turn, from the picked Territorials who slipped across Channel last night to the six-week-old Service battalion maturing itself in mud. It is balanced by the ineradicable English instinct to understate, detract, and decry – to mask the thing done by loudly drawing attention to the things undone.

The more one sees of the camps the more one is filled with facts and figures of joyous significance, which will become clearer as the days lengthen and the less one hears of the endurance, decency, self-sacrifice, and utter devotion which have made, and are hourly making, this wonderful new world. The camps take this for granted – else why should any man be there at all? He might have gone on with his business, or – watched 'soccer.' But having chosen to do his bit, he does it, and talks as much about his motives as he would his religion or his love-affairs. He is eloquent over the shortcomings of the authorities, more pessimistic as to the future of his next neighbour battalion than would be safe to print, and lyric on his personal needs – baths and drying-rooms for choice. But when the grousing gets beyond a certain point – say at three a.m., in steady wet, with the tent-pegs drawing like false teeth – the nephew of the insurance-agent asks the cousin of the baronet to inquire of the son of the fried-fish vendor what the stevedore's brother and the tutor of the public school joined the Army for. Then they sing 'Somewhere the Sun is Shining' till the Sergeant Ironmonger's assistant cautions them to drown in silence or the Lieutenant Telephone-appliances-manufacturer will speak to them in the morning.

The New armies have not yet evolved their typical private, N.C.O., and officer, though one can see them shaping. They are humorous because, for all our long faces, we are the only genuinely humorous race on earth; but they all know for true that there are no excuses in the Service. 'If there were,' said a three-month-old under-gardener-private to me, 'what 'ud become of Discipline?'

They are already setting standards for the coming millions, and have sown little sprouts of regimental tradition which may grow into age-old trees. In one corps, for example, though no dubbin is issued a man loses his name for parading with dirty boots. He looks down scornfully on the next battalion where they are not expected to achieve the impossible. In another – an ex-Guards sergeant brought 'em up by hand – the drill is rather high-class. In a third they fuss about records for route-marching, and men who fall out have to explain themselves to their sweating companions. This is entirely right. They are all now in the Year One, and the meanest of them may be an ancestor of whom regimental posterity will say: 'There were giants in those days!'

The Real Question

This much we can realise, even though we are so close to it. The old safe instinct saves us from triumph and exultation. But what will be the position in years to come of the young man who has deliberately elected to outcaste himself from this all-embracing brotherhood? What of his family, and, above all, what of his descendants, when the books have been closed and the last balance struck of sacrifice and sorrow in every hamlet, village, parish, suburb, city, shire, district, province, and Dominion throughout the Empire?

France at War (1915)

Broke to every known mischance,
lifted over all
By the light sane joy of life, the buckler
of the Gaul,
Furious in luxury, merciless in toil,
Terrible with strength that draws from
her tireless soil,
Strictest judge of her own worth, gentlest
of men's mind,
First to follow truth and last to leave
old truths behind –
France beloved of every soul that loves
its fellow-kind.
Ere our birth (rememberest thou?) side
by side we lay
Fretting in the womb of Rome to begin
the fray.
Ere men knew our tongues apart, our one
taste was known –
Each must mould the other's fate as he
wrought his own.
To this end we stirred mankind till all
earth was ours,

Till our world-end strifes began wayside
thrones and powers,
Puppets that we made or broke to bar
the other's path –
Necessary, outpost folk, hirelings of our
wrath.
To this end we stormed the seas, tack for
tack, and burst
Through the doorways of new worlds,
doubtful which was first.
Hand on hilt (rememberest thou?), ready
for the blow.
Sure whatever else we met we should
meet our foe.
Spurred or baulked at ev'ry stride by the
other's strength,
So we rode the ages down and every ocean's
length;
Where did you refrain from us or we
refrain from you?
Ask the wave that has not watched war
between us two.
Others held us for a while, but with
weaker charms,
These we quitted at the call for each
other's arms.
Eager toward the known delight, equally
we strove,
Each the other's mystery, terror, need,
and love.
To each other's open court with our
proofs we came,

Where could we find honour else or men
to test the claim?
From each other's throat we wrenched
valour's last reward,
That extorted word of praise gasped
'twixt lunge and guard.
In each other's cup we poured mingled
blood and tears,
Brutal joys, unmeasured hopes,
intolerable fears,
All that soiled or salted life for a thousand
years.
Proved beyond the need of proof, matched
in every clime,
O companion, we have lived greatly
through all time:
Yoked in knowledge and remorse now we
come to rest,
Laughing at old villainies that time has
turned to jest,
Pardoning old necessity no pardon can
efface –
That undying sin we shared in Rouen
market-place.
Now we watch the new years shape,
wondering if they hold
Fiercer lighting in their hearts than we
launched of old.
Now we hear new voices rise, question,
boast or gird,
As we raged (rememberest thou?) when
our crowds were stirred.

France at War (1915)

Now we count new keels afloat, and new
hosts on land,
Massed liked ours (rememberest thou?)
when our strokes were planned.
We were schooled for dear life sake, to
know each other's blade:
What can blood and iron make more than
we have made?
We have learned by keenest use to know
each other's mind:
What shall blood and iron loose that we
cannot bind?
We who swept each other's coast, sacked
each other's home,
Since the sword of Brennus clashed on
the scales at Rome,
Listen, court and close again, wheeling
girth to girth,
In the strained and bloodless guard set
for peace on earth.
Broke to every known mischance,
lifted over all
By the light sane joy of life, the buckler
of the Gaul,
Furious in luxury, merciless in toil,
Terrible with strength renewed from a tireless soil,
Strictest judge of her own worth, gentlest
of men's mind,
First to follow truth and last to leave
old truths behind,
France beloved of every soul that loves
or serves its kind.

On the Frontier of Civilisation

'It's a pretty park,' said the French artillery officer. 'We've done a lot for it since the owner left. I hope he'll appreciate it when he comes back.'

The car traversed a winding drive through woods, between banks embellished with little chalets of a rustic nature. At first, the chalets stood their full height above ground, suggesting tea-gardens in England. Further on they sank into the earth till, at the top of the ascent, only their solid brown roofs showed. Torn branches drooping across the driveway, with here and there a scorched patch of undergrowth, explained the reason of their modesty.

The chateau that commanded these glories of forest and park sat boldly on a terrace. There was nothing wrong with it except, if one looked closely, a few scratches or dints on its white stone walls, or a neatly drilled hole under a flight of steps. One such hole ended in an unexploded shell. 'Yes,' said the officer. 'They arrive here occasionally.'

Something bellowed across the folds of the wooded hills; something grunted in reply. Something passed overhead, querulously but not without dignity. Two clear fresh barks joined the chorus, and a man moved lazily in the direction of the guns.

'Well. Suppose we come and look at things a little,' said the commanding officer.

An Observation Post

There was a specimen tree – a tree worthy of such a park – the sort of tree visitors are always taken to admire. A ladder ran up it to a platform. What little wind there was swayed the tall top, and the ladder creaked like a ship's gangway. A telephone bell tinkled 50-foot overhead. Two invisible guns spoke fervently for half a minute, and broke off like terriers choked on a leash. We climbed till the topmost platform swayed sicklily beneath us. Here one found a rustic shelter, always of the tea-garden pattern, a table, a map, and a little window wreathed with living branches that gave one the first view of the Devil and all his works. It was a stretch of open country, with a few sticks like old toothbrushes which had once been trees round a farm. The rest was yellow grass, barren to all appearance as the veldt.

'The grass is yellow because they have used gas here,' said an officer. 'Their trenches are— You can see for yourself.'

The guns in the woods began again. They seemed to have no relation to the regularly spaced bursts of smoke along a little smear in the desert earth two thousand yards away – no connection at all with the strong voices overhead coming and going. It was as impersonal as the drive of the sea along a breakwater.

Thus it went: a pause – a gathering of sound like the race of an incoming wave; then the high-flung heads of breakers spouting white up the face of a groyne. Suddenly, a seventh wave broke and spread the shape of its foam like a plume overtopping all the others.

'That's one of our *torpilleurs*—what you call trench-sweepers,' said the observer among the whispering leaves.

Someone crossed the platform to consult the map with its ranges. A blistering outbreak of white smokes rose a little beyond the large plume. It was as though the tide had struck a reef out yonder.

Then a new voice of tremendous volume lifted itself out of a lull that followed. Somebody laughed. Evidently the voice was known.

'That is not for us,' a gunner said. 'They are being waked up from —' he named a distant French position. 'So-and-so is attending to them there. We go on with our usual work. Look! Another *torpilleur*.'

'The Barbarian'

Again a big plume rose; and again the lighter shells broke at their appointed distance beyond it. The smoke died away on that stretch of trench, as the foam of a swell dies in the angle of a harbour wall, and broke out afresh half a mile lower down. In its apparent laziness, in its awful deliberation, and its quick spasms of wrath, it was more like the work of waves than of men; and our high platform's gentle sway and glide was exactly the motion of a ship drifting with us toward that shore.

'The usual work. Only the usual work,' the officer explained. 'Sometimes it is here. Sometimes above or below us. I have been here since May.'

A little sunshine flooded the stricken landscape and made its chemical yellow look fouler. A detachment of men moved out on a road which ran toward the French trenches, and then vanished at the foot of a little rise. Other men appeared moving toward us with that concentration of purpose and bearing shown in both Armies when – dinner is at hand. They looked like people who had been digging hard.

'The same work. Always the same work!' the officer said.

'And you could walk from here to the sea or to Switzerland in that ditch – and you'll find the same work going on everywhere. It isn't war.'

'It's better than that,' said another. 'It's the eating-up of a people. They come and they fill the trenches and they die, and they die; and they send more and those die. We do the same, of course, but – look!'

He pointed to the large deliberate smoke-heads renewing themselves along that yellowed beach. 'That is the frontier of civilization. They have all civilization against them – those brutes yonder. It's not the local victories of the old wars that we're after. It's the barbarian – all the barbarian. Now, you've seen the whole thing in little. Come and look at our children.'

Soldiers in Caves

We left that tall tree whose fruits are death ripened and distributed at the tingle of small bells. The observer returned to his maps and calculations; the telephone-boy stiffened up beside his exchange as the amateurs went out of his life. Someone called down through the branches to ask who was attending to – Belial, let us say, for I could not catch the gun's name. It seemed to belong to that terrific new voice which had lifted itself for the second or third time. It appeared from the reply that if Belial talked too long he would be dealt with from another point miles away.

The troops we came down to see were at rest in a chain of caves which had begun life as quarries and had been fitted up by the army for its own uses. There were underground corridors, ante-chambers, rotundas, and ventilating shafts with a bewildering play of cross lights, so that wherever you looked you saw Goya's pictures of men-at-arms.

Every soldier has some of the old maid in him, and rejoices in all the gadgets and devices of his own invention. Death and wounding come by nature, but to lie dry, sleep soft, and keep yourself clean by forethought and contrivance is art, and in all things the Frenchman is gloriously an artist.

Moreover, the French officers seem as mother-keen on their men as their men are brother-fond of them. Maybe the possessive form of address: '*Mon general*,' '*mon capitaine*,' helps the idea, which our men cloke in other and curter phrases. And those soldiers, like ours, had been welded for months in one furnace. As an officer said: 'Half our orders now need not be given. Experience makes us think together.' I believe, too, that if a French private has an idea – and they are full of ideas – it reaches his C.O. quicker than it does with us.

The Sentinel Hounds

The overwhelming impression was the brilliant health and vitality of these men and the quality of their breeding. They bore themselves with swing and rampant delight in life, while their voices as they talked in the side-caverns among the stands of arms were the controlled voices of civilization. Yet, as the lights pierced the gloom they looked like bandits dividing the spoil. One picture, though far from war, stays with me. A perfectly built, dark-skinned young giant had peeled himself out of his blue coat and had brought it down with a swish upon the shoulder of a half-stripped comrade who was kneeling at his feet with some footgear. They stood against a background of semi-luminous blue haze, through which glimmered a pile of coppery straw half covered by a red blanket. By divine accident of light and pose it looks like St Martin giving his cloak to the beggar. There were scores of pictures in these galleries – notably a rock-hewn chapel where the red of the cross on the rough canvas altar-cloth glowed like a ruby. Further inside the caves we found a row of little rock-cut kennels, each inhabited by one wise, silent dog. Their duties begin at night with the sentinels and listening-posts. 'And believe me,' a proud instructor, 'my fellow here knows the difference between the noise of our shells and the Boche shells.'

When we came out into the open again there were good opportunities for this study. Voices and wings met and passed in the air, and, perhaps, one strong young tree had not been bending quite so far across the picturesque park-drive when we first went that way.

'Oh, yes,' said an officer, 'shells have to fall somewhere, and,' he added with fine toleration, 'it is, after all, against us that the Boche directs them. But come you and look at my dug-out. It's the most superior of all possible dug-outs.'

'No. Come and look at our mess. It's the Ritz of these parts.' And they joyously told how they had got, or procured, the various fittings and elegancies, while hands stretched out of the gloom to shake, and men nodded welcome and greeting all through that cheery brotherhood in the woods.

Work in the Fields

The voices and the wings were still busy after lunch, when the car slipped past the tea-houses in the drive, and came into a country where women and children worked among the crops. There were large raw shell holes by the wayside or in the midst of fields, and often a cottage or a villa had been smashed as a bonnet-box is smashed by an umbrella. That must be part of Belial's work when he bellows so truculently among the hills to the north.

We were looking for a town that lives under shell-fire. The regular road to it was reported unhealthy – not that the women and children seemed to care. We took byways of which certain exposed heights and corners were lightly blinded by wind-brakes of dried tree-tops. Here the shell holes were rather thick on the ground. But the women and the children and the old men went on with their work with the cattle and the crops; and where a house had been broken by shells the rubbish was collected in a neat pile, and where a room or two still remained usable, it was inhabited, and the tattered window-curtains fluttered as proudly as any flag. And time was when I used to denounce young France because it tried to kill itself beneath my car wheels; and the fat old women who crossed roads without warning; and the especially deaf old men who slept in carts on the wrong side of the road! Now, I could take off my hat to every single soul of them, but that one cannot traverse a whole land bareheaded. The nearer we came to our town the fewer were the people, till at last we halted in a well-built suburb of paved streets where there was no life at all …

A Wrecked Town

The stillness was as terrible as the spread of the quick busy weeds between the paving-stones; the air smelt of pounded mortar and crushed stone; the sound of a footfall echoed like the drop of a pebble in a well. At first the horror of wrecked apartment-houses and big shops laid open makes one waste energy in anger. It is not seemly that rooms should be torn out of the sides of buildings as one tears the soft heart out of English bread; that villa roofs should lie across iron gates of private garages, or that drawing-room doors should flap alone and disconnected between two emptinesses of twisted girders. The eye wearies of the repeated pattern that burst shells make on stone walls, as the mouth sickens of the taste of mortar and charred timber. One quarter of the place had been shelled nearly level; the facades of the houses stood doorless, roofless, and windowless like stage scenery. This was near the cathedral, which is always a favourite mark for the heathen. They had gashed and ripped the sides of the cathedral itself, so that the birds flew in and out at will; they had smashed holes in the roof; knocked huge cantles out of the buttresses, and pitted and starred the paved square outside. They were at work, too, that very afternoon, though I do not think the cathedral was their objective for the moment. We walked to and fro in the silence of the streets and beneath the whirring wings overhead. Presently, a young woman, keeping to the wall, crossed a corner. An old woman opened a shutter (how it jarred!), and spoke to her. The silence closed again, but it seemed to me that I heard a sound of singing – the sort of chant one hears in nightmare-cities of voices crying from underground.

In the Cathedral

'Nonsense,' said an officer. 'Who should be singing here?' We circled the cathedral again, and saw what pavement-stones can do against their own city, when the shell jerks them upward. But there was singing after all – on the other side of a little door in the flank of the cathedral. We looked in, doubting, and saw at least a hundred folk, mostly women, who knelt before the altar of an unwrecked chapel. We withdrew quietly from that holy ground, and it was not only the eyes of the French officers that filled with tears. Then there came an old, old thing with a prayer-book in her hand, pattering across the square, evidently late for service.

'And who are those women?' I asked.

'Some are caretakers; people who still have little shops here. (There is one quarter where you can buy things.) There are many old people, too, who will not go away. They are of the place, you see.'

'And this bombardment happens often?' I said.

'It happens always. Would you like to look at the railway station? Of course, it has not been so bombarded as the cathedral.'

We went through the gross nakedness of streets without people, till we reached the railway station, which was very fairly knocked about, but, as my friends said, nothing like as much as the cathedral. Then we had to cross the end of a long street down which the Boche could see clearly. As one glanced up it, one perceived how the weeds, to whom men's war is the truce of God, had come back and were well established the whole length of it, watched by the long perspective of open, empty windows.

The Nation's Spirit and a New Inheritance

We left that stricken but undefeated town, dodged a few miles down the roads beside which the women tended their cows, and dropped into a place on a hill where a Moroccan regiment of many experiences was in billets.

They were Mohammedans bafflingly like half a dozen of our Indian frontier types, though they spoke no accessible tongue. They had, of course, turned the farm buildings where they lay into a little bit of Africa in colour and smell. They had been gassed in the north; shot over and shot down, and set up to be shelled again; and their officers talked of North African wars that we had never heard of – sultry days against long odds in the desert years ago. 'Afterward – is it not so with you also? – we get our best recruits from the tribes we have fought. These men are children. They make no trouble. They only want to go where cartridges are burnt. They are of the few races to whom fighting is a pleasure.'

'And how long have you dealt with them?'

'A long time – a long time. I helped to organise the corps. I am one of those whose heart is in Africa.' He spoke slowly, almost feeling for his French words, and gave some order. I shall not forget his eyes as he turned to a huge, brown, Afreedee-like Mussulman hunkering down beside his accoutrements. He had two sides to his head, that bearded, burned, slow-spoken officer, met and parted within an hour.

The day closed – (after an amazing interlude in the chateau of a dream, which was all glassy ponds, stately trees, and vistas of white and gold saloons. The proprietor was somebody's chauffeur at the front, and we drank to his excellent health) – at a little village in a twilight full of the petrol of many cars and the wholesome flavour of healthy troops. There is no better guide to camp than one's own thoughtful nose; and though I poked mine everywhere, in no place then or later did it strike that vile betraying taint of underfed, unclean men. And the same with the horses.

The Line That Never Sleeps

It is difficult to keep an edge after hours of fresh air and experiences; so one does not get the most from the most interesting part of the day – the dinner with the local headquarters. Here the professionals meet – the Line, the Gunners, and the Intelligence with stupefying photo-plans of the enemy's trenches; the Supply; the Staff, who collect and note all things, and are very properly chaffed; and, be sure, the Interpreter, who, by force of questioning prisoners, naturally develops into a *Sadducee*. It is their little asides to each other, the slang, and the half-words which, if one understood, instead of blinking drowsily at one's plate, would give the day's history in little. But tire and the difficulties of a sister (not a foreign) tongue cloud everything, and one goes to billets amid a murmur of voices, the rush of single cars through the night, the passage of battalions, and behind it all, the echo of the deep voices calling one to the other, along the line that never sleeps.

The ridge with the scattered pines might have hidden children at play. Certainly a horse would have been quite visible, but there was no hint of guns, except a semaphore which announced it was forbidden to pass that way, as the battery was firing. The Boches must have looked for that battery, too. The ground was pitted with shell holes of all calibres – some of them as fresh as mole-casts in the misty damp morning; others where the poppies had grown from seed to flower all through the summer.

'And where are the guns?' I demanded at last.

They were almost under one's hand, their ammunition in cellars and dug-outs beside them. As far as one can make out, the 75 gun has no pet name. The bayonet is

Rosalie the virgin of Bayonne, but the 75, the watchful nurse of the trenches and little sister of the Line, seems to be always '*soixante-quinze*.' Even those who love her best do not insist that she is beautiful. Her merits are French – logic, directness, simplicity, and the supreme gift of 'occasionality.' She is equal to everything on the spur of the moment. One sees and studies the few appliances which make her do what she does, and one feels that anyone could have invented her.

Famous French 75s

'As a matter of fact,' says a commandant, 'anybody – or, rather, everybody did. The general idea is after such-and-such system, the patent of which had expired, and we improved it; the breech action, with slight modification, is somebody else's; the sighting is perhaps a little special; and so is the traversing, but, at bottom, it is only an assembly of variations and arrangements.'

That, of course, is all that Shakespeare ever got out of the alphabet. The French Artillery make their own guns as he made his plays. It is just as simple as that.

'There is nothing going on for the moment; it's too misty,' said the Commandant. (I fancy that the Boche, being, as a rule methodical, amateurs are introduced to batteries in the Boche's intervals. At least, there are hours healthy and unhealthy which vary with each position. 'But,' the Commandant reflected a moment, 'there is a place – and a distance. Let us say ...' He gave a range.

The gun-servers stood back with the bored contempt of the professional for the layman who intrudes on his mysteries. Other civilians had come that way before – had seen, and grinned, and complimented and gone their way, leaving the gunners high up on the bleak hillside to grill or mildew or freeze for weeks and months. Then she spoke. Her voice was higher pitched, it seemed, than ours – with a more shrewish tang to the speeding shell. Her recoil was as swift and as graceful as the shrug of a French-woman's shoulders; the empty case leaped forth and clanged against the trail; the tops of two or three pines 50 yards away nodded knowingly to each other, though there was no wind.

'They'll be bothered down below to know the meaning of our single shot. We don't give them one dose at a time as a rule,' somebody laughed.

We waited in the fragrant silence. Nothing came back from the mist that clogged the lower grounds, though no shell of this war was ever launched with more earnest prayers that it might do hurt.

Then they talked about the lives of guns; what number of rounds some will stand and others will not; how soon one can make two good guns out of three spoilt ones, and what crazy luck sometimes goes with a single shot or a blind salvo.

Lesson from the 'Boche'

A shell must fall somewhere, and by the law of averages occasionally lights straight as a homing pigeon on the one spot where it can wreck most. Then earth opens for yards around, and men must be dug out, – some merely breathless, who shake their ears, swear, and carry on, and others whose souls have gone loose among terrors. These have to be dealt with as their psychology demands, and the French officer is a good psychologist. One of them said: 'Our national psychology has changed. I do not recognise it myself.'

'What made the change?'

'The Boche. If he had been quiet for another twenty years the world must have been his – rotten, but all his. Now he is saving the world.'

'How?'

'Because he has shown us what Evil is. We – you and I, England and the rest – had begun to doubt the existence of Evil. The Boche is saving us.'

Then we had another look at the animal in its trench – a little nearer this time than before, and quieter on account of the mist. Pick up the chain anywhere you please, you shall find the same observation-post, table, map, observer, and telephonist; the same always-hidden, always-ready guns; and same vexed foreshore of trenches, smoking and shaking from Switzerland to the sea. The handling of the war varies with the nature of the country, but the tools are unaltered. One looks upon them at last with the same weariness of wonder as the eye receives from endless repetitions of Egyptian hieroglyphics. A long, low profile, with a lump to one side, means the field-gun and its attendant ammunition-case; a circle and slot stand for an observation-post; the trench is a bent line, studded with vertical plumes of explosion; the great guns of position, coming and going on their motors, repeat themselves as scarabs; and man himself is a small blue smudge, no larger than a foresight, crawling and creeping or watching and running among all these terrific symbols.

Tragedy of Rheims

But there is no hieroglyphic for Rheims, no blunting of the mind at the abominations committed on the cathedral there. The thing peers upward, maimed and blinded, from out of the utter wreckage of the Archbishop's palace on the one side and dust-heaps of crumbled houses on the other. They shelled, as they still shell it, with high explosives and with incendiary shells, so that the statues and the stonework in places are burned the colour of raw flesh. The gargoyles are smashed; statues, crockets, and spires tumbled; walls split and torn; windows thrust out and tracery obliterated. Wherever one looks at the tortured pile there is mutilation and defilement, and yet it had never more of a soul than it has to-day.

Inside – ('Cover yourselves, gentlemen,' said the sacristan, 'this place is no longer consecrated') – everything is swept clear or burned out from end to end, except two candlesticks in front of the niche where Joan of Arc's image used to stand. There is a French flag there now. (And the last time I saw Rheims Cathedral was in a spring twilight, when the great west window glowed, and the only lights within were those of candles which some penitent English had lit in Joan's honour on those same candlesticks.) The high altar was covered with floor-carpets; the pavement tiles were cracked and jarred out by the rubbish that had fallen from above, the floor was gritty with dust of glass and powdered stone, little twists of leading from the windows, and iron fragments. Two great doors had been blown inwards by the blast of a shell in the Archbishop's garden, till they had bent grotesquely to the curve of a cask. There they had jammed. The windows – but the record has been made, and will be kept by better hands than mine. It will last through the generation in which the *Teuton* is cut off from the fellowship of mankind – all the long, still years when this war of the body is at an end, and the real war begins. Rheims is but one of the altars which the heathen have put up to commemorate their own death throughout all the world. It will serve. There is a mark, well known by now, which they have left for a visible seal of their doom. When they first set the place alight some hundreds of their wounded were being tended in the Cathedral. The French saved as many as they could, but some had to be left. Among them was a major, who lay with his back against a pillar. It has been ordained that the signs of his torments should remain – an outline of both legs and half a body, printed in greasy black upon the stones. There are very many people who hope and pray that the sign will be respected at least by our children's children.

Iron Nerve and Faith

And, in the meantime, Rheims goes about what business it may have with that iron nerve and endurance and faith which is the new inheritance of France. There is agony enough when the big shells come in; there is pain and terror among the people; and always fresh desecration to watch and suffer. The old men and the women and the children drink of that cup daily, and yet the bitterness does not enter into their souls. Mere words of admiration are impertinent, but the exquisite quality of the French soul has been the marvel to me throughout. They say themselves, when they talk: 'We did not know what our nation was. Frankly, we did not expect it ourselves. But the thing came, and – you see, we go on.'

Or as a woman put it more logically, 'What else can we do? Remember, we knew the Boche in '70 when you did not. We know what he has done in the last year. This is not war. It is against wild beasts that we fight. There is no arrangement possible with wild beasts.' This is the one vital point which we in England must realise. We are dealing with animals who have scientifically and philosophically removed themselves inconceivably outside civilization. When you have heard a few – only a few – tales of their doings, you begin to understand a little. When you have seen Rheims, you understand a little more. When you have looked long enough at the faces of the women, you are inclined to think that the women will have a large say in the final judgment. They have earned it a thousand times.

Battle Spectacle and a Review

Travelling with two chauffeurs is not the luxury it looks; since there is only one of you and there is always another of those iron men to relieve the wheel. Nor can I decide whether an ex-professor of the German tongue, or an ex-road-racer who has lived six years abroad, or a *Marechal des Logis*, or a *Brigadier* makes the most thrusting driver through 3-mile stretches of military traffic repeated at half-hour intervals. Sometimes it was motor-ambulances strung all along a level; or supply; or those eternal big guns coming round corners with trees chained on their long backs to puzzle aeroplanes, and their leafy, big-shell limbers snorting behind them. In the rare breathing-spaces men with rollers and road metal attacked the road. In peace the roads of France, thanks to the motor, were none too good. In war they stand the incessant traffic far better than they did with the tourists. My impression – after some 700 miles printed off on me at between 60 and 70 kilometres – was of uniform excellence. Nor did I come upon any smashes or breakdowns in that distance, and they were certainly trying them hard. Nor, which is the greater marvel, did we kill anybody; though we did miracles down the streets to avoid babes, kittens, and chickens. The land is used to every detail of war, and to its grime and horror and make-shifts, but also to war's unbounded courtesy, kindness, and long-suffering, and the gaiety that comes, thank God, to balance overwhelming material loss.

Farm Life Amidst War

There was a village that had been stamped flat, till it looked older than Pompeii. There were not three roofs left, nor one whole house. In most places you saw straight into the cellars. The hops were ripe in the grave-dotted fields round about. They had been brought in and piled in the nearest outline of a dwelling. Women sat on chairs on the pavement, picking the good-smelling bundles. When they had finished one, they reached back and pulled out another through the window-hole behind them, talking and laughing the while. A cart had to be manoeuvred out of what had been a farmyard, to take the hops to market. A thick, broad, fair-haired wench, of the sort that Millet drew, flung all her weight on a spoke and brought the cart forward into the street. Then she shook herself, and, hands on hips, danced a little defiant jig in her sabots as she went back to get the horse. Another girl came across a bridge. She was precisely of the opposite type, slender, creamy-skinned, and delicate-featured. She carried a brand-new broom over her shoulder through that desolation, and bore herself with the pride and grace of Queen Iseult.

The farm-girl came out leading the horse, and as the

two young things passed they nodded and smiled at each other, with the delicate tangle of the hop-vines at their feet.

The guns spoke earnestly in the north. That was the Argonne, where the Crown Prince was busily getting rid of a few thousands of his father's faithful subjects in order to secure himself the reversion of his father's throne. No man likes losing his job, and when at long last the inner history of this war comes to be written, we may find that the people we mistook for principals and prime agents were only average incompetents moving all Hell to avoid dismissal. (For it is absolutely true that when a man sells his soul to the devil he does it for the price of half nothing.)

Watching the Gun-fire

It must have been a hot fight. A village, wrecked as is usual along this line, opened on it from a hillside that overlooked an Italian landscape of carefully drawn hills studded with small villages – a plain with a road and a river in the foreground, and an all-revealing afternoon light upon everything. The hills smoked and shook and bellowed. An observation-balloon climbed up to see; while an aeroplane which had nothing to do with the strife, but was merely training a beginner, ducked and swooped on the edge of the plain. Two rose-pink pillars of crumbled masonry, guarding some carefully trimmed evergreens on a lawn half buried in rubbish, represented an hotel where the Crown Prince had once stayed. All up the hillside to our right the foundations of houses lay out, like a bit of tripe, with the sunshine in their square hollows. Suddenly a band began to play up the hill among some trees; and an officer of local Guards in the new steel anti-shrapnel helmet, which is like the seventeenth century sallet, suggested that we should climb and get a better view. He was a kindly man, and in speaking English had discovered (as I do when speaking French) that it is simpler to stick to one gender. His choice was the feminine, and the Boche described as 'she' throughout made me think better of myself, which is the essence of friendship. We climbed a flight of old stone steps, for generations the playground of little children, and found a ruined church, and a battalion in billets, recreating themselves with excellent music and a little horseplay on the outer edge of the crowd. The trouble in the hills was none of their business for that day.

Still higher up, on a narrow path among the trees, stood a priest and three or four officers. They watched the battle and claimed the great bursts of smoke for one side or the other, at the same time as they kept an eye on the flickering aeroplane. 'Ours,' they said, half under their breath. 'Theirs.' 'No, not ours that one – theirs! ... That fool is banking too steep ... That's Boche shrapnel. They always burst it high. That's our big gun behind that outer hill ... He'll drop his machine in the street if he doesn't take care ... There goes a trench-sweeper. Those last two were theirs, but that' – it was a full roar – 'was ours.'

Behind the German Lines

The valley held and increased the sounds till they seemed to hit our hillside like a sea.

A change of light showed a village, exquisitely pencilled atop of a hill, with reddish haze at its feet.

'What is that place?' I asked.

The priest replied in a voice as deep as an organ: 'That is

Saint —. It is in the Boche lines. Its condition is pitiable.'

The thunders and the smokes rolled up and diminished and renewed themselves, but the small children romped up and down the old stone steps; the beginner's aeroplane unsteadily chased its own shadow over the fields; and the soldiers in billet asked the band for their favourite tunes.

Said the lieutenant of local Guards as the cars went on: 'She – play – Tipperary.'

And she did – to an accompaniment of heavy pieces in the hills, which followed us into a town all ringed with enormous searchlights, French and Boche together, scowling at each other beneath the stars.

It happened about that time that Lord Kitchener with General Joffre reviewed a French Army Corps.

We came on it in a vast dip of ground under grey clouds, as one comes suddenly on water; for it lay out in misty blue lakes of men mixed with darker patches, like osiers and undergrowth, of guns, horses, and wagons. A straight road cut the landscape in two along its murmuring front.

Veterans of the War

It was as though Cadmus had sown the dragon's teeth, not in orderly furrows but broadcast, till, horrified by what arose, he had emptied out the whole bag and fled. But these were no new warriors. The record of their mere pitched battles would have satiated a Napoleon. Their regiments and batteries had learnt to achieve the impossible as a matter of routine, and in twelve months they had scarcely for a week lost direct contact with death. We went down the line and looked into the eyes of those men with the used bayonets and rifles; the packs that could almost stow themselves on the shoulders that would be strange without them; at the splashed guns on their repaired wheels, and the easy-working limbers. One could feel the strength and power of the mass as one feels the flush of heat from off a sun-baked wall. When the Generals' cars arrived there, there was no loud word or galloping about. The lakes of men gathered into straight-edged battalions; the batteries aligned a little; a squadron reined back or spurred up; but it was all as swiftly smooth as the certainty with which a man used to the pistol draws and levels it at the required moment. A few peasant women saw the Generals alight. The aeroplanes, which had been skimming low as swallows along the front of the line (theirs must have been a superb view) ascended leisurely, and 'waited on' like hawks. Then followed the inspection, and one saw the two figures, tall and short, growing smaller side by side along the white road, till far off among the cavalry they entered their cars again, and moved along the horizon to another rise of grey-green plain.

'The army will move across where you are standing. Get to a flank,' someone said.

An Army in Motion

We were no more than well clear of that immobile host when it all surged forward, headed by massed bands playing a tune that sounded like the very pulse of France.

The two Generals, with their Staff, and the French Minister for War, were on foot near a patch of very green Lucerne. They made about twenty figures in all. The cars were little grey blocks against the grey skyline. There was nothing else in all that great plain except the army; no sound but the changing notes of the aeroplanes and the blunted impression, rather than noise, of feet of men on soft ground. They came over a slight ridge, so that one saw the curve of it first furred, then grassed, with the tips of bayonets, which immediately grew to full height, and then, beneath them, poured the wonderful infantry. The speed, the thrust, the drive of that broad blue mass was like a tide-race up an arm of the sea; and how such speed could go with such weight, and how such weight could be in itself so absolutely under control, filled one with terror. All the while, the band, on a far headland, was telling them and telling them (as if they did not know!) of the passion and gaiety and high heart of their own land in the speech that only they could fully understand. (To hear the music of a country is like hearing a woman think aloud.)

'What is the tune?' I asked of an officer beside me.

'My faith, I can't recall for the moment. I've marched to it often enough, though. *Sambre-et-Meuse*, perhaps. Look! There goes my battalion! Those *Chasseurs* yonder.'

He knew, of course; but what could a stranger identify in that earth-shaking passage of 30,000?

Artillery and Cavalry

The note behind the ridge changed to something deeper.

'Ah! Our guns,' said an artillery officer, and smiled tolerantly on the last blue waves of the Line already beating toward the horizon.

They came twelve abreast – 150 guns free for the moment to take the air in company, behind their teams.

And next week would see them, hidden singly or in lurking confederacies, by mountain and marsh and forest, or the wrecked habitations of men – where?

The big guns followed them, with that long-nosed air of detachment peculiar to the breed. The Gunner at my side made no comment. He was content to let his Arm speak for itself, but when one big gun in a sticky place fell out of alignment for an instant I saw his eyebrows contract. The artillery passed on with the same inhuman speed and silence as the Line; and the Cavalry's shattering trumpets closed it all.

They are like our Cavalry in that their horses are in high condition, and they talk hopefully of getting past the barbed wire one of these days and coming into their own. Meantime, they are employed on 'various work as requisite,' and they all sympathise with our rough-rider of Dragoons who flatly refused to take off his spurs in the trenches. If he had to die as a damned infantryman, he wasn't going to be buried as such. A troop-horse of a flanking squadron decided that he had had enough of war, and jibbed like Lot's wife. His rider (we all watched him) ranged about till he found a stick, which he used, but without effect. Then he got off and led the horse, which was evidently what the brute wanted, for when the man remounted the jibbing began again. The last we saw of him was one immensely lonely figure leading one bad but happy horse across an absolutely empty world. Think of his reception – the sole man of 40,000 who had fallen out!

The Boche as Mr Smith

The Commander of that Army Corps came up to salute. The cars went away with the Generals and the Minister for War; the Army passed out of sight over the ridges to the north; the peasant women stooped again to their work in the fields, and wet mist shut down on all the plain; but one tingled with the electricity that had passed. Now one knows what the solidarity of civilization means. Later on the civilized nations will know more, and will wonder and laugh together at their old blindness. When Lord Kitchener went down the line, before the march past, they say that he stopped to speak to a General who had been Marchand's Chief of Staff at the time of Fashoda. And Fashoda was one of several cases when civilization was very nearly manoeuvred into fighting with itself 'for the King of Prussia,' as the saying goes. The all-embracing vileness of the Boche is best realised from French soil, where they have had large experience of it. 'And yet,' as someone observed, 'we ought to have known that a race who have brought anonymous letter-writing to its highest pitch in their own dirty Court affairs would certainly use the same methods in their foreign politics. Why didn't we realise?'

'For the same reason,' another responded, 'that society did not realise that the late Mr Smith, of your England, who married three wives, bought baths in advance for each of them, and, when they had left him all their money, drowned them one by one.'

'And were the baths by any chance called Denmark, Austria, and France in 1870?' a third asked.

'No, they were respectable British tubs. But until Mr Smith had drowned his third wife people didn't get suspicious. They argued that "men don't do such things." That sentiment is the criminal's best protection.'

The Spirit of the People

We passed into the zone of another army and a hillier country, where the border villages lay more sheltered. Here and there a town and the fields round it gave us a glimpse of the furious industry with which France makes and handles material and troops. With her, as with us, the wounded officer of experience goes back to the drill-ground to train the new levies. But it was always the little crowded, defiant villages, and the civil population waiting unweariedly and cheerfully on the unwearied, cheerful army, that went closest to the heart. Take these pictures, caught almost anywhere during a journey: A knot of little children in difficulties with the village water-tap or high-handled pump. A soldier, bearded and fatherly, or young and slim and therefore rather shy of the big girls' chaff, comes forward and lifts the pail or swings the handle. His reward, from the smallest babe swung high in air, or, if he is an older man, pressed against his knees, is a kiss. Then nobody laughs.

Or a fat old lady making oration against some wicked young soldiers who, she says, know what has happened to a certain bottle of wine. 'And I meant it for all – yes, for all of you – this evening, instead of the thieves who stole it. Yes, I tell you – stole it!' The whole street hears her; so does the officer, who pretends not to, and the amused half-battalion up the road. The young men express penitence; she growls like a thunderstorm, but, softening at last, cuffs and drives them affectionately before her. They are all one family.

Or a girl at work with horses in a ploughed field that is dotted with graves. The machine must avoid each sacred plot. So, hands on the plough-stilts, her hair flying forward, she shouts and wrenches till her little brother runs up and swings the team out of the furrow. Every aspect and detail of life in France seems overlaid with a smooth patina of long-continued war – everything except the spirit of the people, and that is as fresh and glorious as the sight of their own land in sunshine.

A City and Woman

We found a city among hills which knew itself to be a prize greatly coveted by the Kaiser. For, truly, it was a pleasant, a desirable, and an insolent city. Its streets were full of life; it boasted an establishment almost as big as Harrods and full of buyers, and its women dressed and shod themselves with care and grace, as befits ladies who, at any time, may be ripped into rags by bombs from aeroplanes. And there was another city whose population seemed to be all soldiers in training; and yet another given up to big guns and ammunition – an extraordinary sight.

After that, we came to a little town of pale stone which an Army had made its headquarters. It looked like a plain woman who had fainted in public. It had rejoiced in many public institutions that were turned into hospitals and offices; the wounded limped its wide, dusty streets, detachments of Infantry went through it swiftly; and utterly bored motor-lorries cruised up and down roaring, I suppose, for something to look at or to talk to. In the centre of it I found one Janny, or rather his marble bust, brooding over a minute iron-railed garden of half-dried asters opposite a shut-up school, which it appeared from the inscription Janny had founded somewhere in the arid Thirties. It was precisely the sort of school that Janny, by the look of him, would have invented. Not even French adaptability could make anything of it. So Janny had his school, with a faint perfume of varnish, all to himself in a hot stillness of used-up air and little whirls of dust. And because that town seemed so barren, I met there a French General whom I would have gone very far to have encountered. He, like the others, had created and tempered an army for certain work in a certain place, and its hand had been heavy on the Boche. We talked of what the French woman was, and had done, and was doing, and extolled her for her goodness and her faith and her splendid courage. When we parted, I went back and made my profoundest apologies to Janny, who must have had a mother. The pale, overwhelmed town did no longer resemble a woman who had fainted, but one who must endure in public all manner of private woe and still, with hands that never cease working, keeps her soul and is cleanly strong for herself and for her men.

French Officers
The guns began to speak again among the hills that we dived into; the air grew chillier as we climbed; forest and wet rocks closed round us in the mist, to the sound of waters trickling alongside; there was a tang of wet fern, cut pine, and the first breath of autumn when the road entered a tunnel and a new world – Alsace.

Said the Governor of those parts thoughtfully: 'The main thing was to get those factory chimneys smoking again.' (They were doing so in little flats and villages all along.) 'You won't see any girls, because they're at work in the textile factories. Yes, it isn't a bad country for summer hotels, but I'm afraid it won't do for winter sports. We've only a metre of snow, and it doesn't lie, except when you are hauling guns up mountains. Then, of course, it drifts and freezes like Davos. That's our new railway below there. Pity it's too misty to see the view.'

But for his medals, there was nothing in the Governor to show that he was not English. He might have come straight from an Indian frontier command.

One notices this approximation of type in the higher ranks, and many of the juniors are cut out of the very same cloth as ours. They get whatever fun may be going: their performances are as incredible and outrageous as the language in which they describe them afterward is bald, but convincing, and – I overheard the tail-end of a yarn told by a child of twenty to some other babes. It was veiled in the obscurity of the French tongue, and the points were lost in shouts of laughter – but I imagine the subaltern among his equals displays just as much reverence for his elders and betters as our own boys do. The epilogue, at least, was as old as both Armies:

'And what did he say then?'

'Oh, the usual thing. He held his breath till I thought he'd burst. Then he damned me in heaps, and I took good care to keep out of his sight till next day.'

But officially and in the high social atmosphere of Headquarters their manners and their meekness are of the most admirable. There they attend devoutly on the wisdom of their seniors, who treat them, so it seemed, with affectionate confidence.

Front that Never Sleeps

When the day's reports are in, all along the front, there is a man, expert in the meaning of things, who boils them down for that cold official digest which tells us that 'There was the usual grenade fighting at —. We made appreciable advance at —,' etc. The original material comes in sheaves and sheaves, where individual character and temperament have full and amusing play. It is reduced for domestic consumption like an overwhelming electric current. Otherwise we could not take it in. But at closer range one realises that the Front never sleeps; never ceases from trying new ideas and weapons which, so soon as the Boche thinks he has mastered them, are discarded for newer annoyances and bewilderments.

'The Boche is above all things observant and imitative,' said one who counted quite a few Boches dead on the front of his sector. 'When you present him with a new idea, he thinks it over for a day or two. Then he presents his riposte.'

'Yes, my General. That was exactly what he did to me when I – did so and so. He was quite silent for a day. Then – he stole my patent.'

'And you?'

'I had a notion that he'd do that, so I had changed the specification.'

Thus spoke the Staff, and so it is among the junior commands, down to the semi-isolated posts where boy-Napoleons live on their own, through unbelievable adventures. They are inventive young devils, these veterans of twenty-one, possessed of the single ideal – to kill – which they follow with men as single-minded as themselves. Battlefield tactics do not exist; when a whole nation goes to ground there can be none of the 'victories' of the old bookish days. But there is always the killing – the well-schemed smashing of a full trench, the rushing out and the mowing down of its occupants; the unsuspicious battalion far in the rear, located after two nights' extreme risk alone among rubbish of masonry, and wiped out as it eats or washes itself; and, more rarely, the body to body encounter with animals removed from the protection of their machinery, when the bayonets get their chance. The Boche does not at all like meeting men whose womenfolk he has dishonoured or mutilated, or used as a protection against bullets. It is not that these men are angry or violent. They do not waste time in that way. They kill him.

The Business of War

The French are less reticent than we about atrocities committed by the Boche, because those atrocities form part of their lives. They are not tucked away in reports of Commissions, and vaguely referred to as 'too awful.' Later on, perhaps, we shall be unreserved in our turn. But they do not talk of them with any babbling heat or bleat or make funny little appeals to a 'public opinion' that, like the Boche, has gone underground. It occurs to me that this must be because every Frenchman has his place and his chance, direct or indirect, to diminish the number of Boches still alive. Whether he lies out in a sandwich of damp earth, or sweats the big guns up the crests behind the trees, or brings the fat, loaded barges into the very heart of the city, where the shell-wagons wait, or spends his last crippled years at the harvest, he is doing his work to that end.

If he is a civilian he may – as he does – say things about his Government, which, after all, is very like other popular governments. (A lifetime spent in watching how the cat jumps does not make lion-tamers.) But there is very little human rubbish knocking about France to hinder work or darken counsel. Above all, there is a thing called the Honour of Civilization, to which France is attached. The meanest man feels that he, in his place, is permitted to help uphold it, and, I think, bears himself, therefore, with new dignity.

A Contrast in Types

This is written in a garden of smooth turf, under a copper beech, beside a glassy mill-stream, where soldiers of Alpine regiments are writing letters home, while the guns shout up and down the narrow valleys.

A great wolf-hound, who considers himself in charge of the old-fashioned farmhouse, cannot understand why his master, aged six, should be sitting on the knees of the *Marechal des Logis*, the iron man who drives the big car.

'But you are French, little one?' says the giant, with a yearning arm round the child.

'Yes,' very slowly mouthing the French words; 'I – can't – speak – French – but – I – am – French.'

The small face disappears in the big beard.

Somehow, I can't imagine the *Marechal des Logis* killing babies – even if his superior officer, now sketching the scene, were to order him!

The great building must once have been a monastery. Twilight softened its gaunt wings, in an angle of which were collected fifty prisoners, picked up among the hills behind the mists.

They stood in some sort of military formation, preparatory to being marched off. They were dressed in khaki, the colour of gassed grass, which might have belonged to any army. Two wore spectacles, and I counted eight faces of the fifty which were asymmetrical – out of drawing on one side.

'Some of their later drafts give us that type,' said the Interpreter. One of them had been wounded in the head and roughly bandaged. The others seemed all sound. Most of them looked at nothing, but several were vividly alive with terror that cannot keep the eyelids still, and a few wavered on the grey edge of collapse.

They were the breed which, at the word of command, had stolen out to drown women and children; had raped women in the streets at the word of command; and, always at the word of command, had sprayed petrol, or squirted flame; or defiled the property and persons of their captives. They stood there outside all humanity. Yet they were made in the likeness of humanity. One realised it with a shock when the bandaged creature began to shiver, and they shuffled off in response to the orders of civilized men.

Life in Trenches on the Mountain Side

Very early in the morning I met Alan Breck, with a half-healed bullet-scrape across the bridge of his nose, and an Alpine cap over one ear. His people a few hundred years ago had been Scotch. He bore a Scotch name, and still recognised the head of his clan, but his French occasionally ran into German words, for he was an Alsatian on one side.

'This,' he explained, 'is the very best country in the world to fight in. It's picturesque and full of cover. I'm a gunner. I've been here for months. It's lovely.'

It might have been the hills under Mussoorie, and what our cars expected to do in it I could not understand. But the demon-driver who had been a road-racer took the 70-h.p. Mercedes and threaded the narrow valleys, as well as occasional half-Swiss villages full of Alpine troops, at a restrained 30 miles an hour. He shot up a new-made road, more like Mussoorie than ever, and did not fall down the hillside even once. An ammunition-mule of a mountain-battery met him at a tight corner, and began to climb a tree.

'See! There isn't another place in France where that could happen,' said Alan. 'I tell you, this is a magnificent country.'

The mule was hauled down by his tail before he had reached the lower branches, and went on through the woods, his ammunition-boxes jinking on his back, for all the world as though he were rejoining his battery at Jutogh. One expected to meet the little Hill people bent under their loads under the forest gloom. The light, the colour, the smell of wood smoke, pine-needles, wet earth, and warm mule were all Himalayan. Only the Mercedes was violently and loudly a stranger.

'Halt!' said Alan at last, when she had done everything except imitate the mule.

'The road continues,' said the demon-driver seductively.

'Yes, but they will hear you if you go on. Stop and wait. We've a mountain battery to look at.'

They were not at work for the moment, and the Commandant, a grim and forceful man, showed me some details of their construction. When we left them in their bower – it looked like a Hill priest's wayside shrine – we heard them singing through the steep-descending pines. They, too, like the 75s, seem to have no pet name in the service.

It was a poisonously blind country. The woods blocked all sense of direction above and around. The ground was at any angle you please, and all sounds were split up and muddled by the tree-trunks, which acted as silencers. High above us the respectable, all-concealing forest had turned into sparse, ghastly blue sticks of timber – an assembly of leper-trees round a bald mountain top. 'That's where we're going,' said Alan. 'Isn't it an adorable country?'

Trenches

A machine-gun loosed a few shots in the fumbling style of her kind when they feel for an opening. A couple of rifle shots answered. They might have been half a mile away or a hundred yards below. An adorable country! We climbed up till we found once again a complete tea-garden of little sunk houses, almost invisible in the brown-pink recesses of the thick forest. Here the trenches began, and with them for the next few hours life in two dimensions – length and breadth. You could have eaten your dinner almost anywhere off the swept dry ground, for the steep slopes favoured draining, there was no lack of timber, and there was unlimited labour. It had made neat double-length dug-outs where the wounded could be laid in during their passage down the mountain side; well-tended occasional latrines properly lined; dug-outs for sleeping and eating; overhead protections and tool-sheds where needed, and, as one came nearer the working face, very clever cellars against trench-sweepers. Men passed on their business; a squad with a captured machine-gun which they tested in a sheltered dip; armourers at their benches busy with sick rifles; fatigue-parties for straw, rations, and ammunition; long processions of single blue figures turned sideways between the brown sunless walls. One understood after a while the nightmare that lays hold of trench-stale men, when the dreamer wanders for ever in those blind mazes till, after centuries of agonising flight, he finds himself stumbling out again into the white blaze and horror of the mined front – he who thought he had almost reached home!

In the Front Line

There were no trees above us now. Their trunks lay along the edge of the trench, built in with stones, where necessary, or sometimes overhanging it in ragged splinters or bushy tops. Bits of cloth, not French, showed too, in the uneven lines of debris at the trench lip, and some thoughtful soul had marked an unexploded Boche trench-sweeper as 'not to be touched.' It was a young lawyer from Paris who pointed that out to me.

We met the Colonel at the head of an indescribable pit of ruin, full of sunshine, whose steps ran down a very steep hillside under the lee of an almost vertically plunging parapet. To the left of that parapet the whole hillside was one gruel of smashed trees, split stones, and powdered soil. It might have been a rag-picker's dump-heap on a colossal scale.

Alan looked at it critically. I think he had helped to make it not long before.

'We're on the top of the hill now, and the Boches are below us,' said he. 'We gave them a very fair sickener lately.'

'This,' said the Colonel, 'is the front line.'

There were overhead guards against hand-bombs which disposed me to believe him, but what convinced me most was a corporal urging us in whispers not to talk so loud. The men were at dinner, and a good smell of food filled the trench. This was the first smell I had encountered in my long travels uphill – a mixed, entirely wholesome flavour of stew, leather, earth, and rifle-oil.

Front Line Professionals

A proportion of men were standing to arms while others ate; but dinner-time is slack time, even among animals, and it was close on noon.

'The Boches got their soup a few days ago,' someone whispered. I thought of the pulverized hillside, and hoped it had been hot enough.

We edged along the still trench, where the soldiers stared, with justified contempt, I thought, upon the civilian who scuttled through their life for a few emotional minutes in order to make words out of their blood. Somehow it reminded me of coming in late to a play and incommoding a long line of packed stalls. The whispered dialogue was much the same: 'Pardon!' 'I beg your pardon, *monsieur*.' 'To the right, *monsieur*.' 'If *monsieur* will lower his head.' 'One sees best from here, *monsieur*,' and so on. It was their day and night-long business, carried through without display or heat, or doubt or indecision. Those who worked, worked; those off duty, not 5 feet behind them in the dug-outs, were deep in their papers, or their meals or their letters; while death stood ready at every minute to drop down into the narrow cut from out of the narrow strip of unconcerned sky. And for the better part of a week one had skirted hundreds of miles of such a frieze!

The loopholes not in use were plugged rather like old-fashioned hives. Said the Colonel, removing a plug: 'Here are the Boches. Look, and you'll see their sandbags.' Through the jumble of riven trees and stones one saw what might have been a bit of green sacking. 'They're about 7 metres distant just here,' the Colonel went on. That was true, too. We entered a little fortalice with a cannon in it, in an embrasure which at that moment struck me as unnecessarily vast, even though it was partly closed by a frail packing-case lid. The Colonel sat him down in front of it, and explained the theory of this sort of redoubt. 'By the way,' he said to the gunner at last, 'can't you find something better than that?' He twitched the lid aside. 'I think it's too light. Get a log of wood or something.'

Handy Trench-Sweepers

I loved that Colonel! He knew his men and he knew the Boches – had them marked down like birds. When he said they were beside dead trees or behind boulders, sure enough there they were! But, as I have said, the dinner-hour is always slack, and even when we came to a place where a section of trench had been bashed open by trench-sweepers, and it was recommended to duck and hurry, nothing much happened. The uncanny thing was the absence of movement in the Boche trenches. Sometimes one imagined that one smelt strange tobacco, or heard a rifle-bolt working after a shot. Otherwise they were as still as pig at noonday.

We held on through the maze, past trench-sweepers of a handy light pattern, with their screw-tailed charge all ready; and a grave or so; and when I came on men who merely stood within easy reach of their rifles, I knew I was in the second line. When they lay frankly at ease in their dug-outs, I knew it was the third. A shot-gun would have sprinkled all three.

'No flat plains,' said Alan. 'No hunting for gun positions – the hills are full of them – and the trenches close together and commanding each other. You see what a beautiful country it is.'

The Colonel confirmed this, but from another point of view. War was his business, as the still woods could testify – but his hobby was his trenches. He had tapped the mountain streams and dug out a laundry where a man could wash his shirt and go up and be killed in it, all in a morning; had drained the trenches till a muddy stretch in them was an offence; and at the bottom of the hill (it looked like a hydropathic establishment on the stage) he had created baths where half a battalion at a time could wash. He never told me how all that country had been fought over as fiercely as Ypres in the West; nor what blood had gone down the valleys before his trenches pushed over the scalped mountain top. No. He sketched out new endeavours in earth and stones and trees for the comfort of his men on that populous mountain.

And there came a priest, who was a sub-lieutenant, out of a wood of snuff-brown shadows and half-veiled trunks. Would it please me to look at a chapel? It was all open to the hillside, most tenderly and devoutly done in rustic work with reedings of peeled branches and panels of moss and thatch – St Hubert's own shrine. I saw the hunters who passed before it, going to the chase on the far side of the mountain where their game lay.

A Bombarded Town

Alan carried me off to tea the same evening in a town where he seemed to know everybody. He had spent the afternoon on another mountain top, inspecting gun positions; whereby he had been shelled a little – marmite is the slang for it. There had been no serious *marmitage*, and he had spotted a Boche position which was *marmitable*.

'And we may get shelled now,' he added, hopefully. 'They shell this town whenever they think of it. Perhaps they'll shell us at tea.'

It was a quaintly beautiful little place, with its mixture of French and German ideas; its old bridge and gentle-minded river, between the cultivated hills. The sand-bagged cellar doors, the ruined houses, and the holes in the pavement looked as unreal as the violences of a cinema against that soft and simple setting. The people were abroad in the streets, and the little children were playing. A big shell gives notice enough for one to get to shelter, if the shelter is near enough. That appears to be as much as any one expects in the world where one is shelled, and that world has settled down to it. People's lips are a little firmer, the modelling of the brows is a little more pronounced, and, maybe, there is a change in the expression of the eyes; but nothing that a casual afternoon caller need particularly notice.

Cases for Hospital

The house where we took tea was the 'big house' of the place, old and massive, a treasure house of ancient furniture. It had everything that the moderate heart of man could desire – gardens, garages, outbuildings, and the air of peace that goes with beauty in age. It stood over a high cellarage, and opposite the cellar door was a brand-new blindage of earth packed between timbers. The cellar was a hospital, with its beds and stores, and under the electric light the orderly waited ready for the cases to be carried down out of the streets.

'Yes, they are all civil cases,' said he.

They come without much warning – a woman gashed by falling timber; a child with its temple crushed by a flying stone; an urgent amputation case, and so on. One never knows. Bombardment, the Boche text-books say, 'is designed to terrify the civil population so that they may put pressure on their politicians to conclude peace.' In real life, men are very rarely soothed by the sight of their women being tortured.

We took tea in the hall upstairs, with a propriety and an interchange of compliments that suited the little occasion. There was no attempt to disguise the existence of a bombardment, but it was not allowed to overweigh talk of lighter matters. I know one guest who sat through it as near as might be inarticulate with wonder. But he was English, and when Alan asked him whether he had enjoyed himself, he said: 'Oh, yes. Thank you very much.'

'Nice people, aren't they?' Alan went on.

'Oh, very nice. And – and such good tea.'

He managed to convey a few of his sentiments to Alan after dinner.

'But what else could the people have done?' said he. 'They are French.'

The Common Task of a Great People

'This is the end of the line,' said the Staff Officer, kindest and most patient of chaperons. It buttressed itself on a fortress among hills. Beyond that, the silence was more awful than the mixed noise of business to the westward. In mileage on the map the line must be between 4 and 500 miles; in actual trench-work many times that distance. It is too much to see at full length; the mind does not readily break away from the obsession of its entirety or the grip of its detail. One visualises the thing afterwards as a white-hot gash, worming all across France between intolerable sounds and lights, under ceaseless blasts of whirled dirt. Nor is it any relief to lose oneself among wildernesses of piling, stoning, timbering, concreting, and wire-work, or incalculable quantities of soil thrown up raw to the light and cloaked by the changing seasons – as the unburied dead are cloaked.

Yet there are no words to give the essential simplicity of it. It is the rampart put up by Man against the Beast, precisely as in the Stone Age. If it goes, all that keeps us from the Beast goes with it. One sees this at the front as clearly as one sees the French villages behind the German lines. Sometimes people steal away from them and bring word of what they endure.

Where the rifle and the bayonet serve, men use those tools along the front. Where the knife gives better results, they go in behind the hand-grenades with the naked 12-inch knife. Each race is supposed to fight in its own way, but this war has passed beyond all the known ways. They say that the Belgians in the north settle accounts with a certain dry passion which has varied very little since their agony began. Some sections of the English line have produced a soft-voiced, rather reserved type, which does its work with its mouth shut. The French carry an edge to their fighting, a precision, and a dreadful knowledge coupled with an insensibility to shock, unlike anything one has imagined of mankind. To be sure, there has never been like provocation, for never since the Aesir went about to bind the Fenris Wolf has all the world united to bind the Beast.

The last I saw of the front was Alan Breck speeding back to his gun-positions among the mountains; and I wondered what delight of what household the lad must have been in the old days.

Supports and Reserves

Then we had to work our way, department by department, against the tides of men behind the line – supports and their supports, reserves and reserves of reserves, as well as the masses in training. They flooded towns and villages, and when we tried short-cuts we found them in every by-lane. Have you seen mounted men reading their home letters with the reins thrown on the horses' necks, moving in absorbed silence through a street which almost said 'Hush!' to its dogs; or met, in a forest, a procession of perfectly new big guns, apparently taking themselves from the foundry to the front?

In spite of their love of drama, there is not much 'window-dressing' in the French character. The Boche, who is the priest of the Higher Counter-jumpery, would have had half the neutral Press out in cars to advertise these vast spectacles of men and material. But the same instinct as makes their rich farmers keep to their smocks makes the French keep quiet.

'This is our affair,' they argue. 'Everybody concerned is taking part in it. Like the review you saw the other day, there are no spectators.'

'But it might be of advantage if the world knew.'

Mine was a foolish remark. There is only one world today, the world of the Allies. Each of them knows what the others are doing and – the rest doesn't matter. This is a curious but delightful fact to realise at first hand. And think what it will be later, when we shall all circulate among each other and open our hearts and talk it over in a brotherhood more intimate than the ties of blood!

I lay that night at a little French town, and was kept awake by a man, somewhere in the hot, still darkness, howling aloud from the pain of his wounds. I was glad that he was alone, for when one man gives way the others sometimes follow. Yet the single note of misery was worse than the baying and gulping of a whole ward. I wished that a delegation of strikers could have heard it.

That a civilian should be in the war zone at all is a fair guarantee of his good faith. It is when he is outside the zone unchaperoned that questions begin, and the permits are looked into. If these are irregular – but one doesn't care to contemplate it. If regular, there are still a few counter-checks. As the sergeant at the railway station said when he helped us out of an impasse: 'You will realise that it is the most undesirable persons whose papers are of the most regular. It is their business you see. The Commissary of Police is at the Hotel de Ville, if you will come along for the little formality. Myself, I used to keep a shop in Paris. My God, these provincial towns are desolating!'

Paris – And No Foreigners

He would have loved his Paris as we found it. Life was renewing itself in the streets, whose drawing and proportion one could never notice before. People's eyes, and the women's especially, seemed to be set to a longer range, a more comprehensive gaze. One would have said they came from the sea or the mountains, where things are few and simple, rather than from houses. Best of all, there were no foreigners – the beloved city for the first time was French throughout from end to end. It felt like coming back to an old friend's house for a quiet talk after he had got rid of a houseful of visitors. The functionaries and police had dropped their masks of official politeness, and were just friendly. At the hotels, so like school two days before the term begins, the impersonal valet, the chambermaid of the set two-franc smile, and the unbending head-waiter had given place to one's own brothers and sisters, full of one's own anxieties. 'My son is an aviator, *monsieur*. I could have claimed Italian nationality for him at the beginning, but he would not have it.' ... 'Both my brothers, *monsieur*, are at the war. One is dead already. And my fiancé, I have not heard from him since March. He is cook in a battalion.' ... 'Here is the wine-list, *monsieur*. Yes, both my sons and a nephew, and – I have no news of them, not a word of news. My God, we all suffer these days.' And so, too, among the shops – the mere statement of the loss or the grief at the heart, but never a word of doubt, never a whimper of despair.

'Now why,' asked a shopkeeper, 'does not our Government, or your Government, or both our Governments, send some of the British Army to Paris? I assure you we should make them welcome.'

'Perhaps,' I began, 'you might make them too welcome.'

He laughed. 'We should make them as welcome as our own army. They would enjoy themselves.' I had a vision of British officers, each with ninety days' pay to his credit, and a damsel or two at home, shopping consumedly.

'And also,' said the shopkeeper, 'the moral effect on Paris to see more of your troops would be very good.'

But I saw a quite English Provost-Marshal losing himself in chase of defaulters of the New Army who knew their Paris! Still, there is something to be said for the idea – to the extent of a virtuous brigade or so. At present, the English officer in Paris is a scarce bird, and he explains at once why he is and what he is doing there. He must have good reasons. I suggested teeth to an acquaintance. 'No good,' he grumbled. 'They've thought of that, too. Behind our lines is simply crawling with dentists now!'

A People Transfigured

If one asked after the people that gave dinners and dances last year, where everyone talked so brilliantly of such vital things, one got in return the addresses of hospitals. Those pleasant hostesses and maidens seemed to be in charge of departments or on duty in wards, or kitchens, or sculleries. Some of the hospitals were in Paris. (Their staff might have one hour a day in which to see visitors.) Others were up the line, and liable to be shelled or bombed.

I recalled one Frenchwoman in particular, because she had once explained to me the necessities of civilized life. These included a masseuse, a manicurist, and a maid to look after the lapdogs. She is employed now, and has been for months past, on the disinfection and repair of soldiers' clothes. There was no need to ask after the men one had known. Still, there was no sense of desolation. They had gone on; the others were getting ready.

All France works outward to the Front – precisely as an endless chain of fire-buckets works toward the conflagration. Leave the fire behind you and go back till you reach the source of supplies. You will find no break, no pause, no apparent haste, but never any slackening. Everybody has his or her bucket, little or big, and nobody disputes how they should be used. It is a people possessed of the precedent and tradition of war for existence, accustomed to hard living and hard labour, sanely economical by temperament, logical by training, and illumined and transfigured by their resolve and endurance.

You know, when supreme trial overtakes an acquaintance whom till then we conceived we knew, how the man's nature sometimes changes past knowledge or belief. He who was altogether such a one as ourselves goes forward simply, even lightly, to heights we thought unattainable. Though he is the very same comrade that lived our small life with us, yet in all things he has become great. So it is with France today. She has discovered the measure of her soul.

The New War

One sees this not alone in the – it is more than contempt of death – in the godlike preoccupation of her people under arms which makes them put death out of the account, but in the equal passion and fervour with which her people throughout give themselves to the smallest as well as the greatest tasks that may in any way serve their sword. I might tell you something that I saw of the cleaning out of certain latrines; of the education and antecedents of the cleaners; what they said in the matter and how perfectly the work was done. There was a little *Rabelais* in it, naturally, but the rest was pure devotion, rejoicing to be of use.

Similarly with stables, barricades, and barbed-wire work, the clearing and piling away of wrecked house-rubbish, the serving of meals till the service rocks on its poor tired feet, but keeps its temper; and all the unlovely, monotonous details that go with war.

The women, as I have tried to show, work stride for stride with the men, with hearts as resolute and a spirit that has little mercy for short-comings. A woman takes her place wherever she can relieve a man – in the shop, at the posts, on the tramways, the hotels, and a thousand other businesses. She is inured to field-work, and half the harvest of France this year lies in her lap. One feels at every turn how her men trust her. She knows, for she shares everything with her world, what has befallen her sisters who are now in German hands, and her soul is the undying flame behind the men's steel. Neither men nor women have any illusion as to miracles presently to be performed which shall 'sweep out' or 'drive back' the Boche. Since the Army is the Nation, they know much, though they are officially told little. They all recognise that the old-fashioned 'victory' of the past is almost as obsolete as a rifle in a front-line trench. They all accept the new war, which means grinding down and wearing out the enemy by every means and plan and device that can be compassed. It is slow and expensive, but as deadly sure as the logic that leads them to make it their one work, their sole thought, their single preoccupation.

A Nation's Confidence

The same logic saves them a vast amount of energy. They knew Germany in '70, when the world would not believe in their knowledge; they knew the German mind before the war; they know what she has done (they have photographs) during this war. They do not fall into spasms of horror and indignation over atrocities 'that cannot be mentioned,' as the English papers say. They mention them in full and book them to the account. They do not discuss, nor consider, nor waste an emotion over anything that Germany says or boasts or argues or implies or intrigues after. They have the heart's ease that comes from all being at work for their country; the knowledge that the burden of work is equally distributed among all; the certainty that the women are working side by side with the men; the assurance that when one man's task is at the moment ended, another takes his place.

Out of these things is born their power of recuperation in their leisure; their reasoned calm while at work; and their superb confidence in their arms. Even if France of today stood alone against the world's enemy, it would be almost inconceivable to imagine her defeat now; wholly so to imagine any surrender. The war will go on till the enemy is finished. The French do not know when that hour will come; they seldom speak of it; they do not amuse themselves with dreams of triumphs or terms. Their business is war, and they do their business.

The Fringes of the Fleet (1916)

In Lowestoft a boat was laid,
Mark well what I do say!
And she was built for the herring trade,
But she has gone a-rovin', a-rovin', a-rovin',
The Lord knows where!

They gave her Government coal to burn,
And a Q.F. gun at bow and stern,
And sent her out a-rovin', etc.

Her skipper was mate of a bucko ship
Which always killed one man per trip,
So he is used to rovin', etc.

Her mate was skipper of a chapel in Wales,
And so he fights in topper and tails –
Religious tho' rovin', etc.

Her engineer is fifty-eight,
So he's prepared to meet his fate,
Which ain't unlikely rovin', etc.

Her leading-stoker's seventeen,

So he don't know what the Judgments mean,
Unless he cops 'em rovin', etc.

Her cook was chef in the Lost Dogs' Home,
Mark well what I do say!
And I'm sorry for Fritz when they all come
A-rovin', a-rovin', a-roarin' and a-rovin',
Round the North Sea rovin',
The Lord knows where!

The Auxiliaries I

The Navy is very old and very wise. Much of her wisdom is on record and available for reference; but more of it works in the unconscious blood of those who serve her. She has a thousand years of experience, and can find precedent or parallel for any situation that the force of the weather or the malice of the King's enemies may bring about.

The main principles of sea-warfare hold good throughout all ages, and, so far as the Navy has been allowed to put out her strength, these principles have been applied over all the seas of the world. For matters of detail the Navy, to whom all days are alike, has simply returned to the practice and resurrected the spirit of old days.

In the late French wars, a merchant sailing out of a Channel port might, in a few hours, find himself laid by the heels and under way for a French prison. His Majesty's ships of the Line, and even the big frigates, took little part in policing the waters for him, unless he were in convoy. The sloops, cutters, gun-brigs, and local craft of all kinds were supposed to look after that, while the Line was busy elsewhere. So the merchants passed resolutions against the inadequate protection afforded to the trade, and the narrow seas were full of single-ship actions; mail-packets, West Country brigs, and fat East Indiamen fighting, for their own hulls and cargo, anything that the watchful French ports sent against them; the sloops and cutters bearing a hand if they happened to be within reach.

The Oldest Navy

It was a brutal age, ministered to by hard-fisted men, and we had put it a hundred decent years behind us when – it all comes back again! Today there are no prisons for the crews of merchantmen, but they can go to the bottom by mine and torpedo even more quickly than their ancestors were run into Le Havre. The submarine takes the place of the privateer; the Line, as in the old wars, is occupied, bombarding and blockading, elsewhere, but the sea-borne traffic must continue, and that is being looked after by the lineal descendants of the crews of the long extinct cutters and sloops and gun-brigs. The hour struck, and they reappeared, to the tune of 50,000 odd men in more than 2,000 ships, of which I have seen a few hundred. Words of command may have changed a little, the tools are certainly more complex, but the spirit of the new crews who come to the old job is utterly unchanged. It is the same fierce, hard-living, heavy-handed, very cunning service out of which the Navy as we know it today was born. It is called indifferently the Trawler and Auxiliary Fleet. It is chiefly composed of fishermen, but it takes in every one who may have maritime tastes – from retired admirals to the sons of the sea-cook. It exists for the benefit of the traffic and the annoyance of the enemy. Its doings are recorded by flags stuck into charts; its casualties are buried in obscure corners of the newspapers. The Grand Fleet knows it slightly; the restless light cruisers who chaperon it from the background are more intimate; the destroyers working off unlighted coasts over unmarked shoals come, as you might say, in direct contact with it; the submarine alternately praises and – since one periscope is very like another – curses its activities; but the steady procession of traffic in home waters, liner and tramp, six every sixty minutes, blesses it altogether.

Since this most Christian war includes laying mines in the fairways of traffic, and since these mines may be laid at any time by German submarines especially built for the work, or by neutral ships, all fairways must be swept continuously day and night. When a nest of mines is reported, traffic must be hung up or deviated till it is cleared out. When traffic comes up Channel it must be examined for contraband and other things; and the examining tugs lie out in a blaze of lights to remind ships of this. Months ago, when the war was young, the tugs did not know what to look for specially. Now they do. All this mine-searching and reporting and sweeping, plus the direction and examination of the traffic, plus the laying of our own ever-shifting mine-fields, is part of the Trawler Fleet's work, because the Navy-as-we-knew-it is busy elsewhere. And there is always the enemy submarine with a price on her head, whom the Trawler Fleet hunts and traps with zeal and joy. Add to this, that there are boats, fishing for real fish, to be protected in their work at sea or chased off dangerous areas whither, because they are strictly forbidden to go, they naturally repair, and you will begin to get some idea of what the Trawler and Auxiliary Fleet does.

The Ships and the Men

Now, imagine the acreage of several dock-basins crammed, gunwale to gunwale, with brown and umber and ochre and rust-red steam-trawlers, tugs, harbour-boats, and yachts once clean and respectable, now dirty and happy. Throw in fish-steamers, surprise-packets of unknown lines and indescribable junks, sampans, lorchas, catamarans, and General Service stink-pontoons filled with indescribable apparatus, manned by men no dozen of whom seem to talk the same dialect or wear the same clothes. The mustard-coloured jersey who is cleaning a 6-pounder on a Hull boat clips his words between his teeth and would be happier in Gaelic. The whitish singlet and grey trousers held up by what is obviously his soldier brother's spare regimental belt is pure Lowestoft. The complete blue-serge-and-soot suit passing a wire down a hatch is Glasgow as far as you can hear him, which is a fair distance, because he wants something done to the other end of the wire, and the flat-faced boy who should be attending to it hails from the remoter Hebrides, and is looking at a girl on the dock-edge. The bow-legged man in the ulster and green-worsted comforter is a warm Grimsby skipper, worth several thousands. He and his crew, who are mostly his own relations, keep themselves to themselves, and save their money. The pirate with the red beard, barking over the rail at a friend with gold earrings, comes from Skye. The friend is West Country.

The noticeably insignificant man with the soft and deprecating eye is skipper and part-owner of the big slashing Iceland trawler on which he droops like a flower. She is built to almost Western Ocean lines, carries a little boat-deck raft with tremendous stanchions, has a nose cocked high against ice and sweeping seas, and resembles a hawk-moth at rest. The small, sniffing man is reported to be a 'holy terror at sea.'

Hunters and Fishers

The child in the Pullman-car uniform just going ashore is a wireless operator, aged nineteen. He is attached to a flagship at least 120 feet long, under an admiral aged twenty-five, who was, till the other day, third mate of a North Atlantic tramp, but who now leads a squadron of six trawlers to hunt submarines. The principle is simple enough. Its application depends on circumstances and surroundings. One class of German submarines meant for murder off the coasts may use a winding and rabbit-like track between shoals where the choice of water is limited. Their career is rarely long, but, while it lasts, moderately exciting. Others, told off for deep-sea assassinations, are attended to quite quietly and without any excitement at all. Others, again, work the inside of the North Sea, making no distinction between neutrals and Allied ships. These carry guns, and since their work keeps them a good deal on the surface, the Trawler Fleet, as we know, engages them there – the submarine firing, sinking, and rising again in unexpected quarters; the trawler firing, dodging, and trying to ram. The trawlers are strongly built, and can stand a great deal of punishment. Yet again, other German submarines hang about the skirts of fishing-fleets and fire into the brown of them. When the war was young this gave splendidly 'frightful' results, but for some reason or other the game is not as popular as it used to be.

Lastly, there are German submarines who perish by ways so curious and inexplicable that one could almost credit the whispered idea (it must come from the Scotch skippers) that the ghosts of the women they drowned pilot them to destruction. But what form these shadows take – whether of 'The *Lusitania* Ladies,' or humbler stewardesses and hospital nurses – and what lights or sounds the thing fancies it sees or hears before it is blotted out, no man will ever know. The main fact is that the work is being done. Whether it was necessary or politic to re-awaken by violence every sporting instinct of a sea-going people is a question which the enemy may have to consider later on.

Dawn off the Foreland – the young flood making
Jumbled and short and steep –
Black in the hollows and bright where it's breaking –
Awkward water to sweep.
'Mines reported in the fairway,
'Warn all traffic and detain.
'Sent up Unity, Claribel, Assyrian, Stormcock, and Golden
Gain.'

Noon off the Foreland – the first ebb making
Lumpy and strong in the bight.
Boom after boom, and the golf-hut shaking
And the jackdaws wild with fright!
'Mines located in the fairway,

'Boats now working up the chain,
'Sweepers – Unity, Claribel, Assyrian, Stormcock and
Golden Gain.'

Dusk off the Foreland – the last light going
And the traffic crowding through,
And five damned trawlers with their syreens blowing
Heading the whole review!
'Sweep completed in the fairway.
'No more mines remain.
'Sent back Unity, Claribel, Assyrian, Stormcock, and
Golden Gain.'

The Auxiliaries II

The Trawlers seem to look on mines as more or less
fairplay. But with the torpedo it is otherwise. A Yarmouth
man lay on his hatch, his gear neatly stowed away below,
and told me that another Yarmouth boat had 'gone up,'
with all hands except one. ''Twas a submarine. Not a
mine,' said he. 'They never gave our boys no chance.
Na! She was a Yarmouth boat – we knew 'em all. They
never gave the boys no chance.' He was a submarine
hunter, and he illustrated by means of matches placed at
various angles how the blindfold business is conducted.
'And then,' he ended, 'there's always what he'll do. You've
got to think that out for yourself – while you're working
above him – same as if 'twas fish.' I should not care to
be hunted for the life in shallow waters by a man who
knows every bank and pothole of them, even if I had
not killed his friends the week before. Being nearly all

fishermen they discuss their work in terms of fish, and put in their leisure fishing overside, when they sometimes pull up ghastly souvenirs. But they all want guns. Those who have 3-pounders clamour for sixes; sixes for twelves; and the 12-pound aristocracy dream of 4-inchers on anti-aircraft mountings for the benefit of roving Zeppelins. They will all get them in time, and I fancy it will be long ere they give them up. One West Country mate announced that 'a gun is a handy thing to have aboard – always.' 'But in peacetime?' I said. 'Wouldn't it be in the way?'

'We'm used to 'em now,' was the smiling answer. 'Niver go to sea again without a gun – I wouldn't – if I had my way. It keeps all hands pleased-like.'

They talk about men in the Army who will never willingly go back to civil life. What of the fishermen who have tasted something sharper than salt water – and what of the young third and fourth mates who have held independent commands for nine months past? One of them said to me quite irrelevantly: 'I used to be the animal that got up the trunks for the women on baggage-days in the old *Bodiam Castle*,' and he mimicked their requests for 'the large brown box,' or 'the black dress basket,' as a freed soul might scoff at his old life in the flesh.

'A Common Sweeper'

My sponsor and chaperon in this Elizabethan world of eighteenth-century seamen was an A.B. who had gone down in the Landrail, assisted at the Heligoland fight, seen the *Blücher* sink and the bombs dropped on our boats when we tried to save the drowning ('Whereby,' as he said, 'those Germans died gottstrafin' their own country because we didn't wait to be strafed'), and has now found more peaceful days in an Office ashore. He led me across many decks from craft to craft to study the various appliances that they specialise in. Almost our last was what a North Country trawler called a 'common sweeper,' that is to say, a mine-sweeper. She was at tea in her shirt-sleeves, and she protested loudly that there was 'nothing in sweeping.' 'See that wire rope?' she said. 'Well, it leads through that lead to the ship which you're sweepin' with. She makes her end fast and you make yours. Then you sweep together at whichever depth you've agreed upon between you, by means of that arrangement there which regulates the depth. They give you a glass sort o' thing for keepin' your distance from the other ship, but that's not wanted if you know each other. Well, then, you sweep, as the sayin' is. There's nothin' in it. You sweep till this wire rope fouls the bloomin' mines. Then you go on till they appear on the surface, so to say, and then you explodes them by means of shootin' at 'em with that rifle in the galley there. There's nothin' in sweepin' more than that.'

'And if you hit a mine?' I asked.

'You go up – but you hadn't ought to hit 'em, if you're careful. The thing is to get hold of the first mine all right, and then you go on to the next, and so on, in a way o' speakin'.'

'And you can fish, too, 'tween times,' said a voice from the next boat. A man leaned over and returned a borrowed mug. They talked about fishing – notably that once they caught some red mullet, which the 'common sweeper' and his neighbour both agreed was 'not natural in those waters.' As for mere sweeping, it bored them profoundly to talk about it. I only learned later as part of the natural history of mines, that if you rake the tri-nitro-toluol by hand out of a German mine you develop eruptions and skin-poisoning. But on the authority of two experts, there is nothing in sweeping. Nothing whatever!

A Block in the Traffic

Now imagine, not a pistol-shot from these crowded quays, a little Office hung round with charts that are pencilled and noted over various shoals and soundings. There is a movable list of the boats at work, with quaint and domestic names. Outside the window lies the packed harbour – outside that again the line of traffic up and down – a stately cinema-show of six ships to the hour. For the moment the film sticks. A boat – probably a 'common sweeper' – reports an obstruction in a traffic lane a few miles away. She has found and exploded one mine. The Office heard the dull boom of it before the wireless report came in. In all likelihood there is a nest of them there. It is possible that a submarine may have got in last night between certain shoals and laid them out. The shoals are being shepherded in case she is hidden anywhere, but the boundaries of the newly discovered mine-area must be fixed and the traffic deviated. There is a tramp outside with tugs in attendance. She has hit something and is leaking badly. Where shall she go? The Office gives her her destination – the harbour is too full for her to settle down here. She swings off between the faithful tugs. Down coast someone asks by wireless if they shall hold up their traffic. It is exactly like a signaller 'offering' a train to the next block. 'Yes,' the Office replies. 'Wait a while. If it's what we think, there will be a little delay. If it isn't what we think, there will be a little longer delay.' Meantime, sweepers are nosing round the suspected area – 'looking for cuckoos' eggs,' as a voice suggests; and a patrol-boat lathers her way down coast to catch and stop anything that may be on the move, for skippers are sometimes rather careless. Words begin to drop out of the air into the chart-hung Office. 'Six and a half cables south, fifteen east' of something or other. 'Mark it well, and tell them to work up from there,' is the order. 'Another mine exploded!' 'Yes, and we heard that too,' says the Office. 'What about the submarine?' '*Elizabeth Huggins* reports ...'

Elizabeth's scandal must be fairly high flavoured, for a torpedo-boat of immoral aspect slings herself out of harbour and hastens to share it. If *Elizabeth* has not spoken the truth, there may be words between the parties. For the present, a pencilled suggestion seems to cover the case, together with a demand, as far as one can make out, for 'more common sweepers.' They will be forthcoming very shortly. Those at work have got the run of the mines now, and are busily howking them up. A trawler-skipper wishes to speak to the Office. 'They' have ordered him out, but his boiler, most of it, is on the quay at the present time, and 'ye'll remember, it's the same wi' my foremast an' port rigging, sir.' The Office does not precisely remember, but if boiler and foremast are on the quay the rest of the ship had better stay alongside. The skipper falls away relieved. (He scraped a tramp a few nights ago in a bit of a sea.) There is a little mutter of gun-fire somewhere across the grey water where a fleet is at work. A monitor as broad as she is long comes back from wherever the trouble is, slips through the harbour mouth, all wreathed with signals, is received by two motherly lighters, and, to all appearance, goes to sleep between them. The Office does not even look up; for that is not in their department. They have found a trawler to replace the boilerless one. Her name is slid into the rack. The immoral torpedo-boat flounces back to her moorings. Evidently what Elizabeth Huggins said was not evidence. The messages and replies begin again as the day closes.

The Night Patrol

Return now to the inner harbour. At twilight there was a stir among the packed craft like the separation of dried tea-leaves in water. The swing-bridge across the basin shut against us. A boat shot out of the jam, took the narrow exit at a fair 7 knots and rounded in the outer harbour with all the pomp of a flagship, which was exactly what she was. Others followed, breaking away from every quarter in silence. Boat after boat fell into line – gear stowed away, spars and buoys in order on their clean decks, guns cast loose and ready, wheelhouse windows darkened, and everything in order for a day or a week or a month out. There was no word anywhere. The interrupted foot-traffic stared at them as they slid past below. A woman beside me waved her hand to a man on one of them, and I saw his face light as he waved back. The boat where they had demonstrated for me with matches was the last. Her skipper hadn't thought it worthwhile to tell me that he was going that evening. Then the line straightened up and stood out to sea.

'You never said this was going to happen,' I said reproachfully to my A.B.

'No more I did,' said he. 'It's the night-patrol going out. Fact is, I'm so used to the bloomin' evolution that it never struck me to mention it as you might say.'

Next morning I was at service in a man-of-war, and even as we came to the prayer that the Navy might 'be a safeguard to such as pass upon the sea on their lawful occasions,' I saw the long procession of traffic resuming up and down the Channel – six ships to the hour. It has been hung up for a bit, they said.

> Farewell and adieu to you, Greenwich ladies,
> Farewell and adieu to you, ladies ashore!
> For we've received orders to work to the eastward
> Where we hope in a short time to strafe 'em some
> more.

> We'll duck and we'll dive like little tin turtles,
> We'll duck and we'll dive underneath the North Seas,
> Until we strike something that doesn't expect us,
> From here to Cuxhaven it's go as you please!

> The first thing we did was to dock in a mine-field,
> Which isn't a place where repairs should be done;
> And there we lay doggo in twelve-fathom water
> With tri-nitro-toluol hogging our run.

> The next thing we did, we rose under a Zeppelin,
> With his shiny big belly half blocking the sky.
> But what in the Heavens can you do with six-pounders?
> So we fired what we had and we bade him good-bye.

Submarines I

The chief business of the Trawler Fleet is to attend to the traffic. The submarine in her sphere attends to the enemy. Like the destroyer, the submarine has created its own type of officer and man – with language and traditions apart from the rest of the Service, and yet at heart unchangingly of the Service. Their business is to run monstrous risks from earth, air, and water, in what, to be of any use, must be the coldest of cold blood.

The commander's is more a one-man job, as the crew's is more team-work, than any other employment afloat. That is why the relations between submarine officers and men are what they are. They play hourly for each other's lives with Death the Umpire always at their elbow on tiptoe to give them 'out.'

There is a stretch of water, once dear to amateur yachtsmen, now given over to scouts, submarines, destroyers, and, of course, contingents of trawlers. We were waiting the return of some boats which were due to report. A couple surged up the still harbour in the afternoon light and tied up beside their sisters. There climbed out of them three or four high-booted, sunken-eyed pirates clad in sweaters, under jackets that a stoker of the last generation would have disowned. This was their first chance to compare notes at close hand. Together they lamented the loss of a Zeppelin – 'a perfect mug of a Zepp,' who had come down very low and offered one of them a sitting shot. 'But what can you do with our guns? I gave him what I had, and then he started bombing.'

'I know he did,' another said. 'I heard him. That's what brought me down to you. I thought he had you that last time.'

'No, I was 40 foot under when he hove out the big 'un. What happened to you?'

'My steering-gear jammed just after I went down, and I had to go round in circles till I got it straightened out. But wasn't he a mug!'

'Was he the brute with the patch on his port side?' a sister-boat demanded.

'No! This fellow had just been hatched. He was almost sitting on the water, heaving bombs over.'

'And my blasted steering-gear went and chose then to go wrong,' the other commander mourned. 'I thought his last little egg was going to get me!'

Half an hour later, I was formally introduced to three or four quite strange, quite immaculate officers, freshly shaved, and a little tired about the eyes, whom I thought I had met before.

Labour and Refreshment

Meantime (it was on the hour of evening drinks) one of the boats was still unaccounted for. No one talked of her. They rather discussed motor-cars and Admiralty constructors, but it felt like that queer twilight watch at the front, when the homing aeroplanes drop in. Presently a signaller entered. 'V 42 outside, sir; wants to know which channel she shall use.' 'Oh, thank you. Tell her to take so-and-so.' ... Mine, remember, was vermouth and bitters, and later on V 42 himself found a soft chair and joined the committee of instruction. Those next for duty, as well as those in training, wished to hear what was going on, and who had shifted what to where, and how certain arrangements had worked. They were told in language not to be found in any printable book. Questions and answers were alike Hebrew to one listener, but he gathered that every boat carried a second in command – a strong, persevering youth, who seemed responsible for everything that went wrong, from a motor cylinder to a torpedo. Then somebody touched on the mercantile marine and its habits.

Said one philosopher: 'They can't be expected to take any more risks than they do. I wouldn't, if I was a skipper. I'd loose off at any blessed periscope I saw.'

'That's all very fine. You wait till you've had a patriotic tramp trying to strafe you at your own back-door,' said another.

Someone told a tale of a man with a voice, notable even in a Service where men are not trained to whisper. He was coming back, empty-handed, dirty, tired, and best left alone. From the peace of the German side he had entered our hectic home-waters, where the usual tramp shelled, and by miraculous luck, crumpled his periscope. Another man might have dived, but Boanerges kept on rising. Majestic and wrathful he rose personally through his main hatch, and at 2,000 yards (have I said it was a still day?) addressed the tramp. Even at that distance she gathered it was a Naval officer with a grievance, and by the time he ran alongside she was in a state of coma, but managed to stammer: 'Well, sir, at least you'll admit that our shooting was pretty good.'

'And that,' said my informant, 'put the lid on!' Boanerges went down lest he should be tempted to murder; and the tramp affirms she heard him rumbling beneath her, like an inverted thunder-storm, for fifteen minutes.

'All those tramps ought to be disarmed, and we ought to have all their guns,' said a voice out of a corner.

'What? Still worrying over your 'mug'?' someone

replied.

'He was a mug!' went on the man of one idea. 'If I'd had a couple of twelves even, I could have strafed him proper. I don't know whether I shall mutiny, or desert, or write to the First Sea Lord about it.'

'Strafe all Admiralty constructors to begin with. I could build a better boat with a 4-inch lathe and a sardine-tin than —,' the speaker named her by letter and number.

'That's pure jealousy,' her commander explained to the company. 'Ever since I installed – ahem! – my patent electric washbasin he's been intriguin' to get her. Why? We know he doesn't wash. He'd only use the basin to keep beer in.'

Underwater Works

However often one meets it, as in this war one meets it at every turn, one never gets used to the Holy Spirit of Man at his job. The 'common sweeper,' growling over his mug of tea that there was 'nothing in sweepin',' and these idly chaffing men, new shaved and attired, from the gates of Death which had let them through for the fiftieth time, were all of the same fabric – incomprehensible, I should imagine, to the enemy. And the stuff held good throughout all the world – from the Dardanelles to the Baltic, where only a little while ago another batch of submarines had slipped in and begun to be busy. I had spent some of the afternoon in looking through reports of submarine work in the Sea of Marmora. They read like the diary of energetic weasels in an overcrowded chicken-run, and the results for each boat were tabulated something like a cricket score. There were no maiden overs. One came across jewels of price set in the flat official phraseology.

For example, one man who was describing some steps he was taking to remedy certain defects, interjected casually: 'At this point I had to go under for a little, as a man in a boat was trying to grab my periscope with his hand.' No reference before or after to the said man or his fate. Again: 'Came across a show with a Turkish skipper. He seemed so miserable that I let him go.' And elsewhere in those waters, a submarine overhauled a steamer full of Turkish passengers, some of whom, arguing on their allies' lines, promptly leaped overboard. Our boat fished them out and returned them, for she was not killing civilians. In another affair, which included several ships (now at the bottom) and one submarine, the commander relaxes enough to note that: 'The men behaved very well under direct and flanking fire from rifles at about 15 yards.' This was not, I believe, the submarine that fought the Turkish cavalry on the beach. And in addition to matters much more marvellous than any I have hinted at, the reports deal with repairs and shifts and contrivances carried through in the face of dangers that read like the last delirium of romance. One boat went down the Straits and found herself rather canted over to one side. A mine and chain had jammed under her forward diving-plane. So far as I made out, she shook it off by standing on her head and jerking backwards; or it may have been, for the thing has occurred more than once, she merely rose as much as she could, when she could, and then 'released it by hand,' as the official phrase goes.

Four Nightmares

And who, a few months ago, could have invented, or having invented, would have dared to print such a nightmare as this: There was a boat in the North Sea who ran into a net and was caught by the nose. She rose, still entangled, meaning to cut the thing away on the surface. But a Zeppelin in waiting saw and bombed her, and she had to go down again at once – but not too wildly or she would get herself more wrapped up than ever. She went down, and by slow working and weaving and wriggling, guided only by guesses at the meaning of each scrape and grind of the net on her blind forehead, at last she drew clear. Then she sat on the bottom and thought. The question was whether she should go back at once and warn her confederates against the trap, or wait till the destroyers which she knew the Zeppelin would have signalled for, should come out to finish her still entangled, as they would suppose, in the net? It was a simple calculation of comparative speeds and positions, and when it was worked out she decided to try for the double event. Within a few minutes of the time she had allowed for them, she heard the twitter of four destroyers' screws quartering above her; rose; got her shot in; saw one destroyer crumple; hung round till another took the wreck in tow; said good-bye to the spare brace (she was at the end of her supplies), and reached the rendezvous in time to turn her friends.

And since we are dealing in nightmares, here are two more – one genuine, the other, mercifully, false. There was a boat not only at, but in the mouth of a river – well home in German territory. She was spotted, and went under, her commander perfectly aware that there was not more than 5 feet of water over her conning-tower, so that even a torpedo-boat, let alone a destroyer, would hit it if she came over. But nothing hit anything. The search was conducted on scientific principles while they sat on the silt and suffered. Then the commander heard the rasp of a wire trawl sweeping over his hull. It was not a nice sound, but there happened to be a couple of gramophones aboard, and he turned them both on to drown it. And in due time that boat got home with everybody's hair of just the same colour as when they had started!

The other nightmare arose out of silence and imagination. A boat had gone to bed on the bottom in a spot where she might reasonably expect to be looked for, but it was a convenient jumping-off, or up, place for the work in hand. About the bad hour of 2.30 a.m. the commander was waked by one of his men, who whispered to him: 'They've got the chains on us, sir!' Whether it was pure nightmare, a hallucination of long wakefulness, something relaxing and releasing in that packed box of machinery, or the disgustful reality, the commander could not tell, but it had all the makings of panic in it. So the Lord and long training put it into his head to reply! 'Have they? Well, we shan't be coming up till nine o'clock this morning. We'll see about it then. Turn out that light, please.'

He did not sleep, but the dreamer and the others did, and when morning came and he gave the order to rise, and she rose unhampered, and he saw the grey, smeared seas from above once again, he said it was a very refreshing sight.

Lastly, which is on all fours with the gamble of the chase, a man was coming home rather bored after an uneventful trip. It was necessary for him to sit on the bottom for a while, and there he played patience. Of a sudden it struck him, as a vow and an omen, that if he worked out the next game correctly he would go up and strafe something. The cards fell all in order. He went up at once and found himself alongside a German, whom, as he had promised and prophesied to himself, he destroyed. She was a mine-layer, and needed only a jar to dissipate like a cracked electric-light bulb. He was somewhat impressed by the contrast between the single-handed game 50 feet below, the ascent, the attack, the amazing result, and when he descended again, his cards just as he had left them.

> The ships destroy us above
> And ensnare us beneath.
> We arise, we lie down, and we move
> In the belly of Death.
>
> The ships have a thousand eyes
> To mark where we come ...
> And the mirth of a seaport dies
> When our blow gets home.

Submarines II

I was honoured by a glimpse into this veiled life in a boat which was merely practising between trips. Submarines are like cats. They never tell 'who they were with last night,' and they sleep as much as they can. If you board a submarine off duty you generally see a perspective of fore-shortened fattish men laid all along. The men say that except at certain times it is rather an easy life, with relaxed regulations about smoking, calculated to make a man put on flesh. One requires well-padded nerves. Many of the men do not appear on deck throughout the whole trip. After all, why should they if they don't want to? They know that they are responsible in their department for their comrades' lives as their comrades are responsible for theirs. What's the use of flapping about? Better lay in some magazines and cigarettes.

When we set forth there had been some trouble in the fairway, and a mined neutral, whose misfortune all bore with exemplary calm, was careened on a near-by shoal.

'Suppose there are more mines knocking about?' I suggested.

'We'll hope there aren't,' was the soothing reply. 'Mines are all Joss. You either hit 'em or you don't. And if you do, they don't always go off. They scrape alongside.'

'What's the etiquette then?'

'Shut off both propellers and hope.'

We were dodging various craft down the harbour when a squadron of trawlers came out on our beam, at that extravagant rate of speed which unlimited Government coal always leads to. They were led by an ugly, upstanding, black-sided buccaneer with 12-pounders.

'Ah! That's the King of the Trawlers. Isn't he carrying dog, too! Give him room!' one said.

We were all in the narrowed harbour mouth together.

'There's my youngest daughter. Take a look at her!' someone hummed as a punctilious navy cap slid by on a very near bridge.

'We'll fall in behind him. They're going over to the neutral. Then they'll sweep. By the bye, did you hear about one of the passengers in the neutral yesterday? He was taken off, of course, by a destroyer, and the only thing he said was: "Twenty-five time I 'ave insured, but not this time ... 'Ang it!'"

The trawlers lunged ahead toward the forlorn neutral. Our destroyer nipped past us with that high-shouldered, terrier-like pouncing action of the newer boats, and went ahead. A tramp in ballast, her propeller half out of water, threshed along through the sallow haze.

'Lord! What a shot!' somebody said enviously. The men on the little deck looked across at the slow-moving silhouette. One of them, a cigarette behind his ear, smiled at a companion.

Then we went down – not as they go when they are pressed (the record, I believe, is 50 feet in fifty seconds from top to bottom), but genteelly, to an orchestra of appropriate sounds, roarings, and blowings, and after the orders, which come from the commander alone, utter silence and peace.

'There's the bottom. We bumped at fifty – fifty-two,' he said.

'I didn't feel it.'

'We'll try again. Watch the gauge, and you'll see it flick a little.'

The Practice of the Art

It may have been so, but I was more interested in the faces, and above all the eyes, all down the length of her. It was to them, of course, the simplest of manoeuvres. They dropped into gear as no machine could; but the training of years and the experience of the year leaped up behind those steady eyes under the electrics in the shadow of the tall motors, between the pipes and the curved hull, or glued to their special gauges. One forgot the bodies altogether – but one will never forget the eyes or the ennobled faces. One man I remember in particular. On deck his was no more than a grave, rather striking countenance, cast in the unmistakable petty officer's mould. Below, as I saw him in profile handling a vital control, he looked like the Doge of Venice, the Prior of some sternly ruled monastic order, an old-time Pope – anything that signifies trained and stored intellectual power utterly and ascetically devoted to some vast impersonal end. And so with a much younger man, who changed into such a monk as Frank Dicksee used to draw. Only a couple of torpedo-men, not being in gear for the moment, read an illustrated paper. Their time did not come till we went up and got to business, which meant firing at our destroyer, and, I think, keeping out of the light of a friend's torpedoes.

The attack and everything connected with it is solely the commander's affair. He is the only one who gets any fun at all – since he is the eye, the brain, and the hand of the whole – this single figure at the periscope. The second in command heaves sighs, and prays that the dummy torpedo (there is less trouble about the live ones) will go off all right, or he'll be told about it. The others wait and follow the quick run of orders. It is, if not a convention, a fairly established custom that the commander shall inferentially give his world some idea of what is going on. At least, I only heard of one man who says nothing whatever, and doesn't even wriggle his shoulders when he is on the sight. The others soliloquise, etc., according to their temperament; and the periscope is as revealing as golf.

Submarines nowadays are expected to look out for themselves more than at the old practices, when the destroyers walked circumspectly. We dived and circulated under water for a while, and then rose for a sight – something like this: 'Up a little – up! Up still! Where the deuce has he got to – Ah! (Half a dozen orders as to helm and depth of descent, and a pause broken by a drumming noise somewhere above, which increases and passes away.) That's better! Up again! (This refers to the periscope.) Yes. Ah! No, we don't think! All right! Keep her down, damn it! Umm! That ought to be 19 knots ... Dirty trick! He's changing speed. No, he isn't. He's all right. Ready forward there! (A valve sputters and drips, the torpedo-men crouch over their tubes and nod to themselves. Their faces have changed now.) He hasn't spotted us yet. We'll ju-ust – (more helm and depth orders, but specially helm) – 'Wish we were working a beam-tube. Ne'er mind! Up! (A last string of orders.) 600, and he doesn't see us! Fire!'

The dummy left; the second in command cocked one ear and looked relieved. Up we rose; the wet air and spray spattered through the hatch; the destroyer swung off to retrieve the dummy.

'Careless brutes destroyers are,' said one officer. 'That fellow nearly walked over us just now. Did you notice?'

The commander was playing his game out over again – stroke by stroke. 'With a beam-tube I'd ha' strafed him amidships,' he concluded.

'Why didn't you then?' I asked.

There were loads of shiny reasons, which reminded me that we were at war and cleared for action, and that the interlude had been merely play. A companion rose alongside and wanted to know whether we had seen anything of her dummy.

'No. But we heard it,' was the short answer.

I was rather annoyed, because I had seen that particular daughter of destruction on the stocks only a short time ago, and here she was grown up and talking about her missing children!

In the harbour again, one found more submarines, all patterns and makes and sizes, with rumours of yet more and larger to follow. Naturally their men say that we are only at the beginning of the submarine. We shall have them presently for all purposes.

The Man and the Work

Now here is a mystery of the Service.

A man gets a boat which for two years becomes his very self –

> His morning hope, his evening dream,
> His joy throughout the day.

With him is a second in command, an engineer, and some others. They prove each other's souls habitually every few days, by the direct test of peril, till they act, think, and endure as a unit, in and with the boat. That commander is transferred to another boat. He tries to take with him if he can, which he can't, as many of his other selves as possible. He is pitched into a new type twice the size of the old one, with three times as many gadgets, an unexplored temperament and unknown leanings. After his first trip he comes back clamouring for the head of her constructor, of his own second in command, his engineer, his cox, and a few other ratings. They for their part wish him dead on the beach, because, last commission with So-and-so, nothing ever went wrong anywhere. A fortnight later you can remind the commander of what he said, and he will deny every word of it. She's not, he says, so very vile – things considered – barring her 5-ton torpedo-derricks, the abominations of her wireless, and the tropical temperature of her beer-lockers. All of which signifies that the new boat has found her soul, and her commander would not change her for battle-cruisers. Therefore, that he may remember he is the Service and not a branch of it, he is after certain seasons shifted to a battle-cruiser, where he lives in a blaze of admirals and aiguillettes, responsible for vast decks and crypt-like flats, a student of extended above-water tactics, thinking in tens of thousands of yards instead of his modest but deadly 3 to 1,200.

And the man who takes his place straight-way forgets that he ever looked down on great rollers from a 60-foot bridge under the whole breadth of heaven, but crawls and climbs and dives through conning-towers with those same waves wet in his neck, and when the cruisers pass him, tearing the deep open in half a gale, thanks God he is not as they are, and goes to bed beneath their distracted keels.

Expert Opinions

'But submarine work is cold-blooded business.' (This was at a little session in a green-curtained 'wardroom' cum owner's cabin.)

'Then there's no truth in the yarn that you can feel when the torpedo's going to get home?' I asked.

'Not a word. You sometimes see it get home, or miss, as the case may be. Of course, it's never your fault if it misses. It's all your second-in-command.'

'That's true, too,' said the second. 'I catch it all round. That's what I am here for.'

'And what about the third man?' There was one aboard at the time.

'He generally comes from a smaller boat, to pick up real work – if he can suppress his intellect and doesn't talk "last commission."'

The third hand promptly denied the possession of any intellect, and was quite dumb about his last boat.

'And the men?'

'They train on, too. They train each other. Yes, one gets to know 'em about as well as they get to know us. Up topside, a man can take you in – take himself in – for months; for half a commission, p'rhaps. Down below he can't. It's all in cold blood – not like at the front, where they have something exciting all the time.'

'Then bumping mines isn't exciting?'

'Not one little bit. You can't bump back at 'em. Even with a Zepp—'

'Oh, now and then,' one interrupted, and they laughed as they explained.

'Yes, that was rather funny. One of our boats came up slap underneath a low Zepp. Looked for the sky, you know, and couldn't see anything except this fat, shining belly almost on top of 'em. Luckily, it wasn't the Zepp's stingin' end. So our boat went to windward and kept just awash. There was a bit of a sea, and the Zepp had to work against the wind. (They don't like that.) Our boat sent a man to the gun. He was pretty well drowned, of course, but he hung on, choking and spitting, and held his breath, and got in shots where he could. This Zepp was strafing bombs about for all she was worth, and – who was it? – Macartney, I think, potting at her between dives; and naturally all hands wanted to look at the performance, so about half the North Sea flopped down below and – oh, they had a Charlie Chaplin time of it! Well, somehow, Macartney managed to rip the Zepp a bit, and she went to leeward with a list on her. We saw her a fortnight later with a patch on her port side. Oh, if Fritz only fought clean, this wouldn't be half a bad show. But Fritz can't fight clean.'

'And we can't do what he does – even if we were allowed to,' one said.

'No, we can't. 'Tisn't done. We have to fish Fritz out of the water, dry him, and give him cocktails, and send him to Donnington Hall.'

'And what does Fritz do?' I asked.

'He sputters and clicks and bows. He has all the correct motions, you know; but, of course, when he's your prisoner you can't tell him what he really is.'

'And do you suppose Fritz understands any of it?' I went on.

'No. Or he wouldn't have Lusitaniaed. This war was his first chance of making his name, and he chucked it all away for the sake of showin' off as a foul Gottstrafer.'

And they talked of that hour of the night when submarines come to the top like mermaids to get and give information; of boats whose business it is to fire as much and to splash about as aggressively as possible; and of other boats who avoid any sort of display – dumb boats watching and relieving watch, with their periscope just showing like a crocodile's eye, at the back of islands and the mouths of channels where something may someday move out in procession to its doom.

Be well assured that on our side
Our challenged oceans fight,
Though headlong wind and heaping tide
Make us their sport to-night.
Through force of weather, not of war,
In jeopardy we steer.
Then, welcome Fate's discourtesy
Whereby it shall appear
How in all time of our distress
As in our triumph too,
The game is more than the player of the game,
And the ship is more than the crew!

Be well assured, though wave and wind
Have mightier blows in store,
That we who keep the watch assigned
Must stand to it the more;
And as our streaming bows dismiss
Each billow's baulked career,
Sing, welcome Fate's discourtesy
Whereby it is made clear
How in all time of our distress
As in our triumph too,
The game is more than the player of the game,
And the ship is more than the crew!

Be well assured, though in our power
Is nothing left to give

But time and place to meet the hour
And leave to strive to live,
Till these dissolve our Order holds,
Our Service binds us here.
Then, welcome Fate's discourtesy
Whereby it is made clear
How in all time of our distress
And our deliverance too,
The game is more than the player of the game,
And the ship is more than the crew!

Patrols I

On the edge of the North Sea sits an Admiral in charge of a stretch of coast without lights or marks, along which the traffic moves much as usual. In front of him there is nothing but the east wind, the enemy, and some few our ships. Behind him there are towns, with M.P.s attached, who a little while ago didn't see the reason for certain lighting orders. When a Zeppelin or two came, they saw. Left and right of him are enormous docks, with vast crowded sheds, miles of stone-faced quay-edges, loaded with all manner of supplies and crowded with mixed shipping.

In this exalted world one met Staff-Captains, Staff-Commanders, Staff-Lieutenants, and Secretaries, with Paymasters so senior that they almost ranked with Admirals. There were Warrant Officers, too, who long ago gave up splashing about decks barefoot, and now check and issue stores to the ravenous, untruthful fleets. Said one of these, guarding a collection of desirable things, to a cross between a sick-bay attendant and a junior writer (but he was really an expert burglar), 'No! An' you can tell Mr So-and-so, with my compliments, that the storekeeper's gone away – right away – with the key of these stores in his pocket. Understand me? In his trousers pocket.'

He snorted at my next question.

'Do I know any destroyer-lootenants?' said he. 'This coast's rank with 'em! Destroyer-lootenants are born stealing. It's a mercy they's too busy to practise forgery, or I'd be in gaol. Engineer-Commanders? Engineer-Lootenants? They're worse! ... Look here! If my own mother was to come to me beggin' brass screws for her own coffin, I'd – I'd think twice before I'd oblige the old lady. War's war, I grant you that; but what I've got to contend with is crime.'

I referred to him a case of conscience in which everyone concerned acted exactly as he should, and it nearly ended in murder. During a lengthy action, the working of a gun was hampered by some empty cartridge-cases which the lieutenant in charge made signs (no man could hear his neighbour speak just then) should be hove overboard. Upon which the gunner rushed forward and made other signs that they were 'on charge,' and must be tallied and accounted for. He, too, was trained in a strict school. Upon which the lieutenant, but that he was busy, would have slain the gunner for refusing orders in action. Afterwards he wanted him shot by court-martial. But everyone was voiceless by then, and could only mouth and croak at each other, till somebody laughed, and the pedantic gunner was spared.

'Well, that's what you might fairly call a naval crux,' said my friend among the stores. 'The Lootenant was right. Mustn't refuse orders in action. The Gunner was right. Empty cases are on charge. No one ought to chuck 'em away that way, but … Damn it, they were all of 'em right! It ought to ha' been a marine. Then they could have killed him and preserved discipline at the same time.'

A Little Theory

The problem of this coast resolves itself into keeping touch with the enemy's movements; in preparing matters to trap and hinder him when he moves, and in so entertaining him that he shall not have time to draw clear before a blow descends on him from another quarter. There are then three lines of defence: the outer, the inner, and the home waters. The traffic and fishing are always with us.

The blackboard idea of it is always to have stronger forces more immediately available everywhere than those the enemy can send. x German submarines draw a English destroyers. Then x calls $x + y$ to deal with a, who, in turn, calls up b, a scout, and possibly a^2, with a fair chance that, if $x + y + z$ (a Zeppelin) carry on, they will run into $a^2 + b^2 + c$ cruisers. At this point, the equation generally stops; if it continued, it would end mathematically in the whole of the German Fleet coming out. Then another factor which we may call the Grand Fleet would come from another place. To change the comparisons: the Grand Fleet is the 'strong left' ready to give the knock-out blow on the point of the chin when the head is thrown up. The other fleets and other arrangements threaten the enemy's solar plexus and stomach. Somewhere in relation to the Grand Fleet lies the 'blockading' cordon which examines neutral traffic. It could be drawn as tight as a Turkish bowstring, but for reasons which we may arrive at after the war, it does not seem to have been so drawn up to date.

The enemy lies behind his mines, and ours, raids our coasts when he sees a chance, and kills seagoing civilians at sight or guess, with intent to terrify. Most sailor-men are mixed up with a woman or two; a fair percentage of them have seen men drown. They can realise what it is when women go down choking in horrible tangles and heavings of draperies. To say that the enemy has cut himself from the fellowship of all who use the seas is rather understating the case. As a man observed thoughtfully: 'You can't look at any water now without seeing "*Lusitania*" sprawlin' all across it. And just think of those words, "North-German Lloyd," "Hamburg-Amerika" and such things, in the time to come. They simply mustn't be.'

He was an elderly trawler, respectable as they make them, who, after many years of fishing, had discovered his real vocation. 'I never thought I'd like killin' men,' he reflected. 'Never seemed to be any o' my dooty. But it is – and I do!'

A great deal of the East Coast work concerns mine-fields – ours and the enemy's – both of which shift as occasion requires. We search for and root out the enemy's mines; they do the like by us. It is a perpetual game of finding, springing, and laying traps on the least as well as the most likely runaways that ships use – such sea snaring and wiring as the world never dreamt of. We are hampered in this, because our Navy respects neutrals; and spends a great deal of its time in making their path safe for them. The enemy does not. He blows them up, because that cows and impresses them, and so adds to his prestige.

Death and the Destroyer

The easiest way of finding a mine-field is to steam into it, on the edge of night for choice, with a steep sea running, for that brings the bows down like a chopper on the detonator-horns. Some boats have enjoyed this experience and still live. There was one destroyer (and there may have been others since) who came through twenty-four hours of highly compressed life. She had an idea that there was a mine-field somewhere about, and left her companions behind while she explored. The weather was dead calm, and she walked delicately. She saw one Scandinavian steamer blow up a couple of miles away, rescued the skipper and some hands; saw another neutral, which she could not reach till all was over, skied in another direction; and, between her life-saving efforts and her natural curiosity, got herself as thoroughly mixed up with the field as a camel among tent-ropes. A destroyer's bows are very fine, and her sides are very straight. This causes her to cleave the wave with the minimum of disturbance, and this boat had no desire to cleave anything else. None the less, from time to time, she heard a mine grate, or tinkle, or jar (I could not arrive at the precise note it strikes, but they say it is unpleasant) on her plates. Sometimes she would be free of them for a long while, and began to hope she was clear. At other times they were numerous, but when at last she seemed to have worried out of the danger zone lieutenant and sub together left the bridge for a cup of tea. ('In those days we took mines very seriously, you know.') As they were in act to drink, they heard the hateful sound again just outside the wardroom. Both put their cups down with extreme care, little fingers extended ('We felt as if they might blow up, too'), and tip-toed on deck, where they met the foc'sle also on tip-toe. They pulled themselves together, and asked severely what the foc'sle thought it was doing. 'Beg pardon, sir, but there's another of those blighters tap-tapping alongside, our end.' They all waited and listened to their common coffin being nailed by Death himself. But the things bumped away. At this point they thought it only decent to invite the rescued skipper, warm and blanketed in one of their bunks, to step up and do any further perishing in the open.

'No, thank you,' said he. 'Last time I was blown up in my bunk, too. That was all right. So I think, now, too, I stay in my bunk here. It is cold upstairs.'

Somehow or other they got out of the mess after all. 'Yes, we used to take mines awfully seriously in those days. One comfort is, Fritz'll take them seriously when he comes out. Fritz don't like mines.'

'Who does?' I wanted to know.

'If you'd been here a little while ago, you'd seen a Commander comin' in with a big 'un slung under his counter. He brought the beastly thing in to analyse. The rest of his squadron followed at two-knot intervals, and everything in harbour that had steam up scattered.'

The Admirable Commander

Presently I had the honour to meet a Lieutenant-Commander-Admiral who had retired from the service, but, like others, had turned out again at the first flash of the guns, and now commands – he who had great ships erupting at his least signal – a squadron of trawlers for the protection of the Dogger Bank Fleet. At present prices – let alone the chance of the paying submarine – men would fish in much warmer places. His flagship was once a multi-millionaire's private yacht. In her mixture of stark, carpetless, curtainless, carbolised present, with voluptuously curved, broad-decked, easy-stairwayed past, she might be Queen Guinevere in the convent at Amesbury. And her Lieutenant-Commander, most careful to pay all due compliments to Admirals who were midshipmen when he was a Commander, leads a congregation of very hard men indeed. They do precisely what he tells them to, and with him go through strange experiences, because they love him and because his language is volcanic and wonderful – what you might call 'Popocatapocalyptic.' I saw the Old Navy making ready to lead out the New under a grey sky and a falling glass – the wisdom and cunning of the old man backed up by the passion and power of the younger breed, and the discipline which had been his soul for half a century binding them all.

'What'll he do this time?' I asked of one who might know.

'He'll cruise between Two and Three East; but if you'll tell me what he won't do, it 'ud be more to the point! He's mine-hunting, I expect, just now.'

Wasted Material

Here is a digression suggested by the sight of a man I had known in other scenes, despatch-riding round a fleet in a petrol-launch. There are many of his type, yachtsmen of sorts accustomed to take chances, who do not hold masters' certificates and cannot be given sea-going commands. Like my friend, they do general utility work – often in their own boats. This is a waste of good material. Nobody wants amateur navigators – the traffic lanes are none too wide as it is. But these gentlemen ought to be distributed among the Trawler Fleet as strictly combatant officers. A trawler skipper may be an excellent seaman, but slow with a submarine shelling and diving, or in cutting out enemy trawlers. The young ones who can master Q.F. gun work in a very short time would – though there might be friction, a court-martial or two, and probably losses at first – pay for their keep. Even a hundred or so of amateurs, more or less controlled by their squadron commanders, would make a happy beginning, and I am sure they would all be extremely grateful.

Where the East wind is brewed fresh and fresh every
morning,
And the balmy night-breezes blow straight from the
Pole,
I heard a destroyer sing: 'What an enjoyable life does
one
lead on the North Sea Patrol!

'To blow things to bits is our business (and Fritz's),
Which means there are mine-fields wherever you stroll.
Unless you've particular wish to die quick, you'll avoid
steering
close to the North Sea Patrol.

'We warn from disaster the mercantile master
Who takes in high dudgeon our life-saving role,
For every one's grousing at docking and dowsing
The marks and the lights on the North Sea Patrol.'

[Twelve verses omitted.]

So swept but surviving, half drowned but still driving,
I watched her head out through the swell off the shoal,
And I heard her propellers roar: 'Write to poor fellers
Who run such a Hell as the North Sea Patrol!'

Patrols II

The great basins were crammed with craft of kinds never
known before on any Navy List. Some were as they were
born, others had been converted, and a multitude have
been designed for special cases. The Navy prepares against
all contingencies by land, sea, and air. It was a relief to
meet a batch of comprehensible destroyers and to drop
again into the little mouse-trap ward-rooms, which are
as large-hearted as all our oceans. The men one used
to know as destroyer-lieutenants ('born stealing') are
serious Commanders and Captains today, but their sons,
Lieutenants in command and Lieutenant-Commanders,
do follow them. The sea in peace is a hard life; war only
sketches an extra line or two round the young mouths.
The routine of ships always ready for action is so part of
the blood now that no one notices anything except the
absence of formality and of the 'crimes' of peace. What
Warrant Officers used to say at length is cut down to a
grunt. What the sailor-man did not know and expected
to have told him, does not exist. He has done it all too
often at sea and ashore.

I watched a little party working under a leading hand at
a job which, eighteen months ago, would have required a
Gunner in charge. It was comic to see his orders trying to
overtake the execution of them. Ratings coming aboard

carried themselves with a (to me) new swing – not swank, but consciousness of adequacy. The high, dark foc'sles which, thank goodness, are only washed twice a week, received them and their bags, and they turned-to on the instant as a man picks up his life at home. Like the submarine crew, they come to be a breed apart – double-jointed, extra-toed, with brazen bowels and no sort of nerves.

It is the same in the engine-room, when the ships come in for their regular looking-over. Those who love them, which you would never guess from the language, know exactly what they need, and get it without fuss. Everything that steams has her individual peculiarity, and the great thing is, at overhaul, to keep to it and not develop a new one. If, for example, through some trick of her screws not synchronising, a destroyer always casts to port when she goes astern, do not let any zealous soul try to make her run true, or you will have to learn her helm all over again. And it is vital that you should know exactly what your ship is going to do three seconds before she does it. Similarly with men. If anyone, from Lieutenant-Commander to stoker, changes his personal trick or habit – even the manner in which he clutches his chin or caresses his nose at a crisis – the matter must be carefully considered in this world where each is trustee for his neighbour's life and, vastly more important, the corporate honour.

'What are the destroyers doing just now?' I asked.

'Oh – running about – much the same as usual.'

The Navy hasn't the least objection to telling one everything that it is doing. Unfortunately, it speaks its own language, which is incomprehensible to the civilian.

But you will find it all in 'The Channel Pilot' and 'The Riddle of the Sands.'

It is a foul coast, hairy with currents and rips, and mottled with shoals and rocks. Practically the same men hold on here in the same ships, with much the same crews, for months and months. A most senior officer told me that they were 'good boys' – on reflection, 'quite good boys' – but neither he nor the flags on his chart explained how they managed their lightless, unmarked navigations through black night, blinding rain, and the crazy, rebounding North Sea gales. They themselves ascribe it to Joss that they have not piled up their ships a hundred times.

'I expect it must be because we're always dodging about over the same ground. One gets to smell it. We've bumped pretty hard, of course, but we haven't expended much up to date. You never know your luck on patrol, though.'

The Nature of the Beast

Personally, though they have been true friends to me, I loathe destroyers, and all the raw, racking, ricocheting life that goes with them – the smell of the wet 'lammies' and damp wardroom cushions; the galley-chimney smoking out the bridge; the obstacle-strewn deck; and the pervading beastliness of oil, grit, and greasy iron. Even at moorings they shiver and sidle like half-backed horses. At sea they will neither rise up and fly clear like the hydroplanes, nor dive and be done with it like the submarines, but imitate the vices of both. A scientist of the lower deck describes them as: 'Half switchback, half water-chute, and Hell continuous.' Their only merit, from a landsman's point of view, is that they can crumple themselves up from stem to bridge and (I have seen it) still get home. But one does not breathe these compliments to their commanders. Other destroyers may be – they will point them out to you – poisonous bags of tricks, but their own command – never! Is she high-bowed? That is the only type which over-rides the seas instead of smothering. Is she low? Low bows glide through the water where those collier-nosed brutes smash it open. Is she mucked up with submarine-catchers? They rather improve her trim. No other ship has them. Have they been denied to her? Thank Heaven, we go to sea without a fish-curing plant on deck. Does she roll, even for her class? She is drier than Dreadnoughts. Is she permanently and infernally wet? Stiff; sir – stiff: the first requisite of a gun-platform.

'Service as Requisite'

Thus the Caesars and their fortunes put out to sea with their subs and their sad-eyed engineers, and their long-suffering signallers – I do not even know the technical name of the sin which causes a man to be born a destroyer-signaller in this life – and the little yellow shells stuck all about where they can be easiest reached. The rest of their acts is written for the information of the proper authorities. It reads like a page of Todhunter. But the masters of merchant-ships could tell more of eyeless shapes, barely outlined on the foam of their own arrest, who shout orders through the thick gloom alongside. The strayed and anxious neutral knows them when their searchlights pin him across the deep, or their sirens answer the last yelp of his as steam goes out of his torpedoed boilers. They stand by to catch and soothe him in his pyjamas at the gangway, collect his scattered lifeboats, and see a warm drink into him before they turn to hunt the slayer. The drifters, punching and reeling up and down their ten-mile line of traps; the outer trawlers, drawing the very teeth of Death with water-sodden fingers, are grateful for their low, guarded signals; and when the Zeppelin's revealing star-shell cracks darkness open above him, the answering crack of the invisible destroyers' guns comforts the busy mine-layers. Big cruisers talk to them, too; and, what is more, they talk back to the cruisers. Sometimes they draw fire – pinkish spurts of light – a long way off, where Fritz is trying to coax them over a mine-field he has just laid; or they steal on Fritz in the midst of his job, and the horizon rings with barking, which the inevitable neutral who saw it all reports as 'a heavy fleet action in the North Sea.' The sea after dark can be as alive as the woods of summer nights. Everything is exactly where you don't expect it, and the shyest creatures are the farthest away from their holes. Things boom overhead like bitterns, or scutter alongside like hares, or arise dripping and hissing from below like otters. It is the destroyer's business to find out what their business may be through all the long night, and to help or hinder accordingly. Dawn sees them pitch-poling insanely between head-seas, or hanging on to bridges that sweep like scythes from one forlorn horizon to the other. A homeward-bound submarine chooses this hour to rise, very ostentatiously, and signals by hand to a lieutenant in command. (They were the same term at Dartmouth, and same first ship.)

'What's he sayin'? Secure that gun, will you? Can't hear oneself speak.' The gun is a bit noisy on its mountings, but that isn't the reason for the destroyer-lieutenant's short temper.

'Says he's goin' down, sir,' the signaller replies. What the submarine had spelt out, and everybody knows it, was: 'Cannot approve of this extremely frightful weather. Am going to bye-bye.'

'Well!' snaps the lieutenant to his signaller, 'what are you grinning at?' The submarine has hung on to ask if the destroyer will 'kiss her and whisper good-night.' A breaking sea smacks her tower in the middle of the insult. She closes like an oyster, but – just too late. *Habet*! There must be a quarter of a ton of water somewhere down below, on its way to her ticklish batteries.

'What a wag!' says the signaller, dreamily. 'Well, 'e can't say 'e didn't get 'is little kiss.'

The lieutenant in command smiles. The sea is a beast, but a just beast.

Racial Untruths

This is trivial enough, but what would you have? If Admirals will not strike the proper attitudes, nor Lieutenants emit the appropriate sentiments, one is forced back on the truth, which is that the men at the heart of the great matters in our Empire are, mostly, of an even simplicity. From the advertising point of view they are stupid, but the breed has always been stupid in this department. It may be due, as our enemies assert, to our racial snobbery, or, as others hold, to a certain God-given lack of imagination which saves us from being over-concerned at the effects of our appearances on others. Either way, it deceives the enemies' people more than any calculated lie. When you come to think of it, though the English are the worst paper-work and *viva voce* liars in the world, they have been rigorously trained since their early youth to live and act lies for the comfort of the society in which they move, and so for their own comfort. The result in this war is interesting.

It is no lie that at the present moment we hold all the seas in the hollow of our hands. For that reason we shuffle over them shame-faced and apologetic, making arrangements here and flagrant compromises there, in order to give substance to the lie that we have dropped fortuitously into this high seat and are looking round the world for someone to resign it to. Nor is it any lie that, had we used the Navy's bare fist instead of its gloved hand from the beginning, we could in all likelihood have shortened the war. That being so, we elected to dab and peck at and half-strangle the enemy, to let him go and choke him again. It is no lie that we continue on our inexplicable path animated, we will try to believe till other proof is given, by a cloudy idea of alleviating or mitigating something for somebody – not ourselves. (Here, of course, is where our racial snobbery comes in, which makes the German gibber. I cannot understand why he has not accused us to our Allies of having secret commercial understandings with him.) For that reason, we shall finish the German eagle as the merciful lady killed the chicken. It took her the whole afternoon, and then, you will remember, the carcase had to be thrown away.

Meantime, there is a large and unlovely water, inhabited by plain men in severe boats, who endure cold, exposure, wet, and monotony almost as heavy as their responsibilities. Charge them with heroism – but that needs heroism, indeed! Accuse them of patriotism, they become ribald. Examine into the records of the miraculous work they have done and are doing. They will assist you, but with perfect sincerity they will make as light of the valour and fore-thought shown as of the ends they have gained for mankind. The Service takes all work for granted. It knew long ago that certain things would have to be done, and it did its best to be ready for them. When it disappeared over the sky-line for manoeuvres it was practising – always practising; trying its men and stuff and throwing out what could not take the strain. That is why, when war came, only a few names had to be changed, and those chiefly for the sake of the body, not of the spirit. And the Seniors who hold the key to our plans and know what will be done if things happen, and what lines wear thin in the many chains, they are of one fibre and speech with the Juniors and the lower deck and all the rest who come out of the undemonstrative households ashore. 'Here is the situation as it exists now,' say the Seniors. 'This is what we do to meet it. Look and count and measure and judge for yourself, and then you will know.'

It is a safe offer. The civilian only sees that the sea is a vast place, divided between wisdom and chance. He only knows that the uttermost oceans have been swept clear, and the trade-routes purged, one by one, even as our armies were being convoyed along them; that there was no island nor key left unsearched on any waters that might hide an enemy's craft between the Arctic Circle and the Horn. He only knows that less than a day's run to the eastward of where he stands, the enemy's fleets have been held for a year and four months, in order that civilisation may go about its business on all our waters.

Tales of 'The Trade' (1916)

'The Trade'

They bear, in place of classic names,
Letters and numbers on their skin.
They play their grisly blindfold games
In little boxes made of tin.
Sometimes they stalk the Zeppelin,
Sometimes they learn where mines are laid
Or where the Baltic ice is thin.
That is the custom of 'The Trade.'

Few prize-courts sit upon their claims.
They seldom tow their targets in.
They follow certain secret aims
Down under, far from strife or din.
When they are ready to begin
No flag is flown, no fuss is made
More than the shearing of a pin.
That is the custom of 'The Trade.'

The Scout's quadruple funnel flames
A mark from Sweden to the Swin,
The Cruiser's thundrous screw proclaims

Her comings out and goings in:
But only whiffs of paraffin
Or creamy rings that fizz and fade
Show where the one-eyed Death has been.
That is the custom of 'The Trade.'

Their feats, their fortunes and their fames
Are hidden from their nearest kin;
No eager public backs or blames,
No journal prints the yarns they spin
(The Censor would not let it in!)
When they return from run or raid.
Unheard they work, unseen they win.
That is the custom of 'The Trade.'

Some Work in the Baltic

No one knows how the title of 'The Trade' came to be
applied to the Submarine Service. Some say that the
cruisers invented it because they pretend that submarine
officers look like unwashed chauffeurs. Others think it
sprang forth by itself, which means that it was coined
by the Lower Deck, where they always have the proper
names for things. Whatever the truth, the Submarine
Service is now 'the trade'; and if you ask them why, they
will answer: 'What else could you call it? The Trade's "the
trade," of course.'

It is a close corporation; yet it recruits its men and
officers from every class that uses the sea and engines,
as well as from many classes that never expected to deal
with either. It takes them; they disappear for a while and

return changed to their very souls, for the Trade lives in a world without precedents, of which no generation has had any previous experience – a world still being made and enlarged daily. It creates and settles its own problems as it goes along, and if it cannot help itself no one else can. So the Trade lives in the dark and thinks out inconceivable and impossible things which it afterwards puts into practice.

It keeps books, too, as honest traders should. They are almost as bald as ledgers, and are written up, hour by hour, on a little sliding table that pulls out from beneath the commander's bunk. In due time they go to my Lords of the Admiralty, who presently circulate a few carefully watered extracts for the confidential information of the junior officers of the Trade, that these may see what things are done and how. The juniors read but laugh. They have heard the stories, with all the flaming detail and much of the language, either from a chief actor while they perched deferentially on the edge of a mess-room fender, or from his subordinate, in which case they were not so deferential, or from some returned member of the crew present on the occasion, who, between half-shut teeth at the wheel, jerks out what really happened. There is very little going on in the Trade that the Trade does not know within a reasonable time. But the outside world must wait until my Lords of the Admiralty release the records. Some of them have been released now.

Submarine and Ice-breaker

Let us take, almost at random, an episode in the life of H.M. Submarine E9. It is true that she was commanded by Commander Max Horton, but the utter impersonality of the tale makes it as though the boat herself spoke.

(Also, never having met or seen any of the gentlemen concerned in the matter, the writer can be impersonal too.) Some time ago, E9 was in the Baltic, in the deeps of winter, where she used to be taken to her hunting grounds by an ice-breaker. Obviously a submarine cannot use her sensitive nose to smash heavy ice with, so the broad-beamed pushing chaperone comes along to see her clear of the thick harbour and shore ice. In the open sea apparently she is left to her own devices. In company of the ice-breaker, then, E9 'proceeded' (neither in the Senior nor the Junior Service does anyone officially 'go' anywhere) to a 'certain position.'

Here – it is not stated in the book, but the Trade knows every aching, single detail of what is left out – she spent a certain time in testing arrangements and apparatus, which may or may not work properly when immersed in a mixture of block-ice and dirty ice-cream in a temperature well towards zero. This is a pleasant job, made the more delightful by the knowledge that if you slip off the superstructure the deadly Baltic chill will stop your heart long before even your heavy clothes can drown you. Hence (and this is not in the book either) the remark of the highly trained sailor-man in these latitudes who, on being told by his superior officer in the execution of his duty to go to Hell, did insubordinately and enviously reply: 'D'you think I'd be here if I could?' Whereby he caused the entire personnel, beginning with the Commander, to say 'Amen,' or words to that effect. E9 evidently made things work.

Next day she reports: 'As circumstances were favourable decided to attempt to bag a destroyer.' Her 'certain position' must have been near a well-used destroyer-run, for shortly afterwards she sees three of them, but too far off to attack, and later, as the light is failing, a fourth destroyer towards which she manoeuvres. 'Depth-keeping,' she notes, 'very difficult owing to heavy swell.' An observation balloon on a gusty day is almost as stable as a submarine 'pumping' in a heavy swell, and since the Baltic is shallow, the submarine runs the chance of being let down with a whack on the bottom. None the less, E9 works her way to within 600 yards of the quarry; fires and waits just long enough to be sure that her torpedo is running straight, and that the destroyer is holding her course. Then she 'dips to avoid detection.' The rest is deadly simple: 'At the correct moment after firing, forty-five to fifty seconds, heard the unmistakable noise of torpedo detonating.' Four minutes later she rose and 'found destroyer had disappeared.' Then, for reasons probably connected with other destroyers, who, too, may have heard that unmistakable sound, she goes to bed below in the chill dark till it is time to turn homewards. When she rose she met storm from the north and logged it accordingly. 'Spray froze as it struck, and bridge became a mass of ice. Experienced considerable difficulty in keeping the conning-tower hatch free from ice. Found it necessary to keep a man continuously employed on this work. Bridge screen immovable, ice six inches thick on it. Telegraphs frozen.' In this state she forges ahead till midnight, and anyone who pleases can imagine the thoughts of the continuous employee scraping and hammering round the hatch, as well as the delight of his friends below when the ice-slush spattered down the conning-tower. At last she considered it 'advisable to free the boat of ice, so went below.'

'As Requisite'

In the Senior Service the two words 'as requisite' cover everything that need not be talked about. E9 next day 'proceeded as requisite' through a series of snowstorms and recurring deposits of ice on the bridge till she got in touch with her friend the ice-breaker; and in her company ploughed and rooted her way back to the work we know. There is nothing to show that it was a near thing for E9, but somehow one has the idea that the ice-breaker did not arrive any too soon for E9's comfort and progress. (But what happens in the Baltic when the ice-breaker does not arrive?)

That was in winter. In summer quite the other way, E9 had to go to bed by day very often under the long-lasting northern light when the Baltic is as smooth as a carpet, and one cannot get within a mile and a half of anything with eyes in its head without being put down. There was one time when E9, evidently on information received, took up 'a certain position' and reported the sea 'glassy.' She had to suffer in silence, while three heavily laden German ships went by; for an attack would have given away her position. Her reward came next day, when she sighted (the words run like Marryat's) 'enemy squadron coming up fast from eastward, proceeding inshore of us.' They were two heavy battleships with an escort of destroyers, and E9 turned to attack. She does not say how she crept up in that smooth sea within a quarter of a mile of the leading ship, 'a three-funnel ship, of either the *Deutschland* or *Braunschweig* class,' but she managed it, and fired both bow torpedoes at her.

'No. 1 torpedo was seen and heard to strike her just before foremost funnel: smoke and debris appeared to go as high as masthead.' That much E9 saw before one of the guardian destroyers ran at her. 'So,' says she, 'observing her I took my periscope off the battleship.' This was excusable, as the destroyer was coming up with intent to kill and E9 had to flood her tanks and get down quickly. Even so, the destroyer only just missed her, and she struck bottom in 43 feet. 'But,' says E9, who, if she could not see, kept her ears open, 'at the correct interval (the 45 or 50 seconds mentioned in the previous case) the second torpedo was heard to explode, though not actually seen.' E9 came up twenty minutes later to make sure. The destroyer was waiting for her a couple of hundred yards away, and again E9 dipped for life, but 'just had time to see one large vessel approximately 4 or 5 miles away.'

Putting courage aside, think for a moment of the mere drill of it all – that last dive for that attack on the chosen battleship; the eye at the periscope watching 'No. 1 torpedo' get home; the rush of the vengeful destroyer; the instant orders for flooding everything; the swift descent which had to be arranged for with full knowledge of the shallow sea-floors waiting below, and a guess at the course that might be taken by the seeking bows above, for assuming a destroyer to draw 10 feet and a submarine on the bottom to stand 25 feet to the top of her conning-tower, there is not much clearance in 43 feet salt water, especially if the boat jumps when she touches bottom. And through all these and half a hundred other simultaneous considerations, imagine the trained minds below, counting, as only torpedo-men can count, the run of the merciless seconds that should tell when that second shot arrived. Then 'at the correct interval' as laid down in the table of distances, the boom and the jar of No. 2 torpedo, the relief, the exhaled breath and untightened lips; the impatient waiting for a second peep, and when that had been taken and the eye at the periscope had reported one little nigger-boy in place of two on the waters, perhaps cigarettes, while the destroyer sickled about at a venture overhead.

Certainly they give men rewards for doing such things, but what reward can there be in any gift of Kings or peoples to match the enduring satisfaction of having done them, not alone, but with and through and by trusty and proven companions?

Defeated by Darkness

E1, also a Baltic boat, her Commander F. N. Laurence, had her experiences too. She went out one summer day and late – too late – in the evening sighted three transports. The first she hit. While she was arranging for the second, the third inconsiderately tried to ram her before her sights were on. So it was necessary to go down at once and waste whole minutes of the precious scanting light. When she rose, the stricken ship was sinking and shortly afterwards blew up. The other two were patrolling nearby. It would have been a fair chance in daylight, but the darkness defeated her and she had to give up the attack.

It was E1 who, during thick weather, came across a squadron of battle-cruisers and got in on a flanking ship – probably the Moltke. The destroyers were very much on the alert, and she had to dive at once to avoid one who only missed her by a few feet. Then the fog shut down and stopped further developments. Thus do time and chance come to every man.

The Trade has many stories, too, of watching patrols when a boat must see chance after chance go by under her nose and write – merely write – what she has seen. Naturally they do not appear in any accessible records. Nor, which is a pity, do the authorities release the records of glorious failures, when everything goes wrong; when torpedoes break surface and squatter like ducks; or arrive full square with a clang and burst of white water and fail to explode; when the devil is in charge of all the motors, and clutches develop play that would scare a shore-going mechanic bald; when batteries begin to give off death instead of power, and atop of all, ice or wreckage of the strewn seas racks and wrenches the hull till the whole leaking bag of tricks limps home on six missing cylinders and one ditto propeller, plus the indomitable will of the red-eyed husky scarecrows in charge.

There might be worse things in this world for decent people to read than such records.

Business in the Sea of Marmara

This war is like an iceberg. We, the public, only see an eighth of it above water. The rest is out of sight and, as with the berg, one guesses its extent by great blocks that break off and shoot up to the surface from some underlying out-running spur a quarter of a mile away. So with this war sudden tales come to light which reveal unsuspected activities in unexpected quarters. One takes it for granted such things are always going on somewhere, but the actual emergence of the record is always astonishing.

Once upon a time, there were certain E type boats who worked the Sea of Marmara with thoroughness and humanity; for the two, in English hands, are compatible. The road to their hunting-grounds was strewn with peril, the waters they inhabited were full of eyes that gave them no rest, and what they lost or expended in wear and tear of the chase could not be made good till they had run the gauntlet to their base again. The full tale of their improvisations and 'make-do's will probably never come to light, though fragments can be picked up at intervals in the proper places as the men concerned come and go. The Admiralty gives only the bones, but those are not so dry, of the boat's official story.

When E14, Commander E. Courtney-Boyle, went to her work in the Sea of Marmara, she, like her sister, 'proceeded' on her gas-engine up the Dardanelles; and a gas-engine by night between steep cliffs has been described by the Lower-deck as a 'full brass band in a railway cutting.' So a fort picked her up with a searchlight and missed her with artillery. She dived under the minefield that guarded the Straits, and when she rose at dawn in the narrowest part of the channel, which is about one mile and a half across, all the forts fired at her. The water, too, was thick with steamboat patrols, out of which E14 selected a Turkish gunboat and gave her a torpedo. She had just time to see the great column of water shoot as high as the gunboat's mast when she had to dip again as 'the men in a small steamboat were leaning over trying to catch hold of the top of my periscope.'

'Six Hours of Blind Death'

This sentence, which might have come out of a French exercise book, is all Lieutenant-Commander Courtney-Boyle sees fit to tell, and that officer will never understand why one taxpayer at least demands his arrest after the war till he shall have given the full tale. Did he sight the shadowy underline of the small steamboat green through the deadlights? Or did she suddenly swim into his vision from behind, and obscure, without warning, his periscope with a single brown clutching hand? Was she alone, or one of a mob of splashing, shouting small craft? He may well have been too busy to note, for there were patrols all around him, a minefield of curious design and undefined area somewhere in front, and steam trawlers vigorously sweeping for him astern and ahead. And when E14 had burrowed and bumped and scraped through six hours of blind death, she found the Sea of Marmara crawling with craft, and was kept down almost continuously and grew hot and stuffy in consequence. Nor could she charge her batteries in peace, so at the end of another hectic, hunted day of starting them up and breaking off and diving – which is bad for the temper – she decided to quit those infested waters near the coast and charge up somewhere off the traffic routes.

This accomplished, after a long, hot run, which did the motors no good, she went back to her beat, where she picked up three destroyers convoying a couple of troopships. But it was a glassy calm and the destroyers 'came for me.' She got off a long-range torpedo at one transport, and ducked before she could judge results. She apologises for this on the grounds that one of her periscopes had been damaged – not, as one would expect, by the gentleman leaning out of the little steamboat, but by some casual shot – calibre not specified – the day before. 'And so,' says E14, 'I could not risk my remaining one being bent.' However, she heard a thud, and the depth-gauges – those great clock-hands on the white-faced circles – 'flicked,' which is another sign of dreadful certainty down under. When she rose again she saw a destroyer convoying one burning transport to the nearest beach. That afternoon she met a sister-boat (now gone to Valhalla), who told her that she was almost out of torpedoes, and they arranged a rendezvous for next day, but 'before we could communicate we had to dive, and I did not see her again.' There must be many such meetings in the Trade, under all skies – boat rising beside boat at the point agreed upon for interchange of news and materials; the talk shouted aloud with the speakers' eyes always on the horizon and all hands standing by to dive, even in the middle of a sentence.

Annoying Patrol Ships

E14 kept to her job, on the edge of the procession of traffic. Patrol vessels annoyed her to such an extent that 'as I had not seen any transports lately I decided to sink a patrol-ship as they were always firing on me.' So she torpedoed a thing that looked like a mine-layer, and must have been something of that kidney, for it sank in less than a minute. A tramp-steamer lumbering across the dead flat sea was thoughtfully headed back to Constantinople by firing rifles ahead of her. 'Under fire the whole day,' E14 observes philosophically. The nature of her work made this inevitable. She was all among the patrols, which kept her down a good deal and made her draw on her batteries, and when she rose to charge, watchers ashore burned oil-flares on the beach or made smokes among the hills according to the light. In either case there would be a general rush of patrolling craft of all kinds, from steam launches to gunboats. Nobody loves the Trade, though E14 did several things which made her popular. She let off a string of very surprised dhows (they were empty) in charge of a tug which promptly fled back to Constantinople; stopped a couple of steamers full of refugees, also bound for Constantinople, who were 'very pleased at being allowed to proceed' instead of being Lusitaniaed as they had expected. Another refugee-boat, fleeing from goodness knows what horror, she chased into Rodosto Harbour, where, though she could not see any troops, 'they opened a heavy rifle fire on us, hitting the boat several times. So I went away and chased two more small tramps who returned towards Constantinople.'

Transports, of course, were fair game, and in spite of the necessity she was under of not risking her remaining eye, E14 got a big one in a night of wind and made another hurriedly beach itself, which then opened fire on her, assisted by the local population. 'Returned fire and proceeded,' says E14. The diversion of returning fire is one much appreciated by the lower-deck as furnishing a pleasant break in what otherwise might be a monotonous and odoriferous task. There is no drill laid down for this evolution, but etiquette and custom prescribe that on going up the hatch you shall not too energetically prod the next man ahead with the muzzle of your rifle. Likewise, when descending in quick time before the hatch closes, you are requested not to jump directly on the head of the next below. Otherwise you act 'as requisite' on your own initiative.

When she had used up all her torpedoes E14 prepared to go home by the way she had come – there was no other – and was chased towards Gallipoli by a mixed pack composed of a gunboat, a torpedo-boat, and a tug. 'They shepherded me to Gallipoli, one each side of me and one astern, evidently expecting me to be caught by the nets there.' She walked very delicately for the next eight hours or so, all down the Straits, underrunning the strong tides, ducking down when the fire from the forts got too hot, verifying her position and the position of the minefield, but always taking notes of every ship in sight, till towards teatime she saw our Navy off the entrance and 'rose to the surface abeam of a French battleship who gave us a rousing cheer.' She had been away, as nearly as possible, three weeks, and a kind destroyer escorted her to the base, where we will leave her for the moment while we consider the performance of E11 (Lieutenant-Commander M.E. Nasmith) in the same waters at about the same season.

E11 'proceeded' in the usual way, to the usual accompaniments of hostile destroyers, up the Straits, and meets the usual difficulties about charging-up when she gets through. Her wireless naturally takes this opportunity to give trouble, and E11 is left, deaf and dumb, somewhere in the middle of the Sea of Marmara, diving to avoid hostile destroyers in the intervals of trying to come at the fault in her aerial. (Yet it is noteworthy that the language of the Trade, though technical, is no more emphatic or incandescent than that of top-side ships.)

Then she goes towards Constantinople, finds a Turkish torpedo-gunboat off the port, sinks her, has her periscope smashed by a 6-pounder, retires, fits a new top on the periscope, and at 10.30 a.m. – they must have needed it – pipes 'all hands to bathe.' Much refreshed, she gets her wireless linked up at last, and is able to tell the authorities where she is and what she is after.

Mr Silas Q. Swing

At this point – it was off Rodosto – enter a small steamer which does not halt when requested, and so is fired at with 'several rounds' from a rifle. The crew, on being told to abandon her, tumble into their boats with such haste that they capsize two out of three. 'Fortunately,' says E11, 'they are able to pick up everybody.' You can imagine to yourself the confusion alongside, the raffle of odds and ends floating out of the boats, and the general parti-coloured hurrah's-nest all over the bright broken water. What you cannot imagine is this: 'An American gentleman then appeared on the upper deck who informed us that his name was Silas Q. Swing, of the Chicago Sun, and that he was pleased to make our acquaintance. He then informed us that the steamer was proceeding to Chanak and he wasn't sure if there were any stores aboard.' If anything could astonish the Trade at this late date, one would almost fancy that the apparition of Silas Q. Swing ('very happy to meet you, gentlemen') might have started a rivet or two on E11's placid skin. But she never even quivered. She kept a lieutenant of the name of D'Oyley Hughes, an expert in demolition parties; and he went aboard the tramp and reported any quantity of stores – a 6-inch gun, for instance, lashed across the top of the forehatch (Silas Q. Swing must have been an unobservant journalist), a 6-inch gun-mounting in the forehold, pedestals for 12-pounders thrown in as dunnage, the afterhold full of 6-inch projectiles, and a scattering of other commodities. They put the demolition charge well in among the 6-inch stuff, and she took it all to the bottom in a few minutes, after being touched off.

'Simultaneously with the sinking of the vessel,' the E11 goes on, 'smoke was observed to the eastward.' It was a steamer who had seen the explosion and was running for Rodosto. E11 chased her till she tied up to Rodosto pier, and then torpedoed her where she lay – a heavily laden store-ship piled high with packing-cases. The water was shallow here, and though E11 bumped along the bottom, which does not make for steadiness of aim, she was forced to show a good deal of her only periscope, and had it dented, but not damaged, by rifle-fire from the beach. As she moved out of Rodosto Bay she saw a paddle-boat loaded with barbed wire, which stopped on the hail, but 'as we ranged alongside her, attempted to ram us, but failed owing to our superior speed.' Then she ran for the beach 'very skilfully,' keeping her stern to E11 till she drove ashore beneath some cliffs. The demolition-squad were just getting to work when 'a party of horsemen appeared on the cliffs above and opened a hot fire on the conning tower.' E11 got out, but owing to the shoal water it was some time before she could get under enough to fire a torpedo. The stern of a stranded paddle-boat is no great target and the thing exploded on the beach. Then she 'recharged batteries and proceeded slowly on the surface towards Constantinople.' All this between the ordinary office hours of 10 a.m. and 4 p.m.

Her next day's work opens, as no pallid writer of fiction dare begin, thus: 'Having dived unobserved into Constantinople, observed, etc.' Her observations were rather hampered by cross-tides, mud, and currents, as well as the vagaries of one of her own torpedoes which turned upside down and ran about promiscuously. It hit something at last, and so did another shot that she fired, but the waters by Constantinople Arsenal are not healthy to linger in after one has scared up the whole sea-front, so 'turned to go out.' Matters were a little better below, and E11 in her perilous passage might have been a lady of the harem tied up in a sack and thrown into the Bosporus. She grounded heavily; she bounced up 30 feet, was headed down again by a manoeuvre easier to shudder over than to describe, and when she came to rest on the bottom found herself being swivelled right round the compass. They watched the compass with much interest. 'It was concluded, therefore, that the vessel (E11 is one of the few who speaks of herself as a 'vessel' as well as a 'boat') was resting on the shoal under the Leander Tower, and was being turned round by the current.' So they corrected her, started the motors, and 'bumped gently down into 85 feet of water' with no more knowledge than the lady in the sack where the next bump would land them.

The Preening Perch
And the following day was spent 'resting in the centre of the Sea of Marmara.' That was their favourite preening perch between operations, because it gave them a chance to tidy the boat and bathe, and they were a cleanly people both in their methods and their persons. When they boarded a craft and found nothing of consequence they 'parted with many expressions of good will,' and E11 'had a good wash.' She gives her reasons at length; for going in and out of Constantinople and the Straits is all in the day's work, but going dirty, you understand, is serious. She had 'of late noticed the atmosphere in the boat becoming very oppressive, the reason doubtless being that there was a quantity of dirty linen aboard, and also the scarcity of fresh water necessitated a limit being placed on the frequency of personal washing.' Hence the centre

of the Sea of Marmara; all hands playing overside and as much laundry work as time and the Service allowed. One of the reasons, by the way, why we shall be good friends with the Turk again is that he has many of our ideas about decency.

In due time E11 went back to her base. She had discovered a way of using unspent torpedoes twice over, which surprised the enemy, and she had as nearly as possible been cut down by a ship which she thought was running away from her. Instead of which (she made the discovery at 3,000 yards, both craft all out) the stranger steamed straight at her. 'The enemy then witnessed a somewhat spectacular dive at full speed from the surface to 20 feet in as many seconds. He then really did turn tail and was seen no more.' Going through the Straits she observed an empty troopship at anchor, but reserved her torpedoes in the hope of picking up some battleships lower down. Not finding these in the Narrows, she nosed her way back and sank the trooper, 'afterwards continuing journey down the Straits.' Off Kilid Bahr something happened; she got out of trim and had to be fully flooded before she could be brought to her required depth. It might have been whirlpools under water, or other things. (They tell a story of a boat which once went mad in these very waters, and for no reason ascertainable from within plunged to depths that contractors do not allow for; rocketed up again like a swordfish, and would doubtless have so continued till she died, had not something she had fouled dropped off and let her recover her composure.)

An hour later: 'Heard a noise similar to grounding. Knowing this to be impossible in the water in which the boat then was, I came up to 20 feet to investigate, and observed a large mine preceding the periscope at a distance of about 20 feet, which was apparently hung up by its moorings to the port hydroplane.' Hydroplanes are the fins at bow and stern which regulate a submarine's diving. A mine weighs anything from hundredweights to half-tons. Sometimes it explodes if you merely think about it; at others you can batter it like an empty sardine-tin and it submits meekly; but at no time is it meant to wear on a hydroplane. They dared not come up to unhitch it, 'owing to the batteries ashore,' so they pushed the dim shape ahead of them till they got outside Kum Kale. They then went full astern, and emptied the after-tanks, which brought the bows down, and in this posture rose to the surface, when 'the rush of water from the screws together with the sternway gathered allowed the mine to fall clear of the vessel.'

Now a fool, said Dr Johnson, would have tried to describe that.

Ravages and Repairs

Before we pick up the further adventures of H.M. Submarine E14 and her partner E11, here is what you might call a cutting-out affair in the Sea of Marmara which E12 put through quite on the old lines.

E12's main motors gave trouble from the first, and she seems to have been a cripple for most of that trip. She sighted two small steamers, one towing two, and the other three, sailing vessels; making seven keels in all. She stopped the first steamer, noticed she carried a lot of stores, and, moreover, that her crew – she had no boats

– were all on deck in life-belts. Not seeing any gun, E12 ran up alongside and told the first lieutenant to board. The steamer then threw a bomb at E12, which struck, but luckily did not explode, and opened fire on the boarding-party with rifles and a concealed 1-inch gun. E12 answered with her 6-pounder, and also with rifles. The two sailing ships in tow, very properly, tried to foul E12's propellers and 'also opened fire with rifles.'

It was as Orientally mixed a fight as a man could wish: The first lieutenant and the boarding-party engaged on the steamer, E12 foul of the steamer, and being fouled by the sailing ships; the 6-pounder methodically perforating the steamer from bow to stern; the steamer's 1-inch gun and the rifles from the sailing ships raking everything and everybody else; E12's coxswain on the conning-tower passing up ammunition; and E12's one workable motor developing 'slight defects' at, of course, the moment when power to manoeuvre was vital.

The account is almost as difficult to disentangle as the actual mess must have been. At any rate, the 6-pounder caused an explosion in the steamer's ammunition, whereby the steamer sank in a quarter of an hour, giving time – and a hot time it must have been – for E12 to get clear of her and to sink the two sailing ships. She then chased the second steamer, who slipped her three tows and ran for the shore. E12 knocked her about a good deal with gun-fire as she fled, saw her drive on the beach well alight, and then, since the beach opened fire with a gun at 1,500 yards, went away to re-tinker her motors and write up her log. She approved of her first lieutenant's behaviour 'under very trying circumstances' (this probably refers to the explosion of the ammunition by the six-pounder which, doubtless, jarred the boarding-party) and of the cox who acted as ammunition-hoist; and of the gun's crew, who 'all did very well' under rifle and small-gun fire 'at a range of about ten yards.' But she never says what she really said about her motors.

A Brawl at a Pier

Now we will take E14 on various work, either alone or as flagship of a squadron composed of herself and Lieutenant-Commander Nasmith's boat, E11. Hers was a busy midsummer, and she came to be intimate with all sort of craft – such as the two-funnelled gunboat off Sar Kioi, who 'fired at us, and missed as usual'; hospital ships going back and forth unmolested to Constantinople; 'the gunboat which fired at me on Sunday,' and other old friends, afloat and ashore.

When the crew of the Turkish brigantine full of stores got into their boats by request, and then 'all stood up and cursed us,' E14 did not lose her temper, even though it was too rough to lie alongside the abandoned ship. She told Acting Lieutenant R.W. Lawrence, of the Royal Naval Reserve, to swim off to her, which he did, and after a 'cursory search' – Who can be expected to Sherlock Holmes for hours with nothing on? – set fire to her 'with the aid of her own matches and paraffin oil.'

Then E14 had a brawl with a steamer with a yellow funnel, blue top and black band, lying at a pier among dhows. The shore took a hand in the game with small guns and rifles, and, as E14 manoeuvred about the roadstead 'as requisite' there was a sudden unaccountable explosion which strained her very badly. 'I think,' she muses, 'I must have caught the moorings of a mine with my tail as I was turning, and exploded it. It is possible that it might have been a big shell bursting over us, but I think this unlikely, as we were 30 feet at the time.' She is always a philosophical boat, anxious to arrive at the reason of facts, and when the game is against her she admits it freely.

There was nondescript craft of a few hundred tons, who 'at a distance did not look very warlike,' but when chased suddenly played a couple of 6-pounders and 'got off two dozen rounds at us before we were under. Some of them were only about 20 yards off.' And when a wily steamer, after sidling along the shore, lay up in front of a town she became 'indistinguishable from the houses,' and so was safe because we do not *löwestrafe* open towns.

Sailing dhows full of grain had to be destroyed. At one rendezvous, while waiting for E11, E14 dealt with three such cases and then 'towed the crews inshore and gave them biscuits, beef, and rum and water, as they were rather wet.' Passenger steamers were allowed to proceed, because they were 'full of people of both sexes,' which is an uncultured way of doing business.

Here is another instance of our insular type of mind. An empty dhow is passed which E14 was going to leave alone, but it occurs to her that the boat looks 'rather deserted,' and she fancies she sees two heads in the water. So she goes back half a mile, picks up a couple of badly exhausted men, frightened out of their wits, gives them food and drink, and puts them aboard their property. Crews that jump overboard have to be picked up, even if, as happened in one case, there are twenty of them and one of them is a German bank manager taking a quantity of money to the Chanak Bank. Hospital ships are carefully looked over as they come and go, and are left to their own devices; but they are rather a nuisance because they force E14 and others to dive for them when engaged in stalking warrantable game. There were a good many hospital ships, and as far as we can make out they all played fair. E11 boarded one and 'reported everything satisfactory.'

Strange Messmates

A layman cannot tell from the reports which of the duties demanded the most work – whether the continuous clearing out of transports, dhows, and sailing ships, generally found close to the well-gunned and attentive beach, or the equally continuous attacks on armed vessels of every kind. Whatever else might be going on, there was always the problem how to arrange for the crews of sunk ships. If a dhow has no small boats, and you cannot find one handy, you have to take the crew aboard, where they are horribly in the way, and add to the oppressiveness of the atmosphere – like 'the nine people, including two very old men,' whom E14 made honorary members of her mess for several hours till she could put them ashore after dark. Oddly enough she 'could not get anything out of them.' Imagine nine bewildered Moslems suddenly decanted into the reeking clamorous bowels of a fabric obviously built by Shaitan himself, and surrounded by — but our people are people of the Book and not dog-eating Kaffirs, and I will wager a great deal that that little company went ashore in better heart and stomach than when they were passed down the conning-tower hatch.

Then there were queer amphibious battles with troops who had to be shelled as they marched towards Gallipoli along the coast roads. E14 went out with E11 on this job, early one morning, each boat taking her chosen section of landscape. Thrice E14 rose to fire, thinking she saw the dust of feet, but 'each time it turned out to be bullocks.' When the shelling was ended 'I think the troops marching along that road must have been delayed and a good many killed.' The Turks got up a field-gun in the course of the afternoon – your true believer never hurries – which out-ranged both boats, and they left accordingly.

The next day she changed billets with E11, who had the luck to pick up and put down a battleship close to Gallipoli. It turned out to be the *Barbarossa*. Meantime E14 got a 5,000-ton supply ship, and later had to burn a sailing ship loaded with 200 bales of leaf and cut tobacco – Turkish tobacco! Small wonder that E11 'came alongside that afternoon and remained for an hour' – probably making cigarettes.

Refitting under Difficulties

Then E14 went back to her base. She had a hellish time among the Dardanelles nets; was, of course, fired at by the forts, just missed a torpedo from the beach, scraped a mine, and when she had time to take stock found electric mine-wires twisted round her propellers and all her hull scraped and scored with wire marks. But that, again, was only in the day's work. The point she insisted upon was that she had been for seventy days in the Sea of Marmara with no securer base for refit than the centre of the same, and during all that while she had not had 'any engine-room defect which has not been put right by the engine-room staff of the boat.' The commander and the third officer went sick for a while; the first lieutenant got gastro-enteritis and was in bed (if you could see that bed!)

'for the remainder of our stay in the Sea of Marmara,' but 'this boat has never been out of running order.' The credit is ascribed to 'the excellence of my chief engine-room artificer, James Hollier Hague, O.N. 227715,' whose name is duly submitted to the authorities 'for your consideration for advancement to the rank of warrant officer.'

Seventy days of every conceivable sort of risk, within and without, in a boat which is all engine-room, except where she is sick-bay; 12,000 miles covered since last overhaul and 'never out of running order' – thanks to Mr Hague. Such artists as he are the kind of engine-room artificers that commanders intrigue to get hold of – each for his own boat – and when the tales are told in the Trade, their names, like Abou Ben Adhem's, lead all the rest.

I do not know the exact line of demarcation between engine-room and gunnery repairs, but I imagine it is faint and fluid. E11, for example, while she was helping E14 to shell a beached steamer, smashed half her gun-mounting, 'the gun-layer being thrown overboard, and the gun nearly following him.' However, the mischief was repaired in the next twenty-four hours, which, considering the very limited deck space of a submarine, means that all hands must have been moderately busy. One hopes that they had not to dive often during the job.

But worse is to come. E2 carried an externally mounted gun which, while she was diving up the Dardanelles on business, got hung up in the wires and stays of a net. She saw them through the conning-tower scuttles at a depth of 80 feet – one wire hawser round the gun, another round the conning-tower, and so on. There was a continuous crackling of small explosions overhead which she thought were charges aimed at her by the guard-boats who watch the nets. She considered her position for a while, backed, got up steam, barged ahead, and shore through the whole affair in one wild surge. Imagine the roof of a navigable cottage after it has snapped telegraph lines with its chimney, and you will get a small idea of what happens to the hull of a submarine when she uses her gun to break wire hawsers with.

Trouble with a Gun

E2 was a wet, strained, and uncomfortable boat for the rest of her cruise. She sank steamers, burned dhows; was worried by torpedo-boats and hunted by Hun planes; hit bottom freely and frequently; silenced forts that fired at her from lonely beaches; warned villages who might have joined in the game that they had better keep to farming; shelled railway lines and stations; would have shelled a pier, but found there was a hospital built at one end of it, 'so could not bombard'; came upon dhows crowded with 'female refugees' which she 'allowed to proceed,' and was presented with fowls in return; but through it all her chief preoccupation was that racked and strained gun and mounting. When there was nothing else doing she reports sourly that she 'worked on gun.' As a philosopher of the lower deck put it: ''Tisn't what you blanky do that matters, it's what you blanky have to do.' In other words, worry, not work, kills.

E2's gun did its best to knock the heart out of them all. She had to shift the wretched thing twice; once because the bolts that held it down were smashed (the wire hawser must have pretty well pulled it off its seat), and again because the hull beneath it leaked on pressure. She went down to make sure of it. But she drilled and tapped and adjusted, till in a short time the gun worked again and killed steamers as it should. Meanwhile, the whole boat leaked. All the plates under the old gun-position forward leaked; she leaked aft through damaged hydroplane guards, and on her way home they had to keep the water down by hand pumps while she was diving through the nets. Where she did not leak outside she leaked internally, tank leaking into tank, so that the petrol got into the main fresh-water supply and the men had to be put on allowance. The last pint was served out when she was in the narrowest part of the Narrows, a place where one's mouth may well go dry of a sudden.

Here for the moment the records end. I have been at some pains not to pick and choose among them. So far from doctoring or heightening any of the incidents, I have rather understated them; but I hope I have made it clear that through all the haste and fury of these multiplied actions, when life and death and destruction turned on the twitch of a finger, not one life of any non-combatant was wittingly taken. They were carefully picked up or picked out, taken below, transferred to boats, and despatched or personally conducted in the intervals of business to the safe, unexploding beach. Sometimes they part from their chaperones 'with many expressions of good will,' at others they seem greatly relieved and rather surprised at not being knocked on the head after the custom of their Allies. But the boats with a hundred things on their minds no more take credit for their humanity than their commanders explain the feats for which they won their respective decorations.

Destroyers at Jutland (1916)

'Have you news of my boy Jack?'
Not this tide.
'When d'you think that he'll come back?'
Not with this wind blowing, and this tide.

'Has anyone else had word of him?'
Not this tide.
For what is sunk will hardly swim,
Not with this wind blowing and this tide.

'Oh, dear, what comfort can I find?'
None this tide,
Nor any tide,
Except he didn't shame his kind
Not even with that wind blowing and that tide.

Then hold your head up all the more,
This tide,
And every tide,
Because he was the son you bore,
And gave to that wind blowing and that tide!

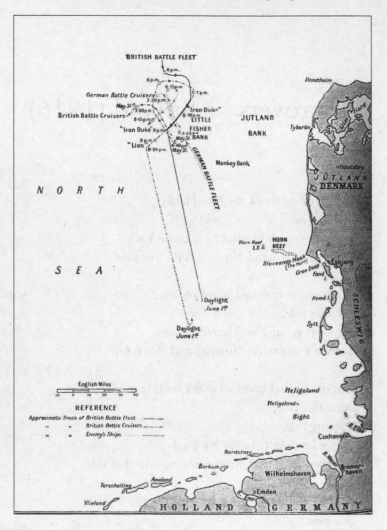

Stories of the Battle

Cripple and Paralytic

There was much destroyer-work in the Battle of Jutland. The actual battle field may not have been more than 20,000 square miles, but the incidental patrols, from first to last, must have covered many times that area. Doubtless the next generation will comb out every detail of it. All we need remember is there were many squadrons of battleships and cruisers engaged over the face of the North Sea, and that they were accompanied in their dread comings and goings by multitudes of destroyers, who attacked the enemy both by day and by night from the afternoon of May 31 to the morning of June 1, 1916. We are too close to the gigantic canvas to take in the meaning of the picture; our children stepping backward through the years may get the true perspective and proportions.

To recapitulate what everyone knows.

The German fleet came out of its North Sea ports, scouting ships ahead; then destroyers, cruisers, battle-cruisers, and, last, the main battle fleet in the rear. It moved north, parallel with the coast of stolen Schleswig-Holstein and Jutland. Our fleets were already out; the main battle fleet sweeping down from the north, and our battle-cruiser fleet feeling for the enemy. Our scouts came in contact with the enemy on the afternoon of May 31, about 100 miles off the Jutland coast, steering north-west. They satisfied themselves he was in strength, and reported accordingly to our battle-cruiser fleet, which engaged the enemy's battle-cruisers at about half-past three o'clock. The enemy steered south-east to rejoin their own fleet, which was coming up from that quarter.

We fought him on a parallel course as he ran for more than an hour.

Then his battle-fleet came in sight, and Beatty's fleet went about and steered north-west in order to retire on our battle-fleet, which was hurrying down from the north. We returned fighting very much over the same waters as we had used in our slant south. The enemy up till now had lain to the eastward of us, whereby he had the advantage in that thick weather of seeing our hulls clear against the afternoon light, while he himself worked in the mists. We then steered a little to the north-west bearing him off towards the east till at six o'clock Beatty had headed the enemy's leading ships and our main battle-fleet came in sight from the north. The enemy broke back in a loop, first eastward, then south, then south-west as our fleet edged him off from the land, and our main battle-fleet, coming up behind them, followed in their wake. Thus for a while we had the enemy to the westward of us, where he made a better mark; but the day was closing and the weather thickened, and the enemy wanted to get away. At a quarter past eight the enemy, still heading south-west, was covered by his destroyers in a great screen of grey smoke, and he got away.

Night and Morning

As darkness fell, our fleets lay between the enemy and his home ports. During the night our heavy ships, keeping well clear of possible mine-fields, swept down south to south and west of the Horns Reef, so that they might pick him up in the morning. When morning came our main fleet could find no trace of the enemy to the southward, but our destroyer-flotillas further north had been very busy with enemy ships, apparently running for the Horns Reef Channel. It looks, then, as if when we lost sight of the enemy in the smoke screen and the darkness he had changed course and broken for home astern our main fleets. And whether that was a sound manoeuvre or otherwise, he and the still flows of the North Sea alone can tell.

But how is a layman to give any coherent account of an affair where a whole country's coast-line was background to battle covering geographical degrees? The records give an impression of illimitable grey waters, nicked on their uncertain horizons with the smudge and blur of ships sparkling with fury against ships hidden under the curve of the world. One sees these distances maddeningly obscured by walking mists and weak fogs, or wiped out by layers of funnel and gun smoke, and realises how, at the pace the ships were going, anything might be stumbled upon in the haze or charge out of it when it lifted. One comprehends, too, how the far-off glare of a great vessel afire might be reported as a local fire on a near-by enemy, or vice versa; how a silhouette caught, for an instant, in a shaft of pale light let down from the low sky might be fatally difficult to identify till too late. But add to all these inevitable confusions and mis-reckonings of time, shape, and distance, charges at every angle of squadrons through and across other squadrons; sudden shifts of the centres of the fights, and even swifter restorations; wheelings, sweepings, and re-groupments such as accompany the passage across space of colliding universes. Then blanket the whole inferno with the darkness of night at full speed, and see what you can make of it.

Three Destroyers

A little time after the action began to heat up between our battle-cruisers and the enemy's, eight or ten of our destroyers opened the ball for their branch of the service by breaking up the attack of an enemy light cruiser and fifteen destroyers. Of these they accounted for at least two destroyers – some think more – and drove the others back on their battle-cruisers. This scattered that fight a good deal over the sea. Three of our destroyers held on for the enemy's battle-fleet, who came down on them at ranges which eventually grew less than 3,000 yards. Our people ought to have been lifted off the seas bodily, but they managed to fire a couple of torpedoes apiece while the range was diminishing. They had no illusions. Says one of the three, speaking of her second shot, which she loosed at fairly close range, 'This torpedo was fired because it was considered very unlikely that the ship would escape disablement before another opportunity offered.' But still they lived – three destroyers against all a battle-cruiser fleet's quick-firers, as well as the fire of a batch of enemy destroyers at 600 yards. And they were thankful for small mercies. 'The position being favourable,' a third torpedo was fired from each while they yet floated.

At 2,500 yards, one destroyer was hit somewhere in the vitals and swerved badly across her next astern, who 'was obliged to alter course to avoid a collision, thereby failing to fire a fourth torpedo.' Then that next astern 'observed signal for destroyers' recall,' and went back to report to her flotilla captain alone. Of her two companions, one was 'badly hit and remained stopped between the lines.' The other 'remained stopped, but was afloat when last seen.' Ships that 'remain stopped' are liable to be rammed or sunk by methodical gun-fire. That was, perhaps, fifty minutes' work put in before there was any really vicious 'edge' to the action, and it did not steady the nerves of the enemy battle-cruisers any more than another attack made by another detachment of ours.

'What does one do when one passes a ship that "remains stopped"?' I asked of a youth who had had experience.

'Nothing special. They cheer, and you cheer back. One doesn't think about it till afterwards. You see, it may be your luck in another minute.'

Luck

There were many other torpedo attacks in all parts of the battle that misty afternoon, including a quaint episode of an enemy light cruiser who 'looked as if she were trying' to torpedo one of our battle-cruisers while the latter was particularly engaged. A destroyer of ours, returning from a special job which required delicacy, was picking her way back at 30 knots through batches of enemy battle-cruisers and light cruisers with the idea of attaching herself to the nearest destroyer-flotilla and making herself useful. It occurred to her that as she 'was in a most advantageous position for repelling enemy's destroyers endeavouring to attack, she could not do better than to remain on the "engaged bow" of our battle-cruiser.' So she remained and considered things.

There was an enemy battle-cruiser squadron in the offing; with several enemy light cruisers ahead of that squadron, and the weather was thickish and deceptive. She sighted the enemy light cruiser, 'class uncertain,' only a few thousand yards away, and 'decided to attack her in order to frustrate her firing torpedoes at our Battle Fleet.'

(This in case the authorities should think that light cruiser wished to buy rubber.) So she fell upon the light cruiser with every gun she had, at between two and four thousand yards, and secured a number of hits, just the same as at target practice. While thus occupied she sighted out of the mist a squadron of enemy battle-cruisers that had worried her earlier in the afternoon. Leaving the light cruiser, she closed to what she considered a reasonable distance of the newcomers, and let them have, as she thought, both her torpedoes. She possessed an active Acting Sub-Lieutenant, who, though officers of that rank think otherwise, is not very far removed from an ordinary midshipman of the type one sees in tow of relatives at the Army and Navy Stores. He sat astride one of the tubes to make quite sure things were in order, and fired when the sights came on.

But, at that very moment, a big shell hit the destroyer on the side and there was a tremendous escape of steam. Believing – since she had seen one torpedo leave the tube before the smash came – believing that both her tubes had been fired, the destroyer turned away 'at greatly reduced speed' (the shell reduced it), and passed, quite reasonably close, the light cruiser whom she had been hammering so faithfully till the larger game appeared. Meantime, the Sub-Lieutenant was exploring what damage had been done by the big shell. He discovered that only one of the two torpedoes had left the tubes, and 'observing enemy light cruiser beam on and apparently temporarily stopped,' he fired the providential remainder at her, and it hit her below the conning-tower and well and truly exploded, as was witnessed by the Sub-Lieutenant himself, the Commander, a leading signalman, and several other ratings. Luck continued to hold! The Acting

Sub-Lieutenant further reported that 'we still had three torpedoes left and at the same time drew my attention to enemy's line of battleships.' They rather looked as if they were coming down with intent to assault. So the Sub-Lieutenant fired the rest of the torpedoes, which at least started off correctly from the shell-shaken tubes, and must have crossed the enemy's line. When torpedoes turn up among a squadron, they upset the steering and distract the attention of all concerned. Then the destroyer judged it time to take stock of her injuries. Among other minor defects she could neither steam, steer, nor signal.

Towing under Difficulties

Mark how virtue is rewarded! Another of our destroyers an hour or so previously had been knocked clean out of action, before she had done anything, by a big shell which gutted a boiler-room and started an oil fire. (That is the drawback to oil.) She crawled out between the battleships till she 'reached an area of comparative calm' and repaired damage. She says: 'The fire having been dealt with it was found a mat kept the stokehold dry. My only trouble now being lack of speed, I looked round for useful employment, and saw a destroyer in great difficulties, so closed her.' That destroyer was our paralytic friend of the intermittent torpedo-tubes, and a grateful ship she was when her crippled sister (but still good for a few knots) offered her a tow, 'under very trying conditions with large enemy ships approaching.' So the two set off together, *Cripple* and *Paralytic*, with heavy shells falling round them, as sociable as a couple of lame hounds. *Cripple* worked up to 12 knots, and the weather grew vile, and the tow parted. *Paralytic*, by this time, had raised steam in a boiler or two, and made shift to get along slowly on her own, *Cripple* hirpling beside her, till *Paralytic* could not make any more headway in that rising sea, and *Cripple* had to tow her once more. Once more the tow parted. So they tied *Paralytic* up rudely and effectively with a cable round her after bollards and gun (presumably because of strained forward bulkheads) and hauled her stern-first, through heavy seas, at continually reduced speeds, doubtful of their position, unable to sound because of the seas, and much pestered by a wind which backed without warning, till, at last, they made land, and turned into the hospital appointed for brave wounded ships. Everybody speaks well of *Cripple*. Her name crops up in several reports, with such compliments as the men of the sea use when they see good work. She herself speaks well of her Lieutenant, who, as executive officer, 'took charge of the fire and towing arrangements in a very creditable manner,' and also of Tom Battye and Thomas Kerr, engine-room artificer and stoker petty officer, who 'were in the stokehold at the time of the shell striking, and performed cool and prompt decisive action, although both suffering from shock and slight injuries.'

Useful Employment

Have you ever noticed that men who do Homeric deeds often describe them in Homeric language? The sentence 'I looked round for useful employment' is worthy of Ulysses when 'there was an evil sound at the ships of men who perished and of the ships themselves broken at the same time.'

Roughly, very roughly, speaking, our destroyers enjoyed three phases of 'prompt decisive action' – the first, a period of daylight attacks (from 4 to 6 p.m.) such as the one I have just described, while the battle was young and the light fairly good on the afternoon of May 31; the second, towards dark, when the light had lessened and the enemy were more uneasy, and, I think, in more scattered formation; the third, when darkness had fallen, and the destroyers had been strung out astern with orders to help the enemy home, which they did all night as opportunity offered. One cannot say whether the day or the night work was the more desperate. From private advices, the young gentlemen concerned seem to have functioned with efficiency either way. As one of them said: 'After a bit, you see, we were all pretty much on our own, and you could really find out what your ship could do.'

I will tell you later of a piece of night work not without merit.

The Night Hunt

Ramming an Enemy Cruiser
As I said, we will confine ourselves to something quite sane and simple which does not involve more than half-a-dozen different reports.

When the German fleet ran for home, on the night of May 31, it seems to have scattered – 'starred,' I believe, is the word for the evolution – in a general *sauve qui peut*, while the Devil, livelily represented by our destroyers, took the hindmost. Our flotillas were strung out far and wide on this job. One man compared it to hounds hunting half a hundred separate foxes.

I take the adventures of several couples of destroyers who, on the night of May 31, were nosing along somewhere towards the Schleswig-Holstein coast, ready to chop any Hun-stuff coming back to earth by that particular road. The leader of one line was *Gehenna*, and the next two ships astern of her were *Eblis* and *Shaitan*, in the order given. There were others, of course, but with the exception of one *Goblin* they don't come violently into this tale. There had been a good deal of promiscuous firing that evening, and actions were going on all round. Towards midnight our destroyers were overtaken by several three-and four-funnel German ships (cruisers they thought) hurrying home. At this stage of the game anybody might have been anybody – pursuer or pursued. The Germans took no chances, but switched on their searchlights and opened fire on *Gehenna*. Her acting sub-lieutenant reports: 'A salvo hit us forward. I opened fire with the after-guns. A shell then struck us in a steam-pipe, and I could see nothing but steam. But both starboard torpedo-tubes were fired.'

Eblis, *Gehenna*'s next astern, at once fired a torpedo at the second ship in the German line, a four-funnelled cruiser, and hit her between the second funnel and the mainmast, when 'she appeared to catch fire fore and aft simultaneously, heeled right over to starboard, and undoubtedly sank.' *Eblis* loosed off a second torpedo and turned aside to reload, firing at the same time to distract the enemy's attention from *Gehenna*, who was now ablaze fore and aft. *Gehenna*'s acting sub-lieutenant (the only executive officer who survived) says that by the time the steam from the broken pipe cleared he found *Gehenna* stopped, nearly everybody amidships killed or wounded, the cartridge-boxes round the guns exploding one after the other as the fires took hold, and the enemy not to be seen. Three minutes or less did all that damage. *Eblis* had nearly finished reloading when a shot struck the davit that was swinging her last torpedo into the tube and wounded all hands concerned. Thereupon she dropped torpedo work, fired at an enemy searchlight which winked and went out, and was closing in to help *Gehenna* when she found herself under the noses of a couple of enemy cruisers. 'The nearer one,' he says, 'altered course to ram me apparently.' The Senior Service writes in curiously lawyer-like fashion, but there is no denying that they act quite directly. 'I therefore put my helm hard aport and the two ships met and rammed each other, port bow to port bow.' There could have been no time to think and, for *Eblis*'s commander on the bridge, none to gather information. But he had observant subordinates, and he writes – and I would humbly suggest that the words be made the ship's motto for evermore – he writes, 'Those aft noted' that the enemy cruiser had certain marks on her funnel and certain arrangements of derricks on each side which, quite apart from the evidence she left behind her, betrayed her class. Says *Eblis*: 'I consider I must have considerably damaged this cruiser, as 20 feet of her side plating was left in my foc'sle.' 20 feet of ragged rivet-slinging steel, razoring and reaping about in the dark on a foc'sle that had collapsed like a concertina! It was very fair plating too. There were side-scuttle holes in it – what we passengers would call portholes. But it might have been better, for *Eblis* reports sorrowfully, 'by the thickness of the coats of paint (duly given in 32nds of the inch) she would not appear to have been a very new ship.'

A Fugitive on Fire

New or old, the enemy had done her best. She had completely demolished *Eblis*'s bridge and searchlight platform, brought down the mast and the fore-funnel, ruined the whaler and the dinghy, split the foc'sle open above water from the stem to the galley which is abaft the bridge, and below water had opened it up from the stem to the second bulkhead. She had further ripped off *Eblis*'s skin-plating for an amazing number of yards on one side of her, and had fired a couple of large-calibre shells into *Eblis* at point-blank range, narrowly missing her vitals. Even so, *Eblis* is as impartial as a prize-court. She reports that the second shot, a trifle of 8 inches, 'may have been fired at a different time or just after colliding.' But the night was yet young, and 'just after getting clear of this cruiser an enemy battle-cruiser grazed past our stern at high speed' and again the judgmatic mind – 'I think she must have intended to ram us.' She was a large three-funnelled thing, her centre funnel shot away and 'lights were flickering under her foc'sle as if she was on fire forward.' Fancy the vision of her, hurtling out of the dark, red-lighted from within, and fleeing on like a man with his throat cut!

[As an interlude, all enemy cruisers that night were not keen on ramming. They wanted to get home. A man I know who was on another part of the drive saw a covey bolt through our destroyers; and had just settled himself for a shot at one of them when the night threw up a second bird coming down full speed on his other beam. He had bare time to jink between the two as they whizzed past. One switched on her searchlight and fired a whole salvo at him point blank. The heavy stuff went between his funnels. She must have sighted along her own beam of light, which was about 1,000 yards.

'How did you feel?' I asked.

'I was rather sick. It was my best chance all that night, and I had to miss it or be cut in two.'

'What happened to the cruisers?'

'Oh, they went on, and I heard 'em being attended to by some of our fellows. They didn't know what they were doing, or they couldn't have missed me sitting, the way they did.]

The Confidential Books

After all that *Eblis* picked herself up, and discovered that she was still alive, with a dog's chance of getting to port. But she did not bank on it. That grand slam had wrecked the bridge, pinning the commander under the wreckage. By the time he had extricated himself he 'considered it advisable to throw overboard the steel chest and dispatch-box of confidential and secret books.' These are never allowed to fall into strange hands, and their proper disposal is the last step but one in the ritual of the burial service of His Majesty's ships at sea. *Gehenna*, afire and sinking, out somewhere in the dark, was going through it on her own account. This is her Acting Sub-Lieutenant's report: 'The confidential books were got up. The First Lieutenant gave the order: "Every man aft," and the confidential books were thrown overboard. The ship soon afterwards heeled over to starboard and the bows went under. The First Lieutenant gave the order: "Everybody for themselves." The ship sank in about a minute, the stern going straight up into the air.'

But it was not written in the Book of Fate that stripped and battered *Eblis* should die that night, as *Gehenna* died. After the burial of the books it was found that the several fires on her were manageable, that she 'was not making water aft of the damage,' which meant two-thirds of her were, more or less, in commission, and, best of all, that three boilers were usable in spite of the cruiser's shells. So she 'shaped course and speed to make the least water and the most progress towards land.' On the way back the wind shifted eight points without warning – it was this shift, if you remember, that so embarrassed *Cripple* and *Paralytic* on their homeward crawl – and, what with one thing and another, *Eblis* was unable to make port till the scandalously late hour of noon on June 2, 'the mutual ramming having occurred about 11.40 p.m. on May 31.' She says, this time without any legal reservation whatever, 'I cannot speak too highly of the courage, discipline, and devotion of the officers and ship's company.'

Her recommendations are a Compendium of Godly Deeds for the Use of Mariners. They cover pretty much all that man may be expected to do. There was, as there always is, a first lieutenant who, while his commander was being extricated from the bridge wreckage, took charge of affairs and steered the ship first from the engine-room, or what remained of it, and later from aft, and otherwise manoeuvred as requisite, among doubtful bulkheads. In his leisure he 'improvised means of signalling,' and if there be not one joyous story behind that smooth sentence, I am a Hun!

The Art of Improvising
They all improvised like the masters of craft they were. The chief engine-room artificer, after he had helped to put

out fires, improvised stops to the gaps which were left by the carrying away of the forward funnel and mast. He got and kept up steam 'to a much higher point than would have appeared at all possible,' and when the sea rose, as it always does if you are in trouble, he 'improvised pumping and drainage arrangements, thus allowing the ship to steam at a good speed on the whole.' There could not have been more than 40 feet of hole.

The surgeon – a probationer – performed an amputation single-handed in the wreckage by the bridge, and by his 'wonderful skill, resource, and unceasing care and devotion undoubtedly saved the lives of the many seriously wounded men.' That no horror might be lacking, there was 'a short circuit among the bridge wreckage for a considerable time.' The searchlight and wireless were tangled up together, and the electricity leaked into everything.

There were also three wise men who saved the ship whose names must not be forgotten. They were Chief Engine-room Artificer Lee, Stoker Petty Officer Gardiner, and Stoker Elvins. When the funnel carried away it was touch and go whether the foremost boiler would not explode. These three 'put on respirators and kept the fans going till all fumes, etc., were cleared away.' To each man, you will observe, his own particular Hell which he entered of his own particular initiative.

Lastly, there were the two remaining Quartermasters – mutinous dogs, both of 'em – one wounded in the right hand and the other in the left, who took the wheel between them all the way home, thus improvising one complete Navy-pattern Quartermaster, and 'refused to be relieved during the whole thirty-six hours before the

ship returned to port.' So *Eblis* passes out of the picture
with 'never a moan or complaint from a single wounded
man, and in spite of the rough weather of June 1 they all
remained cheery.' They had one Hun cruiser, torpedoed,
to their credit, and strong evidence abroad that they had
knocked the end out of another.

But *Gehenna* went down, and those of her crew who
remained hung on to the rafts that destroyers carry till
they were picked up about the dawn by *Shaitan*, third
in the line, who, at that hour, was in no shape to give
much help. Here is *Shaitan*'s tale. She saw the unknown
cruisers overtake the flotilla, saw their leader switch
on searchlights and open fire as she drew abreast of
Gehenna, and at once fired a torpedo at the third German
ship. *Shaitan* could not see *Eblis*, her next ahead, for, as
we know, *Eblis* after firing her torpedoes had hauled off
to reload. When the enemy switched his searchlights off
Shaitan hauled out too. It is not wholesome for destroyers
to keep on the same course within 1,000 yards of big
enemy cruisers.

She picked up a destroyer of another division, *Goblin*,
who for the moment had not been caught by the enemy's
searchlights and had profited by this decent obscurity to
fire a torpedo at the hindmost of the cruisers. Almost
as *Shaitan* took station behind *Goblin* the latter was
lighted up by a large ship and heavily fired at. The enemy
fled, but she left *Goblin* out of control, with a grisly
list of casualties, and her helm jammed. *Goblin* swerved,
returned, and swerved again; *Shaitan* astern tried to
clear her, and the two fell aboard each other, *Goblin*'s
bows deep in *Shaitan*'s fore-bridge. While they hung
thus, locked, an unknown destroyer rammed *Shaitan*

aft, cutting off several feet of her stern and leaving her rudder jammed hard over. As complete a mess as the Personal Devil himself could have devised, and all due to the merest accident of a few panicky salvoes. Presently the two ships worked clear in a smother of steam and oil, and went their several ways. Quite a while after she had parted from *Shaitan*, *Goblin* discovered several of *Shaitan*'s people, some of them wounded, on her own foc'sle, where they had been pitched by the collision. *Goblin*, working her way homeward on such boilers as remained, carried on a one-gun fight at a few cables' distance with some enemy destroyers, who, not knowing what state she was in, sheered off after a few rounds. *Shaitan*, holed forward and opened up aft, came across the survivors from *Gehenna* clinging to their raft, and took them aboard. Then some of our destroyers – they were thick on the sea that night – tried to tow her stern-first, for *Goblin* had cut her up badly forward. But, since *Shaitan* lacked any stern, and her rudder was jammed hard across where the stern should have been, the hawsers parted, and, after leave asked of lawful authority, across all that waste of waters, they sank *Shaitan* by gun-fire, having first taken all the proper steps about the confidential books. Yet *Shaitan* had had her little crumb of comfort ere the end. While she lay crippled she saw quite close to her a German cruiser that was trailing homeward in the dawn gradually heel over and sink.

This completes my version of the various accounts of the four destroyers directly concerned for a few hours, on one minute section of one wing of our battle. Other ships witnessed other aspects of the agony and duly noted them as they went about their business. One of our battleships, for instance, made out by the glare of burning *Gehenna* that the supposed cruiser that *Eblis* torpedoed was a German battleship of a certain class. So *Gehenna* did not die in vain, and we may take it that the discovery did not unduly depress *Eblis*'s wounded in hospital.

Asking for Trouble

The rest of the flotilla that the four destroyers belonged to had their own adventures later. One of them, chasing or being chased, saw *Goblin* out of control just before *Goblin* and *Shaitan* locked, and narrowly escaped adding herself to that triple collision. Another loosed a couple of torpedoes at the enemy ships who were attacking *Gehenna*, which, perhaps, accounts for the anxiety of the enemy to break away from that hornets' nest as soon as possible. Half a dozen or so of them ran into four German battleships, which they set about torpedoing at ranges varying from half a mile to a mile and a half. It was asking for trouble and they got it; but they got in return at least one big ship, and the same observant battleship of ours who identified *Eblis*'s bird reported three satisfactory explosions in half an hour, followed by a glare that lit up all the sky. One of the flotilla, closing on what she thought was the smoke of a sister in difficulties, found herself well in among the four battleships. 'It was too late to get away,' she says, so she attacked, fired her torpedo, was caught up in the glare of a couple of searchlights, and pounded to pieces in five minutes, not even her rafts being left. She went down with her colours flying, having fought to the last available gun.

Another destroyer who had borne a hand in *Gehenna*'s trouble had her try at the four battleships and got in a torpedo at 800 yards. She saw it explode and the ship take a heavy list. 'Then I was chased,' which is not surprising. She picked up a friend who could only do 20 knots. They sighted several Hun destroyers who fled from them; then dropped on to four Hun destroyers altogether, who made great parade of commencing action, but soon afterwards 'thought better of it, and turned away.' So you see, in that flotilla alone there was every variety of fight, from the ordered attacks of squadrons under control, to single ship affairs, every turn of which depended on the second's decision of the men concerned; endurance to the hopeless end; bluff and cunning; reckless advance and red-hot flight; clear vision and as much of blank bewilderment as the Senior Service permits its children to indulge in. That is not much. When a destroyer who has been dodging enemy torpedoes and gun-fire in the dark realises about midnight that she is 'following a strange British flotilla, having lost sight of my own,' she 'decides to remain with them,' and shares their fortunes and whatever language is going.

If lost hounds could speak when they cast up next day, after an unchecked night among the wild life of the dark, they would talk much as our destroyers do.

The doorkeepers of Zion,
They do not always stand
In helmet and whole armour,
With halberds in their hand;
But, being sure of Zion,
And all her mysteries,
They rest awhile in Zion,
Sit down and smile in Zion;

Ay, even jest in Zion,
In Zion, at their ease.

The gatekeepers of Baal,
They dare not sit or lean,
But fume and fret and posture
And foam and curse between;
For being bound to Baal,
Whose sacrifice is vain,
Their rest is scant with Baal,
They glare and pant for Baal,
They mouth and rant for Baal,
For Baal in their pain.

But we will go to Zion,
By choice and not through dread,
With these our present comrades
And those our present dead;
And, being free of Zion
In both her fellowships,
Sit down and sup in Zion –
Stand up and drink in Zion
Whatever cup in Zion
Is offered to our lips!

The Meaning of 'Joss'

A Young Officer's Letter

As one digs deeper into the records, one sees the various temperaments of men revealing themselves through all the formal wording. One commander may be an expert in torpedo-work, whose first care is how and where his shots went, and whether, under all circumstances of pace, light, and angle, the best had been achieved. Destroyers do not carry unlimited stocks of torpedoes. It rests with commanders whether they shall spend with a free hand at first or save for night-work ahead – risk a possible while he is yet afloat, or hang on coldly for a certainty. So in the old whaling days did the harponeer bring up or back off his boat till some shift of the great fish's bulk gave him sure opening at the deep-seated life.

And then comes the question of private judgment. 'I thought so-and-so would happen. Therefore, I did thus and thus.' Things may or may not turn out as anticipated, but that is merely another of the million chances of the sea. Take a case in point. A flotilla of our destroyers sighted six (there had been eight the previous afternoon) German battleships of Kingly and Imperial caste very early in the morning of the 1 June, and duly attacked. At first our people ran parallel to the enemy, then, as far as one can make out, headed them and swept round sharp to the left, firing torpedoes from their port or left-hand tubes. Between them they hit a battleship, which went up in flame and debris. But one of the flotilla had not turned with the rest. She had anticipated that the attack would be made on another quarter, and, for certain technical reasons, she was not ready. When she was, she turned, and single-handed – the rest of the flotilla having finished and gone on – carried out two attacks on the five remaining battleships. She got one of them amidships, causing a terrific explosion and flame above the masthead, which signifies that the magazine has been touched off. She counted the battleships when the smoke had cleared, and there were but four of them. She herself was not hit, though shots fell close. She went her way, and, seeing nothing of her sisters, picked up another flotilla and stayed with it till the end. Do I make clear the maze of blind hazard and wary judgment in which our men of the sea must move?

Saved by a Smoke Screen

Some of the original flotilla were chased and headed about by cruisers after their attack on the six battleships, and a single shell from battleship or cruiser reduced one of them to such a condition that she was brought home by her sub-lieutenant and a midshipman. Her captain, first lieutenant, gunner, torpedo coxswain, and both signalmen were either killed or wounded; the bridge, with charts, instruments, and signalling gear went; all torpedoes were expended; a gun was out of action, and the usual cordite fires developed. Luckily, the engines were workable. She escaped under cover of a smoke-screen, which is an unbearably filthy outpouring of the densest smoke, made by increasing the proportion of oil to air in the furnace-feed. It rolls forth from the funnels looking solid enough to sit upon, spreads in a searchlight-proof pat of impenetrable beastliness, and in still weather hangs for hours. But it saved that ship.

It is curious to note the subdued tone of a boy's report when by some accident of slaughter he is raised to command. There are certain formalities which every ship must comply with on entering certain ports. No fully striped commander would trouble to detail them any more than he would the aspect of his Club porter. The young 'un puts it all down, as who should say: 'I rang the bell, wiped my feet on the mat, and asked if they were at home.' He is most careful of the port proprieties, and since he will be sub again tomorrow, and all his equals will tell him exactly how he ought to have handled her, he almost apologises for the steps he took – deeds which ashore might be called cool or daring.

The Senior Service does not gush. There are certain formulae appropriate to every occasion. One of our destroyers, who was knocked out early in the day and lay helpless, was sighted by several of her companions. One of them reported her to the authorities, but, being busy at the time, said he did not think himself justified in hampering himself with a disabled ship in the middle of an action. It was not as if she was sinking either. She was only holed forward and aft, with a bad hit in the engine-room, and her steering-gear knocked out. In this posture she cheered the passing ships, and set about repairing her hurts with good heart and a smiling countenance. She managed to get under some sort of way at midnight, and next day was taken in tow by a friend. She says officially, 'his assistance was invaluable, as I had no oil left and met heavy weather.'

What actually happened was much less formal. Fleet destroyers, as a rule, do not worry about navigation. They take their orders from the flagship, and range out and return, on signal, like sheep-dogs whose fixed point is their shepherd. Consequently, when they break loose on their own they may fetch up rather doubtful of their whereabouts – as this injured one did. After she had been so kindly taken in tow, she inquired of her friend ('Message captain to captain') – 'Have you any notion where we are?' The friend replied, 'I have not, but I will find out.' So the friend waited on the sun with the necessary implements, which luckily had not been smashed, and in due time made: 'Our observed position at this hour is thus and thus.' The tow, irreverently, 'Is it? Didn't know you were a navigator.' The friend, with hauteur, 'Yes; it's rather a hobby of mine.' The tow, 'Had no idea it was as bad as all that; but I'm afraid I'll have to trust you this time. Go ahead, and be quick about it.' They reached a port, correctly enough, but to this hour the tow, having studied with the friend at a place called Dartmouth, insists that it was pure Joss.

Concerning Joss

And Joss, which is luck, fortune, destiny, the irony of Fate or Nemesis, is the greatest of all the Battle-gods that move on the waters. As I will show you later, knowledge of gunnery and a delicate instinct for what is in the enemy's minds may enable a destroyer to thread her way, slowing, speeding, and twisting between the heavy salvoes of opposing fleets. As the dank-smelling waterspouts rise and break, she judges where the next grove of them will sprout. If her judgment is correct, she may enter it in her report as a little feather in her cap. But it is Joss when the stray 12-inch shell, hurled by a giant at some giant ten miles away, falls on her from Heaven and wipes out her and her profound calculations. This was seen to happen to a Hun destroyer in mid-attack. While she was being laboriously dealt with by a 4-inch gun something immense took her, and she was not.

Joss it is, too, when the cruiser's 8-inch shot, that should have raked out your innards from the forward boiler to the ward-room stove, deflects miraculously, like a twig dragged through deep water, and, almost returning on its track, skips off unbursten and leaves you reprieved by the breadth of a nail from three deaths in one. Later, a single splinter, no more, may cut your oil-supply pipes as dreadfully and completely as a broken wind-screen in a collision cuts the surprised motorist's throat. Then you must lie useless, fighting oil-fires while the precious fuel gutters away till you have to ask leave to escape while there are yet a few tons left. One ship who was once bled white by such a piece of Joss, suggested it would be better that oil-pipes should be led along certain lines, which she sketched. As if that would make any difference to Joss when he wants to show what he can do!

Our sea-people, who have worked with him for a thousand wettish years, have acquired something of Joss's large toleration and humour. He causes ships in thick weather, or under strain, to mistake friends for enemies. At such times, if your heart is full of highly organised hate, you strafe frightfully and efficiently till one of you perishes, and the survivor reports wonders which are duly wirelessed all over the world. But if you worship Joss, you reflect, you put two and two together in a casual insular way, and arrive – sometimes both parties arrive – at instinctive conclusions which avoid trouble.

An Affair in the North Sea

Witness this tale. It does not concern the Jutland fight, but another little affair which took place a while ago in the North Sea. It was understood that a certain type of cruiser of ours would not be taking part in a certain show. Therefore, if anyone saw cruisers very like them he might blaze at them with a clear conscience, for they would be

Hun-boats. And one of our destroyers – thick weather as usual – spied the silhouettes of cruisers exactly like our own stealing across the haze. Said the Commander to his Sub., with an inflection neither period, exclamation, nor interrogation-mark can render – 'That – is – them.'

Said the Sub. in precisely the same tone – 'That is them, sir.' 'As my Sub.,' said the Commander, 'your observation is strictly in accord with the traditions of the Service. Now, as man to man, what are they?' 'We-el,' said the Sub., 'since you put it that way, I'm d—d if I'd fire.' And they didn't, and they were quite right. The destroyer had been off on another job, and Joss had jammed the latest wireless orders to her at the last moment. But Joss had also put it into the hearts of the boys to save themselves and others.

I hold no brief for the Hun, but honestly I think he has not lied as much about the Jutland fight as people believe, and that when he protests he sank a ship, he did very completely sink a ship. I am the more confirmed in this belief by a still small voice among the Jutland reports, musing aloud over an account of an unaccountable outlying brawl witnessed by one of our destroyers. The voice suggests that what the destroyer saw was one German ship being sunk by another. Amen!

Our destroyers saw a good deal that night on the face of the waters. Some of them who were working in 'areas of comparative calm' submit charts of their tangled courses, all studded with notes along the zigzag – something like this:

8 p.m. – Heard explosion to the N.W. (A neat arrow-head points that way.) Half an inch farther along, a short change of course, and the word Hit explains the meaning

of— 'Sighted enemy cruiser engaged with destroyers.'
Another twist follows. '9.30 p.m. – Passed wreckage.
Engaged enemy destroyers port beam opposite courses.
A long straight line without incident, then a tangle, and—
Picked up survivors So-and-So. A stretch over to some
ship that they were transferred to, a fresh departure, and
another brush with Single destroyer on parallel course.
Hit.' '0.7 a.m. – Passed bows enemy cruiser sticking up.'
'0.18. – Joined flotilla for attack on battleship squadron.'
So it runs on – one little ship in a few short hours passing
through more wonders of peril and accident than all the
old fleets ever dreamed.

A 'Child's' Letter

In years to come naval experts will collate all those
diagrams, and furiously argue over them. A lot of the
destroyer work was inevitably as mixed as bombing
down a trench, as the scuffle of a polo match, or as the
hot heaving heart of a football scrum. It is difficult to
realise when one considers the size of the sea, that it is
that very size and absence of boundary which helps the
confusion. To give an idea, here is a letter (it has been
quoted before, I believe, but it is good enough to repeat
many times), from a nineteen-year-old child to his friend
aged seventeen (and minus one leg), in a hospital:

'I'm so awfully sorry you weren't in it. It was rather
terrible, but a wonderful experience, and I wouldn't have
missed it for anything, but, by Jove, it isn't a thing one
wants to make a habit of.

'I must say it is very different from what I expected.
I expected to be excited, but was not a bit. It's hard to
express what we did feel like, but you know the sort of

feeling one has when one goes in to bat at cricket, and rather a lot depends upon your doing well, and you are waiting for the first ball. Well, it's very much the same as that. Do you know what I mean? A sort of tense feeling, not quite knowing what to expect. One does not feel the slightest bit frightened, and the idea that there's a chance of you and your ship being scuppered does not enter one's head. There are too many other things to think about.'

Follows the usual 'No ship like our ship' talkee, and a note of where she was at the time.

'Then they ordered us to attack, so we bustled off full bore. Being navigator, also having control of all the guns, I was on the bridge all the time, and remained for twelve hours without leaving it at all. When we got fairly close I sighted a good-looking Hun destroyer, which I thought I'd like to strafe. You know, it's awful fun to know that you can blaze off at a real ship, and do as much damage as you like. Well, I'd just got their range on the guns, and we'd just fired one round, when some more of our destroyers coming from the opposite direction got between us and the enemy and completely blanketed us, so we had to stop, which was rather rot. Shortly afterwards they recalled us, so we bustled back again. How any destroyer got out of it is perfectly wonderful.

'Literally there were hundreds of progs (shells falling) all round us, from a 15-inch to a 4-inch, and you know what a big splash a 15-inch bursting in the water does make. We got washed through by the spray. Just as we were getting back, a whole salvo of big shells fell just in front of us and short of our big ships. The skipper and I did rapid calculations as to how long it would take them to reload, fire again, time of flight, etc., as we had to go right through the spot. We came to the conclusion that, as they were short a bit, they would probably go up a bit, and (they?) didn't, but luckily they altered deflection, and the next fell right astern of us. Anyhow, we managed to come out of that row without the ship or a man on board being touched.'

What the Big Ships Stand

'It's extraordinary the amount of knocking about the big ships can stand. One saw them hit, and they seemed to be one mass of flame and smoke, and you think they're gone, but when the smoke clears away they are apparently none the worse and still firing away. But to see a ship blow up is a terrible and wonderful sight; an enormous volume of flame and smoke almost 200 feet high and great pieces of metal, etc., blown sky-high, and then when the smoke clears not a sign of the ship. We saw one other extraordinary sight. Of course, you know the North Sea is very shallow. We came across a Hun cruiser absolutely on end, his stern on the bottom and his bow sticking up about 30 feet in the water; and a little farther on a destroyer in precisely the same position.

'I couldn't be certain, but I rather think I saw your old ship crashing along and blazing away, but I expect you have heard from some of your pals. But the night was far and away the worse time of all. It was pitch dark, and, of course, absolutely no lights, and the firing seems so much more at night, as you could see the flashes lighting up the sky, and it seemed to make much more noise, and you could see ships on fire and blowing up. Of course we showed absolutely no lights. One expected to be surprised any moment, and eventually we were. We suddenly found ourselves within 1,000 yards of two or three big Hun cruisers. They switched on their searchlights and started firing like nothing on earth. Then they put their searchlights on us, but for some extraordinary reason did not fire on us. As, of course, we were going full speed we lost them in a moment, but I must say, that I, and I think everybody else, thought that that was the end, but one does not feel afraid or panicky. I think I felt rather cooler then than at any other time. I asked lots of people afterwards what they felt like, and they all said the same thing. It all happens in a few seconds; one hasn't time to think; but never in all my life have I been so thankful to see daylight again – and I don't think I ever want to see another night like that – it's such an awful strain. One does not notice it at the time, but it's the reaction afterwards.

'I never noticed I was tired till I got back to harbour, and then we all turned in and absolutely slept like logs. We were seventy-two hours with little or no sleep. The skipper was perfectly wonderful. He never left the bridge for a minute for twenty-four hours, and was on the bridge or in the chart-house the whole time we were out (the chart-house is an airy dog-kennel that opens off the bridge) and I've never seen anybody so cool and unruffled. He stood there smoking his pipe as if nothing out of the ordinary were happening.

'One quite forgot all about time. I was relieved at 4 a.m., and on looking at my watch found I had been up there nearly twelve hours, and then discovered I was rather hungry. The skipper and I had some cheese and biscuits, ham sandwiches, and water on the bridge, and then I went down and brewed some cocoa and ship's biscuit.'

Not in the thick of the fight,
Not in the press of the odds,
Do the heroes come to their height
Or we know the demi-gods.

That stands over till peace.
We can only perceive
Men returned from the seas,
Very grateful for leave.

They grant us sudden days
Snatched from their business of war.
We are too close to appraise
What manner of men they are.

And whether their names go down
With age-kept victories,
Or whether they battle and drown
Unreckoned is hid from our eyes.

They are too near to be great,
But our children shall understand
When and how our fate
Was changed, and by whose hand.

Our children shall measure their worth.
We are content to be blind,
For we know that we walk on a new-born earth
With the saviours of mankind.

The Minds of Men

How It Is Done

What mystery is there like the mystery of the other man's job – or what world so cut off as that which he enters when he goes to it? The eminent surgeon is altogether such a one as ourselves, even till his hand falls on the knob of the theatre door. After that, in the silence, among the ether fumes, no man except his acolytes, and they won't tell, has ever seen his face. So with the unconsidered curate. Yet, before the war, he had more experience of the business and detail of death than any of the people who condemned him. His face also, as he stands his bedside-watches – that countenance with which he shall justify himself to his Maker – none have ever looked upon. Even the ditcher is a priest of mysteries at the high moment when he lays out in his mind his levels and the fall of the water that he alone can draw off clearly. But catch any of these men five minutes after they have left their altars, and you will find the doors are shut.

Chance sent me almost immediately after the Jutland fight a Lieutenant of one of the destroyers engaged. Among other matters, I asked him if there was any particular noise.

'Well, I haven't been in the trenches, of course,' he replied, 'but I don't think there could have been much more noise than there was.'

This bears out a report of a destroyer who could not be certain whether an enemy battleship had blown up or not, saying that, in that particular corner, it would have been impossible to identify anything less than the explosion of a whole magazine.

'It wasn't exactly noise,' he reflected. 'Noise is what you take in from outside. This was inside you. It seemed to lift you right out of everything.'

'And how did the light affect one?' I asked, trying to work out a theory that noise and light produced beyond known endurance form an unknown anaesthetic and stimulant, comparable to, but infinitely more potent than, the soothing effect of the smoke-pall of ancient battles.

'The lights were rather curious,' was the answer. 'I don't know that one noticed searchlights particularly, unless they meant business; but when a lot of big guns loosed off together, the whole sea was lit up and you could see our destroyers running about like cockroaches on a tin soup-plate.'

'Then is black the best colour for our destroyers? Some commanders seem to think we ought to use grey.'

'Blessed if I know,' said young Dante. 'Everything shows black in that light. Then it all goes out again with a bang. Trying for the eyes if you are spotting.'

Ship Dogs

'And how did the dogs take it?' I pursued. There are several destroyers more or less owned by pet dogs, who start life as the chance-found property of a stoker, and end in supreme command of the bridge.

'Most of 'em didn't like it a bit. They went below one time, and wanted to be loved. They knew it wasn't ordinary practice.'

'What did Arabella do?' I had heard a good deal of Arabella.

'Oh, Arabella's *quite* different. Her job has always been to look after her master's pyjamas – folded up at the head of the bunk, you know. She found out pretty soon the bridge was no place for a lady, so she hopped downstairs and got in. You know how she makes three little jumps to it – first, on to the chair; then on the flap-table, and then up on the pillow. When the show was over, there she was as usual.'

'Was she glad to see her master?'

'*Ra-ather*. Arabella was the bold, gay lady-dog *then*!'

Now Arabella is between 9 and 11½ inches long.

'Does the Hun run to pets at all?'

'I shouldn't say so. He's an unsympathetic felon – the Hun. But he might cherish a dachshund or so. We never picked up any ships' pets off him, and I'm sure we should if there had been.'

That I believed as implicitly as the tale of a destroyer attack some months ago, the object of which was to flush Zeppelins. It succeeded, for the flotilla was attacked by several. Right in the middle of the flurry, a destroyer asked permission to stop and lower dinghy to pick up ship's dog which had fallen overboard. Permission was granted, and the dog was duly rescued. 'Lord knows what the Hun made of it,' said my informant. 'He was rumbling round, dropping bombs; and the dinghy was digging out for all she was worth, and the Dog-Fiend was swimming for Dunkirk. It must have looked rather mad from above. But they saved the Dog-Fiend, and then everybody swore he was a German spy in disguise.'

The Fight

'And – about this Jutland fight?' I hinted, not for the first time.

'Oh, that was just a fight. There was more of it than

any other fight, I suppose, but I expect all modern naval actions must be pretty much the same.'

'But what does one do – how does one feel?' I insisted, though I knew it was hopeless.

'One does one's job. Things are happening all the time. A man may be right under your nose one minute – serving a gun or something – and the next minute he isn't there.'

'And one notices that at the time?'

'Yes. But there's no time to keep on noticing it. You've got to carry on somehow or other, or your show stops. I tell you what one does notice, though. If one goes below for anything, or has to pass through a flat somewhere, and one sees the old wardroom clock ticking, or a photograph pinned up, or anything of that sort, one notices that. Oh yes, and there was another thing – the way a ship seemed to blow up if you were far off her. You'd see a glare, then a blaze, and then the smoke – miles high, lifting quite slowly. Then you'd get the row and the jar of it – just like bumping over submarines. Then, a long while after p'raps, you run through a regular rain of bits of burnt paper coming down on the decks – like showers of volcanic ash, you know.' The door of the operating-room seemed just about to open, but it shut again.

'And the Huns' gunnery?'

'That was various. Sometimes they began quite well, and went to pieces after they'd been strafed a little; but sometimes they picked up again. There was one Hun-boat that got no end of a hammering, and it seemed to do her gunnery good. She improved tremendously till we sank her. I expect we'd knocked out some scientific Hun in the controls, and he'd been succeeded by a man who knew how.'

It used to be 'Fritz' last year when they spoke of the enemy. Now it is Hun or, as I have heard, 'Yahun,' being a superlative of Yahoo. In the Napoleonic wars we called the Frenchmen too many names for any one of them to endure; but this is the age of standardisation.

'And what about our Lower Deck?' I continued.

'They? Oh, they carried on as usual. It takes a lot to impress the Lower Deck when they're busy.' And he mentioned several little things that confirmed this. They had a great deal to do, and they did it serenely because they had been trained to carry on under all conditions without panicking. What they did in the way of running repairs was even more wonderful, if that be possible, than their normal routine.

The Lower Deck nowadays is full of strange fish with unlooked-for accomplishments, as in the recorded case of two simple seamen of a destroyer who, when need was sorest, came to the front as trained experts in first-aid.

'And now – what about the actual Hun losses at Jutland?' I ventured.

'You've seen the list, haven't you?'

'Yes, but it occurred to me – that they might have been a shade under-estimated, and I thought perhaps—'

A perfectly plain asbestos fire-curtain descended in front of the already locked door. It was none of his business to dispute the drive. If there were any discrepancies between estimate and results, one might be sure that the enemy knew about them, which was the chief thing that mattered.

It was, said he, Joss that the light was so bad at the hour of the last round-up when our main fleet had come down from the north and shovelled the Hun round on his tracks. *Per contra*, had it been any other kind of weather, the odds were the Hun would not have ventured so far. As it was, the Hun's fleet had come out and gone back again, none the better for air and exercise. We must be thankful for what we had managed to pick up. But talking of picking up, there was an instance of almost unparalleled Joss which had stuck in his memory. A soldier-man, related to one of the officers in one of our ships that was put down, had got five days' leave from the trenches which he spent with his relative aboard, and thus dropped in for the whole performance. He had been employed in helping to spot, and had lived up a mast till the ship sank, when he stepped off into the water and swam about till he was fished out and put ashore. By that time, the tale goes, his engine-room-dried khaki had shrunk half-way up his legs and arms, in which costume he reported himself to the War Office, and pleaded for one little day's extension of leave to make himself decent. 'Not a bit of it,' said the War Office. 'If you choose to spend your leave playing with sailor-men and getting wet all over, that's your concern. You will return to duty by tonight's boat.' (This may be a libel on the W.O., but it sounds very like them.) 'And he had to,' said the boy, 'but I expect he spent the next week at Headquarters telling fat generals all about the fight.'

'And, of course, the Admiralty gave you all lots of leave?'

'Us? Yes, heaps. We had nothing to do except clean down and oil up, and be ready to go to sea again in a few hours.'

That little fact was brought out at the end of almost every destroyer's report. 'Having returned to base at such and such a time, I took in oil, etc., and reported ready for sea at — o'clock.' When you think of the amount of work a ship needs even after peace manoeuvres, you can realise what has to be done on the heels of an action. And, as there is nothing like housework for the troubled soul of a woman, so a general clean-up is good for sailors. I had this from a petty officer who had also passed through deep waters. 'If you've seen your best friend go from alongside you, and your own officer, and your own boat's crew with him, and things of that kind, a man's best comfort is small variegated jobs which he is damned for continuous.'

The Silent Navy

Presently my friend of the destroyer went back to his stark, desolate life, where feelings do not count, and the fact of his being cold, wet, sea-sick, sleepless, or dog-tired had no bearing whatever on his business, which was to turn out at any hour in any weather and do or endure, decently, according to ritual, what that hour and that weather demanded. It is hard to reach the kernel of Navy minds. The unbribable seas and mechanisms they work on and through, have given them the simplicity of elements and machines. The habit of dealing with swift accident, a life of closest and strictest association with their own caste as well as contact with all kinds of men all earth over, have added an immense cunning to those qualities; and that they are from early youth cut out of all feelings that may come between them and their ends, makes them more incomprehensible than Jesuits, even to their own people. What, then, must they be to the enemy?

Here is a Service which prowls forth and achieves, at the lowest, something of a victory. How far-reaching a one only the war's end will reveal. It returns in gloomy silence, broken by the occasional hoot of the long-shore loafer, after issuing a bulletin which though it may enlighten the professional mind does not exhilarate the layman. Meantime the enemy triumphs, wirelessly, far and wide. A few frigid and perfunctory-seeming contradictions are put forward against his resounding claims; a Naval expert or two is heard talking 'off'; the rest is silence. Anon, the enemy, after a prodigious amount of explanation which not even the neutrals seem to take any interest in, revises his claims, and, very modestly, enlarges his losses. Still no sign. After weeks there appears a document giving our version of the affair, which is as colourless, detached, and scrupulously impartial as the findings of a prize-court. It opines that the list of enemy losses which it submits 'give the minimum in regard to numbers though it is possibly not entirely accurate in regard to the particular class of vessel, especially those that were sunk during the night attacks.' Here the matter rests and remains – just like our blockade. There is an insolence about it all that makes one gasp.

Yet that insolence springs naturally and unconsciously as an oath, out of the same spirit that caused the destroyer to pick up the dog. The reports themselves, and tenfold more the stories not in the reports, are charged with it, but no words by any outsider can reproduce just that professional tone and touch. A man writing home after the fight, points out that the great consolation for not having cleaned up the enemy altogether was that 'anyhow those East Coast devils' – a fellow-squadron, if you please, which up till Jutland had had most of the fighting – 'were not there. They missed that show. We were as cock-ahoop as a girl who had been to a dance that her sister has missed.'

This was one of the figures in that dance:

'A little British destroyer, her midships rent by a great shell meant for a battle-cruiser; exuding steam from every pore; able to go ahead but not to steer; unable to get out of anybody's way, likely to be rammed by any one of a dozen ships; her syren whimpering: "Let me through! Make way!"; her crew fallen in aft dressed in life-belts ready for her final plunge, and cheering wildly as it might have been an enthusiastic crowd when the King passes.'

Let us close on that note. We have been compassed about so long and so blindingly by wonders and miracles; so overwhelmed by revelations of the spirit of men in the basest and most high; that we have neither time to keep tally of these furious days, nor mind to discern upon which hour of them our world's fate hung.

The Neutral

Brethren, how shall it fare with me
When the war is laid aside,
If it be proven that I am he
For whom a world has died?

If it be proven that all my good,
And the greater good I will make,
Were purchased me by a multitude
Who suffered for my sake?

That I was delivered by mere mankind
Vowed to one sacrifice,
And not, as I hold them, battle-blind,

But dying with opened eyes?

That they did not ask me to draw the sword
When they stood to endure their lot,
What they only looked to me for a word,
And I answered I knew them not?

If it be found, when the battle clears,
Their death has set me free,
Then how shall I live with myself through the years
Which they have bought for me?

Brethren, how must it fare with me,
Or how am I justified,
If it be proven that I am he
For whom mankind has died;
If it be proven that I am he
Who being questioned denied?

War in the Mountains

The Roads of an Army

When one reached the great Venetian plain near Army Headquarters, the Italian fronts were explained with a clearness that made maps unnecessary.

'We have three fronts,' said my informant. 'On the first, the Isonzo front, which is the road to Trieste, our troops can walk, though the walking is not good. On the second, the Trentino, to the north, where the enemy comes nearest to our plains, our troops must climb and mountaineer, you will see.'

He pointed south-east and east across the heat haze to some evil-looking ridges a long way off where there was a sound of guns debating ponderously. 'That is the Carso, where we are going now,' he said; then he turned north-east and north where nearer, higher mountains showed streaks of snow in their wrinkles.

'Those are the Julian Alps,' he went on. 'Tolmino is behind them, north again. Where the snow is thicker – do you see? – are the Carnic Alps; we fight among them. Then to the west of them come the Dolomites, where tourists use to climb and write books. There we fight, also. The Dolomites join on to the Trentino and the Asiago Plateau,

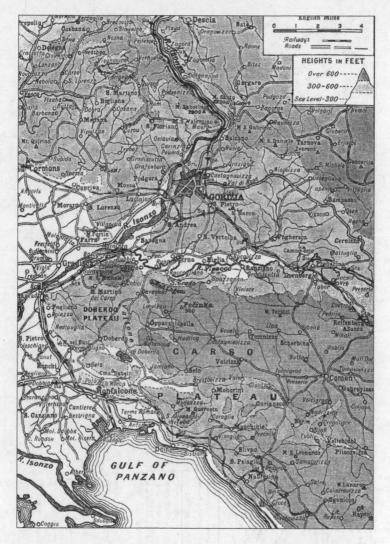

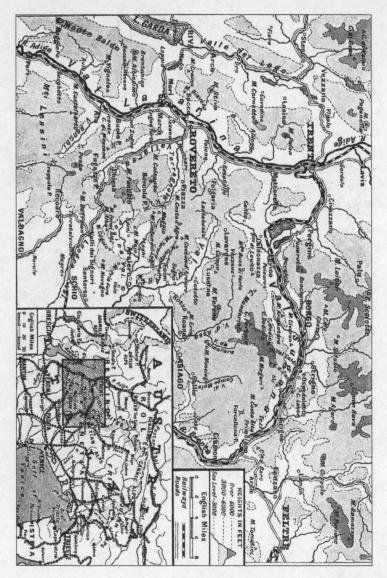

and there we fight. And from there we go round north till we meet the Swiss border. All mountains, you see.'

He picked up the peaks one after another with the ease of a man accustomed to pick up landmarks at any angle and any change of light. A stranger's eyes could make out nothing except one sheer rampart of brooding mountains – 'like giants at a hunting' – all along the northern horizon.

The glass split them into tangled cross-chains of worsted hillocks, hollow-flanked peaks cleft by black or grey ravines, stretches of no-coloured rock gashed and nicked with white, savage thumbnails of hard snow thrust up above cockscombs of splinters, and behind everything an agony of tortured crags against the farthest sky. Men must be borne or broke to the mountains to accept them easily. They are too full of their own personal devils.

The plains around Udine are better – the fat, flat plains crowded with crops – wheat and barley patches between trim vineyards, every vine with her best foot forwards and arms spread to welcome spring. Every field hedged with old, strictly pollarded mulberry-trees for the silkworms, and every road flanked with flashing water-channels that talk pleasantly in the heart.

At each few score yards of road there was a neat square of limestone road-metal, with the water-channel led squarely round it. Each few hundred yards, an old man and a young boy worked together, the one with a long spade, the other with a tin pot at the end of a pole. The instant that any wear showed in the surface, the elder padded the hollow with a spoonful of metal, the youth sluiced it, and at once it was ready to bind down beneath the traffic as tight as an inner-tube patch.

There was curiously little traffic by our standards, but all there was moved very swiftly. The perfectly made and tended roads do most of the motor's work. Where there are no bumps, there can be no strain, even under maximum loads. The lorries glide from railhead to their destination, return, and are off again without overhaul or delay. On the simple principle that transportation is civilisation, the entire Italian campaign is built, and every stretch of every road proves it.

But on the French front, Providence does not supply accommodating river-beds whence the beautiful self-binding stuff can be shovelled ready-made into little narrow-gauge trucks all over the landscape. Nor have we in France solid mountains where man has but to reach out his hand to all the stone of all the pyramids. Neither, anywhere, have we populations, expert from birth at masonry. To parody Macaulay, what the axe is to the Canadian, what the bamboo is to the Malay, what the snow-block is to the Esqimaux, stone and cement is to the Italian, as I hope to show later.

They are a hard people habituated to handling hard stuffs, and, I should imagine, with a sense of property as keen as the Frenchman's. The innumerable grey-green troops in the bright fields moved sympathetically among the crops and did not litter their surroundings with rubbish. They have their own pattern of steel helmet, which differs a little from ours, and gives them at a distance a look of Roman Legionaires on a frieze of triumph. The infantry and, to a lesser extent, other arms are not recruited locally but generally, so that the men from all parts come to know each other, and losses are more evenly spread. But the size, physique, and, above all, the poise of the men struck one at every step. They seem more supple in their collective movements and less loaded down with haberdashery than either French or British troops. But the indescribable difference lay in their tread – the very fall of their feet and the manner in which they seemed to possess the ground they covered. Men whose life runs normally in the open, own and are owned by their surroundings more naturally than those whom climate and trade keep housed through most of the year. Space, sunlight, and air, the procession of life under vivid skies, furnish the Italian with a great deal of his mental background, so when, as a soldier, he is bidden to sit down in the clean dust and be still as the hours while the shells pass, he does so as naturally as an Englishman draws a chair to the fire.

The Belly of Stones

'And that is the Isonzo River,' said the officer, when we reached the edge of the Udine plain. It might have come out from Kashmir with its broad sweeps of pale shoals that tailed off downstream into dancing haze. The milky jade waters smelt of snow from the hills as they plucked at the pontoon bridges' moorings which were made to allow for many feet rise and fall. A snow-fed river is as untrustworthy as a drunkard.

The flavour of mules, burning fuels, and a procession of high-wheeled Sicilian carts, their panels painted with Biblical stories, added to the Eastern illusion. But the ridge on the far side of the river that looked so steep, and was in reality only a small flattish mound among mountains, resembled no land on earth. If the Matoppos had married the Karroo they might have begotten some such abortion of stone-speckled, weather-hacked dirt. All along the base of it, indifferent to the thousands of troops around, to the scream of mules, the cough of motors, the whirr of machinery and the jarring carts, lay in endless belts of cemeteries those Italian dead who had first made possible the way to the heights above.

'We brought them down and buried them after each fight,' said the officer. 'There were many fights. Whole regiments lie there – and there – and there. Some of them died in the early days when we made war without roads, some of them died afterwards, when we had the roads but the Austrians had the guns. Some of them died at the last when we beat the Austrians. Look!'

As the poet says, the battle is won by the men who fall. God knows how many mothers' sons sleep along the river before Gradisca in the shadow of the first ridge of the wicked Carso. They can hear their own indomitable people always blasting their way towards the east and Trieste. The valley of the Isonzo multiplies the roar of the heavy pieces around Gorizia and in the mountains to the north, and sometimes enemy aeroplanes scar and rip up their resting-places. They lie, as it were, in a giant smithy where the links of the new Italy are being welded under smoke and flame and heat – heat from the dry shoals of the river-bed before, and heat from the dry ridge behind them.

The road wrenched itself uphill among the dead trenches, through wire entanglements red-rusted on the ground – looking like 'harrows fit to reel men's bodies out like silk' – between the usual mounds of ruptured sand-bags, and round empty gun-pits softened at their angles by the passage of the seasons.

Trenches cannot be dug, any more than water can be found, on the Carso, for a spade's depth below the surface the unkindly stone turns to sullen rock, and everything must be drilled and blasted out. For the moment, because spring had been wet, the stones were greened over with false growth of weeds which wither utterly in the summer, leaving the rocks to glare and burn alone. As if all this savagery were not enough, the raw slopes and cusps of desolation were studded with numberless pits and water-sinks, some exquisitely designed by the Devil for machine-gun positions, others like small craters capable of holding eleven-inch howitzers, which opened at the bottom through rifts into dry caverns where regiments can hide – and be dug out.

We wound under the highest rise of the ridge and came out on its safest side, on to what the Arabs would call a belly of stones. There was no pretence of green – nothing but rock, broken and rebroken, as far as the eye could carry, by shell-fire, as though it were the far end of Lydd ranges. Earth, however battered, one can make some sort of shift to walk on, but here there was no more foothold than in a nightmare. No two splinters were the same size, and when a man stumbled on the edge of a shell-crater, its sides rolled down with the rattle of a dried tongue in the mouth. Great communal graves were heaped up and walled down their long sides with stone, and on one such stack of death's harvest someone had laid an old brown thigh-bone. The place shivered with ghosts in the hot daylight as the stones shivered in the heat. Dry, ragged points, like a cow's hips, rose along the ridge which we had overlooked. One of them only a few feet lower than we stood had been taken and lost six times. 'They cleared us out with machine-guns from where we are now,' said the officer, 'so we had to capture this higher point first. It cost a good deal.'

He told us tales of regiments wiped out, reconstituted and wiped out anew, who achieved, at their third or fourth resurrection, what their ancestors had set out to win. He told us of enemy dead in multitudes put away somewhere beneath the ringing stones, and of a certain Austrian Honved division which by right of blood claim that this section of the Carso is specially theirs to defend. They, too, appear out of the rocks, perish, and are born again to be slain.

'If you come into this shell-hole – I don't think I should stand up too much – I'll try to show you what we want to do at our next push,' the officer said. 'We're just getting ready for it' – and he explained with a keen forefinger how it was intended to work along certain hills that dominate certain roads which lead, at last, towards the head of the Adriatic – one could see it, a patch of dull silver to the southward – under some dark, shadowy hills that covered Trieste itself.

A sun-warmed water-pipe crossed our shell-hole at about the height of one's chin, and the whirr of a distant shell. The officer's explanation was punctuated by the grumble of single big guns on the Italian side, ranging in anticipation of the serious work to come. Then the ground hiccupped a few yards in front of us, and stones – the poisonous edged stones of the Carso – whirred like partridges. 'Mines,' said the officer serenely, while the civils automatically turned up their collars. 'They are working up the steep side of the ridge, but they might have warned us!'

The mines exploded in orderly line, and it being impossible to run away over the stones, one had to watch them with the lively consciousness that those scores of thousands of dead beneath and around and behind were watching too. A pneumatic drill chattered underground, as teeth chatter.

'I didn't know there were so many loose stones in the world,' I said.

'They are not all loose. We wish they were. They're very solid. Come and see!'

Out of the ginning sunshine we walked into a great rock-cut gallery with rails running underfoot and men shovelling rubbish into trucks. Half-a-dozen embrasures gave light through thirty feet of rock. 'These are some of the new gun-positions,' said the officer. 'For 6-inch guns perhaps! Perhaps for 11.'

'And how'd you get 11-inch guns up here?' I asked.

He smiled a little – I learned the meaning of that smile up in the mountains later.

'By hand,' said he, and turned to the engineer in charge to reprove him for exploding the mines without warning.

We came off the belly of stones, and when we were on the flat lands beyond the Isonzo again, looked back at it across its girdling line of cemeteries. It was the first obstacle Italy found at her own threshold, after she had forced the broad uneasy Isonzo, 'where troops can walk, though the walking is not good.' It seemed enough.

Podgora

'We have finished with stones for a little,' said the officer. 'We are going to a mountain of mud. It is dry now, but this winter it never stayed quiet.'

An acre or so of the climbing roadside was still uneasy, and had slid face-down in a splatter of earth and tree-roots which men were shovelling off.

'It's rather a fresh road. Altogether we have about four thousand miles of new roads – and old roads improved – on a front of about 600 kilometres. But you see, our kilometres are not flat.'

The landscape, picked out in all the greens of spring, was that of early Italian holy pictures – the same isolated, scarred hummocks rising from enamelled meadows or drifts of bloom into the same elaborate entablatures of rock, crowned by a campanile or tufted with dark trees. On the white roads beneath us the lines of motors and mule transport strung out evenly to their various dumps. At one time we must have commanded 20 full miles, all working at once, but never could we spy a breakdown. The Italian transport system has been tried out by war long ago.

The more the road sunk to the plains, the more one realised the height of the mountains dominating us all round. Podgora, the mountain of mud, is a little Gibraltar about 800 feet high, almost sheer on one side, overlooking the town of Gorizia, which, in civil life, used to be a sort of stuffy Cheltenham for retired Austrian officers. Anywhere else, Podgora hill might be noticeable, but you could set down half-a-dozen Gibraltars among this upheaval of hills, and in a month the smooth Italian roads would overrun them as vine tendrils overrun rubbish-heaps. The lords of the military situation round Gorizia are the 4- and 5,000-foot mountains, crowded one behind the other, every angle, upland and valley of each offering or masking death.

The mountains are vile ground for aeroplane work, because there is nowhere to alight in comfort, but none the less the machines beat over them from both sides, and the anti-aircraft guns which are not impressive in the open plains fill the gorges with multiplied coughings more resembling a lion's roar than thunder. The enemy fly high, over the mountains, and show against the blue, like bits of whirling ash off a bonfire. They drop their bombs generously, and the rest is with fate – either the blind crack on blank rock, or the long harmless whirr of slivered stone, or that ripe crash which tells that timber, men and mules have caught it full this time. If all the settings were not so lovely, if the lights, the leafage, the blossom, and the butterflies mating on the grassy lips of old trenches were not allowed to insult the living workmen of death, their work would be easier to describe without digressions.

When we had climbed on foot up and up and into the bowels of the mountain of mud, through galleries and cross-galleries, to a discreetly veiled observation-point, Gorizia, pink, white, and bluish, lay, to all appearance, asleep beneath us amid her full flowering chestnut-trees by the talking Isonzo. She was in Italian hands – won after furious fights – but the enemy guns from the mountains could still shell her at pleasure, and the next move, said our officer, would be to clear certain heights – 'Can you see our trenches creeping up to them?' – from their menace. There and there, he pointed, the Italian troops would climb and crawl, while thus and thus would the fire of our guns cover them, till they came to that bare down and must make their rush – which is really a climb – alone. If that rush failed, then they must dig in among the rocks. And lie out under the bitter skyline, for this was war among the mountains where the valleys were death-traps and only heights counted.

Then we turned to the captured hills behind us that had lived so unconsidered since they were made, but now, because of the price paid for them, would stand forth memorable as long as Italy was remembered. The heathen mountains in front had yet to be baptized and entered on the roll of honour, and one could not say at that moment which one of them would be most honourable, or what cluster of herdsmen's huts would carry the name of a month's battle through the ages.

The studied repose that heralds a big push cloaked both lines. No one, except a few pieces who were finishing some private work, was saying anything. The Austrians had their own last touches to put in too. They were ranging on a convent up a hillside – one deliberate shell at a time. A big gun beneath us came lazily into the game on our side, shaking the whole mountain of mud, and then asking questions of its observing officer across the valley.

Suddenly a boy's voice, that had been taking corrections, spoke quite unofficially at the receiver in the gloom under our feet. 'Oh! Congratulations!' it cried. 'Then you dine with us tonight, and you'll pay for the wine.'

Everyone laughed.

'Rather a long walk,' said our guide and friend. 'The observing officer – he is down near Gorizia – has just telephoned that he has been promoted to Aspirant – Sub-Lieutenant, don't you say? He will have to climb up here to the artillery Mess tonight and stand drinks on his promotion.'

'I bet he'll come,' someone said. There were no takers. So you see, youth is always immortally the same.

Gorizia

We dropped from Podgora into Gorizia by a road a little more miraculous than any we had yet found. It was in the nature of a toboggan-run, but so perfectly banked at the corners that the traffic could have slid down by itself if it had been allowed.

As we entered the town, men were mending the bridge across the river – for a reason. They do a great deal of mending in Gorizia. Austrians use heavy pieces on the place – 12-inch stuff sometimes – dealt methodically and slowly from far back, out of the high hills. I tried to find a house that did not carry that monotonous stippling of shrapnel, but it was difficult. The guns reach everywhere.

There was no air in the still hollow where the place lay – hardly a whisper among the domed horse-chestnuts. Troops were marching through to their trenches far up the hillside beyond, and the sound of their feet echoed between the high garden-walls where the service wires were looped among pendants of wisteria in full flower.

There are several hundred civilians in the city who have not yet cared to move, for the Italian is as stubborn in these things as the Frenchman. In the main square where the house-fronts are most battered and the big electric-light standard bows itself to the earth, I saw a girl bargaining for some buttons on a card at a shop door – hands, eyes, and gesture, all extravagantly employed, and the seller as intently absorbed as she. It must be less distracting than one thinks to live under the knowledge one is always being watched from above – breathed upon in the nape of the neck, so to speak, by invisible mouths.

A little later I was being told confidentially by some English woman among a garden of irises, who owned a radiographic installation and a couple of shrapnel-dusted cars, that they had been promised, when the push came, that they and their apparatus might go into Gorizia itself, to a nice underground room, reasonably free from shells which disconcert the wounded and jar the radiograph, and 'wasn't it kind of the authorities?'

The Ridge of the Waiting Guns

The amazing motor-lorries were thicker on the more amazing road than they had been. Our companion apologised for them. 'You see, we have been taking a few things up to the Front in this way in the last few days,' he said.

'Are all Italians born driving motors?' I demanded, as a procession of high-hooded cars flopped down the curve we were breasting, pivoted on its outside edge, their bonnets pointing over a 400-foot drop, and slid past us with a 3-inch clearance between hub and hub.

'No,' he replied. 'But we, too, have been at the game a long time. I expect all the bad chauffeurs have been killed.'

'And bad mules?' One of them was having hysterics on what I thought – till I had climbed a few thousand higher – was the edge of a precipice. 'Oh, you can't kill a mule,' and sure enough, when the beast had registered its protest, it returned to the dignity of its sires. The muleteer said not a word.

We bored up and into the hills by roads not yet mapped, but solid as lavish labour can make them against the rolling load of the lorries, and the sharp hoofs of the mule, as well as the wear and tear of winter, who is the real enemy. Our route ran along the folded skirts of a range not more than 3 or 4,000 feet high, more or less parallel with the Isonzo in its way from the north. Rivers that had roared level beside us dropped and shrunk to blue threads half visible through the forest. Mountains put forward hard shaly knees round which we climbed in a thousand loops that confused every sense of direction. Then, because the enemy, 7 miles off, could see, stretches of the crowded road were blinded with reed mats while torn holes above or below us proved that he had searched closely.

After that, the colossal lap of a mountain alive with dripping waters would hide us in greenery and moisture, till the sight of a cautious ash-tree still in bud – her sister ten minutes ago had been clothed from head to foot – told us we had risen again to the heights of the naked ridge. And here were batteries upon batteries of the heaviest pieces, so variously disposed and hidden that finding one gave you no clue to the next. Elevens, eights, fours – sixes, and elevens again, on caterpillar wheels, on navy mountings adapted for land work, disconnected from their separate tractors, or balanced and buttressed on their own high speed motors, were repeated for mile after mile, with their ammunition caves, their shops, and the necessary barracks for their thousand servants studded or strung out on the steep drop behind them. Obscure pits and hollows hid them pointing to heaven, and how they had been brought up to be lowered, there passed imagination as they peeped out of the merest slits in green sod. They stood back under ledges and eaves of the ground where no light could outline them, or became one with a dung-heap behind a stable. They stalled themselves in thick forest growth, like elephants at noon, or, as it were, crawled squat on their bellies to the very bows of crests overlooking seas of mountains. They, like the others down the line, were waiting for the hour and the order. Not half-a-dozen out of a multitude opened their lips.

When we had climbed to a place appointed, the shutter of an observation-post opened upon the world below. We saw the Isonzo almost vertically beneath us, and on the far side were the Italian trenches that painfully climbed to the crest of the bare ridges where the infantry live, who must be fed under cover of night until the Austrians are driven out of their heights above.

'It is just like fighting a burglar across housetops,' said the officer. 'You can spot him from a factory chimney, but he can spot you from the spire of the cathedral – and so on.'

'Who sees those men down yonder in the trenches?' I asked.

'Everybody on both sides, but our guns cover them. That is the way in our war. Height is everything.'

He said nothing of the terrific labour of it all, before a man or a gun can come into position – nothing of the battle that was fought in the gorge below when the Isonzo was crossed and the Italian trenches clawed and sawed their red way up the hillside, and very little of the blood-drenched snout of the height called the Sabotino that was carried, lost and recarried most gloriously in the old days of the War, and now lay out below as innocent-seeming as a mountain pasture.

They are a hard people, these Latins, who have had to fight the mountains and all that is in them, metre by metre, and are thankful when their battlefields do not slope at more than 45 degrees.

A Pass, A King, and A Mountain

A falcon swooped off the hill-top and hung below us searching the valley at the head of the pass, which was a broad grassy funnel dipping out into space, exactly like the Muttianee behind Simla. The usual roughly paved caravan track led over it between hummocks of board, rock, and earth, whence it seemed only right that Hillmen would presently come out with brick-tea. But it was a gunner with kindly offers of coffee – a weather-worn commander whose eyes were set to views of very distant horizons. He and his guns lived up there all the year, and on the highest grazing-grounds on either side of his lair were black shell-holes by the score, where the enemy had hunted for him. The snow had just gone, neatly turning in the winter-killed grass-stems around the edge of the older shell-holes as it melted away. This Commandant, like the others, controlled an observation post. When he clicked back its shutter, we looked down as the falcons do, into an Austrian town with a broken bridge over a river, and lines of Italian trenches, crawling towards it across river flats – all laid out mapwise, 3,000 feet below. The town waits – as Gorizia waits – while decisions of which it knows nothing are being taken overhead, whether it shall live or die. Meanwhile, the Commandant pointed out its beauties, for it was his possession, you see, by right of eminent domain, and he dispensed the high, the low, and the middle justice over it.

When we were at coffee, a subaltern came with word that the Austrians, 10,000 metres away, were shifting something that looked like a gun. (Guns take all sorts of shapes when they have to be moved.) The Commandant excused himself, and the telephones called up observers laid out somewhere among the tangled steeps and hanging woods below.

'No,' he said presently, shaking his head, 'it's only a cart – not worth a shot just now.'

There was much bigger game afoot elsewhere, and I fancy that the orders were not to flush it too soon.

The keen wind whooped over the grass and drummed on the boards of the huts. A soldier at a bench fitted nails into his boot, and crooned to himself as he tapped. A blast or two exploded somewhere down the new-made screened road along which we had come, and the echoes clamoured through the valley. Then a motor-horn with a distinctive note rang fierce and piercing.

'That's the King's bugle,' someone said. 'He may be coming here. Listen. No ... he's going on to look at some of the new batteries. You never know where he'll turn up, but he's always somewhere along the line, and he never leaves anything unseen.'

The remark was not addressed to the private with the boot, but he grinned as men do as the name of a popular general. Many pleasant tales are current in his armies concerning the King of Italy. The gist of them all is that he is very much of a man as well as a statesman. Kings and ammunition-dumps are fair targets for aeroplanes, but, if the tale be true, and it squares with all the others, there is one King at least who shoots back and shoots straight. No fear or circumstance distinguish him from any other general in field kit, down to the single ribbon that testifies to a year's war service. He moves temperate, loyal, keen, in stark simplicity among his men and full hazards of war.

All that day a triangular snow peak had risen like a master wave, now to one side, now to the other, of our road. On the steepest slopes of its topmost snows it carried a broad, open V, miles long on either limit, which appeared in the changing lights like a faint cattle-brand, or giant ski-tracks, or those dim canals of Schiaparelli which mark the face of the red planet Mars. That was Monte Nero, and the mark was the line of the Italian trenches on it. They are cut through snow that melts, into packed snow that never melts, into packed snow that never softens; and where the snow cannot lie on the sheer rocks, they are blasted in and out among the frost-ridden rubbish of the mountain crest. Up there, men fight with field-guns, machine-guns, and rifles, and more deadly shoots of stones heaped together and sent sliding down at the proper time. Up there, if a man is wounded and bleeds only a little before he is found, the cold kills him in minutes, not hours. Whole companies can be frostbitten and crippled even while they lie taking cover in the pauses of a rush, and the wandering mountain gusts take sentries from under the lee of their rock as they stand up to be relieved, and flick them into space.

The mountain draws its own supplies and troops for miles and miles back, over new roads that break off from the main arteries of traffic and split into mule-trails and man-tracks, emerging, at last, against the bare rocks, as thin and threadlike as the exposed roots of a botanical diagram to illustrate capillary attraction. There has never been a greater work of invention, preparation, and endurance among fantastic horrors than the winning and holding of this one post. And it has passed almost unnoticed by nations, each absorbed in its own hell.

'We climbed! We climbed! We carried the approaches. Now we are up there, and the Austrians are a little to the right just above that sinking cloud under that cliff. When they are dislodged we get full command of that height,' etc., etc. The officer spoke without emotion. He and a few million others had been goaded out of their known life to achieve the incredible. They had left the faculty of wonder at home with the pictures and the wallpapers and the unfit.

Armies and Avalanches

'But if you make a road, you must make a road,' the officer insisted.

'Admitted. But can all these tremendous works be necessary?'

'Believe me, we do not lay one stone more than we have to. You are seeing the roads in spring. We make them for winter in the mountains. They must be roads to stand everything.'

They clung to the hillside on hanging arches of concrete, they were riveted and sheathed 30 or 40 feet down with pointed masonry; protected above by stonewallings that grew out of the rock itself, and above that again, by wing walls to part and divert uneasy snow-slides or hopping stones a quarter of a mile uphill. They were pierced by solid bridges and culverts at every turn where drainage might gather, or flanked with long aprons of pitched stone, where some mountain's soaked side slid down in broad fans of stony trash which, when the snows melt, delivers sudden blasts of racing pebbles and water.

Every few hundred yards on the road were the faithful old man and the boy, the stone-heap and the spade, and the 20-mile-an-hour lorries rolled as smoothly over the flawless surface as they had in the plains.

We passed a Touring Club notice, of peace times, bidding people 'pay attention' to avalanches. A tangle of pines, snapped like straws underneath one drunken boulder about the size of a house, underlining the warning.

'Yes, before the War, people used to whisper and hold their breath when they passed some of these corners in winter. And now! Hear what a noise that string of cars makes in these gorges! Imagine it in winter! Why, a single motor-bus sometimes would start an avalanche! We've lost many men that way. But transport can't stop for snow.'

It did not. We ran, as the lorries ran, into patches of melting snow, fringed with gentian clumps, heath, and crocus! These patches thickened to sheets, till at the head of a pass we found ten foot of packed snow, all newly shovelled back from the dry, perfectly graded road-bed. It trailed after us brokenly, through villages whose gutters danced with bright water, and closed up abreast of us in sheets once more when we reached Cortina.

This was an ex-health and pleasure resort, which of

late belonged to the Austrians, who filled it with 'new-art' hotels, each more villainous in design than its neighbour. Today, as the troops and transport come and go, the jigsaw and coloured-glass atrocities look like bedizened ladies, standing distracted in the middle of a police raid. The enemy do not shell the hotels much, because they are owned by Austrian heyducs who hope to come back and resume their illustrious trade.

In the old days, whole novels were written about Cortina. The little-used mountains round made an impressive background for love-tales and climbing adventures. Love has gone out of this huge basin of the Dolomites now, and the mountaineering is done by platoons in order to kill men, not by individuals who read papers before Alpine Clubs.

On most of the other Fronts war is waged in hot contact with all man's work and possessions. The slayer and the slain keep each other company at least in a world that they themselves created. But here one faces the immense scorn of the hills preoccupied with their own affairs; for between frost, snow, and undermining waters, the hills are always busy. Men, mules, and motors are busy too! The roads are alive with them. They inhabit cities inside dim forests of pine whose service paths are cut through stale snow and whose aisles ring with machinery! They march out, marshal, and distribute themselves among the snowfields above, by whole regiments and arsenals at a time. Take your eye off them for an instant, and they are swallowed up in the vastness of things long before they reach the upthrusting rock walls where the mountains and the fighting begin.

There is no scale to lay hold on. The largest shells make a smudge no bigger than a midge in a corner of a fold of a swell on the edge of a snowfield's bank. A barracks for 200 men is a swallow's nest plastered beneath the overhanging eaves, only visible when the light is good – the same light that reveals the glancing spider-web of steel wire strung across the abysses, which is the aerial railway feeding that post. Some of these lines work only by night when travelling cradles that hang from the wires cannot be shrapnelled. Others spin and whisper busily all day, against rifts and chimneys of the rock, with their loads of building material, food, ammunition, and the blessed letter from home, or a still burden of wounded, two at a time, slung down after some fight on the very crest itself. From the wire rope and its cradle, to the mule who carries 200 pounds, to the 5-ton lorry or the cart, to the rail-head, is the way of it for every ounce of weight that travels up or down this battle-front. Except the big guns. They arrive at their proper place by the same means that Rome was built.

Men explained and re-explained their transport to me, giving weights, sizes, distances, and average allowance per head of troops. Their system is not like ours. It seems to lack our abundance of forms and checks, as well as palaces full of khakied clerks initialling bits of paper in quadruplicate.

'Oh, but we have forms and paper enough,' they protested. 'Any amount of forms. You'll find them in the cities. They don't grow well in the snow here.'

'That sounds reasonable,' I replied, 'but it is the infinite labour imposed on you by your mere surroundings that impresses me most of all. Everything you handle seems to end in a 200-pound package taken up the side of a house, and yet you have heavy artillery on the edge of glaciers. It's a new convention.'

'True. But these are our surroundings, and our people are used to them. They are used to getting load up and down hill; used to handling things and straps and gears and harness and beasts and stones all their lives; besides, we've been at it for two years. That is why the procession moves.'

Yet I came on one ghastly break in it, nevertheless.

There had been a battery with guns, mules, barracks, and stables complete, established on a mountain side, till it had seemed good to the mountain to brush them away as a woman brushes off snow from her skirt. 'Ninety are down below in the valley with the mules and the rest. Those we shall never find. How did it happen? A very little thing starts an avalanche when the snow is ripe for it. Perhaps a rifle-shot. And yet,' he added grimly, 'we must go on and shake all this atmosphere with our guns. Listen!'

There was nothing doing, at the moment, on this front any more than the others – only a hidden piece here or there answering its opponent. Sometimes the discharge sounded like a triumphant whoop across the snows! Then like the fall of trees far off in the thick woods! But it was most awful when it died down to a dumbed beat no louder than the pulse of blood in one's ears after a climb, or that hint which a mountain-slide might give before it chose to move into action on its own

'Only a Few Steps Higher Up'

For a special job, specialists, but for all jobs, youth above everything! That portion of the Italian frontier where men must mountaineer as well as climb is held with the Alpine regiments. The corps is recruited from the people who inhabit, and know what is in the mind of, the mountains – men used to carrying loads along 18-inch paths round 1,000-foot drops. Their talk is the slang of mountains, with a special word for every mood and state of snow, ice, or rock, as elaborately particular as a Zulu's talk when he is describing his cattle. They wear a smash hat adorned with one eagle feather (worn down to an honourable stump, now); the nails upon their boots resemble, and are kept as sharp as, the fangs of wolves; their eyes are like our airman's eyes; their walk on their own ground suggests the sea; and a more cheery set of hard-bitten, clean-skinned, steady-eyed young devils I have never yet had the honour to meet.

'What do you do?' I was foolish enough to demand of them from the security of a Mess-room 7,000 feet up among pines and snows. For the moment, the forest cut off the oppression of the mountain view.

'Oh, come and see,' said these joyous children. 'We are working a few steps higher up the road. It is only a few steps.'

They took me by car above the timber-line on the edge of the basin, to the steep foot of a dominant rock wall which I had seen approaching, for hours back, along the road. 20 or 30 miles away the pillared mass of it had looked no more than implacably hostile – much as Mont Blanc looks from the lake. Coming nearer it had grown steeper, and a wilderness of wrathful crags and fissures had revealed itself. At close range from almost directly below, the thing, one perceived, went up sheer, where it did not bulge outward, like a ship's side at launching.

Every monstrous detail of its face, etched by sunshine through utterly clear air, crashed upon the sight at once, overwhelming the mind as a new world might, wearying the eye as a gigantically enlarged photograph does.

It was hidden by a snow tunnel, wide enough for a vehicle and two mules. The tunnel was dingy brown where its roof was thick, and lighted by an unearthly blue glare where it was thin, till it broke into blinding daylight where the May heat had melted out the arch of it. But there was graded gravel underfoot all the way, and swilling gutters carried off the snow-drip on either side. In the open or in the dark, Italy, makes but one kind of road.

'This is our new road,' the joyous children explained. 'It isn't quite finished, so if you'll sit on this mule, we'll take you the last few steps, only a few steps higher.'

I looked up again between the towering snowbanks. There were not even wrinkles on the face of the mountain now, but horrible, smooth honey-coloured thumbs and pinnacles, clustered like candle-drippings round the main core of unaffected rock, and the whole framing of it bent towards me.

The road was a gruel of gravel, stones, and working-parties. No one hurried; no one got in his neighbour's way; there were very few orders; but even as the mule hoisted herself up and round the pegged-out turns of it, the road seemed to be drawing itself into shape.

There are little engine-houses at the foot of some of the Swiss bob-runs which, for fifty centimes, used to hoist sportsmen and their bob-sleds up to the top again by funicular. The same arrangement stood on a platform nicked out of rock with the very same smell of raw planks, petrol, and snow, and the same crunch of crampons on slushy ground. But instead of the cog-railway, a steel wire, supported on frail struts and carrying a two steel-latticed basket, ran up the face of the rock at an angle which need not be specified. Qua railway, it was nothing – the merest grocery line, they explained – and, indeed, one had seen larger and higher ones in the valleys lower down; but a certain nakedness of rock and snow beneath, and side-way blasts of air out of funnels and rifts that we slid past, made it interesting.

At the terminus, 4 or 500 feet overhead (we were more than 2,000 feet above the Mess-house in the pines), there was a system – it suggested the marks that old ivy prints on a wall after you peel it off – of legends and paths of slushy trampled snow, connecting the barracks, the cook-house, the Officers' Mess and, I presume, the parade ground of the garrison. If the cook dropped a bucket, he had to go down 600 feet to retrieve it. If a visitor went too far round a corner to admire the panoramas, he became visible to unartistic Austrians who promptly loosed off a shrapnel. All this eagle's nest of a world in two dimensions boiled with young life and energy, as the planks and girders, the packages of other stuff came up the aerial; and the mountain above leaned outward over it all, hundreds of feet yet to the top.

'Our real work is a little higher up – only a few steps,' they urged.

But I recalled that it was Dante himself who says how bitter it is to climb up and down other people's stairs. Besides, their work was of no interest to anyone except the enemy round the corner. It was just the regular routine of these parts. They outlined it for the visitor.

You climb up a fissure of a rock chimney – by shoulder or knee work such as mountaineers understand – and at night for choice, because, by day, the enemy drops stones down the chimney, but then they had to carry machine-guns, and some other things, with them. ('By the way, some of our machine-guns are of French manufacture, so our Machine Gun Corps' souvenir – please take it, we want you to have it – represents the heads of France and Italy side by side.')

And when you emerge from your chimney – which it is best to do in a storm or a gale, since nailed boots on rock make a noise – you find either that you command the enemy's post on the top, in which case you destroy him, or cut him off from supplies by gunning the only goat-path that brings them; or you find the enemy commands you from some unsuspected cornice or knob of rock. Then you go down again – if you can – and try elsewhere. And that is how it is done all along that section of frontier where the ground does not let you do otherwise.

Special work is somewhat different. You select a mountain-top which you have reason to believe is filled with the enemy and all his works. You effect a lodgement there with your teeth and toe-nails; you mine into the solid rock with compressed-air drills for as many hundred yards as you calculate may be necessary. When you have finished, you fill your galleries with nitro-glycerine and blow the top off the mountain. Then you occupy the crater with men and machine-guns as fast as you can. Then you secure your dominating position from which you can gain other positions, by the same means.

'But surely you know all about this. You've seen the Castelletto,' someone said.

It stood outside in the sunshine, a rifted bastion crowned with peaks like the roots of molar-teeth. The largest peak had gone. A chasm, a crater and a vast rock slide took its place.

Yes, I had seen the Castelletto, but I was interested to see the men who had blown it up.

'Oh, he did that. That's him.'

A man with the eyes of a poet or musician laughed and nodded. Yes, he owned, he was mixed up in the affair of the Castelletto – had written a report on it, too. They had used 35 tons of nitro-glycerine for that mine. They had brought it up by hand – in the old days when he was a second lieutenant and men lived in tents, before the wire-rope railways were made – a long time ago.

'And your battalion did it all?'

'No – no: not at all, by any means, but – before we'd finished with the Castelletto we were miners and mechanics and all sorts of things we never expected to be. That is the way of this war.'

'And this mining business still goes on?'

Yes: I might take it that the mining business did go on.

And now would I, please, come and listen to a little music from their band? It lived on the rock ledges – and it would play the Regimental and the Company March; but – one of the joyous children shook his head sadly – 'those Austrians aren't really musical. No ear for music at all.'

Given a rock wall that curves over in a sounding-board behind and above a zealous band, to concentrate the melody, and rock ribs on either side to shoot the tune down 1,000 feet on to hard snowfields below, and thunderous echoes from every cranny and cul-de-sac along half a mile of resonant mountain-face, the result, I do assure you, reduces Wagner to a whisper. That they wanted Austria was nothing – she was only just round the corner – but it seemed to me that all Italy must hear them across those gulfs of thin air. They brayed, they neighed, and they roared; the bandsmen's faces puckered with mirth behind the brasses, and the mountains faithfully trumpeted forth their insults all over again.

The Company March did not provoke any applause – I expect the enemy had heard it too often. We embarked on national anthems. The Marsellaise was but a success *d'estime*, drawing a perfunctory shrapnel or so, but when the band gave them and the whole accusing arch of heaven the Brabanconne the enemy were much moved.

'I told you they had no taste,' said a young faun on a rock shelf; 'still, it shows the swine have a conscience.'

But some folk never know when to stop; besides, it was time for the working-parties to be coming in off the roads. So an announcement was made from high overhead to our unseen audience that the performance was ended and they need not applaud any longer. It was put a little more curtly than this, and it sounded exactly like ears being boxed.

The silence spread with the great shadows of the rock towers across the snow: there was tapping and clinking and an occasional stone-slide far up the mountain side; the aerial railway carried on as usual; the working parties knocked off, and piled tools, and the night shifts began.

The last I saw of the joyous children was a cluster of gnome-like figures a furlong overhead, standing, for there was no visible foothold, on nothing. They separated, and went about their jobs as single dots, moving up or sideways on the face of the rock, till they disappeared into it like ants. Their real work lay 'only a few steps higher up' where the observation-posts, the sentries, the supports and all the rest live on ground compared with which the baboon-tracks round the Mess and the barracks are level pavement. Those rounds must be taken in every weather and light; that is, made at 11,000 feet, with death for company under each foot, and the width of a foot on each side, at every step of the most uneventful round. Frosty glazed rock where a blunt-nailed boot slips once and no more; mountain blasts round the corner of ledges before the body is braced to them; a knob of rotten shale crumbling beneath the hand; an ankle twisted at the bottom of a 90-foot rift; a roaring descent of rocks loosened by snow from some corner the sun has undermined through the day – these are a few of the risks they face going from and returning to the coffee and gramophones at the Mess, 'in the ordinary discharge of their duties.'

A turn of the downward road shut them and their world from sight – never to be seen again by my eyes, but the hot youth, the overplus of strength, the happy, unconsidered insolence of it all, the gravity, beautifully maintained over the coffee cups, but relaxed when the band played to the enemy, and the genuine, boyish kindness, will remain with me. But, behind it all, fine as the steel wire ropes, implacable as the mountain, one was conscious of the hardness of their race.

The Trentino Front

It does not need an expert to distinguish the notes of the several Italian fronts. One picks them up a long way behind the lines, from the troops in rest or the traffic on the road. Even behind Browning's lovely Asolo where, you will remember, Pippa passed, seventy-six years since, announcing that 'All's right with the world,' one felt the tightening in the air.

The officer, too, explained frankly above his map:

'See where our frontier west of the Dolomites dips south in this V-like spearhead. That's the Trentino. Garibaldi's volunteers were in full possession of it in our War of Independence. Prussia was our ally then against Austria, but Prussia made peace when it suited her – I'm talking of 1864 – and we had to accept the frontier that she and Austria laid down. The Italian frontier is a bad one everywhere – Prussia and Austria took care of that – but the Trentino section is specially bad.'

Mist wrapped the plateau we were climbing. The mountains had changed into rounded, almost barrel-shaped heights, steep above dry valleys. The roads were many and new, but the lorries held their pace; the usual old man and young boy were there to see to that. Scotch moors, red uplands, scarred with trenches and punched with shell-holes, a confusion of hills without colour and, in the mist, almost without shape, rose and dropped behind us. They hid the troops in their folds – always awaiting troops – and the trenches multiplied themselves high and low on their sides.

We descended a mountain smashed into rubbish from head to heel, but still preserving the outline, like wrinkles on a forehead, of trenches that had followed its contours. A narrow, shallow ditch (it might have been a water-main) ran vertically up the hill, cutting the faded trenches at right angles.

'That was where our men stood before the Austrians were driven back in their last push – the Asiago push, don't you call it? It took the Austrians ten days to work half-way down from the top of the mountain. Our men drove that trench straight up the hill, as you see. Then they climbed, and the Austrians broke. It's not as bad as it looks, because, in this sort of work, if the enemy uphill misses his footing, he rolls down among your men, but if you stumble, you only slip back among your friends.'

'What did it cost you?' I whispered.

'A good deal. And on that mountain across the gorge – but the mist won't let you see it – our men fought for a week – mostly without water. The Austrians were the first people to lay out a line of 12-inch shell-holes on a mountain's side to serve as trenches. It's almost a regulation trick on all the fronts now, but it's annoying.'

He told tales of the long, bitter fight when the Austrians thought, till General Cadorna showed them otherwise, they had the plains to the south at their mercy. I should not care to be an Austrian with the Boche behind me and the *exercitus Romanus* in front.

It was the quietest of fronts and the least ostentatious of armies. It lived in great towns among forests where we found snow again in dirty, hollow-flanked drifts, which were giving up all the rubbish and refuse that winter had hidden. Labour battalions dealt with the stuff, and there were no smells. Other gangs mended shell-holes with speed; the lorries do not like being checked.

Another township, founded among stones, stood empty except for the cooks and a bored road-mender or two. The population was up the hill digging and blasting; or in wooded park-like hollows of lowland. Battalions slipped like shadows through the mists between the pines. When we reached the edge of everything, there was, as usual, nothing whatever, except uptorn breadths of grass and an 'unhealthy' house – the battered core of what had once been human – with rain-water dripping through the starred ceilings. The view from it included the sight of the Austrian trenches on pale slopes and the noise of Austrian guns – not lazy ones this time, but eager, querulous, almost questioning.

There was no reply from our side. 'If they want to find out anything, they can come and look,' said the officer.

One speculated how much the men behind those guns would have given for a seat in the car through the next few hours that took us along yet another veiled line of arms. But perhaps by now the Austrians have learned.

The mist thickened around us, and the far shoulders of mountains, and the suddenly seen masses of men who loomed out of it and were gone. We headed upwards till the mists met the clouds, by a steeper road than any we had used before. It ended in a rock gallery where immense guns, set to a certain point when a certain hour should come, waited in the dark.

'Mind how you walk! It's rather a sharp turn there.'

The gallery came out on a naked space, and a vertical drop of hundreds of feet of striated rock tufted with heath in bloom. At the wall-foot the actual mountain, hardly less steep, began, and, far below that again, flared outward till it became more reasonable slopes, descending in shoulders and knolls to the immense and ancient plains 4,000 feet below.

The mists obscured the northern views, but to the southward one traced the courses of broad rivers, the thin shadows of aqueducts, and the piled outlines of city after city whose single past was worth more than the future of all the barbarians clamouring behind the ranges that were pointed out to us through the observatory windows. The officer finished his tales of year-long battles and bombardments among them.

'And that nick in the skyline to the right of that smooth crest under the clouds is a mine we sprung,' said he.

The observation shutter behind its fringe of heather-bells closed softly. They do everything without noise in this hard and silent land.

The New Italy

Setting aside the incredible labour of every phase of the Italian war, it is this hardness that impresses one at every turn – from the stripped austerity of General Cadorna's headquarters, which might be a monastery or a laboratory, down to the wayside muleteer, white with dust, but not a bead of sweat on him, working the ladder-like mountain trails behind his animal, or the single sentry lying-out like a panther pressed against a hump of rock, and still as the stone except for his shadowed eyes. There is no pomp, parade, or gallery play anywhere, nor even, as far as can be seen, a desire to turn the best side of things to the light. 'Here,' everybody seems to imply, 'is the work we do. Here are the men and the mechanisms we use. Draw your own conclusions.' No one is hurried or over-pressed, and the 'excitable Latin' of the Boche legend does not appear. One finds, instead, a balanced and elastic system, served by passionate devotion, which saves and spares in the smallest details as wisely and with as broad a view as it drenches the necessary position with the blood of 20,000 men.

Yet it is not inhuman nor oppressive, nor does it claim to be holy. It works as the Italian, or the knife, works – smoothly and quietly, up to the hilt, maybe. The natural temperateness and open-air existence of the people, their strict training in economy, and their readiness to stake life lightly on personal issues have evolved this system or, maybe, their secular instinct for administration had been reborn under the sword.

When one considers the whole massed scheme of their work one leans to the first opinion; when one looks at the faces of their generals, chiselled out by war to the very cameos of their ancestors under the Roman eagles, one inclines to the second.

Italy, too, has a larger number than most countries of men returned from money-getting in the western republics, who have settled down at home again. (They are called Americanos. They have used the new world, but love the old.) Theirs is a curiously spread influence which, working upon the national quickness of mind and art, makes, I should imagine, for invention and faculty. Add to this the consciousness of the New Italy created by its own immense efforts and necessities – a thing as impossible as dawn to express in words or to miss in the air – and one begins to understand what sort of future is opening for this oldest and youngest among the nations. With thrift, valour, temperance, and an idea, one goes far.

They are fighting now, as all civilisation fights, against the essential devildom of the Boche, which they know better than we do in England, because they were once his ally.

To that end they give, not wasting or sparing, the whole

of their endeavour. But they are under no illusions as to guarantees of safety necessary after the War, without which their own existence cannot be secured. They fight for these also, because, like the French, they are logical and face facts to the end.

Their difficulties, general and particular, are many. But Italy accepts these burdens and others in just the same spirit as she accepts the cave-riddled plateaux, the mountains, the unstable snows and rocks and the inconceivable toil that they impose upon her arms. They are hard, but she is harder.

Yet, what man can set out to judge anything? In a hotel waiting for a midnight train, an officer was speaking of some of d'Annunzio's poetry that has literally helped to move mountains in this war. He explained an allusion in it by a quotation from Dante. An old porter, waiting for our luggage, dozed crumpled up in a chair by the veranda. As he caught the long swing of the verse, his eyes opened! His chin came out of his shirt-front, till he sat like a little hawk on a perch, attentive to each line, his foot softly following its cadence.